EMPIRE OF ASH BOOK 3

LORD
⊷ OF ⊷
BATTLE

R.J. VICKERS

ISBN-13: 9798853389960

www.rjvickers.com

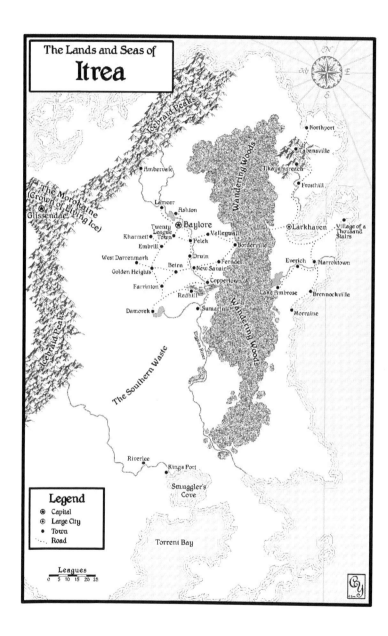

The Lands and Seas of
Itrea

Icebraid Peaks

Northport

Labansville

Wandering Woods

Ilkajumsreach

Ambervale

Frosthill

The Morokaine
(Crown of Living Ice)
Glissendae

Lameer

Ashton

Baylore

Twenty
League
Town

Kharmett

Pelch

Valleywall

Larkhaven

Village of a
Thousand
Stairs

Embrill

Borderville

West Darrenmark

Druin

Beirn

Ferndell

Everich

Marroktown

Golden Heights

New Savair

Icebraid Peaks

Farrinton

Coppertown

Lake Ambrose

Brennockville

Redhill

Damorek

Sumarin

Wandering Woods

Morraine

The Southern Waste

Erglunn River

Riverlee

Kings Port

Smuggler's
Cove

Legend
- ⊛ Capital
- ⊙ Large City
- • Town
- ⋯ Road

Torrent Bay

Leagues
0 5 10 15 20 25

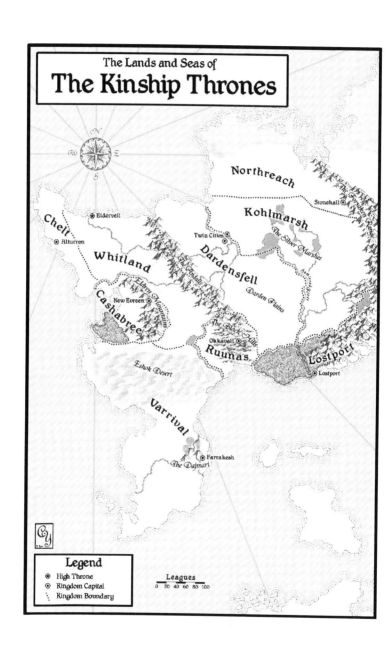

The Lands and Seas of
The Kinship Thrones

Northreach

Kohlmarsh

Stonehall

The Silver Marshes

The Forsaken Range

Eldervell

Chelt

Alturren

Twin Cities

Whitland

Dardensfell

Darden Plains

The Spinals

Sweetwater River

Eldren Mountains

New Evreen

Cashabree

The Black Falls

Okkavell

Ruunas

Lostport

Lostport

Eshok Desert

Varrival

Farrakesh

The Dajmari

Legend

⊕ High Throne
⊙ Kingdom Capital
⋰ Kingdom Boundary

Leagues

0 20 40 60 80 100

I

Evacuation

Baylore looked like the aftermath of a hurricane.

Daymin could barely pick his way down the main street, so crowded it was with furniture and foodstuffs and clothing, strewn about as if by a violent wind. His people were throwing themselves into preparing for evacuation, though he wasn't sure they had taken his orders about only bringing what they could carry to heart. Some enterprising townspeople had even begun disassembling their own houses to re-purpose the wooden joists and bearers and struts for wagons.

Daymin glanced back to make sure his scouts were keeping up. One had stopped to help an old lady move her oven down the step onto the street, while the others were close at his heel.

As the main road curved and began dropping gradually toward the gates, a handful of townspeople realized their king was in their midst and shouted greetings. Daymin acknowledged them with a smile and a raised hand—he was glad they were not making a fuss on his account. After getting locked out of his own palace, with dozens of nobles joining him in the city, the lines between royalty and commoners had blurred in a gratifying way. As he passed the Weavers' Guild, he saw Tarak and Zahira's mother helping a handful of Weavers stack warming tapestries in a wagon, while several nobles from his own Reycoran family entertained a gaggle of young children further down the road.

Daymin clambered over a pile of stone blocks that had toppled off the side of a house, likely destabilized when its floors were removed, and came across a line of wagons backed up from the gates.

"It's the king!" a man shouted. He stumped over to Daymin, brow furrowed. "These here wagons are blocking the whole street. None of us can get anything in and out of our houses. Tell 'em to park somewhere else, would you? Yer Majesty?"

"We can't move them outside the gates or the Whitish will realize we're evacuating," Daymin said. "This is the only street wide enough for them. What do you need to get through the door that won't fit around them?"

The man grumbled something under his breath. "It's an antique chest. Good for keeping vermin outta grain stores, ye know?"

"I'm afraid we can't afford the extra weight. We won't be able to bring all of our grain stores as it is. However, each sack has been enchanted to deter rodents, so our supplies should be safe."

He threw Daymin a dirty look. "Easy for you to say. I bet you've got a whole army of wagons carrying yer valuables."

"No," Daymin said shortly, "seeing as they're trapped

within the palace, which I'm barred from entering. I imagine my preparations will be far easier than yours, since I've already lost everything."

"Oh. Sorry, Yer Majesty. But my neighbor's got a really useful wood cabinet…"

By the time they reached the city walls, it was past noon, the spring sun hot on Daymin's head. He was getting hungry, and did not relish the idea of walking all the way back through the chaotic streets to the main square.

At the gates, Daymin and his scouts climbed the stairs to the guard tower, which looked out over the circle of farmland surrounding Baylore. Stepping onto the wall, Daymin gazed past the farmland to the ring of churned-up earth where the ancestor trees had once stood. He wasn't sure he would ever grow accustomed to the sight of the barren landscape, still brown from winter. The farmland seemed naked and somehow much smaller than before, as if Baylore was nothing more than a dot in the vast plains, rather than the beating heart of a tiny kingdom. And without the forest wall, Baylore was dangerously exposed.

Beyond lay empty grassland, and far off he could see a column of smoke rising from the Whitish stronghold at Twenty-League Town.

"They haven't attacked yet, Your Majesty," one of the scouts said, shuffling her feet nervously. "That has to be a good sign, doesn't it?"

"They'll be taking stock of the situation after the battle of Darkland Fort," Daymin said. "Making plans for their next move. I can't imagine that will take long. I'll get my Cloudmages to send a few snowstorms to delay them as long as possible."

Daymin turned away from the plains to size up his scouts.

Most were men and women he recognized from previous assignments, but the one who had spoken was young, barely out of her teens. It was a reminder of the casualties they had taken at the battle of Darkland Fort. He had bought more time for the Wandering Woods, but at what cost?

Daymin sighed, forcing away these dark thoughts. "I need you to stake out the perimeter of Twenty-League Town. At the first sign the Whitish are making moves to attack, I need to know. You were chosen because you're my fastest runners, so show us what you're made of. Even a six-hour head start could save countless lives."

"Yes, Your Majesty," a few of his scouts murmured.

"And—thank you. I know you're risking your lives out there. We are humbled by your sacrifice." It was something he thought Uncle Cal might have said; the words sounded odd coming from his mouth, but the scouts bowed their heads in gratitude.

Stepping around his scouts, Daymin leaned over the inner wall to look back up Market Street. Especially now, with so many people thronging the streets, Baylore looked like a bustling metropolis. Vibrant colors tumbled over the bricks from haphazard piles of clothing, delicious smells wafted from intermittent stalls where vendors handed out free food and drinks, and the streets rang with chatter and song.

And soon it would fall silent. In less than two quarters— twenty days—the whole city would empty. The streets would sit skeletal and cold until the Whitish marched in and seized Baylore.

2

Stragmouth

As Kalleah's fleet cut through the silvery waters toward Stragmouth, at the terminus of the Lodren River, she was highly conscious of the fact that there were no other oceangoing ships docked in town.

Though it was just past dawn, a cluster of townspeople emerged to watch their approach. They must have made quite the sight—a fleet of eight ships with a mix of the usual white, grey, and tan sails along with a red-sheeted pirate and a black smuggler. This was not a typical destination for either pirates or smugglers; Kalleah wouldn't have been surprised if the townspeople thought they were under attack.

Kalleah's small, unusually-designed Whitish ship was the first to slip into a vacant berth along the docks. The river delta stretched inland to her left, while the waterfront was less sheltered than most Cheltish and Whitish port cities they had passed, with large swells lifting her ship even here between the floating docks. Elu lost his footing when he jumped down to tie them in place, and Nidawi caught his shoulder to steady herself as she followed.

A rotund man with buttons bulging at his stomach hurried down the dock, his footing steady.

"Ah—welcome to Stragmouth." He cleared his throat. "We—ah—charge a daily mooring fee for any ships stopping here. And—er—we can arrange transport up the river for any goods carried by ships who don't—ah—wish to make the inland journey."

Kalleah was about to step up to the rail when Mellicante laid a hand on her arm.

"You might be recognized," she whispered.

Kalleah and Leoth backed away, taking a few steps down the stairs until they could no longer see the onlookers, while Baridya emerged from the wheelhouse to join Mellicante.

"Thank you for your kind greeting," Baridya said warmly. "I know we must make an alarming sight. But we are nothing more than common merchants who have banded together to avoid being requisitioned by the Whitish army. Some of us are from King's Port, legally outside the High King's jurisdiction, yet we have all been preyed on by his royal fleet."

"Ah. Of course. Well, a very warm welcome to you all, my lady. We haven't had much in the way of trade lately, so it's not just you who's been feeling the bite of the High King's war. Is the captain of your ship around?"

Kalleah expected Baridya to introduce herself as captain, but instead she said, "He's just below. I'll have him sign your mooring documents when he comes up."

"Good, good. Plenty of room for all, and don't forget to

restock for the journey upriver while you're here!"

Leoth took Kalleah's hand and tugged her down the stairs while Mellicante and Baridya followed. Abeytu was already waiting below, frowning at Elu and Nidawi, who would have been wise to remain hidden.

"So," Baridya said, stepping up to the dining table and planting her hands on the back of a chair. "This is going to be a very different experience than Chelt. Under Whitish law, women have no right to own property, operate businesses, or even open a bank account without a man to sign off on the documents. I imagine Dardensfell follows similar rules. Assume you will be treated like an underage child, and you won't be disappointed."

"We won't stay long," Kalleah said. "We just need to learn more about the situation in the Twin Cities. Decide if there's any point continuing upriver."

"The harbormaster didn't sound pleased with the High King's war," Leoth said. "That bodes well."

"Do we stay on board?" Abeytu asked.

"I think you should," Kalleah said. "We don't want to draw more attention than we already have."

Nidawi groaned quietly. She, Abeytu, and Elu were highly conspicuous, with a leopardine pattern of spots around their chins and necks and brown hair that hung in coiled ropes. The spots could have been hidden beneath scarves and heavy layers of facepaint, but the odd angles of their faces and the catlike slits of their pupils could not be disguised.

"Speaking of which," Leoth said, "we need to think of disguises for ourselves."

"I can lighten your faces," Baridya said. "And a bit of dramatic kohl and eyeshadow could draw attention away from your features."

"If only we had wigs," Leoth said.

"You'd need to dip your face in chalk to suit a lighter-colored wig," Mellicante said grimly. Her face was twisted with a bad-tempered frown.

"Do what you can," Kalleah told Baridya. "I'd like to explore the city this afternoon and possibly spend the night somewhere along the waterfront. See if we can loosen a few tongues over drinks in a tavern."

While the rest of Kalleah's followers disembarked and spread throughout the city, Kalleah and Leoth sat at the dining table nursing mugs of wine while Baridya worked on their faces. Through a window at the end of the hall, Kalleah could make out glimpses of the scene outside—local vendors swarming the new arrivals, setting up food stalls by the waterfront and trying to tempt them into their establishments.

Baridya started with Leoth, lightening his face a few shades and adding convincing wrinkles around his mouth and forehead. When she dusted his hair with white powder, Kalleah tried not to laugh at the old man who was suddenly sitting across from her.

"What?" Leoth asked with a confused smile.

"Oh, go on, give him the mirror," Kalleah told Baridya.

Smirking, Baridya passed him a hand mirror.

"Nine plagues! You've turned me into someone's decrepit grandfather."

"You're old enough for it," Mellicante said, lips twitching. "Anyway, who knows? Daymin might have already sired a bastard in your absence and neglected to tell you about it."

"Bloody Varse. Don't say that." Leoth swatted at Mellicante

with the mirror. "At least promise you'll do the same to Kalleah."

"Oh, I had something else in mind for her," Baridya said.

Kalleah tilted her chin back and closed her eyes as Baridya leaned toward her with the brush. Her whole face was covered liberally with a paste followed by a powder, and once that was finished, she could feel a cold, wet paint being applied to her eyelids.

"Open your eyes," Baridya said, pressing the mirror into her hand.

Kalleah blinked past a heavy crust on her eyelids. Her whole face was paler, closer to Baridya's shade of tan, and the shadows on her cheekbones were different now, giving her Baridya's exotic, angular Ruunan features. But most of her attention was drawn to her eyes, which were heavily lined in black, the lids painted a lurid blue that rose nearly to her brows.

"Well, no one is going to recognize me," Kalleah said, a bit taken aback by the flashy paint. "I could probably walk through the streets of Baylore without being identified."

"That's not fair," Leoth said. "She doesn't look bad at all! I could be her father."

Kalleah turned a skeptical look on him. "Would you prefer if I painted my face this way all the time?" She had a hard time keeping a straight face when she looked so ridiculous.

"Gods, no! Imagine if I tried kissing you. I'd end up with that—" he gestured at her face—"smeared all over my forehead."

Mellicante snorted. "You must have an interesting way of kissing her."

Kalleah and Leoth both laughed.

"My mother always told me the best way to draw attention away from your own face when in disguise is to draw it *to* something else," Baridya said. "So I've turned you into a travelling performer from Ruunas. As soon as word of the attack on Eidervell spreads, the world will know you're abroad and gathering a fleet. You have to be careful."

Kalleah looked around at her friends—Mellicante, looming behind a chair and tapping her feet with impatience; Baridya, frowning as she put away the makeup; and Leoth, still trying to catch glimpses of himself in the hand mirror. Baridya was the only one who was truly familiar with the Kinship Thrones, and she seemed more worried than the rest of them put together.

"What happens if this goes badly?" Kalleah asked no one in particular.

Leoth gave her a grim look. "We pepper the town with cannonfire and make a hasty retreat."

"Giving up on Dardensfell and Kohlmarsh in the process?" Kalleah said dubiously.

"I suppose. We ought to try not to get into trouble, then."

Baridya nodded solemnly. "Agreed."

They split up when they reached the shore, Mellicante and Baridya heading for a likely-looking tavern, Leoth making a beeline for a customs office, and Kalleah setting off into the maze of streets with no particular direction in mind.

Stragmouth sloped gently away from the waterfront before leveling out. Where many Cheltish and Whitish cities became more imposing the further you retreated from the harbor, Stragmouth appeared uniform throughout—low wood buildings lining narrow streets built without apparent design, some alleys barely wide enough for a grown man to pass sideways, others narrowing as they went until they reached a slot at the end like a keyhole. She could discern no government buildings or manors or anything larger or more solidly built than the sprawl of wooden houses and shops and inns.

It was not long before she lost sight of the handful of her followers she had chanced across; the city seemed to swallow them up effortlessly. Alone now, Kalleah felt a creeping unease descending over her like fog. She was far beyond the waterfront now, hoping to find a tavern or teahouse where she could speak to someone who had not yet noticed the arrival of her fleet, but these looked like private homes, with only the odd fishmonger or butcher on a corner. There were scores of beggars about as well, huddling under cloaks in narrow alleys and hassling passersby with hands extended; Kalleah wondered if they had once been tradespeople whose livelihoods had dried up with the slowing of trade upriver.

Kalleah received stares everywhere she went. Some ogled her face, where she could feel the heavy layers of paint crusted on her eyelids like cement, but more gaped at her legs. Eventually she realized she was the only woman in the entire town wearing trousers rather than skirts—and, indeed, the only woman walking unaccompanied. Some of the women from her fleet had wandered off alone as well, but they didn't appear to have penetrated this far into the city. Kalleah wore her enchanted Weaver's armor, so she was protected from attack, yet the stares made her feel naked.

At long last, she came across a dingy doorway with a sign reading "The Wayfarer's Rest." It sounded promising, so she ducked inside, blinking until her eyes adjusted to the gloom.

"What're you doing here, lady?" a man's voice demanded

from the shadows.

"I'm hoping for a drink," Kalleah said. "I've just arrived in town."

"I'll say. Where's your man?"

Kalleah ventured forward another step, her foot scuffing the dirt floor, until she could make out the square-jawed proprietor who was giving her a confrontational stare. "I'm traveling with a troupe of performers from Ruunas."

"Where's your troupe, then?"

"They've gone ahead to resupply."

He grunted. "We don't allow ladies in here unaccompanied, and we don't have the sort of drinks that'd suit a lady anyhow. Move along."

"I've heard trade has been slow of late," Kalleah said, taking another step forward. "Surely any coin is better than none."

"Not if the city guard catch me. You're not meant to set foot in here at all, so get you gone before we're both in trouble." He made a shooing motion at her.

"Please, sir. This is my first time in Dardensfell, and I'm not accustomed to being treated this way. Are women not allowed to visit taverns unaccompanied anywhere in this kingdom? It seems rather unfair."

"It's treason to question the will of the High King, little lady." He pushed himself to his feet, a dangerous glint in his eyes, and raised a butcher's knife from behind the counter. "I'm not asking you again. Leave and don't come back."

With a sigh, Kalleah turned and stalked from the tavern. It was galling to be treated like a child, especially by people who had never left their small town and knew nothing of the world beyond their borders.

Outside, she found a small crowd watching her from the periphery, including a knot of children peeking from the end of a shadowed alley and a pair of beggars gazing up at her from beneath their hoods.

Though she tried to ignore them, the prickle of unease grew stronger than before. She would be wise to return to the waterfront and try again another day, this time with Leoth at her side.

Several streets down, she reached an alley that dead-ended. Turning to retrace her steps, she found a larger crowd following her, though most ducked down side streets as soon as she spotted them.

Kalleah flexed her left wrist, where her concealed dagger was strapped in place, heartbeat speeding up. She hurried back up the street and took a turn at random, sending a group of beggars scattering. She would be able to kill them all in a heartbeat if it came to that, calling on her power to rip the life from them, but that was exactly the sort of maneuver that would give her away. She would never be able to find allies in the Twin Cities if King Edreon's loyal subjects were expecting her.

It took all her self-control not to break into a run as the footsteps behind her grew louder. At least the streets were now sloping down more dependably; she must be getting closer to the waterfront.

Then, just as she stepped from a narrow alley onto a wide main street, the sort that she had hoped to find in her original foray, a man's voice shouted, "Halt!"

Kalleah whirled. Men with swords belted around their waists were jogging down the street toward her, and in the split second she had to flee before they were upon her, she froze, unable to decide whether they were official guards or something less savory.

Then the men surrounded her, one gripping her by the shoulder while another held a sword to her throat.

"What're you doing wandering our streets without an escort?" one of the men demanded.

"I—" Kalleah's excuse about looking for a drink died in her throat. What was an acceptable activity for a woman to undertake here? "I was just—I lost my way when I—"

Before she could come up with anything convincing, a gloriously familiar face rounded the corner at a run.

"Take your hands off my wife!" Leoth shouted.

The men turned to frown at him, several others drawing swords.

"I've been searching for her," he panted, slowing to a halt just out of range. "She was looking for cloth for a new dress, but she must have lost her way."

"I did," Kalleah said, relief coloring her voice. "I'm so glad you found me! I promise I won't go wandering alone again."

Leoth put a hand on his hilt, jerking his head at the guards, and they finally retreated.

Kalleah hurried to Leoth's side, and they hastened back down the curving main street, neither talking until they reached the waterfront. Kalleah's heart was still hammering against her ribs, though her lingering fear was now mixed with anger.

"How did you find me?" she whispered once they had drawn alongside the docks.

"The city guards had come down and started patrolling the waterfront, but then they suddenly dashed off into the city. I thought it must have been one of our people in trouble, so I followed."

"Thank the cloudy gods." Kalleah scraped the corner of her eye with a nail where the paint was beginning to itch. "How do women live like this? I was practically told I'd be arrested for entering a tavern without a male escort."

"We'll be more careful next time," Leoth said. "We need to find appropriate clothing for you and stick together."

"You do realize this is what Itrea would be like if the Whitish took over, don't you?"

Leoth gave her a grim look. The fall of Baylore was nigh inevitable; if they were looking at their kingdom's future, Kalleah was not sure she ever wanted to return.

She hoped the Twin Cities would not prove as hostile as Stragmouth.

3

Devotees of Tabanus

Edreon wondered if this was how his father had felt close to the end of his life—too weak to stand, his clothes clammy with sweat and pus, his once-loyal servants regarding him with a mixture of pity and scorn. Militarily, he was poised to catapult Whitland to more eminence than it had enjoyed in centuries, but in a nation that glorified physical prowess above all else, no one would follow a cripple.

Queen Kalleah's attack on Eidervell had been wholly unexpected—which, he realized now, was a result of his own shortsightedness—and now her fleet had vanished without a trace. A few sightings had been reported from so many different corners of the Kinship Thrones that he could not give them credence, though he suspected they were on their way to seize Larkhaven or King's Port. The worst part was that they had taken his enchanted ship, removing any possibility of healing his wounded leg with magic.

And holy Varos, his leg hurt. Queen Kalleah had sliced deep into his flesh, perhaps even sawing at his bone, and the slightest twitch of his muscles sent agony knifing through his whole body.

When he was alone, Edreon spent his time drifting in and out of fitful sleep and harassing his various informants for more news through the linked journals. Preparations for the attack on Baylore seemed to be proceeding smoothly, and Chelt was no longer causing trouble now that he held thousands of their women hostage outside Eidervell, but his troops in Baylore Valley were close to starvation and the Wandering Woods remained impenetrable.

Edreon's dark thoughts were interrupted by a knock at the door. Many of his visitors had incensed him by acting as though he were on his deathbed, but just now he would welcome anything that might take his mind off the pain.

"Enter," he called.

A physician in black robes pushed open the door, hefting a bulky case at his side.

"I've been sent to care for you, Your Majesty," he said with a bow and a furtive glance at Edreon.

"I hope you know what you're doing," Edreon said sourly. "I need to be up and walking in a quarter or two. Can you promise me that?"

The physician's thin lips pressed together. "Only Varos is given leave to work miracles, Your Majesty. I will need to examine your leg before I can give you a prognosis."

"Do what you must."

The physician folded back Edreon's heavy quilt and lifted his nightgown to expose the festering wound above his knee. The bandages were soaked through with blood and pus, and when the physician lifted his leg to unwrap them, Edreon spat out a curse. He was lightheaded with pain, and he realized now would be the perfect time for a rival to assassinate him. He had never been more vulnerable.

Soon the physician reached the final layer of bandages, peeling it off in one swift, excruciating movement. Edreon gripped the covers and clamped his jaw shut, tears leaking from the corners of his eyes.

The skin underneath did not look like living flesh, but rather the severed neck of a deer brought back from the hunt. Only he had never made such a mess of his kills. The sight was nauseating; Edreon was abruptly confronted with the possibility that he might lose his leg.

No. If I become a cripple, I might as well toss my crown into the sea.

After wiping away the worst of the crusted blood from around the gash, the physician set his case on Edreon's desk without asking permission and rummaged inside. He returned with a vial of maggots that were wriggling about in a disconcerting way. Uncorking the top, he poured them carefully into the wound.

At once the agony multiplied tenfold. The tiny movements of the maggots aggravated the already-throbbing wound, wracking Edreon with such intense pain he feared he would seize up and die. His father's Truthbringers had reported back on healing methods in Baylore, and even those without magic did not resort to anything so crude as hideous burrowing insects.

When a yell ripped from his throat, Edreon turned on the thin, berobed man who leaned over him.

"You call yourself a physician?" he shouted, voice raw with agony. "This is peasant medicine! How can you inflict such punishment on your king? I could have you burned for this!"

"This is standard practice, Your Majesty," the physician said with a slight tremor in his voice. "We used the same treatment on your father, and his father before him. The maggots help consume the rot so it does not overtake your flesh."

"They don't do this in Itrea!" Edreon roared. "And hardly anyone dies from rot there!"

The physician paled. "The Gods of Sin watch over their progeny, Your Majesty. Rot and ruin come from them, so it follows that the children of Sin are guarded against it."

"Would that I were a Makhori, then, and protected from your clumsy ministrations!"

Just as he finished speaking, the door swung open quietly to admit Naresha, looking subdued in a forest-green gown that hung straight to the floor without hoops or flounces.

While Edreon was distracted, the physician used a wooden spoon to hastily scoop the maggots back into their vial. Edreon turned to strike at him, but he darted away just in time, shoving the cork back onto the vial.

"Your Majesty," Naresha said demurely. "I wished to enquire after your health."

"I was in better health before this charlatan began ministering to me!" Edreon said loudly.

"Do—do you wish me to proceed, Your Majesty?" he ventured.

"What torment have you next devised for me?"

"We must chill the wound to preserve the flesh before laying a poultice into the lesion. We can arrange an ice bath for Your Majesty, or else I have brought a compress of snow."

Catching a look from Naresha, Edreon said from between

clenched teeth, "The compress, if you will." From the doorway, he saw Naresha nod imperceptibly.

The compress of snow did at least dull the pain, numbing his leg in a way that burned almost pleasantly, but it did not last long. Soon the melting snow and its towel were lifted away and the physician pressed a brown poultice into the gash. This was swiftly bandaged, and by the time the numbness wore off and Edreon could feel the way the poultice irritated his flesh, it was too late to do anything about it.

"Keep your leg still, Your Majesty. I will return soon to assess whether the healing process is going smoothly."

"And my prognosis?" Edreon asked wearily.

The physician blinked several times in rapid succession. "The will of Varos will prevail, Your Majesty."

Then he bowed his way from Edreon's bedchamber, his movements twitchy.

"I'm going to lose my leg," Edreon said as soon as he and Naresha were alone. "That bastard is going to ruin me."

With a sigh, Naresha settled on the edge of Edreon's bed. Anyone else would have been frightened of him in this mood, but she knew him well enough to tolerate it. "You should not have said what you did about Itrea," she said quietly. "The physician will talk. Your position is precarious enough as it is without people suspecting you of sympathizing with Makhori."

"They know I can't tolerate those demon-spawn," Edreon snapped.

"Do they?"

Edreon glared at her.

"You're counting on their corruption to win the war in Itrea, harvesting their enchanted trees, and wavering on your commitment to Varos. What are people supposed to think?"

"I am using a valuable resource from the land I have conquered," Edreon hissed. "They don't know the rest of it."

"And if they find out? It's a rather large secret to keep hidden, especially while you're ailing. What if someone else takes over communications with Twenty-League Town?"

"I will not allow myself to grow so weak as that." Edreon knew he was being unreasonable, but his temper had been sparked by the physician's ministrations. It seemed insane that the Itreans in their dying city could enjoy more competent medical attention than he, in the heart of the Kinship Thrones.

Then he recalled something he had heard as a boy, something his father had taken pains to do away with. "Some devotees of Tabanus are healers, are they not?"

"Yes." Naresha sounded wary.

"Bring one to me. Surely they can do no worse than that oaf."

"But that would—"

"Do it in secret, woman. Are you an assassin or not?"

With a sigh and a fleeting caress of Edreon's cheek, Naresha was gone, leaving behind the scent of roses.

Edreon let his eyes drift closed, praying for a release from the pain. He had always respected Varos for his glorification of battle, but maybe Edreon's predecessors had been mistaken to stamp down on worship of the Nine. Much of their devotion was shown through dedication to the pursuits each god oversaw—merchants to noonday Sullivim, the god of growth and bounty; mapmakers to Totoleon, the god of stars known; charitable workers to the moon, Ilkayum, who watched over those neglected by daylight; and so on.

Edreon wondered how much knowledge had been lost when the Alldrosants were driven underground more than a century ago. Their temples and priests still existed, but it was considered heresy to worship them, so no commoners devoted themselves openly to the Nine as they once had. And more than one temple had been sacked over the years.

This drew his thoughts back to the Itreans, godless demon-spawn who were seen as little more than savages. But Edreon had heard the Truthbringers' reports when he was a child and Baylore was first being infiltrated. They had found a city far more densely packed than Eidervell, yet, paradoxically, cleaner and healthier than the Whitish capital.

Maybe, instead of crushing Baylore in his attack, Edreon should be trying to learn more from the Itreans. If their secrets came down to magic, that would be the end of it. But if they were simply using knowledge the Varonites had lost, maybe he could improve Eidervell in ways that would elevate it above the other Kinship Thrones. Then Whitland would deserve its supremacy.

Edreon worried at the bandages, which were painfully tight. This was why Naresha had been concerned. He was straying dangerously close to heresy himself.

No, he corrected himself. *I've long since crossed that line.*

4

To Stand and Fight

Daymin found himself in an odd frame of mind. He should have been panicking about the impending Whitish attack and the subsequent loss of Baylore, but instead he was enjoying himself more than ever. He liked staying outside the palace and mingling with the townspeople, with whom he had much more in common than the courtiers and royalty; he liked the joyful bustle of the city, which was infused with an odd sort of optimism, perhaps because everyone was glad to finally have a purpose again; and though he had always been a solitary person who needed to retreat from society when it became overwhelming, he inexplicably found Idorii's company preferable to solitude.

He and Idorii were still staying together—and sharing a bed, though Daymin tried to think about that as little as possible—and they had written a list of preparations they needed to tackle, which each had claimed with a little "D" or "I" beside the item.

Daymin stood in front of this list now, scanning the remaining items, while Idorii's nimble fingers ran down the buttons on Daymin's coat. He could easily have dressed himself, but they both liked the excuse to linger together a while longer before launching off in separate directions for the day.

"What are you doing today?" Daymin asked idly, his gaze flicking between *Arrange storms with Cloudmages* and *Speak to Ellarie and Falsted*.

"I'll round up your Weavers and see if I'm allowed in to see the ones still living in the palace," Idorii said. "I don't know if you remember, but I was surprised that the enchanted machines hadn't been warded against shattering. What we did in our last battle won't work well in a siege, so I'm hoping we can figure out a better way to bring them down. Maybe we can break through the enchantment with a freezing spell, chill the entire structure until it's brittle, and then slam it with a rock."

"That sounds complicated," Daymin said.

"Less complicated than sending our own soldiers down to cut small holes in the metal."

"True."

Idorii moved behind Daymin to straighten his collar, catching Daymin's eye in the mirror and giving him a brief smile. Daymin could just make out where the root-like markings of corruption had spread up Idorii's neck and onto his chin, concealed beneath a scarf and a layer of face paint. His hair was loose today, hanging past his shoulders in silver sheets threaded with black, and his dark eyes were full of warmth.

"Are you assuming a decent force will stay behind to fight?" Daymin asked.

Idorii's hands lingered on Daymin's shoulders. "Even a

handful of soldiers could fire crossbows and catapults."

"I suppose." Daymin did not want anyone to remain in Baylore, but he was still facing resistance from several groups, particularly the holden monarchs who had captured the palace and the mob that had previously agitated for violence.

"And what are you doing today?" Idorii asked. "Your options are getting limited, I see."

"I was planning to speak to the Cloudmages."

Idorii nudged him over toward the window. With surprise, Daymin realized a few stray snowflakes were beginning to fall.

"What—?"

"I already spoke to them yesterday. Or rather, they came up to me, expecting we would need help keeping the Whitish at bay. You were away."

"Plagues. I was hoping to put off talking to Ellarie and Falsted a bit longer."

Idorii laughed. "Maybe you can politely request that no one shoots me when I try to visit the palace."

"They wouldn't kill a Weaver. Me, on the other hand…"

"Why would they kill you? They have exactly what they want."

"And that's the problem," Daymin grumbled.

Idorii tugged a lock of Daymin's hair into place, and then neither could delay any longer. They headed down the stairs to the dining room of The Queen's Bed, which was empty aside from a table where Uncle Cal and his wife Nyla were in deep discussion with a pair of tradesmen.

On their way past the bar, Idorii called out to the innkeeper, "Good morning! Have you found it?"

"Young master!" the man shouted from the kitchen in the

back. "One moment, please."

"What's this about?" Daymin asked with a frown.

"You'll see."

A few minutes later, the innkeeper appeared with a steaming mug of tea. Daymin could smell it before he set it on the counter—cinnamon, his favorite variety, which had been virtually impossible to find in the city since his return from Darkland Fort. Far better than the thick, bitter hot cocoa most courtiers enjoyed in the morning.

Daymin reached for it, a sense of calm spreading through him as he breathed in the sharp aroma. "Did you arrange this?" he asked Idorii in wonder.

Idorii nudged Daymin with his elbow. "I thought, as your valet, I was supposed to see to your comfort."

Out of sight beneath the bar, Daymin brushed his knuckles against Idorii's. "You're incredible."

Then they passed through the door into the swirling snow, Daymin cupping his mug in both hands, the fragrant steam billowing around his face. They crossed the square together; Idorii tried to walk a step behind Daymin, but Daymin found this irksome, so he kept waiting until Idorii had caught up. Finally Idorii relented and they closed the last distance to the palace gates side by side.

A pair of guards in Dellgrain livery stepped up to confront them.

"Your Highness," one said sourly, giving him the title of a holden monarch rather than a king. "What is it this time?"

"This Weaver requires access to the Makhori still stationed in the palace. He wishes to help arrange the defense of Baylore."

"We cannot allow it."

Daymin took a step closer, until his face was nearly touching the bars. "Do I understand you correctly? Are Holden King Falsted and Holden Queen Ellarie intending to stage a mass suicide?"

"What? No, of course not, that's absurd."

"Then why would they reject the help of someone hoping to protect Baylore? Perhaps you don't recognize Idorii. This is the Weaver who discovered the counterspell that defeated the enchanted towers, the man who won the battle of Darkland Fort for us." Daymin gave him a grim smile. "I think you should let him in."

Still the guards hesitated.

"Search me for weapons, if you want," Idorii said, "and keep me under guard at all times. It makes no difference to me."

At last, a third guard approached and unbolted the gates. The other two stepped aside, seemingly glad someone else had taken responsibility.

"I'll escort him, Your Highness." She took Idorii by the shoulder and marched him up the steps; near the top, Idorii threw an amused look back at Daymin. In his absence, Daymin felt colder than before, and less confident. He tightened his grip around the mug of tea.

"Well?" the first guard said. "Are you finished?"

"No," Daymin said. "I wish to request an audience with Holden King Falsted and Holden Queen Ellarie."

The guard sighed. "Hand over your sword, and I'll show you in."

"I'm not going in there without an army at my back."

"Very well, then. Stand in the snow and wait, and I'll see if they're willing to honor you with their presence."

Daymin waited so long his feet grew numb. He finished his tea and set the mug on the cobblestones, where it began collecting a fine sheen of snow, while a few of the townspeople paused in their work to watch him. The main square was overrun with supplies just like the rest of the city; it was the collection point for any dry stores individual families had kept but were unable to carry. People from all quarters traipsed through, overseen and helped by a significant number of his own soldiers.

He was about to give up and retire to the warmth of The Queen's Bed when the side door of the palace finally swung open to admit Ellarie and Falsted. Ellarie was dressed in a formal gown, her greying hair pinned beneath a net, a small crown perched on her brow. She was Cal's mother, but she shared very little of his appearance, save the shape of her ears and the curve of her lip. Falsted was younger, his skin paler than most Itreans', his sandy hair speckled with grey. His eyes narrowed at the sight of Daymin.

"Have you come to surrender to us?" Falsted asked sardonically.

"No."

"In that case, why are you wasting our time?"

Daymin drew a breath. "I want you to evacuate Baylore with us."

Falsted gave a short, derisive laugh. "How could you expect such cowardice of us? Oh, yes—because you are the most cowardly of all."

"I don't understand how you can abandon Baylore without a fight," Ellarie said. "The city has held before. Our chances outside are far worse than they are here, yet you'd gladly throw away our most fortified position on the continent?"

"That was before the Whitish had enchanted towers."

"We fought them off before," Falsted said. "In your absence, may I remind you. With a severely diminished force."

"They were just testing our defenses," Daymin said. "If they had been serious about their attack, they wouldn't have withdrawn after losing a single tower."

"Has the High King confided in you, then?" Falsted said, his voice thick with derision.

"We've always known we couldn't hold Baylore without the forest wall."

"Mere conjecture," Falsted said. "We ought to stand and fight. It's what any sane leader would do."

"You're dooming us all, you know," Ellarie said tightly. "If your armies stayed behind, and Morrisse and Pollard's as well, we would have a chance at holding Baylore. Instead you've chosen to give up before the war has truly started."

"This is very different from the position you took just after my mother left," Daymin said.

"Oh?"

"You told me Baylore was clearly doomed, because my mother wouldn't have made such a dangerous gamble if we had any chance of winning the war."

"The situation has changed," Ellarie said.

"Yes—we've lost the forest wall. We're in a much worse state than we were last year."

"But we found a way to defeat the enchanted machines."

"Which we didn't know about back then."

Ellarie just glared at him.

"Daymin is grasping at excuses for his cowardice," Falsted said imperiously. "We must not pay him any heed. If he wishes to doom the population of Itrea and his capital along with it, he is now free to make that choice. Thankfully, the throne is now in the hands of more competent rulers."

The throne and nothing else, Daymin thought angrily. How could they delude themselves into thinking it meant anything?

Falsted turned and strode away, but Ellarie lingered a moment longer, frowning at Daymin. He thought he could see a hint of fear in her eyes.

Before he could say anything privately to her, she turned and hastened after Falsted, leaving Daymin wondering if she had been coerced into throwing her support behind him.

5

Letto's Ward

Confinement felt comfortable to Jakovi. He had been staying in the narrow room adjoining King Daymin's for several days now, and he was hesitant to leave. Idorii had been bringing him meals; he was quite happy to eat alone and pass his time watching the square below, where a pretty kitchen girl emerged from time to time to pick herbs from a little planter.

But worry was beginning to gnaw at him. From the snatches of conversation he'd heard, he gathered a large number of people had decided to stay behind to defend Baylore. He was afraid King Daymin would leave him in the city to save Baylore if all else failed, not realizing the consequences of using his magic would be worse than anything the Whitish could unleash.

When Jakovi heard the door to the king's room open and a single pair of footsteps enter, he pulled his own door open a crack and peered out. It was Idorii, just as he'd hoped, his cheeks bright red from the cold outside and a fine layer of snow dusting his coat.

"Jakovi," Idorii said in surprise. He unwound the damp scarf at his neck, and Jakovi winced when he saw the mark of corruption there. He would never forgive himself for that.

"Can I talk to you?" Jakovi asked nervously.

"Please! I've ordered tea sent up, and there should be enough scones for us both."

Idorii draped his coat over the back of a chair, which he pulled away from the desk to face Jakovi.

Hesitantly, Jakovi crept into the room and perched on a cushioned stool at the foot of the bed.

"You don't need to hide in there if you don't want to, you know," Idorii said. "If you wish to explore the city, I can arrange a guide."

"No, no, that's fine." Jakovi worried at the embroidery on the stool. "No, it's—I wanted to make sure I'll be allowed to evacuate. I don't want King Daymin to leave me here."

"He wouldn't do that, Jakovi!"

Jakovi glanced up and met Idorii's eyes. "You're positive?"

"I—"

"Please?"

Idorii sighed. "Listen. I know Letto is definitely evacuating, so if I give you into his care, he'll make sure you're nowhere near Baylore when the Whitish attack. It's the most I can do. If Daymin changes his mind and orders you to stay, I won't be able to counteract that, but this way at least you'll be out of sight."

"Thank you," Jakovi said quietly.

When the tea and scones arrived, Jakovi ate three rosemary-flecked scones, still in awe at how delicious food could taste. He was not as fond of the herbal tea Idorii had selected, so he returned to his room to pack while Idorii finished his cup. He had very few belongings—only one change of clothes and his pan flute—and from the look of the storm outside, he would need to wear every warm layer he owned.

Before they left, Idorii arranged his scarf carefully once more. He handed Jakovi a wool hat and gloves from the hook behind the door, which Jakovi took gratefully, wondering if they belonged to King Daymin.

In the dining room downstairs, Idorii made enquiries with one of the army captains while Jakovi peered through the glass at the chaos in the main square. Then they both ventured into the storm, heads down.

Only a thin layer of snow had accumulated, and it had done nothing to thin the crowds hurrying in every direction. Jakovi shrank closer to Idorii as they plowed through a mob of woodworkers constructing a frame for a wagon, and when they turned down the main street, the press of bodies grew tighter still. Here there was wind to contend with as well, howling between the buildings and scraping Jakovi's cheeks raw, tossing stray bundles of plant matter and scraps of cloth across the mounded supplies.

Thankfully they didn't have too far to walk, though Jakovi was still coming to terms with the concept of distance. Most of his life had been spent in a tiny cell beneath Darkland Fort, immediately followed by a long trek across a featureless plain; compared to those, Baylore felt at once vast and far more cramped than the outside world was meant to be.

Eventually they reached a long, featureless warehouse ringing with noise. Inside were many dozens of soldiers sorting through a mountain of crates; judging by the sleeping rolls lining the far wall, the space was also serving as their living quarters.

Jakovi spotted Letto before Idorii did. The Whitish soldier had let his hair get longer since they left Darkland Fort, and he wore a loose white shirt and black pants rather than the uniform Jakovi was familiar with.

Letto was not looking their way, so Jakovi started through the warehouse, Idorii close behind. It wasn't until they were right behind him that Letto turned, stumbling back in surprise when he recognized them.

"What are you doing here?" he asked blankly.

"I have a favor to ask of you," Idorii said, sounding reluctant.

"Oh, really?"

"I'm sorry. But aren't you glad to be here?"

Letto let Idorii's words hang in the air for a moment before answering. "Yes."

"Anyway, Jakovi doesn't want to be left behind in Baylore. I was hoping you could take him under your wing, get him out of the public eye for a while. Make sure he gets to the mountains safely."

"Keep him away from the king?" Letto asked under his breath.

"Yes, that's part of it."

"Aren't you and the king—" Letto made an odd gesture. "Can't you ask a favor of him, since you have his ear?"

"Please, Letto."

The man sighed, his shoulders sagging. "Fine. I'll do it."

Idorii gave him a grim smile. Clapping Jakovi on the shoulder, he walked off, leaving the two staring at each other.

"So, you're my ward now, huh? Sorry about all that—it's

nothing to do with you. Idorii and I have a bit of a—a complicated history."

"Oh," Jakovi said, not understanding in the slightest what he was talking about. "I won't get in the way. I promise."

"Don't worry about it. Are you looking forward to it, then? Leaving Baylore and traveling to the Icebraid Peaks?"

Jakovi nodded. "The further from Baylore we go, the better."

6

Trinkets

This time Kalleah was prepared. After staying two nights at the waterfront tavern, she and Leoth ventured into Stragmouth once again, heavily disguised as before and with Kalleah in skirts. The innkeeper had drawn them a map that showed the sole main street winding its way through the chaos of smaller alleys, and they were following this toward a square said to be bustling with trade even with oceangoing business greatly reduced.

The main street still meandered in a confusing way, but at least there were shops and inns here, and many were even open. The beggars kept to the shadowed alleyways, perhaps out of fear of the guards who occasionally patrolled the street; Kalleah could not believe how many beggars there were. Was it possible the town had once supported all these people, or were they refugees from elsewhere?

Eventually they reached the square, which was busier than

Kalleah had expected. From the carts and mules tied up beside most stalls, she could tell they had traveled from the far-flung regions of Dardensfell and perhaps Kohlmarsh, visiting Stragmouth to sell their wares on to merchants who would take them further abroad.

Kalleah took Leoth's arm as they stepped into the square. At second glance, most of the traffic in the square was the merchants and their families, the children chasing stray cats and climbing crates. Many of the merchants had abandoned their stalls to swap news with their neighbors, all wearing grim expressions. A few traders inspected the goods; many of them were Ruunan, though a few looked Whitish with a hint of Varrilan blood, indicating they had likely traveled from Lostport.

Leoth started toward a stall where a white-haired merchant sat alone, and Kalleah had no choice but to follow. Upon closer inspection, the merchant was selling odd wooden and metal objects set with large gemstones—definitely not a product she had encountered elsewhere in the Kinship Thrones.

"Good morning," Leoth said.

The merchant's eyes flicked up nervously to Leoth's face before returning to the wares spread before him.

"What are these?" Kalleah asked before she could help herself.

"They're just trinkets," the merchant said, his voice wispy and halting. "Display curiosities. You—you wind them up, and—" He seized a metal sphere perched on a stand and cranked something at the base. When he replaced it on the table, several small metal stars extended out from the main body and began orbiting the sphere while a series of gem-studded metal bands rotated in place, giving the whole object the appearance of constant motion. If she hadn't seen him wind it, Kalleah would have assumed it was a piece of Weavers' magic.

"Where was that made?" Kalleah asked with excitement. "We've heard whispers about a settlement in the mountains selling unusual goods, and this looks like the sort of thing they might have been referring to."

"It's made not—not far from the Twin Cities." For some reason, the merchant kept glancing at Leoth rather than Kalleah as he spoke. "I don't know why you would've heard about—about such useless trinkets."

"We have clients who might be interested in such a thing," Leoth said. "We've traveled from King's Port, and now that trade with Chelt is getting tricky, we're after a new venture that might be worth our while."

"But if we decide to take on a product like this, we need to speak directly to the craftspeople," Kalleah said. "We would gladly pick up future shipments in Stragmouth, but we need to discuss the full details with the makers. It might be our market supports a different variety of trinket. One that might be…*enhanced*."

Now the merchant looked deeply uncomfortable. He seized a metal dolphin and began polishing it vigorously as he spoke. "I'm afraid I—I don't know what you're referring to. And we don't usually make arrangements like—like that." Once again, he acted as though only Leoth had spoken. Kalleah found it irritating.

"In that case, I'm afraid we'll have to move on," Leoth said. "I'm sorry for wasting your time."

Kalleah wanted to ask more, but Leoth clamped a hand over where hers rested lightly on his arm and dragged her away from the table.

"Let's go back to the waterfront," he said under his breath.

As they followed the meandering main street back down toward the harbor, Kalleah muttered, "He's definitely hiding something. Did you think his trinkets were enchanted?"

"I don't know. There aren't supposed to be any Weavers left in the Kinship Thrones, so if there was magic involved, it must be a type we don't recognize. It might just be very clever workmanship."

"Done by a community of artisans hidden in the mountains. I'd wager the wealth of Baylore on it."

Leoth nodded.

"And if they're selling those here, it means even Stragmouth is hiding part of its activities from the high throne. On the surface, it appears to be a perfect Whitish society, yet underneath..." Kalleah paused. "Though I can't believe he refused to look at me when addressing us."

"Maybe it means something different here," Leoth said. "Maybe it's lewd to look at another man's wife."

"That's absurd."

"I didn't make the rules. Anyway, you know how you can solve it, right?"

Kalleah looked sideways to see Leoth grinning cheekily. "What?"

"Dress as a man."

Kalleah snorted. "You know, I might just try that. It's no more ridiculous than my current disguise."

7

A Joint Response

Daymin woke to find his window streaked with rain. A persistent drizzle was falling, and when he climbed from bed to peer outside, he found most of the snow melted away.

"Plagues," he muttered.

Worse still, Idorii had not returned the previous night; though he knew he was likely just caught up in his work, he couldn't help but worry. It felt odd to dress himself alone, and strange to descend the stairs to breakfast without a companion.

There were a few small groups already dining, but he didn't want to impose his company on them, so he slid into a seat at an unoccupied table in the corner. He had never understood the people who feared solitude, the courtiers who had pestered him out of boredom when they were children even though he was poor company, but now he felt the same way. There were too many thoughts rattling around inside his head; he wanted to discuss them with Idorii before they drove him mad.

The innkeeper stopped by Daymin's table with a smile. "What can I get for you this morning, Your Majesty? Eggs and potatoes? Potatoes and eggs? Possibly a millet scone, if I can find the wagon where the flour has been packed away?"

"Whatever's easiest. Though—you don't happen to have any of that cinnamon tea left, do you?"

The innkeeper chuckled. "Enough for one cup, Your Majesty. Would you like to enjoy it today or save it for another day?"

Daymin shrugged. "Might as well have it today. We could be dead tomorrow for all I know."

"That's the spirit, Your Majesty."

Still chuckling, the innkeeper returned to the kitchen, leaving Daymin alone once more to stare out at the rain. He would even be grateful for Tarak, Zahira, and Lalaysha's company right now, though he wasn't sure he could keep up with their banter this early in the morning.

Maybe it was this bloody rain ruining his mood. With the snow gone, he wouldn't be able to delay the Whitish much longer. They could be marching from Twenty-League Town at this very moment. Baylore could be under siege in a matter of hours.

If your scouts are still alive, you'd have heard of it before now. Even a short head start would make a difference.

The door to The Queen's Bed swung open with a jingle, interrupting his thoughts. Daymin's heart leapt when a hooded figure stumped into the dining room, his cloak dripping.

Tugging off his hood, Idorii headed directly for Daymin's table, leaving a trail of wet footprints on the floor. He looked exhausted, his eyes bloodshot and rimmed with dark circles, but there was a gleam of fanaticism about him. With him here, warmth and air flooded back into the room; Daymin could not keep a grin from his face.

"Hey," Idorii said with an affectionate smile.

"Where have you been?"

"Working. On top of the Weavers who fought at Darkland Fort, I managed to drag a few dozen more out of the palace, and half the Guild has joined us as well. We've commandeered a warehouse that used to store wagons."

"And?"

Idorii dropped into the chair opposite Daymin, smile widening. "We've figured it out. It wasn't that hard, really—the biggest problem was intensifying our freezing spell. But with several hundred Weavers working together, we were able to test variations in no time."

"So you can bring down the towers?"

"I think so."

They fell silent as the innkeeper approached with Daymin's tea and breakfast. "Cocoa for you, Master Idorii?" he asked.

"Please. And make it as strong as you can. I can't remember when I last slept."

Daymin started on his scrambled eggs and roasted potatoes, neither speaking until the innkeeper had returned to the kitchen.

"Listen," Idorii said, so quietly Daymin could hardly hear him. "I want you to hear me out before you argue."

Daymin frowned at him in confusion.

"I've been thinking a lot about this evacuation and the holden monarchs and what comes next for Itrea." Idorii reached across the table and snatched a piece of potato from Daymin's plate, pausing for a moment as he chewed. "I know you're not going to like this, but just think about it. Now that we have a way to bring down the enchanted towers from behind the safety of our walls, maybe it's worth mounting a real defense of Baylore. It could make a big difference for everyone who's evacuating."

"You're not asking me to leave my army behind, are you?"

"No! Not at all. But if Ellarie and Falsted are determined to remain in Baylore, maybe you should work with them. Give them what they need to put up a good fight. If they're successful, maybe they'll weaken the Whitish army enough that they won't come after us in a hurry."

Daymin let out a heavy breath. "It would mean throwing away the lives of tens of thousands of soldiers."

"I know."

"And the worst part is, I don't think most of them realize it. They're still listening to the lies Ellarie and Falsted are telling. They think they'll be able to save Baylore."

Idorii gave a half-shrug. "Maybe they will. If we really can defeat their towers…"

"You as well! Why is everyone so Varse-damned optimistic?"

Idorii nudged Daymin's leg with his foot. "I don't actually think that. But we won't know how the battle will play out until it happens."

"This is the problem! Everyone was so quick to criticize me for how bad a state Baylore was in when I first came to power, making it sound like I'd personally brought about our ruin, but now that we actually are doomed, they'll cling to even the most misguided hope! I'd gladly leave behind a small army if they were willing to commit to a suicide mission in full awareness of—"

Daymin cut his rant short when the innkeeper approached with hot cocoa and another plate of eggs and potatoes for Idorii.

"Here," Idorii said, spearing a cube of potato with his fork and depositing it on Daymin's plate.

Daymin snorted.

Both were quiet for a few minutes as they ate, Daymin playing through the different scenarios in his head.

The problem was, he really did need someone to distract the Whitish while his people evacuated. If the Whitish realized immediately that the city was unoccupied, they could chase him down and slaughter his entire population long before they reached the mountains. But if Ellarie and Falsted remained behind, they could keep up the appearance of a fully populated and defended city.

It's just too many lives on the line.

Daymin pushed aside his plate. "If there was some way to make sure they knew what they were committing to, I'd do it. But Ellarie and Falsted won't let me get anywhere near their troops."

"What if you just…start treating them as if they were willingly making that sacrifice? Guards will talk. Word will get around somehow. There might be defectors, or they might all be stubborn, but at least you'll know you did what you could."

"I suppose I could talk to them again today. See how they take it." Daymin did not relish the idea of approaching Ellarie and Falsted once more, but with this rain replacing the snow, his time was running out. He couldn't delay.

"Oh, and I've found different lodgings for Jakovi," Idorii said offhandedly, reaching for his cocoa. "So you have your bed back."

"Oh." Daymin's voice came out flat and emotionless. "That's—great." He should be relieved. He could never return Idorii's affection the way he deserved; it was cruel of him to lead Idorii on as he was doing. So why did this news hit like a fist to the chest?

* * *

That afternoon, Daymin ventured into the persistent drizzle to speak with Ellarie and Falsted once more. The weather had driven all but the hardiest townspeople inside, which could not be helping their evacuation efforts. Daymin had half a mind to tell the Cloudmages to abandon their attempt to delay the Whitish altogether.

When Daymin asked to speak to the holden monarchs once more, Ellarie appeared in the palace doorway only minutes later, standing far enough back that the rain didn't dampen her skirts.

"Come inside!" she called down. "I'm not speaking to you out there!"

Daymin hesitated.

"Don't be ridiculous, Daymin! We're not going to kill you or capture you or anything." She paused. "And even if we did, I'm sure my son would carry on in your absence, so it wouldn't change anything."

She had a point. When the guards unbolted the palace gates, Daymin climbed the steps to join Ellarie, who waved him inside impatiently. "Oh, take your coat off. You'll drip all over the floors."

As he followed her down the hallway, leaving his coat with

a guard at the door, he was struck anew at how vast and impersonal the palace was. It was like a miniature city in itself, only one that discouraged its residents from congregating in throughways and left the largest communal spaces vacant most of the time. Until his recent quarters in the city, Daymin had never fully realized how removed it was from reality.

When they passed the stairs leading down to the dining hall and ballroom, he realized the palace was empty no longer. Soldiers had filled every available space, breakfasting perched on benches and barrels in the dining hall and running through sword drills in the cleared spaces between mounded sleeping rolls in the ballroom. As they passed the Mountain wing, which Holden King Pollard's family had vacated after the palace takeover, Daymin heard laughter and rowdy talk spilling from the doorway—more soldiers.

Eventually they made their way to the war room, where Falsted was poring over a map of Baylore's defenses with an oversized ceremonial crown on his brow.

"What is he doing here?" Falsted snapped.

"He wanted to speak to us again," Ellarie said tiredly. "Apparently he has a different proposal to make."

"Oh?" Falsted's cold eyes turned on Daymin. "We've heard your drivel more times than I can count. Unlike you, we have a battle to prepare for, so we can't afford to waste time."

"I—wanted to help you with that," Daymin said. "I've realized we do actually need a significant force to remain behind in Baylore, enough to convince the Whitish the city is still fully populated and guarded. We want to give them a good fight, and when we lose, we don't want them to immediately chase after our refugees. It's a very serious commitment, one that will likely cost you your lives, but if you want to take that route, I won't stop you."

"I see," Falsted said, the beginnings of a smile curling his lip. "And if we do manage to hold Baylore, are you willing to cede any claim to the throne to us? Given you are abandoning your only strategic position and dooming your population to a lifetime of vagrancy?"

"Yes." Daymin did not hesitate; he knew without a doubt that Baylore would fall. "If you hold Baylore against the Whitish attack, the kingdom is yours."

"You'll help us prepare, then?" Ellarie asked.

"My Weavers are already working on that. They've found a way to defeat the enchanted towers from a distance, and they'll create as many weapons as possible before they leave the city."

Ellarie and Falsted shared a look; from their expressions, Daymin guessed their joint ruling was not going as smoothly as they wished it to appear.

"That's wonderful," Ellarie said. "Would you send a representative to speak with us about a few of the weaknesses we encountered when they last attacked? Your Weavers might have a way to strengthen our defenses."

"Of course," Daymin said. "And there's one more thing…"

"What?" Falsted asked peevishly.

"When—if—the Whitish do take Baylore, I need you to destroy all the remaining food stores, books of magic, and enchanted items remaining in the city. I don't want the Whitish to get their hands on them."

"It's almost as if you want our kingdom to burn," Ellarie said, her face hardening. "You've given up, and you want to take all of Itrea with you when you fall. But nothing is lost until it's lost. We still have hope."

"We don't," Daymin said. "That's what I keep trying to tell you! My mother knew it when she left, and I'm just trying to save what we can before our kingdom goes up in flames around us."

"We're not going to lose the city," Falsted snapped. "And we're certainly not destroying anything that might come in useful in the future. Now get out of here before I change my mind and take you hostage just to silence you."

8

The Trade Ambassador

When Kalleah ventured off her ship two nights later, this time disguised as a man, the difference was remarkable. She still drew looks because of her dark skin and hair, but they were curious rather than disdainful, and a few of the sailors working around the docks nodded as she passed.

She had not planned to spend so much time in Stragmouth, but if her initial impression was correct, sailing into the Twin Cities would be as good as handing herself over to High King Edreon. While the hidden mountain settlements seemed more promising, their populations could not be large, which meant they would not have much to offer her in the way of troops or political clout. She had to be certain of what she would face before she made her decision.

The tavern she was heading toward now had been the establishment of choice for several crews who had disembarked from riverboats recently, one flying a Ruunan flag and two sporting the colors of Lostport, so Kalleah hoped its clientele might be a bit better versed in world affairs.

As soon as she ducked through the door into the noisy, dim room, lit only by candles sitting in pools of wax on the rough tables, she knew she had come to the right place. A full-blooded Varrilan man with dark skin and tightly-coiled hair sat alone in a corner, while two Ruunan women in unusual dresses laughed and joked with the barkeeper. Most of the other patrons were of mixed blood; some looked part-Itrean, which meant they had Makhori blood somewhere in their ancestry.

She stumped up to the bar and ordered an ale, doing her best attempt at a man's voice, before choosing an empty table near the center of the room. It allowed her to catch snatches of conversation from several groups, though her eyes kept going back to the Varrilan, whose face was now shadowed beneath his hood as he surveyed the room.

Eventually he rose and ordered another drink from the bar; instead of returning to his seat in the corner, he dropped onto the bench opposite Kalleah.

"You're Itrean," he said without preamble. His accent was jumbled, more Whitish than Varrilan.

"And you're Varrilan," Kalleah said.

He lowered his hood. "What is an Itrean doing in Stragmouth?"

"I could ask you the same question."

"I'm a trade ambassador. We used to ship goods up to Chelt, but the High King captured one of our ships recently, so we're trying to decide if the inland route is a worthwhile alternative."

"Why wouldn't it be?" Kalleah asked.

"It's a lot more work. Our ships can travel up some rivers, but not the Samiread, which you follow all the way from Lostport nearly to the Twin Cities. And after that you have to travel by land before dropping into the Lodren River for the final distance. Lots of tariffs paid at each transfer, plus a substantial cost to hire the riverships and wagons. And all that to sell goods to the Twin Cities, which aren't anything compared to the Cheltish ports."

"They aren't?" Kalleah asked with interest.

"They're the largest cities in Dardensfell and Kohlmarsh—largest cities east of the Andalls—but they're a dead end. Neither kingdom has any significant cities apart from their capitals. Stragmouth is probably the next-largest city in Dardensfell, and as you can see, it's just a backwater trading port. If you sell to the Twin Cities, that's it. Your goods aren't traveling any further. Whereas with Chelt, you'd be working with merchants traveling inland to Whitland and overseas to King's Port and Larkhaven."

"This war really has strangled the Kinship Thrones, hasn't it?" Kalleah asked softly.

He nodded. "But I'm still curious what an Itrean is doing way out here. The real fight is in Itrea, you know."

"It's hardly a fight any longer."

"I wouldn't say that. Most of the High King's army is still committed in your homeland. As long as Itrea holds out, we're all hoping his power might break. It's the only chance we have. Even Varrival—we like to think we're separate from the Kinship Thrones, but our economy is largely supported by the goods we export."

Kalleah wrapped both hands around her mug, meeting the

man's somber gaze. "Itrea is lost. Don't hold out hope. Even King's Port is slipping away—I've been living there for many years now, but the Whitish influence is growing too strong. That's part of why we've left."

"Are you planning to sail upriver, then?"

"I'm considering it. What was it like in the Twin Cities? Would they be hostile to a crew from King's Port?"

He gave her a fleeting smile. "They might be. Especially if the rest of your crew looks like you. And especially if you're all women trying to pass as men."

"I beg your pardon!" In her indignation, her voice rose, betraying her.

The man's smile grew. "You won't see any judgment from me, I promise. Our merchants do the same when trading with the more backward kingdoms."

Kalleah gave a huff of annoyance. "Well, what is it like in the Twin Cities, then?"

"Have you been in Stragmouth long?"

"A few days."

"Well, you've seen most of what's wrong with the Twin Cities, then. Trade has almost dried up over the past twenty years, especially now the High King keeps seizing ships, so plenty of people have lost their livelihoods. Crime and poverty are rampant, so there isn't much of a market for the sort of exotic goods you would've sold in Chelt. But Stragmouth is lucky in some ways, because it doesn't have to deal with the Lord's Men."

"What are those?" Kalleah asked warily.

"I'm not entirely sure. They appear to be some sort of brutal law-enforcement gang someone dispatched to the Twin Cities, but no one is completely sure who they answer to. They're the ones to watch out for. You'll find a warm welcome from the actual residents, but with skin that dark, you'll be targeted straightaway by the Lord's Men."

"Plagues."

"I know. I'm about to sail back to Farrakesh without a single realistic trade proposal. It's a messy situation all around. No one is happy with Whitland at the moment, least of all the kings of Dardensfell and Kohlmarsh."

A spark of hope lit in Kalleah's chest. "Wait. Are you saying the kings aren't backing these Lord's Men?"

"Not at all. They're as trapped as the rest of their populations. Which is why we're all counting on Itrea, you see. If Whitland's stranglehold on the rest of the Kinship Thrones is broken, things will swiftly return to normal."

Kalleah sipped at her ale, eyes sliding out of focus as she let her gaze drift over the crowd near the tavern bar. It sounded like the Twin Cities were more dangerous than she'd bargained on, but at the same time, the idea of meeting with two kings who might back her was a strong temptation.

"Where are you headed next?" she asked her unlikely ally.

"Back home. There's no point continuing any further—it's just backwater settlements until you hit Whitland."

"Maybe I'll run across you again someday, then," she said.

He raised his mug to her, smiling. "Safe travels, my friend."

9

A Deadly Proposition

When Daymin returned from a long day of inspecting weaknesses in the city wall with his Weavers, he found a crowd of thuggish men and women loitering outside The Queen's Bed.

"We want to talk to you, Your Majesty," said a man with a puckered scar on his forehead. Daymin thought he'd seen him before; he had to be part of the group that kept agitating for violence against Whitland.

"What is it?" Daymin asked warily, glancing around to see if he had support nearby. Several dozen of his soldiers were busy constructing a trebuchet in the main square, using salvaged timbers from a house they had demolished, but The Queen's Bed was empty behind him.

"We don't like the idea of fleeing like cowards. We've got magic, we've got troops ready to fight, so why don't we use them?"

"Are you planning to stay behind to support Holden Queen Ellarie and Holden King Falsted, then?" Daymin asked.

"No. I'm talking about using the rest of your Varse-damned army for more than carrying sacks of grain."

"What do you mean?"

"The Whitish haven't just abandoned the rest of Itrea to hole up in Twenty-League Town, have they?"

"No."

"Well, there aren't walls around every town they've taken. We'd like you to use that massive bloody army of yours to attack the Whitish wherever they're undefended. Give them some of the same as we're getting. It'd make a difference, I'll bet. Stretch them thin. Buy the rest of our people more time to get to safety."

Daymin's first instinct was to dismiss the proposal at once, but the idea of buying more time for his evacuees was valid. He worried Baylore wouldn't hold for more than a day or two, which could mean the army would chase his civilians down just outside the city.

"Thank you for bringing this up," he said at last. "I'll think about it."

The scarred man took a step toward Daymin, rolling a shoulder threateningly as he loomed over him. "I'd do that, Your Majesty. If you don't do anything with that army of yours, we'll make it very challenging for you when it comes time to leave. Don't forget it."

* * *

Back at her ship, Kalleah found her small crew clustered around a scrap of paper on the dining table.

"What's this?" she asked, pulling off her hat and letting her braid fall against her back.

"Read it," Leoth said.

She stepped up to the table and bent over the paper.

We are working to destabilize the Whitish throne and believe you might be interested in joining us. You can find us at the Temple of Totoleon outside Darrenmark.

"Do they know who we are?" she asked in alarm.

"It almost sounds like they do," Mellicante said. "If someone here has a means of communicating with Eidervell, they might very well have heard about our fleet. Anyone who saw the attack will know exactly who our ships belong to."

"But how did someone get in here without us noticing?" Baridya asked, eyes round with worry.

"Abeytu and the others have been staying out of sight, not guarding our ship," Mellicante said. "It wouldn't have been hard for someone to slip past them."

"I think the more important question is whether this is a trap or a useful lead," Leoth said.

Kalleah wondered if it was the man in the tavern who had given them away. If he had heard any news at all in the past six spans, he might have been able to guess at her identity. Certainly there were not many Itrean women sailing around the Kinship Thrones in these times.

"It could be worth—"

Mellicante broke off at the sound of running footsteps along the dock. All four piled up the steps onto the deck, Kalleah stuffing her hair hastily under her hat once more.

It was her friend from the tavern, his hood fallen back, his eyes glinting in the lights from the oil lamps lining the waterfront.

"I thought this was yours," he panted as he slowed at the foot of their gangplank. "Have you seen the ship that just anchored offshore?"

Kalleah stepped around the others, trying to read in his expression whether he was involved with whatever group had left that message. "No. Why?"

"It looks like it belongs to the Lord's Men. When they dock tomorrow morning, they'll make trouble for you. They have the authority to seize your ships and arrest you for defying the High King's orders."

"Do you know this man?" Leoth asked from Kalleah's shoulder.

She ignored him. "Thank you for telling us. Do you know anything about the Temple of Totoleon in Darrenmark?"

"What?" The look he gave her was perfectly blank. She knew at once that he was not related to the strange invitation.

"Never mind. Thank you again. And safe travels."

He gave her an Itrean salute, fist to his chest, before jogging back along the docks.

"I spoke to him earlier," Kalleah said, in response to the confused looks of her companions. "He was telling me more about the situation in the Twin Cities. It sounds...tricky, to say the least."

"Gods," Baridya said hollowly. "If he's right, we'd better get out of here straightaway."

"But where do we go?" Mellicante asked. "Back out to sea? Or on to the Twin Cities?"

10

A Diversionary Force

Alone in his room, Daymin ransacked his desk for all the maps he'd brought from the palace. Normally he would have dismissed the suggestion of attacking Whitish-occupied settlements without a second thought, but the idea had taken root in his mind and wouldn't let him rest. Ellarie and Falsted's accusations of cowardice had rattled him; even though he was certain his army could not hold Baylore, he didn't want to give up completely if he still had a chance of evening the odds.

Unfurling his most accurate map of Itrea on his bed, with its many annotations and symbols indicating Whitish occupation, he traced the route from Baylore to the Icebraid Peaks. It didn't look too far, but with no roads to follow and large numbers of children and elderly among the refugees, it could take more than a span. Forty days in which Daymin had to hope the Whitish would not realize what he'd done. If they decided to chase his population down, their cavalry could surround them and cut them down in a matter of days.

But if Daymin took a force south, attacking major Whitish-occupied settlements as he went, he could draw the High King's forces out of Twenty-League Town and away from Baylore. He could torch the bridge at Pelek, cutting off the main supply route from Larkhaven, and ransack the most significant farming towns along the Elygian River. Further south, he could even collapse the mines around Redhill and Coppertown, hampering the army's ability to expand its occupation.

It could work. The bulk of the Whitish army was stationed in Twenty-League Town, so as long as Daymin's forces stayed ahead of those troops, they could wreak havoc without ever coming up against the full Whitish army. And surely the High King wouldn't allow tens of thousands of Daymin's troops to rampage through the countryside unchecked. King Edreon would have to deal with that threat before focusing on Baylore.

When Idorii joined him later that evening, Daymin was still poring over the map. He'd even laid out a few coins to denote the movement of troops, playing out different scenarios based on whether the reinforcements from Chelt arrived unexpectedly while his army was elsewhere. He wasn't certain he wanted to commit to the idea, but it was looking more and more attractive.

"What's this?" Idorii asked, coming up beside Daymin to survey his work.

Daymin raked a hand through his hair. "The group that keeps agitating for violence wants my army to attack Whitish-occupied settlements while the rest of our population flees. They've promised to cause trouble if we don't agree to it. I didn't like the idea at first, but the more I think about it, the more sense it makes."

Idorii studied the map with a frown. "Were you thinking of following the Elygian River south?"

"It makes sense. Those are some of the most strategically significant towns, and if we torched all the bridges, the Cheltish reinforcements would have a much harder time joining the main body of the Whitish army."

"And if the troops from Twenty-League Town caught up with us? Our city wall has been the only reason we've held out so long against them. If we met them on an open field, no amount of magic would save us."

Daymin dug the heels of his hands into his eyes in frustration. "I know. But is it worth taking that risk?"

Idorii took him by the shoulders and turned him away from the map, which was already imprinted in his vision. His nimble fingers ran swiftly down the buttons on Daymin's coat before he pulled it off his shoulders and hung it on the rack near the door. "You were unwilling to sacrifice Ellarie and Falsted's troops a few days ago," Idorii said at last, his voice quiet. "This would be a much greater loss."

"Only if they catch up to us."

"You don't think they will?"

Daymin swept the pile of coins off the map and deposited them on his desk. "I don't know." He rolled up the map and left it on the desk as well, reaching for his nightclothes even though he was far too agitated to sleep.

Idorii slipped away to his adjoining room, leaving the door open, and Daymin heard the sheets rustle as he climbed into bed. He tapped the lights in his own room to extinguish them before climbing into bed, restless energy making him twitchy, as though he'd just drunk a full pot of hot cocoa.

After a few minutes of staring at the slat of moonlight that slipped through his curtains to illuminate the ceiling, Daymin said, "What if this was the only way to keep our evacuees safe? Would it be worth sacrificing my entire army to give them a chance?"

"It's not that straightforward, is it?" Idorii said from the other room, his voice slightly muffled. "You've swept up all of your young, healthy population to serve in the army, so if every one of them died, who would be left? Those who couldn't look after themselves very well."

"There are fit, capable teenagers among the evacuees who could look after the others," Daymin said without conviction.

"And you want to give them that responsibility?"

Daymin sighed. "No."

"Besides, even if every one of our soldiers died, we wouldn't be able to kill off a meaningful portion of the Whitish army. They'd still come after our evacuees, and who would defend them then?"

Daymin sat up in bed, dragging his fingers roughly through his hair in frustration. "I hate this."

"I know."

Both were silent for a moment.

"I'm not keeping you up, am I?" Daymin asked.

"No. I can't sleep either."

"Do you want to come over here? It's hard talking around the wall."

He heard sheets rustling, followed by the soft pad of Idorii's feet as he came through the door. Daymin could barely make out his features in the sliver of moonlight, but he thought Idorii was smiling wanly. After a moment's hesitation, Idorii settled on the bed beside him, both of them leaning against the headboard.

"What would you do if you were king, then?" Daymin asked softly.

Idorii leaned his shoulder against Daymin's. "I have no idea." He was quiet for a moment, his gaze distant. "I'll respect whatever choice you make. It's an ugly situation no matter how it plays out."

"Maybe the Whitish won't catch us. We'll have a head start if we leave before they realize what we're doing."

"True."

"Or maybe the Cheltish reinforcements will come at us from the other direction, and we'll be pinned between two forces."

"Maybe Ellarie and Falsted will hold Baylore and we won't need to distract the Whitish in the first place," Idorii said.

Daymin snorted. "Wouldn't that be useful."

Idorii slipped an arm behind Daymin's back, and Daymin rested his head on Idorii's shoulder. His nerves were feeling frayed; the buoyant energy of the city preparing for departure juxtaposed with their imminent demise was making him feel a bit manic. Idorii's closeness helped ground him, even if wasn't wise.

"You've done the most anyone could do for Itrea," Idorii murmured. "If we all die, it won't be your fault."

"Is that supposed to be reassuring?"

"Maybe." Idorii toyed with Daymin's hair, smoothing his loose curls and tugging a lock into place. Daymin had never liked being touched, even as a child, and had rarely tolerated grooming by his parents or servants. But he liked this. It stirred something in him, something intoxicating yet bewildering.

"I'm glad you're here," he said softly.

Idorii rested his head against Daymin's. "We should try to get some sleep. This won't be any easier in the morning if we're both exhausted."

"Will you stay?"

"Of course."

11

Upriver

At the dark end of one of the docks, Kalleah and Leoth met with representatives from each ship in their fleet. Distant lights from her ships and the lamps on shore danced off the waves, while the stars were muffled beneath a layer of clouds.

"We've been warned that a ship belonging to a brutal law enforcement group from the Twin Cities has just anchored offshore," Kalleah said quietly. "They'll make trouble for us if we aren't gone by morning. The time has come to decide on our next move."

"I saw someone dropping anchor just before sundown," Nandra said grimly. "But what's this group you mentioned?"

"They call themselves the Lord's Men, it seems," Kalleah said, "and they've been working on behalf of King Edreon to make life miserable for everyone in the Twin Cities."

"Brilliant," Captain Jezwick said sarcastically. A brawny

man with a short beard and moustache, he was the merchant from King's Port who had joined Kalleah's fleet just after Nandra. "I'm definitely tempted to make the journey upriver now."

"It could be a good sign, in a way," Kalleah said. "If people in the Twin Cities hate these Lord's Men as much as it appears, they might be angry with King Edreon and eager to throw off his influence."

"Yes, as long as we can survive the encounter," said the pirate captain from King's Port. "Fighting on a river is very different from fighting out at sea. There's nowhere to retreat to if your ship starts taking on too much damage."

"This is why I've gathered you," Kalleah said. "I want to hear your thoughts before we commit to a course of action. Based on what we've seen in Stragmouth, we'd likely have a difficult time in the Twin Cities, but this could also represent exactly the opportunity we'd hoped for."

Kalleah looked around the tight huddle of captains, seven in all, who had abandoned their own lives and followed her for hundreds of leagues. In addition to Nandra and Jezwick, there were three other Cheltish merchants, a smuggler, and a pirate. She could barely make out their faces in the darkness.

"My crew had a hard time even walking around Stragmouth," one of the Cheltish captains said. She was a short woman with a boyish figure and a braid twisted up at the back of her head. "If the Twin Cities are similar, I don't think a boatload of women will do you any good."

"I found the same," Kalleah said grimly.

"I wouldn't risk it," Captain Jezwick said. "Too many unknowns. And no easy way to retreat if harm befalls us inland."

"Where else would we go, then?" Kalleah asked. "We have no other potential allies to turn to if we leave Dardensfell and Kohlmarsh."

"Back to King's Port," Captain Jezwick said; the smuggler and the pirate nodded. "We still have a good chance of ousting the Whitish. Then we could defend the harbor and keep them away from the southern coast altogether."

"To what end?" Kalleah asked. "I like the idea of securing King's Port as much as you, but it wouldn't make any difference to the war as a whole. Sooner or later, King Edreon will sweep through your city and take it along with the rest of the continent."

"Maybe you're thinking a bit too ambitious for the force we have," the pirate captain said gruffly. "We have eight ships crewed by sailors who've barely learned to handle a sword, yet you somehow think we'll be able to turn the tides of war. We can't capture a single town, let alone defeat King Edreon's armies."

"You forget this is Queen Kalleah you're speaking to," Leoth said. "Her voice resonates throughout the known world."

"Not if she's locked away," the pirate said stubbornly.

Kalleah stepped on Leoth's foot when he opened his mouth for a retort. She didn't want him staking too much on her power as queen; her influence in the Kinship Thrones was illusory at best.

"I had envisioned a diplomatic mission, not a military assault," Kalleah said. "And if we were to approach the Twin Cities, we would do it in a way that did not raise undue attention. We would need to approach as a single ship, not as a fleet."

"You'll be delivering yourself right to the Lord's Men," the pirate said.

"Maybe," Kalleah said. "But that would leave the rest of our fleet free to continue our work if we fell into trouble."

"King Leoth is right," the short Cheltish captain said. "We can't do much without you, Your Majesty. And your power. It's the only reason we survived Eidervell."

"King's Port would be easy enough to retake, even without Kalleah's support," Leoth said. "If you wanted to fight, that would be your safest target."

The more they argued against traveling to the Twin Cities, the more Kalleah was convinced that this was their only option. None of the alternatives would make a difference to the war as a whole. Now that Chelt was subdued, Dardensfell and Kohlmarsh were the only remaining kingdoms with populations and wealth significant enough to challenge Whitland.

And if she truly wanted to topple Whitland and ensure they would never attack Itrea again, she had to get a better grasp on the politics of the Kinship Thrones. The more she learned, the less sense it made; each of the kingdoms appeared to present very different faces depending on whom they were dealing with, and at the moment all were making a show of subservience to Whitland. But as long as their kings groveled and hid the truth, none would be able to forge alliances that might change their fates.

It was a many-faceted puzzle, and Kalleah would not be able to make progress without discovering how the pieces fit together.

Kalleah waited for Nandra to finish speaking before rejoining the debate.

"I've decided to take the Whitish ship upriver with a small

crew," she said.

The short Cheltish woman had opened her mouth as if to reply to Nandra, but she snapped it closed and looked at Kalleah in surprise.

"I will travel with Leoth, Mellicante, and Baridya, while our crewmembers from Cashabree will join a different ship. We can take as many as seven volunteers with us, one from each of your ships. Men, if at all possible. Though if you don't want to send a representative, I won't be offended. The rest of you will follow the coast of Kohlmarsh until you find some friendly port where you can wait for us to rejoin you."

"And if you don't return?" Captain Jezwick asked.

"Give us three spans. If we don't appear in that time, sail to King's Port and reclaim the city to make your stand there."

12

A Bid for Supplies

The Varos-damned physician had only made Edreon's wound worse.

He felt sore and achy all over, and when his own attendants unwrapped the bandages, he glimpsed a bright red halo of skin indicating infection. Though none brought the matter up with him directly—perhaps fearing his wrath—he overheard their worried muttering as they redressed the wound. Unless his shipment of enchanted trees arrived soon, he was almost certain to lose the leg. Or perhaps die; he wasn't sure which was more likely.

As soon as his attendants bowed their way from his room, leaving the air reeking from the foul wound, Edreon dragged himself into a sitting position. He reached for the journal linked to Lord Juriel, the general who had formerly presided over Darkland Fort. His most recent communications indicated the army from Darkland Fort had settled in at Twenty-League

Town.

When he lifted his quill and wrote, his handwriting was uneven in places, growing crabbed and shaky whenever a wave of pain gripped him.

Lord Juriel —

When can we expect the next shipment of wood to arrive in Whitland? Our need has grown dire. If there is any way to speed this along, make it your priority.

High King Edreon Desterial

The reply did not come until much later that afternoon, following a luncheon Edreon could barely stomach and a visit from Marviak, who treated him as if he were on his deathbed.

At last Edreon opened his journal to find a lengthy missive from Lord Juriel.

Your Majesty —

We have chosen to send the first of the logs floating down the Elygian River to King's Port, which should be far more expedient than transporting them by land. Our men scouted the route on the previous trip and did not find any obstacles that appeared unsurpassable. A troop of soldiers will follow on horseback to ensure their safe delivery. At this rate, they could arrive in King's Port in a matter of days, and thence on to Eidervell.

Begging your pardon, but the transportation of logs will not strike your men at Twenty-League Town as a priority. We are running dangerously low on foodstuffs, and despite heavy rationing and requisitioning of stores from nearby settlements, we have at most a quarter before our supplies run out altogether. Our soldiers are weakening; seven have already collapsed after overexerting themselves. It is a dangerous situation all around, and unless we can either take Baylore or cut a path through the Wandering Woods in a matter of days, we may be forced to retreat to King's Port.

We await your orders with desperation.

Your faithful servant,
Lord General Juriel

Edreon let the journal fall shut with a thud. *Hunter's blood.* Caught up in his own convalescence, he had fully neglected his troops in Itrea.

Pain lanced through his leg once again. Edreon dug his fingers into the uninjured flesh below the wound, desperate for any relief. He felt trapped in this useless body.

When the pain subsided at last, he slumped back against his pillow and reached for the journal. As High King, he was not supposed to be beholden to the weaknesses of mortal flesh. That was part of why he had scorned his father at the end of his life; instead of seeing the war in Itrea through to completion, he had allowed his physical weakness to undermine his military strategy.

But Edreon had now done the same. He had let the pain become everything, and in doing so, he had lost sight of his grand vision for Whitland.

Pull yourself together, you Varos-damned fool. You're not dying.

Twisting at an uncomfortable angle to hold the quill without shifting his leg, Edreon wrote a painstaking reply.

> *Baylore is our quickest path to seizing provisions. The fight against the Wandering Woods will be much slower.*
>
> *Prepare for immediate attack. Without the forest guarding Baylore, we won't have any trouble toppling their defenses, even if they defeat our towers.*
>
> *However, you must damage the city itself as little as possible. There are valuable secrets to learn from Itrea—secrets that do not involve magic—including medical practices and the delivery of water into homes in Baylore. I wish to study their manuscripts and infrastructure to take what we can for Whitland. The Truthbringers were reluctantly impressed by the cleanliness and health of the city, and I see no reason why the seat of the High King should not enjoy similar standards.*
>
> *If the fight stalls, use the deadly gases prepared by your captives to exterminate the population without resorting to trebuchets.*
>
> *I await news of your success.*

Edreon did not like to refer to any of the magic races involved in his work at Darkland Fort, in case his writing was read by someone who wished him ill; when he had set up the experiment in the years before his father's death, he had been careful to burn each correspondence as it was sent or received. The parchment in the holy relics could be replaced without the link being destroyed as long as both journals were re-bound at the same time. Edreon did not doubt they were magical artifacts rather than holy relics, but since the same art did not seem to exist in Baylore, it was a convenient story for the royal family to continue telling themselves.

"Holy Varos," Edreon muttered, sliding down in his bed once more as he let the journal fall to his side. The pain in his leg spiked yet again, and he wondered if it was possible to die of sheer agony.

Before he could sink back into a feverish sleep, the door opened without a warning knock to admit Naresha and a hooded man.

"What's this?" Edreon mumbled, peering at them through half-lidded eyes.

Naresha shut the door swiftly. "This is the healer you asked for," Naresha said quietly. "The devotee of Tabanus."

As Naresha bolted the door, the healer lowered his hood and bowed deeply. "Your servant, Your Majesty. We have all been grateful for your lenience toward the Alldrosants."

Edreon grunted. "So? Can you help me?"

The healer approached, and Edreon got a better look at him—a thin, grey-haired man with a pointed beard, slight enough for a gust of wind to knock him over. "That depends on the injury, Your Majesty. May I examine your leg?"

Edreon locked his hands over his stomach, trying not to groan when Naresha and the healer rolled down his blankets. As the healer began unwinding the bandages, a putrid odor filled the room, so foul that Edreon gagged. To his amazement, Naresha remained unflinchingly by his side. She was no ordinary woman.

"The infection has spread nearly to your groin, Your Majesty," the healer said with a pinched expression. "I can treat the surface infection, but that deep, we will have to see if your body mends itself. If I had been brought in from the start…"

"Even this could lose me my throne," Edreon said tightly. "I couldn't risk seeing a heretic before my own royal physician tended to me."

"Their methods are crude at best," the healer said. "Ours have been rigorously tested on all manner of wounds."

"Can you help, then?" Edreon asked.

"I'll do what I can, Your Majesty. But I worry you won't survive the infection unless we amputate your leg."

"I won't allow it. Do what you must, but leave my leg intact."

The healer paused a beat. "Very well, Your Majesty."

As the old man worked, Edreon prayed to whatever god would listen that the trees would arrive before the infection claimed his life.

The healer gave Edreon a fibrous chunk of willow bark to chew on, which helped dull the pain, before pouring vinegar over the gash on his leg.

Edreon roared in agony before he could stop himself. He dragged a pillow over his mouth to muffle the sound while Naresha took his hand and gripped it hard.

Then came a dash of fresh water, though the wound continued to burn for several more ragged breaths. At last the pain subsided and Edreon relaxed his crushing grip on Naresha's hand.

"Please consider his advice," Naresha said quietly while the healer packed something that smelled of honey into the wound. "I know losing your leg could compromise your authority, but dying would do so far more expediently. And you still have no heir…"

"Silence, woman," Edreon hissed. It was dangerous to speak of these matters in front of a stranger.

Naresha leaned closer so the healer would not hear. "Why have you not sought a wife?" she whispered. "You have gone to extraordinary measures to secure Whitland's glory. Why do you care so little for extending your legacy beyond your death? You are not immortal, Edreon."

Edreon was not certain of the answer, except that the very idea of marriage repulsed him. He did not like women, as a rule—weak, sniveling creatures that they were—and loathed the idea of sharing his private living quarters with another. He had always been solitary and secretive; he even preferred his dalliances with courtesans to take place away from Eidervell Castle, so as not to intrude on his privacy.

Naresha was an exception. He respected and—and—

Don't mistake lust for affection, Edreon reminded himself sternly.

Besides, even if she were a wealthy noblewoman, he would not want to wed her. He liked keeping their lives separate.

"I'll consider your advice," he said at last, through gritted teeth.

Little though he wished to admit it, Naresha was right. He could not afford to leave his inheritance contested at a time like this.

13

Striking Into the Heart of Itrea

Daymin's scouts found him in the dining room of The Queen's Bed, where he and Idorii were poring over the map of Itrea once more; they had laid claim to a large table in the middle of the room, and Daymin had used coins to mark estimated troop numbers in each settlement and stronghold.

Both looked up, startled, when three scouts dashed through the doors together. All were out of breath and red in the face, and they stopped before him, gasping.

"The Whitish—are readying—for attack," one panted. "Their armies—are assembling—outside Twenty-League Town. They'll likely march—tomorrow."

Daymin and Idorii exchanged a horrified look. Then Daymin pushed back his chair and rose.

"Are you certain?"

"There's a line of those enchanted towers—outside the

town," a different scout said, kneading at his side. "Along with trebuchets and regular siege towers. Soldiers moving everywhere. It'll take a while—to get the towers to Baylore, but they might be planning to march—through the night."

"Thank you," Daymin said. He looked around for his generals, but the dining room was empty aside from a group of teenage Weavers who were playing cards at a booth in the corner. "Get yourselves something to drink and rest for a spell. As for the rest of us…we can't delay any longer."

As the scouts limped off to the bar, Daymin turned back to the map. He and Idorii had been running through a whole list of scenarios, trying to find a route that might not put his troops in as much danger; the problem was, unless he attacked the most strategically significant settlements, the High King was likely to disregard him and keep his attention focused on Baylore.

"I thought we'd have more time," Idorii said hollowly. "Our city can't evacuate in a day, can it?"

"No," Daymin said. "Plagues. This is a mess."

"We have to try to distract them," Idorii said. "There's no other way the refugees will get out in time."

"You really think so?"

Idorii nodded grimly.

Daymin had been second-guessing the suggestion to attack Whitish-held settlements ever since it had been proposed, but he had thought that was only because Idorii deemed it too great a risk. Yet now that Idorii agreed with the idea, he still wasn't convinced it was wise. The Whitish might decide to ignore his army altogether and attack Baylore while it was poorly defended, which wouldn't delay them much at all.

"If the Whitish decide to attack Baylore instead of chasing

us," Daymin said slowly, "we might still be able to buy the refugees time. As long as they can get out of the city before the Whitish attack, King Edreon will surely pursue our army before he chases down our civilians. It will give them a chance either way."

"I just wouldn't count on surviving," Idorii said with a bleak smile.

"No. I won't."

Abandoning the map on the table, still covered in piles of worthless coins, Daymin turned to the door. "Come with me. I'm going to make the announcement."

As soon as he spoke, his stomach began to squirm. There would be no going back from a decision like this.

Idorii followed him to the door, which swung open to admit a gust of warm air. The square baked under a relentless sun, warm for spring, with not a cloud in the sky. The Cloudmages had been unable to continue their work, explaining with much hand-wringing that an odd pressure system had settled over the continent, a force too strong for them to counteract.

At least it had sped along the preparations. The piles of goods had mostly been removed from the streets, either stacked on the supply wagons or returned to their owners' houses. With their own belongings ready to go, many townspeople had joined the effort to build as many new wagons and carts as possible to transport the vast quantities of grains and pulses that would not fit in the existing wagons. They would have to abandon that effort when they fled; Daymin hoped the remaining stores would not mean the difference between survival and starvation for his evacuees.

"I have an announcement to make," Daymin called to the

cartwrights hard at work in the main square.

While he and Idorii crossed to the fountain, those within earshot abandoned their work and drew near. Others were emerging from Market Street; they would have seen the scouts running up from the gates. They knew something was amiss.

When he reached the fountain, Daymin climbed onto the rim and turned to face the small crowd. There were several contingents of troops scattered amongst the townspeople, and Daymin knew they would help spread the word. He could not wait for a larger audience to assemble.

"The Whitish troops in Twenty-League Town are preparing to march on Baylore," Daymin said in a ringing voice. "We can't evacuate our civilians before they arrive. So, to give our people more time, the majority of my army will march forth tomorrow morning to draw the Whitish away from Baylore. As soon as their attention is diverted, our evacuees will start making their way from the city as swiftly as possible. Only a small contingent of troops will travel with them to guard them from attack."

Dozens more had piled into the square as he spoke, pushing the existing crowd inward, and Daymin caught sight of the scarred man who had proposed the idea in the first place. He gave Daymin a fierce grin.

"Why not leave tonight?" shouted one of Daymin's generals.

"We need to march out while it's light," Daymin said. "Our army needs to draw attention if we want to turn the Whitish from Baylore."

"Can't the refugees start fleeing now, at the very least?"

"I want to make sure our ploy works before sending civilians beyond the city wall. If King Edreon decides to ignore our army and proceed with the capture of Baylore, our civilians will fare better within the city."

Still more civilians were pouring into the main square.

"What's this I hear about fighting?" called Jassor, one of the minor nobles in the Reycoran family.

Daymin was reminded again of Uncle Cal's way of handling matters. He ought to be inspiring his people, not discussing logistics. Taking a deep breath, he forced aside the part of himself that objected to stretching the truth.

"We're marching forth to deal a great blow against Whitland!" Daymin called out over the rising chorus of voices. "While our civilians flee, our army will strike deep into the heart of Baylore Valley. The Whitish will struggle to hold Itrea with their farming towns razed, their bridges burned, and their mines collapsed. They will not forget us!"

This coaxed a cheer from the crowd.

"Prepare to leave tomorrow! Our army will march out at dawn, and our civilians later that day. This is it! This is the night we farewell Baylore."

14

Revelry

As the sun went down, Baylore descended into chaos. While harried-looking groups rushed around making last-minute preparations, others brought forth whatever they could not carry from the city for one final, hedonistic celebration.

Countless barrels of wine and mead and ale and rum flowed freely in the main square; when a barrel fell from the back of a cart and cracked open, a great gush of wine ran down Market Street, staining the cobblestones blood-red. Butchers slaughtered any goats and chickens and pigs that could not travel with the army, and a bonfire in the center of the main square sizzled with grease as the meat roasted on a great spit.

While the night deepened, the population grew steadily more inebriated. Bawdy music drifted from every street, townspeople tossed what looked like precious heirlooms into the bonfire in the main square, and more than one civilian seized a soldier at random for a kiss.

Daymin and Idorii watched the revelry from the edge of the main square, accompanied by Tarak, Zahira, and Lalaysha. At the beginning of the night, Daymin had tried to keep his soldiers from indulging along with the civilians, but that attempt had been swiftly abandoned. This might be the last time any of them set foot in their homes, the last night families spent together, the last chance to feast before spans of privation.

Zahira had procured drinks for the five of them, and despite Daymin's best intentions, his head was swimming. Only Idorii seemed to be restraining himself.

Eventually the last of the meat was pulled from the spit and sawed into pieces—Daymin and his friends could not resist pushing their way forward for a slab of searing-hot ham—and then a potion was poured into the fire to make it burn green. When a gang of Flamespinners coaxed the bonfire into a flickering tableau, several groups of musicians congregated in one corner of the square and struck up a popular folk dance.

"Oh, you must dance with me," Zahira said, grabbing Daymin by the arm and shoving her mug into Tarak's hand.

"D'you even know this dance?" Daymin asked.

"I learned it while I was staying in the city. Come on, it's easy!"

Throwing a pleading look at Idorii, who just laughed, Daymin followed Zahira to the space that was clearing between The Queen's Bed and the bonfire. He shoved the last of the ham into his mouth and wiped his greasy hand on his coat.

Before he was ready, Zahira dragged him into the tangle of pairs who were already dancing to the lively tune. It wasn't the least bit easy, but as long as he followed wherever Zahira led,

Daymin was able to keep up.

When the dance slowed to a walking pace, Daymin searched the square for the others. Idorii had retreated to the awning outside The Queen's Bed, where he stood alone, while Tarak and Lalaysha were nowhere in sight. Eventually he spotted them refilling their mugs at one of the nearby barrels.

As the dance picked up pace again, Daymin's gaze kept going back to Idorii. He was watching Daymin with a small, unreadable smile; their eyes met again and again, and each time they did, Daymin felt an odd wrenching in his chest. What was wrong with him?

He needed something more to drink.

The next song was a familiar Bashard, so Zahira convinced him to stay, though he gulped down a mug of spiced rum before complying.

"What're you trying to accomplish?" he slurred when he rejoined her.

"I'm not trying to seduce you, if that's what you're worried about," Zahira said with a sly grin. "I'd say you're already spoken for, hmm?"

Daymin had no idea what she was talking about, but he didn't question it. "Don't you have hundreds of suitors to choose from?"

"No, and even if I did, they're not out here dancing to folk songs. You're much more persuadable than most of the courtiers I know."

Daymin grunted.

"I just enjoy dancing. And this might be the last time I'll ever do this. Has it really hit home that we're leaving? Because it didn't seem real to me until tonight. All of this—it's going to be gone."

Daymin realized with surprise that Zahira's eyes were sparkling with tears. "I'm sorry."

"It's not your fault," Zahira said. "We never could've won."

The dance started, so Daymin pulled Zahira into the familiar steps, finding comfort in the movement. "Are you coming with the army, then?"

"Yes. I might not know how to fight very well, but I can learn. I'm not cowering in the mountains while everyone I love risks their lives in the plains."

Daymin looked at Zahira with renewed respect. Why couldn't he fall in love with her? She was less intimidating now that he'd grown accustomed to her sense of humor, and she was the perfect example of an elegant courtier, though she didn't place any importance in that sort of thing.

Again Daymin felt the odd wrenching somewhere deep in his chest. As he and Zahira turned slowly, he searched for Idorii once more.

He was no longer standing outside The Queen's Bed.

Daymin fumbled his steps, his boot colliding with Zahira's ankle. He found his place in the dance quickly enough, but he felt adrift. He couldn't stop searching the crowd for Idorii, eyes sweeping across the square each time they rotated. At last he spotted a head of silvery hair disappearing down an alleyway that led off the main square.

As soon as the dance finished, Daymin mumbled something about looking for a toilet. Then he slipped away from Zahira.

He shoved his way through the crowd, none of whom realized who he was, until he reached the alleyway. It was lit only by the light spilling from upstairs windows, and as he ventured down the narrow walkway, the Weavers' crystals and flames from the square quickly faded to darkness.

Daymin was beginning to worry he had been mistaken. If he had any enemies still in the city, this was the perfect place for an ambush. But he couldn't turn back yet.

At last he rounded a small woodshed that blocked half the alleyway. Idorii leaned against the wall, one foot propped on the bricks, his eyes dark and intense.

Daymin stopped, breath catching in his throat.

"Daymin?" Idorii asked. "What are you doing here?"

Daymin could only stare at him. He was so beautiful, with his deep brown eyes and high cheekbones and thin lips, which were now pressed together in a resolute way. Daymin felt like a moth drawn to a flame; he would sooner singe his wings and drop crippled to the ground than leave.

With a graceful movement, Idorii pushed off the wall with his foot and straightened. "Were you not enjoying the dancing?" he asked softly.

"No, that was Zahira's—I wasn't—" Idorii's face was very close to his, and Daymin could see his long eyelashes, could feel his breath against his cheeks. He was having a hard time thinking straight. It was probably just the rum. That last mug had been too much.

Then Idorii slid a gentle hand behind Daymin's neck and kissed him.

Oh.

At the touch of Idorii's lips, fire spread through Daymin, burning away the cold of the night and the fog of alcohol, igniting something wild and unknowable deep within him. He hadn't been sure why he had followed Idorii until this moment.

Without thinking, Daymin reached up and dug his fingers into Idorii's hair, drowning in his touch. His lips were soft and warm, his hands—the same long, elegant fingers that had dressed Daymin so many times—now raising goose pimples down his neck. Their bodies collided as Idorii backed Daymin against the wall, and he groaned to feel Idorii's arousal. Daymin gripped the collar of Idorii's coat, pulling him closer, terrified that he might lose him.

All those days of wanting Idorii in his bed, of craving his closeness, of stealing any touch he could manage; how had he denied this for so long?

At last Idorii released him. Both were breathing hard, Idorii's face flushed. Daymin trapped his gaze in the shadows and saw his own openness, his own giddy hunger, mirrored back at him.

But as the cold night air flooded the space between them, reality slammed back into place. As long as he intended to call himself king, he had to follow the rules of his station. He was required to marry a woman and produce an heir; Idorii could have no part in that.

It seemed laughable to worry about such things now, on the eve of their evacuation, since he would soon have neither crown nor throne to claim. Yet with the future of Itrea resting on his already-questionable right to rule, he could not risk casting any further doubt on his legitimacy. Choosing his own happiness over the survival of his people was pure selfishness.

Could he keep Idorii by his side as a lover, posing outwardly as his valet?

Daymin cringed at the thought. He couldn't ask that of

Idorii. He had already ruined his friendship with Lalaysha by taking things too far; he would not do the same here. He would rather spend the rest of his life yearning for something he couldn't have than risk losing Idorii.

But Lalaysha had not accepted that line of reasoning, not until it was too late. Daymin had to make sure Idorii didn't face the same temptation.

Cloudy gods, if I could have just one more kiss...

Steeling himself, he stepped back, withdrawing his hand from Idorii's arm.

"I'm sorry," he said quietly. "I can't do this. I—"

I love you, Idorii.

Idorii's expression closed over. "Of course," he said, voice tight and controlled. "I'm so sorry. I never meant it to go this far—I know it's been me pushing you all along, and I've stepped way past what was appropriate."

"No, that's not—"

Idorii backed away. "Daymin, I—I need to stay in Baylore. To help protect the city as much as I can. Most of your Weavers will be remaining behind, so it's only right."

"No!" Daymin reached out to grab Idorii's arm, but he stepped out of reach. "That's too dangerous! Please. Stay with me."

Idorii shook his head. "Goodbye, Daymin. Safe travels."

Then he was gone.

Daymin slid to the ground, the cobblestones icy beneath him, and wrapped his arms around his knees. He felt like the earth had been wrenched out from under his feet. If Idorii died when Baylore fell, it would be because of him. He wanted to cry.

Dropping his head back against the wall with a thump, he

stared up at the narrow slit of sky he could see between the two roofs. Stars winked overhead, hazy behind a sheen of smoke from the bonfire. The city felt cold and empty without Idorii by his side.

15

The King's Departure

Idorii stumbled back to The Queen's Bed in a haze of misery. From the very start, he had vowed not to get too invested in the idea of a relationship that could never happen, but that did nothing to ease the pain of Daymin's rejection.

What did you expect, you idiot?

Up in the room he had shared with Daymin, he shoved his belongings into a bag and hurried back down the stairs before Daymin returned.

As he shouldered his way through the crowd in the main square, he downed a mug of spiced rum, hoping to dull the ache in his chest; usually he preferred to remain clear-headed, but he was desperate to erase the past hour from his memory. It had hurt even more because Daymin had seemed to welcome his kiss at first.

By the time he reached the palace, Idorii's vision was beginning to waver.

"I've come to help secure the city against the Whitish," he told the guards at the gate, their faces swimming in the darkness. "You know who I am, don't you?"

Someone unlatched the gates and stood back to admit Idorii. He was in no mood to speak to anyone right now, so he followed the familiar route up the stairs to the Makhori quarters under the roof, where he collapsed into his old bed. No one had claimed it, thank the cloudy gods, but it smelled faintly of rat droppings.

It's better this way, Idorii told himself firmly. *Easiest to remove yourself from temptation before it goes too far.*

He'd already proven himself unable to resist. It had started out innocently enough, with flirtatious banter in the messages he had written to Daymin on his arm, but somehow that had led to sharing a bed with someone who had made it clear he was not attracted to men.

I don't believe that, he thought grimly. *Not after tonight.*

But oh, it hurt.

* * *

In the morning, Idorii's head was pounding when he dragged himself out of bed.

He ran into several of the palace Weavers as he stumbled down to the washroom; they had moved back to their former quarters to help guide Ellarie and Falsted's resistance. Etriona did a double-take when she saw him, and Idorii realized with horror that he had forgotten to wrap a scarf around the mark of corruption on his neck.

"What are you doing here?" she asked, reaching for his

shoulder before he slipped away. "Aren't you marching out with King Daymin's troops?"

"Change of plans," Idorii muttered. "I'm staying to help defend Baylore."

"Are you well?" Etriona asked with concern.

"Bloody fantastic."

Idorii pulled free of her grip and hurried to the washroom, where he glared at the spreading pattern of roots that had crept from his shoulder up to his jaw. At least the spikes—now ground to nubs—were only on his arm. He couldn't have shown his face in public if those were visible.

He splashed water over his face and combed out his hair, half-hoping he could delay long enough that he would emerge from the palace to find Daymin already gone.

But he had to see him one last time. No matter how much it killed him.

Turning up the collar of his coat and pulling it tight around his neck, Idorii hurried back to his room to fetch the light scarf he had been wearing to conceal the markings.

Then he followed the river of Weavers and soldiers and courtiers through the palace to the entrance hall. Bodies spilled down the steps and along the wedge of flagstones encircling the palace, many unable to see the square beyond the wall, but Idorii pushed his way right to the wrought-iron gates.

The main square stood empty apart from rows of troops in careful formation.

As he watched, a handful of people emerged from The Queen's Bed—Daymin at the front, in a simple black coat of Weavers' armor, flanked by Prince Calden and Princess Nyla. Behind them trailed Daymin's friends—Tarak, Zahira, and

Lalaysha.

Horses stood waiting outside the inn, and Daymin, Prince Calden, and Princess Nyla mounted, while the others followed on foot. When Daymin nudged his horse forward, the whole column of troops began moving down Market Street, cheers rising from onlookers in every upstairs window.

Idorii's heart tore at his chest as he watched Daymin riding away. But at the same time, the spectacle reminded him how untouchable the king of Itrea truly was. He had allowed himself to forget whom he had fallen in love with; removed from the palace, it had been easy to let convention drop away. Now, as Daymin stepped into the public eye once more, Idorii remembered the guards at the entrance to the Cheltish wing, the vast suite of rooms he presided over, the difficulty of ever sharing a conversation with Daymin away from the watchful eye of the court. He should be grateful for what they had shared. It was more than he could ever have hoped for.

When Daymin reached Market Street, he turned to look up at the palace, hands loose on his reins. He scanned the crowd before his gaze locked on Idorii; his eyes widened, and Idorii could see longing there, as well as fear.

Then Daymin's face hardened. He turned away and followed the gentle curve of Market Street until he was out of sight, leaving Idorii clutching the gates, his insides brittle and hollowed-out.

16

A Scant Lead

Down Market Street Daymin rode, his head pounding at the noise that assailed him from all sides. There were cheers from onlookers and shouts as his soldiers readied the last of the wagons, shrieks of children darting into his column of troops to farewell their parents, and beneath it all the relentless thunder of thousands of marching feet.

He had nearly lost his resolve when he saw Idorii watching him from the palace gates. If not for the audience, he would have ordered Idorii to accompany him, and damn the consequences. Better that Idorii resented him than ended up dead.

But it was too late for that now.

He and probably the rest of the city was suffering from a murderous hangover, the wine-stained streets a vivid reminder of the excesses of the night before. It felt fitting, somehow. A shadow of the blood that would soon be spilled on those same cobblestones.

As they passed through the city gates, the noise finally relented, though Daymin's head continued to throb. No one was speaking much. The cheers of the evacuees had only served to remind him how much their survival depended on his success, unlikely as that was.

"Which way are we going?" Uncle Cal asked quietly. From his bloodshot eyes and haggard expression, he was suffering as much as Daymin.

"Well away from Twenty-League Town," Daymin said. "I don't want to tempt the Whitish army to engage with us before we've even made it to Pelek. But we need to be seen. We'll cut past the guard tower just north of the main road."

The sun glared down from a cloudless sky, aggravating Daymin's headache, though at least the good weather had dried the ground enough to offer solid footing to his army. It was much better to travel in spring than in the dead of winter, especially since he had no hot bath to look forward to at the end of his campaign.

Daymin glanced over his shoulder toward the Icebraid Peaks. The distant range was snow-locked until midsummer, which would not be easy for his refugees. Leaving Baylore did not hit him as hard as it had Zahira, since he had spent most of his life feeling like a stranger there, but facing the vast, open plains without a stronghold to retreat to was unsettling.

As soon as they reached the edge of the circle of farmland surrounding Baylore and crossed the churned-up ring of earth where the ancestor trees had once stood, Daymin turned off the main road. The remains of a toppled Whitish tower lay nearby, and if they traveled directly southeast from there, they would run across the next tower before hitting the main road.

Behind him, Daymin's army snaked all the way back to the city gates. For the first time, he had been forced to take supply wagons on a military campaign, which would slow his progress and limit the terrain he was able to cross. With any luck, he would be able to resupply at settlements along the way, and he intended to abandon the wagons once empty.

By the time the last of his army slipped through the city gates, Daymin had lost sight of them behind the rolling plains.

As the day wore on, a series of scouts on horseback rode past with reports of the Whitish army's movements at Twenty-League Town.

"The Whitish are assembling outside the town wall, Your Majesty."

"No progress toward Baylore yet."

"They must've seen your army, Your Majesty. The troops seem to be in chaos."

Then, before another scout arrived, shouts came from the back of the army. A young man in the dark blue tunic and black trousers of a reserve soldier jogged up, calling out, "Your Majesty! Your Majesty!"

Daymin guided his horse out of the line of soldiers and waited for the young man, who staggered to a halt before him, dropping onto one knee.

"Your Majesty! Whitish riders just captured two of our wagons! They galloped in and seized our supplies before we could move against them, Your Majesty!"

Varse. They had needed those supplies.

"Slow our progress and bring the wagons into the middle of our column," Daymin said. "And we'll turn east, away from the road. The Whitish clearly know our army has mobilized."

But will they take the bait?

As the young man fell back, accompanied by Dellik and a few of her best soldiers, Daymin kneed his horse into a canter to resume his place at the front of the column. Unease churned in his stomach as he shifted their progress eastward at a now-plodding pace—they were much closer to Twenty-League Town than he'd wanted to be when the enemy discovered his maneuver. The Whitish could catch up to them in no time.

But the Whitish cavalry was not large enough to do more than heckle his army. With any luck, the main body of the Whitish army would need time to gather supplies for what could be a longer campaign, which would slow them long enough to give Daymin the advantage.

Unless they decided to proceed with the capture of Baylore…

* * *

The rest of the day passed in tense silence as Daymin's army waited for word from Twenty-League Town. The steady thud of marching footsteps vibrated across the plains with a grim finality. With each step they took from Baylore, they sealed their commitment to what was increasingly appearing to be a suicide mission.

Three more supply wagons were captured before his troops managed to surround the remaining wagons, which would now barely last them past Pelek. Thank the cloudy gods he had ordered his troops to carry two quarters—twenty days—of supplies on their backs. Most of the wagons had remained with the refugees now waiting to leave Baylore.

At last, just as he called a halt to the day's march and ordered his troops to set up camp, a figure came streaking through the grasses. She seemed to burn a fiery orange in the light of the setting sun, and she startled a flock of starlings into the air as she drew near.

"They've given orders to pursue your army!" she shouted as she slowed before Daymin, who was still mounted. "The siege towers are withdrawing into Twenty-League Town, and the army is preparing to chase us down!"

A triumphant roar went up from a group of soldiers nearby.

"When did they set out?" Daymin asked.

"It can't have been long ago. I left before they marched out, so it would've been only an hour or two before sunset. I don't know if they'll march through the night—"

Hoofbeats pounded over the dry earth as Dellik approached, reining her horse in beside Daymin. "Varse-damned bastards. We'll camp in a ring around the wagons." Glancing at the scout, she said, "News from Twenty-League Town?"

"They've decided to chase us."

Dellik smiled grimly. "Well done, Your Majesty."

Daymin tried and failed to return the smile. He still wasn't sure they would last a quarter out here in the plains. Not with the Whitish directly on their tail.

"Another scout has ridden to Baylore with the news, Your Majesty," the scout said. "I imagine the refugees will start moving out tonight. I don't know if the Whitish intend to do the same."

"Not if they hope to pick up our trail," Dellik said. "But if they decide to cut around us and fortify Pelek…"

"We need to get ahead of them," Daymin said. "We'll rise before dawn tomorrow to gain more distance." This whole scheme was starting to seem more and more a disaster.

Uncle Cal approached, saddlebags slung over his arm, and Daymin dismounted beside him.

"Did I hear something about the Whitish pursuing us?" Cal asked.

Daymin nodded, mouth pressed in a thin line.

"They'll catch us before we reach Pelek at this rate."

"I know."

Cal grimaced. "I could gather a handful of Flamespinners and set fire to the grasses around them—chase them back a ways. What do you say?"

"We need to draw them further from Twenty-League Town before we try something like that," Daymin said. "Otherwise they might give up on us and march straight back to Baylore."

"True."

"But if we can keep ahead of them for a few days, that could buy us the time we need. We just need to push ourselves as hard as possible. Maintain the half-day lead we have on them at all costs."

And if they didn't manage it…

Daymin was loath to contemplate what failure would mean.

17

Darrenmark

The further she journeyed upriver from Stragmouth, the more Kalleah felt she had stumbled across a slice of Itrea in the heart of the Kinship Thrones. Apart from the Andalls to the west, which were more jagged and sheer-faced than the Icebraid Peaks, the landscape was remarkably familiar. Wild grasslands stretched into the distance on both sides of the river, just beginning to blush green from the spring rains, and the mud-brick architecture of the towns lining both banks resembled that of many Itrean settlements.

The Lodren River flowed clean and cold, fed by countless streams draining from the Andalls. Unlike the turbulent Elygian River in Itrea, it was gentle, with only the occasional riffles disturbing the glassy surface.

With a favorable wind at their back, Kalleah and her crew were able to sail easily upriver in the small Whitish ship. They had left Abeytu and the two young Ma'oko behind with a

Cheltish merchant ship, instead taking on three volunteers: Desh, a grey-haired smuggler from King's Port; Triyam, a fashionable young merchant from King's Port who wore his hair pulled back in a tail; and Luc, a young sailor from a Cheltish merchant ship who immediately befriended Triyam. The pirates had refused to send a representative, while the other ships had no suitable men aboard.

Baridya tracked their progress on a map they had procured from Stragmouth, and as they neared the Twin Cities, the settlements on both banks grew denser and more developed, until they were traveling past what looked like one long, narrow city split down the middle by the Lodren River. No bridges spanned the water, but countless ferries and fishing boats tied to docks on both sides spoke of a closely intertwined relationship between the two kingdoms. Indeed, Kalleah had heard the Twin Cities referred to by that name far more often than their separate titles, Darrenmark and Kohldar. Though they were ruled over by two different kings, it seemed they operated as a single sprawling metropolis.

At last Kalleah glimpsed the trappings of a city in the distance—spires and domes rising from a hill on the right bank and a more imposing Whitish-style castle dominating the skyline on the left.

Closer still, she was surprised when they passed a substantial wall enclosing the heart of Darrenmark, ending at the riverbank. Kohldar, on the left bank, had no wall of its own. It seemed an odd decision to fortify a city like this while leaving such a long stretch of riverway undefended.

When she commented on it, Leoth said, "Maybe Kohldar was once walled as well. The Twin Cities haven't faced attack in many centuries. It could have fallen into disrepair."

"Before we came here, I'd been under the impression the Kinship Thrones were constantly fighting amongst themselves," Kalleah said.

"I think a lot of that happens within Whitland and around the border between Whitland and Varrival these days," Leoth said, his eyes fixed on the distant towers of Darrenmark. "The kingdoms themselves haven't fought in a couple hundred years."

Leoth had been acting odd ever since they started inland, alternating between coarse humor and introspection; right now he had withdrawn again, his eyes dark, expression unreadable.

"Are you all right?" Kalleah asked quietly, taking Leoth's hand.

He frowned at her. "What are you talking about?" Even with his eyes on her, his gaze was still distant, as if he looked through her.

"Never mind."

She did not release his hand until their small ship glided up to a row of docks on the Darrenmark side. The river traffic was heavier here, with dozens of smaller boats bobbing back and forth like ducks, while the docks were already half-filled with oceangoing ships and riverboats. It was a relief to see that trade had not been cut off altogether; they would have a much easier time escaping the attention of the Lord's Men if they could blend in with other merchant crews.

Triyam and Luc jumped down to tie off their ship as soon as they nudged against the dock—the two were always willing to help, despite Triyam's somewhat prim manner—while Kalleah hurried belowdecks to prepare. The faces around the docks were more diverse than those in Stragmouth, so she didn't need to disguise her Itrean blood this time, but she tucked her hair into a cap once more and wore a heavy coat that hid her curves. Even if she didn't make a convincing man, it would lower the chances of anyone recognizing her.

When she emerged from her room, she found Mellicante similarly attired, with a satchel over one shoulder and a sword beneath her coat. The others were waiting up on deck, so they left Desh behind to guard the ship and ventured onto the shore.

Here, by the docks, a wide street ran along the riverfront, backed by the usual assortment of taverns, inns, fishmongers, and tariff offices. The stench was unbelievable, especially without a sea breeze to clear the air. Rotting fish entrails had caught in the reeds under the docks, the smell so rank she could hardly register anything else, but as they moved away from the water, Kalleah caught the distinct odor of urine and sour ale.

"Bloody varse, that's foul," Mellicante said with a grimace.

"What happened to the harbor rat I used to know?" Baridya teased.

"Larkhaven wasn't like this at all. Well, maybe the stale piss from drunkards, but that washed away when it rained."

"It definitely stank of fish more often than not," Baridya said. "You would've gotten used to it, living there, but I was always shocked after a few spans at sea."

"Not like the Kinship Thrones," Mellicante said. "This is on a completely different scale. Desden was tolerable, but even King's Port was vastly better than that, and my senses weren't dulled when we stayed there."

"King's Port smelled strongly of fish," Baridya said.

"But in a good way. A clean way."

"Because it rained before we went down to the harbor,

remember?"

"Hmph."

"Maybe we should be the ones doing the conquering, not the other way around," Leoth said. "Then we could clean up these sorry excuses for cities."

Kalleah nudged him. "Don't talk like that," she whispered. "We don't know who might be listening."

They ducked into a tavern called The Lost Sailor and found the place packed with all manner of people. There were Varrilans and Ruunans and others with features she did not recognize, but most seemed to have Whitish blood. To her relief, there were a few women scattered around the room; Baridya did not draw attention the way she had in Stragmouth.

Kalleah and her party cut their way through to the bar, Triyam and Luc nearly stepping on her heels. They seemed to think they might be abducted if they strayed too far from her protection.

"Any recommendations for a reputable inn where we might spend the night?" Leoth asked the barkeeper.

He smiled from beneath his beard. "Newly landed, are you? That's brave. I've got a few rooms upstairs, and of course I'll say they're the best in town, eh?"

"Why do you say it's brave?" Mellicante asked sharply.

His smile faded. "Haven't you been warned?"

"About the Lord's Men?" Leoth asked.

"Bane of our lives, they are," the barkeeper said under his breath. "And they're not friendly to merchants neither. Keep your heads down and don't look their way if you can avoid it, is all I'm saying."

They ordered a round of drinks, wanting to learn more, but

the barkeeper refused to discuss the Lord's Men any further. "Not 'round this crowd, I won't. Never know who's keeping watch."

After the initial impression of a bustling waterfront, unease settled in Kalleah's stomach, making the hairs on the back of her neck stand up. At second glance, she realized the tavern crowd was far from the rowdy gathering she would have expected from such a place. Patrons huddled in groups, speaking quietly, and any bursts of laughter were quickly silenced.

"Let's move on," Kalleah said under her breath when Leoth looked as if he was about to order a second round of drinks. "See if any of the other taverns are friendlier."

They wove their way back through the subdued crowd to the waterfront, which now seemed abnormally quiet given the size of the crowd in the tavern. People were keeping off the streets, it seemed.

"Varse," Mellicante swore loudly.

Following her gaze, Kalleah reeled in shock.

Their ship was gone.

"What the plagues is this?" Leoth demanded, striding up to the nearest official-looking passerby. "Our ship has just vanished!"

The man cast a surprised look over the rest of their party before shrugging. "It's the jurisdiction of the Lord's Men to seize merchant ships for King Edreon's army. Didn't they warn you in Stragmouth?"

"But we've sailed from King's Port!" Kalleah said, almost forgetting to keep her voice low in her anger. "The High King has no authority over us!"

"As an unrecognized pirate port, I'd imagine he can do what

he wants with you lot." He grimaced. "We've all been taken aback by how much the Lord's Men are allowed to get away with."

"What about all the other ships here, then?" Kalleah demanded.

"They've either bribed the Lord's Men or worked out deals with them. It's the way of the times, I'm afraid."

Mellicante was still muttering a string of curses.

Kalleah felt dizzy, as if the ground had vanished underfoot.

"What now?" Baridya asked anxiously.

"Where's Desh?" Luc asked.

The name cut through her panic, and Kalleah tried to pull herself together. Her friends were counting on her. "Plagues. I hope he's safe."

"We're stuck in bloody Darrenmark," Leoth said under his breath. "None of us are safe."

Kalleah looked around at her small group, chest knitted tight with worry. They had nothing but what they'd carried, which included only enough coin for a night or two at an inn, and they had no way to escape if they ran into trouble with the Lord's Men. Kalleah couldn't even rely on her powers to keep them safe, because if she revealed who she was, King Edreon might send a full army to hunt her down.

The man who had spoken to them was already walking away, pulling a notebook from his coat pocket as he approached a mountain of crates being unloaded from a nearby riverboat.

"This is it, then," Kalleah said. "We can't back out."

"Gods help us," Baridya whispered.

18

The Borderlands Academy

After so much time spent crossing Whitland by foot, Jayna was overjoyed to ride the ocean swells once again. The Varrilan pirate ship cut smoothly through the water, and the days were brisk and sunny, a constant breeze lending them speed.

Jayna and Hanna tried to stay out of the way as much as possible, never knowing where they stood with the pirate crew, so they had more than enough time to watch the horizon and guess at what awaited them in Itrea.

Yakov had been keeping busy, and Jayna missed his company. Especially since he was the only one who spoke Whitish, aside from the gruff translator. Where Yakov had come across as mature and worldly as he traveled through Whitland, he now deferred to the other pirates, and Jayna could see he didn't fully belong here.

Several days after leaving the Whitish coast behind, Yakov

joined Jayna and Hanna for lunch at the bow. Jayna and Hanna were perched on crates with their bowls on their knees, the salty breeze toying with their hair. Much of what the Varrilan pirates ate was pickled in strange spices, and there seemed to be endless barrels of pungent pickled fish and vegetables she did not recognize. Ordinarily Jayna doubted she would have liked it, but after spans of eating increasingly bland rations on Queen Kalleah's ship, she welcomed the change.

As soon as Yakov settled onto a barrel beside them, Hanna—who was normally so reticent—said, "Jayna told me you attended the Borderlands Academy?"

"I did," Yakov said with a faint smile.

"What was it like? I was originally hoping to attend the academy in Cashabree, but I'm beginning to think the Borderlands Academy might be a more interesting choice."

"Interesting is the right word to describe it," Yakov said, his smile growing. "It certainly gave me a unique insight into the intricacy of politics in the Kinship Thrones."

"Who attends the Academy?"

Jayna shoveled a spoonful of pickled fish and buckwheat into her mouth, disgruntled. Yakov was supposed to be *her* friend. Why was Hanna so determined to monopolize his attention?

But Yakov was warming to the subject. "All sorts. I've never seen such a fascinating mix of cultures, and it's the only place in Whitland where women are allowed to study the same subjects as men."

"What do they study?" Hanna asked.

"A number of disciplines. The Academy isn't just one institution—there are several schools joined under the one name, and I don't fully know what they get up to. A good deal of it is subversive in one way or another."

"What do you mean?" Jayna asked, interested in spite of herself.

Yakov laughed. "Finally caught your attention, have I?"

Jayna scowled at him.

"You would love it. The Academy is a breeding ground for all sorts of international schemes and conspiracies, and plenty of influential people attend. Not royalty, but the people who surround them."

"But what do they actually study?" Hanna asked.

"Never mind that," Jayna said. "I want to know more about these schemes."

Yakov paused for a bite of his meal before setting it aside. "There are several factions that often draw students into their webs. One is made up of women who learn the fighting arts and create secret networks of conspirators throughout Whitland, in hopes they will someday have a chance to overthrow the men who oppress them. Another practices the mystical Ruunan religion, while the Prophet's Eyes are devotees of Totoleon, one of the nine Whitish Gods of Light. Oh, and the assassins who give their services to various kings but ultimately answer to the leaders of the Borderlands Academy."

"So much religion," Hanna said quietly, looking troubled.

"Whitland is deeply religious," Yakov said. "I didn't grasp the extent of it until I enrolled."

"Is Varrival religious?" Jayna asked.

Yakov's eyes went distant, and Jayna sensed he was uncomfortable with the question. "We do worship a god, but she is less...*meddling* than the Whitish gods. She doesn't drive us to war, nor demand the extreme level of devotion I saw at the Academy."

As Hanna pressed him for more details on the different schools and the subjects on offer, Jayna set aside her bowl and rose to stroke Tika's scarlet feathers. The firehawk was perched on the rail, one wing still hanging lopsidedly. She had healed well enough to hold her balance against the wind, but she could not yet fly, so Hanna had been rinsing the vinegar off the pickled fish and feeding them to her until she could hunt again.

Ahead, Dragon wheeled on the thermals high above the ocean, her brown feathers rendering her unremarkable from this distance. Jayna could not get her to scout for other ships the way Tika had done, but Yakov had assured her the pirate ship could outrun any enemy they might encounter.

Jayna glanced back at Hanna and Yakov, sitting so cozily together at the bow, and felt a surge of resentment. Hadn't she and Yakov shared something special in all those days they had walked together through Whitland? Yet here he was, turning all his charm and good looks on Hanna.

She turned her back on them, crossing her arms. She shouldn't let it bother her. When she and Hanna reached Itrea, they would be parting ways with the pirates, never to see them again.

Even so, it was an uncomfortable feeling. She had never been jealous of her friend before.

Eventually Jayna returned to the crate to finish her lunch. When Yakov paused for a breath, she asked, "What were you doing at the Borderlands Academy, anyway? You weren't part of some crazy conspiracy, were you?"

He smiled. "No. It was more a matter of curiosity for me.

I'd always wanted to learn more about the world, and this was one of the only opportunities I had to meet people from every kingdom without getting caught up in the war."

"And you think that would be the place for you?" Jayna asked Hanna with a frown. "All those schemes and such? Would you actually go to the Borderlands Academy?"

Hanna turned her gaze to the horizon ahead, where the waves were a vivid blue beneath the cloudless sky, jostling and splashing as their ship plunged forward. "It doesn't really matter, does it? Because we're heading for Itrea, and even if we survive our journey, I can't see us ever making it back home. Can you?"

Hanna's words sent a thrill of excitement through Jayna. "No," she said. "I can't. And if we do, you'll be far too old to study somewhere like that. Why are you so curious, then?"

Hanna's cheeks reddened, and she threw an embarrassed glance at Yakov. "I suppose because I could see myself taking that route instead of following you to Itrea."

"What—are you regretting this?" Jayna's voice rose in alarm.

"No, it's too late for that. I just wanted to know what I could have been missing."

Jayna thought that was a good way for Hanna to drive herself mad, but before she could say this, Yakov spoke.

"With this war spreading, the Academy may not be around much longer. If King Edreon gets wind of its involvement in subversive activities, he might shut it down before it becomes a threat to his reign."

"Oh," Hanna said in a small voice.

"Are you sad that a school you can't even attend might shut down in some hypothetical future?" Jayna asked incredulously.

Hanna laughed softly. "It sounds stupid when you say it that way."

"No, I know what you mean," Yakov said, and his eyes were distant, his hand trailing from the rail to catch sprays of seawater as they shot up beneath the bow. "Before the war, the world was such a vibrant place, and I could dream of traveling to far-off lands and connecting all the major trade routes in a big loop on land and at sea. Even if I had never achieved it, I liked knowing the possibility was there. Now I'd be asking to be captured or killed if I tried anything of the sort. It hurts, knowing how much we've lost."

Though she was annoyed that Yakov had taken Hanna's side against her, Jayna had to admit his words rang true. She had always dreamed of visiting Baylore because of what it had been before the war, not because she had truly wanted to get herself trapped in a city under siege.

And now that she was on her way to Itrea, she knew she would soon confront the reality that none of the beautiful places she expected to find were as she had imagined. The picturesque port city of Larkhaven was under Whitish occupation and too dangerous to approach, the famous forest road would be patrolled heavily, the inns that had once lined the trade route would be derelict or in enemy hands, and Baylore was on the brink of collapse.

Why couldn't she have lived fifty years earlier, when her father would have readily agreed to her taking the position as record-keeper of Baylore?

But that wasn't the world they lived in. Not any longer.

Jayna was still determined to see what remained of Itrea. If she could not chronicle the kingdom's final days, it would slide quietly into oblivion. And that would be the saddest loss of all.

19

The First to Leave

Jakovi was glad to leave the city. Staying with Letto had not been as easy as he had imagined—the constant bustle of the warehouse where they had slept was fraying at his nerves, and he worried he might lose control if he couldn't escape before long.

Thankfully, Letto would be guarding the front of the line of refugees, which meant he and Jakovi were among the first to leave Baylore.

Wagons and civilians were already spilling onto the road outside Baylore when the front guard reached the city gates. No one was on horseback, since all the horses had left with King Daymin's army, so it was difficult to see who was in charge and make sense of the chaos. Jakovi clung to Letto like a burr, following a half-step behind him and accidentally catching his heel more than once. Thankfully, Letto did not seem annoyed.

While Letto pushed his way through the crowd, Jakovi tried

to take everything in, still overwhelmed by so much *life* all packed into one space. Wagons and carts were flooding through the gates, clogging the road and jostling for space along the wall, and the oxen and donkeys pulling them added to the clamor. There were countless hand-drawn carts as well, with their goods lashed tightly in place since they tipped at a precarious angle when set down. Between these flowed rivers of people, some in finery, most in simple garb. Jakovi spotted dozens of refugees in tattered clothes, the same he had seen huddled in the streets, and he wondered if they regretted leaving their homes now that Baylore was no longer a safe haven.

Soon he couldn't take in anything more, so he fixed his eyes on Letto's back and tried to ignore the blur of color and movement that passed on either side. Harder to block out was the magic that swarmed him, buzzing in his ears and pulsing against his skin, begging him to let it in. The magic and the crowd and the noise were all wrapped up in one, a building intensity that made his heart pound and his forehead sweat.

When they turned off the main road, Jakovi held his breath, desperate to escape the ceaseless clamor. Maybe here he would find relief.

But now they were walking between a pair of stone walls just barely wide enough for the wagons, and the bodies were packed tighter than ever.

Jakovi sucked in a breath, head spinning, and nearly succumbed to the magic.

Stumbling to the side, he fell against one of the stone walls, planting both palms on the sun-warmed rocks. For a moment he just stood there, taking shuddering breaths and trying to calm himself. He could smell the flowers from the nearby field, but beneath that was the reek of manure, which reminded him of all the animals shoving their way past him and trapping him in the narrow lane.

It wasn't working. He had to escape.

He pushed himself upright again, surprised to see how far Letto had drawn ahead.

He broke into a run, boots scrabbling against the dirt underfoot. He skirted around a cart laden with sacks and brushed against the warm flank of an ox, and then he was past Letto and sprinting around the last clump of wagons and evacuees.

At last he was free. Ahead lay nothing but farmland, muddy and full of weeds, and the lane stretched empty before him, all the way to the place where the farms gave way to wild grasslands.

Jakovi slowed, heartbeat thudding in his ears. He could do this. If he stayed at the front of the column, the emptiness would be enough to temper his magic.

Pounding footsteps behind him made him stiffen, and he fought back the instinct to flee. Instead he turned and saw Letto jogging his way, looking alarmed.

"What was that?" he demanded, slowing to walk beside Jakovi. "You're not trying to run off, are you?"

Jakovi still wasn't sure why Letto had changed sides; he worried the man might be spying on the Itreans. Though if that were the case, he would have tried to follow King Daymin's army, wouldn't he?

Either way, Idorii seemed to trust him. And since Letto would be watching over him while they traveled, he needed to know a few things about how Jakovi's magic worked. To keep everyone safe.

"If I did want to run off, you wouldn't be able to stop me," Jakovi said. "I have to fight all the time to keep from letting the magic in, and it's exhausting. Back there, all those people, and the animals, and the tight spaces…it was too much. When I get overwhelmed, I have a hard time holding the magic back."

Letto was looking at him with a sort of fascinated horror. "When you got us out of Darkland Fort, how did you know what to do? You'd never done anything like that before, had you?"

"No," Jakovi said. "But it was easy." He didn't want to answer any more questions about his magic, especially not from Letto. It was enough for him to know what precautions to take. "If we can, I want to walk at the very front of the evacuees. So I don't have to feel trapped around all those people."

"Of course," Letto said, his mind clearly somewhere else. Then, abruptly, he said, "Could King Edreon have used you as a weapon against your will?"

"I don't know." Jakovi definitely did not want to discuss this with Letto. The Whitish had tortured his father for years, and it had been enough to break his spirit and bend him to their will. Jakovi could not say for sure what would have happened if they had given him the same treatment. Would he have fought back with his magic, leaving the whole fortress riddled with corruption? Or would he have resisted, and instead lost his mind?

He never wanted to put that question to the test.

They lapsed into silence, their boots scuffing the dirt, the parade of animals and people and carts groaning away behind them.

When they reached the end of the farm fields and left the narrow lane behind, Jakovi felt like he could breathe deeply for the first time in quarters. The air was fresh out here, the intensity of the throng of bodies tempered by emptiness.

And for the first time, he was able to appreciate the view of the distant Icebraid Peaks rising like teeth from the horizon. There was something about seeing a landmark so far away that filled him with hope.

Hope that maybe somewhere in this vast world, he would find a place where he could hide. Away from the war, away from the kings who thought they could twist his power to their benefit, away from the horrors that would unleash.

20

Bennett

After making the rounds through the waterfront taverns, Kalleah's group had ended up back at The Lost Sailor. Mellicante had found Desh cowering in an alleyway with a red mark down the side of his face, and in his embarrassment at being found in such a state, he had been so ungrateful that Mellicante had suggested he hire himself out on the next riverboat heading downstream.

He had apologized, and they had used the last of their coin to hire an entire wing of the inn behind the tavern for the night, so Kalleah had enough space that she would not endanger anyone with her power.

Unfortunately, they could only afford the one night, so the next morning they were all on the edge of panic as they shared the bowls of gruel provided to guests in the dining room. Unless they were able to find a different way to finance their stay, they would be sleeping on the streets tonight.

"I think we should try the palace first," Kalleah said. "If we can find a way to speak directly to King Rodarin, and he is as sympathetic to our cause as we've been led to believe, he might put us up as guests. Then our lack of funds would be irrelevant."

"Wouldn't that be lovely," Baridya said wistfully.

"Do you really want to risk revealing who you are this quickly?" Leoth asked. "Maybe we should keep some of our cards hidden, at least until we know more about the situation."

"We won't have a chance to do that if we end up sleeping on the streets," Mellicante said flatly. "I've seen the Lord's Men harassing beggars, and if we draw their attention, we're done for."

"Come look for employment with me, then," Leoth said. "There are always jobs at the docks that pay a few coins for hard labor."

"Good idea," Mellicante said. "You boys can join us." She nodded at Triyam, Luc, and Desh.

"I still want to scope out the palace," Kalleah said. "We need to know what we're dealing with."

Leoth shot her a hard look. "I don't want you going off on your own."

There was still something *off* about his manner, and the way he spoke irked her. It was as though he was starting to believe women were as useless as they had been treated in Stragmouth.

"I can take care of myself better than any of you," she said sharply. "Or have you forgotten Eidervell?"

"I thought we were trying to avoid that," Leoth said. "Given how far inland we are, without any way to escape."

"I can defend myself in other ways, too." Kalleah shoveled down the last of her gruel—it was bland and lumpy, but it was the last meal they were guaranteed to receive—and stood with a huff. She was already dressed as a man, with her hair tucked under her hat and a coat and baggy trousers hiding her curves, so she stalked to the door and let herself onto the street that followed the riverbank.

As before, the smell overwhelmed her, setting her breakfast churning in her stomach. But she quickly left the worst of it behind as she started up the road winding toward the palace.

The city sloped gradually up from the river, the houses growing larger and more imposing the further she climbed, and at the top perched the palace, surrounded on three sides by sheer cliffs. Most of the buildings were two stories, built of grey stone, and the narrow, curving main street was lined with businesses of every sort. There were cafes, tailors, spice merchants, jewelers, bakeries, bookshops, glass merchants, and much more, though a surprising number of the shops were dark, their doors locked.

Kalleah enjoyed walking alone, especially since she could blend into the crowd here. It gave her the space to think.

Leoth's behavior was worrying her. There was something about being around these people, with their backward ways, that seemed to trigger the behavior she'd seen when she first met him all those years ago. And she wasn't sure whether he was doing it out of fear or instinct, because this was how he'd been raised to act. To think less of those with magic, especially the forbidden races, and to give credence to the cruel teachings of the Whitish gods.

She didn't blame him for it, because she knew how hard he had fought to escape his parents' influence—and how much he had suffered for it. But it scared her.

The street grew steeper underfoot, and the shops finer.

Here there were no boarded-up storefronts; these establishments were frequented by well-dressed gentry who seemed unaffected by the slowing of trade. Kalleah caught a whiff of incense drifting from a store that sold fine furniture and tableware, and everywhere the clatter of footsteps was accompanied by swishing skirts.

Now she was starting to attract a few odd looks. The foot traffic in this part of town was not nearly as diverse as what she had seen lower down, and her brown skin stood out like a stain.

Kalleah moved to the side of the street, hugging the shadows, and kept her head down as she skirted around a gaggle of noblewomen with feathered hairpieces.

At last the street gave way to a wide stairway ascending to the palace gates. The stairs were heavily guarded on either side by Whitish brutes—they had to be the Lord's Men. They wore leather vests and jerkins in place of armor, with no uniform to distinguish them, though each wore the same thick black belt with a wolf's head worked in silver on the buckle.

Kalleah doubted they would grant her an audience with the king, and she was just trying to decide which side street running along the base of the cliff she wanted to explore first when one marched down the steps and seized her by the wrist.

"Unhand me!" Kalleah demanded, pitching her voice as low as she could.

"What is an Itrean doing in Darrenmark?" the man growled.

While Kalleah twisted her arm, trying to free it from his grasp, more of the Lord's Men descended the steps to surround her. His grip was painfully tight, his fingers digging into the soft flesh on the inside of her wrist. "I'm a merchant from King's Port," she gasped, her pitch rising as she panicked.

Varse—if they realized she was a woman, she would be in deep trouble. How had she gotten herself into this mess? Was she that conspicuous?

The brute twisted her arm to stop her from struggling, and Kalleah hissed in pain.

"What is a piece of demon spawn doing at our palace?"

"I was—hoping to make new contacts in the Twin Cities, now that trade with Chelt is getting challenging. The street ended at the palace, and I was—trying to remember the way back to—"

Kalleah broke off with a grunt as he twisted her arm further.

"Your place is down by the docks, with the rest of the scum," another guard spat. "We don't welcome Itreans here. You're nothing but vermin."

The first guard shoved Kalleah forward, releasing her arm as he did, and she fell to her knees, grazing her palms.

Every instinct told her to jump to her feet and face her enemy head-on, but she suspected that would be as dangerous as approaching the palace in the first place. So she stayed on her hands and knees, saying, "I'm sorry. I'll leave right now."

When she tried to crawl forward, a booted foot came flying toward her, connecting with her ribs.

She collapsed sideways, curling around the place he'd kicked her, and her hat nearly slipped as she fell.

"That'll teach you to bring your filth to Darrenmark," the man said coldly.

Another boot came swinging her way, but this time Kalleah was able to twist out of the way and avoid the worst of the impact.

She shrank in on herself, frantically trying to find a way out.

Fighting back would make the situation worse, but she couldn't let them keep beating her up until they tired of it. She felt as though she was back in Baylore in the days before her coronation, the crowd on Market Street pelting her with rotten fruit.

Only this time there was no palace to escape to.

Before the Lord's Men could abuse her any further, a man's shout rang out from the street.

Kalleah unfolded enough to see the circle of guards parting before a handsome man. He was a handful of years younger than her, dressed in subdued finery, and his brown hair hung in waves to his shoulders.

"Pardon me," he said, bowing graciously to the brutes. "I believe there has been a misunderstanding. I invited this charming new arrival to speak with me about a business venture, and he seems to have lost his way."

"Yes, of course," Kalleah said, jumping to her feet and dusting off the grit from the road. "Apologies for the scene I've caused."

"No harm done," he said, waving a hand dismissively. "Now, if you'll follow me this way…"

Kalleah hurried after him, the Lord's Men scowling at her retreating back. It infuriated her that she had needed to be saved by a man yet again.

As soon as they rounded the corner, Kalleah hissed, "Who are you, and why did you try to protect me back there?"

"I saw you at the tavern this morning, with your companions," he said, bending at the waist in a slight bow without slowing his pace. "My name is Bennett, and I've been staying at The Lost Sailor for several quarters now. I saw your ship taken just after you arrived, and I know you've disguised yourself as a man."

Kalleah shot him a disgruntled look.

"What can I say? I was intrigued. We don't see many Itreans in these parts, especially not ones traveling on such an interesting vessel."

"Did you follow me?" Kalleah asked coldly.

"I may have."

"Why?"

Bennett shrugged, giving her an apologetic half-smile. "I thought you might come to harm." When Kalleah glared at him, he said, "Well, I was right, wasn't I?"

They fell quiet as they passed through a crowd of raucous noblemen who looked as though they had been drinking. As they skirted around the last of the group, Bennett did an odd pirouette and cut in front of Kalleah, handing her a leather pouch as he did.

"What—?" Kalleah's eyes widened as she heard coins jingling within the pouch. It was laden with money. "You're a thief!"

This time Bennett gave her a sweeping bow, eyes glinting with humor. "Your servant."

"How did you get the palace guards to leave me alone, then? I thought you were a nobleman!"

"It's all about knowing the right people."

There was something in his flirtatious manner that reminded her of Ricardin, the emissary from King's Port who had been close to her family for many years, and while she did not trust him, she was intrigued.

And as much as she disliked accepting stolen money, she

could see no other way to remain safely in the Twin Cities. She slipped the coin purse into her pocket without thanking Bennett.

When they reached the door to The Lost Sailor, Kalleah was just wondering how she was going to explain the man to her companions when he slipped down a side street and disappeared.

She immediately put a hand to her pocket to check that the purse was still there. It was, and when she untied the drawstrings and drew out a handful of coins, she was relieved to see that the coins were genuine.

With a sigh, she stepped through the door, glad to escape the clamor and stench of the docks. Her bruised ribs were beginning to ache, and the whole experience had left her rattled.

Nothing about this is going to be easy, is it? she thought grimly.

21

Mountains of Books

In the days since Daymin's army had marched from Baylore, Idorii had been combing through every library in the city in search of a spell that might help their forces defeat the enchanted siege towers more readily.

At the moment, toppling the towers required three separate attacks—first the freezing enchantment that would render the towers brittle, next a stone enchanted with the counterspell so it could shatter the steel, and finally an assault with either a Potioneer's explosive or a Flamespinner's fire to destroy the internal mechanisms that powered the siege engines.

It would be challenging to pull off, especially if the towers attacked in many different places at once. Even with a full army of Makhori, they would have struggled to coordinate their defense well enough to keep the city safe; now they were working with a skeleton force, the city virtually drained of the magic races apart from the Weavers who had stayed to help

Idorii. There were fewer than ten Flamespinners among Ellarie and Falsted's troops, and their supplies of Potioneers' explosives were dangerously low after the recent battles at both Darkland Fort and Baylore.

What they needed was an enchantment that bundled all three attacks in one—a spell they could embed in the heavy rocks thrown by their trebuchets, strong enough to bring down a tower with a single hit.

Unfortunately, he could find no freezing spell that would work instantaneously, so it was his job to hunt down the next best option.

At least it kept him busy. Idorii had felt miserable and heartsick ever since Daymin had pushed him away, and his search prevented him from dwelling on it constantly.

It's your own damn fault, he reminded himself for the hundredth time. *You knew all along he could never be yours.*

With a sigh, Idorii pushed aside the book he had been skimming. He was in the University library, piling up likely-looking volumes to investigate more carefully later. The light from the windows was growing dim, so he ought to think about returning home and scrounging up a meal.

When he stood, he discovered a persistent ache in his back. He stretched and twisted, groaning as the knots popped, the sound loud in the silent stacks.

The solitude was starting to weigh on him. Not wanting to interact with Holden Queen Ellarie and Holden King Falsted more than absolutely necessary, he had taken up residence in an abandoned mansion in the Gilded Quarter. It was a relief to have his own living quarters, especially now that he was so hideously disfigured, but he had grown used to having Daymin and Jakovi around.

He wouldn't have minded it if he could have lost himself in his work, but digging through dusty old tomes was more mind-numbing than satisfying. He would have given anything to get his magic back.

Loading the stack of books into his arms, Idorii stumbled from the library, not bothering to lock the door. Only food held value to thieves these days, and besides, most of them had evacuated along with the rest of the population.

Outside, Idorii blinked several times, waiting for his eyes to adjust to the twilit streets. Staring at cramped text all day was making his vision blur, and he felt the beginnings of a headache.

His manor was just a block from the University gates, so Idorii let himself in a few minutes later, his footsteps echoing through the cavernous entryway. He had turned the spacious sitting room into a warren of book piles, which he had organized by source, and he stooped to add his latest finds to the collection.

In the kitchen, which was designed for a chef working with multiple assistants, Idorii lit the fire in the stove. He had never cooked for himself before, instead indulging in the generous feasts prepared for palace staff, so his skills were limited to boiling millet and potatoes and frying eggs on a skillet. There was little else to choose from these days—though he had been grateful to find salad greens planted in the manor garden—and his own lack of skill made him appreciate the creative ways the palace kitchens had served their meager rations.

While he waited for the water to boil, Idorii rolled up his sleeve without thinking and wrote, *You would not believe how many Varse-damned libraries this city has. If we combined them all, they might amount to the largest library in the world. Not the most useful, mind.*

How goes the campaign?

Then he threw aside his pen in annoyance. Writing to Daymin was exactly what had gotten him into this mess in the first place. He had sworn not to reach out unless he had something valuable to communicate, and this was certainly not that.

Seizing a dish towel, he wetted it and scrubbed off the ink.

Plagues, he missed Daymin.

Once his boiled potato and fried egg were ready, Idorii sloped back to the sitting room to eat, sinking into an armchair overlooking the mountains of books.

Before him lay hundreds of volumes on Weaver's magic and on combining the various magical disciplines. They represented only the barest fraction of what Baylore held. The city was a vast repository of knowledge—not equal to Cashabree, perhaps, yet representing centuries of magical study.

And when the Whitish took Baylore, all would be destroyed.

Idorii's mood, already bleak, darkened further. Their people could evacuate, and the city could be rebuilt, but this was a loss they could not recover from.

Without the knowledge contained within these libraries, they would be set back to the days of the First Fleet, relying on memory and oral records to preserve fragments of the whole.

Worse, if the refugees were forced into battle as they fled, the Makhori with the deepest understanding of their craft could die before they had a chance to pass their knowledge on.

Idorii took a bite of his egg, no longer seeing the room before him.

What if there was a way to preserve the most valuable

knowledge Baylore held? What if he could carry those irreplaceable volumes to safety, to give his people a better chance at rebuilding what they had lost?

If there was a way to do it, he had to try.

22

Grassfires

Daymin's army was nearing Pelek at last. The supply wagons had slowed their pace to a crawl, and they had only maintained their lead on the Whitish army because the wagons had traveled through the night, their drivers swapping out oxen for warhorses when they began to tire.

Only Daymin and his commanders remained on horseback. Dellik had ridden forward with a small force guarding the supply wagons, while Uncle Cal formed the rear guard along with the rest of the army's Flamespinners.

Rather than marching, his army shuffled along despondently, the wild grasses rustling as they passed. After a wet early spring, the plains were unusually verdant, and large flocks of birds wheeled in the sky overhead.

Riding alone amidst a sea of foot soldiers, Daymin had far too much time to think. Again and again he envisioned the path of destruction he would carve through Baylore Valley, trying to foresee every possible place where his army might be trapped, though without the map before him, this exercise was more paranoia-inducing than useful.

And when he wasn't envisioning his army's downfall, he was missing Idorii so much it hurt. He had received no word from Idorii since he had left Baylore, and he was furious with himself for handling the situation so badly. This was exactly what he had wanted to avoid—taking things too far and ruining his friendship with Idorii when he was unable to offer him a true partnership.

But maybe it was too late for that.

Until Idorii had kissed him, Daymin hadn't realized how deep his own feelings ran. Without understanding what he was doing, he had pulled Idorii into his life in countless ways—he had become a confidant, a friend, a bedfellow; someone to bounce ideas off, to commiserate with, to come home to at the end of a long day.

And when he had rejected Idorii's kiss, Idorii must have taken it as a rejection of everything they had shared.

Plagues.

Daymin wanted him back desperately.

But Idorii was trapped in a doomed city while Daymin marched to war, and if they were both alive in a span's time, it would be a miracle.

A shout from the rear of the army dragged Daymin from his miserable thoughts.

He twisted in his saddle, looking over his shoulder, but the army was stretched out in such a long column that he couldn't see the end behind the gently undulating plains.

Then a man on horseback thundered into view, galloping at

full speed along the edge of the column. Even before he could see the man's face, Daymin knew it was Uncle Cal.

"The Whitish are closing in on us!" Cal shouted, leaning forward over his horse's neck. "They'll have us cornered by nightfall!"

Daymin guided his horse to the edge of the column, pulse racing. He knew what he had to do next, and if it backfired, the Whitish might turn around and attack Baylore instead of pursuing his army.

Uncle Cal reined in his horse just before he reached Daymin. The beast was breathing hard, prancing restlessly as though it sensed its rider's agitation.

"Are you ready for me to give the orders?" Cal asked grimly.

"We can't wait any longer," Daymin said. "Are you sure the fires won't endanger our troops?"

"The greater danger is that the grasses are too wet to hold a flame."

"Do what you can," Daymin said. "And see if you can force the Whitish army northeast, away from Baylore and away from us. The rest of our troops can pick up speed until we catch up to the wagons."

"Yes, Your Majesty." Cal gave Daymin a salute, fist to his chest. "We will meet you in Pelek."

When Cal spurred his horse back the way he had come, Daymin guided his own mount up a short rise that gave him a better vantage over his troops.

"The Whitish are near!" he called out. "We need to make haste to Pelek while our Flamespinners hold their forces at bay. Forward march, as fast as you can manage, or we may not reach Pelek alive!"

He regretted the dire words as soon as they left his mouth, but at least his army was listening—those within earshot began jogging, despite the heavy packs on their backs, while the rest of the column quickened their pace as his commanders passed the orders down the line.

Daymin kicked his horse into a gallop, streaking past the disordered ranks of soldiers, the heavy thudding of hoofbeats rattling through him and drowning out the clatter of his jogging troops. Soon he had passed the front of his army and was closing the distance to the plodding supply wagons. The sun was dropping low in the sky, so if they could force the Whitish back far enough, they might have another night to reach Pelek and orchestrate their attack.

When he caught up to the supply wagons, Dellik cantered over to intercept him.

"What's happening?" she demanded.

"The Whitish have nearly reached us. Prince Calden is going to try to hold them off while the rest of our troops catch up to you."

"We're still a few hours from Pelek," Dellik said, "and the sun will set before then. Are you planning to attack at night?"

"That depends on how successful we are at diverting the Whitish troops. If there are Itreans in Pelek, I would rather attack in daylight so we don't risk harming civilians. But we might not have a choice."

Dellik nodded grimly.

After a pause, she asked, "How far off are the Whitish?"

"I'm not sure."

Dellik inclined her head toward a granite boulder jutting from the top of a knoll. "Would we be able to see them from there?"

Dismounting swiftly, Daymin handed his reins to one of Dellik's soldiers and set off at a run toward the boulder. He was surprised to hear heavy footsteps behind him a moment later.

He and Dellik dashed up the hillock and scrambled their way up the boulder, the rough granite providing easy purchase. Then they stood side by side, looking back the way they had come.

From here, they could see Daymin's full column of soldiers, and—less than a league behind that—their Whitish pursuers.

Daymin's heart flew into his throat. It seemed his ploy had been more successful than he'd imagined—the army at his tail was nearly equal in size to his own. King Edreon had committed a substantial chunk of his army to stopping Daymin.

It meant he was unlikely to launch an attack against Baylore until Daymin's army had been stopped.

But it also meant his forces could crush Daymin's if the two armies met on the field.

They had to keep ahead of the Whitish. No matter the cost.

"Bloody Varse," Dellik said in a hushed voice.

They watched in silence as a tiny contingent of Itrean soldiers approached the sea of Whitish, the figures no bigger than ants. The wind picked up, ruffling Daymin's hair and whistling through the grasses below, and still the armies moved forward, like ink staining a page.

Then, as Cal's troops neared the front ranks of the Whitish army, a wall of fire sprang up before them.

From this distance, it looked no more substantial than a candle flame. But the Whitish army slowed, and as the Flamespinners spread out along their front line, the wall of fire stretched and grew.

At first, Daymin couldn't tell whether it was the Flamespinners sustaining the fire or if the grass itself had caught alight.

Little by little, the band of flames grew wider, until it was unmistakably a grassfire. As the fire spread, the Flamespinners stretched out their line, lengthening the wall of fire until it stretched past the Whitish army on both ends.

After a confused moment of retreating before the spreading flames, the Whitish army made a frantic charge toward the eastern end of the fire, trying to pass around the wall. But the Flamespinners were extending the blaze faster than they could clear it, and Daymin spotted bursts of fire flaring up directly in the path of the cavalry, spooking the horses and scattering the ranks.

Before long, the Flamespinners had extended the fire all the way northeast to the Elygian River, cutting off any way through.

Now the natural fire was picking up speed, the band of flames growing as the wind drove it on. And at last the Whitish army was forced backward.

"You don't think they'll march straight back to Baylore?" Daymin asked as the Whitish forces picked up speed, their ranks scattering as they fled. "Wasn't there once an old road between Pelek and Baylore?"

"It washed away more than a century ago," Dellik said. "The floods carved a deep gorge in the land running down to the river, so they'll get trapped against that if they head much further north." She hesitated. "It might make sense to attack Pelek in the dark, so the Whitish are sure to see the flames. Once they realize what we're doing, they'll have to stop us."

"I hope you're right," Daymin said.

They watched for a while longer as smoke began billowing from the fires and choking the sky, the setting sun staining the smoke a vivid orange. The Elygian River glowed like a ribbon of gold as the sun dropped toward the horizon, and little by little Daymin's army drew closer to the supply wagons.

Eventually Daymin climbed down from the boulder, stiff after standing on the uneven surface for so long. He and Dellik mounted and spurred their horses in the direction of the wagons, the setting sun blinding them.

When they reached the wagons, Daymin could see a wooden stronghold rising in the distance, which must be attached to Pelek. He hoped the wood had not been harvested from the dead ancestor trees. They rode a short distance further before stopping just outside Pelek. If there were sentries posted at the stronghold, they would have long since spotted Daymin's army, but there was little they could do to defend themselves against such a substantial force.

Daymin left his horse with the wagon-drivers to be fed and watered, and he wandered off into the grasses, desperate for a moment alone. Not far ahead were the first of the stone walls marking the edge of farm fields, but where he stood, the grasslands were still untamed.

They were not far from Darkland Fort. Though they had approached from a different angle, the landscape felt familiar.

Returning so soon after the battle brought memories flooding to the surface. The ring of dead trees that had trapped the harvesting towers so Daymin and Idorii could fell them. The sickening moment when the fortress had collapsed on the Makhori captives in their cells underground. The human casualties that had barely registered in the fight between giants. The way Idorii had risked his life to learn the counterspell.

Idorii…

Daymin ground the heels of his hands into his eyes, furious with himself for letting Idorii stay in Baylore. He should have ordered him to join his army. He should have chased after him and apologized while he still had the chance.

Sinking onto a rock that lay exposed in the grasses, Daymin pushed up his left sleeve. Out of habit, he still carried a pen with him everywhere he went, even though it had been a while since he last wrote to Idorii.

He pressed a thumb to the round symbol embedded in his arm, knowing it was useless but wishing nonetheless.

Nothing happened.

So he bent over his arm and began to write.

Idorii—

We are camped outside Pelek, and being this close to Darkland Fort is bringing back all sorts of memories. Most of them include you. And I can't stop thinking about how wonderful it was when you escaped with Jakovi and I got to see you properly for the first time after writing to you for so many spans.

I am so sorry for how I handled the situation the other night. I was afraid of losing you, but it seems I've gone and done exactly that. I miss you so much it's tearing me apart, and you must know how deeply I care for you, even if I can't be with you that way.

I hope you can find a way to forgive me.

Yours, as always,
Daymin

He read the message over several times before pressing the tattoo. The ink sank into his skin, leaving no trace of the scrawl that had covered his wrist moments before.

He remained where he was for a long time, watching the fields darken as the sun set and the sky deepened to turquoise. From here, he could smell the smoke from the distant fires, and he thought he could make out an orange glow on the northern horizon.

More than once, he pushed up his sleeve to check for a reply. The tattoo hadn't flashed cold, which it did whenever Idorii sent a message, but he expected to hear something soon. At this time of night, Idorii would be eating dinner in the palace dining hall, so it would be easy for him to scribble a response under the table.

Yet nothing came. As the minutes stretched on, Daymin began to worry Idorii no longer wanted anything to do with him. It was Lalaysha all over again.

Plagues. Why am I so useless at this?

He was rubbing his arm in agitation when he heard someone swishing through the grass behind him.

Jumping to his feet, he turned to see Tarak, Zahira, and Lalaysha approaching. They were chewing on strips of jerky as they walked, and when they stopped before Daymin, Tarak held out a hard biscuit and another strip of jerky.

"What are you doing out here?" Zahira asked, peering through the gloom. "You're not trying to scout the town, are you?"

Daymin felt his face heat up, and he was thankful for the darkness. "I was just…remembering the battle of Darkland Fort. So much has changed since then, and it's barely been a couple quarters."

"I know what you mean," Tarak said solemnly. "It's hard to believe we're here again, preparing for another battle. And this is just the beginning."

Daymin nodded.

"How will it happen?" Lalaysha asked.

"Dellik thinks we should attack before sunrise, so the Whitish see the fires from the town," Daymin said. "I don't want to hurt civilians, but everything the Whitish have built needs to burn. If we don't survive this campaign, I want our work to have made a difference, and not just in buying our civilians time to escape."

Tarak and Lalaysha were nodding, while Zahira folded her arms over her chest with an uncharacteristically grim expression.

"How are you feeling?" Daymin asked her.

She shot him a surprised look. "Why do you ask?"

"Because I've dragged you into this ill-conceived suicide mission along with my army, and you've never trained properly, and this is your first time facing the enemy outside the city walls. I—"

"You haven't dragged me anywhere," Zahira said. "Everyone I love is marching to war along with me, and if we don't survive, so be it. This is exactly where I want to be."

As she spoke, her usual certainty returned, her posture straightening. Daymin was not fooled, though. Zahira was as worried as he was.

"Let's try to get a bit of sleep while our Flamespinners catch up to us," Daymin said.

"Can we join you in your tent?" Lalaysha asked quietly.

Tarak hugged her to his side, and Lalaysha leaned into his embrace.

"Of course." Daymin's voice was choked up. With Idorii's absence still eating at him, their company might help stave off the darkness of his thoughts.

23

The Libraries of Baylore

Idorii was digging through a private collection of books in the Weavers' Guild when his tattoo flashed cold.

He felt a swoop of joy, quickly followed by cramping pain.

What did Daymin want from him now?

Plagues, he was desperate for anything Daymin was willing to give him.

And this is why you stayed behind, he reminded himself.

Idorii rolled up his sleeve and pressed the tattoo, chest constricting at the familiar, beloved script.

Cloudy gods. Daymin was apologizing.

What did he mean by it?

Idorii read the final lines over and over, until the words were imprinted in his vision.

I miss you so much it's tearing me apart, and you must

know how deeply I care for you, even if I can't be with you that way.

   I hope you can find a way to forgive me.

Yours, as always,
Daymin

Idorii rose from the stool he had been squatting on and paced the length of the room, working out the cramps in his muscles.

After the initial joy of hearing how much Daymin cared for him, the pain of rejection crept back, stronger than before. When he had kissed Daymin, he had taken a terrible risk, knowing he had sworn not to throw himself at the king yet daring to hope that his affection might be returned.

And Daymin had wanted none of it.

Now, reading Daymin's message for the twentieth time, Idorii began to wonder if Daymin did love him after all. Perhaps he was confused about his feelings, afraid of entering a relationship with a man. Among royalty, it held certain implications of deviance, and Daymin was not one to raise eyebrows if he could avoid it.

Well, he would not push it any further. He had made his own feelings clear, and now it was up to Daymin to decide whether or not he wished to reciprocate.

Besides, he might never see Daymin again. None of this would matter if Idorii died when Baylore fell.

At that cheerful thought, Idorii pulled his sleeve back down. He wasn't ready to write back to Daymin yet, not when the ache was still so raw.

It was getting late, so Idorii gathered up the pile of books he had set aside and extinguished the lights in the library. It was no more than a narrow room that spanned several houses, with doors through to three separate Weavers' shops, yet it had contained countless spells Idorii had never come across before. He supposed he had been trained for a very particular use of magic during his upbringing in the palace, and spells for keeping out vermin, warding cloth against stains, and heating water more efficiently had not come into it.

Arms loaded with books, Idorii pushed open the shop door with his shoulder and stepped onto the dark street. With so many homes lying empty, the only lights came from streetlamps on the main throughfares. Here and there, the odd window glowed jewel-bright against the gloom, but they were outnumbered by dwellings that lay half in ruins, their frames raided to build wagons.

Idorii picked his way through the mess, which included the remains of the final celebration. The street-cleaners were gone, as were the shopkeepers who would have kept their storefronts tidy and well-presented, and in their absence, no one seemed to care. The air was bitter, and Market Street still smelled of wine, stronger after drying and baking to the cobblestones.

The abandoned city filled Idorii with melancholy. This was the end of an age, and it had never been so apparent as it was in the bones of their once-great capital.

He picked up his pace, the heels of his boots echoing eerily in the deserted alleyways. Rats scrabbled into the shadows before him, and unlatched shutters creaked in the breeze.

When Idorii finally reached the manor he had taken over, he shut the door and latched it quickly, leaning against the doorframe in relief. Even though he knew there was very little danger while the city stood deserted, walking through the empty streets unnerved him. He needed to return home while it was still light next time.

Once he had tapped the Weavers' crystals by the door to light the main room, Idorii felt much better. He dropped his new stack of books beside the rapidly expanding collection and started a pot of water boiling in the kitchen before returning to survey his work.

Until Daymin's message had arrived, Idorii had finally been distracting himself successfully with his work. He was determined to gather every book on Weavers' magic in Baylore; though he could not carry an entire library's worth of knowledge to the Icebraid Peaks, he could at least collate any spells that were unique to a particular source. That way, Itrea would not lose any irreplaceable knowledge.

He worked with a feverish determination, going systematically through Weavers' guild libraries and personal collections; he would leave the more substantial libraries at the palace, the cathedral, and the University for last, since they would be better-organized and more likely to contain duplicates.

Already he had stumbled across several ancient tomes that looked as though they had not been touched in centuries. These were the jewels of his collection, even if he had not been brave enough to crack the spines yet.

From the kitchen, he heard the water beginning to boil, so he paced back through the too-empty house to cook whatever he could find for supper.

It was good to be useful again. Though he had lost everything that mattered—his magic, his home, and Daymin—

he would still leave a mark on this world.

24

Pelek

Daymin had still heard nothing from Idorii. That meant he was still angry with Daymin—either that, or he wanted nothing more to do with him. He and his friends had crawled into their sleeping rolls in the royal tent, but Daymin was far from sleep, and he could tell from their stirring that the others were no better.

It was late at night when Uncle Cal finally returned with the Flamespinners who had forced back the Whitish troops. Their clothes reeked of smoke, and those on foot stumbled drunkenly into camp. Daymin had been counting on them to lead the attack on Pelek, but he wasn't sure they would be able to use their magic when they were this exhausted.

"Dellik said we're attacking before sunrise?" Cal asked wearily.

"If possible. How are you holding up?"

Cal sank onto a sack of dried lentils, looking at once older and more vulnerable than Daymin had ever seen. "None of us have pushed ourselves that hard before. It took ages for the grass to catch alight, and as soon as it did, we were sprinting to the end of the line to spread the fire. Creating fire that powerful, and sustaining it for so long, is not something we've ever trained for. We usually try for distance and accuracy, not brute strength." Cal massaged his temples. "Two of the younger ones collapsed on the way back, and we tied them to my horse since none of us were strong enough to carry them."

"Did Dellik tell you she wanted to burn the town?" Daymin asked worriedly.

"She did. She said she wanted our attack to be visible to the Whitish army, but we can do that with torches and target a few carefully-selected buildings. I…think I need to lie down."

Daymin could see how much he hated admitting weakness. "I'll have a few wagons prepared for you," he said gently. "You and your team can skirt around the town and meet us at the southern end."

"Thank you," Uncle Cal said hoarsely.

Daymin spoke to one of the drivers, and a set of wagons were quickly prepared for the Flamespinners to rest in. As Cal rose and staggered over to the nearest wagon, Daymin was struck by how the dynamic had changed between the two of them. For the first time, Cal seemed to be deferring to him out of true belief in his authority, not simply as a show of respect.

Dellik jogged up to him, calling, "Are we moving out, Your Majesty?"

"Yes. We'll be attacking without the Flamespinners, so the front guard will need to carry torches."

"We don't have torches," Dellik said.

Varse. "Are there any Flamespinners who stayed behind?"

"A few children, Your Majesty."

"Then we'll save the fires for after we've captured Pelek," Daymin said.

Hurrying back to his tent, he told his friends, "We're marching for Pelek now. Let's go."

All three sat up at once, and Lalaysha scrambled to her feet, looking worried.

"Do you have your armor here?" Daymin asked.

"I think so," Tarak said.

While they readied themselves, Daymin pulled on his Weavers' armor—a new enchanted gambeson that was now padded to soften any hits he took, enchanted trousers that could not be penetrated by any ordinary blade, and boots that dulled pain and boosted his stamina. The others were similarly attired, though they wore enchanted coats instead of gambesons.

Last of all, he strapped his sword belt around his waist and tucked his helmet under one arm.

"Be safe," he told his friends before ducking from the tent.

It took him a moment to find his horse in the chaos outside. Weavers' crystals glowed from wagons and necklaces and bridles, illuminating the field with a soft white radiance, and everywhere there were guards packing away tents and soldiers readying for battle.

Swinging into his saddle, Daymin guided his horse to the front of his troops, where Dellik waited with the other commanders.

"Are you riding at the front with us?" she asked, kneeing her horse closer.

"Of course," Daymin said.

155

With the clamor they were making, not to mention the smoke from the distant fires that choked the air, the residents of Pelek would have more than enough time to prepare for their approach. Daymin hoped that would not matter.

For the first time, he would be facing the Whitish without much magic on his side. The Flamespinners were out of action, the last of the Potioneers' explosives and flammable mist had been left behind to guard Baylore, and he had no ancestor trees to call upon if his need was dire. Many of his soldiers would be equipped with enchanted swords and clothing, but the Weavers' armor was less effective than plate metal—which Baylore had lacked the resources to forge in large quantities—and the enchanted swords could only cut through Whitish armor with great effort.

He would be relying on sheer numbers to trample his way through the Whitish defense.

Behind him, the first of his ranks were beginning to form up, so Daymin turned to address his army.

"We march now for Pelek! Do no harm to the civilians, but destroy any Whitish fortifications you find. Fight for your loved ones who are still fleeing Baylore. Fight to buy them time. Here, tonight, we begin our last, desperate campaign against Whitland. We have lost so much, but we will not go quietly into the night."

An answering roar rose from his army, full of vengeful fury.

Daymin let the sound carry him forward as he nudged his horse into a trot. He was no longer isolated in his palace, removed from the suffering of his city; his grandmother was among the refugees, and Idorii still in Baylore, so he felt the weight of their campaign as much as any of his soldiers.

As Daymin's commanders fell into line on either side of

him, their horses' hooves thundering along the road, the rest of his army broke into a run. Their ranks disintegrated, and they yelled as they ran, the roar swelling to fill the quiet night.

Closer to Pelek, Daymin saw that the Whitish were indeed prepared for him.

Lines of soldiers stood waiting where the main street of Pelek branched off the highway. Torchlight illuminated their ranks in flickering orange, and Daymin saw a few dozen in plate armor, spears bristling from the front of the formation.

Closer still, he realized that even the Whitish soldiers who lacked plate armor were wearing white uniforms.

All but those who knelt at the front of the line.

Daymin reined in his horse, falling momentarily behind his generals.

"Stop!" he shouted. "Those are civilians at the front!"

Dellik and the rest of the generals slowed, horses whinnying as they pranced to a halt. Behind them, his army jogged up to meet them before stopping, packing the space more densely than before.

"We can't charge into their ranks," Daymin said. "We have to do this slowly, or we'll trample the civilians."

He dismounted and handed his reins to the nearest soldier. "Take my mount around the western edge of Pelek, and wait for us where the supply wagons have stopped."

"They have archers," Dellik said, dismounting beside him. "If we approach slowly, they'll pick us off one by one."

She was right.

"Anyone who carries a shield, come forward!" Daymin shouted into his ranks. He had not been able to requisition shields for his army, lacking the wood or steel necessary, so those soldiers who carried shields had scavenged materials and crafted them independently.

"I want only those soldiers with helmets and enchanted armor to join the initial charge," he called while the shield-bearers jostled their way forward. "Everyone else, stay back or approach from the side of town. The Whitish will fire on us as we approach, and I don't want their volleys catching anyone who is unprotected."

One of the soldiers who pushed her way close to Daymin held a wooden shield painted with a black fox against a pale blue background. They were the Bastray colors, and when Daymin peered through the slit in the helmet, he recognized Zahira's brown eyes.

"Give me your shield," Daymin said, holding out his hand. "I don't want you in the front line."

Zahira's eyes narrowed. "I want to be here."

"While I admire your determination, I need experienced soldiers by my side," Daymin said sternly. "This is going to get messy, and I can't afford to be worrying about you."

"You would worry about me?" Daymin caught a teasing glint in Zahira's eyes.

"Of course. Just as I would worry about Tarak—please tell me he's not here as well? None of us are experienced enough for this."

"What do you need my shield for, then?"

Daymin held out his hand for it with amused exasperation. "Because I'm king. It doesn't matter if I'm terrible at fighting. I need to be here."

With a sigh, Zahira handed over her shield. "I *am* going to join the initial charge, though. I'm not handing over my helmet."

Before Daymin could argue, she stalked away.

Eventually a couple hundred shield-bearers had gathered at the front of his army.

"Form a wall of shields," Daymin called out. "We'll push through the civilians and knock the spears out of the way to reach the Whitish soldiers. The sooner we can crush their defense, the less time they'll have to fire into our ranks."

As he spoke, his shield-bearers began stretching out to form a line on either side of him. Several of his generals had handed off their horses and joined Daymin at the front, while Dellik and the rest rode back to organize the rear of his army.

Eventually the shield wall was in place, Daymin at the center. Those soldiers with helmets packed in behind him, jostling together without any hint of a formation. A restless clatter rose from his army, sending adrenaline humming through him.

The whole thing didn't quite seem real—he still could not believe he was leading his army on a campaign of destruction through Itrea. It was something his mother would have done, not him. In the darkness, the soft light of Weavers' crystals illuminating his forces, the scene had taken on a dreamlike haze.

Daymin shoved his helmet on and slid his left arm through the leather strap on his shield. Adjusting his grip on the cold metal handle, he tried to ground himself in the moment. When he clashed with the waiting Whitish forces, he knew the battle would abruptly feel very real.

Shifting on his feet, he surveyed the Whitish ranks one last time. There were only a few hundred, and the spears told him they had not been equipped as well as the main part of the Whitish army, but he could not guess how he would fare against their numbers.

Finally he raised his shield to match those on either side. It was not a tidy wall, what with every shield varying in size and design, but it was better than nothing.

"Ready?" he asked those on either side of him.

Murmurs of agreement rippled down the line.

Raising his voice, he shouted, "Charge!"

Then he broke into a run, his shield-bearers matching his pace, the rest of his army pouring down the road after him.

As he ran, his helmet slipped sideways, narrowing his vision. He shoved his helmet back into place one-handed, the palm gripping his shield already sweaty.

The road ahead was dark, but ahead lay the row of dancing torches, and Daymin stared at them until the light was seared into his vision. All around him was chaos—feet pounding on the dirt road, light flickering in and out of view as Weavers' crystals swung on chains, and heavy breathing rasping in his ear. And beneath it all was the drum of his own pulse.

Closer, Daymin could smell the acrid smoke rising from the torches.

Then, with a *thwack*, the first volley of arrows flew from the back of the Whitish ranks.

Daymin jerked his shield up, but the arrows streaked over him to land amongst the soldiers that followed. Shouts made him twist his head to search for casualties, but all he could see was the river of bodies pounding after him. It was impossible to tell what was happening further back.

Another volley of arrows flew, and another, and finally Daymin was within a few paces of the waiting soldiers.

He slowed, his shield wall fragmenting as his soldiers

followed suit at different times, and for a moment they shifted and shoved against the soldiers at their back as they re-formed.

Lowering his shield, Daymin could see the Itrean townspeople watching him with fear plain on their faces. A few held daggers and spears, but most were serving as no more than a human wall.

Daymin stepped out in front of his shield wall. "Your king has not forsaken you!" he called to his civilians. "Shelter behind my ranks, and we will protect you."

At his words, his shield-bearers shifted to create gaps in the wall.

"Go! Run!" a man shouted from the line of civilians.

He pelted forward, head down, and streaked toward Daymin's army. In his wake, a dozen others followed, including a handful of children.

Thwack.

An arrow buried itself in the man's back, and he howled in pain, dropping to his hands and knees.

One of the children screamed, "Da!"

An older girl grabbed the boy's hand and dragged him forward, leaving the man twitching on the dirt.

"If anyone else deserts, we'll kill the rest of your town!" a Whitish soldier shouted.

A glint of torchlight on metal revealed that many of the townspeople were chained together, manacles around their wrists.

"Forward! Slowly!" Daymin called out.

He marched the final distance to meet the Whitish forces, shield raised.

Arrows began flying once more, and he heard shouts as they

found their marks. He hoped they were bruising rather than slicing through skin.

As soon as Daymin found his shield pressed up against the first of the Itreans, he turned sideways, allowing them to slip into his ranks.

"Run," he whispered. "Get as far from the Whitish arrows as you can."

He felt his soldiers jostling aside to allow the townspeople through, and all around, his shield-bearers were pushing more civilians to safety.

Then a spear slammed against Daymin's shield, throwing him momentarily off-balance. He tried shoving at it and parrying it aside with his shield, but it would not budge.

His enchanted sword would cut through the wood, but when he glanced around the edge of his shield, he realized the spear was jutting from between two civilians. There was no way to strike at it without injuring his own people.

Plagues.

It was clever, what the Whitish had done. They couldn't win against such odds, but they had positioned themselves to slow Daymin's forces and deal as much damage as possible before his army pushed through their line.

"We could do with a bloody Flamespinner right about now," a soldier growled from beside him.

It was true. He had not realized how much he had come to rely on magic for his battle strategies.

While his front ranks pushed against the Whitish, Daymin heard a commotion from behind. Glancing back, he saw a knot of his soldiers without helmets dashing forward, laden sacks over their shoulders.

"What's this?" Daymin shouted.

Ignoring him, the soldiers pushed their way forward until they stood right behind his shield wall. Then they started hurling their sacks over the heads of Daymin's shield-bearers and the Itrean civilians to land in the ranks of Whitish.

Confused shouts rose from the Whitish, and the soldiers drew to either side to avoid being hit by the sacks.

The spear that had held Daymin at bay withdrew.

With a roar, he shoved his way forward, breaking through the last of the civilians. Trusting that his soldiers would follow, he raised his sword and charged at the first of the Whitish soldiers.

As Daymin's blow connected with the soldier's pauldron, slicing into the armor before jamming in place, the man threw aside his spear and drew a sword.

Daymin let go of his shield and shook his arm free of the leather strap before grabbing his hilt with both hands. He braced himself, trying to yank it free of the man's shoulder guard.

While he fought to free his sword, the soldier grabbed Daymin's helmet and ripped it off. The night air chilled the sweat that had dampened his hair.

Daymin finally managed to dislodge his sword from the metal, and he took a step back, feeling very vulnerable.

But before he could engage the soldier again, his army swelled around him, pushing him back to safety.

Daymin scanned the ground for his discarded helmet. There—it was rolling sideways after a soldier had kicked it in passing. He lunged for it and jammed it back onto his head before shoving his way to the front once again.

By the time he rejoined the fight, most of the Whitish

soldiers had been killed or subdued. With arrows no longer flying, the rest of his army swarmed forward to flood the streets of Pelek, the civilians clustering off to one side.

"What should we do with the captives, Your Majesty?" Dellik called out, galloping toward him.

"Bring them to the stronghold," Daymin said, indicating the wooden structure at the southern end of town. "We need to round up any who have escaped."

His soldiers began going around to each house in town, hammering on doors and forcing their way through any that did not open, dragging out the handful of Whitish soldiers they found within. Most of the dwellings belonged to Itreans, some of whom had been enslaved, others who still kept businesses but must have lived in perpetual fear of the Whitish army turning against them.

Daymin hung back as his soldiers worked, listening to the residents thanking his army and describing in hurried snatches their time under Whitish occupation. Pelek had been one of the first towns captured by the Whitish, so its residents had not been given the opportunity to flee to Baylore.

When the last of the Whitish had been rounded up, Daymin followed his soldiers as they herded the captives to their stronghold. He was not planning to leave any survivors.

At the doors to the stronghold, Daymin called out, "Let us in or we'll light your wall on fire!"

After a minute, the doors creaked open.

"Stay out here," Dellik ordered Daymin. "I don't want you risking yourself."

He nodded and stepped back while a company of soldiers filed past with the Whitish captives. With the doors open, he could see that the stronghold was nothing more than a set of wooden barracks and a practice yard surrounded by a high wooden fence. He watched as Dellik and her company barged into the buildings one by one, emerging with a few Itrean slaves and a pair of cows. Next they returned for several barrels of dry goods and sacks of potatoes.

Daymin's soldiers withdrew, closing the stronghold doors on the remaining Whitish soldiers. The dry goods piled outside the wall did not seem enough to sustain the soldiers that had occupied Pelek for more than a quarter; now that he looked closer, Daymin realized the townspeople were emaciated, their clothes hanging loose on their frames.

Were the Whitish suffering from food shortages, just as Baylore was? Was this why they had been so quick to capture his supply wagons?

"Give the orders to move my army out of Pelek," Daymin said. "Leave a couple Flamespinners here with me."

"And the Whitish soldiers, Your Majesty?" Dellik asked.

Daymin lowered his voice. "I'll deal with them. I don't want everyone here when it happens."

"Understood, Your Majesty."

25

The Whitish Stronghold

Daymin stood watching as his army marched from town, dirt from the main road choking the air in their wake. Three young Flamespinners approached, and Daymin recognized two of them as the siblings who had helped finish off the enchanted towers at the battle of Darkland Fort.

"We meet again," he said, giving them a bleak smile.

"Prince Calden didn't let us help force the Whitish back," the girl said with a scowl.

"Well, thank the cloudy gods for that. I want you to set fire to this stronghold and make sure everything inside burns. Can you do that?"

The Flamespinners shared a surprised look.

"But...aren't there men inside there?" asked the unfamiliar Flamespinner, who was younger than the other two.

"Whitish men," Daymin said grimly. "Never forget that this is war."

The two siblings approached the stronghold. The girl said something in an undertone, and as they raised their hands, flames sprang from the ground to trail their way up the wall.

Soon the wood was burning, giving off a thick column of smoke. Daymin stepped back from the heat as the Flamespinners worked their way around the wall, setting more and more of the stronghold ablaze.

While he watched, an older man approached Daymin, twisting his hands together.

"Are you the king?" he asked nervously.

"I am," Daymin said.

"We wanted to thank you for freeing us," he said. "But is it true there's a Whitish army at our backs?"

"Yes. A significant force is pursuing us."

The man cleared his throat. "Pardon me, Your Majesty, but don't you think they'll burn Pelek to the ground when they see what you've done?"

"I hope not," Daymin said, guilt tightening his throat. When he had orchestrated his campaign to free Whitland, he had not thought past distracting and weakening the Whitish. Of course his own civilians would face retribution for what he had done; why had he not considered it before now?

He had to offer some form of hope, however pitiful.

"The people of Baylore are evacuating, even now," Daymin said quietly. "We don't want the Whitish to discover this, or our civilians will never make it safely away. If you want to join them, they are heading for the Icebraid Peaks. Otherwise, do what you can to survive under Whitish rule. Itrea is no more."

The man's eyes clouded over with pain. "Yes, Your Majesty. Thank you."

The fires consuming the stronghold were growing faster than ever, and above the crackling of flames, Daymin heard men shouting. His heart ached at the sound. After killing men in battle and seeing the evil Whitland had brought to Itrea, Daymin had thought the death of Whitish men would no longer affect him.

But they were men nonetheless. He stood and watched with a grim sense of duty, flames searing across his vision, eyes stinging from the smoke.

When the Flamespinners finished their circuit and rejoined Daymin, all three were flushed from the heat of the fires.

"Make sure it doesn't spread to the town," Daymin said. "And one of you, come with me."

The siblings looked at each other, and then the girl approached Daymin. "What do you need me to do?"

"We're going to burn the bridge at the northern end of Pelek," Daymin said. "That will cut off the Whitish army's supply route and slow the reinforcements that landed in Larkhaven."

The girl followed Daymin through the town, past townspeople who had emerged from their homes to watch the fires consuming the fortress. Dawn was approaching, tinging the sky a hazy grey-blue, and the stars were winking out.

When they reached the end of town, Daymin could make out a distant red-orange glow where the grassfires still burned.

Approaching the bridge, Daymin asked the Flamespinner, "Can you do it?"

"Easily."

He stood back and watched as she sent a jet of fire at the bridge. The flames quickly caught in the wood and clawed their way up the railings, the angry orange glow reflecting off the river. The fire crackled and sparked as it grew, sending yet another column of smoke billowing skyward.

And behind him, he could still hear the screams from the stronghold.

* * *

Daymin and the young Flamespinners rejoined his army just outside the remains of Darkland Fort. As the sun rose, he could see the sheen of smoke lying over Baylore Valley like gauze; even here, south of Pelek, the smell was pervasive.

It was eerie returning to the old battlefield so soon after the fight. The fortress lay in ruins, scattered stones flattening the surrounding grasses where they had not been ripped apart by the ancestor trees' roots. Daymin could see the remnants of a bonfire where the Whitish must have burned the human casualties; the destroyed harvesting machines had been removed, and the dead ancestor trees chopped down. Vast stumps marked where the trees had died, some with roots sprawling across the ground, others planted firmly in place. Scattered around these were branches and dead leaves the Whitish would have discarded when preparing the logs for transport.

It was a sobering reminder of how much they had already sacrificed in the war for Itrea.

And their losses were far from over.

Tents sprang from the battlefield like flowers growing from ashes, and Daymin picked his way through these until he found Dellik conferencing with Morrisse and Pollard.

169

"Get some rest," Dellik said gruffly. "We'll move out in a few hours."

"Thank you," Daymin said, relieved that someone else had taken charge.

He stumbled off to his tent, which was empty this time save for his bedroll and waterskin. After he had gulped down enough water to soothe the burn in his throat, Daymin pushed up his sleeve. He didn't care if Idorii read what he wrote; he just needed a way to process his thoughts, and this was the best he could come up with.

Idorii –

> *Don't bother to read this if you don't wish to. I just miss the comfort of having someone to write to when it all becomes too much.*
>
> *We took Pelek today, and I burned the surviving Whitish soldiers alive in their wooden stronghold. Does that make me a monster? Is this how my mother felt when she had to use her power to save Baylore?*
>
> *We're now camped beside the ruins of Darkland Fort, and it's making me question everything. At what point is the cost of fighting no longer worth the reward? How many more battles will we need to fight—how many will die—before we admit we have nothing left to fight for? Would our civilians have fared better under Whitish rule than they will in the mountains? Have I sent my people there to die?*
>
> *But if we do give up, who will stop the Whitish from slaughtering every last Makhori and Allakoash and ancestor tree? Aren't their lives worth any sacrifice?*

Apologies for the rambling. I'm running out of space, so I'll end this here.

Yours,
Daymin

He pressed the tattoo and pulled down his sleeve, and then he wrapped his arms around his legs and pressed his face into his knees, trying to forget the screams of the Whitish soldiers.

26

The Raid

The thief's purse was nearly empty. Kalleah's companions had been venturing out each day to seek employment, but no one was hiring—like Stragmouth, the Twin Cities had been hit hard by the decline in trading, and their economy was crippled further by the Lord's Men. When riverboats pulled up to the docks, a virtual army of beggars descended to help offload goods in hopes of earning a drav, and Kalleah's companions had been unable to compete with their desperation.

Kalleah spent her time wandering the streets near the docks in disguise, hoping she might come across someone who could help get her closer to King Rodarin without approaching the palace itself. More than once, she glimpsed Bennett keeping an eye on her in a way that always appeared as though he was there by coincidence—chatting to the dockworkers, examining wares in nearby shops, or accompanying finely-dressed ladies to the waterfront.

She would have been impressed if it wasn't so annoying. She still did not trust him, and resented that he knew they were surviving on his charity.

On the last day before their coin ran out, Kalleah was making her way back to the tavern when she heard a shout behind her.

She flinched, still on edge after being attacked outside the palace.

Turning, she saw a gang of Lord's Men jogging toward a tailor's shop.

"Where is the proprietor?" shouted the brute at the front.

Kalleah darted to the end of an alleyway to watch. She was not alone; a small crowd of passersby and beggars gathered around her, gravitating to the scene.

When a thin, wiry man stepped up to the shop doorway, two of the Lord's Men seized him by the shoulders.

"Show us your coin," one bellowed. "You've had a full quarter to pay your fine, and we've seen nothing! Cough up now, or we'll seize your business."

"I've nothing to pay!" the man said desperately. "All our coin went to ordering a new shipment of cloth, and it never arrived!"

"Search the premises and seize anything of value," one of the Lord's Men commanded.

While the tailor stood wide-eyed on the street, the thugs pushed past him into the shop.

Kalleah would have given a great deal for the chance to kill those brutes where they stood. Even as she thought this, the street blurred around her, the golden threads of life swimming into view from every living body within range.

She tore her eyes from the shop, falling back against the stone wall. As the mortar grazed her knuckles, the threads vanished, the street coalescing into sharp lines once more. Now was not the time to be reckless. If she used her power in that way, she would have to flee the Twin Cities. She would only take such a risk if it could tip the balance of the war.

Leaning forward to glance around the corner once more, Kalleah saw that the Lord's Men were tossing bolts of cloth and half-finished garments into a pile in the street, heedless of the foul runoff that was already ruining the fabric.

At last the Lord's Men stalked from the shop, releasing the tailor. One gathered the bolts of cloth into his arms and rested them on his shoulder, while another threw a heavy spool of thread at the window as he passed. The glass shattered, falling to the ground in a clinking rain.

Disgusted, Kalleah turned away and started down the alley. As she did, she caught the eyes of a beggar who had been watching her.

Plagues. It was Bennett again.

Knowing he would follow her, she paused at the end of the alley. When she looked back at him, he scurried to her side, grinning toothily.

"What was that about?" she asked, too disturbed by the scene the Lord's Men had caused to question the thief. "What did they mean about a fine?"

"How much do you know about the Lord's Men?" Bennett asked quietly, steering her to a quieter street that ran directly to the waterfront.

"Only that they've been making trouble in the Twin Cities."

"That's an understatement," he said, glancing both ways

before hurrying across an intersection. "They've come to enforce the High King's law by any means necessary, or so they say, but it's just a cover to harass civilians. Whitish laws are so strict that virtually everyone in Darrenmark has broken them in some way or another, so they can hand-pick their targets."

The reek of the waterfront was rising to meet them; Kalleah didn't know how they could stand it. "What laws are you referring to?"

"Where to begin?" Bennett's smile was bitter. "Nothing except royal dwellings and places of worship can be built out of stone. Women aren't allowed to own businesses or work. Only goods from Lostport are allowed to be traded upriver through the Twin Cities, and all other goods must pass through Whitish ports first." He ticked them off on his fingers as he spoke. "None with Makhori blood are allowed within the city walls. No language except Whitish is to be spoken. All foreigners must register with the authorities and submit to regular searches of both homes and businesses. And so on."

"Were the Twin Cities always this strict?"

"Not at all. This is what rankles the most—we're used to enjoying certain freedoms, and the Twin Cities only exist because of them. We don't know if High King Edreon wants to cripple us because he sees us as a threat, or if the Lord's Men are acting of their own volition."

They reached the waterfront, and Kalleah paused. "Thank you for telling me this. But why do you persist in following me?"

Bennett leaned his back against a stone wall, hood low over his face as he gazed across to the opposite bank of the river. "Curiosity, I suppose. What are you really doing in the Twin Cities?"

Kalleah nearly lied, but she stopped short. If Bennett was as well-connected as he appeared, he might be able to help. So she offered up a sliver of truth. "I need to speak to King Rodarin."

"That's a tricky proposition," Bennett said, kicking his heel against the cobblestones. "Especially for a woman, and a foreigner at that. You saw what happened when you tried to approach the palace looking as you do."

"Yes," Kalleah said shortly.

"However, I do have my contacts. If you were willing to work with me, I could get you in. Of course, I couldn't guarantee your safety beyond the gates. I'm no lost princeling." His teeth glinted beneath his hood as he grinned.

Kalleah leaned against the wall beside him, watching the river slide past. She could see where the streets drained into the water, staining it brown, but upstream of the Twin Cities it ran clear. Across the bank, Kohldar was far less imposing than its twin, sprawling across the flat plains with few taller buildings to draw the eye.

She thought about the Lord's Men and the clockwork trinkets she had seen in Stragmouth, and about the invitation she had received to visit the Temple of Totoleon. It seemed everyone here was hiding something.

"I'll consider your offer," she said at last. "But I would still be grateful if you stopped following me."

Bennett whisked off his beggar's cloak, revealing finer clothes beneath, and finished his outfit by donning a wide-brimmed velvet hat that he must have clutched beneath the folds of the cloak. "I can make no promises, good sir. Have a lovely day."

Then he strode off, whistling as he followed the river upstream.

Kalleah made her way slowly back to The Lost Sailor, deep in thought. How could anyone eke out a living in such a hostile place? She had seen no reason for the Lord's Men to target that particular tailor; he had been neither foreign nor a woman, and his business did not appear to be successful. Maybe that was the point—King Edreon's lackeys wanted to remind the people of Darrenmark that no one was safe.

When she pushed open the door of the tavern, Kalleah scanned the room, half-expecting to find Bennett lounging at a table in the corner.

Instead she saw only Leoth, who sat with his head bowed over a mug of ale.

"How long have you been here?" she asked, dropping into the seat opposite him.

Leoth blinked at her, his eyes hazy. For a second, she thought she saw something like guilt—or was it pain? Then he gave her a bitter smile.

"I've found a job."

"What?" Kalleah was taken aback. "How did you manage that?"

"I was desperate enough to consider any option that came my way."

"What do you mean?"

"I've been hired by the Lord's Men." Leoth's smile grew grimmer still.

"No!" Kalleah was so startled she forgot how dire their situation had become. "You can't do that! I just saw them tear apart the shop of a tailor whose only crime was that his premises were built from stone, just like the rest of the town."

"I know," Leoth said flatly. "But I couldn't find anything else, and neither could the others. It's the only way we can stay in the Twin Cities, unless you would rather we give up and walk back to the coast?"

Kalleah just stared at him. It was all her fears come to life. She had worried this kingdom was a bad influence on Leoth, and it must have been, because how else could he have considered joining such a brutal organization? This went beyond scraping by.

As she studied him—he must have been drinking for a while now, by the smell of alcohol on his breath, and it had deadened something in his eyes—she was assaulted by memories of the Truthbringers who had tormented her in Baylore. Leoth had been one of them when she first met him. His parents had forced him into their ranks, but she worried there was a part of him that still felt kinship with that brutal order.

And the Lord's Men were worse by several degrees.

"Will you stand by as they assault civilians?" Kalleah asked coldly. "Or will you join in their work?"

Leoth flinched. "I'll do only as much as necessary to play the part."

Needing a moment to think, Kalleah stalked over to the bar to order a cider for herself. When they had parted ways many spans ago, Leoth had been terrified at the thought of traveling inland. Was this not far more dangerous? She could not imagine what horrors he might face if his forbidden blood was discovered by such an unforgiving organization.

The barkeeper handed Kalleah her cider, and she took a

drink, grimacing at the sour taste. If not for the way Leoth had behaved since leaving Stragmouth, she would have worried he was facing the same fears now.

But he had been abrasive and distant for quarters now. If this was some sort of coping strategy, it was not endearing him to Kalleah.

When she turned back to Leoth's table, she saw Mellicante and Baridya entering the tavern, Triyam and Luc at their heels.

"Why so grim?" Mellicante asked, tugging off her cloak and draping it over the back of a chair. She was dressed as a man, like Kalleah, though she was doing a much more convincing job of it. "Is it just our impending homelessness? Or has something happened to Desh?"

"I ran across the Lord's Men again," Kalleah said, "this time terrorizing a poor shopkeeper. And when I returned, Leoth told me he's managed to secure a job with those brutes."

"Well, that's good, isn't it?" Mellicante asked, while Baridya's mouth twisted in displeasure. "Will it earn you enough to keep us off the streets?"

"It should," Leoth said darkly. "And if my official pay falls short, it sounds like I can use my newfound authority to seize whatever the plagues I want."

"Don't you dare try anything like that," Baridya said, looking horrified.

"Bloody Varse," Leoth said. "I did this to protect us, and suddenly you're all acting like I'm the enemy. I'll see you later."

He downed the rest of his drink and stalked off toward the back door leading to the inn.

Mellicante and Baridya dropped onto the chairs beside Kalleah while Triyam and Luc ordered drinks. They had been helping the tavern-keeper with small tasks around the inn—cleaning and hauling crates and chasing down patrons who forgot to pay—and in exchange they could drink cheap alcohol as they wished.

While they were away, Mellicante leaned close and whispered, "What's going on with Leoth?"

"I don't know," Kalleah said. "I really don't. He's been acting strange ever since we left Stragmouth, and now this…"

"You don't think the Lord's Men will influence him, do you?" Baridya asked quietly.

"I honestly can't say," Kalleah said.

"No," Mellicante said firmly. "I know what he did when he was younger, but in all the years since, he's been nothing but honest and gentle. He's a good man, Kalleah. You should trust him."

Kalleah stared into the dregs of her cider. "I do, logically. But a part of me is still afraid I'll lose the support I've won over the years. Remember how my dearest friends voted against my rule, knowing I would be thrown to the Truthbringers if I failed to secure the crown? That could happen again. My followers might wake up one morning and realize they've been led astray by a demon queen whose brutality is unmatched in all the world."

She hesitated, reluctant to voice her deepest fears. "And what if Leoth has realized he can't support me any longer?" *What if he sees me for the monster I'm becoming?*

"We all believe in your cause," Baridya said. "You're the only hope we have of overthrowing Whitland."

"She's right," Mellicante said. "Whatever this is, it's about Leoth, not about you."

Kalleah hoped she was right.

27

Vultures at Court

As Edreon continued to battle the infection in his leg, he grew steadily more paranoid. He could tell his support was waning, and with fevers and pain keeping him abed most days, there was little he could do to bolster his presence at court.

Worried as he was, he checked his communications from Itrea obsessively, discarding any evidence that might point toward the use of magic overseas. If he lost consciousness or slipped into a feverish delirium, he did not want any mark of heresy to seal his doom.

It was late one night, when he woke with sweat drenching his bedsheets, that Edreon rolled over in search of something to calm his racing heart and instead discovered an alarming new missive from Lord Juriel. He read by the light of a flickering candle, eyes aching from lack of sleep.

Your Majesty,

> *An Itrean army has recently marched from Baylore and taken Pelek. They are now on their way to Druin and may have already captured the town. We sent a sizeable army to chase them down and hoped to resolve the situation before we needed to involve you, but our troops were stalled by a company of Flamespinners, and King Daymin's forces have moved several days beyond us.*

> *Should we leave the Itrean army to tear through the countryside, capturing smaller towns and mines, and proceed with the planned attack on Baylore? Or ought we to focus our attention on stopping the Itrean forces before laying siege to Baylore?*

> *May I also note that the Itrean army is similar in size to the one that met our forces at Darkland Fort, which indicates they have left a considerable defense behind in Baylore.*

> *And there is of course the timing of our attack on the Wandering Woods to factor into the decision.*

> *We await your advice.*

Your faithful servant,
Lord General Juriel

Edreon threw the journal onto his covers, jostling the bandages as he did and sending a fresh wave of agony up his leg. That was what his life had been reduced to—fevers and pain.

Did King Daymin know?

Was he making such an aggressive move because he realized his enemy lay on his deathbed, a horde of claimants ready to fight for the throne in the event of his downfall?

No. Surely not. There was no way that information could have reached Itrean ears.

In truth, the Itrean army was the least of his worries. Without the trees on their side, his forces would crush them without trouble, and they had even done him the favor of exposing themselves outside the walls of Baylore.

This was a problem he could solve, thank Varos.

He reached for his pen and bent over the journal, his handwriting crabbed and uneven. His hand shook as he wrote, which filled him with impotent fury. He had become a worthless invalid.

Lord Juriel —

Continue pursuing King Daymin's army until they have been dealt with. I would prefer not to lose our mines, and it certainly appears he is heading that direction. Send only the forces necessary to subdue his army.

In the meantime, send another army to the border of the Wandering Woods to prepare to reconnect Larkhaven to the central plains. Our harvesting machines are in place, the poison seeded in the Elysian River, and I have requisitioned additional catapults that should be waiting in both Twenty-League Town and Larkhaven to assist in dispersing further poison over the trees themselves. If we break through the forest quickly enough, the timing of our attack on Baylore will no longer matter. Their food stores are unlikely to be substantial, especially now that they have lost the last of their farmland.

Speaking of which, maintain enough troops in Twenty-

League Town to monitor the situation in Baylore. If you see any sign of another force mobilizing, prepare to attack without delay. Without the trees on his side, King Daymin should not be able to mount a significant resistance.

I wish to receive daily updates until the situation has been resolved.

High King Edreon Desterial

Edreon read over his words several more times, head pounding. The candlelight threw disconcerting shadows around his room, and in his exhausted delirium, he kept imagining he saw assassins lurking behind the drapes.

He had tested the journals before Lord Juriel left Whitland all those years ago, and he knew the words appeared on the linked journal exactly as he wrote in his. He was now safe to tear the page free of the binding and destroy all mention of harvesting machines and poison, both of which had magical origins.

With no way of reaching the embers of his fire unaided, Edreon crumpled up the page and doused it in his water glass, blurring and dissolving the ink. He then shoved it beneath his mattress, along with several other pages he had disposed of similarly. When he was next alone with Naresha, he would order her to burn them properly.

Then he sank back into a fitful, feverish half-sleep, his body a prison around him.

* * *

In the morning, Edreon felt well enough to sit upright for a time, so he decided to make his presence known at court once again.

He called for a noonday feast and invited the city planners to report on the recovery work taking place around Eidervell Harbor, and Naresha visited him midway through the morning to report on how the arrangements were proceeding.

"Everyone who is anyone plans to attend," Naresha told him. "I hope you don't intend to make a spectacle of yourself, because that is exactly what they expect."

"I plan to sit in one place for the duration of the feast and remind my enemies that I am still alive and well," Edreon said sharply. "Is that too much to ask?"

Naresha raised her perfectly-sculpted eyebrows. "Perhaps we should send someone to improve your complexion. You won't convince anyone of your health looking as you do."

"Must you remind me how wretched I've become?" Edreon snapped.

"I'm looking after your best interests, darling. Also, are you intending to walk to your throne, or should we arrange a palanquin?"

"You know I can do nothing of the sort. Have you come here to needle me, or is there another purpose for your visit?"

Naresha sighed. "You've been letting details slide of late. Someone has to see to them if you won't. I really do want to help, Edreon. Let me do what I can. If you think you'll have the stamina for it, we could arrange you on your throne before the guests arrive so no one will have to see your entrance."

"And what about my exit?" Edreon asked sourly, not wanting to admit that Naresha had a point.

"After the feast is over, we could ask the city planners to

invite the guests onto the castle wall, to survey the progress they have made. That should ensure the hall clears swiftly."

So it was that Edreon found himself propped painfully in his throne while his staff finished setting out the great hall for the feast. Naresha, Luvoli and his wife, and Marviak had accompanied Edreon and were trying their best to distract him from his discomfort. Naresha had powdered his cheeks with rouge to give them a lifelike color, and his hair had been fixed carefully.

Luvoli and his wife had claimed seats a couple along from Edreon, and Luvoli said, "If you need us to rescue you from the feast early, simply flutter a handkerchief over your plate." He tugged one from his sleeve and demonstrated.

"I am not the sort who *flutters handkerchiefs*," Edreon said with gritted teeth.

"Then tell us what signal you would prefer."

They were all trying to be so *helpful*, and it set Edreon on edge. He did not like accepting help. Hunter's blood, he did not like needing help in the first place.

At last, because all four were watching expectantly, he said, "If I raise my goblet and toast the city planners, it will mean I need to leave this godforsaken hall."

"Were you not planning to toast the city planners regardless?" Naresha asked.

"No. Certainly not. They are not doing their job quickly enough, and in the meantime all our water tastes of ash."

From the door, a butler called out, "The first of the guests are arriving, Your Majesty. Should we show them in?"

Edreon waved a hand in acknowledgment, and the doors creaked open to reveal the first group of nobility. As he had expected, all stared at him unashamedly, whispering to one another as they crossed the floor to their seats.

It took every shred of his energy to smile and greet his court with a strong voice and steady smile. His inner circle, bless them, stayed close to his side, Luvoli and Marviak more boisterous than usual, their enthusiasm offsetting his own painful attempts at normalcy.

The meal came out very soon after his guests were seated, and by the time he was served, Edreon felt his fever returning and wanted nothing more than to crawl back into his bed. Instead he sampled every dish laid before him, forcing down the meal, determined to make the most of his display. And indeed, the stares lessened as the luncheon feast wore on, his guests moving on to different subjects of gossip.

At one point, through his haze of misery, he spotted Odelia cozying up with a group of his detractors. She was acting very familiar with them, displaying her full innocent charm, and Edreon immediately suspected her of defecting to the enemy now that his own power was waning.

He needed to speak to Naresha about the girl. He would have her removed from court if she showed any signs of betraying his trust.

But he couldn't worry about that now. The rich dishes were making his stomach turn, and Edreon scanned the room to gauge how much longer he had before his court naturally moved on to the next stage of the event.

Too long, he decided.

Well, he had done his part. He had made an appearance before court and reminded his people that he was still alive and capable of ruling, and with any luck they would not suspect how far his power had slipped.

He just had to hold onto his throne until the next shipment of logs arrived. Then he would be restored to his full health.

As long as the infection did not claim his life in the meantime.

Edreon raised his goblet and said, "A toast! To the city planners who have labored tirelessly to restore Eidervell to its former glory. Queen Kalleah thought she had dealt a major blow on our capital, but her attack was no more effective than a storm blowing down a stick house."

The gathered nobility lifted their goblets in response, and as the murmur of voices subsided, Marviak got to his feet.

"On that note, we now invite you to join us for pleasant stroll along the castle wall, to survey the work of our good city planners."

On the opposite side of Edreon, Luvoli stood as well, holding out a hand to his wife. As the three made their way around the trestle tables to the entrance, the rest of the guests pushed back the benches and followed, raising a clamor that resounded through the great hall. No one seemed to notice that Edreon remained seated on his throne, and even if they did, it was perfectly acceptable for a king to remain behind while his subjects went on a frivolous excursion.

Eventually no one remained but Naresha and his serving staff.

"Well?" he asked Naresha when she approached, skirts swishing. She was as ravishing as always, her golden hair twisted into a knot at the back of her head with a few curls falling artfully down the side of her face, her crimson gown cut low.

"You've done admirably," she said. "No one will imagine

you are on your deathbed after that display. But even so, the gossip is worrying. Your power is eroding, and those who wish to take advantage of the situation are growing bold."

"On that note, I want to speak with your daughter once she returns," Edreon said with a frown.

"Why?"

"I may decide to tell you later. In the meantime, get me out of this blasted chair before I collapse into my pudding."

* * *

Edreon was woken from a fever dream when someone knocked tentatively on his door. He clawed his way back to consciousness, trying to pick out what was real and what was part of his dream. Whoever was at the door continued knocking, the sound quiet but irritatingly persistent.

Edreon dragged himself to a sitting position, gritting his teeth against the waves of agony that tore through him. Where was his Varos-damned valet? He must have allowed this unwanted visitor into his quarters, damn the man. And now there was no one to make sure he looked decent.

Little by little, his brain ground back into action, and he remembered he had asked Naresha to send her daughter to see him this afternoon. Which was why she had made it past his security so effortlessly.

Edreon raked his fingers through his hair and mopped the sweat on his brow with his sleeve. Then he barked out, "Come in."

The knocking finally ceased, and the door swung open to admit Odelia, whose cheeks were flushed. From her windblown hair, he guessed she had just come down from the castle wall.

"Apologies, Your Majesty. My mother said you summoned me?" She dropped into an elegant curtsey, eyes lowered.

"I saw you trying to sweet-talk your way into the confidence of my enemies at court," Edreon said coldly. "What do you mean by this? Have you turned traitor so quickly? You see my power waning and seek a rising star to latch onto?"

Odelia rose from her curtsey, looking surprised. "Was I not supposed to keep an eye on your opponents, Your Majesty? I have been ingratiating myself with many different factions while you have lain on your sickbed, in hopes that I might hear any whispers of dissent before they spread too far."

She was right. He truly was growing paranoid in his sickness. "And what have you heard?"

"Today I learned that Prince Navaire, who I believe was stationed in Chelt—"

"That's right," Edreon said gruffly.

"He has returned to Whitland, along with his army. It seems he's raising a force against you, Your Majesty. He sees you going down the same path as your father, delaying the war and weakening our kingdom's power as you do so, and he wants to seize control before Whitland has fallen too far. He believes if he were in power, he could quickly crush Itrea and Chelt and focus his attention on subduing the rest of the Kinship Thrones."

"Then he is a fool," Edreon muttered, speaking more to himself than to Odelia. Raising his voice, he said, "Thank you for bringing this to my attention. I expect you to report back to me every time you hear a similar piece of intelligence, do you understand?"

"Of course, Your Majesty." Odelia dropped into a low curtsey.

"Begone with you, then, and tell your mother she raised you well."

He caught a hint of a smile tugging at Odelia's lips as she turned and retreated from his bedchamber.

Alone again, Edreon tried to summon up the energy to deal with Prince Navaire's threat today, but failed. He would alert his inner circle of the danger on the morrow.

What a fool, he thought grimly. Prince Navaire had no idea how vulnerable the situation was in both Itrea and Chelt. If he thought he could bring a swift end to a conflict that had dragged out over decades, he was more arrogant than Edreon had realized.

The troublesome prince could be dealt with, but he was only one of many who had swooped in like vultures to feast on Edreon's pain. His position in Itrea was as fragile as it had ever been, with food shortages to contend with on top of King Daymin's new push to reclaim the countryside, and difficulties at home were the last thing he needed right now.

Of course, none of that mattered if he did not survive the infection still eating away at him. If he died without an heir, Whitland would fall to chaos.

28

Archery Lessons

A quarter out from Baylore, the Whitish army was beginning to feel distant. Jakovi knew the end of the line of refugees was still several days behind them, especially those pulling handcarts, but it was hard to give credence to their original fears of Whitish pursuit when the only thing they had seen in days were coyotes and the odd herd of buffalo.

Letto's company at the front of the line traveled at a leisurely pace, not wanting to draw too far ahead of the civilians, so they were left with many hours to fill each afternoon after they set up camp.

Letto had already taught Jakovi a gambling game, saying it had helped win him the friendship of the soldiers he served alongside, and Jakovi had joined them for three evenings of games. Money was worthless out here, so they bet with a combination of coins and pebbles; Jakovi quickly picked up the rules, and Letto teased him good-naturedly for his intensity.

Little by little, Jakovi was beginning to feel safe enough to let his guard down. With the population of Baylore behind him, he was no longer overwhelmed to the point that his magic was on the brink of tearing free; instead he drank in the views of the Icebraid Peaks gradually rising before them.

He was growing accustomed to company as well. With nowhere to hide, Jakovi found himself trading words with dozens of people each day. And each time he did, the experience grew less unsettling. The soldiers were unfailingly friendly, always making jokes and asking after his well-being, while Letto seemed determined to expose him to as many new experiences as possible.

One of the first had been caffeine, in the form of thick, bitter hot cocoa. Jakovi had drunk a mug with breakfast a few days out from Baylore, and all that morning he had found himself wide-eyed and filled with energy. It thrummed through him in a way similar to his magic, but to his relief, it hadn't stirred his power to life.

Now, with the afternoon sun shining hot over their finished camp, Letto had pulled out a couple bows and a set of arrows from the army supplies.

"We're meant to do archery practice in any case," he said, "seeing as we don't know what we'll encounter in the Icebraid Peaks, but I thought it would be fun to give you a lesson while we're at it."

"Thank you," Jakovi said uncertainly. He wasn't sure if Idorii would want him handling weapons, but then again, it hardly mattered.

Letto paced through the grass, taking longer strides than usual, as though measuring the distance. At last he stopped and stabbed an arrow into the dirt. "We'll put the target here."

"What were you planning to use for a target?" one of the other soldiers called.

"A stump, I suppose?" Letto said.

A third soldier barked a laugh. "When did you last see a tree? C'mon, throw me the sack we finished off yesterday."

The first soldier tossed over a burlap sack, and the other man leaned over and began ripping up handfuls of grass before stuffing them in. "We'll join you, if you don't mind," he said as he worked.

Soon Jakovi was hovering behind a cluster of soldiers who had gravitated toward the archery practice, evidently bored. The burlap sack sat twenty paces away, firm enough to hold its form, though Jakovi expected it would fall over the first time someone struck it.

"Do you want to have a try first?" Letto asked Jakovi.

He felt the weight of the soldiers' stares as all turned to regard him.

"Um…I'd rather watch you first," he said nervously.

Letto plucked an arrow from the quiver he'd set on the ground and slid the notch at the end onto his bowstring. "I'm actually terrible at this," he said. "I specialized in swordplay, not archery."

"Stop stalling!" one of the soldiers teased good-naturedly.

Letto lifted the bow and bent his elbow, pulling the string back until the end of the arrow was level with his eye. "You sight your target along the line of the bow," he said. "Then, to fire, all you do is remove the two fingers holding the string. Observe."

Letto released the bowstring, and a second later Jakovi heard a *thwack* as the arrow buried itself in the target. He had been too busy watching Letto's fingers to see the arrow fly.

"Your turn," Letto said.

"What about everyone else?" Jakovi asked.

Letto chuckled. "These bastards are much better at archery than me. You need to give it a try before you're intimidated by their talent."

"That's not reassuring," Jakovi muttered, too quiet for the others to hear.

But he didn't want to cause a scene by arguing, so he stepped up and took the bow from Letto. It took a moment to notch the arrow onto the string, and then he had a hard time maneuvering the opposite end of the arrow to rest properly on his left hand.

"Now draw the bow, aiming this hand for your ear."

Jakovi did as he was told, feeling an answering pulse from the magic hanging all around. He shoved it back, trying to ignore the itching sensation on the back of his neck. Maybe this had been a mistake.

"Elbow up," Letto said, nudging his arm into the right place.

Jakovi looked down the length of the arrow, watching the grasses rippling in the light breeze. Letto's arrow had knocked the target back just slightly, so the arrow now tilted upward at an improbable angle.

"When you're ready, release," Letto said. "Remember, just move the two fingers holding the string. Nothing else changes position."

When his fingers twitched on the string, Jakovi felt an overwhelming urge to correct his aim with magic. He could make the arrow fly true, if he wanted. It would only take the tiniest nudge.

And that way lies madness, he told himself firmly.

Then, because the temptation was too great to push down, he closed his eyes. When he lifted his fingers from the string, his whole arm reverberated as the arrow flew from the bow with a *swish*.

He snapped his eyes open just in time to see the arrow plop into the grass well short of the target.

"Did you just close your eyes?" Letto asked in amusement.

"I blinked," Jakovi said defensively.

Letto held out another arrow. "Have another try. I don't even know where to begin with the advice, except that maybe watching what you're doing will help."

"I'll keep that in mind," Jakovi said, voice heavy with sarcasm.

But this time he managed to focus on the chatter of the soldiers behind him and the glint of the sun off the peaks, and the distractions helped hold his walls in place.

He drew the bow swiftly this time, sighting his line for only a heartbeat. Then he released the string before temptation had a chance to creep back in.

The arrow still flew wide, but this time it sailed past the target, only missing by a few handsbreadths.

"Much better!" Letto said. "That's something I can work with."

"The rest of you can have a turn now," Jakovi said quickly. "I need a break."

By the time they abandoned their practice, he was getting better at suppressing the temptation to correct his aim with magic, though his shots were not improving. Even when he spent a minute eyeing the target with what the soldiers considered perfect form, his arrows flew in wildly different directions every time.

"You'll get there," Letto said, clapping Jakovi on the shoulder as the other soldiers started rounding up their arrows.

"Sure," Jakovi said.

But as he headed to dinner, he felt a comforting rush of familiarity. Of ease. He knew how Letto's company functioned, and he knew the people who moved around him. The routine was giving him confidence in moving through the outside world. He was finally learning to live like a normal person—he could put his clothes on without puzzling over the different items and fastenings, and he could join in conversations without feeling hunted.

It was a jovial dinner that night, with Letto's company dining on a hearty stew that included a few rabbits they had shot during archery practice.

Jakovi perched on his sleeping roll as he ate, bowl resting on his knees. The warmth fled as soon as the sun went down, and he was already wearing his heavy coat. Several of the soldiers were drinking, but Letto did not partake, perhaps because he didn't want to tempt Jakovi. One had pulled out an odd instrument Letto called a harmonica, and its wailing melody drifted over the camp. It made Jakovi want to bring out his pan flute, only he wasn't brave enough yet.

Soon, he promised himself.

When Letto settled back onto his sleeping roll beside Jakovi with a second helping of stew, Jakovi realized he trusted the former Whitish soldier as much as anyone he had known. It still did not make sense to him, yet Letto had been nothing but kind from the day he had first approached Jakovi's cell.

"You were asking about my magic the other day?" Jakovi said in a low voice.

Letto looked at him in surprise. "What's this about?"

"I wanted to answer your questions. I was nervous, at first, that—"

"What—that I'd betray you?" Letto asked with a grim smile.

"Well, yes."

"Have you forgotten that I was the one who got you out of Darkland Fort in the first place?"

Jakovi shifted uncomfortably. "I know. But I didn't understand why you would betray the Whitish…"

"I like to lie with men," Letto said flatly. "Among my own people, that's a crime punishable by death. Idorii told me it was different here. And it is."

"Oh." Jakovi tried to get his head around that information and found himself more confused than before. During his time living in the Makhori quarters of Baylore Palace, he had found himself admiring one of the young Weaver women whom he glimpsed in passing from time to time. But he had never felt anything of the sort before, and hadn't known what to do with the sensation. He had never met a woman in all his years at Darkland Fort, and he knew nothing about them except that some men were expected to partner up with them eventually, not including the soldiers who lived all their days in fortresses without access to female company.

Anyway, it made a lot of sense for men to partner with men in some situations, especially at war, since there were so many men to go around.

Jakovi did not want to admit how ignorant he was, so

instead of saying any of this, he returned to his original purpose. "Well, since you have the job of watching me, I want you to know more about my magic. I can't tell you much, since I know very little, but if you have any questions, I'll answer honestly."

Letto stared at him for a moment, several confusing emotions playing across his face. Eventually he blinked and seemed to return to himself. "Yes. That would be good. What *do* you know about how your magic works? I'm familiar with the magic races from my work at Darkland Fort, and it seems many of them need to study for years to master their skills. Yet…you spent your entire life locked away in a cell, only to break free and give us an impressive display of magic without any practice."

"I think…" Jakovi hesitated. This was all conjecture, a theory he had begun to put together after spending time observing the palace Makhori. But maybe if he voiced it, he could work out his thoughts more clearly. "The way I use magic—the world is buzzing with power for me. Especially when I'm around lots of people, and I can feel it even more strongly in certain places. I draw on that when I work spells, and it's easy because there's so much magic out there that it takes nothing to shape it to my will. The harder part is keeping the magic *out*."

"And the other magic races don't work that way?"

Jakovi shook his head. "I think their power is bound up inside them somehow. For Weavers, it's in their hair. They don't reach outside themselves at all. So it's a smaller fragment of magic, with more limited uses, and that's why they need to study to learn how it works."

Someone came around with drinks, but Letto waved him off. Jakovi finished the last bites of his stew and set aside his bowl, marveling that even out here, leagues from civilization, he was eating far better than he had in Darkland Fort.

"My father didn't tell me any of this," Jakovi said once they were alone again. "I don't think he understood my power at all. He just told me it was very dangerous and that long ago someone with my powers had caused great destruction."

"Morvain," Letto said quietly.

The name sent a chill through Jakovi. If even the Whitish knew the name of the man who had shared his power, he must have been terrible indeed.

He slid off the sleeping roll and wrapped his arms around his knees, looking across the darkening grasslands to where moonlight now bathed the snowy mountaintops in a soft glow. Stars were appearing overhead, and bats flitted through the twilight.

"I don't think Morvain's magic had the same consequences as mine, or we would know about it," Jakovi said at last. "The more I use, the more I corrupt. I think I could finish off the Whitish army singlehandedly, but I would destroy Itrea in the process. This is why I can't afford to use my power."

"Like what happened to Idorii?" Letto asked softly.

"Exactly. Only much, much worse."

Letto set aside his bowl and gave Jakovi a grim smile. "I'll protect you as best I can, so you never find yourself in that situation. Idorii nearly died, didn't he?"

Jakovi nodded.

"Then you're right. It's not worth the risk."

29

The Open Markets

Kalleah hurried up the lane to the open markets. Set on a wide, flat street that wound around the base of the hill, the open markets were packed daily with stalls offering the city's freshest source of produce, fish, meat, and cheese.

She had come here because she expected that, similar to the chefs at Baylore Palace, those employed by King Rodarin would be here first thing each morning to purchase the best of the delicacies available.

The sun was still below the horizon, the sky a hazy blue, yet the market was already bustling. And the market-goers were not just servants—noblemen haggled over fresh eels, ladies' maids filled baskets with field mushrooms and walnuts in their shells, and commoners perused the selection of fresh greens and root vegetables and squash. There were live chickens in cages, and baskets of eggs on the tables beside them, and stall after stall of freshly-baked breads and rolls and pastries.

For the first time, Kalleah found herself admiring Darrenmark. Other than the Sullimsday Market, which packed the main street of Baylore once a quarter, the fresh produce in her own capital was generally sold in smaller markets on squares dotting the Market District. But those lacked the energy she sensed here. She could tell this was the heart of Darrenmark, where all else fell away before the appreciation of good food.

She pretended to take her time browsing the stalls as she scanned the streets for a likely-looking shopper. Several of the market-goers were clearly chefs of some repute, but none bore any markings distinguishing them as palace employees. Pausing to buy a roll studded with walnuts, Kalleah finally glimpsed someone who might fit the description. He was just disappearing around the corner, so she dropped her coins on the table and snatched up her roll before hurrying after him.

He was tall and wiry, with a close-cropped grey beard, and several others followed in his wake, purchasing and loading the goods he had selected into baskets. The stallholders deferred to him, some even bowing; as she drew closer, Kalleah overheard them asking after the day's menu.

Yes. He was the one.

Now that she had found him, he was easy to follow. Kalleah kept her back to the man as she moved up the street, pretending to browse more intently as she listened to his conversations. It seemed he was either a chef or a head of kitchen staff, for he spoke as though he was involved in preparing meals in some way.

When they neared the end of the market, Kalleah turned the corner in the direction she expected him to take and stood waiting for him, hoping she could catch him alone long enough to speak with him. This was the only way she had been able to devise to speak with someone in King Rodarin's household, and if she was to consider working with Bennett to infiltrate the palace, she needed to be certain the king would listen to her.

She stood for several minutes in the dark street, cloak pulled tight against the chill of the early morning. The sky was growing bluer by the minute, but if the sun had already peeked over the horizon, it was impossible to tell in this warren of buildings.

At last the man turned the corner, his long legs carrying him swiftly down the street.

Kalleah stepped into his path.

"A word, if you please," she said quietly.

The man stumbled in surprise; when he had caught his balance, he drew himself up to his full height, which was taller than Kalleah by at least a hand. His expression of anger changed to confusion as he peered closer. "You look like one of the marsh folk, but your accent is wrong. Are you Itrean?" he asked.

"I am."

"What is an Itrean doing in the Twin Cities?"

"I am not at liberty to say. But please, I want to know if King Rodarin is a willing accomplice in what the Lord's Men are doing to your city."

"Why do you ask me?" he shot back.

"I know you work for him. I could find no other way to learn more about his position on this mess without going through the Lord's Men."

When he hesitated, Kalleah said, "Please. This could be very important for the future of your kingdom. King Rodarin may have allies willing to help him if he wants to free himself of the influence of the Lord's Men, but I need to know what he thinks of them first."

The man's mouth twisted. "He despises the lot of them," he said in a low growl. "As do we all. Not that we're allowed to say it."

"And—" She had to risk asking; she might not get another chance. "What does he think of High King Edreon? Does he resent the way Whitland is meddling in other kingdoms?"

"I won't speak ill of my king," he said in a warning tone. "But I can't think of any monarch who welcomed High King Edreon's push for tighter control over the Kinship Thrones."

It was answer enough. "And do you know any way I could seek an audience with King Rodarin, without being turned away at the gates by the Lord's Men?"

"An Itrean like you? Never."

Footsteps at the end of the road made them both whirl. The servants carrying baskets had caught up to the chef, and at their curious looks, Kalleah slunk back into the shadows, drawing her hood up so it obscured her eyes.

"What was that?" asked an old woman balancing a basket on her head.

"Just a beggar who thought he could corner me," the chef said gruffly.

Still hugging the deep shadows beside the wall, Kalleah shuffled her way back down the street to the market. She didn't need to hear any more.

This time she retraced her steps quickly, weaving her way through the growing crowd and eating her bun as she went. She had nearly reached the road she had taken from the riverfront when she saw them.

The Lord's Men.

Kalleah's heartbeat quickened, and not because she expected to be harassed in a market like this. No—she was afraid she would see Leoth among their number.

She finished her bun in two bites and slunk into a shadowed alley behind the chicken cages to watch.

As the Lord's Men strode down the street, civilians scurried out of their way. Soon the stretch ahead of them lay empty. The man at the front carried a solid-looking club over his shoulder, and the men behind him were scanning the street, eyeing the stallowners and passersby as though they were searching for a criminal suspect.

When the Lord's Men passed the alley Kalleah had ducked down, she didn't dare blink, searching their faces one by one for Leoth's familiar features.

There.

Her heart stuttered as she recognized Leoth, grim-faced and clad in the same black uniform as the rest, the wolf's head belt around his waist. His eyes darted around the market, cold and accusing, searching for any hint of trouble.

He looked like a stranger.

Kalleah slumped against the stone wall behind her, pulse racing. She *knew* he had only taken the job to provide for them. She should have been grateful for the risk he was taking.

But there was a part of her that couldn't forget the abuse she had suffered at the hands of the Truthbringers, no matter how many years had passed.

And in that moment, Leoth had become the enemy. Everything about his demeanor frightened her; she could not rationalize away that instinctive response.

Plagues. She had to get out of here.

She didn't know where this alley led, but it sloped downward, so she hoped it would eventually spit her out at the waterfront. She started walking quickly, letting the momentum carry her forward until she was nearly running. Her hood fell back, and her braid came free of her cap, which drew a few stares. Kalleah didn't care.

She needed to speak to King Rodarin soon. If she stayed her much longer, she might find herself married to a stranger.

30

A Visit to the Palace

Idorii was at his manor house, skimming through the books he had collected in an attempt to narrow down the stack of volumes worth preserving, when he ran across a spell that allowed Weavers to fix potions in the objects they were enchanting.

The spell was similar to what he had done when he had included ink in the tattoo he shared with Daymin, except several extra steps had to be taken to preserve the qualities of the potion even while rendering it solid.

Sitting back and rubbing his eyes, Idorii dragged his thoughts away from the cataloguing of books. His mind was stuffed with spells he had never heard of before; he had begun to devise a system to categorize them by rarity and usability, only it had several glaring flaws, so his mind was churning away at the problem in the background on top of all the rest. As a result, he'd passed several sleepless nights.

There was a reason why this spell was more useful than the rest. If his brain didn't hurt so much, maybe he would be able to figure it out.

Idorii stood and shook out his legs. This work was making him feel like a decrepit old man, and the solitude didn't help either. He was deep in the same obsessive streak that had made him work on spells without stopping for meals or sleep, except this time, the more he worked, the more panicked he felt.

There was no way he could possibly save enough knowledge to make a difference in the long run. It was folly to assume he could singlehandedly preserve centuries of Weavers' art.

But the idea of stopping now—of giving up…

That was even worse.

As he paced around the piles of books to the kitchen, Idorii finally remembered why that spell was so important.

The defense of Baylore.

They needed to find a way to bring down the towers more efficiently, and if they could embed a Potioneer's explosive in the same rock that cracked the enchanted outer surface of the siege towers, they could destroy the whole thing in two hits instead of three.

Idorii glanced out the window. It was still mid-afternoon, so he had time to bring the spell to the Weavers at the palace.

He gulped down some of the cold millet porridge he had abandoned at breakfast, wondering if he would have a chance to steal a few bites from the palace dining hall while he was there. He had never realized there was a wrong way to cook millet porridge until he had tried doing it himself.

Idorii fetched his coat and wrapped the usual scarf over his markings. He paused to eye himself in the bathroom mirror, grateful at least that the root-like pattern had not spread any further since the battle of Darkland Fort. Then he tucked the book under his arm and let himself onto the street.

Outside, he gulped in the fresh air, still unnerved by the silent streets. His footsteps rang out loudly as he followed the wide lane past the University gates and onto the main square.

Here at last he found other people. A surprisingly large complement of guards still stood around the palace gates, which seemed like a waste given the only people remaining in Baylore were supporters of the two holden monarchs, though Idorii supposed they had nowhere better to spend their time. Several soldiers watched over a pile of metal implements scavenged from abandoned houses, and Idorii could hear distant clanging echoing from a forge in the Market District.

When he approached the palace gates, one of the soldiers said, "Good afternoon, Master Idorii. What business do you have here?"

Idorii held out the book he had brought. "I found something that might make a big difference in our defense of Baylore. I've come to deliver this to your Weavers."

"Go on, then," the soldier said, stepping forward to unlatch the gates. She had been there when Idorii first approached the palace with Daymin, and she had never tried to turn him away since.

Idorii jogged up the steps and through the side door into the palace. It was strange how familiar the place still felt, overrun as it was by soldiers, even though Idorii no longer called it home.

He paused to peer down the steps to the dining hall—no food to scavenge yet, alas—and then raced along the familiar route to the Makhori quarters. At the top, he half-expected to find Etriona and Lyanna waiting with reports on the progress they had made on the counterspell.

Except they had gone with Daymin's army. The Weavers who had remained were mostly elderly men and women who were willing to die when the city fell. Many were from the Weavers' Guild, so Idorii had never met them formally, though he recognized a few from the palace. And there were a handful of Weavers in their twenties, Weavers who—like Idorii—hoped to do their part and then leave before the Whitish attacked.

Idorii wasn't even sure who was in charge of the work here. He wandered the familiar halls, glancing into his old study and pausing to watch the work that went on in the smaller workshops, before turning back to the largest of the Weavers' workshops.

When he strode through the door, several Weavers turned to look at him, and soon he had the attention of the whole workshop. Even though he had not spoken of what happened at Darkland Fort, everyone seemed to know he was behind the successful discovery of the counterspell, and it had given him an odd sort of fame.

Idorii hated it. He was not the one who had devised the spell; he had merely benefitted from the work Jakovi's father had done. And if they were talking about him, he feared they would learn about the corruption that had marked him. Few knew about it, but he doubted something as grotesque as that would remain a secret for long.

Pushing aside these worries, Idorii stepped forward and set the book on a workbench.

"I've found a spell that could help us finish off the

enchanted siege towers more efficiently," he said, flipping to the right page. "It allows us to embed potions alongside Weavers' enchantments. If we could combine the explosives with the rocks designed to shatter the steel, it would give us a better chance of felling the towers."

"Thank you," said one of the old Weavers, stepping forward to take the book. "We will experiment with this and see what we can devise."

"Good," Idorii said. "Let me know if you need any help."

As soon as the words left his mouth, he cursed himself for his arrogance. Of course the Weavers here didn't need help from someone without magic. Did he think they were such idiots they could not figure out a simple spell without his input?

"Very good," the old Weaver said, smiling gently. "You know, your old rooms are still available here, if you want to stay with us."

Looking at the man closer, Idorii realized he knew him from the palace. He had followed his daughter into Queen Kalleah's service, years ago, but his wife and other children had remained in the city, so he had stayed in the palace for part of the week and returned to the Weavers' Guild for the other part.

"Thank you," Idorii said quietly, hoping the others would stop staring at him. "I do miss the food here. But I've been busy collecting books from around the city, and I don't like the idea of carrying them up so many stairs."

The old man chuckled. "Very well, suit yourself."

On his way out of the palace, Idorii turned toward the Cheltish wing on a whim. The base of the stairs was no longer guarded, and when he crossed the raised walkway to the common area beyond, he found soldiers coming and going with no regard for security.

The doors to Daymin's old suite hung open, and Idorii saw with a pang that the furniture had been pushed aside to create a dumping-ground for boots and coats.

Seeing this again, walking the halls of the palace, made Idorii miss Daymin so much his chest ached.

Daymin had written several more times since the first, each time in a rambling way as he processed his thoughts on their campaign, and the unselfconsciousness of it all made Idorii love him more than ever.

But Idorii still hadn't responded.

Each time, he had promised himself he would write back that evening, but invariably he found himself dizzy with exhaustion after digging through books until past midnight. He had left Daymin's words on his arm, returning to them whenever he needed comfort, only wiping them away when a new message came.

Now, after spending so much time alone, Idorii could no longer deny how desperately he wanted Daymin back in his life.

He might not be able to have a true relationship with him, but plagues, Idorii was willing to be whatever Daymin wanted, as long as it kept him close.

Still, he had to be cautious. This was the king he was thinking about, and he wasn't about to push things like he had done before. If Daymin wanted him in his life in any way, it had to be Daymin who asked for it. Not Idorii.

"Can I help you?" a soldier asked gruffly, dragging Idorii out of his thoughts.

"Sorry. I was looking for someone, but I don't think they're here. I'll just be going…"

He walked away quickly before he could be questioned further.

As soon as he reached his manor, which felt emptier than ever after the palace, Idorii dampened a rag and wiped away Daymin's most recent message. Then he sank into his favorite easy chair and dug the pen from his pocket.

Now that he was here, though, he didn't know what to say. He tapped his pen against his arm and traced the tattoo, half-wanting to put into words how he felt, though he was too nervous to expose himself in that way.

Dearest Daymin, let me be your plaything. I will chain myself to you and follow you to the ends of the earth, at least until you tire of me.

No. That wouldn't do at all.

Cloudy gods, this was a mess. Why had he gone and let himself care about the one person he could never have?

Finally, painstakingly, he began to write.

Daymin –

> *I miss you too. More than I want to admit.*
>
> *Though I deeply regret leaving your side, I have been doing valuable work here in Baylore, far more valuable than anything I could have accomplished on a battlefield. In fact, I may have made a breakthrough in our efforts to combat the siege towers. Well, I wasn't the one who figured it out. I just found the right book. But without me, no one else would have dug through enough libraries to stumble across the right information.*
>
> *I've enjoyed hearing of your progress through Baylore Valley. I can just imagine it—the scholar king turned great warlord. Please don't overthink the casualties. I know I would*

do the same, and it's very easy for me to rationalize it from afar, but you mustn't forget that this war has shaped the fate of our entire world. It is the Whitish who have done this, and nothing you do to push back against their power will come close to the brutality they have wrought.

Remember that every town you capture buys more time for your people to reach safety. The line of refugees took more than a day to leave Baylore, and those pushing handcarts at the back of the column were still visible from the wall two days later. They need as much time as we can give them.

Take care of yourself, Daymin. I know nothing is certain in times like these, but I dearly hope I will be able to see you again before we meet our fate.

Yours,
Idorii

Without reading the message back through, Idorii pressed the tattoo and watched the ink sink into his skin. He had forgotten to scavenge food from the palace, and his stomach was now grumbling hollowly, but it no longer seemed to matter.

His work searching through old books had pushed aside the reality of his situation, at least temporarily; now it confronted him once again, more daunting than ever.

Would his mother make it safely to the Icebraid Peaks with Daymin's army? What about the children who had fled with the refugees? Would they find food there, or would they starve? And how quickly would Baylore fall when Whitland finally attacked?

But all of it blurred to insignificance beneath the fear that Idorii would never see Daymin again.

31

The Village of a Thousand Stairs

The pirate ship made much quicker progress than Jayna had expected. There was something in the Varrilan design—she almost suspected it was magic, except she knew of no brand of magic that could accomplish such a feat— that cut through the water like a shark.

Now they were drawing up to the Larkhaven coast, far enough south of the harbor that the Whitish shouldn't notice them.

"How will we get up the cliffs?" Jayna asked Yakov, who was standing at the prow with her and Hanna.

"The Village of a Thousand Stairs is built into the cliffs themselves, with access to the water," Yakov said.

"Is that where we're headed?" Hanna asked, eyes glinting with excitement.

Yakov grinned. "Just wait until you see the place. I've never been myself, but the stories I've heard…"

Once again, Jayna felt a stab of resentment at the way Yakov responded to Hanna's enthusiasm. The longer they had traveled together, the fonder she had grown of Yakov, who was an endless font of epic tales and obscure knowledge.

But over time, she had watched with jealousy as Hanna claimed more and more of Yakov's attention. Hanna's thirst for knowledge was more than Jayna could keep up with, and she could tell Yakov appreciated speaking to a fellow scholar.

She couldn't even resent Hanna for it. She had never seen Hanna break out of her shell this way, and the more Yakov encouraged her questions, the more confident she grew.

Anyway, it didn't matter. They were about to part ways with the Varrilans, and neither she nor Hanna would ever see Yakov again.

Gradually they plunged closer to the cliffs. Lush emerald grass started where the grey rock ended, sweeping inland as far as she could see, but Jayna could make out no sign of the Wandering Woods or the mountains beyond. She was in the habit of visualizing Itrea as a small kingdom, akin to Cashabree, though she knew from maps that the continent was larger than Whitland, Chelt, and Cashabree put together. She knew it would be hard to grasp the true size until she had crossed the land on foot.

As they drew closer, the pirates hoisted a red flag with a yellow sun at the center.

"It means we're approaching with friendly intentions," Yakov explained. "Varrival has a bad enough reputation with some of the Kinship Thrones that we prefer not to attack ports, but this guarantees us a good reception. Possibly because everyone is too frightened to do anything else." His eyes were sparkling with humor.

Closer still, they passed into a small bay where the waves calmed to a gentle lapping. From here, Jayna could make out the stairs that gave this settlement its name. They zigzagged back and forth across the cliff face, connecting a series of caves that appeared as dark holes vanishing into the rock. Several of the stairways dropped down to the water, where floating docks jutted away from the cliffs, and here Jayna could see people congregating, some drifting away from shore in small sailboats and dinghies.

Sooner than she had expected, Jayna heard the anchor creaking as it lowered, dropping into the water with a splash. It took several more minutes for the anchor to catch, during which time they drifted much closer to shore, sails luffing; she realized the ocean must plunge to a considerable depth just offshore.

As soon as the line pulled tight, dragging the ship to a halt, the sailboats and dinghies picked up speed, cutting across the gentle water toward the Varrilan ship.

"Welcome!" called a man from the deck of a sailboat. "We haven't seen a Varrilan ship this close to Larkhaven in years!"

"We have two very valuable passengers here," Yakov said, pushing Jayna and Hanna forward. Hanna's cheeks reddened at his words.

"What's this?" the man asked.

Jayna didn't respond, instead waiting for the fleet of small boats to reach the Varrilan ship. Soon a gaggle of villagers stood on deck, looking around in amazement.

"Well?" a woman prompted, eyeing Jayna and Hanna. "You don't look like anyone I've seen before. What's brought you all the way to Itrea?"

"We were traveling with Queen Kalleah, until recently," Jayna said.

Gasps rose from the villagers.

"Queen Kalleah is still alive?" an old man asked in a hushed voice.

"She is. And she's seeking allies in the Kinship Thrones."

The villagers whispered excitedly amongst themselves, and a woman said, "We haven't heard word from Baylore in spans now. Not since the forest road closed."

Jayna shot Hanna a surprised look. This was news to her.

"Has she sent you here, then?" the old man asked.

"She has," Jayna said proudly. "We've come to negotiate with the Icelings and arrange safe passage for her people through the Icebraid Peaks."

"Does this mean—"

"We heard word from King Daymin that Baylore is evacuating," Hanna said quietly. "I'm sorry."

Another wave of whispers swept through the crowd.

"We knew it would happen in the end," a woman said sadly.

"Come, come," another woman said. "You must be eager to stand on solid ground again. Come ashore, and we'll see what you need for your journey. You are the last hope of our people, and we'd like to help you on your way as best we can."

Jayna turned to Yakov, who swept her into a fierce embrace. He smelled of exotic spices and something else, something purely Yakov, and she breathed in deeply, trying to memorize it.

"It's been wonderful traveling with you, Jayna," he said quietly. "I'd like to imagine our paths might cross again someday in the future."

Then he kissed her cheek, the touch of his lips sparking fire in her. Sweet Mianda, she couldn't believe she was about to lose the first man she'd ever fallen for.

"You're more likely to run across Hanna," Jayna said, trying her hardest to quash the jealousy that bubbled up when Yakov embraced Hanna in the same way. "Maybe she can hitch a ride with you to the Borderlands Academy."

"We all know how likely that is," Hanna said, giving Yakov a look of longing that spoke of more than just affection.

All too quickly, it was time to leave. Jayna and Hanna shouldered their small packs and climbed down the ship's ladder to the nearest sailboat, which bobbed wildly as they stepped onboard.

The smell of brine was stronger than ever down here, and as they started toward the cliffs, Jayna caught sight of a vast school of fish darting just beneath the surface. No wonder these people were able to survive in such a precarious location.

Soon they drew up to the small docks, which were dwarfed by the cliffs. From the Varrilan ship, she had not appreciated how high they rose before giving way to gentle fields.

"Will you stay with us tonight?" asked the woman who sailed their ship.

"Gladly," Jayna said. It was still hours before sundown, but they would need to make a plan before embarking on a cross-country trek through enemy territory.

"Very good, then. My name is Pochra, and I'd be delighted to show you a map of Itrea my daughter painted many years ago."

As soon as their ship nudged against the dock, a boy grabbed the rope and tied them in place. Pochra then led Jayna and Hanna up the dock and to the stairs.

From this angle, Jayna realized the stairs were narrower than she'd realized, with no rails or other handholds to help with balance. Her stomach gave a swoop that was part nerves, part excitement. *This* was the sort of thing she'd hoped to see when she set off for Itrea.

The woman paused at the foot of the steps. "How do you feel about climbing? We can send someone down with a rope if you'd prefer."

"We'll manage," Jayna said.

Pochra gave them an indulgent smile.

Jayna glanced up and saw children running along the stairs as though unafraid of the drop, and her determination solidified.

Slowly they began to climb. There was no room to pass on the steps, but there were frequent ledges and caves with wide mouths, and several times they drew aside to let others hurry ahead.

At first Jayna ascended with confidence, the rough stone giving her better grip than she'd expected. But as they climbed past the third cave entrance, she began to feel a flutter of nerves that told her it was a long way down.

"Nearly there," Pochra said. "As soon as we reach the first cave, we can climb a few levels inside."

"Thank Diona," Hanna breathed from behind her.

"I thought you were some brave mountaineer," Jayna teased, not daring to look back at Hanna.

"That was terrifying, and I'd happily never do it again," Hanna said.

Just then, their guide ducked into a cave. Jayna hastened after her, glad to stand on a wider surface again, only to find her eyes struggling to adjust to the dim light. Unlike the caverns in

221

her own realm, these did not appear lit, and it was a minute before she realized a door stood in the rock just two paces before her.

She and Hanna followed Pochra deeper into the cave, and as the stone door swung open, light flooded the passageway. Where the entrance had smelled of brine and seaweed, beyond the door Jayna caught the smell of fish sizzling over a fire. The white glow emanated from Weavers' crystals placed in sconces on the walls, illuminating a circular room with a fire pit in the center and a hole in the ceiling to vent the smoke. Animal skins hung across doorways all around the room, and a ladder led up the wall and through a second hole in the ceiling.

"My home is two levels up," Pochra said. "Take care on the ladders. It's a rough landing if you fall."

"And it wasn't dangerous on the stairs outside?" Jayna asked dubiously.

"Oh, they're designed to drop straight into the water. Our children learn to run the steps by falling more than once, and they quickly figure out how to land in a way that doesn't sting."

Jayna glanced at Hanna, eyebrows raised in amusement.

They followed Pochra up the ladder, Jayna's backpack scraping against the rough rock. After the stairs, this felt easy, and she scampered up as fast as she could just for fun.

When they reached the woman's house, she sat on a woven grass mat and started building a fire. Jayna and Hanna sat beside her, watching in wonder, as she struck a fire from a spark thrown off a small rock. Once the fire was burning merrily, eating through the grasses used as kindling and catching on the smooth driftwood, Pochra fetched a kettle of water and sat it on the fire.

"While we wait for that to heat up, I'll show you the map,"

she said, getting to her feet.

Jayna followed her eagerly through one of the deerskin flaps. Beyond lay a larger room with a domed ceiling, and on one wall was a painted map that was unmistakably Itrea. It was stylized, more an artist's impression than an accurate representation, but she could see the Wandering Woods and Baylore Valley and the Icebraid Peaks.

"We're here," said Pochra, pointing to a small indent in the coast that lay much closer to Larkhaven than Jayna had realized. In fact, they were near the end of a wide peninsula, and the quickest route back along the peninsula to the main body of the continent passed right beneath Larkhaven.

"And we want to go…" Jayna walked over to the opposite end of the map, where a line of mountains rose from the western side of the continent. Towns were illustrated as collections of houses, most lacking names, and the trade road around Baylore Valley was much more circular than she remembered. "I don't actually know where the Itreans are evacuating. Do you think they would've headed directly west, aiming for the Iceling capital, or taken the quicker route toward that settlement up there?"

"They were heading directly west," Hanna said shyly. "Queen Kalleah drew a rough sketch for me before we left, and King Daymin confirmed it. I think they're worried about snow in the mountains, and the farther north they go, the later it will linger."

"Well, we need to reach the Iceling capital in any case, so that will make our job easier," Jayna said.

"Very good," said Pochra. "Now, this is going to be complicated. There aren't many landmarks to follow in the open countryside, so you may need to walk within sight of the roads. But keep well enough away that the Whitish don't catch sight of you. They never travel the road to our village past the intersection with Marroktown, so you'll be safe to there, and after that you'll cut directly toward the forest."

"And…will the forest let us through?" Hanna asked nervously.

Pochra shrugged. "I can't say. I know the situation has changed greatly in the past year, but we've been cut off from any news from Baylore. And the trees are all bound up in the conflict. I will tell you this, though. You won't find your way through the forest without the Drifters helping you."

"And past that?" Jayna asked.

"I can't help you much with the central plains, I'm afraid. The Whitish occupation is expanding too fast for us to keep up with, so I couldn't tell you which settlements are still in Itrean hands. Just keep in mind that you'll need to find a bridge across the Elygian River, as it's too deep and swift to cross any other way, and the only bridges are near Ashton, Pelek, New Savair, Coppertown, and Sumarin." She pointed out the settlements as she spoke, and indeed, many included fanciful illustrations of bridges. "Oh, and the biggest Whitish strongholds are at Twenty-League Town and Darkland Fort, so I'd stay clear of those if I were you."

"Darkland Fort has fallen," Jayna said. "King Daymin destroyed it. We heard from him just before we parted ways with Queen Kalleah."

Pochra's eyes widened. "If that's true, our people are stronger than I'd realized! So why are they fleeing?"

"Something about the trees leaving Baylore," Jayna said.

"But I'm sure there's more to the story. There's a lot about this conflict that we don't know."

"We feel the same way," Pochra said gravely. "Now, would you like a cup of seaweed broth?"

* * *

Hours later, Jayna and Hanna curled on furs on the floor to sleep, taking a room that Pochra said had once belonged to her daughter, who was now living in King's Port. Though the smell was all wrong, there was something comfortingly familiar about the caves and the furs. It sparked a curious nostalgia in Jayna—something about being far away from home made her appreciate it more than usual.

"I'm going to miss Yakov," she said glumly, staring up at the dark ceiling.

"I know," Hanna whispered.

"And you're not?"

Hanna was quiet for a moment. "I…did admire him."

"You were constantly following him around!"

Even though it was dark, Jayna knew Hanna would be blushing. "He knew so much! But no, you knew him longer than I did. I wasn't about to try to steal him from you."

"He wasn't mine to begin with," Jayna muttered.

"Anyway, he was far too clever for me. Well-traveled, but also witty. I couldn't keep up." Hanna paused. "Would you have followed him? If the circumstances had been different?"

"I don't know," Jayna said.

For a while, both lay in silence, though Jayna could tell Hanna was still far from sleep.

At last, Hanna said, "It will be hard for you, you know. Finding a partner. You've chosen a very difficult life for yourself, and you'll need someone who is willing to follow wherever you lead."

"And that's not Yakov," Jayna said grimly.

"No."

"What about you? You're following me, and I never would've imagined you as the adventurous type. That means it can't be that hard to come across a person like that."

"I don't know," Hanna said. "I think that's different. You've always dreamed of travel, whereas I just needed direction. I wanted to get involved in the conflict somehow, without fighting, and you had a way to do that. If we make it through the war alive, I think we'll end up parting ways eventually. This is just a temporary alignment of paths."

Jayna pulled the furs up closer to her chin, probing at the bittersweet ache that was all she had left of Yakov. She had finally reached Itrea, a land she had always dreamed of. She was becoming a great adventurer, welcomed like a hero come to turn the tides of war, readying to embark on a great journey across hostile territory.

So why did she feel the loss of Yakov—of home—so keenly?

32

The Forges of New Savair

Daymin could smell the forges of New Savair long before his army came within sight of the town. Located north of the mines at Redhill and Coppertown, New Savair had been closely guarded ever since it fell under Whitish occupation, so he had no recent intelligence to tell him what to expect.

New Savair marked the southernmost reaches of Baylore Valley, before the ground grew arid and rocky, and he could already see signs that the land here was less fertile than around Baylore. Large rocks jutted from freshly-plowed fields, and instead of the tall wild grasses he was accustomed to, the uncultivated land was colonized by scrubby plants and shrubs.

He had easily captured Druin, several days south of Pelek, and the Whitish army was now far enough behind that Daymin hoped he would never have to face them directly. He intended to take back the mines before crossing the river at Coppertown and stranding the Whitish on the opposite bank, which would only be possible if he kept a good lead on the Whitish.

As the smell of scorched metal grew stronger, Daymin kicked his horse into a trot, cutting off the road to summit a gentle hill.

Then he tensed at the sight before him.

New Savair had become a small metropolis under Whitish control. Houses sprawled for leagues along the opposite riverbank, and at the southern end of town lay dozens upon dozens of forges and warehouses. A steady line of donkey-drawn wagons carried chunks of ore up the road from the mines, and a cloud of black smoke lay thick over the town.

Though no stronghold guarded the town, this fight could turn messy, especially if New Savair had a sizeable population.

Daymin guided his horse back down to the road, where he caught up with Dellik, Morrisse, and Pollard.

"Could you see the town?" Dellik asked.

"We're nearly there," Daymin said, "and it's bigger than I'd expected. It looks like a manufacturing hub for the metals mined nearby."

"The Whitish won't want to lose such a valuable asset," Morrisse said grimly.

"No," Daymin said. "And they must know we're on our way. So why haven't they mounted a defense?"

"Maybe they underestimate us," Morrisse said.

Daymin doubted that, but he said nothing.

"We should move quickly, before they have a chance to prepare," Pollard said.

"Agreed," Daymin said. "Dellik, summon the cavalry and Flamespinners to the front, and give orders to set up camp behind this hill. We'll leave our supply wagons behind and return after we capture the town."

"You don't think they plan to bring down the bridge before we can cross, do you?" Dellik asked worriedly.

Daymin grimaced. "If they do, we'll head south and rejoin the wagons closer to the mines. But keep out of sight, just in case. I don't want to give them much of a warning."

While the three rode off to pass along his orders, Daymin pushed up his sleeve to check if he'd received a new message from Idorii. He had finally received a reply a couple days ago, and seeing Idorii's familiar handwriting—the way he had admitted that he missed Daymin too—had made the distance more painful than ever. Since then, he and Idorii had exchanged messages multiple times each evening, and the secret of their communication was like a fire that warded off his dark thoughts.

Idorii hadn't written anything, so he pulled his sleeve back down and tried to focus on the upcoming battle.

What worried him most was that the Whitish might tear through each of the villages he had recaptured and punish their residents for Daymin's actions. His mother had been accused of focusing more on the residents of Baylore than on the Itreans outside the forest border, and now Daymin could see he was going down the same path. He was placing farmers and rural villages in the path of the Whitish army in exchange for evacuating Baylore's population.

The numbers alone told him it was worth the sacrifice, but war was never that simple. These people had suffered far more than any who had made it safely to Baylore—many had spent years in slavery, watching their loved ones killed or captured one by one.

But it was too late to be worrying about this now. He was deep into his campaign, leading the Whitish army through the heart of Baylore Valley, and the only way to safety was to push forward.

The pounding of hooves drew his attention; when he turned, he saw Dellik returning with his cavalry.

"Shall we sweep through the town and quickly deal with any in our path?" she asked.

"I'm not sure we'll be able to tell civilians apart from Whitish," Daymin said. "We can fell anyone who raises a sword against us, but otherwise we should leave the rest of the population for my foot soldiers to capture."

"Noted," Dellik said. "Are you ready, Your Majesty?"

Daymin nodded tersely.

Once Dellik, Cal, and the various commanders had assembled with their troops, Pollard and Morrisse stationed further back in the column, Daymin tugged his helmet over his curls and spurred his horse into a canter. Around him, the rest of his cavalry fell into line, sweeping down the hill and into view of the town that sprawled across the opposite riverbank.

Daymin urged his horse faster as he neared the bridge, still half-expecting it to collapse underfoot, but his horse's hooves thundered safely over the boards. The river was swollen from the spring melt, and Daymin could see evidence of past floods rising higher still along the bank, so the town sat a hundred paces back from the water's edge.

Soon he reached the eastern side of the river, his cavalry surging forward around him.

Shouts were now rising from the streets nearest the bridge, and Daymin could see people running in every direction. A small knot of soldiers dashed down the main street and formed a pitiful line where the town ended, while others filled in behind them, most in civilian clothes.

Daymin leaned forward over the neck of his horse and urged him faster still. They would plow right through the pitiful defense. He hardly needed to bother with his sword.

They thundered up to the edge of town, ready to tear down the main street—

The next thing Daymin knew, he was flying over his horse's head, yelling in surprise.

His shoulder slammed into the ground, and he skidded, helmet slipping so he couldn't see. Pain tore through him, and for a moment he lost all sense of his surroundings, overcome by a wave of dizziness.

All around him, soldiers were shouting and cursing, while their horses whinnied in pain.

As the dizziness subsided, Daymin wrenched his helmet back into place. He was lying where dirt ground gave way to cobblestones, and his sword had skidded away from him when he fell.

Pushing himself into a sitting position with one hand, his shoulder throbbing hideously, he realized what had happened.

The Whitish had dug a long pit like a moat in the ground outside New Savair, hiding it beneath clods of grass balanced on a thin latticework of twigs. And Daymin's cavalry had ridden right into the pit.

Even after the first wave of soldiers had revealed the pit, momentum must have carried the rest of his cavalry forward; Daymin could hardly see a horse that didn't appear injured by the fall. The sight sickened him.

A few had leapt safely across and were even now driving back the Whitish soldiers, but the rest were trying to recover from the shock, just as Daymin was.

He grabbed his sword and stumbled to his feet, wincing as pain lanced through his shoulder once more.

Plagues. He could hardly fight in this condition.

"Orders, Your Majesty!" Dellik's voice shouted. Turning, Daymin was relieved to see she was among those who had made it through safely.

"Spread out and take the town quickly," Daymin said. "There don't seem to be many soldiers around. But stop before the forges—we might find a stronger resistance there."

Dellik saluted.

As Daymin turned back toward the pits, he heard her shouting directions to the other generals. The foot soldiers were faring better than his cavalry, balancing on the rods that had lain across the pit at intervals to support the grass on top, and they were soon flooding the street.

Without a mount, Daymin had no easy way of leading troops, so he gritted his teeth against the pain in his shoulder and let the swelling tide of soldiers carry him down the main street.

Buildings loomed over him on both sides, most two stories tall, almost all built of wood. Daymin had no idea where the Whitish would have found such vast quantities of wood, unless they had harvested it from around King's Port. The style was uniform and lifeless, more like rows of barracks than a true city.

And as they drew closer to the forges, Daymin began to understand why this was. There were bars on many of the windows, and down a side street he glimpsed men with ankles chained together.

New Savair was a city of slaves. *Itrean* slaves.

Now he knew why the Whitish defense had been so weak—because there were very few Whitish soldiers based here. Just enough to keep the slaves in line as they refined the ore delivered from the mines and worked the forges.

"Careful!" he shouted, his voice nearly lost beneath the clamor of running footsteps. "These are mostly Itreans here! Don't harm anyone unless you're certain they're Whitish!"

Soon the main street turned a corner and carried them toward the southern end of town. Here the smoke lay thicker than ever, and above the sounds of his army, Daymin could hear clanging from the forges.

His army slowed as they reached the end of the street. Daymin pushed his way forward to see what was waiting for them, angling sideways to protect his shoulder.

Between the main town and the forges lay a vast square, and it was here the carts of ore were unloaded. Another few dozen soldiers had gathered between Daymin's army and the industrial workings, a laughable force set against his tens of thousands of troops.

But as he watched, a man jogged from one of the warehouses with a torch in hand. The clanging from the forges had finally fallen silent.

"There are several thousand Itreans inside the forges," he shouted, "and we've doused the floors in oil. Take one step closer and we'll send them up in flames."

Daymin glanced sideways at Dellik, who was within earshot. "Bring the Flamespinners forward," he muttered.

He saw a ripple of movement as she passed on his orders

on.

Now Daymin needed to distract the Whitish long enough for Uncle Cal's troops to reach his side.

After scanning the square quickly to make sure there were no archers within range, he pulled off his helmet.

"Why are you doing this?" Daymin demanded, his voice ringing through the square. "Does King Edreon not care about the loss of his metalworking industry?"

"Our forges fueled the takeover of Itrea," the soldier said dismissively, "and that work is nearly done. If we lose New Savair, we don't intend to leave behind anything that you might find useful."

"Your king is so confident in his victory?" Daymin asked, still stalling.

"Taking back a few small towns changes nothing," the soldier said. "Baylore will fall any day now."

Daymin felt movement at his back and glanced sideways to see Uncle Cal squeezing his way between the front line of soldiers.

"What do you want me to do?" he whispered.

"He's threatening to set those buildings on fire with Itrean slaves inside," Daymin muttered, trying not to move his lips. "Could your Flamespinners get the fire under control quickly enough to keep them safe?"

"Depends on how fast the fire spreads," Cal whispered.

Daymin grimaced. "He says he's doused the floors in oil."

Cal was silent for a long moment. As Daymin waited, pulse racing, the Whitish soldier stalked forward.

"Well?" he demanded. "What are you going to do?"

"Are you expecting us to surrender?" Daymin asked

incredulously. "My army of thousands, lay down our swords before a dozen enemies?"

"We should try," Cal whispered. "He might be bluffing."

"Unless you want to slaughter your own civilians," said the Whitish soldier.

They had nothing to lose, which made them dangerous. But Daymin couldn't leave such a valuable town in Whitish hands. And he certainly couldn't walk away after seeing so many of his people in chains.

"Very well," Daymin said. Raising his voice, he shouted, "Archers!" He hadn't given orders for his archers to stand ready, but to his relief, a haphazard volley immediately soared from his ranks.

The Whitish in the square scattered, and in the confusion, nothing happened to the forges. Daymin jammed his helmet on once again and charged forward, no longer caring about the pain in his shoulder. There couldn't be many Whitish soldiers guarding the forges—he just had to fell the ones with torches, and then his people would be safe.

But before he reached the opposite end of the square, orange firelight bloomed from within the nearest forge. The flames spread rapidly, crackling and sending out sparks, and Daymin could feel the heat washing across his face.

"Cal!" he shouted. "Tell us how we can help!"

"Clear a path," Uncle Cal's voice yelled back from somewhere in the chaos.

Daymin's troops were already slowing, held at bay by the heat of the growing inferno.

"Make room for our Flamespinners!" Daymin shouted, holding out his arms to either side to slow the soldiers behind him. His shoulder throbbed in protest, but he was too panicked to care. "Archers, aim for the soldiers with torches!"

The Whitish soldiers in the square had vanished, cut down in Daymin's initial charge, but he could still make out figures waiting in each of the forges and warehouses with torches in hand. They were stalling—he hoped they might second-guess their orders now the soldier in charge was gone.

In the space that opened before him, Cal and at least fifty other Flamespinners dashed forward to meet the blaze. As they raised their arms, Daymin could see the flames bending beneath their will.

But it wasn't going to be enough. He could already see that. The Flamespinners had a limited range, and the fire was tearing deep into the forge. Besides, from what he knew about Flamespinners, they had a much harder time controlling fires that had latched onto other materials.

While he watched, Daymin edged sideways, ducking behind other soldiers to keep a low profile. His archers were shooting from several points in the square and had already felled three of the soldiers with torches, their flames rolling safely onto the cobblestones, but one stood in the shadows of a warehouse near where Daymin waited. He was half-hidden behind the doorway, out of reach of Daymin's archers, and no one else seemed to have noticed him.

When Daymin was close enough, he brought his sword to his shoulder and readjusted his grip on the hilt, palm sweaty.

Then he charged out from his own ranks, toward the Whitish soldier.

For a split second, the man didn't move.

Then he drew his own sword, torch dangling from his left

hand.

Daymin sprinted through the warehouse doorway, bringing his sword down in a swinging arc as he did.

The soldier caught it on his own blade. The clash of metal rang out in the hollow space, and the blow reverberated through Daymin's arm.

"You've made—a big mistake," the soldier grunted as he struck out at Daymin. His teeth were bared in a terrible grin.

"I don't know what you're talking about," Daymin said, struggling to block the soldier's strikes. He was not as skilled a foe as the soldiers Daymin had faced at Darkland Fort, but he was still a better swordsman than Daymin.

"Oh, you'll find out."

His words gnawed at Daymin, distracting him from the fight. Maybe he was simply referring to the way Daymin had engaged him in a fight he couldn't win.

Daymin blocked a great overhand swing, attempting to twist his sword around for another attack, but the soldier shoved his blade aside.

Maybe he should focus on forcing the man into the square, where one of his archers could fell him.

Trying not to be obvious about it, Daymin twisted his body with his next strike so his back was against the open doorway.

The Whitish soldier parried his blow easily. When he lashed out again, Daymin stepped backward, out of range of the blade.

And the Whitish soldier followed.

They exchanged more blows, blades clacking together, while Daymin pretended to be forced backward. Soon the soldier stood fully exposed in the doorway.

Daymin couldn't risk a glance to the side to see if anyone

had noticed his fight. The Whitish soldier was growing more aggressive, blows raining on Daymin without a pause, though thankfully most were standard forms he knew how to block. It was responding quickly enough that was the challenge, and Daymin was grateful for his recent battlefield experience that had taught him to react more instinctively.

Even so, he fumbled a few blocks, and the sword struck more than once on his helmet and his enchanted gambeson.

Then, with a loud *twang* that made Daymin flinch, an arrow materialized in the Whitish soldier's arm. Daymin hadn't seen it until it struck.

The man dropped his sword with a roar of pain and clutched at his arm. He wore no armor, and the arrow had pierced deep into his flesh.

Taking advantage of his distraction, Daymin whipped his own blade up to the man's throat. "Drop that torch. Now."

The soldier twisted backward, away from Daymin's sword. As he did, he took the torch in his uninjured hand and flung it toward the nearest wall of the forge.

Daymin shoved the man backward, toppling him, and plunged his sword into his chest.

At the sight of blood pouring from the wound, revulsion rose up in his throat, but he swallowed it back and yanked his blade free.

A crackling sound behind him made him whirl. The fire was already spreading up the wall, following a line of oil staining the faded wood.

"No," Daymin said frantically. "Not this one too."

He dropped his sword and dashed over to the spreading flames, pulling off his gambeson as he went.

Ignoring the way the burgeoning heat seared at his face, he threw his coat over the flames, pressing it against the wall to smother the fire.

Still the flames darted upward.

Daymin slammed his coat against the wall again and again, slapping at the flames, hardly noticing when he singed his palm.

Then, at last, the fire sizzled out.

Daymin let his gambeson fall to the ground, the fabric smoking faintly. It hadn't been fireproofed, since he had assumed his own side would be the only ones using fire in battle, which he realized now was folly. A section of the wall was scorched black—Daymin was lucky he hadn't hesitated a moment longer, or the fire would have climbed beyond his reach.

He felt winded. And humiliated.

He was posing as a great warlord, leading his army on one last, desperate campaign as if they were truly equal to the Whitish army, yet he had been unable to hold his own against an unarmored soldier. Without the archer who had noticed his fight, he never could have brought the man down on his own.

Reaching for his coat, he stumbled back toward the bulk of his forces. The Flamespinners had finally brought the fires in the first forge under control, and he could see no sign of their enemies guarding the industrial buildings.

In fact, he couldn't see any Itrean slaves, either.

Daymin jogged over to Dellik, who was watching the Flamespinners with a frown. The fires around the doorway had been extinguished, and Uncle Cal had led his forces into the smoke-filled building to put out the last of the blaze. As Daymin watched, several Flamespinners staggered out of the building, coughing, their hair grey with ash.

"Where are the slaves?" Daymin asked Dellik.

"I don't know," she said, still frowning. "Maybe the Whitish were just bluffing."

"Soldiers, split up and search the warehouses and forges!" Daymin shouted. "We need to find the civilians!"

Several contingents broke off and jogged toward the open doorways, keeping away from the remnants of the fire.

That was when he heard the screams.

33

Fire in the City

Daymin whirled.

The screams rose from behind him, echoing through the streets of New Savair. As he looked closer, he noticed something that he had missed in his preoccupation with the forges.

Towering plumes of smoke billowed from every direction, encircling the town. The Whitish had set fire to New Savair, and from the look of the smoke, the blaze had spread far enough that Daymin's army would struggle to break free.

"Bloody Varse," Dellik said under her breath. "They've trapped us."

When Daymin hesitated, paralyzed with horror, Dellik raised her voice and shouted, "Run! Find the quickest way out and reassemble by the riverbank! We can't let the fires trap us!"

At her words, Daymin's army descended into chaos. Some of the better-trained soldiers remained in companies, holding formation as they dashed toward the nearest streets leading off the square, while the rest scattered.

Daymin still couldn't force his feet to move. His blood was pounding in his ears, his vision wavering.

Then he realized the Flamespinners didn't know what was happening.

"Cal! Get out of there!" Daymin bellowed.

When he heard no response, he finally managed to uproot himself. Dashing toward the forge, he yelled, "Cal! Flamespinners! Abandon your work! The city is burning!"

The last of the flames still flickered at the back of the warehouse, but the Flamespinners must have heard, because they began jogging out to the entrance. All looked exhausted and starved for oxygen, and many were coughing heavily.

When Uncle Cal approached Daymin, he was gasping for breath.

"We can't—fight the fires—around the city," he said.

"I know," Daymin said. "Get yourselves to safety. Go!"

Then he sprinted back out to the square, where Dellik was bellowing orders at the soldiers who remained by her side.

Pausing to draw breath, she noticed Daymin. "You need to get out of here," she said sharply.

"What about the civilians?"

Dellik hesitated, and he thought she bit back the first words that had come to mind. Then she sighed. "Leave that to me. But we can't save everyone."

"I know."

"Now get the plagues out of here, Daymin!" she barked.

Daymin flinched at her tone. He wanted to stay behind until he was certain his army had made it to safety, but Dellik was right—he had to get out of New Savair alive. If something happened to him, their campaign would lose its momentum. The army was following *him*, not Uncle Cal or Pollard or Morrisse, and the population of Baylore was counting on his success.

"*Go!*" Dellik shouted.

Daymin jogged off in the direction of a group of soldiers that had ducked down a side street. He had gotten turned around in the city, but he thought they were heading roughly west, in the direction of the river.

As he ran, he saw panicked civilians emerging from the wooden buildings, some slowed by chains around their ankles. The soldiers he followed tore past the civilians without glancing their way, driven on by instinctive fear, but Daymin couldn't do it.

Knowing what Dellik would say if she saw him, Daymin slowed and approached the nearest civilians. Without asking permission, he drew his enchanted sword and sliced through the chains with a swift downward stroke.

"Get out of the town!" he shouted at them. "My army will protect you!"

Then he broke into a run, not waiting for them to follow. When he reached a corner and glanced back, he saw them stumbling after him, picking up their pace as they went.

Each time he reached a group of slaves in chains, Daymin stopped to break the links with his sword. As he went, the smoke clogging the streets grew thicker and thicker, until each breath clawed at his lungs. He thought the air was warmer than it had been, and ahead he could see flickers of orange illuminating the smoke-blackened sky.

He was fully lost now. The last of the soldiers had long since fled, so the only people in the streets were civilians.

Daymin quickened his pace, lungs searing. This was exactly what Dellik had wanted to avoid. If he died in the fires, along with all the civilians he had freed from their chains, he would have thrown everything away for the sake of his own conscience.

Bloody plagues. Why was it always so hard to see the big picture when he was fighting?

Cursing himself, he tore around another corner. He was feeling lightheaded, coughing every time he drew breath, and the air was definitely warmer now.

Then, for a single heartbeat, the smoke before him parted and he could see where the city ended. He just had to keep running this way, and he would be free.

As he ran faster than before, head pounding, vision clouding over, he could see flames billowing from the wooden structures on either side of the street.

He had to make a dash for it.

Yelling hoarsely, Daymin sprinted the final distance down the street. Fire seared his cheek, and he smelled burning hair.

Still he ran, blinded by the smoke, eyes stinging.

At last the heat eased. Daymin slowed, coughing violently, and realized the air was clean out here. He still couldn't see; rubbing at his eyes, he blinked until the scene came clear.

His army had gathered along the riverbank, many with singed uniforms, and there were civilians among their number as well. This didn't seem to be his full force—how many had he lost?

Dellik was nowhere in sight, nor was Uncle Cal, and Daymin felt momentarily directionless without them.

He felt wretched, but he pushed the sensation aside. He had

to deal with the fallout from this disastrous battle before he could afford to think about it.

Scanning the riverbank, he found Pollard and Morrisse seeing to their own troops. He jogged toward them, lungs still burning.

"Your Majesty!" Morrisse shouted when he noticed Daymin. "We didn't realize you were still in the city! By the time we made it out, the streets were nearly impassable."

"I know," Daymin said woodenly. "Do you have any idea how our army has fared?"

"Many would have escaped on the opposite side of town," Pollard said. "We won't have a true idea of the casualties until they rejoin us."

Daymin turned to look back at the burning city. The Whitish must have torched every building on the perimeter, sacrificing their city for the sake of weakening Daymin's army.

It had been a very clever trap. Daymin never would have expected the Whitish to take such drastic action, torching their own metalworks for the sake of defeating him, but then again, this was exactly the sort of brutality the Whitish were known for.

As he watched, a few civilians dashed from the same street Daymin had followed.

His chest tightened. Maybe his efforts hadn't been in vain after all.

Then one fell, and the others left him behind, running clumsily to join the army beside the river.

"Organize your forces to move across the river, back to our camp," Daymin said. "Mine will follow."

As Morrisse and Pollard passed on his orders, Daymin jogged off in search of his friends. Tarak, Zahira, and Lalaysha had been among his foot soldiers, and he had not seen them since before the fight began. They could be anywhere in this mess of an army—or in the burning city—and he cursed himself again for falling into such a deadly trap.

Morrisse's troops were beginning to move toward the bridge, so Daymin followed them, intending to inventory his army as they crossed. He wouldn't leave this bank until Dellik, Uncle Cal, and his friends had made it to safety.

Daymin stopped at the eastern end of the bridge, planting his feet in the reedy grass. His shoulder was still aching dully, but it no longer seemed to matter in the face of everything else he had lost. From here he could see the bodies of the horses that had fallen in the initial charge, and again the sick feeling rose in his stomach.

He swallowed it back. *Not now.*

After Morrisse's troops came Pollard's, followed by Daymin's reserve army. His main army remained behind, organizing the civilians and scooping up any stragglers who managed to escape the inferno; Daymin was grateful his lesser generals had taken the initiative even without Dellik there to give orders.

Little by little, civilians and wounded soldiers began straggling over the bridge. Many of the freed slaves still had chains trailing from manacles around their ankles, though Daymin's soldiers had cut through the links just as he had done. There were children as well, including a few babies, and many of the civilians ducked their heads respectfully to Daymin as they passed.

He hated it. If he hadn't marched on New Savair, none of them would have lost their lives. They should be spitting at his feet, not thanking him.

Little by little, more soldiers and civilians circled around from the opposite side of town, and Daymin began to hope he had only lost a few thousand. It was still a terrible blow, but it would not cripple his army.

Then, at last, he spotted the faces he had searched for. Tarak, Zahira, and Lalaysha walked together, all seemingly uninjured, though Lalaysha's clothes were charred.

"Meeko!" Lalaysha cried when she saw him. She broke into a run and threw herself into his arms; Daymin hugged her fiercely, fighting back tears.

Then Tarak and Zahira were hugging him as well, Zahira's eyes glistening.

"You're safe," Daymin said, again and again. "You're all safe."

Lalaysha gave him a last squeeze before letting him go. "I was so worried when I didn't see you leaving the city."

"Where were you when the fires started spreading?" Daymin asked.

"We were somewhere in the middle of the city," Tarak said.

"It was horrible," Zahira said.

Tarak nodded. "We smelled smoke and heard fighting, but it wasn't until the soldiers ahead of us started dashing off in every direction that we realized what had happened."

"I'm sorry," Daymin said. "I'm so sorry."

"You didn't do this," Lalaysha said.

Daymin shook his head, too weary to argue the point. "Go on. Get back to camp, and I'll join you there in a bit."

Lalaysha looked like she wanted to argue, but Zahira took her by the elbow and dragged her onto the bridge.

Alone again, Daymin watched with increasing worry as the stream of people from the opposite side of the town dried up.

Where were the Flamespinners? And where was Dellik?

The whole town was ablaze now, smoke pouring off the buildings so thickly he could barely make out the remains of the wooden structures. Distant crashes sounded as the buildings collapsed, and soon the outermost ring lay in smoldering ruins.

Then a knot of people emerged from the smoke-clogged streets.

It was the Flamespinners. And they were escorting a crowd of several hundred civilians.

Daymin's heart leapt. He couldn't make out their faces through the smoke, but the one at the front, organizing the group, had to be Uncle Cal.

As they staggered to the waterfront, the group scattered, and one of the Flamespinners broke into a jog toward the bridge.

When he drew near, Daymin recognized Cal. His clothes were charred, his face smeared with soot, and his eyes were red with exhaustion.

"I think we were the last ones alive in there," Cal said hoarsely, slowing to a halt. "How did the rest of your army fare?"

"I don't know yet," Daymin said. "Have you seen Dellik?"

Cal shook his head.

Daymin's throat closed up. "Then—she must not have made it."

34

Dellik

Alone in his too-large tent that night, Daymin finally allowed the pain of his losses to consume him.

So many dead. Such wanton destruction. All because New Savair had been a convenient target for him to recapture.

He lay on his sleeping roll, staring sightlessly at the top of his tent as the battle played through his mind once again.

The smoke. The screams. The injured horses, cast away like carrion. The duel he had been unable to win.

Dellik.

It had been Daymin's orders that kept her in the city. If she hadn't stayed behind to rescue civilians, she would have made it out alive.

He had killed her.

His eyes burned, tears leaking from the corners. Dellik had always been there for him, ever since his mother left Baylore.

She had looked out for him. Kept him honest. Organized his troops when Daymin hadn't known what he was doing.

And until he had stepped from the city alone, he hadn't realized how much he had depended on her and Uncle Cal. They had been the voices of authority that guided his army, not him. Without them, Daymin had felt powerless.

Thousands had died in New Savair, not including the countless slaves who hadn't made it out alive.

Plagues. When had his simple campaign twisted into such a brutal death march?

A final storm of fire and blood—wasn't that how he had thought of his last strike against the Whitish?

His words were proving truer than he'd guessed.

We knew there would be casualties, he reminded himself. *We marched to war knowing we would give everything to grant safe passage to our families as they fled to the Icebraid Peaks.*

Yet still it hurt.

Had he made a mistake? Had his own stupidity led them right into the trap?

He didn't know, and the uncertainty tore at him like a knife in his gut.

At last he sat up, head spinning. He dug the pen from his pocket and rolled up his sleeve, shoulder twinging as he did.

Should he put this burden on Idorii? He wasn't sure he deserved a sympathetic ear after what he had done.

But he had to find a way past this. Writing to Idorii was the only way he could imagine moving forward.

Idorii —

Our battle for New Savair was a disaster. The Whitish lured our army into the city and distracted us by setting fire to their forges, pretending they had trapped civilians inside. While our attention was diverted, they lit the whole city on fire. We barely made it out alive—thousands were lost, including General Dellik. You didn't know her well, but she was the reason my army functioned as well as it did. I don't know what I'll do without her.

And the worst part is, she wouldn't have died if I hadn't asked her to stay behind to help the civilians. Very few made it out alive, so she died needlessly.

I'll be expected to emerge from my tent tomorrow morning and lead my army onward, but I don't know if I can do it. This campaign is turning into a disaster, and I'm no longer sure if pushing south is the right move. Should we give up now? Turn around and face our pursuers on the field and take down as many as we can before they slaughter us?

Anything is better than killing more civilians needlessly.

Daymin

While he waited for Idorii's reply, he stared listlessly at the flap of his tent, the camp beyond coming to him in confused snatches as the breeze tugged it open. Darkness had fallen, but the space was lit by Weavers' crystals placed at uneven intervals, and he caught sight of many boots passing outside, underlaid by the quiet murmur of voices.

At last his tattoo flashed cold, and Daymin pressed the circular pattern inlaid in his skin.

Just the sight of Idorii's familiar handwriting solidifying on his arm gave him strength, and he took a deep breath, steadying himself.

Oh, Daymin, I wish I could be there with you. I would embrace you and remind you that you are loved by so many, and that we all still believe in you.

The battle sounds grim, but it doesn't change the fact that you have drawn a significant portion of the Whitish army away from Baylore and bought us the time we needed to save our population. You knew, going into it, that this campaign would be bloody. But you decided—and I agreed with you—that it was the right decision regardless.

It takes a strong leader to push through despite such challenges, and I know you are that leader.

Yours,
Idorii

Daymin raked a hand through his hair, which still smelled of smoke. Idorii's words *had* helped. He was right—Daymin's army would see this as just one setback of many along the brutal path they had taken.

It hurt, but war was supposed to hurt.

And plagues, he was no warlord.

Thank you. I needed to hear that.

But what am I supposed to do without Dellik? She was always the one who took charge when I hesitated. I'm trying, I swear I am, but I still can't get out of my head sometimes. I need to act first, think later, but my first instinct is to freeze up when

I don't know what to do.

I miss you so damn much, Idorii. I feel like I would be better able to face the ugliness of it all with you by my side.

Yours,
Daymin

Moments later, Idorii wrote back, *I miss you too, and I'm trying not to dwell on it, or I'll drive myself mad.*

You said you found the spell you needed! Can you not leave Baylore and rejoin my army now?

What—should I follow the Whitish army at your tail until I meet up with you? No. I'll wait until you circle back past Baylore, and then I'll leave at the opportune moment.

Unless the Whitish attack first, Daymin wrote back.

Yes. But I can get out easily enough when they do.

It feels like an eternity before we make our way north to Baylore again. How am I going to endure such a long wait to see you again?

At least we can write, Idorii replied. *Imagine how hard this would be if we had no way to communicate.*

True. Cloudy gods, Idorii. Sometimes I think you're the only reason I've kept my sanity. I wish I hadn't been so Varse-

damned stupid and pushed you away.

You know I've forgiven you for it, right?

That doesn't change the fact that you're in Baylore and I'm out here.

Idorii's response took a while to appear, so Daymin prodded at the ache in his shoulder, wincing when he hit the sensitive spot. He knew he could never marry Idorii, so it was selfish to keep leading him on this way. He still hadn't decided what he was going to do when they were together again—he only knew that he craved the touch of Idorii's lips, the warmth of his embrace.

And for now, he couldn't hide the way he felt. With everything else falling apart around him, Idorii was the one thing he had that remained steady and true and good.

I'm counting down the days until I see you again, Idorii wrote at last. *You know my heart is yours.*

And mine is yours, Daymin wrote back.

35

Guides

The distance from the Village of a Thousand Stairs to the Wandering Woods was longer than Jayna had expected. *Much* longer.

Pochra had arranged horses for them, borrowed from a farmer who lived near the top of the cliffs, and the farmer's daughter had acted as their guide. Even so, it was a three-day gallop to the forest border, with Jayna and Hanna clinging to the saddles in fear of their lives.

Tika was well enough to fly again, so she and Dragon wheeled overhead, occasionally swooping down to catch a rodent. The landscape stretching out from the coast was lush and rolling, and apart from pockets of tilled fields surrounding farmhouses and settlements, most of the land was grazed by sheep. Jayna and her companions startled more than one flock of sheep into stampeding away when they galloped over a hillock at full speed.

They reached the outskirts of the Wandering Woods with the sun dropping low in the sky before them. Where the forest in Cashabree began gradually, here there was nothing but emerald grasses and then, suddenly, a line of towering trees.

Jayna reined in her horse just before the trees, an earthy, *alive* smell rising to meet her. She dismounted—or more accurately, fell off her horse—grateful to feel solid ground underfoot once more.

"Never again," she said, massaging the tender place where her buttocks had been slammed repeatedly against the saddle.

Hanna was moving gingerly as well, though she had yet to voice a complaint about the discomfort of horseriding.

Instead, Hanna turned to their guide and ducked her head, putting a hand to her forehead in a gesture of deep gratitude. "We would have walked for spans without your help," she said. "On behalf of Queen Kalleah and King Daymin, we thank you."

Merciful Jesha—when had Hanna gotten better at interacting with people than Jayna?

"Yes," Jayna said hurriedly. "The role you have played in your kingdom's survival will go down in the official records of Cashabree."

The girl giggled. She was only twelve, yet she was a highly competent horsewoman, and her parents clearly trusted her to send her on such a dangerous mission unaccompanied.

"Good luck," she said. "Come visit again, if you make it back this way."

"We will," Jayna said, knowing she would never follow this exact route again.

Hanna whistled for Tika—Dragon swooped after, as always—and the two birds landed on their wrists. Then, with a final wave at their guide, they stepped beneath the trees.

Jayna could immediately feel a watchful presence. She knew the stories—that the trees themselves were sentient and able to move about—but she didn't know what to believe. Her people claimed to keep records for every civilization in the known world, but their record-keepers were only installed at official courts, which did not include loosely-organized, tribal societies like this one.

In fact, she might be the first Mountain Lord ever to observe the Allakoash directly. At the thought, excitement bubbled up in her chest.

"I wonder when we'll run across the people," she whispered to Hanna.

"Shh," Hanna said.

As they crept forward, Jayna swore she could see the trees moving out of their path, realigning subtly to create a clear way forward. Dragon shifted restlessly on her arm, pecking at the leather brace in agitation, so she cradled her close to her chest.

They had walked for perhaps thirty minutes when a movement ahead made Jayna freeze. She grabbed Hanna's sleeve, stopping her from going any further.

Then a figure stepped from behind a tree.

He was paler than any Itreans Jayna had known, with black hair braided down his back, and there was something familiar about the shape of his eyes. Sweet Mianda—were her own people related to the Allakoash?

As he approached, hands held out, he spoke in an unfamiliar tongue. His eyes were wide as he took in the girls and their birds. After a moment, he smiled and beckoned them to follow.

They started after him, picking their way over moss-covered roots and through glades filled with ferns, and as they walked, the last of the sunlight filtered through the trees, dappling the ground in gold.

Before the sun set, they reached a camp set in a clearing in the woods. A fire stood in the middle of the grassy space, with a hare roasting on a spit, and at first Jayna couldn't see any evidence of houses. Then she saw someone emerging from a hollow tree, pushing aside a curtain of moss, and realized each tree had a similar entrance. Some were covered by animal skins, while others had doorways of bark or moss that draped like cobwebs from the tree.

No one seemed to speak Whitish, but the Allakoash beckoned Jayna and Hanna to join them around the fire. Over a dinner of rabbit and pheasant and roasted fern fronds, Jayna and Hanna tried to explain themselves with gestures, failing spectacularly. Word of their arrival must have spread, because others emerged from the dark woods while they ate, watching and listening with sharp curiosity.

* * *

In the morning, an unfamiliar woman approached them. Though her hair was grey, her skin was unlined—Jayna couldn't begin to guess her age.

"Hello," the woman said in Whitish. "I was summoned by this tribe, who guessed you spoke Whitish."

"We do," Jayna said.

The woman smiled. "Welcome. From what this tribe was able to piece together, you have traveled from across the sea?"

"Yes," Jayna said, "from Cashabree. We were sailing with Queen Kalleah until recently."

The woman's eyes widened. "Truly?"

"She sent us to help King Daymin," Hanna said.

The woman beckoned another to her side and spoke quickly in Allakoash. All at once, they had an audience—everyone within earshot hurried over to listen, while more materialized from the nearby trees. Their expressions showed wonder and...hope?

Jayna had known of the alliance between the Itreans and the Allakoash guarding Baylore, but she also knew from Queen Kalleah's description that the Allakoash were secretive and did not want to get involved in affairs beyond their borders.

But the way they reacted to this news...

If Jayna wasn't mistaken, the Allakoash were counting on King Daymin, even if they did not want to admit it.

How would they react if they learned he was evacuating Baylore?

She wouldn't say anything, just in case.

"Where are you headed?" the old woman asked.

"Baylore," Jayna lied. "We need to find a safe way across the central valley."

"You will want to travel north of the road. I will lead you to the place where the forest road once ended, and you can continue from there."

"Has the forest road really closed?" Hanna asked shyly.

"Yes. The Whitish were attacking our trees, so we cut them off from the coast. Some worried it would drive them to more aggression, but we have seen no sign that their armies plan to fight us. They are intimidated by the Wandering Woods, it seems."

"That's good," Jayna said.

"Why are you offering to guide us?" Hanna asked.

Jayna elbowed her. "Don't question their kindness!" she hissed.

Hanna flushed. "Sorry. It's just—ever since we arrived in Itrea, everyone we meet has been going out of their way to show us kindness and hospitality. Is it just Itrean culture, or…?"

"We have been without hope for a very long time. When Queen Kalleah left Itrea, we thought we would never hear of her again. But to learn now that she is in the Kinship Thrones, still doing her best to save our home, and that she has sent envoys to aid King Daymin…" The old woman smiled sadly. "It is like a new shoot growing from scorched earth. A shooting star when all else has gone dark. You see why we welcome you?"

Jayna understood what she meant, but the words rang hollow in her ears. She and Hanna were not bringers of life in a deadened land. They were the shepherds who would guide King Daymin's people to their funeral pyres.

36

The Teahouse

Kalleah was whiling away the hours in The Lost Sailor with Mellicante, Triyam, and Luc, who had joined her to play the much-abused game of Kins the innkeeper kept behind his bar. Triyam and Luc were both happily sipping away at tankards of ale, while Kalleah and Mellicante had nothing but water to occupy them.

"I'm still furious that I left the journal behind," Kalleah muttered to Mellicante while Triyam executed an unnecessarily elaborate maneuver. She had lost the book linked with Daymin when their ship had been captured, and while she had made a habit of ripping out pages once they were read, she had not done so for several quarters now.

"If they suspected you were here, they would have come for you already," Mellicante whispered back.

"It's not that. What if Baylore has fallen and Daymin is dead? What if we're risking our lives here for nothing?"

"You know what Baridya would say about that," Mellicante said with a grim smile. "Our work is still worthwhile as long as there are kingdoms oppressed by Whitland."

"Hah! I've captured your port!" Triyam said, placing his piece on the southernmost port of Chelt with a flourish.

"Very good," Luc said drily. "And you've bankrupted yourself to do it."

"On the contrary, it was an excellent move."

Before Luc could reply, the bell on the door jingled, drawing Kalleah's eyes. She kept half-expecting Leoth to show up in the uniform of the Lord's Men, but no—this was Baridya, dressed only somewhat convincingly as a man.

She looked flustered, and her hair was falling down from the hat she had tucked it beneath.

Mellicante was immediately by her side, taking her hand and patting at her as if checking for injuries.

"What happened?" Mellicante asked in a low voice.

Baridya cast a wary glance at Luc and Triyam, so Kalleah rose and led her friends over to a quieter table in a corner where they would not be overheard.

"You aren't injured, are you?" Mellicante helped Baridya into a chair and drew off Baridya's hat, running her fingers through her hair as it fell around her shoulders.

"No, and that's part of the problem," Baridya said, her expression pinched with worry.

"Explain," Kalleah said.

Baridya sighed. "I was scoping out a shop that sells Cheltish goods when a man attacked me."

"The Varse-damned bastard!" Mellicante spat.

"He must have recognized me as a woman."

"But he didn't hurt you?"

"No! How many times do I have to tell you?" From Baridya's amused exasperation, Kalleah could tell she appreciated Mellicante's concern. "No, the problem was that I pulled a sword on him and fought him off. That was when the Lord's Men got involved, and they nearly arrested me. It's illegal for a woman to wield a sword."

"Of course," Mellicante said drily. "Next thing you know, it will be illegal for us to gut fish or eat fruit or—"

"Set our feet on the ground," Baridya said.

"Exactly."

"How did you get out of that?" Kalleah asked.

Baridya turned to Kalleah, worry lining her face once more. "I was saved by a stranger. A man wearing a chain with a diamond-shaped pendant engraved with stars. Likely a reference to Totoleon."

The words of the invitation she had received flashed through Kalleah's mind. *We are working to destabilize the Whitish throne and believe you might be interested in joining us. You can find us at the Temple of Totoleon outside Darrenmark.*

Was Baridya's mysterious savior part of the group that had contacted Kalleah? Were they watching her somehow? Following her?

Was *Bennett* a member of this group?

This was becoming too strange to ignore. Kalleah had to speak to Bennett again and see if she could prise out some of his secrets.

And if he truly did have a way for her to enter the palace, she had to at least consider his suggestion. If someone in this city knew who she was and had been keeping an eye on her, she was not safe.

"It's your turn, Cad!" Luc said, calling Mellicante by the name she had taken when disguised as a man.

Kalleah, Mellicante, and Baridya rose, sharing wary looks.

"I don't want you walking the streets alone again," Mellicante told Baridya sternly.

"Then you'll have to pose as my husband again." Baridya hooked a finger through Mellicante's belt and pulled her close for a swift kiss.

"And what about you?" Mellicante asked Kalleah. "I don't want you risking yourself unnecessarily."

"I can take care of myself," Kalleah said.

* * *

It was easy enough to track down Bennett the following day—she merely had to stray close to the Lord's Men while they were on their usual bullying patrol, and he swept from the shadows to lead her away.

He carried the strong scent of perfume, one Kalleah did not recognize, and as usual, he was in disguise. This time he wore a starched wig and a lace collar, and he walked with an odd affectation.

"Good sir," he said, bowing ebulliently. "What a pleasure to chance upon you."

"We need to talk," she said out of the corner of her mouth.

"Ah! The very words I hoped to hear. I know just the place, if you will be so kind as to follow me?"

Kalleah followed him warily up the street into the wealthier part of town. This was a quarter she had never chanced across before, with fine storefronts and restaurants and wine bars attracting a well-dressed clientele.

Bennett stopped at last at a teahouse scattered with small tables painted in bright geometrical patterns. Harp music drifted from one corner of the room, blurring the low murmur of voices, and the servers wore an unfamiliar style of dress that Kalleah thought might be Ruunan.

Bennett led Kalleah to a booth at the far side of the teahouse, where they were unlikely to be overheard. As she scanned the other patrons, she realized the majority were pairs of men, some dressed in the garb of wealthy merchants, others minor nobility, and many had stacks of documents at their tables. This was a common meeting place for making business deals, it seemed.

"Your menu," Bennett said, handing Kalleah a slim, leather-bound menu.

She opened it and was surprised to find that it listed nothing but tea, arranged by country of origin. There was cinnamon tea from Varrival, chamomile tea from Whitland, spiced tea from Chelt, manuka tea from Lostport, nine treasures tea from Kohlmarsh, hibiscus tea from King's Port, and many more. She had never heard of half of them.

Bennett ordered a black tea from Ruunas, while Kalleah selected a rose hip tea from Dardensfell.

"Not tempted by the more exotic selections?" Bennett asked with a smile once their server had left.

"As a newcomer to Dardensfell, I feel I should sample the local specialties," Kalleah said. "Now. You spoke of a way you could get me into the palace?"

Bennett's smile grew lopsided, which added to his good

looks. "I did. And I can say for certain that you won't like it."

"If it won't end with me locked in a cell, I have to consider it. Tell me."

Bennett paused as their waiter returned with two pots of tea and two delicate porcelain cups. Kalleah caught the bitter aroma of Bennett's unfamiliar brew, while her own sparked a wave of nostalgia. She wasn't certain, but she might have drunk something similar as a child.

"This is how it would work," he said at last, speaking quietly enough that his voice would not carry to the next table over. "King Rodarin will soon host the usual spring festival, and while his guest list is tightly controlled, he always invites a set of performers and…other entertainments."

Removing the tea infuser from his pot and setting it aside, Bennett poured himself a cup. The drink was dark, the strong smell overwhelming the more delicate scent of Kalleah's tea, and Bennett paused with the teapot still in one hand. "Would you like a taste?"

"Why not," Kalleah said, holding out her cup.

Bennett stirred sugar into his tea before drinking, while Kalleah sampled hers as it was. The taste was bitter, even more so than the hot cocoa she drank at home, but there was something enjoyable about it. She liked how overpowering it was.

Holding his teacup daintily, Bennett sat back in his chair and continued. "With the right disguise, you could pose as one of the courtesans hired to entertain guests at the festival. You would need a wig, and pastes to lighten your skin, but the shape of your face is pleasing enough that you would pass."

Kalleah wasn't sure if he was trying to flatter her.

"And…what would be expected of me?"

"Nothing onerous," Bennett said. "At least, from what I've heard. Your job would mainly be to dance and flirt with partnerless men. In that guise, you would even be able to approach King Rodarin without drawing attention."

Was this what she had stooped to? Disguising herself as a courtesan and flirting her way to King Rodarin's side?

But she could see no other way into the palace, not with the Lord's Men keeping such tight control of the city. And unless she had the support of King Rodarin, there was little she could accomplish here without resorting to wanton murder.

To give herself time to think, she finished off the bitter tea and poured a cup of her own rose hip tea. Once again, the scent stirred a bittersweet nostalgia in her, and she thought perhaps this was something she had shared with a childhood friend whose father had later forbidden her from seeing Kalleah.

She sipped at the tea, wondering if she had made a mistake in traveling to the Twin Cities. Should she cut her losses and start the trek back to the sea before her friends got into any further trouble?

Yet there was something more to discover here, beyond the potential ally she might find in King Rodarin. If the group who had contacted her truly believed they could destabilize the Whitish throne, they must have considerable power. And if she intended to tangle herself in the same conflict, she could not ignore such influential playing pieces.

Besides, she was beginning to suspect Bennett was involved in the same group. She could not see a pendant like the one Baridya had described beneath his lacy collar, but the circumstances were too suspicious to dismiss.

"What about the Kohldar palace?" Kalleah asked, setting aside her tea with a soft *chink*. "Would I be able to seek an audience with the king who sits the Kohlmarsh throne?"

"I don't doubt King Parvell would be willing to speak to you, but Kohldar is patrolled just as heavily as Darrenmark. And my own influence does not extend that far."

"Oh."

Kalleah folded her arms across her chest, wishing she had been able to drag her fleet back to Itrea to join the fight there. This had been so much easier when she was leading troops on a mission where her enemies were obvious and the risk straightforward. Now she was forced to resort to humiliating measures just to figure out who her allies were.

At least she would be able to escape using her powers if it came to that.

Kalleah sighed. "Very well. I'll do it."

37

The First Shipment

The news came from Jormund, who burst into Edreon's sickroom with an indecent grin.

"What are you doing here?" Edreon snapped. He was not in the mood for gaiety—his infection had now crept past his groin, and when Naresha's healer had last visited him, he had said with deepest apologies that he did not think it possible for a man to survive such a virulent disease of the flesh.

Edreon spent most of his days in a feverish stupor, clawing his way back to himself whenever someone disturbed his sleep. The pain was so persistent, so overwhelming, that he almost craved death.

Almost.

He was not so far gone that he had forgotten the state he would leave Whitland in if he passed without an heir.

"Apologies, Your Majesty," Jormund said. He was still grinning, the bastard. "The first shipment of logs has arrived!

They make an arresting sight, and certainly your citizenry is impressed. They are singing your praises all across town."

Relief swept through Edreon, so powerful he felt dizzy. "Are you certain?"

"I've seen the logs myself! And with the spring festival nearly here, we have cause to celebrate."

"Order the logs delivered to the castle," Edreon said. He was invigorated enough by the news to push himself to a sitting position. "They can wait in the armory until my creditors return to claim them. I would not wish any ill to befall such a valuable piece of material."

"Begging your pardon, but I'm not sure there is an easy way to transport the logs through the city. Not without widening the streets."

"Then have them widened," Edreon said curtly. "My soldiers in Itrea managed to transport them all the way from Baylore down to King's Port. If my guards cannot manage the short journey up from the docks, they are more useless than I realized."

Jormund gave him another broad smile. "Of course. Right away!"

"Oh—and send Luvoli to me, would you?"

Jormund bowed on his way out.

Alone again, Edreon pushed back the bedcovers and eyed the inflamed skin of his leg. The gentle brush of fabric against his skin was enough to make him hiss in pain, but if the enchanted logs might heal him in a matter of days, he could endure.

Varos save me, he thought. He was digging himself deeper and deeper into the pit of heresy.

When Luvoli arrived, he looked as excited as Jormund.

"Your star is rising once again," he said, filling the room with his perfume as he strode to Edreon's bedside. "Did you hear the news?"

"Yes, which is why I summoned you," Edreon said. "I want to make an appearance on the castle wall as the logs approach."

"A splendid idea," Luvoli said. "But...when did you last walk?"

Edreon's mouth twisted. He had stumbled from his palanquin to his throne at the feast more than a quarter back, and since then he had been bed-bound, relying on his footman to change his sweat-drenched nightshirt and help him use the bedpan.

"I'll manage," he said sourly.

"I very much doubt that," Luvoli said. "Now, I *did* hear about a marvelous Itrean invention, a type of boot enchanted to dull pain—"

"No more of your foolishness," Edreon growled. "I'll use the same palanquin as before."

"I only wondered if you would need another pair of hands to help."

"You'll do," Edreon said.

"Very well," Luvoli said. "In any case, it will do you some good to venture outside again. The weather is warming up at last, and the city is bursting with flowers in preparation for the spring festival."

Hunter's balls. Edreon had forgotten about the spring festival. He would be expected to dance, as usual; if the trees had not worked their magic by then, no one would be able to deny that he was a cripple.

"The decorations at the cathedral have gone a little heavy on the religious iconography this time, though." As he spoke, Luvoli strode over to Edreon's wardrobe and searched through the garments. "It almost seems they are trying to make a point."

"They don't like my tolerance for the Alldrosants," Edreon said.

"A shame, that. Think of how many kingdoms we might have conquered if not for the centuries of squabbling between sects!"

"You only say that because you've spent enough time around me," Edreon said gruffly. "Had you been asked when you first arrived in Eidervell, you would have staunchly defended the Varonites and called the Alldrosants backwater heathens."

"True." Luvoli busied himself with Edreon's clothes, pulling out doublets and shirts to examine them before shoving them back onto the rack. At last he chose a yellow brocade doublet with puffed sleeves slashed to reveal a deep green.

Edreon tugged off his nightshirt and held out his arms for Luvoli to help him with a simple cream shirt followed by the doublet.

His trousers were going to be more of a challenge. He had not worn anything on his legs aside from bandages since the feast, and with the swelling, he was not even sure he would fit his usual trousers.

Luvoli seemed to be puzzling over the same dilemma, because he eyed Edreon's legs critically.

"Something dark," he muttered at last. "In case anything leaks from your wound. Do we need to fix your bandages first?"

"No," Edreon snapped. "No one touches the bandages."

He did not want Luvoli to see how disgusting the wound had become, especially if it would heal soon enough.

Varos grant it works.

Luvoli dug in Edreon's drawers until he found a set of black trousers that looked roomier than the rest.

"You will need to lie down," Luvoli said, face pinched in worry.

Edreon shifted until he was lying back on his pillow, grimacing at the pain stirred up by each movement.

Luvoli worked carefully as he pulled up the trousers, but the sensation was still agony. When he reached the injury, Edreon writhed and shouted out in pain.

Luvoli jumped back as though burned. "I'm sorry! That was clumsy of me."

"No," Edreon said through gritted teeth. "It's not your fault."

He reached for one of the clean cloths that he kept on hand to mop up the pus that leaked from his wound and shoved it into his mouth, biting down hard.

Warily, Luvoli returned to his work, flinching whenever Edreon gave a muffled howl.

At last the trousers were on.

"I pray that I never have to do such a thing again," Luvoli said, giving Edreon's hand a brief squeeze. "I hate to say this, but—the infection looks grim, does it not? Are you likely to—to—"

"Varos will decide my fate," Edreon said bleakly. "And with it, the fate of all Whitland."

* * *

By the time he reached his position on the castle walls, the logs were already approaching. Each had been laid across several wagons whose sides had been removed, pulled by a team of twenty oxen.

When his people caught sight of King Edreon in his festive doublet, crown sparkling in the sunlight, a cheer rose from the watching crowd. As Luvoli had described, there were flowers everywhere—growing from window boxes outside houses, hanging in garlands, and adorning the hair of young maidens. Some had even been strewn across the vast flanks of the logs.

Below, the gates ground open to make way for the wagons. Edreon wasn't certain the logs would fit, but the first one passed through without incident. Excitement hummed through him, dampening the pain and the feverish ache.

Soon. If he could but endure another day, his ordeal might end.

One by one, the logs passed through the castle gates into the courtyard beyond. A team of sailors followed the wagons, preparing to lever the logs down from the wagons. They would hardly fit in the armory; Edreon hoped he would not face questions as to why he had chosen to store them here rather than at the warehouses by the docks.

But the festive atmosphere had swept away all doubts in his leadership. Folk music floated up from the square, and women called out his name, waving bouquets and handkerchiefs. Edreon lifted a hand to them, granting them a regal smile, and all was as it should be.

* * *

Once the logs had been deposited in the armory and the wagons driven carefully away, Edreon directed his guards to carry his palanquin down to the armory. He pretended he had made arrangements for his own attendants to collect him once he had inspected the logs, but instead he planned to sleep there in the armory.

And when he woke the next morning, the floor cold and unforgiving against his back, Edreon felt more himself than he had in quarters. His fever had broken, and the ache running all down his leg had subsided.

When he sat up, the wound gave a throb, so he pulled up the leg of his trousers and unwrapped the bandages.

The smell that assaulted him made him gag. Edreon turned his head away and held his breath as he yanked off the last of the gauze.

Though the wound itself was still there, deep as ever, the infection was gone. The angry red that had stained Edreon's leg had cleared away, which meant he had bought himself time.

Perhaps he needed to seal himself inside a structure made of enchanted planks to allow for a more thorough healing. He could not cut into these logs, since they did not belong to him, but he would live, thank Varos.

Yet he was far from regaining the use of his leg.

38

The Road to Redhill

On the advice of the freed slaves, Daymin's army was now following a new road west of the Elygian River that cut straight from New Savair toward Redhill. The road did not exist on any map he had seen, yet it was deeply rutted from use.

According to the former slaves, Redhill was the central settlement of what had become a major mining region, occupied almost exclusively by enslaved Itreans who worked the mines. Many of the people they had rescued had spent time in the mines themselves, and they told stories of the Whitish who lived like lords in manors removed from the filth of the mines.

Two days south of New Savair, a hailstorm caught Daymin's army unprepared, so they hastily set up camp to shelter from the storm. Tarak, Zahira, and Lalaysha joined Daymin in his tent, where they sipped at mint tea to ward away the cold.

"How are you faring?" Daymin asked his friends. He had found precious little time to speak with them after the recent battle, and once he had dragged himself away from the bleak spiral of his own thoughts, he had realized the experience would have been traumatic for others as well.

"Don't worry about us," Tarak said.

Zahira shot him an annoyed look. "Easy for you to say. I hate to admit it, but this campaign has been a lot more than I'd bargained on."

"I know," Daymin said quietly. "I had envisioned sweeping through under-fortified settlements and scooping them up without a true fight. What happened in New Savair…"

They were silent for a moment.

"I don't like fire," Lalaysha said. "It is all I see when I close my eyes now."

"I'm sorry," Daymin said.

"No, I chose to follow you. But Zahira is right. I thought this would be easier."

Tarak looked at Daymin, his eyes full of concern. "And you? I can't imagine it was easy losing General Dellik."

Daymin's eyes stung. He hated his own weakness, especially since he had been the one who killed her.

But Zahira set aside her tea and sat beside Daymin on the rug, draping an arm around his back, and Tarak squeezed his other shoulder.

"You must miss Idorii, too," Zahira murmured. Something in the way she spoke told him she knew what Idorii meant to him.

"I do," he admitted, his voice coming out strangled. "Cloudy gods, I do."

277

"And he's still in Baylore…" Zahira gave him a grim look. "If Tarak had decided to stay behind, I would've knocked him unconscious and dragged him along with me. We might be struggling out here, but it's nothing compared to how Baylore will fare when the Whitish attack."

Daymin's chest ached at the thought. As much as Idorii claimed he would be able to escape easily enough when the Whitish attacked, the risk was still there.

"He's not going to stay and fight," Daymin said. "He'll leave as soon as the Whitish march on Baylore."

"Good," Zahira said.

"Are you able to communicate with him?" Tarak asked. "How did he report to you while he was stationed at Darkland Fort?"

"That's a secret," Daymin said quickly, his face hot.

"Ooh," Lalaysha said with a cheeky grin. "I love a good secret."

Zahira looked like she was struggling with herself; thankfully, she did not say whatever was on her mind.

Instead, they sipped their tea in silence for a moment, the rain hammering away at the tent above their heads.

At last Daymin said, "I wish I wasn't such a useless fighter. Of everything that's been bothering me since the battle, that's the one that irritates me the most. I got into a fight with an average, unarmored Whitish soldier, and I couldn't even defeat him without an archer injuring him first. What kind of warrior am I if I can barely hold my own in battle?"

"I feel the same way," Tarak said. "Our skills were enough back in Baylore, but out here, we're like children against the Whitish."

"You're ones to talk," Zahira said. "Lalaysha and I never lifted a sword until a few spans ago. We want to help, but right now we're just getting in the way."

"I'm glad you finally acknowledge that," Tarak said drily.

Zahira narrowed her eyes at him.

"We should practice," Lalaysha said, eyes sparkling with enthusiasm. "Please. I want to learn more."

Daymin looked around at his friends, their expressions a mixture of bleak and hopeful. He knew they were craving distraction, just as he was.

"We'll find someone experienced to train under," he said at last. "With Dellik gone, I could use all the help I can get."

* * *

That afternoon, shortly before sundown, the rain finally ceased. The clouds still hung menacingly over the plains, but off on the eastern horizon, Daymin could see a narrow strip of teal sky.

He and his friends emerged from his tent to find the ground muddy and still running with rivulets of water. While the camp cooks prepared dinner, Daymin sought out Uncle Cal and asked for his recommendation of the most skilled general who was willing to take students.

So it was that they found themselves trailing a tall, swarthy man named General Vask to the edge of camp. When Daymin had made his request, he had acquiesced with a grunt that made Daymin worry he resented the task.

But he needed to improve. There was no way around it.

Where the camp ended, they came to a place where the dirt gave way to a slab of sandstone. The stone was pocked with holes that held water, but at least there was no mud to slip on. Daymin drew his sword and stood awkwardly, shifting his balance from one foot to the other, while the women hung back.

"You say you don't consider yourself an adequate fighter?" General Vask asked gruffly.

"That's right," Daymin said.

"Nothing to be ashamed of. Most of our army wouldn't hold up against the Whitish. I've seen that firsthand, and it's humiliating. Which is why I've pushed myself to become as skilled as their elite soldiers. If you want to achieve something similar, it's going to be hard work. No way around that."

"We're willing to do the work," Daymin said, while Zahira nodded emphatically.

General Vask grunted. "Then let's see what we're working with. Show me the basic sequence of strikes."

Standing side by side at the edge of the sandstone slab, Daymin and Tarak raised their swords to their shoulders. Then, while General Vask barked out the numbers, they ran through the sixteen basic strikes. The first four carried them forward, one step matching each blow, and then they pivoted to return for the next four, retracing their steps for the final eight.

"Your turn, girls," General Vask said once they finished.

Daymin had never seen either Zahira or Lalaysha fight before, so he watched with interest. Lalaysha had the form down well, though she hesitated before each stroke, while Zahira was quicker and sloppier.

"And now. King Daymin, opposite me."

Daymin stepped up to face General Vask, who raised his sword. The man had a good hand of height on him, and was much more strongly-built as well. Daymin would not want to face him in a real duel.

"Block me," he said.

He ran through the same sequence of strikes, while Daymin met each one.

"A solid foundation," General Vask said, "but that only goes so far. Again."

This time, when Daymin blocked his first strike, General Vask twisted his sword to strike again from an unexpected direction.

Daymin recognized the move, but he couldn't remember how to block it. Instead he hopped backward, out of range, disengaging their blades as he did.

"You'll never win a duel if you resort to moves like that," General Vask said grimly.

Daymin flushed.

"This is where prowess with the sword makes itself evident. Each soldier knows the basic set of strikes and blocks—it's the reactions that win or lose a fight. For every move, there is a set of possible countermoves, and the more you know, the more likely you are to catch your opponent unaware. You need to drill these until you can do them in your sleep. Until you respond instinctively to every possible attack. Only then can you win against a Whitish soldier."

General Vask eyed Daymin and his friends critically. "A bit more muscle wouldn't hurt, either. Once your lesson ends each day, return to your tents and do push-ups until you collapse."

They spent the evening running through forms. General Vask pushed Zahira and Lalaysha through the basic sequence again and again, until their forms were correct and they could move without hesitation, while he drilled Daymin and Tarak on the complicated set of countermoves that could be used against the first of the sixteen strikes.

To his surprise, Daymin found great pleasure in the work. It was a relief to have something to focus on instead of his own failures, and he relished the burn in his muscles and the fatigue that meant he would sleep well for once. His shoulder was still sore from where he'd fallen off his horse, but he worked through the ache, not wanting to let it slow him.

By the time they broke for dinner, Zahira and Lalaysha were grinning with their success, while Daymin was feeling tired and satisfied and a bit overwhelmed. He had barely memorized the first set of countermoves, and was far from mastering the forms, let alone making them instinctive; if there were fifteen more sets as grueling as these, he could see why it took a lifetime to master the sword.

When he returned to his tent with his dinner, he collapsed on his rug. Before he started eating, he rolled up his sleeve to write to Idorii.

You'll never guess what I've decided to occupy myself with during our campaign.

Idorii's response came almost immediately. *Do tell!*

I've decided I can't continue leading my army when my own swordsmanship is so shoddy. So my friends and I have apprenticed ourselves to a master of the sword. By the time you next see us, I'll be a true warlord.

You make me feel like I should be working on my own skills as well! What sort of drills would be useful for a valet? Should I challenge myself to speed-buttoning rounds?

Daymin chuckled. Cloudy gods, he loved Idorii. *Admit it. Hairdressing is your weakest point. You need to train under a master hairstylist until you can tame even my curls.*

Alas, you've pinpointed my fatal flaw! I hereby pledge to dress the hair of the first fifty men I can talk into this madness, in hopes I won't let you down so gravely the next time you need my services.

I look forward to hearing of your progress.

And I yours. I can just imagine you vanquishing your enemies on the battlefield in a storm of swords and shining armor.

Daymin snorted. *That doesn't sound much like me, does it?*

My dear scholar king. I'll always see you that way, even if you do become a fearsome warrior.

In all honesty, training this way doesn't feel like something I would choose to do…yet it is satisfying in ways I cannot explain.

Something to take your mind off the battle? Idorii wrote back. *I can't tell you how much I miss my magic, and for the same reason. Because it was something to occupy my mind, something I could put effort into and see results.*

What am I left with now? Piles of books? This work is

valuable, but instead of leaving me energized, I find it exhausting and demoralizing.

Idorii had rarely spoken of how much the loss of his magic hurt. Daymin sensed that it was not solely the magic he missed; Idorii had mastered many crafts in his years of service to the throne, and it was the sort of handiwork he had been able to take pride in. Daymin knew he was drawn to the full act of creation, from beginning to end.

This was why Daymin had originally balked at the idea of Idorii doing menial work for him. No matter how much Idorii joked about wanting to demean himself for the sake of staying close to Daymin, he knew Idorii hated how far he had fallen. He had lost his passion, his pride, his life's work, his obsession.

When you rejoin my army, I want you to seek a new purpose, Daymin wrote. *When I first took the throne, the only purpose I saw for myself was preserving the alliance between Allakoash and Itreans. And once that failed, you convinced me that I was a valid and worthwhile king regardless. I suppose this campaign is partly me trying to prove that I'm able to do my part for Itrea without the ancestor trees backing me. Whether I am succeeding or failing on that account remains to be seen.*

But it's now your turn to find a new path. You have a brilliant mind and skilled hands that can flawlessly execute any craft you turn to, and those talents are valuable in themselves, with or without magic.

You're no valet, Idorii. And you're wasted as a librarian. I want you to find something else that sparks your passion.

Yours,
Daymin

As he set aside his pen and started on his stew, which was lukewarm and beginning to congeal, Daymin reflected that he would not have been capable of giving advice like that a few spans back. He had been so wrapped up in his own feelings of inadequacy that he would have balked at the idea of guiding someone else.

But something was changing. He was finally starting to see himself as a king and a leader, and he was beginning to believe that he was worth following, regardless of his many flaws.

And that meant he had to continue on the path he had chosen, no matter how bloody. His kingdom was counting on him.

39

A Stash of Knowledge

Idorii was coming to crave the nightly exchanges from Daymin. After spending his days alone, that short burst of human contact felt like the only thread tying him to his sanity.

Tonight he had bared his heart more than he usually would have dared, and Daymin's final message had warmed him through.

I want you to find something else that sparks your passion.

Idorii let the words dry on his arm as he carried the remains of his dinner to the kitchen.

When he returned to the sitting room, he abruptly saw it for what it was: an irredeemable mess.

There were hundreds of books lying in piles on the floor.

No, thousands.

He had organized them, of course, but if the Whitish attacked tomorrow, what would that matter? He couldn't carry such a load to the Icebraid Peaks alone. He may as well pick up the whole house and try to lug that on his back.

Bloody Varse.

What had he even been doing? He was delusional to think he could categorize and extract all the Weavers' spells in Baylore before the city fell.

And the more time he had spent searching, the more irreplaceable knowledge he had stumbled across. He could not transcribe it or summarize it without years of labor, nor could he bear the thought of ripping pages from ancient books.

Plagues. He had to think of some other strategy to ensure Itrean civilization would not burn along with Baylore.

Idorii stalked around the room, examining the piles of books. Even now, he had forgotten the specifics of his carefully-devised organization system. Did this pile represent the books with multiple variations of familiar spells? Or were they the volumes that included fewer than five unfamiliar spells?

If he could hide every single book in the city, he would do it.

But what hiding place would be safe from the Whitish?

It had to be somewhere that would neither topple when the city came under siege, nor reveal its secrets when the Whitish rampaged through town seeking evidence of magic to destroy.

Even imagining that fate made Idorii's heart ache. There was so much memory and love bound up in this city—and soon it would all be lost.

It was getting dark outside, but he had the beginnings of an idea he wanted to investigate, so he grabbed his coat from where it lay draped across the back of a chair and strode into the cool evening air.

Baylore University lay at the heart of town, out of range of trebuchets, and Idorii suspected he might be able to find a suitable hiding place there. Perhaps not something large enough for the number of books he hoped to preserve, but even a small cellar could suffice. He could get another Weaver to seal it with spells, so that—what? So Itreans could stumble across it, centuries from now, in the unlikely event they re-captured their former capital?

It was foolish. He knew it was. But he would feel better knowing the books would not be burned as soon as the Whitish took Baylore.

As before, the University was unlocked, so Idorii pushed open the gates and slipped into the quiet courtyard. The glow of the streetlights did not extend here, so he illuminated the crystal pendant on his neck and used that soft white light to see his way forward.

He made a quick circuit of the two courtyards, looking in every unsecured room for a door or flight of stairs that might lead down.

He found nothing, but many of the rooms had been locked, so he decided he would return in daylight with a universal key.

Then, as he was passing beneath the wall to the University gates, the glow of his crystal fell on something he had overlooked before.

There was a door set in the archway.

Idorii knew, somehow, that this was what he wanted. He tried the handle and was surprised to find it unlocked.

Beyond the door, a flight of stairs led down into blackness; Idorii's chest swelled with hope at the sight. This did not look like a small cellar.

As he ventured down the stairs, the air grew staler, thick with dust and the smell of old rat droppings. When he reached the foot of the stairs, his light illuminated a narrow passageway leading forward, with rooms branching off on both sides.

Heart pounding with excitement, Idorii started down the corridor, opening doors and peering into rooms as he went. Some lay empty, while others were storerooms of some sort or another, holding everything from spare furniture to crates of potion ingredients. Still others appeared to be secret laboratories packed with experimental equipment.

Idorii felt a rush of longing. He had received just about the best education a Weaver could under the tutelage of the palace Makhori, but he would have loved to attend Baylore University. There was something about surrounding himself with enquiring minds and learning for the sake of learning, not just in service of the war, that tugged at him.

And now he would never have the chance.

Eventually he came to a dead end, so he retraced his steps and hurried back to his manor. Though it was late, he was eager to begin his work. Besides, the Whitish could attack any day now. Who knew how much time he would have?

He wished for a wagon, but those had all been taken by the evacuees, so instead he loaded books into a crate and staggered back down the street to hide them beneath the University. Back and forth he went, as the night grew later and later, his back aching and arms searing. It was as Daymin had said—the physicality of the work was satisfying in itself. He was so relieved to be making progress again that he did not want to stop.

At last he could carry no more. He collapsed into his chair and surveyed the remaining books, which still made a respectable collection. And now that he had a place to hide them, there were other books he could secure as well. He had focused exclusively on Weavers' magic, but now he could save the other disciplines as well.

There you go, Daymin, he thought with satisfaction. *How is that for a new purpose? And now my decision to stay behind won't have been wasted.*

40

Tainted Blood

Kalleah had barely seen Leoth in days. He returned late, after she had gone to bed, and since they did not share a room, he did not wake her.

The longer this arrangement went on, the more worried she grew. Tonight she was waiting in the tavern close to midnight, wanting to catch him on his way back, though she was half-afraid of what he might say if she confronted him. Was he avoiding her because he was starting to believe their lies once again? Did he think her an abomination, and himself no better?

When Leoth finally stumbled in, Kalleah could tell from his gait that he was drunk. His eyes were bloodshot, and when he approached her table, she could smell the alcohol on his breath.

"What is this?" she asked in a sharp undertone. "Are you avoiding us?"

Leoth focused on her with seeming difficulty. "I'm keeping you safe," he mumbled.

"I'm not sure how drinking yourself into a stupor is helping any of us."

"You don't know the half of it."

"Oh?" Kalleah said coldly. "And why don't you tell me what you've been hiding?"

"You'd hate me for it," Leoth said.

Then he turned and staggered off, leaving Kalleah feeling as if she'd been slapped.

* * *

Kalleah tossed and turned all night, and in the morning she woke with the sun despite staying up late.

Stumbling blearily out to the bar, she wasted a coin on a cup of mint tea, desperate for something to shake her from the fog of exhaustion. Pity they didn't serve hot cocoa here.

Leoth's words had played through her mind all night. What did he mean, he was keeping her safe? Was he just referring to the coin he earned from his brutality? Or was there something more to his employment?

And when he had said Kalleah would hate him if she knew the truth…plagues. That made it sound like he was brutalizing civilians just like the rest of the Lord's Men.

Kalleah gripped her mug as if she could wring answers from the ceramic. She had hated parting ways with Leoth before the attack on Eidervell, but this was worse by several degrees.

She worried she was losing him forever.

Part of it was irrational. She knew that. She had done many terrible things in the name of saving Itrea, and while the Truthbringers had seeded lies and hatred among her people, they were far from the most brutal of the Whitish she had faced. It was the way they had turned her into a pariah that still hurt. They had twisted good people to believe magic was evil—none more so than the forbidden races—and because of his parents' influence, Leoth had bought into that notion wholeheartedly.

And the way he was now avoiding her, pushing her away…

"Morning," a soft voice said from behind Kalleah, making her jump.

She turned to see Bennett approaching, this time clad in black trousers and a simple leather jerkin, like a sailor or laborer.

"What is it?" she asked warily. This was the first time he had spoken to her at The Lost Sailor.

"I thought I might join you for breakfast. Shall I order?"

Kalleah waved him off and then watched his back, frowning, as he requested the daily breakfast and a mug of tea for himself. There was something in his manner that told her he was trying to charm her, and she didn't like it.

Soon he was back, setting down the plates with a flourish. "Not gruel, I see! We ought to thank the chef."

They each had a boiled egg and two slices of buttered toast, which was luxurious for The Lost Sailor.

As they dug in, the door to the inn opened and Leoth strode through.

Kalleah opened her mouth to wish him a good morning, but he shook his head sharply. Instead he threw Bennett a cold look and stalked from the tavern without breakfast.

With a sigh, Kalleah let him go.

"Why are you really here?" she asked Bennett, wondering if Leoth had encountered him elsewhere. Why else had he looked at him with such hatred?

He leaned close, his expression uncomfortable. "You know I've been watching over you since you arrived."

"Yes…"

"Well, I was told you were a friend of ours, someone whose aims aligned with our own."

"Who are you referring to?" Kalleah asked quickly.

"Oh, no one in particular," Bennett said. "Just those of us who wish to be rid of the Lord's Men. Gods know there are enough of us."

Kalleah gave him a sharp look, which he ignored.

"And since you're the first Itreans I have ever come across, I couldn't help but wonder about your stance on this war. As I see it, there are three sides to the conflict—the Whitish, the Itreans, and everyone else who resents the High King's interference."

"Are we not grouped together, since our aims align?" Kalleah asked.

"Nine gods, no. Many of us are still devout followers of Varos or the Nine, and we are hesitant to admit that your people—and the cursed blood they carry—are not a danger to our societies."

"You would advocate slaughtering us, just like the Whitish?" Kalleah said coldly.

"No. Certainly not. But there is a big difference between exterminating a race and welcoming them into our lands with open arms."

He leaned closer still, close enough that Kalleah could smell the honeyed tea on his breath, and she sat back in disgust.

"What did you think of the attack on Eidervell? You sailed from upriver—surely you heard of it."

"Yes," Kalleah said. It seemed he didn't know who she was, or else he was going a roundabout way of convincing her of it.

"And? Did you not find it brutal?"

Kalleah blinked at him. "My own country has been plagued by Whitish brutality for decades. How could such a small counterattack register in comparison with what they have already brought upon us?"

"It was more the way it happened. Did you hear the details? How—" he lowered his voice to a whisper— "Queen Kalleah slaughtered thousands of innocents using her accursed power?"

"I wasn't aware of that part." Kalleah felt a creeping sense of dread. "Was the harbor not set aflame? I heard a good portion of the city was destroyed, but the queen failed to breach the castle."

Bennett waved a hand. "Details. No, it was Queen Kalleah's role in the battle that surprised us most. I had once been a firm supporter of Itrea, but after the attack on Eidervell…well, let's just say the queen's actions gave me pause. Is that really the sort of thing we want to allow in the Kinship Thrones? Monsters like that?"

"No, I suppose not," Kalleah said, endeavoring to keep her tone light.

"Perhaps I shouldn't be surprised. After all, even Itreans recognize the taint of evil magic blood." He leaned in again, speaking as if he shared a great secret. "Did you know that some Alldrosant scholars believe the ban against magic races was misinterpreted? Only those with evil blood bear the taint of the Gods of Sin. Those like Queen Kalleah—forbidden races, I believe you might call them."

"Then you will be disappointed to hear that Itrea has spent

the past few years attempting to integrate the forbidden races into normal society," Kalleah said tartly.

"On the queen's orders, I would imagine?"

"Yes."

Bennett finished off his toast and wiped his hands on his trousers. "I can see I've offended you. Please, I meant no disrespect. We simply come from very different ways of seeing the world, and as an Alldrosant myself, I find it hard to understand how heathens like yourselves can grasp concepts such as morality and evil."

"Did you come here just to criticize my people?" Kalleah asked stiffly. She was growing more uncomfortable with Bennett the longer she spoke to him, and now regretted agreeing to his scheme.

"I do apologize. I let my curiosity run away with me. No, I wanted to go over the plan with you."

Kalleah let him talk, outlining where and when she would meet him to prepare for the spring festival, while she puzzled over what group he had referred to. Surely it was the same one that had invited her to the Temple of Totoleon—and the fact that he was an Alldrosant supported that hypothesis.

But in that case, shouldn't he know who she was? Yet he did not seem to realize he had just criticized the very person sitting across from him. What would he think if he discovered her identity?

To her relief, he soon rose and bid her farewell. Kalleah remained where she was, watching the tavern door with a frown. After what he had said, she no longer felt comfortable knowing he was staying at the same inn as her. But she could hardly relocate—he would find her group again in no time, and then she would have to explain why she had acted so strangely.

Besides, she was still relying on him. At least until the spring festival. Then, if she found a willing ally in King Rodarin, perhaps he would invite her to stay as his guest at the palace. If that happened, she could put an end to this mess. Leoth could abandon the Lord's Men, and she could try to learn more about this mysterious group without relying on one of its members.

Before long, Baridya appeared from the inn wearing skirts, her hair hanging loose around her shoulders.

"Where's Mellicante?" Kalleah asked as Baridya joined her for breakfast.

"She and the boys received a tip about a fishing ship that docked shortly after sunrise, traveling upriver from the ocean," Baridya said tiredly. "They think they can earn a few coins gutting and sorting fish."

Kalleah made a face. "Won't the fish be rotten by now?"

"Mellicante saw another one like it last quarter—apparently they drag the fish behind them in a net, still alive. Anyway, what's wrong? You look worried."

Kalleah sighed. "I'm tired of being useless."

"I know what you mean," Baridya said darkly. "I had known what to expect, but that doesn't make it any easier. How do women live their whole lives this way?"

"I have no idea." Kalleah hesitated. "Can you keep something quiet? I don't want you to say anything to Mellicante or Leoth."

Baridya immediately perked up. "What is this about?"

"You know how you were rescued the other day under strange circumstances?"

"Yes?"

"Well, the same thing happened to me. The man who rescued me has been following me around, occasionally approaching me, and while I haven't seen the same insignia on him, the circumstances are too similar to be coincidence."

"Is he dangerous, do you think?" Baridya asked, eyebrows drawing together.

"I don't know. But he's offered to get me into the palace, and I agreed to his plan. Except…this morning, he started asking me about Itrea and saying he thought Queen Kalleah was a monster. I feel very uncomfortable working with him after that."

"I can imagine," Baridya said darkly. "And I know how you feel." She glanced over at the bar, which was untended, before lowering her voice. "A few days ago, the tavern-keeper told me in a strangely jovial way that he's disgusted by my relationship with Mellicante. He's figured out that we're both women, and—" She grimaced. "The taboos against that run deep in the Kinship Thrones."

"I'm so sorry." Kalleah reached across the table and squeezed Baridya's hand. The tavern-keeper had always come across as friendly and welcoming, so this seemed particularly cruel coming from him.

Then again, she had thought the same about Bennett until he started describing how much he hated her.

"Would you be willing to join me when I infiltrate the palace?" Kalleah asked. She lowered her voice. "Bennett intends to disguise me as a courtesan, and claims I will be able to speak to the king without raising suspicion. It seems a compromising situation to put myself in, but I can't see any other way into the palace."

"Of course I'll join you," Baridya said with a small smile.

"Gods, a few years back I would have loved doing something like this. And the sooner we can leave this place, the better."

41

Borderville

After several days of traveling through the Wandering Woods, Jayna was finally growing accustomed to the dense life all around. The forest in Cashabree was nothing like this, with its narrow-trunked beech trees and sparse undergrowth. Here everything was covered in moss and ferns and vines, and it was impossible to walk in a straight line without climbing over vast roots. Even when the trees shifted branches at their approach, they did not move the roots that lay tangled over one another in a many-layered network.

The firehawks were growing restless—they had trouble finding their way back to Jayna and Hanna when they flew above the canopy, so they spent most of the journey perched on the girls' shoulders, Dragon combing his beak through Jayna's hair in boredom.

Just when Jayna was starting to crave open air again, the forest ended as abruptly as it had begun. One moment, they were walking through a ceaseless tableau of greenery; the next, they stood before a vast open grassland that stretched, featureless, as far as she could see.

"We are just south of the road," said Chanesh, the old woman who had guided them through the woods. "You will want to cross to the northern side when you leave the forest. But first, will you stay the night in Borderville?"

"Is that your home?" Jayna asked with curiosity.

"It is," Chanesh said. "Borderville was once an Itrean settlement with close ties to the forest and many Allakoash residents. Now…well, you will see."

She stepped into the woods once more, and Jayna took a deep breath of the open air, enjoying the smell of sunbaked dirt and flowers and grasses, before following her back into the forest.

Before long, they came to a place where the trees opened up to a grassy clearing filled with thatched cottages. The clearing was surrounded on all sides by forest, and the populace was a collection of Itreans and Allakoash, including many with mixed blood.

"How is this possible?" Hanna asked in wonder.

"When the Whitish first invaded Itrea, the forest closed up around Borderville," Chanesh said with a smile. "We agreed unanimously on the move. And so, we are the last Itrean settlement outside of Baylore that has remained untouched by the Whitish."

As she led them down the grassy lane toward the center of town, residents noticed the strangers in their midst and began approaching, whispering excitedly. Jayna heard Itrean and what must have been Allakoash spoken by people of both races, and she guessed this settlement was similar to her own people in the way it used two languages interchangeably.

"We'll give you maps before you set out," Chanesh said. "They won't be fully accurate, since none of us have ventured beyond the forest border in recent spans, but it's better than what anyone on the Larkhaven coast could have given you."

"Thank you," Jayna said. "You've done so much for us. How can we repay you?"

"King Daymin is an honorary member of one of our tribes," Chanesh said, "and he has done a great deal for our people. If you help him, it will be repayment enough. Come. Let me show you the maps first, and then we want to welcome you properly."

Chanesh led them into what looked like a schoolhouse, with rows of desks and a sizeable collection of books along the walls. When Hanna approached one of the shelves and ran her fingers along the spines, wide-eyed, Chanesh explained with a smile that this was the only true collection of written Allakoash teachings and stories, since their culture followed an oral tradition.

"Are you a teacher, then?" Hanna asked in wonder.

"I am."

Chanesh dug in a drawer of the teacher's desk and pulled out a map, which she unrolled on the desk. "This is the route you'll follow from the forest border," she said, tracing the main road past Valleywall. "The bridge near Pelek is heavily guarded, so I would recommend cutting north to the crossing near Ashton. But I can't say what the Whitish occupation looks like in those parts. Stay clear of any towns you come across—you both look far too foreign to risk stopping at any Whitish-held settlements."

"Thank you," Jayna said, studying the map carefully. West of the bridge at Ashton, she and Hanna would come very close to Baylore before leaving behind any trace of civilization as they cut across the plains toward the Icebraid Peaks. It looked easy enough. Now that she had traveled a portion of the continent, she was getting a better feel for its size, and based on the vast emptiness before them, avoiding Whitish-occupied settlements should be simple.

"What were you doing on the opposite side of the woods?" Hanna asked. "You didn't know to expect us, did you?"

"Of course not," Chanesh said. "No, I was sent there to see if rumors of new troops landing in Larkhaven were true."

"The Cheltish draftees," Jayna said. "Did King Edreon send them here before he knew the forest road would close?"

"The road has been closed for spans," Chanesh said grimly. "If King Edreon sent reinforcements to Larkhaven, he must think he can force us to reopen the forest road."

"Can he?" Jayna asked in alarm.

"Not using any means we've seen before. Still, it doesn't bode well."

Jayna didn't know what to say to this.

"Come. I'll draw you a bath before dinner."

She led them to her house, where her husband—an Itrean—greeted her with a kiss. Chanesh ran water from a tap into a deep metal tub, and her husband lit the fire underneath. Then they left Jayna and Hanna, saying there were preparations to be made.

"There's a lot more to this conflict than I'd realized," Jayna said, leaning forward to test the water.

"I'm sure the same is true in the Kinship Thrones," Hanna

said. "I wish we had known more—then we might have been more of a help to Queen Kalleah."

"If you'd attended the Borderlands Academy, you would've known about every scheme from Whitland to Varrival," Jayna said drily.

"Yakov didn't know what the other factions were involved in," Hanna said.

"Or so he claimed."

Hanna rolled her eyes.

"But the forest road closing? The Allakoash and whatever is going on between them and the Itreans? King Edreon sending Cheltish soldiers to Larkhaven?" Jayna grimaced. "I feel like we were sent to fish for a lobster, only we ended up with a shark and an octopus and an eel, and they're all trying to kill each other, but some of them are secretly allies and just pretending, and the other ones are probably going to kill us instead."

"Yes," Hanna said with an amused smile. "That's exactly how this feels."

* * *

That night, the grassy lane running through the center of Borderville was transformed into an outdoor banquet hall. Tables laid together formed one long buffet, laden with the most varied spread of foods Jayna had ever seen.

Chanesh led them along the table, describing the dishes— partridge and quail and pigeon cooked in rich sauces; wild hog roasted on a spit; poached quail eggs; tender fern shoots and asparagus cooked in butter; salads of chickweed, bittercress, and clover; oyster mushrooms; and the more common Itrean staples of millet scones, cheese, and potatoes.

"I thought Itrea was suffering from food shortages," Jayna said, salivating at the delicious smells rising from the table. She had not eaten so well in spans.

"The Whitish are hungry because they aren't used to cultivating the dry central plains," Chanesh said. "Their crops have failed there, year after year, and they are too ignorant to adapt to the local versions. Instead they relied heavily on the farmland along the Larkhaven coast, which was a more familiar climate. So, as soon as the forest road closed, they were left with very little to eat."

"Didn't you lose your farmland as well?" Jayna asked.

"We did," Chanesh said. "What we have here looks like a bounty, but only because it is mostly foraged. Aside from the small gardens we can keep here, we hunt and gather the rest, so we eat small amounts of a wide range of foods."

"And the millet?" Hanna asked.

Chanesh gave her a fleeting smile. "Well spotted. That grows wild in the plains nearby, so we harvest whatever we can find."

"What are we supposed to eat while we travel across the plains?" Jayna asked warily.

"We will send you with as much as you can carry," Chanesh said. "The rest you will have to hunt or forage. There are hares and prairie dogs and grouse and prairie chickens, so if you have any skill with a bow or slingshot, you should be able to catch these regularly enough."

Jayna and Hanna shared a worried look.

"The wild grasses will just be turning green at this time of year, so you won't find any grains, but there are abandoned orchards north of the road where you might find nuts left from last year's crop. And when you reach the river, you can try fishing."

When Chanesh left them to fill their plates at the buffet, Jayna turned to Hanna and muttered, "I don't like our chances out there."

"Let's wait and see how much food they give us," Hanna said. "If we ration carefully, we might not need to hunt."

"And in the meantime, let's eat enough to keep ourselves going for the next quarter."

"Agreed."

Jayna loaded her plate with a bit of everything, unable to believe so many delicacies grew in the Wandering Woods. From her ignorant perspective, the forest had seemed like nothing but moss and trees and ferns.

While she and Hanna ate, villagers kept approaching and asking if it was true they had traveled with Queen Kalleah. Eventually Chanesh shooed the curious villagers away, saying Jayna would tell the full story after dinner.

With the full population gathered, some sitting on the grass, others leaning against doorframes, Jayna stepped up to speak. Ever since she had joined Queen Kalleah, she had felt like a pretender—a child who had clung to the coattails of the first real adventurer she had come across.

But now, with hundreds of eager eyes watching her, she felt a piece of that glory herself.

"I first met Queen Kalleah when she came to Cashabree to repair her ship," Jayna began.

As she described the way Hanna had sent her bird to hunt down ships before Queen Kalleah captured them for her fleet, she drew gasps and applause from her audience. She told them of the battle for Desden, and how the women of the town had joined Queen Kalleah to march on Eidervell. And she described how Queen Kalleah had stampeded through Eidervell, felling every soldier in her path before dealing a near-fatal blow to High King Edreon. She had not seen any of it herself, but she could imagine how it would have unfolded.

The eyes of her audience shone with awe, and Jayna felt buoyed by their excitement. She had dreamed of chronicling events in the greater world, and here she was, doing just that. No—not just chronicling. She was influencing the very course of Itrea's future.

Or she would be, if she and Hanna made it to the Icebraid Peaks in time.

42

The Battle for the Mines

As his army neared Redhill, Daymin saw the first of the manor houses the freed slaves had described. The land was barren out here, yet the manors had lush gardens brimming with flowers and vines. Despite the Whitish taboo against constructing common buildings of stone, many were constructed of the same sandstone that lay close to the surface in these parts. Perhaps their owners were simply too far from Whitish authority to care about such things.

Knowing he would not be able to stomach the brutality himself, Daymin sent Uncle Cal, General Vask, and a handful of soldiers to kill the Whitish overlords in their homes. He felt guilty, but he could not afford another mental crisis now. Not when he needed to liberate the mines.

He heard the squeak of wheels and the clanging of hammers before he spotted the mines themselves. Ahead lay an expanse of red hills shot through with black ore, and as Daymin followed the road around the first of the hills, he caught sight of a rough settlement built around a spring in the foot of a valley. Around the spring, the land was green and full of life, but beyond lay only rock and more rock.

And the first of the mines.

The valley beside the settlement was an open pit mine with scaffolding built along the ravaged hillsides, and Daymin could see workers chipping away at the stone and gathering what had fallen into carts. Past this, he spotted a hole tunneled in another hill, with a line of wagons waiting outside.

He was not riding—after most of their horses had been crippled at New Savair, he had refused to take one of the few remaining mounts—so he stepped onto a rock beside the road so his soldiers could see him.

"We approach cautiously," he called out over the sound of marching feet. "Only three companies will follow me in the first wave. Our forces are more than strong enough to overwhelm whatever resistance we find here, and we now know the perils of rushing into a dangerous situation with our full army. General Vask, General Tria, General Bendrick—with me."

Daymin stepped down from the rock and started forward again, registering the confusion of running feet as his army reorganized behind him. Ever since Dellik's death, he had found himself taking on more of her role, learning the names of his generals and giving direct orders rather than passing that work on. Though he was nervous about what it would take to get on speaking terms with his generals, he knew it was better this way. His soldiers would be more likely to trust someone who worked with them closely.

When Tarak jogged forward and fell into step beside him,

Daymin did not send him away. Both had been drilling with General Vask every night since that first lesson, and Daymin was eager to test his budding skills against a Whitish foe. He knew Tarak must feel the same way.

Even Lalaysha and Zahira were catching up quickly. Zahira frighteningly so. Tarak had confessed that he'd seen his sister drilling behind her tent until late each night; she was the last person Daymin had ever expected to see wielding a sword, yet there was something in the way she moved that told him she would be unstoppable if she kept at it long enough.

As Daymin and his three companies marched down the slope to Redhill, Whitish soldiers began dashing away from their posts at the mines, forming a line just outside the town. They seemed disorganized and badly-equipped, many with spears instead of swords, their clothes patched and covered in rock dust. This was not a desirable posting, Daymin realized, and the men who drove the slaves in the mines would also answer to the lords who had installed themselves in nearby manors. He wondered what it took to get assigned to the mines—were these criminals and defectors, or were they just unlucky?

When he came within arrow range of Redhill, Daymin donned his helmet, expecting volleys to streak their way.

None came.

He broke into a wary jog, watching the ground carefully for any signs of a hidden pit. But there was no grass here to hide such a thing, and the earth was too hard and rocky to dig into without spending years chipping away at the stone. Uncle Cal and General Vask fell into line beside him, Tarak still on his right, and the rhythmic pounding of footsteps told him the rest of the soldiers were keeping pace.

Just before the line of Whitish, Daymin raised his sword and quickened his pace to a run.

With a shout, he slammed into the wall of bodies, cutting down with his blade in the first strike in the sequence.

To his surprise, his sword connected with a spear, his enchanted blade shearing the wood in half.

His momentum carried him forward, and he barreled into the man holding the broken spear.

The Whitish soldier staggered back, trying to regain his footing.

Daymin's sword was already in position for it, so he followed through with the second strike in the sequence, cutting up in a backhand sweep.

Again the Whitish soldier blocked with his stubby length of his broken spear, and this time Daymin's sword slid up the rod and grazed the man's fingers.

The soldier dropped his broken spear and stumbled back.

Daymin lunged at him once more, artlessly, and his sword plunged through the man's thin shirt, into his stomach.

His momentary wave of nausea was counteracted by a strange thrill. He had won that fight easily, holding his own in the line of Itreans.

Against a man wielding a stick, Daymin thought derisively.

Still. He was improving.

As the fog of concentration cleared, he realized his soldiers had already broken through the line of Whitish. No enemies remained, as far as he could see, and Itreans were emerging from the houses all down the main street to see what the commotion had been.

"We have come to liberate the mines from Whitish

control!" Daymin called out. "Are there any others who would stand against us?"

A woman stepped forward with a toddler on one hip, a baby in a sling sleeping against her chest. "There are Whitish men driving our husbands down in the mines," she said, her accent almost Whitish to Daymin's ears. "Not many, mind."

"Thank you," Daymin said. "We'll proceed carefully, then."

When Daymin started forward, Uncle Cal put a hand on his shoulder. "The mines could be hazardous. Send us in your stead."

Daymin hesitated, wanting to argue. But Cal was right. He couldn't risk himself unnecessarily. "I'll take the pit mine, then. General Tria, I'll need your company to join me. Prince Calden, do as you see fit."

Daymin, Tarak, and General Tria's company split off from the rest, heading for the pit mine. General Tria was a woman perhaps ten years Daymin's senior, too young to have fought in the first war yet skilled enough that she had risen quickly through the ranks, and Daymin found her less intimidating than the older generals.

When they reached the pit mine, they started down the short road carved in the rock. It appeared this had once been a hill, and the rear of the mine still rose above the nearby valley.

The Whitish soldiers at the base of the scaffolding were ready for him. Each restrained an Itrean miner, many of them boys barely in their teens, with a blade to the throat.

"Take another step and we'll kill the captives!" one of the soldiers shouted.

Daymin swallowed against the lump in his throat. He had expected something like this, but not with children.

"Archers?" he said quietly. "Can you hit the Whitish without harming their captives?"

He felt movement behind him; glancing over his shoulder, he saw one of the archers holding a drawn bow behind the cover of Tarak's back, the tip pointed to the ground.

"Now!" he whispered.

A dozen bows rose from his army, twanging as they loosed their arrows.

Many fell short, but three found their mark, one burying itself in the neck of a Whitish soldier.

As the man collapsed backward, blood gushing down the front of his coat, his captive dashed sideways and barreled into the next man in line.

In the confusion, Daymin's archers did not risk shooting again, so Daymin drew his sword and rushed forward with a yell. When he neared the foot of the ramp, he jumped the final distance to the foot of the pit and sprinted across the rough rock toward the last of the Whitish soldiers.

It was over in minutes. Daymin only managed to aim a single blow at a Whitish soldier before his more experienced soldiers took over.

When General Tria's company stepped back, revealing the bodies of eight Whitish soldiers staining the rock with blood, the miners sent up a cheer.

Men started clambering and jumping down from the scaffolding, abandoning the carts they had been filling, excited chatter ringing off the stone.

"King Daymin is here to deal one last blow against Whitland," General Tria called over the clamor.

"King Daymin?" someone shouted. "Is that really King

Daymin?" He was pointing at Tarak.

"I am," Daymin said, stepping forward and pulling off his helmet. He knew he looked anything but regal, with his dirt-caked Weaver's armor and his curls plastered to his head with sweat, yet a gasp went through the crowd when they saw his face.

Then the Itreans were dropping to their knees, some pulling off hats and holding them to their chests.

"Thank you, Your Majesty," said an older man, head bowed. "We never thought we'd merit the attention of the king hisself, here in our humble little mining town."

"I didn't come here just to free you," Daymin said, insides twisting with guilt. "We're on a campaign to distract the Whitish so the population of Baylore can evacuate."

"And we're grateful just the same. Them Whitish bastards drove us like beasts, they did, and we've all lost family in the mines."

"What can we do for you?" Daymin asked.

"Collapse the mines!" another man called from the back of the crowd. "That'll slow the Whitish for sure! What we're digging out here isn't worth much—the underground mines are where most of the ore is at."

"We can do that," Daymin said. "And what of you and your families? Do you want to follow our army or stay here?"

"Where's the people of Baylore going?" asked a boy who was missing one ear.

"To the Icebraid Peaks," Daymin said. "You could try to find them there, but it would be a long, treacherous journey, and we have no guarantee of sanctuary once we reach the mountains."

The miners muttered to each other, some with arms crossed

over their chests.

"What happens after this?" a man asked. "Is Itrea a Whitish colony?"

"More or less," Daymin said. "We can't hold out any longer. So if you choose to stay, I can't offer you any protection. King's Port is still free, but I don't know how long that will last."

"I'm taking my family to the Icebraid Peaks, then," he said, jaw set with determination.

"I'm gonna follow the army!" a boy declared.

"Me too!"

"Not if your mother has anything to say about it," a man said, cuffing the second boy on the side of the head.

"Traveling with my army might be the safest way to the Icebraid Peaks," Daymin said. "We'll be able to resupply as we capture towns, and our army is more than a match for whatever force we might encounter along the way. Then again, if the Whitish army at our tail manages to catch us, we might be slaughtered. It's your choice. We'll move out in the morning."

"The survivors from New Savair are following our army," General Tria said. "So you wouldn't be the only civilians if you choose that route."

Leaving the former slaves debating amongst themselves, Daymin led his troops away from the scaffolding and back up the ramp out of the pit. By the time his company reached the entrance to the mine tunnel, most of the other soldiers were waiting outside as Itreans filed up from underground. There were dozens upon dozens of miners, many of them bearing signs of injury on their arms and hands, and there were countless boys among their number, some as young as eight.

"This is King Daymin," Uncle Cal said gravely as Daymin

stopped before the freed slaves.

Once again, the men dropped to their knees, muttering their thanks.

"I've invited the others to follow our army, if they wish," Daymin said.

"Good," Cal said. Turning to the miners, he said, "We can offer you nothing more if you choose to stay. The Whitish army will recapture Redhill soon enough, so you can follow us to dubious safety or put your fate in Whitish hands."

"We'll follow you," a man said, and others spoke up in agreement.

"Then prepare to move out in the morning," Cal said.

* * *

In the end, the whole town decided to follow Daymin, including several women with babies and young children. He did not imagine the grueling march would be easy for them, but these people had faced years of brutality at the hands of the Whitish. Anything was preferable to that.

The injuries he saw among the miners were sobering. Many were missing fingers or even hands, and some were half-blind or badly scarred. A scattering of children who looked more Whitish than Itrean indicated that rape was commonplace, and some of the mothers Daymin spotted were still in their early teens themselves.

But against such a grim sight, he was warmed to see the way the survivors from New Savair greeted the miners. It seemed the region was closely tied by blood, and there were families sharing tearful reunions and introducing young children to grandparents they had never met.

Daymin's army rounded up the remaining stores in town, loading all they could carry onto the wagons, and prepared the rest for a feast that night. They built a great bonfire in the center of town, burning the scaffolding and mine carts while they cooked the dried stores, and just before sunset, a pair of Potioneers set off explosives all along the mine tunnel.

The distant booms echoed off the hills, and in their wake, Daymin heard the rumble of rocks collapsing.

A cheer rose from the people of Redhill, and Daymin found himself grinning in satisfaction. He finally felt as though he had done some good, and not just for the residents of Baylore.

As darkness set in, the townspeople brought out instruments and struck up unfamiliar folk tunes, luring their fellows into a set of dances.

Daymin ducked into his tent just before dinner to write to Idorii, heart aching at the joy of it all juxtaposed with the suffering his people had faced.

The capture of Redhill was a success, thank the cloudy gods! But plagues, I had no idea how much my people were suffering outside of Baylore. They greeted me as a hero, and I could hardly stand their praise, since I had only thought to aid them in service of those in Baylore.

Any sign that the Whitish are preparing for an attack yet?

Well done, Daymin, Idorii replied almost at once. *You needed a victory like that. You deserve their thanks, even if you freed them in service of a different mission, because who else would have ventured so far south? Your mother had long since forsaken the rest of her kingdom. Only you were willing to make one last push through the countryside.*

No sign of Whitish movement yet, and the evacuees have made good progress away from Baylore. As much as this campaign is troubling you, it has achieved its purpose, has it not?

Yours,
Idorii

Daymin ventured from his tent once again, this time settling on a chair Uncle Cal had fetched from one of the nearby houses. He could feel the heat from the bonfire washing over his face, bringing back unpleasant memories of New Savair, yet beneath these were the memories of his final days in Baylore. Falling in love with the city for the first time. Laughing and drinking and moving among his people as though he was truly one of them. Idorii by his side, sharing his bed, dressing him each day. Kissing him.

Why was it that the same war that had ripped his country apart and claimed so many lives could also bring beauty and joy?

He would never understand it.

Tarak, Zahira, and Lalaysha joined him, sharing around a flask of whiskey plundered from one of the Whitish manors, and Daymin half-expected Zahira to drag him into the unfamiliar dance.

"Could you imagine living out here as a slave, laboring under the Whitish army's thumb, with no hope that anyone might come along to save you?" Zahira asked, watching the dancers with a pensive expression. "How would you keep going? If it had been me, I'm sure I would have given up by now."

"These men had families," Tarak said. "That's reason enough for most of them."

"I feel sick now, thinking of all the frivolous games I used to play back at court," Zahira said. "None of it mattered, did it?"

"You were just having fun," Daymin said. "Making the most of what you were given. Don't lose that joy, Zahira. Please. You help remind me that there's more to life than this war."

"I used to drive you crazy," she said drily.

"I could never tell if you were teasing me," Daymin said. "But I got used to it."

"Thanks. That's very encouraging."

"Daymin is right," Lalaysha said. "He and Tarak are too serious sometimes." She poked Tarak in the chest. "Especially now, with this sword training. Sparring used to be fun, and now Tarak is so grim about it that I'm afraid to challenge him."

Tarak put a hand to the back of his neck, looking embarrassed. "I'll try not to act that way in the future."

"And you are just as bad!" Lalaysha said to Zahira. "When you pick up that blade, you frighten me sometimes. Soon I'll be the only useless fighter here."

Zahira bared her teeth in a fierce grin. "Someday I'll be as great as General Vask. Armies will tremble before my might!"

Tarak laughed. "I'd love to see that."

Just then, Daymin spotted a figure running from the darkness at the eastern end of town into the glowing light cast by Weavers' crystals.

He jumped to his feet, hand going to his sword. Were they under attack?

Then the man's face came into view, and Daymin's heart leapt into his throat.

It was Renok, his childhood friend.

Renok was stopped before he made it far into the camp, so Daymin set off at a jog toward him.

"Unhand that man!" Daymin shouted at his soldiers. Renok couldn't speak Whitish and had no way of explaining himself. "He's a friend of mine!"

The soldiers heard and released Renok, who ventured forward more warily.

Daymin closed the distance and gripped Renok's hand in greeting. Up close, he could see Renok had dark bags under his eyes, and he looked close to collapse.

"What's wrong?" Daymin asked in Allakoash.

"The Whitish—are sending their towers—against the forest," Renok gasped.

Lalaysha skidded up to Daymin's side, eyes wide. "What do you mean?" she asked.

"A whole line of towers—is rolling toward the forest, along with—thousands of soldiers," Renok said, chest heaving. He coughed, and Daymin steadied him with a hand. "And trebuchets, like what they used against Baylore—in the last war. Our tribe recognized them."

Daymin felt as though he was rooted in place. "What are they trying to do?"

"We didn't realize it, but the forest road closed up—many moons ago. I'm sure they intend to cut a way through to Larkhaven." Renok lifted his bloodshot eyes to Daymin's, pleading. "We can't fight off this many machines. This is going to be the end of us."

Daymin looked from Renok to Lalaysha. Then he turned to survey his vast army, which spilled from the town to camp in tiers along the rocky hillsides.

At last he met Renok's eyes once more.

"I made your people a promise," Daymin said, "and I intend to honor it. My army will come to your aid."

43

Varos and the Gods of Light

After her recent conversation with Bennett, Kalleah knew she needed to learn more about Totoleon and the Nine Gods of Light. She had asked Baridya, who had told her Totoleon was the God of Stars, also referred to as the Guide. According to legend, he was the one who drew out the contours of the earth and threw the stars into the sky, and Baridya said many mapmakers and seafaring navigators were devotees of Totoleon.

This was more than she had ever known about the gods who predated Varos, but Kalleah wanted more. She wanted to learn about where the different gods stood on the issue of magic, and what role they had played in the history of the Kinship Thrones.

So she returned to the street with the teahouse she and Bennett had visited, ducking into a bookstore she had noticed the last time she was here.

Inside, the place smelled of parchment and dust, a comfortable, familiar scent.

The shopkeeper greeted her warmly, paying no heed to her dark skin, and asked what he could help with.

"I'm looking for books on the Nine Gods of Light," Kalleah said in her best attempt at a man's deep voice. "Not religious mythology, exactly, but more of the history of the Alldrosants and what role they played in shaping the Kinship Thrones."

She realized as soon as she spoke that it had been a mistake to refer to their religion as "mythology," but the shopkeeper had either missed her slip-up or did not care.

"Of course," he said, leading her through the narrow corridors between shelves. "We have religious texts back here, or you might find more useful answers in the history of the Kinship Thrones as recorded by the most recent Alldrosant king." He handed her a thick volume with gilding on the cover.

"Thank you very much," Kalleah said.

When the shopkeeper left, she scanned the spines of the religious texts, surprised to see volumes referencing belief systems she had never heard of before, including some in different languages. This spoke to her of the other side of the Twin Cities, the side that had once welcomed influences from around the world, and she felt a rush of hope at the sight. Maybe she would find answers here after all.

Settling on a stool in one corner, she soon lost herself in reading, much as she had done in Cashabree.

She began with the history text, scanning until she found references to the various Gods of Light. It seemed their devotees had been less unified before Varos, instead forming different factions that squabbled and chose different means of showing their dedication. Some of the gods were commonly referenced—Sullivim, for example, was the god of growth and plenty, and even in Baylore, the Sullimsday Market must have originally been set on that particular day as a way of giving thanks to Sullivim for a successful harvest.

Others attracted followers based on the pursuits they encouraged. The followers of Totoleon explored and mapped the world; the followers of Ilkayum worked for charitable causes; and the followers of Tenenus were warriors.

Before the time of Varos, it seemed some of the Gods of Light had advocated showing mercy to Makhori, and indeed, some of the miracles described in those early days were clearly the work of specific magic races.

Then, little by little, attitudes had begun to change. The Gods of Light came together into a more cohesive set of beliefs and codes, and as they did, the Gods of Sin—and hence the Makhori who were supposedly their progeny—solidified into the one true enemy.

Much of this had happened in the time before the Kinship Thrones had been declared, when Whitland was a burgeoning power and the rest of the continent was sparsely settled by Makhori and other races. It was the king who had set his sons on the nine Kinship Thrones and declared the continent a unified body under Whitish rule who had also brought the Nine into their true supremacy.

And as Whitland had begun dominating the other races, so had the Gods of Light become more brutal and less tolerant.

So if Bennett spoke of a sect of Alldrosants who did not believe all magic was evil, perhaps he followed an older version of the religion. One that her own people would not find as objectionable.

If she hoped to form a genuine alliance with any of the Kinship Thrones, she had to come to terms with the fact that their societies were deeply enmeshed in religion. Even if she found some of their beliefs objectionable, she had to seek a common ground.

Maybe approaching those who believed that only the forbidden races were evil would be the right way in. After all, Itreans had believed the same, even before the Truthbringers began deepening the divide. She had spent most of her life dealing with prejudice relating to her power. This was something she knew and understood and could accept.

Kalleah realized her back was beginning to ache, so she rose from the stool and twisted from side to side. Then she gathered up the books and returned them carefully to their shelves, feeling guilty that she had entered with no intention of buying anything.

On her way out, she thanked the shopkeeper profusely and tipped him with a coin she had intended to save for dinner, and he smiled and bowed her from the store, not seeming the least bit surprised that she had used his shop as a library. In fact, she had heard of no library since reaching the Twin Cities, so perhaps he was used to his store being treated as an unofficial repository of knowledge.

As she started back down the streets to the waterfront, the familiar reek rising to meet her, she found she was grateful that Bennett had broached the subject of magic. Even if he had gone about it in an offensive way. She had spent the past few quarters loathing the restrictions she faced as a woman and a foreigner in the Twin Cities, but instead of grousing about her loss of freedom, she should have been searching for ways in which their thinking aligned nonetheless. And Bennett had given that to her.

She was feeling more hopeful about their situation as she rounded the corner onto the waterfront.

Then she spotted a company of Lord's Men heading straight for The Lost Sailor.

Bloody Varse.

Kalleah's first instinct was to search the gang for Leoth's face, so she wasted precious seconds scanning the heads of the mob. Thankfully he was not among their number.

There was a back entrance to the inn, so Kalleah retreated into the alley she had just emerged from and raced around the rear of the building to the service doorway. Guests were allowed to use this entrance, but since it was also the delivery point for the kitchens and the closest access to the open sewer where chamber pots were emptied, the hallway was often cluttered and reeking of urine.

Kalleah pushed open the door and squeezed her way past a mountain of crates, narrowly avoiding a tower of chamber pots that awaited scrubbing.

At last she made it to the next doorway leading into the inn proper. Picking up her pace, she dashed up the stairs two at a time to reach her friends' rooms.

Mellicante and Baridya answered the door when Kalleah knocked, Baridya with her hair halfway into a complicated updo.

"What's wrong?" Mellicante demanded.

"The Lord's Men are coming," Kalleah said. "I don't know why, but they're marching up to the tavern right now like they mean trouble."

"Varse. We need to get out of here."

"Meet me by the back entrance," Kalleah called back, already hurrying down the hall to the next room.

Leoth was not in his room, unsurprisingly, so Kalleah raced on in search of the other three. When they didn't answer their doors, Kalleah bounded back down the stairs to the tavern door.

Pushing it open, she caught sight of Triyam and Desh playing cards at a table in one corner. Beyond the windows, she could see the Lord's Men approaching, nearly to the door.

She dashed across the tavern, raising a few surprised cries.

"The Lord's Men are coming!" she called when Triyam and Desh noticed her.

They scrambled to their feet, abandoning their cards and their drinks, and wove their way hurriedly to her side. At her words, the tavern had descended into chaos. Anyone could be a target for the Lord's Men, and no one wanted to be in their path when they decided to carry out a raid.

"Where's Luc?" Kalleah asked breathlessly.

"Washing dishes," Triyam said.

"Meet me outside the back door!" Kalleah said. "I'll find Luc."

Triyam showed signs of wanting to delay, but Desh grabbed him by the shoulder and steered him through the inn door.

When Kalleah approached the tavernkeeper, he slammed the bottle he was holding onto the counter, scowling at her. "You've brought this on us somehow, haven't you?"

"No!" Kalleah said. "I swear, we had nothing to do with this!"

"There's something unnatural about you and your companions," he said sourly. "I wouldn't be surprised if you've attracted the attention of the Lord's Men. You'd better pray they don't trash this place."

"Where's Luc?" Kalleah asked. "Is he washing dishes?"

The barkeeper looked as though he wanted to be unhelpful—to keep Luc as payment for the trouble she had brought to his doorstep. Then he sighed and shouted, "Luc! You're wanted!"

Before Luc emerged from the kitchen, the Lord's Men stomped up to the tavern door.

"Tell him to meet us outside the back entrance," Kalleah said.

Then she turned and dashed away just as the Lord's Men pushed the door open.

She was sure someone would have seen her, so she tore through the inn, past the other panicked guests, to the back entrance. Mellicante, Baridya, Triyam, and Desh were already waiting there, only Mellicante carrying her pack.

"Where's Luc?" Triyam asked, peering behind Kalleah at the chaos filling the hallway.

"He's on his way. I hope." She thought of Bennett just then; she would have given him warning as well if she had known which room he stayed in. Then again, he seemed friendly with the Lord's Men, so she doubted they would harass him. In fact, there was a chance he had set them on her.

Guests were beginning to pour from the back entrance, as well as a few patrons Kalleah had recognized from the tavern. Triyam was bouncing on his heels in worry, craning his neck to see around the corner.

"We can't wait much longer," Kalleah said. "They saw me running from the tavern, and they might send someone after me if they thought I was trying to hide something."

"You and twenty other people," Mellicante said. "They can't chase everyone down."

Kalleah hoped she was right.

Just then, Luc came tearing around the corner, his sleeves rolled up past his elbows, the front of his shirt damp.

"Luc!" Triyam called, seizing him in a one-armed hug.

"They're coming!" Luc panted.

Kalleah broke into a run up the alley, her companions racing after her. They took several turns at random, finally slowing down as they reached a street where they could lose themselves in a heavy flood of pedestrians.

"Plagues," Mellicante said. "What was that about?"

"You don't think they know who we are, do they?" Baridya asked in a hushed voice.

"I don't know," Kalleah said. "We should cross a bridge and see if we can watch them from the opposite bank."

They cut south, following streets Kalleah did not recognize, until eventually they emerged on the waterfront well away from The Lost Sailor. Even here, people were running about in confusion, and Kalleah glimpsed another complement of Lord's Men barging into a different inn.

Soon they reached the closest bridge and hurried across to the Kohlmarsh side, where they hugged the shadowed awnings as they approached The Lost Sailor from the opposite side.

"This can't be about us," Mellicante said, slowing as they came within sight of the Lord's Men hauling barrels of spirits from the tavern. "If they'd received a tip-off, they would have gone after us in a way that didn't give us plenty of time to escape, and they wouldn't have disturbed any other establishments. This might just be a routine raid."

"How can anyone live like this?" Baridya asked.

Kalleah shook her head, and they watched in silence as a few of the brutes descended on the tavern next door. Angry shouts rose across the water, but most of the civilians who crossed paths with the Lord's Men fled without stopping to put up a fight.

"I'm starting to think King Edreon might not be behind this after all," Kalleah said. "Yes, it keeps the people in line, but it has also unified them in their hatred of the Lord's Men. It seems the population here is diverse in its beliefs and loyalties, so there would have been Whitish supporters mixed in among the dissenters. What these men are doing…"

"They've turned all but the most extreme loyalists against King Edreon," Mellicante said.

"Exactly."

Mellicante crossed her arms, frowning. "You don't think this is a scheme by a different power altogether to undermine King Edreon's hold on the Twin Cities, do you?"

"Maybe," Kalleah said slowly. "I just don't understand why anyone would bother. The Twin Cities aren't currently playing a part in the war, so turning the population against King Edreon won't change anything in the rest of the Kinship Thrones."

"Unless King Edreon is counting on reinforcements from the Twin Cities," Mellicante said. "Maybe it will make a big difference when he does finally need to draft the people here. If he was relying on their help, and they refuse—"

"But who would go to such lengths? Who would benefit from pushing the Twin Cities away from Whitish control?"

"The followers of Totoleon," Baridya said. "They said they were working to destabilize the Whitish high throne."

"You're right," Kalleah said. "It's all related somehow. It must be."

And Bennett could be the key to it all.

"Beg pardon," Desh said gruffly, "but I think that man's been watching us for a while. Maybe we ought to get a move on."

Kalleah followed his gaze to see a dockworker staring at her group with sharp-eyed mistrust.

"Good idea," she said. "We need to find somewhere to hide."

She led the way down a street into Kohldar. This side of the river was far more maze-like than Darrenmark, with streets curving and intersecting and splitting seemingly at random, and it did not help that there was no hill to orient her.

Soon they came across a shop that had been ransacked by the Lord's Men. The windows were smashed, the inside charred, and only the counter remained of the shop interior.

Glancing around to make sure no one was watching, Kalleah pushed open the door of the shop, which hung partway off its hinges. Her companions followed her swiftly inside.

"What are we doing here?" Mellicante hissed.

"Staying the night," Kalleah said. "I don't want to go back to the waterfront while the Lord's Men are around. And besides, the innkeeper thought we were responsible for the raid. If we return now, we're likely to attract the wrong sort of attention."

"Why would he suspect us of drawing the Lord's Men to our doorstep?" Triyam asked indignantly. "I thought he appreciated all the free labor we were giving him!"

"Look at us," Mellicante said. "We're the only Itreans in the Twin Cities, and women at that. Of course people are going to

331

be suspicious."

Kalleah ventured toward the back of the shop, where the air was thick with ash. Past a singed half-door that swung open when she gave it a push, she found a back room that might have once been an office. Here again the space was stripped bare, and this far back from the street, she dared to light her Weaver's crystal. There was plenty of room for all of them to stretch out, though they would be lying directly on the floorboards—except perhaps Mellicante, who still had her pack with the sleeping roll she had brought from Baylore.

As she sank to the ground, Kalleah realized with a jolt that Leoth would not be able to find them here. He would return to The Lost Sailor and think them gone.

Kalleah felt a stabbing ache in her side. All at once, she no longer cared what Leoth's work with the Lord's Men had involved; she just wanted him back by her side.

After the spring festival, she promised herself. *As soon as I speak to King Rodarin, I'll hunt him down.*

44

Enemy Territory

Though they had weighed their packs down with as much food and water as they could carry, Jayna and Hanna finished off the last of their water three days out from the Wandering Woods.

Soon after leaving the forest, they had run across a line of strange metal towers rolling across the plains, forcing them to head north to avoid being seen.

"You don't think those are planning to attack the trees, do you?" Hanna had asked Jayna nervously.

"If they are, there's nothing we can do about it," Jayna said. "The Allakoash will see them soon enough anyway."

They had stood watching the towers until they vanished over the horizon, Jayna fighting off the creeping sense of unease that made her want to turn around and chase the towers all the way back to the forest.

By the time they had found the road once more, they

realized they had made very little progress west. Ahead, Jayna could make out a collection of buildings that had to be Valleywall, since they had yet to run across the river.

"How far is the river?" Jayna asked. Her throat was already parched, and her stomach was grumbling hollowly—most of their staple foods needed to be cooked in water, so they had foregone these for the past day, instead chewing on strips of jerky and eating their way through the wilted greens they had strapped outside their packs.

Hanna pulled out the map Chanesh had sketched and squinted at it. "Another…ten leagues, if we get the direction right?"

Jayna groaned. "How many days is that?"

"Two, I think? If we push ourselves."

"I'm not going to survive that long without water," Jayna said.

"No."

They kept walking in silence. Overhead, Dragon and Tika wheeled lazily, scanning the plains for prey. Tika had brought back a few small offerings for Hanna, but the field mice had not been substantial enough to merit the effort it would take to light a fire. And besides, what were they supposed to cook with? Chanesh had mentioned abandoned orchards, but they had yet to run across any of these. Maybe they were further along, in Baylore Valley.

The clouds that had covered the Larkhaven coast were far behind them, and they had seen nothing but clear skies and sun since leaving the Wandering Woods. Even this early in spring, the sun heated the air, making them sweat out everything they drank.

Jayna finally said, "Would it be stupider to die of thirst halfway to the river or get ourselves captured sneaking into Valleywall?"

"I think we have to try Valleywall," Hanna said. "We'll never make it otherwise."

The fact that Hanna was willing to go along with such a crazy idea made Jayna nervous.

Closer they walked, the sun nearly blinding them as it sank low in the west.

"Should we wait until it's dark?" Jayna asked.

"Definitely," Hanna said.

With the sun nearing the horizon, they reached an abandoned farmhouse just north of the road. Here they waited, watching the residents of Valleywall as they returned home from their work in the fields. The town seemed oddly quiet, and most of the houses Jayna could see were dark, some lying in obvious disrepair.

"Where is everyone?" Jayna whispered.

"It's Whitish-occupied, isn't it?" Hanna asked. "Maybe all the original residents left, and the town wasn't important enough for the Whitish to station a larger force here."

"Good. That means we're less likely to be seen."

"Or we'll be even more conspicuous."

Hanna was right. Bother. "Let's leave our packs here, anyway."

They stashed their packs beside the abandoned farmhouse and donned cloaks, pulling up the hoods to hide their faces.

"Stay here," Hanna told Tika, pointing to a rotting fence.

Tika swooped low and landed obligingly on the fence Hanna had indicated, while Dragon took off in a different direction, feathers vanishing against the darkening sky. Jayna shook her head—the bird was still obstinate and strong-willed. But she could look after herself.

Then, in the deepening twilight, Jayna and Hanna set off toward Valleywall.

When they crossed over the main road, they reached a wide street leading into Valleywall, passing between a row of abandoned houses. The fences and gates were of finely-wrought metal, but the houses beyond were falling into disrepair, some with collapsed stones that spoke of deliberate harm, others with weedy gardens and broken windowpanes.

Venturing deeper into Valleywall, more of the houses were lit—particularly the largest and most imposing of the structures. When they reached a central area with a well in the open plaza, they encountered pedestrians visiting alehouses and speaking with neighbors, the space lit by a mix of enchanted crystals and oil lamps. There were no women or Itreans in town, only Whitish soldiers, a few in uniform, most in civilian clothes.

"Look," Jayna whispered, pointing at the well. "Let's go."

"Are we safe walking right up to it?" Hanna asked nervously.

"No idea."

Head down, Jayna led the way directly across the plaza to the well. No one would be able to tell they were women from their clothes, so they were unlikely to be stopped. They could have waited until later that night, but Jayna figured that would be even more suspicious.

Besides, she was about to go mad from thirst.

As she neared the well, she drew her waterskins from beneath her cloak. The well operated by pump, so she uncorked the first of the waterskins and held it under the spout.

When she began pumping, the water flowed easily, gushing forth in a sweet-smelling fountain that made Jayna salivate. Once she had filled her first waterskin, she drank deeply and topped it up before moving on to the next.

It was when Hanna moved forward to take her turn that Jayna noticed the man watching them. He stood outside a nearby alehouse, hand on the hilt of his sword, the shadows making his face seem twisted and menacing.

"Hanna," Jayna whispered. "Someone is watching us."

Hanna kept pumping, though Jayna could see the way she had tensed.

"What should we do?" Jayna asked.

"We can't outrun him, can we?" Hanna whispered.

"No."

"Then we need to finish what we're doing and leave. If we make a sudden move, it will look suspicious."

Just then, the man stepped down onto the plaza and started toward them, moving swiftly. The Whitish were so *tall*; Jayna realized this alone would have singled her and Hanna out.

"Hanna!" she hissed.

Hanna flinched, her grip on the waterskin slipping.

"We need to get out of here!"

Hanna shoved the cork onto the half-filled skin and slipped it under her cloak. Jayna still had the sword she had carried into battle in Eidervell, while Hanna was armed only with a dagger. But Jayna wasn't about to draw her sword—she could never win a fight against an armed Whitish soldier.

Jayna took off toward the opposite end of the square, hoping there was some way out of town from this side.

337

"Stop!" the soldier shouted. "Who are you?"

Jayna broke into a run, Hanna scrambling to keep up, and she heard the soldier's boots clicking on the cobblestones as he picked up his pace as well. Jayna ran so fast she worried she would lose her footing any moment now, but still the soldier gained on them.

Just as they reached the street leading off the plaza, the soldier lunged at Jayna and grabbed her cloak.

Jayna tripped and fell roughly onto the cobblestones, grazing her palms. Her hood slipped off, revealing her braided black hair.

When she tried to twist and scramble back to her feet, she found the soldier stepping on her cloak, pinning her down. Then she felt a blade nudging against the small of her back.

"A woman," the man said coldly. "And a Drifter. Can you speak Whitish?"

"Yes," Jayna gasped, not bothering to correct him.

"What are you doing in Valleywall?"

"We just wanted water," Jayna said, heartbeat thudding in her throat. She threw a desperate look at Hanna, hoping she would do something, but Hanna stood as if frozen.

"What business do you have so far from the woods?"

Jayna said nothing.

"Well, you'll make a pretty pet, even with that strange face of yours. We could do with a woman to warm our beds."

The soldier leaned forward and grabbed Jayna's arm, hauling her roughly to her feet. She could smell the sweat on him, stale and rank.

This finally spurred Hanna into action. She lunged at the soldier, something flashing as she moved—the dagger, which must have been hidden beneath her cloak.

As the soldier stepped aside, Jayna drew her own sword left-handed and flailed it at him. Neither attack was enough to dislodge the man's grip on her arm.

Now he drew his sword, face twisting in anger. "Who gave you a sword? Varos's weapons don't belong in the hands of savages."

With foolish bravado, Jayna said, "We took it from the soldiers we defeated in Desden."

That threw the soldier off for a moment. As he hesitated, confused, Jayna swung wildly at him once more. This time her blow landed, tearing his shirt.

"Fool." The soldier released her arm and slammed his sword into hers, knocking her blade to the ground.

When Jayna dropped to her knees to retrieve her sword, he slashed at her arm.

Jayna yelped in pain, vision going momentarily hazy. He had cut deep into her upper arm, tearing through her flesh, and it was all she could do not to collapse at the searing agony. Waves of pain surged through her, and beneath it Jayna could feel warmth soaking her sleeve as blood poured from the wound.

"Jayna!" Hanna cried. She grabbed Jayna's other arm and dragged her to her feet, but before they could stumble out of the man's reach, his hand closed around Jayna's braid.

"No more of that," he said sharply. "Unless your friend wants a scar to match yours?"

Jayna gasped as he yanked her head back by her braid.

"Our people will come for you if you don't let us go!" Hanna cried.

The soldier's lip curled. "No they won't. Our army is about

to raze your forest to the ground. When we're finished, there will be no one left to save you."

Hanna's eyes widened, and beyond the fog of pain, Jayna felt a stab of worry for Borderville. What would happen to Chanesh? To the people who had welcomed them so warmly?

The man lunged for Hanna, but before he could lay a hand on her, a shriek sounded from overhead.

He looked up just in time to see Dragon diving at his face, talons outstretched.

Relief flooded Jayna. Thank Diona for the disobedient bird.

Dragon landed with a *whump* on the man's forehead, talons digging into his flesh.

He roared in surprise and released Jayna as he staggered backward.

"Run!" Hanna whispered, grabbing Jayna's hand and pulling her down the shadowed street.

Jayna ran.

She looked back once to see Dragon holding tight to the man's hair, wings flapping in a flurry as she pecked at his face.

Then they reached the edge of the town, where the land dropped away in a steep slope to the foot of Baylore Valley. The crescent moon had risen, and it shed enough light to guide them around the town, back toward the main road.

As Jayna's panic subsided, her arm began throbbing so painfully that tears leaked from her eyes. Still she ran. She kept imagining she could smell the man's sweat and feel his powerful hand around her arm.

From the distance, she heard Dragon shriek again, and she prayed the bird hadn't been injured.

"Come back to me, Dragon," she muttered as she ran. "You

beautiful bird."

At last they crossed the main road and jogged the final distance to the barn. They dropped to their knees beside their packs, their ragged breathing loud in the quiet darkness.

Hanna fumbled in her pack for a Weaver's crystal, and when the light fell across Jayna's injured arm, she felt sick. The cut was deeper than she'd imagined, a mess of bloodied flesh, and her sleeve was soaked in blood past the elbow.

"Can you take your shirt off?" Hanna asked. "I need to treat and bind that before you bleed too much."

"Do you know how?" Jayna asked dubiously.

"I had to bandage my uncle's leg when he sliced it open on a rock. I've carried the supplies all the way from home."

Jayna wiped at her eyes. "Which one of us is the true adventurer here?"

She tried to pry her shirt off one-handed, but Hanna ended up helping, finally cutting off the sleeve when Jayna couldn't manage to maneuver her injured arm through. The shirt was ruined anyway.

Then Jayna lay on the ground, hugging her sleeping roll and crying, while Hanna splashed water on the wound and packed something into the cut before wrapping it with linen.

Dragon returned before Hanna was done, and the bird landed beside Jayna's head, polishing her beak on Jayna's hair in a way she supposed was meant to be comforting. Jayna couldn't even summon the energy to greet her bird. The pain was so intense that she wanted to claw her way out of her own skin. Why had she ever left home? This was no adventure. This was agony worse than she had ever imagined.

Finally Hanna smoothed Jayna's hair back from her face.

"I'm done."

Jayna was beginning to shiver in the night air, so she struggled into the only other shirt she owned, hoping blood wouldn't leak through to stain this one as well. She was hiccupping, tears still leaking from her eyes, too miserable to see a way forward.

"How are you doing?" Hanna asked softly.

"It hurts so much," Jayna whimpered. "I hate this. I just want to go home."

"I know," Hanna said. She pulled Jayna's head into her lap and stroked her hair; Jayna finally stopped trembling, and her tears dried up, though her eyes were puffy and swollen.

"This is my own fault," Jayna said. "We have no idea what we're doing. Why did I think we could make it all the way to the Icebraid Peaks on our own? We're going to die out here. I'm so sorry, Hanna."

"I knew what we were getting into," Hanna said, still stroking her hair gently. Jayna felt like a spooked bird that Hanna was slowly coaxing back from its hiding place. "And we're not necessarily going to die. Don't think about the whole journey. Just think about the next step. We're not far from the Elygian River—surely we can make it there."

Jayna sniffed. "I thought I was some brave adventurer. But I'm not. I can't do anything right."

"This would have been dangerous for anyone, no matter how experienced. And if we do make it to the Icebraid Peaks, we'll be heroes. No one will care how good we are at fighting or how scared we were along the way."

Rather than comforting, Jayna found Hanna's words irritating. She was miserable and in pain, and she wanted to wallow. Not listen to logic.

She sat up with difficulty, dislodging Hanna and Dragon, and stumbled to her feet. The movement brought blood rushing to her head, and for a moment she swayed, vision spotting over with black.

Once she recovered her balance, she staggered away from the barn, heading north through the wild grasses. Then she sank to the ground once more and pillowed her head on her knees, gazing bleakly at the moonlit plains. This adventure was nothing like what she'd imagined. She had been so naïve. Such a fool.

Why had she ever wanted to get tangled up in this messy, all-consuming war?

45

The Ruined Bridge

aymin's army was nearing the bridge at Coppertown, the closest route to the forest from Redhill. Ever since Renok had brought word of the harvesting towers' attack on the Wandering Woods, he had driven his army hard, marching from sunrise to sunset.

Now he caught glimpses of the sunlight reflecting off the Elygian River each time the road crested a hill, so they had to be close to the bridge.

Daymin's legs ached from the long days. Their pace was relentless, and with each day they left the civilians and supply wagons further behind, guarded by a smaller force.

At last he rounded a corner and saw Coppertown perched on the opposite bank of the river. Slightly larger than Redhill, Coppertown was a compact town of stone houses, with smaller clusters of buildings perched around the entrances to the nearby mines.

"Varse," Uncle Cal said from beside Daymin.

He looked at Uncle Cal in surprise. Then, following his gaze, he realized what he had overlooked.

The bridge lay in ruins.

"The Whitish were ready for us," Cal said grimly.

Daymin felt dizzy. He had pushed his army so hard, and for what? Leagues of wasted effort. "What are we supposed to do now?"

"The only other bridge is at New Savair. And if we backtrack, the Whitish are likely to catch up to us."

Alarm spiked through Daymin. "Plagues. Do you think we can ford the river?"

"Not here," Cal said. "It looks like it's starting to turn into a gorge. It will be deeper and swifter than it is farther north, and I can't see any safe way up the opposite bank."

Cal was right. The river had cut directly into the rock, and even though it was swollen, the clear water lay several paces below the surrounding land.

"Daymin," Cal said, his voice pitched quietly enough that the nearby soldiers couldn't hear. "Do you think we should abandon this route? I know you promised to help the Allakoash, but their forest forsook Baylore, so they can't hold you to your word. And besides, they have the entire might of the Wandering Woods behind them. That amounts to thousands of trees. Maybe even millions. What can we do compared to them?"

"We have a way of felling the machines," Daymin said. "The Allakoash don't. If we can't stop the harvesting machines, they'll destroy the forest. Since we have means of saving the Allakoash, we have a duty to come to their aid, even beyond any promise I made."

345

When Cal opened his mouth to argue, Daymin said, "Itrea is doomed anyway. Our people are refugees who might die as soon as they reach the mountains, and then everything our army has done here will be wasted. But the Allakoash are still free. If we can bring down the last of the harvesting machines, we will have saved an entire people from destruction. Isn't that a worthwhile goal? No matter the cost?"

Cal sighed. "I don't know. What are your orders?"

Daymin recognized the familiar signs of an advisor who disagreed with him yet would support him nonetheless. So he turned to his army and called out, "The bridge at Coppertown has been destroyed! Turn north and follow the river back to the crossing at New Savair!"

Lowering his voice, he told Cal, "Send scouts on horseback to see how close the Whitish army is. If they catch up to us before we reach New Savair, we'll have to try fording the river."

Cal saluted and jogged back the way they'd come, leaving Daymin to lead his army off the road toward the river. The ground was barren and rocky around here, with nothing to slow him, so he let the momentum of the slope carry him faster and faster until he was running.

Though the impact jolted through his sore legs, Daymin was glad to be moving fast, the speed giving him the illusion of progress. He wanted to scream in frustration. Even without doubling back, he was already taking an insane risk in coming to the aid of the Allakoash; he would be pitting his army against the harvesting machines once again, this time with a force equal to his at his tail.

Cal was right. He could abandon this madness and loop around south to rejoin his evacuees, capturing a few more towns on the way. If he didn't reach New Savair in time, the Whitish army would pin his troops against the river, forcing them into a battle he knew they would lose.

And if they dashed themselves to pieces against the Whitish army, they wouldn't be able to help the Allakoash.

Racing to New Savair was reckless. Unconscionable. Especially since the Whitish had horses and he had none.

But he couldn't abandon the Allakoash. Not when they still had a chance.

Why was the Varse-damned bridge gone? If he could have crossed at Coppertown, the situation would have been vastly different.

Daymin was still running, each footfall juddering through his aching body. Gradually the slope tapered off, and he slowed to a walk, his muscles still vibrating from the impact. On top of everything else, his army wouldn't be capable of fighting if he drove them too hard. He was close to collapse himself; the idea of lifting a sword was daunting. He hadn't practiced since he left Redhill.

The scouts will decide it, he thought. *If we have a hope of beating the Whitish to New Savair, we'll make a dash for it. If not…*

For now, he just had to put one foot in front of the other.

* * *

That evening, instead of passing out the moment he climbed into his tent, Daymin wrote to Idorii to ask what method they intended to use to fight the harvesting machines.

After describing the trebuchets and paired enchantments they had prepared, Idorii wrote, *Why do you ask? Are you hoping*

347

Baylore might hold out after all?

> *Not at all,* Daymin replied. *The harvesting machines are descending on the Wandering Woods, and my army is racing to aid the Allakoash. I was hoping you might offer us a more viable means of defeating the towers.*

> *I'm afraid our enchantments won't do much without trebuchets to provide the necessary force. I wish I could offer more.*

> *Apparently the Whitish are bringing trebuchets to the front as well. If we can capture one, maybe we can use it. Could you write the exact wording and methodology of the spells, so our Weavers can attempt to replicate it?*

Idorii wrote down the spell, and Daymin copied it carefully onto a scrap of paper, making sure to spell the strange words correctly.

After Idorii had finished the spell, he wrote, *Fighting so many harvesting machines sounds like a dangerous prospect. Are you going to be safe?*

> *I don't know,* Daymin wrote back. *It was supposed to be a reasonable plan, until we reached Coppertown to find the bridge destroyed. Now we're doubling back to New Savair, which puts us at risk of running into the Whitish army. As usual, Prince Calden is questioning my judgment. And this time he has a very good point.*

> *But knowing you, you're not about to change your mind.*

No. Does that make me a terrible person?

I…might have to reserve judgment until you explain your reasoning. Sorry, Daymin. But aren't there millions of trees in the Wandering Woods? How can your army make a difference compared to what those trees can do?

Daymin hesitated before writing back. He wasn't going to change his own mind, but knowing he had Idorii's support would make all the difference.

I'm doing this for more than one reason. First, and most simply, I bought Baylore time many spans ago by promising I would ride to the aid of the Wandering Woods if the Whitish ever sent a large force against them. One of my tribe came to us, seeking our help, and I couldn't turn him down. Not knowing what I had sworn.

Second, you remember how badly the trees fared against the machines at Darkland Fort. There are many more trees in the Wandering Woods, but they have never managed to bring down even a single tower without our help. If we don't stop them, they will eat away at the forest until nothing remains. Part of me hopes we can sweep in quickly and deal with the towers without fighting a true battle, especially if we can find a way to use your spells against them.

And finally…I know this sounds silly, but I can't bear to watch the last free peoples east of the Icebraid Peaks fall to the Whitish. We're done for, and King's Port won't be far behind, but the Allakoash are still independent. If I destroy my army in the process of saving them, won't it be worth the cost?

Oh, Daymin. I can see why you're doing it, but when you say it that way…plagues. Promise you'll be safe. I can't bear the thought that you'll throw your life away for a doomed cause.

Isn't that what my whole campaign is? A doomed cause?

Yes, but it was never this foolhardy before. Please. Don't be reckless. I know I'm being selfish to make demands of you, but if you die before I see you again, it will destroy me.

How do you think I felt when you decided to stay behind in Baylore? Daymin wrote back in amused indignation.

I know, I know. I'm a complete hypocrite. And I should have known not to lose my heart to someone so honorable. I love you, Daymin. I hope you know that.

Daymin gave a choked laugh. With a shaking hand, he wrote, *And I love you too.*

Then he lay back on his sleeping roll, legs still throbbing. After what Idorii had said, he was more committed than ever to his decision. But that didn't soften the ache of knowing how much this would hurt those who cared for him.

46

Fortitude

As they trekked the final distance to the Elygian River, Jayna felt dizzy and off-balance. Hanna checked the bandaging on her wound every day, and the poultice she had set in it seemed to be helping it heal swifter than it should, yet it continued to ache fiercely.

When she first glimpsed the river reflecting the sunlight like a beacon in the distance, she thought she was hallucinating. She paused to dig her fingers into her shoulder, just above the wound, the pressure giving her a moment's relief. The pain was wearing at her, until she was ready to collapse. Walking when she was in this state...Merciful Jesha. All she wanted to do was lie down and wait to die. Anything else seemed like too much effort.

She forced herself to stagger on, and soon the river was unmistakable.

The last distance seemed to take a lifetime. Jayna's eyes

stung with tears she furiously blinked back, and her head began to pound.

Willows and reeds grew thick along both banks of the river, and when they reached its banks at last, Hanna led the way through the thick growth to the water. It was flowing fast, the water clear; back in the distant past, before this murderous adventure, she would have been eager for a swim. Now she just wanted to sleep.

"We should camp here a few days," Hanna said. "At least until you've recovered. It's dangerous to push on when you're in this state."

Jayna was too tired to argue. Instead she crawled into her oilskin sleeping roll and fell asleep to the sound of water rushing past.

* * *

She didn't wake until late the next morning. Hanna was already up, cooking something over a small fire, and Jayna's stomach gave a loud rumble at the smell.

"How are you feeling?" Hanna asked.

"Better now there's food," Jayna said grimly. She struggled out of the sleeping roll, wound throbbing with each movement, and staggered over to sit on a log beside Hanna. It was nice to see trees again, and good to camp somewhere hidden enough that they didn't have to be on constant lookout for enemies.

"Dragon brought back a couple prairie dogs," Hanna said. "Since I've already lit the fire, I thought we could cook them up as well."

Jayna watched as Hanna propped a skewer with the two

skinned prairie dogs over the fire. They were larger than rats, so they looked like a veritable feast after so many days of rationing.

While they waited for the prairie dogs to cook, Hanna dished the watery millet porridge into their bowls. Jayna ate greedily, hungry enough to eat another five helpings. The sizzling meat was beginning to give off a delicious aroma, tormenting her with impatience.

"I thought we should discuss our options," Hanna said abruptly.

Jayna tore her eyes from the juicy meat. "What do you mean?"

"We still have a long way to travel to the Icebraid Peaks, and we're starting to see how desperate the situation is here. If we get ourselves tangled up with King Daymin's army, we might not be able to escape the war."

"Unless we make it to the Icebraid Peaks."

"I don't know," Hanna said. "That depends on how determined the Whitish are. If they're happy to conquer Baylore and stop there, we might find refuge with the Icelings. But if not—"

"The Icelings don't have anywhere fortified to hide, do they?" Jayna asked.

"No."

Jayna frowned at Hanna, wondering what she was getting at.

"We could still turn back," Hanna said quietly. "If we travel south to King's Port, we might be able to arrange transport back to Cashabree. We don't have to die for a foreign cause. Not if we don't want to."

The idea was jarring. Jayna leaned forward, staring into the flames, and tried to imagine the journey south to King's Port. It would be a grueling trek, but at least there would be some hope of comfort at the end. *Home.*

What they were doing now was no longer an adventure. Far from it. Traveling with the pirates and venturing into the Wandering Woods and being welcomed as heroes…that was what Jayna had dreamed of when she left home.

Not killing a man while following King Leoth through Whitland. Not getting an injury so painful she could barely think straight. Not pushing on through endless days of hunger and thirst and aching muscles.

She hated the fact that she couldn't cope with it. She had always imagined herself as fearless and strong, yet she was ready to give up at the first sign of adversity?

No, Jayna thought stubbornly. *Getting my arm cut open was never part of the deal. No one would be able to keep going with an injury like this—would they?*

Then she thought of Queen Kalleah, and guilt twisted her insides. *She* was a true hero. Queen Kalleah had never given up, no matter what ordeals she faced. She had braved impossible odds and continued when all seemed lost, and even now she was still fighting for her people.

Queen Kalleah was counting on her. *Itrea* was counting on her.

Hanna was watching her in silence, a troubled look on her face.

Jayna groaned and pulled herself away from her thoughts. "Giving up now would feel like a huge betrayal."

"I know."

"We promised to help King Daymin. We can't turn back

now."

"You're right," Hanna said quietly.

Jayna stared at her. "Wait. Did you want to continue on?"

"Of course. But I'm not the one who is injured, so I didn't want to push you if you didn't feel comfortable with it."

"What? I thought you were skeptical about this whole thing!"

"No," Hanna said. "I agreed to join you because it was the right thing to do. I know it's been hard, but I never expected anything else. I'm here because there are hundreds of thousands of refugees on their way to the Icebraid Peaks right now, and without our help, they might find themselves trapped between two armies. Queen Kalleah and King Daymin are the true heroes here, and the fate of their people is the biggest tragedy anyone has seen in centuries. If we can help them even in the smallest of ways, surely that's worth any amount of suffering."

Jayna stared at Hanna, wondering where the quiet, unassuming girl who had once lurked in the firehawk nesting grounds had gone.

Then again, Hanna had agreed to travel to Chelt in service of Jayna's crazy plan in the first place. Maybe this righteous determination had been there all along, hidden beneath Hanna's shy demeanor. She had just needed a little push from Jayna to find her true path.

Jayna scooted close to Hanna and gave her a hug with her good arm. "I have a funny feeling you're the one who will go down in history someday, not me."

Hanna flushed. "I'm not—"

"You're the true hero. And you're right. We're doing this for Itrea, not just for ourselves. Itrea may be a foreign power, but I can't let myself think the way my father does. Their lives still matter. We have a duty to save their people if we can."

Hanna was still red in the face, but she didn't argue. Instead she lifted the prairie dogs from the fire and prodded at them. "I think these are done."

Jayna pulled hers off the skewer, not caring that it burned her fingers, and tore off a chunk of juicy, tender meat. Then she grinned at Hanna.

Queen Kalleah had not expected them to succeed, but they had made it halfway across Itrea already. They would find King Daymin and negotiate his people's safe refuge in the Icebraid Peaks. Itrea was counting on them.

47

The Spring Festival

W hat are we supposed to do next?" Mellicante asked. They had been hiding out in the ruined shop for several days now, and she had just returned empty-handed from a trip into Kohldar to scavenge for food.

"Something important is at work here," Kalleah said. She paced the small space restlessly, catching snatches of music from the streets beyond. The spring festival was happening this evening, and the city was alive with merriment, though none of it had appeared in the narrow street where they had taken refuge. Mellicante had described dancing and music and flowers throughout the two cities. "But I can't see how we'll grasp it from the heart of the Twin Cities. Not with the Lord's Men keeping such a tight rein on the place."

"Especially not from inside this bloody ruin," Baridya said sourly. Neither she nor Kalleah had ventured out since they had first sought shelter here, and both were growing restless. Until they had a path forward, Kalleah didn't want to risk giving away their hiding place, so only Mellicante was allowed to leave.

"Do you think it's time to visit the Temple of Totoleon?" Mellicante asked.

Kalleah hesitated. That seemed the obvious answer, and for that reason it was likely to be a trap.

More importantly, she had to find a way to meet Bennett that afternoon without Mellicante discovering her plan. "Maybe. But we need to find Leoth first. Would you hunt him down? He'll probably be out patrolling somewhere obvious while the festival is going on."

"Of course," Mellicante said.

"Can we go too?" Luc asked. "I'm hungry, and I bet we'd be able to find something to eat out there."

Perfect. "All three of you can go," Kalleah said, indicating Luc, Triyam, and Desh. "Just make sure you're back by midnight. Baridya and I will wait here."

"Are you sure you'll be all right?" Mellicante asked Baridya with a frown.

"Hungry and bored, yes," Baridya said, "but of course we'll be safe. Look after yourself, will you?"

She pulled Mellicante to her for a fleeting kiss, and then the three were gone.

Kalleah and Baridya waited until the sound of their voices had faded. The music was louder than before, the unfamiliar folk tunes full of a liveliness she had yet to see from the Twin Cities.

"Well?" Baridya asked, raising her eyebrows. "Were you trying to get them out of our way?"

"Yes. I'm still planning to meet Bennett this afternoon, but I understand if you don't want to join me."

"Of course I do! Anything to escape this place."

"Let's go, then."

Baridya was wearing skirts, while Kalleah wore a loose shirt and trousers, so she tucked her braid under her hat to complete her half-hearted disguise as a man. Everyone seemed to see through it, but it would be enough to keep passersby from singling them out as women out walking without a male companion.

They glanced through the broken windows to make sure no one was around before slipping onto the street. One block down, they hit a main street packed with townspeople celebrating the festival. Until now, Kalleah had not realized how large a population the Twin Cities held—the Lord's Men had clearly scared everyone into staying home.

Now, with the festival overtaking the city, people seemed to be trusting in the crowds to keep them safe. There were women and girls strolling around unaccompanied, and more diversity than Kalleah had expected. She spotted Varrilans, Ruunans, and even a sizeable number of people who could almost have passed for Itrean.

Baridya linked her arm with Kalleah's, and together they wove their way through the crowd toward the river. Wherever musicians performed, there were couples and groups dancing, and countless women wore crowns of flowers in their hair. Wine flowed freely, and Kalleah used her last drav to buy a honeyed bun to share with Baridya. The pastry melted on her tongue, sweet and airy and gently spiced with cardamom.

When they reached the bridge, they found the rails garlanded with flowers. Here there were women in matching dresses dancing a complicated sequence while acrobats performed suspended from ropes that dangled toward the water. Kalleah and Baridya stopped to watch for a moment, caught up in the gaiety of the festival, until they heard shouts from behind them.

"Damn them," Baridya muttered, glancing at the Lord's Men pushing their way along the waterfront. They seemed intent on causing trouble, with no particular target, and the crowd scattered around them.

Kalleah and Baridya forged on, past the dancers and the acrobats, into the more familiar streets of Darrenmark.

As they started up the hill toward the wealthier part of town, Kalleah noticed that the women with flower crowns were getting considerable attention from the men nearby.

"What do the crowns mean?" she asked Baridya in an undertone.

"They're for unattached women seeking a partner," Baridya said. "In Chelt, it was customary for young women to wear the flower crowns for the span leading up to the spring festival, which gave men a chance to court them. They would then announce their engagements at the festival. I don't know if the tradition is different here, or if the women just waited until the festival because it was too dangerous to draw attention to themselves before now."

Kalleah watched with interest as a nobleman presented a young woman with a necklace, which she fastened around her neck before taking his arm. "It's sad to see such joy today, knowing most of these people are afraid to go out any other day," Kalleah said.

"I know."

Kalleah turned toward the familiar teahouse, which was

packed with couples today. She and Baridya took one of the only remaining tables, and Baridya looked over the menu with delight. "I haven't seen black tea in years! My father used to order it directly from Ruunas, and he and Mother were addicted to the stuff. I used to love drowning my tea in milk and sugar."

Kalleah laughed. "Let's get a pot, then." They were counting on Bennett showing up as promised, because they had no way to pay for the tea otherwise.

Soon they were sipping cups of black tea with milk and sugar, both with their backs to the wall so they could watch the other patrons and the passersby outside the windows. After so many quarters of sneaking around and looking over their shoulder for the Lord's Men at every turn, it was refreshing to see the city full of life once more, the streets packed with enough people that they didn't need to hide.

There were girls walking in groups up the street, giggling as they chased down men; men uncorking bottles and offering wine to anyone who passed them on the street; townspeople gathering around the nearby musicians and clapping along to the music; and people throwing bouquets from upstairs windows. And inside the teahouse, the couples sitting together represented a diversity Kalleah had never seen outside Baylore. There was a Varrilan man with a Darden woman; a pair of men whom she would have mistaken for business partners if not for their intimate manner; a Ruunan woman with a man whose dark skin almost gave him the appearance of an Itrean, like those she had seen before; and many more besides.

"Where is he from?" Kalleah whispered to Baridya, indicating the brown-skinned man.

"No idea. I've never seen anyone like that before. He

doesn't quite look Itrean, does he?"

"No."

Baridya refilled their teacups, and Kalleah took another sip, smiling at the vibrancy of it all.

"I'm glad we got to see this," she said.

"I know," Baridya said. "It's good to know something this beautiful still exists in the Kinship Thrones."

48

River Crossing

Daymin's scouts thundered up to meet him just after he had glimpsed New Savair in the distance. The Whitish army had not come into view ahead, which boded well, but they were still several hours from the ruined industrial town.

Uncle Cal led the scouts, dust billowing up in the wake of his horse. They had left behind the rocky, barren landscape around the mines and were now marching through an expanse of dry grasses and spiny bushes, which slowed his army's progress and might prove impassable for his supply wagons. Daymin was trying not to think too much about it.

When Uncle Cal drew near, he reined in his horse and dismounted, coughing at the dust that rose up around him.

"The Whitish army is a day north of New Savair," he said with a salute.

"We can still beat them across the bridge, then," Daymin said.

Cal shook his head curtly. "No. The bridge at New Savair has been destroyed as well."

Daymin stumbled back a step, mind buzzing uselessly.

No. That couldn't be true.

All the leagues they had traveled at a punishing pace, and for nothing…

"Can we ford the river?" he asked, ribs knit tight with anxiety.

Cal grimaced. "There's a place where it widens and slows a league north of here. But it's still too deep for us to wade across, and too swift to swim. If we sealed the wagons, we could use them as rafts—"

"They're too far behind us," Daymin said. "I don't know if they'll ever catch up."

Cal beckoned Daymin to follow him off to the side, out of earshot of his army. "You need to give up this madness. How many lives do you intend to waste before you choose a different course?"

"I'm not wasting lives," Daymin snapped. "I'm using my army for the purpose it was intended, distracting the Whitish from Baylore while also defending the Allakoash."

"You're putting us in a position we won't be able to escape from, backed up against a much stronger enemy force. What good will it do if we don't even reach the forest? You will have thrown away your soldiers' lives for nothing."

This gave Daymin pause, because it was the one line of reasoning he could not argue against. If he never reached the Wandering Woods in the first place, his intentions would not matter, however noble.

So he tried a different tack. "The Whitish must be trying to

364

stop us from joining their battle against the forest, which means they're worried. They know we can bring down their harvesting machines."

"Either that, or they're trying to trap us against their army," Cal said.

Daymin blew out a frustrated breath that hissed through his teeth. "Can you think of any other way for us to cross the river?"

"Ropes. Someone could swim across, and the rest of us could follow, holding the rope to keep from getting swept downstream. We'd need to set up a pulley system to get our gear across without it getting soaked. It could take days for our whole army to cross, by which time the Whitish will have caught up to us. Not to mention the civilians and supply wagons you'd be stranding on this side."

"I thought you'd finally decided to trust my leadership," Daymin said in irritation. "Why can't you just follow my orders for once?"

"Because I value the lives of our citizens. These aren't just career soldiers, Daymin. Your army represents everyone who is eligible to serve—most of our country's young, healthy population. They deserve to make it safely to the Icebraid Peaks as much as the rest of our people."

"Then take anyone who wants to follow you and go! I'm not changing my mind. The Allakoash deserve protection as much as our people do, and I won't abandon them when their need is greatest."

"That's not what I was advocating, Daymin!" Cal said angrily.

But Daymin turned and stalked back to his army. Putting a foot in the stirrup of Cal's horse, he swung himself onto the saddle so he could see over the heads of his soldiers. He spotted Tarak, Zahira, and Lalaysha near the front of the column, while his generals each marched at the heads of their companies.

"The bridge at New Savair is gone!" Daymin called out. "Our supply wagons can't make it across the river, so our army will split into two parts. Prince Calden will lead a force back to guard the civilians and the supply wagons, who will cut directly toward the Icebraid Peaks to rejoin our evacuees. Meanwhile, the rest of my army will follow me across the river to the Wandering Woods. Any who wish to abandon our attempt to save the Allakoash, you may join Prince Calden. Heed his authority as if he were your king. All else, follow me upriver."

Daymin spurred the horse forward, shoulders tense, waiting for the uproar to begin. He didn't look back until he heard running footsteps behind him.

"Wait!" Tarak's voice shouted. "We need time to organize!"

Daymin reined in Uncle Cal's horse and turned to watch the army at his back. Pollard and Morrisse's forces had drawn off to one side, while the bulk of Daymin's army was marching upriver after him.

Uncle Cal stood where Daymin had left him, watching in visible disbelief as soldier after soldier passed by without throwing him a glance.

Eventually Pollard and Morrisse's troops rejoined the main column, and soon Daymin's army had caught up to him. Cal was left standing alone in the barren scrubland.

Daymin felt a surge of triumph, though it was tempered with guilt. He shouldn't have pitted Cal against him, not in such a visible way. Though they'd had their disagreements, Cal had always stood firmly by his side.

Now Daymin had used Cal's valid arguments against his plan to paint him as a dissident, and in doing so, he had likely lost another of his most trusted allies.

Plagues. Why did he keep doing this?

But it was too late to turn back.

"General Bendrick, take your company along with three others and help Prince Calden escort the civilians west," Daymin called. "Bring all the remaining horses. If you reach the Icebraid Peaks quickly enough, you might be able to protect our refugees when the Whitish come after them." Now that his army had proved its unshakeable loyalty, he wanted to make it up to Cal by painting his choice as heroic.

From behind, General Bendrick began shouting orders, and gradually a force of several thousand soldiers split away from the main army. Daymin dismounted and handed the reins to one of his soldiers, who jogged off to pass his mount along to Cal's troops.

"We'll cross the river here," Daymin told his remaining troops. "Anyone who has rope, bring it forward now. We'll have to swim."

With much pushing and shouting, his army prepared several ropes long enough to cross the river. A young man in peasant clothing came forward and offered to swim the ropes across, saying he was from New Savair and had spent his childhood swimming in the river, and he was soon stroking across the current with the ropes tied around his waist. Even swimming as powerfully as he was, the current pushed him fiercely downstream, until Daymin feared the ropes wouldn't allow him enough slack to reach the opposite bank.

Just as he thought this, the man found his footing on the

opposite bank, his shoulders and torso rising above the turbulent surface. Leaning his weight upstream, he walked slowly forward, the water curling in a wave against his chest.

When he reached the shore he crawled onto the grassy bank and sat for a moment, water streaming down his skin.

Then he walked upstream until he was directly across the river from where he had started. He fastened the first of the ropes around a sturdy bush and backtracked several paces downstream before tying the next off.

Daymin thought he should cross first, since he was asking his army to plunge into the icy river on his orders, so he stripped down to his trousers and tied everything to his small pack, including his sword belt. The rest of his belongings—including the royal tent—were distributed among his other soldiers.

Leaving his belongings to be transferred across on the pulley system, Daymin stepped barefoot down to the water, wincing at the sharp stones underfoot. He felt as though he was about to take an irreversible step forward.

The icy water lapped at his toes, and as he ventured in up to his knees, his feet tingled as they went numb. He didn't know how the swimmer had made it across.

Then the bank dropped off steeply. He had no choice but to plunge in.

Holding the rope in both hands, Daymin sucked in a breath. Then he lowered himself into the water.

The cold was shocking, like a million needles pricking him at once. He gritted his teeth as he began pulling himself hand over hand along the rope, the current already buffeting him.

Soon he was facing the full brunt of the current, the water fighting to tear him loose. He kicked against the flow, but it seemed to do nothing, so instead he focused his energy on moving hand over hand across the river.

By the time he reached the opposite bank, he was stiff with cold, his hands so clumsy he could barely keep hold of the rope. He lowered his bare feet into the drowned grasses and staggered up the bank, still clutching the rope. As the breeze whisked against his wet skin, he started shivering violently.

When he finally splashed from the water, he found the man from New Savair grinning at him.

"How could you do that for f-fun?" Daymin asked, teeth chattering.

"It's usually not this bad. The water warms up by Sun-span, and it's a completely different river that time of year. Uh, Your Majesty."

Daymin coughed. "No need for formality. Not while I'm standing here shirtless like a fool."

The wind was picking up, raising goose pimples all down his back, and Daymin hugged his arms across his chest for warmth.

Looking back, he saw the next pair of soldiers wading into the river, one with a bundle of ropes to create more lines and set up the pulley system. Daymin wished he had tied his shirt around his neck—he was going to be chilled to the bone by the time his belongings finally made it across.

Half an hour later, they had ten ropes spanning the river, one with a pulley system that Daymin's soldiers were already using to ferry bags across one by one. Daymin's pack was one of the first over, thank the cloudy gods, and he pulled his shirt and boots on gratefully. The breeze had long since dried his skin, but his trousers were still clammy where they clung to his legs.

It was very slow going. Pollard and Morrisse had somehow wormed their way to the front of his army, and their troops were crossing one after another, leaving Daymin's soldiers stranded on the opposite bank. The ropes weren't secured that firmly, which meant no more than two soldiers could cross safely at a time; it felt as though they were trying to grind away a boulder with sandpaper, bits of dust flaking away without making any difference to the stone itself.

As the hours passed, Daymin grew more and more anxious. The Whitish soldiers must be closing in on them—if they knew how close his army was, they might be picking up their pace in hopes of catching him.

North of him lay a bluff where the river entered a gorge for a hundred paces, and from the top, Daymin thought he might be able to see as far north as New Savair. It was certainly the highest point he could see from this vantage.

"I'm going to survey the land upriver," he told General Vask, who frowned at him but did not argue. "I'll be back soon."

Then he strapped on his sword belt and strode off toward the bluff. He wished for the company of his friends, but they were still on the opposite side of the river, trapped behind Morrisse's troops.

The land grew rockier as it climbed toward the bluff, and Daymin picked up his pace as the tangle of scrub cleared away. Soon he was jogging up the step-like layers of the rock formation, filled with a boyish sense of adventure.

At the top, the bluff was steeper than it had looked from a distance, so he used his hands to climb the final distance.

Then he straightened. He was perhaps thirty paces above the river, but with the ground so flat all around, he could see for leagues. There was New Savair, nothing remaining of the town but a few charred husks of buildings. There, to the south, were the distinctive hills surrounding the mining towns they had just left.

And just north of New Savair, much closer than he had expected, was the Whitish army.

Daymin's heartbeat thudded against his ribcage. They would never cross the river in time.

Looking closer, he spotted a smaller force of white-uniformed soldiers streaking toward his army on horseback—the full Whitish cavalry, several hundred horses strong. They would close the distance in less than an hour.

Plagues.

His army couldn't cross the river if they were fighting. And against a heavily-armed cavalry, what could they do?

If they had enough warning, his Flamespinners could hold them at bay. But Daymin knew they couldn't sustain a wall of fire for long, not without something for it to catch on.

He had to warn his army.

They were too far to hear him, so he turned to climb back down the bluff.

Just then, an arrow whizzed past his head.

Daymin flinched.

Another arrow whirred by, this time catching on a lock of his hair.

Daymin scrambled backward in surprise. His foot slipped on a loose piece of rock, and he skidded, scrabbling for purchase. His heartbeat thudded frantically as the rocks came away beneath his hands and he began sliding down the side of the bluff leading toward the river.

Then he slammed to a halt, foot wedged against a rock, just before the bluff dropped away to the water.

Daymin's heartbeat thundered in his ears as he looked at the drop before him. Small rocks were raining down from the slope to splash in the river far below, and the current tore past the face of the cliff.

He looked up, nerves taut.

There. Five soldiers watched him from the opposite bank, only the tops of their heads and their bows rising above the rock they had stationed themselves behind. All five arrows were trained on him.

With a swish of feathers, the first arrow flew.

Daymin flung himself sideways, heart leaping into his throat, and nearly lost his footing. He watched dizzily as a few more rocks crumbled away to splash into the river below.

Then, with a chorus of twanging, the remaining four archers loosed their arrows.

Daymin didn't think. He just flung himself forward, off the cliff, toward the water below.

49

The Whitish Cavalry

For a second, Daymin knew only the sheer panic of falling without any way of stopping himself.

Then his feet slammed into the water.

He plunged underwater, everything vanishing in a swirl of bubbles. The cold forced the air from his lungs, and the current dragged him mercilessly downstream. When he fought his way back to the surface, he could see the bluff already a dozen paces behind him.

He didn't know how to swim, but there was something instinctual about kicking and flailing his arms to stay on the surface. The current alternately buoyed him up and dragged him under, too powerful to fight, so he focused on sucking in gasping breaths whenever his head was above the water. Riffles splashed at him, small wavelets spraying his face with water and blinding him, and the cold burrowed its way deeper and deeper into his bones until he hardly had the energy to stay afloat.

Eventually he became aware of distant voices calling his name.

A wave pushed him under, but he kicked back to the surface, fighting back the fog of exhaustion.

"Daymin! Grab the rope!"

Blinking water from his eyes, he saw the first of the ropes charging toward him at an alarming pace. It was too high for him to reach—he lunged at the rope but missed, and the current swept him on.

Then someone seized him around the waist.

He was dragged to an abrupt stop, the water now pounding against his shoulders as it tried to force him onward.

Again he tried to grab for the rope, but it slipped from his numb hands. Instead his savior began hauling him toward the shore.

Soon his feet collided with the ground. They were on the western bank, where most of his army still waited to cross, and Daymin spotted his friends pushing their way through the ranks of soldiers to his side.

Daymin crawled up the bank, legs too numb to support his weight, and began coughing violently. Water spilled from his lungs, and he gasped for air, shoulders heaving.

Then Tarak was wrapping a blanket around his shoulders, and Daymin hugged it to his chest gratefully, numbness slowly giving way to violent shivering. His savior was a burly man he didn't recognize; he held out a hand and pulled Daymin roughly to his feet, saying, "What the plagues were you doing upriver, Your Majesty?"

"Looking for th-th-the Whitish," Daymin stammered. His thoughts were sluggish—wasn't there something important he was supposed to tell his army?

Looking over his shoulder, he spotted the bluff once more, and everything clicked back into place.

"The Whitish are almost h-here!" he said. "Their cavalry is l-less than an hour away, and th-the rest of the army is almost to N-New Savair."

General Tria had raced over to his side, and she now shouted his news to the waiting army.

"Move faster!" she yelled. "Three to a rope, if you think they'll hold!"

"What happened to you?" Tarak asked Daymin urgently.

"I c-climbed up that bluff, and a company of Whitish archers sh-shot at me." Daymin pointed at the bluff.

Someone else was shoved their way from the crowd—a Weaver. In his confused state, Daymin thought for a moment that it was Idorii, and his lungs tightened with hope.

But it was an unfamiliar man, much older than Idorii, and as he approached, he held out a thick blanket.

"It's enchanted like the heating tapestries," he said. "It will warm you as well as a hot bath."

Daymin shed the blanket Tarak had given him and let the Weaver wrap the enchanted blanket around his shoulders. He was still shivering uncontrollably, but as the warmth settled over him, the tightness in his muscles eased.

Daymin let out his breath. Little by little, his shivering subsided, and his extremities tingled as the feeling returned.

"Did you really jump off that bluff?" Zahira asked skeptically.

"I saw something falling into the water," Lalaysha said. "I thought it was a rock."

"It was the only way to escape the archers," Daymin said. "I wasn't wearing armor or anything."

"You're an idiot, you know that?" Zahira said.

Tarak shot her a warning look.

"It's true! Only a fool would have wandered off alone without armor."

"I know," Daymin said. "And I can't believe I've ended up back on this side of the river. I'd almost rather let the Whitish take me captive than jump back in that water."

Zahira grimaced. "Is it that cold?"

"Imagine rolling around naked in snow, only a hundred times worse."

"Remind me why we didn't follow Prince Calden's forces?" she asked Tarak.

"At least you only have to swim it once," Daymin said. "But in the meantime, we have an army to fight off."

Still clutching the enchanted blanket over his shoulders, warmth radiating through his wet clothes, Daymin scrambled up the riverbank to the flat land beyond.

"The Whitish cavalry is nearly upon us!" he shouted. "Archers and Flamespinners, encircle our army and do what you can to slow their initial charge. If they break through our defenses, they'll trample us without needing to raise swords. The rest of you, get across the river as fast as you can!"

His army scrambled to rearrange themselves, some pushing forward to the riverbank while others formed ranks around the remaining troops. Dozens of Flamespinners spread out to form a narrow band around his army, archers arrayed just behind. None had many arrows in their quivers; they must have run through their stock in recent battles.

Many of his troops pushed their way down the slope to the water's edge, clustering around the ropes, while Daymin and his friends took up positions right before the land dropped away. Unlike Daymin, they wore Weavers' armor; he knew he would have to stay away from the front line so he didn't risk himself unnecessarily.

For a while, his army held their restless formation, troops flowing across the river little by little.

Then a distant thunder echoed from the north.

The Whitish cavalry was near.

Daymin saw the dust before he caught sight of the horses. The reddish-brown plume billowed out behind the cavalry, choking the air.

Soon enough, the column of horses charged into view, their uniformed riders a white streak against the spreading brown. The hoofbeats pounded louder than ever, until the very ground seemed to shake.

Daymin let the enchanted blanket fall from his shoulders. Drawing his sword from its wet sheath, he fell into a fighting stance, pulse thudding in his ears. There was something about the speed of the horses charging toward him that triggered every instinct to flee, even though he knew they would be slowed before they reached him.

Closer the horses thundered, the cloud of dust expanding until everything behind the cavalry ceased to exist.

They were two hundred paces away.

A hundred.

Fifty.

A bolt of flame shot toward the cavalry. Though the Flamespinner was out of range of the Whitish, several of the horses swerved, panicking, and broke the momentum of the charge.

Closer still, a series of flames flared up between the Whitish cavalry and Daymin's army. In their wake, something streaked through the air.

Boom.

Explosions peppered the ground, sending rocks flying and spooking the horses. And now the arrows were flying, some hitting their mark and felling horses that vanished in the stampede.

When another gout of fire erupted in the air just before the cavalry, the front ranks veered off, the horses galloping in a messy, uncontrolled panic.

But the riders behind them had avoided the mess. Even as another wave of arrows and explosives flew, the Whitish cavalry plunged into Daymin's army.

Screams and whinnying rose over the thunder of hooves. The orderly ranks of Daymin's army disintegrated as soldiers fled the stampeding cavalry, many pushing their way toward the river so violently that the nearest soldiers were forced into the water.

Daymin shoved against the crowd, trying to hold his position on the flat ground. Beside him, Lalaysha was pushed downhill by the weight of his army, pinned between two taller men.

The cavalry withdrew and regrouped for another charge, Daymin's army scrambling to re-form ranks in their absence.

When they charged again, a new burst of flames leapt into the air before them, accompanied by a single explosion that made the horses whinny in surprise.

Then, just as the riders reached Daymin's army, a pair of nets unfurled in the air above the first two. These expanded rapidly until they had engulfed the two riders and their horses, the edges of the nets dragging down until they tore the riders from their saddles and forced the horses to their knees.

Excitement shot through Daymin. He had heard of these enchanted nets from the first war; they had helped turn the tide in his mother's battle at Twenty-League Town. His own army had yet to use them, because they had served no purpose in battles between harvesting machines and ancestor trees. Here, though, they had slowed the cavalry's charge and given his soldiers a chance to strike at the enemy before the horses trampled their way through his ranks.

As the horses veered around the ones trapped in nets, Daymin's soldiers dashed forward, swinging at the Whitish while they were distracted with the reins.

More nets flew, catching another set of horses, and soon the battlefield was a mess of riders and foot soldiers.

One of the riders broke loose of the mayhem and charged toward the riverbank, aiming directly for Daymin.

A soldier swung at the horse and cut into its flank; the beast reared, whinnying in pain.

Another soldier slashed at its legs, and the horse fell, sending its rider sprawling.

Before the man could rise, he was set on by dozens of Itrean soldiers, and his scream cut off abruptly.

Soon the cavalry were gone. Daymin's army had been thrown into chaos, soldiers scattered and injured by the stampeding horses, and many had died as well. More than he wanted to admit.

His army seemed to be in shock. They moved slowly, many hurrying to the sides of those who lay injured, and the stream of soldiers crossing the river had slowed.

Daymin searched for Lalaysha, who had been dragged away from him in the madness, and found her trying to push her way out of a knot of bodies near the ropes.

"Go across!" he shouted at her. "We'll meet you on the other side!"

"Are you okay?" Tarak asked.

For a moment, Daymin stared at him blankly. Then he remembered he had been near-hypothermic not long ago. The enchanted blanket and the excitement of battle had shaken away the last of the chill.

"I'm fine," he said briskly. "But my army won't be if we don't hurry up!"

Raising his voice, Daymin yelled, "The rest of the Whitish army is catching up to us! Get across the river *now*! That cavalry attack was nothing compared to what's coming!"

At his words, several companies of soldiers pushed their way toward the riverbank, again shoving those closest to the river into the water up to their ankles. But this time he didn't mind a bit of panic, if it got his army moving faster. He had seen the vast Whitish force from the bluff, and if they charged what remained of his army on this side of the river, his troops would be flattened. No amount of fire or nets or explosives—the supply of which was almost exhausted in any case—could stop such a tide.

Little by little, his soldiers continued across the river. There were still tens of thousands of soldiers on this bank, and each wave that crossed made hardly a dent in those that remained.

Daymin grew more anxious the longer he waited. He sent the enchanted blanket across with their supplies and then stood with his sword unsheathed, going through the strikes and blocks he could do without injuring anyone nearby. He felt jumpy and on edge; he couldn't see how his army would reach safety before the Whitish caught up to him, which meant he had miscalculated.

And with so much of his army across the river, it was too late for him to abandon his plan. He was committed.

At last, white uniforms shimmering like a mirage in the distance, the first of the Whitish soldiers marched into view.

Daymin's heartbeat sped up. He felt like a deer with hunters at his tail, and he had to fight the instinct to turn and run.

"Faster!" Daymin shouted at his soldiers. "Five to a rope! Go!"

His soldiers had already been piling more onto each rope than was safe, and now even more splashed into the water. Soon the first of the ropes sagged into the water beneath the weight of at least twenty bodies.

The rope was dragging downstream, the soldiers kicking those clinging to the next rope down, and Daymin drew in a sharp breath as a woman lost her grip and slipped underwater.

Someone on a rope farther down lunged for her, but too late—she was swept downstream.

Daymin cursed under his breath and took a step in the direction of the river before he caught himself.

There was nothing he could do to help.

The first rope was sagging more than ever, and Daymin knew a second before it happened that it was going to come free.

With a snap, the bush on the opposite bank broke in two,

sending that end of the rope flying down to the water.

Caught in the current, the rope stretched out down the river, its line of soldiers knocking against all the soldiers on ropes downstream as it went. Several lost their grip and were swept away like the first, while the soldiers still clinging to the rope were sinking without the tension to hold it above the water.

Some managed to grab the other ropes, while a few dropped the loose rope and began stroking powerfully toward the opposite bank. A man at the very end of the loose rope clung to it with a look of desperation, the water pushing him under and then thrusting him back to the surface. He didn't seem capable of fighting the current, and the time he spent submerged grew longer and longer.

At last he was towed under and did not reappear. A minute later, the frayed end of the rope bobbed to the surface, no longer weighed down by his body.

Daymin's hands were clammy, and he realized he had been staring at the scene in the river, frozen in place, for the last several minutes. This was the sort of situation where Uncle Cal or Dellik would have jumped in and started shouting orders while Daymin stalled, and when he looked back up the river, he discovered with a jolt that the Whitish army had gained considerable ground while he was distracted.

Plagues. He had to pull himself together.

But how was he supposed to fix this disaster?

"Pull the rope back to the other side," Daymin shouted. "We need to fasten it again. And don't overload the ropes!"

"We're not going to make it," Tarak muttered in his ear.

"I know. What are we supposed to do?"

"We'll have to swim, won't we?"

Panic spiked through Daymin. He had barely made it across last time, and he didn't know what lay downstream. There could be rocks, or rapids, and if his soldiers hit the gorge before they managed to climb out on the opposite bank, there would be no saving them.

But Tarak was right. The Whitish were almost upon them.

"Anyone who can swim, hold back!" Daymin yelled. "Everyone else, get across the river as fast as you can!"

Chaos overtook the riverbank as a portion of his soldiers pushed their way up from the water. Daymin was surprised by how many had willingly turned back to leave space for those who couldn't swim.

Daymin's standing army gravitated toward the outside, where they formed a solid wall against the oncoming Whitish. All wore Weavers' armor, and many had helmets as well, which might allow them to hold out long enough for the rest of his army to escape.

Daymin took up a position behind them, since he still wasn't wearing armor.

A couple hundred paces from Daymin's army, the Whitish broke into a run. They were like a river bursting its banks and flooding the plains, their column stretching so far back Daymin couldn't see the end.

Tarak and Zahira stepped up beside him, and with a spike of fear, Daymin asked, "Can you swim?"

"No," Zahira said, "but you didn't look like you could either. We're staying with you."

Daymin swallowed, touched by their loyalty. "You're bloody fools."

"And so are you."

Adrenaline racing through him, Daymin braced himself for impact. Even behind the front line, he knew he would feel the weight of the Whitish army crashing into his troops.

As they thundered across the barren earth toward him, the Whitish took up a wordless war cry, the sound making the hair on the back of Daymin's neck stand on end.

His army answered in kind, and Daymin found himself shouting along with them, the rising roar turning fear into adrenaline.

Then, with a great *crash,* the Whitish slammed into Daymin's army.

He was shoved back a step as the weight of the Whitish bore down on his front line.

A moment later, his ranks broke under the pressure, and Daymin found himself facing a Whitish soldier in chainmail.

As he struck out at the soldier, adrenaline roared through him, blurring everything beyond the man he faced.

The soldier blocked him effortlessly, and Daymin soon found himself on the defensive, backing up as the soldier struck out again and again.

Then, as he edged back another step, his foot was met with empty air. He lost his footing and fell to his knees—he had stepped over the lip of the riverbank, where the ground sloped away abruptly.

As he scrambled to right himself, the soldier struck out swiftly, slicing Daymin's neck.

He hissed in pain and brought a hand to the cut.

While he was distracted, the soldier lashed out again.

Daymin parried clumsily, but the soldier twisted his blade aside and lunged for his heart.

Just then, someone charged in from the side, yelling, and knocked the soldier off-balance. Zahira.

"Thank you," Daymin gasped.

"Get back!" Zahira yelled, shoving Daymin down the slope. "This is too dangerous for you without armor!"

Daymin staggered back a few steps, out of reach of the fighting, and saw that his soldiers were overwhelmed. They hadn't managed to hold formation, and in the confusion, they were being cut down one by one.

"This is too dangerous for all of us," he said. "Grab Tarak and get across that river. *Now*."

Not waiting to see if Zahira had followed his orders, Daymin pushed his way back up to the flat ground, stepping onto a rock so he could see over the chaos.

"Retreat!" he yelled. "Cut the ropes and swim! We can't hold any longer!"

Then he sprinted down the riverbank and started hacking at the first of the ropes with his sword.

Beside him, other soldiers helped cut the remaining ropes, and those who still clung to the opposite ends were swept a short way downstream before the ropes pulled taut. Then they dragged themselves up the ropes, wavelets crashing over their heads.

Not waiting to see if his army was following, Daymin waded into the river once more. This time the cold hardly registered beneath his frantic adrenaline, and he plunged into the depths of the current without hesitation.

Immediately the current yanked at him, tugging him downstream. He kicked as hard as he could, trying to swim like he'd seen the others do. Sometimes the force of the river pushed him under, and he flailed out for the surface, gasping in air as soon as he emerged. The opposite bank was still so far away; he could see nothing but water and a distant smudge of earth.

As the cold sank in, he grew clumsy, his head slipping under more often than not. He breathed in water and coughed, which only made him swallow more water. Soon he felt lightheaded, the icy water dragging at him and making him sluggish.

No. You have to fight this.

Daymin kicked his way back to the surface and sucked in another breath. This time he glimpsed the opposite bank, and it was much closer—the river was turning a bend, and as it did, the current thrust him in the right direction.

He was going to pass very close to a few willows growing into the water.

This was his only chance.

Daymin kicked fiercely in the direction of the trees, and as the current pushed him toward the bank, he managed to grab one of the roots that hung into the water.

He realized his mistake quickly—the current was stronger than ever here, and as his body was shoved downstream, his numb fingers slipped on the root.

Don't let go.

With a tremendous effort, he hauled himself up so his body draped over the root, out of the wicked current.

Then, moving clumsily, he crawled his way over the network of roots onto the soggy riverbank.

Numb and shaking, Daymin pulled himself to his feet.

Then he turned to look upstream.

He had floated several hundred paces from the crossing, and he could see the mass of bodies on the opposite bank where his soldiers were quickly losing ground. Many had already flung themselves into the water, while others were splashing their way into the current, and Daymin spotted a few who had managed to swim to shore upstream of him.

The Whitish were pushing his army back faster than ever, and his soldiers began throwing themselves into the water in huge waves, the river churning with bodies.

As his army was swept downstream, some broke from the group, stroking toward the opposite bank, while others flailed in the current. Before long, soldiers were floating past Daymin, a few managing to grab the roots near where he had clawed his way to shore.

He stumbled back, leaving room for them to climb up the mess of roots.

More and more were swept past him, and Daymin saw soldier after soldier slipping underwater and failing to resurface. They, like him, would be growing sluggish as the icy water numbed them.

Daymin could hardly draw breath—so few were making it across. His army was drowning, one after another, and once again it was his own foolishness that had led them to their deaths.

Where were Tarak and Zahira?

Panic seized him, and his heartbeat thudded in his ears. He shouldn't have let them stay behind with him.

As he searched the river again, frantic now, a wave of dizziness swept through him. He was shaking from the cold, his legs still half-numb. He had to get back to his army and warm up.

Wretched with cold and guilt, Daymin staggered up from

the bank and started off toward his army. More soldiers were making it safely across, and he joined a stream of sodden men and women stumbling their way upriver.

By the time he reached the main body of his army, the last of his soldiers had thrown themselves into the river. None remained on the opposite bank except the Whitish and the bodies of those who had fallen.

This last wave of soldiers was swimming more powerfully than those before, and Daymin realized it was his standing army—they had stayed until the end, guarding his reserve soldiers until all had entered the water. Most of them managed to cross the river well upstream of where Daymin had dragged himself out, and soon they were stumping up the bank, water dripping from their uniforms.

Lalaysha pushed her way through the crowd and threw her arms around Daymin's neck. "You're safe!" she said in Allakoash. "Where are Tarak and Zahira?"

"I don't know."

Even after she released him, she clung to his arm, searching the crowd anxiously for their friends. Daymin was glad for her presence—he was still shaking from the cold, and he thought Lalaysha's grip was the only thing keeping him from collapsing.

Eventually a soldier brought him the enchanted blanket he had used before, and Daymin draped it around both his and Lalaysha's shoulders, hugging her to his side. He felt as he had after the battle of New Savair, his stomach twisting painfully as he waited for his friends to appear.

"Were they with you?" Lalaysha asked softly.

"When we were fighting. I lost track of them after that."

She pressed her lips together, still clutching at Daymin.

Then, at last, Daymin caught sight of a familiar cloud of black hair in the distance. Zahira and Tarak were stumbling up the river in the direction of his army—they had been swept even farther downstream than Daymin, yet they had somehow managed to drag themselves to safety.

A Camp Across the River

When they drew near, Tarak and Zahira broke into a run, finally throwing their arms around Daymin and Lalaysha. Lalaysha peppered Tarak's face with kisses, while tears spilled from Zahira's eyes.

"You're safe," Daymin said. "You're all safe. Thank the cloudy gods. I never thought I'd see you again."

He drew them all under the blanket, and Zahira put her icy hands against his cheeks, startling a laugh from him.

"There were others still swimming downstream of us when we got out," Tarak said. "They'll catch up to us eventually."

"Plagues," Daymin said. "I can't believe they survived. I could barely move my legs by the time I crawled out."

"You had already been chilled through," Zahira reminded him. "Twice." She wiped tears from her cheeks, smiling.

All four stood there for a long moment, letting the warmth of the blanket seep through them. Daymin was dizzy with relief.

His army had taken heavy casualties, but the vast majority of his troops had made it across. And most importantly, his friends were safe.

When the bulk of the swimmers had stumbled up the bank to join his army, Daymin stepped away from his friends, the breeze immediately chilling his wet clothes.

"We'll move away from the river to set up camp," he called out. "General Vask, stay behind with a company of archers and soldiers to stop any Whitish who try to cross. You can rejoin us tonight."

Sunset was still a couple hours away, and Daymin didn't want to waste time, but he would be endangering the lives of his soldiers if he pushed them on in this condition. They needed to set up camp, dry off, and warm up before hypothermia claimed them.

He and his friends started off in the direction of the Wandering Woods, still dripping onto the arid ground. Zahira clutched the blanket around her shoulders for a while before passing it to Lalaysha, who took a turn before handing it to Tarak. Eventually Daymin ended up with the blanket, and he hugged it gratefully around his back. The warmth of the sun wasn't enough to ward off the chill, not when his clothes were still wet.

When he passed the blanket back to Zahira, Daymin noticed many of the men in his army had stripped off their sodden shirts, so he did the same. His hair dripped cold water down his back, but with the sun beating down on his skin, he began to warm up little by little.

They stopped to set up camp around a shallow stream flowing from the direction of the Wandering Woods. Daymin thought he could see the first of the trees on the horizon, but it could also be smoke rising from Ferndell. It was hard to tell from this distance.

While a group of soldiers erected Daymin's tent, Renok approached, looking grim. He had crossed in the earliest wave of soldiers, so his clothes had long since dried.

"Can you hear that?" he asked in Allakoash.

Daymin paused, listening for something beyond the murmur of voices and scuffing of feet as his soldiers set up camp.

Then, from far away, he thought he heard the creaking of trees.

"Is that—"

"The ancestor trees," Renok said in a hushed voice. "The Whitish must be attacking already."

"I can't push my army any faster," Daymin said. "I'm sorry. We'll lose half our soldiers if we continue on in this state."

"I know," Renok said. "But I worry we'll be too late to help them."

"How much farther do we have to go?"

"Another two days at least. The forest border has pushed west since the war began, so it's not as far as it once was, but the Whitish might not have attacked this far south."

Daymin kneaded his forehead. He had taken so many risks, and still it wasn't enough. "We're doing as much as we can."

"And we're very grateful for that. When I tracked you down, I never expected you to send your full army to help. But—" Renok dropped his eyes to the ground. "I'm afraid. I've never been so afraid. I think the Whitish are strong enough to destroy us."

Daymin squeezed his shoulder. "I'm afraid too."

Renok met his eyes for a long moment, and Daymin could see a desperate hope warring with his fear.

Then he turned and walked away, his shoulders slumped with defeat.

"I can't believe you're doing this for us," Lalaysha said quietly from behind Daymin. She spoke in Allakoash, and her eyes shone with emotion. "I'm sorry I ever doubted you."

"It's fine," Daymin said. "I doubted myself. I still do. But I'm not going to abandon your people at their moment of greatest need."

At last the camp was set, and the cooks were starting on dinner, lighting fire-twists to heat warming stews and gruel.

Surveying their camp, Daymin realized they must have lost a good half of their supplies on the opposite side of the river, since there were far fewer tents than he was accustomed to.

"Do you want to stay with me tonight?" Daymin asked Tarak, Zahira, and Lalaysha. "I think we're short on tents."

"Definitely," Zahira said. "Especially if it means sharing that wonderful blanket."

Soon they were eating dinner, sitting cross-legged between the thorny bushes. Daymin was growing cold again now that he had stopped moving, though thankfully he had been able to dig a dry shirt and trousers from his pack. His friends were not so lucky—their belongings had been lost in the confusion, so they were still wearing the damp clothes they had swum across the river in. When he had offered his sole dry pair of clothes to them, all had refused.

He wrapped his hands around his bowl, savoring the warmth that radiated from the stew. He still felt overwhelmed from everything that had happened that day. His nerves were frayed, his body aching and wrung-out. Where the battle of New Savair had left him mentally wrecked, this one had destroyed him physically.

And what would they find waiting for them at the Wandering Woods? An army bigger than the one they had just faced? Hundreds of harvesting machines slashing their way deep into the forest?

It was discouraging to know that he had pitched his full army against a fraction of the Whitish force and nearly lost, while the Whitish were fighting successfully on two fronts even with most of their soldiers still in Twenty-League Town.

Around camp, soldiers were huddling around the fire-twists, desperate for any scrap of heat they could take from the small fires. The enchanted fire-twists burned hot and smokeless, but their warmth was nothing compared to a proper campfire.

Before Daymin finished eating, he heard the scuffing of footsteps from the direction of the river. General Vask was returning with his troops.

Daymin set aside his bowl and jogged over to greet the general.

"Are the Whitish trying to cross?" he asked.

"No," General Vask said. "They stripped the bodies of fallen soldiers and collected everything we had left behind, and then they turned back upriver. I don't think they intend to chase us any further."

"Thank the cloudy gods," Daymin said, relief flooding through him. His gamble hadn't been a complete disaster after all.

"Several hundred soldiers trekked up to join us while we

waited," General Vask continued, "and they say more survivors are on their way. I left a couple men to camp by the river and direct them on to us."

"Thank you," Daymin said. "Get yourselves some dinner. You've earned it."

He wove his way through the maze of spiny bushes to rejoin his friends and finish his own stew, feeling more drained than ever.

When they finished, they stumbled off to Daymin's tent, which already smelled faintly mildewed from the clothes and Weavers' armor they had hung to dry.

Zahira dangled a Weaver's crystal from the top of the tent, and they sorted through their belongings, checking what they still had. Only Daymin's pack had made it across, with its spare set of clothes and Weaver's armor; his other supplies had been carried by his soldiers, and they had survived as well. In addition to his tent, he had a sleeping roll, a blanket, an extensive set of eating utensils, and his map of Itrea.

The others had only what they had worn—clothes, Weavers' armor, boots, and sword belts. Daymin pulled his sword from his sheath and laid it on the ground to dry, and then he checked the pocket of his trousers for his pen. It was still there, and—he drew on his palm to check—still functional.

"I hope you don't mind cuddling," Zahira said with a teasing smile. "Because there isn't enough bedding to go around."

"I know," Daymin said gruffly. He could feel his face heating up. Lying beside the two women he had slept with was an uncomfortable prospect, though Zahira at least seemed to know his feelings lay elsewhere.

Then Zahira and Lalaysha began stripping down to their underthings, discarding their wet clothes, and the situation grew more uncomfortable still. Tarak turned his back to the wall to give the women privacy as he pulled off his shirt, while Daymin left his own clothes on, suddenly very glad no one had taken up his offer to use his dry garments.

With nothing better to do, Daymin stretched out his sleeping roll and blanket to form a bed of sorts, which they would cover with the enchanted blanket. They ended up with the women in the middle and the men on the outside, Tarak cuddling up to Lalaysha while Daymin tried to keep as much distance as possible from Zahira.

Soon they were tucked comfortably under the warming blanket, and it was so deliciously warm that Daymin forgot his earlier embarrassment. His limbs felt like they were melting, the tension and soreness and exhaustion draining away to leave his muscles as limp as dough. Zahira had extinguished the light, and he thought he might fall asleep, or at least into a mindless stupor…

Then Zahira shattered his peace. "What was that tattoo on your arm?"

Daymin's heart skipped a beat. "What?"

"When you had your shirt off, I saw a circle on your arm, with a strange silver-and-black pattern…"

Varse damn it. He had been too overwhelmed by the battle to think about hiding it.

"Do you really have a tattoo?" Tarak asked with interest. "I wouldn't have expected that of you. It's not some Allakoash thing, is it?"

"No," Lalaysha said.

"Well?" Zahira poked him in the side.

Daymin sighed. He had never wanted to reveal this to anyone else—it felt far too intimate. Too close to his heart.

But after all they had done for him...maybe his friends deserved the truth.

"It's...an enchantment. It's how I've been communicating with Idorii."

"What do you mean?" Zahira asked.

Daymin pressed the heels of his palms into his eyes, hating this. "I write on my arm and press the tattoo, and—the message goes through to his arm."

Zahira made a surprised noise. "Cloudy gods, Daymin. That's the most romantic thing I've ever heard of!"

"Are you and Idorii...together?" Tarak ventured cautiously.

"No. Not really." Daymin buried his head under the blankets, his voice coming out muffled. He wished he could throw himself in the river again. Anything to make this conversation end.

"Did you set that up so he could pass intelligence to you from Darkland Fort?" Zahira asked.

"Yes." Daymin's voice was still muffled.

"Ooh," Zahira said. "Did you love him, even back then?"

"What? No, I didn't even know him!"

Zahira poked him in the side again, making him grunt. "Most kings wouldn't let some random person emb a spell in their arm for the sake of receiving intelligence."

"I didn't trust anyone else with it."

Thinking back, Daymin remembered the intensity of the day he and Idorii had bound themselves together. He knew now that Idorii had admired him from afar long before they became friends; had Daymin sensed that from him, without knowing what it was? Had he agreed to Idorii's suggestion because he had felt the same pull?

He didn't know.

Pulling the blankets off his face, Daymin said, "None of you are to breathe a word of this to anyone else, do you understand? I'm not allowed to marry a man, and I won't ruin Idorii's reputation by taking him as a lover."

"This is what you did to me," Lalaysha said in a quiet voice. "You pushed me away to keep me safe, without asking first whether I wanted it."

Daymin's head whipped sideways, though he couldn't see her face in the dark. "I thought you were happier with Tarak!"

"I am. But you didn't allow me to make the choice for myself."

"What are you planning to do the next time you see him?" Zahira asked. "Pretend you don't care for him? Leave him behind again while you ride to war?"

"It was his choice to stay," Daymin snapped.

"Yes, but I'm sure you had some hand in it, didn't you?"

Daymin bit back his frustrated response, because Zahira was right. Of course she was.

"As king, can't you change that rule?" Tarak asked. "It's outdated anyway."

"Yes, but I still need an heir."

"In an imaginary version of Itrea that no longer exists," Zahira said with exasperation. "You're king of a bunch of refugees and an army that seems determined to dash itself to pieces every chance it gets. Meanwhile, Holden King Falsted and Holden Queen Ellarie sit the real thrones, albeit in a city that will be lost by the end of the span."

"True. But if our people continue to exist in any form, they'll need a leader to follow after me."

"Does the inheritance have to follow your bloodline?" Tarak asked. "The royal families seem a bit absurd now that two of them are about to kill off their entire lines for the sake of a doomed city. Unless you were planning to do the same as your mother, and pass the throne to your direct descendant…"

Daymin rubbed at his eyes. This was too much for tonight, after everything he had gone through today. "Can we think about this some other time? I don't even know if we'll make it to the Icebraid Peaks alive."

"Thank you," Zahira said. "That was my point exactly. You don't know how long any of us will survive, so if you see Idorii again, you should enjoy your time with him while it lasts. It's ridiculous to waste time thinking about rules and heirs when we no longer have a kingdom." She paused. "Anyway, I could carry your heir if it came to that. If you were drunk enough, I'm sure you wouldn't mind."

Lalaysha giggled, while Daymin's face grew hot. *Bloody Varse.* Of course the girls would have swapped stories of the times Daymin had lain with them.

"I feel like I'm missing something," Tarak said warily.

This whole conversation had taken on the feel of a dream. Maybe it was the darkness and the fact that all four of them were lying side by side in their underthings, but Daymin felt like he couldn't hide this any longer.

He groaned. "Since you seem determined to drag out my most embarrassing secrets…I slept with Zahira once. I was very drunk, and she was very persistent."

Zahira snorted. "And also drunk."

"I'm sorry," Daymin said.

After a stunned silence, Tarak laughed. "That explains a lot. I always thought you acted strangely around each other." He paused. "Am I the only one here you haven't lain with, then, Daymin?"

"Bloody Varse. We are *not* discussing this," Daymin groaned.

"Does that mean it's my turn next?"

Daymin heard a thump, followed by a surprised yelp from Tarak. Lalaysha must have hit him.

"You're not interested in men anyway, idiot," Zahira said.

"I didn't think I was either," Daymin admitted.

The bedding rustled beside him, and the blanket was dragged abruptly off his shoulders as Zahira sat up.

"Daymin. Can I write a message to Idorii?"

She lit her Weaver's crystal, and as Daymin squinted past the sudden brilliance, he saw that her eyes were sparkling in a way that meant mischief.

"Why?"

"Because I want to see how it works! Also, it would be fun to surprise Idorii."

Daymin sighed. "Fine. But I need to warn him first."

He sat up and shuffled away from the others so they couldn't see what he was writing. Then he pushed up his sleeve.

Idorii –

After a very long day that involved multiple drenchings in an icy river—I'll explain later—I took off my shirt and accidentally revealed the linked tattoo to my friends. They forced an explanation out of me, so now they know how we are able to communicate. Zahira thinks it's very romantic…and she is determined to write a message to you on my arm.

Consider yourself forewarned.

Yours,
Daymin

A moment later, Idorii wrote back, *Ooh, I can't wait!*

Daymin showed Idorii's reply to Zahira, whose eyes widened in excitement.

"That's incredible. How do you know when he's written to you?"

"The tattoo feels cold for a moment, and then I have to press it to make the words appear."

"So you press it to send the message?"

"Yes."

As Daymin wiped the words from his arm, Zahira reached for the pen. Then Daymin held out his wrist reluctantly. After everything that had happened this evening, he was no longer embarrassed by the sight of Zahira in her underclothes, even when she propped his arm on her bare legs to write. She wrote from his elbow toward his wrist, opposite from what Daymin usually did, and he read her words upside down as she wrote.

Greetings, Idorii! This is Zahira. I'm sure you can tell this isn't Daymin's handwriting. I want you to know we are looking after him out here, even if he insists on getting himself into trouble. He is desperate to see you again.

Then, before Daymin could say anything—he had intended to ask her to wipe off the last sentence—she pressed the tattoo harder than necessary. She, Tarak, and Lalaysha watched with interest as the words sank into his skin.

"Do you know if he's read it?" Zahira asked.

"No," Daymin said.

"What if he took ages to reply?"

"Then I'd worry something had happened to him."

Soon enough, Daymin's tattoo flashed cold. He held out his arm to Zahira, who pressed the symbol again.

Idorii's words emerged and solidified, and after everything his friends had said this evening, the familiar handwriting made his breath catch in his throat.

Zahira –

What an honor. I have not shared the secret of our communication with anyone else, and I am flattered to know Daymin has told his closest friends.

Do take care of him, and I hope to see all of you before too much longer.

Idorii

"What fun!" Zahira said. "And his handwriting is much nicer than yours, Daymin."

Making a face, Daymin wiped the ink from his arm. "Now I'm done making a fool of myself. Let's go to sleep."

Zahira extinguished the Weaver's crystal, and Daymin curled up under the enchanted blanket, glad for the warmth that cocooned him. He thought it would take a few more days to shake the chill that had lodged itself in his bones.

When Zahira molded her body behind his, knees tucked against his legs, Daymin found he welcomed her closeness. After everything he had been through today, it was wonderful to have his friends here by his side.

51

The Foothills

The closer the mountains drew, the less Jakovi could believe such a thing existed. They were taller than should be possible, their tops living in the world of clouds and stars, and the blinding whiteness of the snowy peaks seemed to erase everything else.

Jakovi stared at the mountains until his eyes hurt, until the shape of the sun reflecting off the snow remained burned into his vision long after he looked away.

Eventually the dark green on the slopes of the mountains took on the forms of trees, while the snowy peaks were gradually hidden behind the first row of green foothills. Then, with an abruptness that surprised him, they reached the end of the plains.

The trees were sweet-smelling and grew strange needles instead of leaves, and Jakovi felt compelled to step beneath their wide branches.

"Wait," Letto said when Jakovi started forward.

Jakovi froze.

"Look," Letto said in a whisper.

This time Jakovi spotted what he had missed in his fascination with the forest—there were strange people standing beneath the trees, their skin deathly pale, their white hair streaked faintly with blue.

He felt a creeping unease at the sight. There was something unnatural about them, something that pricked at his awareness in a discomfiting way.

The Icelings stared at the Itreans for several long minutes, their eyes flicking between the faces of the front guard and taking in the long, narrow column of evacuees that stretched far past the horizon toward Baylore.

Then they withdrew. Whether they were still watching from further back or had retreated in the face of such an overwhelming force of Itreans, Jakovi could not tell.

"What happens now?" Jakovi asked.

"We need to find a way into the mountains," Letto said.

Rocks jutted from the faces of the steep, tree-covered foothills, which cut off access to the higher mountains beyond. The notches between peaks seemed likely ways through, but Jakovi had no way of judging where the terrain was too steep for them to attempt.

"Most of the front guard will scout the route," Letto continued. "Do you want to stay behind or join them? I'll go wherever you do."

"I want to go into the mountains," Jakovi said immediately. There was something about the wild places beyond the plains that called to him; maybe the rugged unknowability of it all would help subdue his magic.

"We'll set off in the morning, then," Letto said. "We need to make sure the Icelings aren't planning to attack the refugees first."

* * *

Morning arrived with no further glimpse of the Icelings. Jakovi was filled with a hungry excitement not dissimilar to the way his magic felt running through his veins, and for a moment he worried he would find himself assaulted by power the moment he stepped beneath the trees.

But when he followed Letto and five other soldiers into the woods, he found only a gentle hush. The fallen needles dampened the sound of their footsteps, and the sweet, fresh smell of pine hung in the air.

As the hill steepened, Jakovi ran ahead, grinning breathlessly. He felt freer than he ever had, and it wasn't just the emptiness of the mountains. He had sensed it yesterday, and now he could feel it—his magic seemed less overwhelming here. It was something that nagged at the back of his mind, not something that fought every moment to surge to the surface.

"Wait!" Letto called, and Jakovi turned to grin at him. Letto was red in the face as he charged up the hill, sweat glistening on his forehead.

When he reached the first of the rock formations, Jakovi slowed to catch his breath, giving Letto a chance to catch up. The rocks were great reddish slabs jutting from the mountainsides and rising many paces toward the peaks of the foothills, like the armor of some great beast.

"You're enjoying yourself," Letto said when he staggered to a halt beside Jakovi. "But we need to watch out for the Icelings. They could ambush us anywhere in these woods."

"I can take care of myself," Jakovi said.

Letto gave him a hard look. "Weren't we trying our hardest to prevent you from using magic?"

"I know."

"Besides, what good would your power do if they caught you unawares? If they shot you in the heart before you had time to react? Could you heal yourself of a fatal wound?"

That gave Jakovi pause. "I…think so. But not if I died right away."

"Well, let's not put that to the test. Stay close to me or someone else who knows how to defend themselves."

Jakovi wanted to run alone again, to charge up the mountainside like an antelope. He wanted to stand on top of one of those peaks, nothing around him but the birds and the clouds, and feel the wind buffet him until he believed there was nothing more powerful than the wind itself.

He gave Letto a pleading look. "Will you at least run with me a bit farther?"

Letto laughed. "Fine! I'll leave it to the others to give us a lecture tonight."

Grinning, Jakovi broke into a run again, tearing up the hillside past the slab of stone. It rose higher than he'd realized, and by the time he reached the top, he could see for leagues across the plains.

The line of refugees snaked all the way to the horizon, where people and wagons were nothing more than hazy dots. Even after his time in Baylore, Jakovi still had a hard time believing there could be so many people in the world.

Letto stepped up beside him, a grim look on his face.

"What's wrong?" Jakovi asked.

Letto shook his head. "So many innocent people driven from their homes. I was caught up in the routine of things at Darkland Fort, but as soon as I left, I couldn't understand why we were still fighting. King Warrow started this war to wipe out the last vestiges of magic from the earth, but King Edreon is using the same Varos-damned magic to fight, so he's strayed from his father's original path."

"Is it something to do with the harvesting machines Idorii always talked about?" Jakovi asked, still struggling to grasp the enormity of the war he had found himself tangled in.

"Maybe. But why attack Baylore if he just wants wood? It's such an immense war effort—bigger than anything we've seen in centuries. King Edreon must be trying to expand the Whitish empire, but why? I thought we could hardly keep control of what we had."

Jakovi said nothing. This was all far beyond his understanding.

"There must be more to the situation in Whitland," Letto said, speaking more to himself than anything. "But I don't know why we continue to follow King Edreon's orders when they make no sense. Years of conditioning, I suppose. The soldiers who grew up in Whitland were always more disciplined." Letto sighed. "Don't listen to me. I'm still trying to figure out where I fit in, now that I've deserted the Whitish army and feel great sympathy for my former enemies."

"At least the world makes sense to you," Jakovi said. "Everything just seems so big and confusing to me."

"Yes, but you never thought the Whitish cause was worth fighting for, did you?"

"Only because my father told me I was held captive by the evil Whitish. It was the only thing I knew about the world outside, so of course I believed it."

Letto frowned at him. "What do you think of me, then? Am I evil because of what I did at Darkland Fort? Selfish because I chose my own desires over my country? Capable of redeeming myself if I serve King Daymin well enough? Forever untrustworthy because a deserter might always desert again?"

"You're a hero," Jakovi said. "You saved me and Idorii. And I wouldn't have told you so much about my magic if I didn't trust you."

Then, because Letto's questions were making his head spin, Jakovi turned and bounded up the slope again. He didn't want to think about sides and who was right or wrong and who deserved saving. Because if he started believing too much in the Itrean cause, he might start thinking some situations justified the use of his magic, and where did he stop after that? Before he knew it, the whole world would be in ruin.

He could hear Letto's footsteps just behind him, so he kept going, the ground steepening underfoot. Soon bare dirt and rock lay where dead pine needles had once cushioned the forest floor, and Jakovi slowed, using roots to pull himself up.

At last they came to a saddle between two short peaks. Jakovi walked up to the very edge of the saddle, chest heaving from the effort, and stopped.

Ahead, the ridge dropped straight down, too steep to traverse. And beyond that lay the true Icebraid Peaks.

Countless peaks rose in white-capped splendor, some tall

and jagged, others sloping gently. The ground just beyond the foothills was covered with patchy snow, and within a few hundred paces it overtook the grasses. Yet Jakovi thought he could see a few green valleys in the distance, so there might be a place for the Itreans to camp if they could find the way. And if the cold and the Icelings didn't kill them first.

"We can't make it down this way," Letto said. "We'll have to try a different route. And I can't see how the wagons are supposed to make it through that sort of terrain."

"What if we stopped here, in the foothills?" Jakovi asked. "We could hide in the forest until the Whitish forgot about us."

Letto braced his foot on a rock, leaning out to get a better view along the ridge to the north. "They'll hunt us down in no time. As soon as they realize Baylore has emptied out, they'll come for us. We have to find a way in."

52

The Backing of the Priests

The third time the priest requested a meeting, Edreon knew he could not refuse. As much as his hold over Eidervell had tightened since the logs had arrived, the Varonite priests were continuing to push their weight around, threatening to erode his power if he refused to commit to Varos.

So it was that he found himself waiting in the cavernous throne room, alone save a handful of guards, while he waited for the priest to join him. Ordinarily he was the one who would keep his subjects waiting, but as he still could not walk and was attempting to conceal that fact, he had to position himself on his throne long before any visitors arrived.

At least his fever had not returned. With his mental faculties intact, he felt much more capable of dealing with any trouble that might arise.

Edreon tapped his fingers impatiently on his throne. He had received word this morning that King Daymin's forces had evaded his own at the Elygian River, and he was anxious for an update. If all the bridges south of Baylore truly had been toppled, King Daymin's army would have trouble crossing back to the west side, which meant he was unlikely to attack any other significant Whitish-occupied settlements.

In fact, Edreon had a hard time discerning King Daymin's strategy. Unless he hoped to hide within the Wandering Woods?

Or...did his army plan to aid the forest?

The idea was laughable.

In the meantime, Edreon had ordered his own troops back to Baylore to capture the city once and for all. The attack on the Wandering Woods was underway, King Daymin's army was heading in a direction where it could do little damage to Edreon's forces, and the next shipment of trees had already left King's Port.

The pieces were coming together at last. If he could pull this off, Itrea—no, the entire Whitish-speaking world—would be his for the taking.

As long as he didn't lose his grasp on Whitland in the meantime.

Eventually the priest arrived. He was young and severe-featured, his robes not disguising the physique of a warrior. Edreon was glad; he preferred the pragmatic devotees who embraced Varos's militarism over the spiritual ones who feared for Edreon's soul.

"Your Majesty." The priest paused and bowed halfway to Edreon's throne before striding closer. "Thank you for granting me an audience."

"Of course." Edreon refrained from reminding the man that he had pushed for it relentlessly.

"I wished to bring forward a matter of some urgency, in hopes it might encourage you to cease wavering in your faith."

"Oh?" Edreon said with a cold look.

"Your Majesty, Prince Navaire has recently put forward his claim to the throne, and is gathering followers to support him in this."

"I was aware of his treasonous campaign."

"Certainly, Your Majesty. But were you aware he has dedicated himself firmly to Varos? He is attracting to his side those who cannot abide your failure to commit to Varos." The priest paused, and his expression grew hard. "Including the priests of Varos. We have officially agreed to back Prince Navaire's bid for power if you refuse to declare Varos the one true god and continue to allow those heathens who worship the Nine."

And this is the flaw in my plan, Edreon thought bitterly. His people could not see the wheels moving in Itrea, so they thought he stagnated and weakened while in fact he was on the verge of achieving a victory no previous monarch had dreamed of.

Damn the priests and their meddling. He knew his people were not religious zealots like the priests they followed, and most had welcomed his tolerance. Even those who followed Varos. He could not stomach the thought of condemning the Alldrosants for their beliefs yet again, stirring up the same infighting his father had sought to circumvent by launching his campaign in Itrea, yet if he lost his throne in the process, it would do his kingdom no good.

The priest was still watching him expectantly. Prince Navaire was not a significant threat yet, but losing the support of the priests would be dangerous. He could think of no Whitish monarch who had ever held the throne without the backing of his faith.

"I will consider your words carefully," Edreon said. He planned to do nothing of the sort, but if he could achieve a great victory in Itrea before Prince Navaire challenged him, the influence of the priests would matter less. He needed time.

The priest bowed stiffly. "I thank you for your presence today, Your Majesty. When you have your answer, come to the cathedral. I beg you, do not delay in your commitment. A king who is weak in his faith is too weak to hold the high throne."

Edreon nodded curtly and waved to the man to dismiss him. His shoes clicked as he strode from the throne room, robes fluttering behind him.

"Fetch my footman," Edreon ordered his guards. He did not want even his guards to know he was a cripple; only his footman and his inner circle were aware he had yet to regain the use of his leg.

His guards marched from the room, leaving Edreon fuming on his throne. How could those blasted priests overlook everything he had done for Whitland? Did they prefer a weak, divided kingdom over the mighty empire he was forging?

Just then, soft footsteps startled him from his thoughts.

Edreon whirled to see Odelia emerging from behind a curtain not far from the throne.

"Hunter's blood, girl! What are you doing here?"

"Fulfilling my duties, Your Majesty. My mother has suggested I should be present wherever possible to see if I catch nuances you miss."

Edreon grunted. "And you think you, a newcomer to court, will be able to glean more from situations like this than I?"

Odelia curtseyed, her head down in a submissive gesture that Edreon now knew meant she was about to say something he might not like. "I hear many things that never reach your ears, Your Majesty. Your subjects show you only what they wish you to see. For instance, do you know which members of your court still whisper that you cannot walk and use this to fuel rumors of your declining health?"

"Who is it?" Edreon demanded.

"I will bring you a full list later today. Most prominent among their number is Lord Beshor."

Edreon gripped the arms of his throne. "Curse him. And how do you suggest I silence these rumor-mongers?"

"A display of strength would serve best, Your Majesty. A duel, perhaps, or a promenade through the city."

"If you are so well informed, then you must know I can do no such thing," Edreon hissed.

"I know, Your Majesty," Odelia said quietly.

Edreon frowned at Odelia without seeing her. What would he do if he lost his leg in the end? Could he prove to his people that a crippled king was still strong enough to lead the Kinship Thrones?

He doubted it.

With a sigh, he blinked Odelia's face back into focus. "And what can you tell me about the priest who came before me today?"

"Nothing, Your Majesty. He spoke plainly. But…I have to ask. Have you ever considered converting to the Nine?"

"Keep your voice down," Edreon growled. "My enemies have enough fuel to build my pyre without adding an outright religious takeover to the mix."

"I know," Odelia said. "But I also know you see the value in the Nine. My mother told me you enlisted the help of a healer who follows Tabanus."

"Not because I wished to follow his teachings."

"No, but you recognized that the Alldrosants hold knowledge that the Varonites have cast aside. They value knowledge. Learning. Craftsmanship. Charity. And what does Varos value?"

"War," Edreon said gruffly.

"Exactly."

"It's not that simple," he said. "Varos also speaks of defending the weak and innocent and guarding the sanctity of Whitland. Those are worthwhile aims, especially at a time like this."

"But as a king devoted to Varos, you need to be the defender, not the weak," Odelia said. She was no longer looking down coyly—she met his eyes like an equal, and Edreon could see her passion for the subject. "Whereas an Alldrosant king can find other ways to prove his eminence. Regardless of his physical capabilities."

"A solid argument," Edreon said drily. "You've convinced me—if I lose my leg, I will convert to the Nine."

Odelia narrowed her eyes. "Are you mocking me?"

"No. But you fail to grasp the broader issue here."

"What do you mean?"

Edreon sighed. "Are you a devout believer in the Nine?"

"I believe what serves my ends, Your Majesty, but I can say with full honesty that I admire and respect the teachings of the Nine."

Interesting. It intrigued him that she would push him to

416

convert to a religion she did not wholly believe in.

"Then you might see the truth where others remain blind. Whitland has been a mess for centuries, child. Regardless of which religion held dominance. We have seen nothing but in-fighting and religious persecution ever since the Makhori fled the continent, and while my father's war served as a unifier and a temporary distraction, it won't last forever. The answer is not to choose one religion over another. The answer is to secure the Whitish Empire and assert the dominance of the High Throne, until none of these petty claimants can use religion as an excuse to chip away at my power.

"That was where the trouble started. When the Makhori uprisings weakened the High Throne many centuries ago, every prince and lord with a scrap of royal blood decided to use the opportunity to undermine the High King's authority and seize small pockets of land.

"This has never been about religion. The gods have been used as an excuse for petty rivalries and clumsy grabs for power all along, and until their supporters can learn to coexist, we will never be free of this madness. Whitland will crumble from within."

"And you think *you* can stop it?" Odelia asked softly.

"Little by little, Whitland has gone from the dominant power in the Kinship Thrones to a weak, impoverished mess. If I can build up our wealth with the trees harvested in Itrea and prove our eminence by tightening our hold on both continents, it might be enough to unify our people and stop the meaningless warmongering." Edreon lowered his voice to a whisper. "My father started the war in Itrea because it was the only way to keep Whitland from collapse. I hope to drag us back from the brink and give us a new taste at glory. One that doesn't require the persecution of our own people."

Odelia was watching him with a strange expression.

"What?" Edreon snapped.

"I must admit myself surprised, Your Majesty. You're a good man, even if you try to hide it."

Edreon scowled at her.

"But you have no heir, do you? What happens if you die without a successor? Will all your work fall apart?"

Did she know she might be his bastard? *Varos damn the girl.* She was too clever for him, and here he was spilling out his most private thoughts so she could twist them to her advantage.

Edreon heard footsteps approaching from the hall, so he straightened. "My heir is not your concern. Back to your hiding place, and stay there until I've left this room."

With a swift curtsey, Odelia slipped behind the curtain once more, the fabric swaying behind her.

"As to your earlier question about the Nine," he said to the empty room, "Varos is the god I need to bless my campaign. This war is all-consuming and allows no time for the pursuits favored by the Gods of Light. If I turn my back on Varos now, I will doom my entire kingdom to collapse."

53

King Rodarin

By the time Bennett met them at the teahouse, Kalleah and Baridya had drank their way through three pots of tea. When Baridya had started yawning after too much exposure to Kalleah's power, Kalleah had taken a stroll around the block to give her a reprieve. The festivities outside were growing more raucous as the alcohol flowed freely, and Kalleah caught snatches of drunken singing that clashed with the fiddler's tunes.

She returned just in time to see Bennett pushing open the door.

"You came!" Bennett said in surprise, taking a seat at their table. "When you disappeared from The Lost Sailor, I wondered if you had left town altogether." He was dressed in merchant's garb today, with an embroidered vest and the crossed belts common in Chelt.

"We didn't want to be near when the Lord's Men were

about," Kalleah said. "How did the inn fare?"

"No damage," Bennett said, "but they claimed several bottles of expensive spirits and raided the poor man's safe. I spoke to the innkeeper the other day—apparently most businesses are hiding their money more carefully these days, so he wasn't fully bankrupted."

"Still, that would have hurt," Baridya said.

"Indeed." Bennett smiled grimly at them. "So. Am I to understand you will be joining our scheme, my lady?"

"Yes," Baridya said.

Bennett stood. "Then we have work to do. Come."

"We haven't paid for the drinks," Kalleah said, rising slowly. "We left the inn with nothing."

"Then you're lucky a merchant always keeps a healthy purse on hand." Bennett patted the bulging coin purse strapped across his chest. He pulled out a handful of dravs and left them on the table before leading them from the teahouse.

Outside, the streets were littered with flower petals, many crushed beneath the feet of passersby. Their floral perfume hung thick in the air, mixed with the strong smell of ale.

Bennett led them through a maze of streets Kalleah had not ventured down before, heading away from the waterfront toward the western end of town. Eventually they came to a hairdresser's shop with a door at the back leading to a hidden room.

The air in the hidden room was musty and choked with incense, and as Kalleah and Baridya stepped forward, a woman emerged from the shadows.

"Greetings," she said, her voice lightly accented. "I did not expect two customers, Bennett. You should have allowed more time."

"Apologies," Bennett said. "It was a last-minute change of plans."

"Are you from Ruunas?" Baridya asked with interest.

"Indeed. And you as well?"

"My mother is Ruunan, my father Cheltish."

The woman's eyes glinted in interest. "Delighted to meet you. And you must be the Itrean?" She turned her gaze on Kalleah.

"I am."

"Welcome, welcome. I am called Lady Daara, and I deal in costumes and disguises. Bennett tells me you wish to pass as Darden courtesans for the night? Or perhaps we could disguise you less heavily," she told Baridya. "A Darden and a Ruunan would raise no eyebrows."

She began to walk around them, tongue poking between her lips as she considered them. "And you are on the mature side for courtesans as well, so we must give you a youthful demeanor."

"Are you calling us old?" Baridya asked with a laugh.

"Not at all. You look younger than me, at least. But the more details we change, the more effective the disguise, no?"

"Of course," Baridya said.

The woman pulled up chairs and had them sit side by side, while Bennett stood in the corner with his arms crossed over his chest. Then she wheeled a cart before them and began selecting bottles, frowning and muttering to herself as she worked.

"I'm looking forward to this," Baridya said with a smile. "I've done minor work with disguises in the past, all of it without much direction. It will be intriguing to see a master at work."

"Is that why you decided to join me?" Kalleah teased. "Because you wanted the chance to dress up?"

Baridya laughed.

"You won't be offended if I use an Itrean crystal while I work, will you?" Lady Daara asked.

"No," Kalleah said, though she had no idea what the woman referred to.

She produced a Weaver's crystal, with its intricate casing of metal, and set it in a holder on her cart. When she lit it, the gloomy room was transformed.

"I didn't know you could find such things this deep in the Kinship Thrones," Kalleah said with interest.

"Oh, you would be surprised."

Lady Daara propped up a mirror on the cart so they could watch as she worked. Then she started on Kalleah, spreading a paste across her face and down her neck to lighten her skin. Her eyebrows were tinted white and then brown, and shadows were added to her cheeks and nose to subtly change the shape of her face. Finally, when she could hardly recognize herself beneath the makeup, Lady Daara added the bright tint on her lips and around her eyes that marked her as a courtesan. Blossoms of color like butterfly wings spread from the corners of both eyes, sparkling as it caught the light.

"What are you going to do with my hair?" Kalleah asked.

Lady Daara chuckled. "You'll wear a wig. The color of your hair will be the first mark in your favor. Nothing can be done about your accent, so I would recommend speaking as little as possible, but we can fix the color of your eyes. Tilt your head back, if you will."

"Is this safe?" Kalleah asked as she leaned her head back,

looking up at the wood-paneled ceiling.

"Entirely. It's another Itrean import, I believe."

She spilled a few drops of cool liquid into Kalleah's eyes; Kalleah blinked furiously, the liquid itching as it spread.

When she looked into the mirror again, she saw some of the color bleeding from her irises, leaving them a light brown.

"Now for the gown." Lady Daara beckoned Kalleah to follow her through a curtained doorway to a small room lined with costume racks. Kalleah saw flowing gowns and Whitish armor, travelers' cloaks and priests' robes, Cheltish belts and the patterned silk robes she had worn in King's Port, and much more she did not recognize. This must be where Bennett got his various disguises; she wondered if the two were married or perhaps lovers. Lady Daara was at least fifteen years older than Bennett, but she was not unattractive.

"This will do," Lady Daara said, selecting a low-cut blue gown with laces up the front. "Try not to touch your face as you change."

Kalleah pulled off her shirt but did not shed her trousers— she felt uncomfortable going into a dangerous situation in nothing but skirts. She stepped into the flounced underskirt before pulling on the gown, which had a stiff bodice and billowing skirts.

"What's this?" Lady Daara asked, touching the sheath strapped to Kalleah's wrist.

"A dagger."

"You'll be searched when you enter the palace," Lady Daara said. "Something like this will raise unwanted attention."

Kalleah fingered the sheath. She had worn it for many years, removing it only at night; the hidden blade had served her well before, especially when etiquette prevented her from carrying a sword.

"I don't feel comfortable going into the palace without a weapon," she said.

"Strap it elsewhere, then."

Kalleah unbuckled the sheath and knelt to pull up her trousers. She then loosened the straps and buckled it around her calf, the leather digging into her skin when she straightened.

Lady Daara laughed softly. "Very well, then."

While Kalleah stood still, Lady Daara cinched the laces tight, forcing her breasts up so they nearly spilled from the low neckline. Kalleah was hit by a flash of strange déjà vu—this felt so much like all the times Baridya had dressed her while she was queen, yet there was something jarring about it as well.

Maybe it was because she was no longer that person. She had left behind the niceties of court life, the trappings of queenship, and now they fit her as badly as a discarded snakeskin.

In learning to use her power, she had abandoned any illusion of dignified leadership. She had become a warrior, a weapon. A monster.

And that monster did not wear gowns.

When she finished lacing the stays, Lady Daara selected a wig of light brown hair with a knot at the back fastened with a silver pin, the rest coiled in ringlets. She pinned Kalleah's braid into place and settled the wig carefully over her hair, adjusting the ringlets until they fell just so over Kalleah's shoulders.

"You didn't plan on wearing boots, did you?" Lady Daara asked.

Kalleah hated the idea of leaving her boots behind, but

when she took an experimental step forward, the toe of her boot peeked from beneath her skirts, unmistakable even in the dim light. "No," she said reluctantly.

Lady Daara helped her change into a pair of delicate gold slippers, and then she led the way back into the larger room.

Baridya gasped. "Gods. I can hardly convince myself it's you."

"You've done a brilliant job," Bennett said, beaming at Lady Daara.

Kalleah stepped up to the mirror, intrigued, to find a stranger staring back at her.

The woman in the mirror was indisputably of Whitish descent, from the shape of her face to the color of her hair, and the tightly-laced bodice and bright paint around her eyes gave her a seductive air.

"Remarkable," Kalleah said. "If only we could have hired you from the moment we arrived in the Twin Cities. You could have turned me into a convincing man, I'm sure."

"Plagues," Baridya said. "It's disconcerting hearing your voice coming from that—that creature."

"Are you going to do the same to her?" Kalleah asked.

"Oh, nothing so extreme," Lady Daara said. "Her Ruunan blood will raise no questions, so we simply need to erase a few years and dress her as a courtesan."

Kalleah watched as Lady Daara fixed Baridya's hair and smoothed the lines on her face before adding the same butterfly-wing design stretching out from the corners of her eyes. She was then dressed in a red gown similar to Kalleah's, her more generous bosom spilling from the neckline in an indecent way.

When she was finished, Baridya eyed herself in the mirror

for a moment, a faint frown tugging at the corner of her mouth.

"What is it?" Kalleah asked.

"I still look like myself, just…a whore. Whereas you seem a different person altogether. Your disguise is less personal."

"Courtesans are no common whores," Bennett said. "They are educated women, companions who are known for their conversation and artistry as much as their skill in the bedroom. In fact, the profession has gained respect under the Lord's Men as the only sphere where women of learning are still allowed to move in the same circles as men. I wouldn't be surprised if many are using the guise to protect them from scrutiny without selling their bodies in the bargain."

"I hope you're right," Kalleah said under her breath.

A distant bell began ringing, and Bennett paced to the door. "Come. We must hurry."

Baridya thanked Lady Daara, and with a wide-eyed look at Kalleah, she followed Bennett from the room.

Evening was settling over the town, and the streets were lit with oil lamps that shed a soft golden glow on the cobblestones. Kalleah and Baridya attracted fewer looks than she had expected—many women wore finery, including face paint almost as absurd as theirs.

"How many people has the king invited to his ball?" Baridya asked, lifting her skirts as she hurried to keep up with Bennett.

Bennett chuckled. "These commoners aren't going to the palace. There will be dancing on all the main squares throughout town, and along the waterfront as well."

Kalleah wished she could see that. And she missed Leoth more than ever—festivities like these took her back to her first days in Baylore, when he had danced with her and won her affection long before she trusted him.

Though she was glad he wouldn't see her like this.

Soon they reached the main street leading up to the palace, where the more boisterous crowd gave way to well-dressed gentry.

"Excuse me," Bennett said, pushing his way forward. "I'm accompanying two special guests here. Beg pardon. I do apologize."

When they saw Kalleah and Baridya, the guests moved aside without question, some raising their eyebrows appreciatively. Soon they reached a small crowd of similarly-dressed courtesans who were being fussed over by a grey-haired woman.

"Not the feather! Oh, why will your hair not stay put? You've soiled your gown, silly girl."

Noticing Bennett, she gave him a grateful look. "Good gods, man, what took you so long? And where did this Ruunan specimen come from?" She put a finger under Baridya's chin and tilted it up, examining her with a frown.

"I'm afraid there was a miscommunication," Bennett said. "Two women, not one, and both a tad more mature than I'd anticipated."

"Never mind, they'll do. Hurry along!"

Kalleah and Baridya fell into line with the other women, some of whom gave them keen-eyed looks of scrutiny.

"First time taking on such a role?" one asked Kalleah in a whisper.

"I'm afraid so," she mumbled, trying not to let her accent give her away.

When they reached the palace gates, they found the courtyard heavily guarded by Lord's Men. Several stepped

427

forward to block their way, saying, "We've been given orders to search all hired performers."

Kalleah's heart started racing, even though she knew her fear was irrational. These men were looking for weapons, not for the disguised queen of a foreign country. She bit the inside of her cheek and tried not to flinch as the men patted her down roughly, groping at her chest and pushing aside her skirts to shove a hand between her legs.

Then she was released. Face flushed from anger, she hurried after the other courtesans, trying to lose herself in the crowd of women.

Halfway through the courtyard, she saw Leoth standing in the line of Lord's Men.

She stumbled, heart lurching into her throat.

Baridya elbowed her. "Did you see—?"

Kalleah nodded, unable to speak. Damn him, but he looked handsome in the leather uniform of the Lord's Men—handsome and dangerous.

Leoth's eyes were fixed straight ahead, on the crowd passing through the courtyard, and he did not so much as glance her way.

Soon they reached the palace doors, and it took every bit of Kalleah's resolve not to turn and search for Leoth once more.

Instead she let the crowd sweep her through the entrance hall to the ballroom, where the musicians were playing a light tune. This palace was grander than the one in Baylore, with soaring towers and high, arched ceilings and a sense of unity that Baylore Palace lacked, and the ballroom stood at its heart, directly across from the entrance. Chandeliers gleamed overhead, while heels clicked on the polished marble floor.

"You know your role," the grey-haired woman said, stopping just inside the ballroom. "Make the guests feel special. All are fascinating and irresistible, and none are beneath your notice."

Kalleah and Baridya drew off to one side, watching the guests milling about the ballroom. There were tables set with wineglasses along one wall, while the young women wearing flower wreaths in their hair had gathered along the opposite wall.

"I could do with a glass of wine," Kalleah said. She was completely out of her element.

"I'm not sure we're allowed alcohol," Baridya said.

"Plagues. You're right. How are we supposed to do this?"

"Watch," Baridya said.

With a grace Kalleah would never master, she sashayed off toward a cluster of gentlemen. Within moments, she had them laughing at something she had said, and soon a man laid a hand on the small of her back and drew her close like a favored companion.

Bloody Varse. Of course Baridya would handle herself well. She had always been good at playing the flirt.

Hitching a smile onto her face, Kalleah approached another group of men. These men were younger, perhaps in their twenties, and she immediately felt sick at the thought of what Daymin would think if he saw her here.

But they welcomed her into their circle, asking if she had been at court before and arguing over who would get a turn to dance with her first. Kalleah spoke as little as possible, trying to say, "Yes, Milord," and "No, Milord," in her best Darden accent, and the men certainly didn't seem suspicious.

Soon the ballroom was packed and the first dance began.

None were familiar, and it took most of her attention to keep pace with her partners. Whenever she sat out a dance, she watched King Rodarin, wondering how best to approach him without drawing attention. Several of the courtesans sidled up to his throne in the early evening, before he joined in the dancing, and he seemed to be amenable to their company. Perhaps it would be as easy as walking straight up to him.

But once he started dancing, she found it challenging to get any closer. He partnered with the queen for most of the dances, favoring only a few older women with a turn while his wife rested, and whenever Kalleah started weaving her way through the crowd toward the throne, someone would ask her for a dance.

One man kept approaching her, but though he made her uneasy, she could not turn him down without causing a scene. He had untidy brown hair and a red face, and his breath reeked of alcohol; after the second dance, he kept making lewd comments and trying to weasel information out of her.

"How many men have you lain with?" he asked with a leer.

"I'm not allowed to disclose such information," Kalleah said.

"I bet you're riddled with disease. You're not even Darden, are you? Where is that accent from?"

"The marshlands," she said, remembering that someone had mentioned ancient Makhori settlements in the marshes.

He sniffed. "Those backwater savages? No wonder you're so unrefined. Still, I've got a friend who'll want a piece of you later. Several friends, in fact. They're well-traveled gentlemen who like sampling the goods from every region."

When the dance ended, Kalleah managed to slip away,

weaving hurriedly through the crowd in the direction of the throne. To her relief, an older man stopped her and asked her for a dance, saving her from the attentions of the drunken man. They were preparing for a dance that rotated through a line of partners, it transpired, with the women lining up on one side and the men on the other. Kalleah felt a swoop of relief when she spotted King Rodarin among their number.

As the dance began, Kalleah and her partner stepped up to each other, linking hands and turning in a slow circle.

"You've an unfamiliar face, lass," the man said, drawing her attention away from the king. "Is this your first time in the palace?"

"It's a long time since I've been called 'lass,'" Kalleah said, looking up through her lashes in a way she hoped would be taken for flirtatious. As they rotated the other direction, she glimpsed Baridya at the end of the line, face animated, touch lingering on the man she partnered. It was a good thing Mellicante was not here to see her charming every man within reach.

"I'm old enough to be your grandfather," Kalleah's partner said. "You remind me of one of my brother's grandchildren, in fact. She's a quiet young thing like you."

Then they stepped away from each other, and the dance carried Kalleah to the next man in line. Partner by partner, she moved closer to the king, praying the song would not end before she had a chance to approach him.

At last, heart hammering in her chest, she stepped up and laid her palm against the king's. If she had guessed wrong, this could ruin everything.

As they rotated, eyes locking momentarily, Kalleah whispered, "What would you do if Queen Kalleah offered you an alliance?

A spark of surprise registered in King Rodarin's eyes, so she forged on.

"What if she could free your city from the Lord's Men and stop Whitland from interfering in your kingdom? Would you take that chance?"

They switched hands and rotated the other way, King Rodarin searching her face with a look of hope bordering on desperation.

At last he gave a tiny shake of his head. "My hands are tied," he whispered.

Then they stepped apart and moved on to the next partners in line.

Triumph surged through Kalleah. She knew without a doubt that King Rodarin was hers—if she could just find a way to free the Twin Cities from the Lord's Men.

Now that she had a way forward, she was eager to round up her friends and make a plan. It was time to leave the palace.

When the dance ended, Kalleah stepped away from the line, her original partner nowhere to be seen.

Just then, a hand seized her.

She whirled, heart pounding, and saw the man who had been pursuing her all evening.

"Take your hands off me!" she demanded.

The man dragged her close. Now he looked dangerous rather than drunken, and when Kalleah struggled to free herself from his grasp, he reached up and swiped roughly at her cheek with a wet handkerchief.

She gasped—he had wiped away the paste that had lightened her skin.

"I knew it," he said with a cruel smile. "You're no Marshlander." Raising his voice, he shouted, "Guards! Arrest this woman!"

Kalleah managed to yank her arm free from his grasp.

He lunged for her, seizing a handful of hair.

When Kalleah broke into a run, he kept his grip on the wig, pulling it off to reveal the black braid pinned to the back of her head.

The music faltered as Kalleah dashed through the ballroom, knocking guests aside with her skirts as she pushed her way toward the door. A few men made clumsy grabs for her, but most of the guests hurried out of her way, whispering in surprise.

She veered around the last of the guests and skidded through the ballroom doors—where she found her way blocked by a wall of brutish Lord's Men.

54

The Fight on the Stairs

Kalleah's first instinct was to start ripping the life from her enemies, and as she stood before them, lungs straining beneath the tight bodice, she found herself sinking reflexively into the state of deep concentration needed to control her power.

Running footsteps from behind pulled her from her trance. Kalleah glanced back to see Baridya dashing through the ballroom doors, skirts fisted in her hands.

Still gasping for breath, Kalleah pushed away her instinctive reaction. If she started killing people openly, she would reveal her identity and make an enemy of herself. She still remembered Bennett's distaste when he had described her attack on Eidervell—even if she was doing these people a service by removing the Lord's Men, they would see her as a monster.

When Baridya jogged up to her side, Kalleah put a hand on her shoulder for balance and raised her foot to retrieve the hidden dagger.

"What's the plan?" Baridya whispered.

Kalleah grimaced. "Fight our way through somehow?"

"Two against thirty? I don't like our chances."

"No."

Two of the Lord's Men had been about to seize them, but Kalleah whipped out the dagger and lunged at the nearest man's throat. He stumbled back out of reach, giving them another moment's reprieve.

"You're prepared," Baridya said in surprise.

"Yes, this should even the odds nicely."

Then Kalleah spotted Leoth at the back of the line. He met her eyes and gave her a tiny nod.

When the Lord's Men swarmed forward to surround them, Kalleah grabbed Baridya's hand and barreled forward, right into their midst.

Most of the brutes weren't carrying swords, since they were facing two unarmed women, so the only resistance they met was the wall of solid bodies.

The men grabbed at them as they ran, but Kalleah dove beneath the last of the line and found herself at the palace doors.

"There are more at the palace steps," a wonderfully familiar voice said in Kalleah's ear.

She was dragged to her feet, a sword pressed into her left hand.

"Go!"

Kalleah took off at a run, only looking back once she was halfway across the courtyard. Leoth and Baridya were dashing after her, both holding swords, and the Lord's Men were close at their heels.

The skirts tangled her legs and slowed her, and Kalleah wished she had asked for a gown with a skirt she could easily shed.

But she hadn't expected this to come to a fight.

When she reached the palace gates, where the courtyard opened to the wide flight of stairs leading down to the city, Kalleah slowed.

Another dozen Lord's Men barred her path, these ones armed and waiting for her.

In the few seconds she had before the rest of the brutes closed in on her, Kalleah sawed at the fabric of her skirts with her dagger. The fine material gave way easily, and soon she was yanking away great wads of fabric and stepping out of the underskirt.

At last she stood in nothing but her trousers and uncomfortable bodice, grateful at the very least that she was unlikely to fall down the stairs in a tangle of skirts.

Leoth and Baridya jogged to a halt on either side of her.

"What's your plan?" Leoth asked quietly.

Kalleah threw him a panicked look. "Fight our way out?"

"Then let's go!" he said.

Leoth charged down the steps, straight into the mass of Lord's Men.

As he traded clanging blows with the first of the brutes, Kalleah swapped her sword into her right hand and dashed after him.

She and Baridya plunged into the waiting guards, swords flying.

Kalleah could tell at once that these men were no elite soldiers, and she quickly drove her opponent back, landing more than one blow. But the guards that had chased them across the courtyard were closing in, and they wouldn't be able to hold out against such numbers, no matter how well they fought.

From her left, Baridya shrieked, distracting Kalleah from the fight.

While her attention faltered, her opponent took a wild strike at her neck, slicing open the skin of her collarbone.

Kalleah hissed in pain and took a step backward.

Just then, she spotted another familiar face dashing up the steps from the street—Mellicante had found them and was joining the fight. She must have followed Leoth to the palace.

Kalleah lost track of her friends as the man in front of her lunged once again.

She caught his blade on hers and twisted toward him, plunging her dagger left-handed into his throat. The movement was clumsy—she was accustomed to wielding a longsword with two hands and had never trained with her left hand alone—but it was enough to send him toppling down the steps.

As he fell, a space cleared before her, and Kalleah leapt forward, nearly to the end of the wall of soldiers.

Little by little, she and her friends pushed their way down the stairs. But for every man they felled, three more surged forward to take his place.

Soon they were backed up together on the flat street, surrounded by at least thirty of the Lord's Men. Kalleah could see no way out.

"At what point do you use your power?" Leoth muttered out of the corner of his mouth.

"When we're ready to give up on the Twin Cities altogether."

"Weren't we about to leave anyway?" Mellicante whispered.

"King Rodarin will work with us if we free his city of these brutes," Kalleah whispered. *I hope.* "Besides, if we reveal ourselves now, we might find a whole army descending on us when we try to reach the coast."

One of the Lord's Men stalked forward, waving his sword in Kalleah's direction. "What plot is this?" he demanded. "And why is he fighting for you?"

None of them spoke. Kalleah was trying to find an opening to make a run for it, but the Lord's Men were closing the circle around them, the wall of bodies growing more impenetrable with each step inward.

Soon the men stood just out of range of their swords.

"Seize them!" a man shouted.

Four of the brutes surged forward at Kalleah, and without the space to swing properly, she couldn't hold her ground. While she parried blows from one, another man seized her by the arm and ripped the sword from her grasp. Another seized her dagger, while the last trapped her wrists behind her back.

She flailed out, trying to kick and fight her way free, but the men were too strong. As she struggled, another two men took hold of her shoulders to restrain her, their hands rough against her skin.

Breathing hard, Kalleah straightened. There was no point fighting against such odds.

Looking behind her, she saw that her friends had been similarly restrained; only Mellicante still held her blade, though one of the Lord's Men had seized her left arm.

"Drop that blade or we'll make the whore bleed," one of the Lord's Men growled at Mellicante.

Mellicante glanced sideways to where one of the brutes restrained Baridya, his blade against the soft skin of her throat.

Mellicante dropped her sword with a clatter.

Several of the men laughed coarsely.

"Good. Now don't think about fighting, or we'll carve up that pretty chest."

They shoved Kalleah and her friends down the street, toward a cluster of wide-eyed onlookers.

"Where are you taking us?" Leoth demanded.

"Back to headquarters, of course." A heavyset man with a mustache gave him a sneer. "There'll be plenty who want to take a piece out of the traitor, eh?"

Then they were marched roughly forward.

"Isn't now a good time?" Mellicante hissed when she was dragged close to Kalleah.

"Not in the middle of the city."

The danger was that she would find herself locked up with no one in range of her power, and then she would be as helpless as a common soldier.

But maybe she could kill the Lord's Men when they reached their headquarters, if it was somewhere less visible.

Kalleah kept her head down, her arms twisted at a painful angle behind her back. The delicate slippers were not suited for walking, and they were chafing badly.

Less than two blocks from the palace, something sprang from the shadows and slammed into the Lord's Men.

Kalleah looked up, startled, to see several dozen figures in grey cloaks pushing and fighting their way through the mass of Lord's Men.

One by one, the men restraining her were forced to

relinquish their grip so they could fight, and as she tried to slip free, someone threw a cloak over her.

"This way," a familiar voice hissed.

Kalleah grappled with the cloak, finally pulling it around her shoulders and tugging the hood over her head so her face was in shadow. Then she followed her savior from the tangle of fighting.

When she reached the quiet of a side street, she paused to look back at her friends. Leoth had escaped the melee and was sprinting around the mess of Lord's Men to reach the alley, while several of their cloaked saviors had surrounded Baridya and were escorting her from the battle.

Soon only Mellicante remained. She had found a sword somewhere, and she was facing off against three of the Lord's Men, who had backed her against the wall of a bakery.

When Baridya and Leoth joined Kalleah, Baridya turned and scanned the street until she found Mellicante.

"Mells!" she shouted.

Mellicante heard and paused, long enough for one of her opponents to trap her sword against his hilt.

She shoved back against his blade, but the other two were closing in on her.

Then the men in cloaks encircled her opponents, dropping two of them with a sword to the back.

As soon as she saw an opening, Mellicante fled, dashing through the Lord's Men while they were still distracted by the cloaked attackers.

Once she reached the alley, the familiar voice said, "Run! We need to leave the city before the gates close for the night!"

Kalleah and her friends took off down the street, following

their cloaked saviors without question. Bennett's hood fell down as he ran, as did a few others, though Kalleah did not recognize any of the other men in the group.

They followed a twisting route through back alleys, avoiding the music and laughter that spilled from the wider streets, until at last they came to the city wall. Kalleah had never been here before, since they had entered along the river, and she was surprised by how dingy and neglected this part of the city appeared. There were beggars huddled under lean-tos—not dissimilar to the refugees who had flooded Baylore, she reminded herself—and more than one rundown building overflowing with rubbish.

Eventually they reached a larger street, where the derelict buildings gave way to a collection of inns and stables. Here the city gates stood open, guarded lightly by a handful of soldiers.

The rest of the cloaked men had caught up with Kalleah, and they slipped through the city gates just as the distant bells began ringing. Behind them, the gates creaked closed.

"Thank you," Kalleah said. "I don't understand why you helped us, but we owe our lives to you."

She made to step away from their cloaked saviors, but Bennett blocked her path.

"You're coming with us," he said.

"Where?" Mellicante asked sharply.

"The Temple of Totoleon."

55

Baylore and the Wandering Woods

Daymin's army set up camp where the road disappeared into the woods. They were just south of Borderville, but there was no sign of the village, so it must have been swallowed up by the ancestor trees in the years since the map was drawn.

Daymin could hear the creaking of trees deep in the woods, which meant the attack was already underway; he had wanted to push on in the darkness, but in the absence of Uncle Cal, Tarak and Zahira had managed to talk him out of it.

Now he was pacing the camp, nerves wound tight from stress.

What if he was too late to save the forest? What if the Whitish had more harvesting machines than he had bargained on, and they crushed his army before he could bring them down?

When his tattoo flashed cold, Daymin started, even though he had been expecting a reply. He had told Idorii they would be fighting the harvesting machines in another day or two, and he anticipated a message wishing him luck.

Cutting his way to the edge of camp, Daymin pushed up his sleeve and read by the light of a nearby crystal.

Daymin –

The city is abuzz with the news that the Whitish are preparing for a direct attack on Baylore. Scouts have reported siege towers and trebuchets lining up outside Darkland Fort, and the army that pursued yours has been spotted not far from Pelek.
Wish us luck.

Yours,
Idorii

A cold dagger of uncertainty plunged through Daymin's chest, the ice spreading until he felt numb.

If he abandoned the Allakoash, he still had time to turn around and fight for Baylore.

With the civilians gone, they could take risks they hadn't dared before. Maybe they could hold the city if they gave it everything, knowing there was nothing to lose if they failed.

What would Cal do in his place?

What would his mother do?

Plagues. Daymin knew exactly what his mother would do— she would throw everything she had at the defense of Baylore. She wouldn't let their capital fall to the Whitish until none remained to fight.

But he couldn't do it. He couldn't abandon the Allakoash.

He had already given up Baylore for lost, and turning back now would mean trading the lives of the Allakoash for the defense of a city that had become no more than a symbol of Itrea.

A powerful symbol, though. Once Baylore had fallen, Itrea would be no more.

Did he value the Allakoash more than the very existence of Itrea?

Daymin tugged his sleeve down clumsily. He was glad the news had come directly to him; he couldn't face the rational, well-meaning arguments of his followers. He felt sick enough as it was.

He staggered back through camp to the tent he was still sharing with his friends. When Tarak saw his face, he set aside his sword. "What's wrong?"

Daymin swallowed. This was his own burden to carry.

"I'm just worried how the battle will play out tomorrow," he said quietly. "I hope the harvesting machines don't overwhelm us."

* * *

After a sleepless night, Daymin rose at the first light of dawn. Lalaysha was gone, and he had a feeling he knew where he would find her.

He dressed as quietly as he could, pulling on his Weaver's armor and boots and buckling on his sword belt. Then he pushed open the tent flap to venture out to the still campground, where a thin sheen of mist hung over the ground. The air was chill and damp; he wondered if a nearby stream had fed the mist.

As he had expected, he saw two figures at the edge of the

forest—Lalaysha and Renok. When he drew closer, he realized they were talking to a third, a woman hidden in the shadows of an ancestor tree.

Lalaysha turned at the sound of Daymin's footsteps rustling the grass.

"Meeko!" she called softly. "She's come to describe the battle to us." She spoke in Allakoash, and as she did, the unfamiliar woman's eyes rose to meet Daymin's in surprise.

"Does he speak our tongue?" she asked.

"This is King Daymin," Lalaysha said, and Daymin's chest ached at the pride in her voice. This was why he had been unable to abandon the forest.

"How bad is it?" Daymin asked the woman, who was staring at him in disbelief.

After a moment, she cleared her throat. "The towers are focusing on the part of the forest where the road once stood. This is the narrowest stretch, and they seem determined to carve a way back through to Larkhaven."

"How far have they made it?" Daymin asked.

"You'll reach their towers by midday. Only a small army has come into the trees with them, but there are others along the forest border launching something at our trees with a strange machine."

"Trebuchets," Renok said, using the Whitish word.

"What are the trebuchets doing?" Daymin asked in surprise.

Renok shook his head. "I caught sight of one this morning. Whatever it's throwing doesn't seem to have any effect on the trees."

"We'll leave them for now, then," Daymin said. Turning back to the unfamiliar woman, he said, "Can you lead my army through the trees to the Whitish? I'd like to catch them by surprise."

"Yes, of course."

Daymin glanced from Lalaysha to Renok. "Let's rouse the camp. We don't want to give the harvesting machines too great a head start."

An hour later, Daymin's army was assembled at the edge of the forest. They left their camp standing, guarded by a handful of soldiers; Daymin hoped the Whitish would not stumble across it and raid their dried goods while they were away.

He still felt nauseous at the knowledge that Baylore was about to be attacked and he was doing nothing to stop it. Especially since Idorii was there.

But the Weavers were ready with their enchanted weapons, and his army was here, just a few short leagues from the last of the harvesting machines.

"I don't know what we'll find in the woods," Daymin said to his army, "but the trees are on our side. They will help us and conceal us in any way they can. This will be our last great strike against the Whitish before we join our civilians in the Icebraid Peaks. Let us make it count!"

His soldiers were eyeing the forest with unease, so Daymin led the way beneath the trees, stepping over roots and around ferns. The woods felt at once familiar and unknowable; Daymin had never been able to understand the thoughts of the ancestor trees the way the Allakoash could, but he could sense the ancient, sleepy sentience of these trees who had stood here for centuries.

Deeper in the woods, the sound of thousands of footsteps scuffed the ground behind him, muffled by the layer of decomposing leaves. Distant creaking and shouts rang out from time to time, at odds with the stillness all around, and Daymin caught sight of Allakoash watching his army pass from the branches of trees.

As they drew nearer to the battle, the stillness of the forest evaporated. Every tree seemed to be shifting, and the chorus of creaking and rustling leaves put Daymin on edge. Closer still, he could hear people shouting in Allakoash, along with the grinding of gears as the harvesting machines crawled forward.

At last Daymin caught sight of a swath of dead trees. The harvesting machines had torn a path deep into the forest, leaving rows of lifeless trees standing like sentinels on either side of the cleared earth. In the midst of such greenery, the dead trees and bare earth seemed an unnatural stain.

"So many trees," Lalaysha whispered from his side.

Daymin was more amazed that the harvesting machines had made it so deep into the forest. They were moving quickly—there must be dozens of them to cut through the dense growth at such a rate.

When he caught sight of an Allakoash boy watching from a nearby tree, Daymin called, "How many soldiers are traveling with the towers?"

The boy blinked in confusion before shouting back, "Lots! But the towers are guarding them, so our trees can't touch them."

"Thank you," Daymin said.

Daymin turned to his troops, which had spread out widely as they passed through the trees. General Vask was at the front, looking twitchy and ill at ease, and Daymin beckoned him closer.

"Take five companies and approach the Whitish from the

cleared path," Daymin said when the general stopped before him. "I want them focusing all their attention on your troops. The rest of us will surround the towers from within the forest and attempt to fell them without being seen."

"How many soldiers can we expect to face?" General Vask asked.

"It seems they're traveling within a ring of towers, so there can't be more than a couple thousand."

"Good. Are you ready, Your Majesty?"

Daymin felt a ripple of apprehension down his back. "We'll move out as soon as your troops are organized."

While General Vask drew his companies off to the side, Daymin repeated his orders to his other generals, who passed them in a whisper through the waiting troops.

Daymin stepped onto a root to watch as his army gradually organized itself as well as possible in the forest. Instead of the sick apprehension that often tormented him before a battle, he felt a heady wave of adrenaline.

He was genuinely excited to fight the Whitish.

Here, at last, he would be making a real difference. He wouldn't be harming civilians or battling a force so large his army would be crushed; no, he had come with weapons that could fell the harvesting towers once and for all. His army might not be equal to the Whitish army, but here—for once—he was not outmatched.

And he would be fighting alongside ancestor trees and Allakoash, in a place that felt as familiar as Baylore Palace.

While his troops organized themselves, Tarak and Zahira wove their way through the trees to join Daymin and Lalaysha.

"Daymin walks through the forest like one of your people,"

Tarak told Lalaysha with a smile. "Meanwhile, Zahira and I keep tripping over roots and getting moss tangled in our hair."

"Of course he does," Lalaysha said, nudging Daymin's shoulder. "He *is* one of us."

"Am I no longer an outcast, then?" he asked with amusement.

Lalaysha stepped closer and whispered in Allakoash, "Renok told me what they've been saying. Even before this, the tribes back in the forest saw you as some great legendary hero. The first Itrean king who has ever fought for us. If you manage to defeat the towers, you'll practically be a god." She laughed softly. "Don't let that go to your head."

"Ancestors' breath. I don't need that sort of pressure." Daymin shot her a sideways look. "Wait. Weren't the other tribes always questioning me? I thought the tribes in the Wandering Woods were just as skeptical."

"They heard the stories secondhand," Lalaysha said. "They didn't know about all the delays and the uncertainty. They just knew that you sent your full army to guard the forest around Baylore, and later joined our trees to attack Darkland Fort and destroy as many harvesting machines as possible. What other king would do such a thing for us?"

"What are you whispering about?" Zahira asked, poking Daymin in the shoulder. "Why can't you speak in Whitish?"

"Maybe this just means you need to study Allakoash." Tarak grinned at his sister.

"Don't tell me you could understand all that!"

"I got the general idea."

General Tria approached Daymin, and his friends fell silent.

"Your troops are ready, Your Majesty," she said in a hushed

voice. Unlike Daymin, the rest of his army seemed nervous at the prospect of fighting within a forest that could move.

"Good," Daymin said. "Let's get into place, then."

General Vask led his troops toward the scar of torn-up undergrowth while Daymin started forward again, staying well back from the dead trees as he approached the harvesting machines. As the sound of blades thwacking against wood grew louder, some of his giddy anticipation drained away, tempered by the magnitude of what the harvesting machines had done.

"Stay back," Daymin whispered to General Tria and his friends.

They kept moving forward, heading at what must have been a direct easterly angle parallel to the path of destruction, while Daymin darted closer to the harvesting machines. When he glimpsed the first flash of metal through the trees, he crouched down, letting the ferns and bushes nearer to the ground shield him as he moved closer still.

Soon he was so close to the battlefield that he could hear the shouts of the Whitish soldiers.

"Forward! Forward! Don't let the roots get under you!"

"It's not working!"

"Where's the poison? The duct is empty!"

"It's those bloody Drifters again! Arrows, men!"

Darting behind a towering ancestor tree, Daymin climbed the trunk, careful to stay out of sight of the Whitish.

Once he was safely in the canopy, he crept along a bough until he had a good view over the battlefield.

The scene below was chaos. The harvesting machines were concentrated at the front of the force, some pausing to chop down trees from the path of the army while others stabbed at roots with their spikes and widened the ring of dead trees. There were more than fifty in all, and a few rolled along at the rear of the force to guard the soldiers.

The Whitish soldiers numbered no more than five hundred, but all were fully armored, and even now Daymin saw a volley of arrows flying from the trees to glance uselessly off helmets and breastplates and vambraces. He could see a couple bodies in the wake of the army, so the Allakoash must have landed a few lucky shots through the slits of their visors, and a handful of Allakoash were stripping armor from one of the fallen Whitish.

In the battle at Darkland Fort, the ancestor trees had managed to topple a tower by pushing it from beneath with a root. Here, the towers were guarded against such a possibility—for every tower that had paused to chop down a tree, there were five more stabbing at the ground and catching every root that came near. And the Whitish were firing poisoned arrows into the forest beyond the range of the towers, widening the swath of destruction.

At the sight of so many towers moving in concert, Daymin's heart lurched into his throat.

This would not be as easy as he had hoped.

Yes, he had weapons enchanted with the counterspell overlaid with the other spells Idorii had discovered, but they had been designed to work with trebuchets providing the force to shatter the towers. Daymin worried his soldiers would be reduced to cutting holes in the sides of the towers once more, which would be slow, grueling work with so many towers to defeat.

And in the meantime, the towers would continue on their

path of destruction.

Several of his archers had crossbows, which he hoped would hit the towers with enough force to shatter a small section of frozen steel. The trick would be catching them unawares. From there, his Flamespinners would finish off the towers just as they had done at Darkland Fort.

With another look over the battlefield, memorizing the placement of the machines, Daymin climbed swiftly down from the tree. He remained crouched down until he was out of sight of the Whitish before setting off at a jog toward the front of his army.

"Your Majesty," General Tria greeted him when he rejoined her a few minutes later. Tendrils of black hair were coming out of her braid, and he recognized her look of intense focus from previous battles. "How does it look?"

"There are at least fifty harvesting machines, but no more than five hundred soldiers," Daymin said. "We'll leave General Vask to focus on the soldiers while we take down the machines. The Whitish aren't leaving many openings. It will be hard work, but if our enchantments do what they're meant to, we should be able to stop the towers."

They had drawn abreast of the Whitish army, so Daymin turned to face his army and called softly, "Archers and Flamespinners, to me!"

With a soft rustling of footsteps, the archers threaded their way forward, followed by a knot of Flamespinners. Daymin regretted sending Uncle Cal away—he could have used his leadership in what was sure to be a messy battle.

As the archers gathered around him, Daymin caught sight of different swatches of color marking the various enchantments on arrows and crossbow bolts. All were enchanted with the counterspell and a spell to cut easily through metal, while one set had been imbued with the freezing spell. Another set of arrows had been seeded with explosives designed to shatter the metal, while the crossbow bolts would attempt to do the same with force alone.

It had worked when Daymin's archers tried it on a pair of cooking pots. But the metal sides of the harvesting machines would be many times thicker.

"I want you to form teams of three," Daymin said quietly. "One archer with the freezing enchantment, one with a crossbow or a set of explosive arrows, and one Flamespinner in each team. Every team needs to claim one of the harvesting machines. I want all fifty targeted at once, as far as that is possible, because we'll never get a better chance to hit them from close range."

"What about the rest of your army?" General Tria asked.

"Stay back. We don't want to get in the way of the archers. As soon as the enchanted arrows are exhausted, any soldiers wielding a blade with the counterspell can approach the remaining machines and attempt to cut through the steel."

The archers started through the trees, encircling the Whitish army. As they stretched out along the fringes of the dead forest, the ancestor trees seemed to be dying faster than ever, forcing the archers to retreat. Daymin realized the trees were holding their roots still so they didn't trip up the archers, which made them easier targets; he swallowed against the lump in his throat.

At last they were in place. Daymin's own sword had been enchanted with the counterspell, so he fell into line behind the archers and Flamespinners. General Tria took up position beside him, her company filling in the spaces between trees, while Daymin's friends had long since fallen behind.

From the other side of the Whitish force, he could hear shouts from General Vask's troops. Many of the Whitish soldiers had turned to face their attackers, but the bulk of the army remained exactly where it had been, tightly packing the space between the harvesting machines.

Daymin drew in a ragged breath. Now that the battle was upon them, he realized they were facing far too many unknowns. For all he knew, his own troops could end up crushed beneath the weight of metal and roots.

He was conscious of the way his archers shifted uneasily around him, flinching every time a tree adjusted its branches. They couldn't stay here much longer, pinning the trees in place, or it would be a rout.

He kept hoping the mess of Whitish soldiers might thin or at least gravitate toward the opposite side of the battlefield, but when several minutes passed without any change in their positioning, he decided it was dangerous to wait any longer.

"Archers!" he called softly. "Ready!"

As the archers nearest to him raised their bows, the rest of the circle followed suit, though only a few were visible through the trees.

"First round! Shoot!" he said quietly.

A wave of arrows whirred toward the towers. Daymin could see two towers from his vantage; an arrow lodged into the side of one, while the other fell uselessly to the ground.

"Second round! Shoot!"

The next set of arrows and crossbow bolts flew after them. An arrow seeded with explosive struck the tower that had been hit by the previous arrow, and Daymin's nerves hummed as he tensed, watching.

As soon as the arrowhead buried itself in the tower, an explosion rang out, sending up a small cloud of smoke around the surface of the structure. The *boom* was echoed by many others around the circle.

When the smoke cleared, he could see a narrow gap in the side of the tower where the steel had cracked and warped.

It had worked.

"Flamespinners! Forward!"

Adrenaline thrummed through Daymin as the Flamespinners dashed around the archers and past the dead trees.

When a Flamespinner reached the tower with the cracked exterior, he sent flames shooting through the gap.

The tower swiveled, its driver realizing he was under attack, and the steel spike shot out in the direction of the Flamespinner.

The man threw himself to the side, narrowly avoiding the spike.

As he stumbled back, he tripped over a root and fell.

This time, the spike slammed into his chest.

Daymin wobbled where he stood, the air rushing from his lungs.

The Flamespinner collapsed backward, pinned beneath the crushing weight. Blood leaked from the hole in his Weavers' armor—which had been unable to stand up against the enchanted spike—and his eyes rolled up in his head.

"Look," General Tria said in an undertone. "It worked."

Tearing his eyes from the gruesome sight, Daymin realized smoke was now gushing from the slits at the top of the tower.

The spike did not retract, and Daymin heard panicked shouts echoing from within the tower.

Daymin blinked and wrenched himself from his daze. Uncle Cal and Dellik weren't here to take charge; he had to stay focused.

"Archers! Pair up and chase down any towers that haven't been breached! Flamespinners, find any weakness you can exploit!"

Since they were no longer trying to stay out of sight, the archers jogged closer to the towers. Daymin edged around a tree until he could see more of the battlefield. His archers were firing shot after shot, and from this distance, more had the power needed to sink into the metal.

Several of the crossbow bolts did manage to chip off a small chunk of brittle, frozen steel, and as the Flamespinners swept in behind the archers, smoke billowed from a dozen towers.

As the towers juddered to a halt, the remaining machines closed in their circle around the Whitish soldiers, leaving a strip of cleared earth ahead of them where the trees had been felled. Enormous logs lay on either side of the gash the Whitish had torn through the forest, stripped of leaves and branches, and Daymin realized belatedly that his archers approaching from the sides of the Whitish force would have been unable to hit their targets without climbing over the logs.

Into the space ahead of the machines flooded the Whitish, forcing the Flamespinners away from the remaining towers.

"Archers, keep shooting until your arrows are exhausted!" Daymin shouted. "Soldiers, with me! We need to force the Whitish back to clear a path for the Flamespinners!"

An answering roar rose from his troops.

Daymin jammed his helmet into place and drew his sword. With General Tria at his side, he charged from the band of dead trees into the cleared space before the harvesting machines.

With a great clash of metal and wood, the two armies collided.

The armored Whitish soldiers were like a wall—heavy, impenetrable—but Daymin's army had the advantage of numbers, and the soldiers at his back kept flooding into the space, pushing forward until the Whitish were forced back step by step.

It was too tight a space for Daymin to wield his sword, but he reached up and tore the nearest soldier's helmet off, exposing a mop of blond hair and a surprisingly youthful face.

General Tria lunged, a dagger in her hand, and buried the blade in the man's throat.

Daymin only had time for a brief lurch of unease before they were pushing forward again, the man's body dropping to the ground and disappearing beneath the mass of soldiers.

Soon they had forced the Whitish back to the line of burned-out harvesting machines. From here, Daymin could see what he hadn't before—General Vask's troops had managed to break through the ring of harvesting machines and were now fighting the Whitish soldiers inside the cleared circle. There were fewer Whitish left than Daymin had realized, which was why his army had pushed them back so easily.

The Flamespinners were edging their way forward again, and when they reached the front ranks of Daymin's army, they were nearly within reach of the functioning harvesting machines. The arrows had stopped flying, which must mean their supplies were exhausted, but each machine bristled with arrows, and

Daymin could see cracks and holes in the sides of most.

Daymin's army pushed closer, staying out of range of the deadly spikes, and the Flamespinners started sending bursts of flame toward any towers with weaknesses.

Before Daymin could tell if they had succeeded in setting the towers alight, a bone-jarring grinding sound started from the machine directly to Daymin's right. He had thought it destroyed, but on closer look, there was no sign of damage on the exterior.

"Back!" General Tria shouted, throwing Daymin out of its path.

He scrambled to regain his footing.

With alarming haste, the machine trundled forward, straight into the bulk of Daymin's army.

"Into the trees!" Daymin shouted.

Then the tower turned and aimed the spike directly at him.

Daymin threw himself into the ranks of his soldiers.

The spike grazed his leg with bruising force as it plunged to the ground, but it didn't tear through his armor.

"Back! Back!" Daymin shouted frantically, clawing his way deeper into the mass of soldiers.

Men and women were screaming and stampeding for the trees, but packed as densely as they were, they couldn't run fast enough to avoid the tower.

Eventually Daymin reached the first of the dead trees. While the rest of his army shoved their way past, he ducked behind the tree and waited for the flood to subside.

All the while, the machine creaked closer, until Daymin worried it was aiming directly for the tree he hid behind.

Then a Flamespinner dashed around the tree and stopped when she saw him. It was the same girl who had helped finish off the towers at Darkland Fort. She and her brother were always in the middle of things, it seemed.

She threw Daymin a quick look, not seeming to recognize him, and hauled herself onto a low branch of the dead tree.

"What are you doing?" Daymin called over the roar of the battle.

"Stopping that tower!"

She climbed higher, soon looping around to the opposite side of the tree, and Daymin edged around the tree to see what she was planning.

Daymin froze—the harvesting machine was heading directly toward them.

And it was only a few paces away.

The grinding, clanking sound was deafening, and as it moved closer, the machine began to split down the middle, preparing to fell the tree the Flamespinner was perched atop.

As the tower split, she lodged herself in a fork between two branches and sent flames rippling toward the interior.

Still the tower rolled closer.

"Watch out!" Daymin shouted.

The girl sent another burst of flames toward the tower, this time aimed at the platform where Daymin could see the soldier controlling the levers.

Then the tower engulfed the tree, with the girl still in its branches.

As it started to close, Daymin saw the flames catch on the wooden platform, smoke curling through the dead branches of the tree.

Everything else seemed to slow down around him. Daymin could think of nothing but the girl trapped in the blazing tower.

Daymin could hear when the blades began whacking the branches from the tree, and his stomach lurched. The young Flamespinner was right in the path of those wicked blades.

But the smoke from the slits at the top was growing thicker, and a moment later, the thwack of the blades subsided.

The tower was truly defeated this time.

Still Daymin couldn't move.

He pulled off his helmet, deaf to the fighting around him, and let his sword hang uselessly by his side. That girl was too young to fight at all, and now—

Daymin's eyes stung from the smoke. Abruptly he remembered the stories his mother had told of Cal's reckless daring in battle, when he had been a young boy determined to fight for the queen he loved.

Why is it always the Flamespinners who throw themselves into battle so rashly?

Again Daymin regretted sending Uncle Cal away.

Then, with a metallic twang, a panel at the base of the harvesting machine popped out of place.

Daymin's heart lurched into his throat.

The Flamespinner stumbled from the tower, coughing violently, her clothes and hair black with soot.

Then she lifted her eyes to Daymin and grinned.

56

King Shonameeko

The battle ended quickly after that.

While Daymin's forces had fled the harvesting machine, General Vask's troops had finished off the last of the Whitish soldiers. More than half of the towers had fallen still, and without the Whitish soldiers to push Daymin's army back, his Flamespinners were able to set the remaining towers alight without trouble. A handful had not been compromised by the arrows, but Daymin's soldiers swarmed these and sliced through the metal while the spikes plunged futilely into the masses of bodies.

At last the battlefield fell still. The machines stood motionless, some unblemished, others badly charred, while the bodies of fallen soldiers littered the cleared ground.

Daymin stepped into the middle of the empty battlefield, looking around at the skeletal trees backed by dense greenery, the soldiers clustered around their bases.

Then the Allakoash started emerging from the forest.

First came Renok and Lalaysha and the woman who had guided them to the battlefield, but they were soon joined by dozens of others.

"King Shonameeko promised to come to our aid," Lalaysha said, stepping to Daymin's side. "And he did not forsake his promise. Not even after we left Baylore. Our trees guarded his people for many years, and now his army has defeated the last of the Whitish machines and saved our forest. Maybe this is the start of a true alliance between Itreans and Allakoash."

Hushed voices rose from the Allakoash, many of them watching Daymin with a kind of reverence that made him uncomfortable.

Then Lalaysha knelt before him, followed by Renok. Soon all the Allakoash were kneeling, heads bowed.

Daymin pulled Lalaysha to her feet, stomach squirming at this show of loyalty. "I am no king of yours," he said. "But I was born in this forest, and you are my people as much as the Itreans. If we can salvage any fragment of this continent after the war, I hope our people can enter a new age of cooperation and trust."

An old man with a deeply-lined face rose and approached Daymin.

"In repayment of this service you have done us, your people are welcome to seek refuge in the Wandering Woods."

The words tore at Daymin. He had no idea what his people would find in the Icebraid Peaks, but it was too late to turn from that course. If he were to change his mind now, it would take many more spans for the evacuees to reach the Wandering Woods, giving the Whitish time to track them down and slaughter them.

462

Plagues. He wished this had been an option from the start.

"I thank you for your generosity," Daymin said. "My people have chosen another refuge for now, but we will remember your kind offer."

General Vask and General Tria were stumping over to Daymin, and as they approached, the Allakoash backed away, melting into the woods once more.

"Your Majesty," General Vask said shortly. "What are your orders?"

"We'll return to our camp at the edge of the forest," Daymin said. "General Vask, stay back with a handful of soldiers to make sure the harvesting machines are thoroughly destroyed. General Tria, organize the rest of my troops to move out of the woods. We'll follow the cleared path through the trees."

As the generals moved off to organize his army, Daymin picked his way around the debris of the battlefield, heading toward the gash the Whitish had carved through the forest. It seemed like a highway designed for giants, as wide as a city block and lined by the enormous felled trees, and Daymin wondered what it would take for the woods to heal from such a wound.

At first he walked alone, leaving the clamor of his army behind. The air hung with the smell of disturbed earth, while the ground underfoot was unusually barren, the nearby roots withdrawn in their futile attempt to escape the harvesting machines.

A distant bird trilled, and Daymin realized the woods had been unnaturally silent.

Little by little, more birds took up the chorus, while the living trees beyond the rows of skeletal trunks rustled softly as they shifted in place.

When he looked back to see whether his army was following, Daymin caught sight of the young Flamespinner at the front of his troops. He stopped and waited for her; when she caught him watching her, she grinned.

"Who are you?" Daymin asked, falling into step beside her. "You're too young to be at war, yet you're always in the middle of things."

"I'm not that young," she said defiantly. "I'm seventeen. More than old enough to serve."

"And your name?"

"Veesha, Your Majesty."

"Did you and your brother live in the Market District, then?"

"We did. I always dreamed of fighting for Queen Kalleah, but my parents said I wouldn't be allowed to join the Makhori at the palace until I was twenty."

Daymin laughed shortly. "That doesn't seem to have stopped you from fighting."

She gave him a sly smile. "Well, you put out the call for Flamespinners to join your army. It was all the excuse we needed."

They walked in silence for another minute. On top of everything else, Daymin was impressed that she was willing to speak to him so informally.

At last he said, "When we rejoin the refugees, I want you to train under Prince Calden. I think he'll find you a true asset to our army."

She looked at him in surprise. "Won't we be done fighting when we reach the Icebraid Peaks?"

"No. I'm afraid not. This war is just beginning."

57

The Temple of Totoleon

T he Temple of Totoleon was nothing like what Kalleah had expected.

Built atop a hill, the temple was a round, domed structure open to the elements, the roof supported by stone pillars. A statue of Totoleon—depicted as a strong bearded man casting a handful of stars into the sky—stood on a plinth at the center of the temple, and the ceiling was painted a deep blue speckled with constellations of gold stars.

A door in the hillside led to a series of rooms beneath the temple, including a number of workshops where cartographers mapped the earth. Some rooms were filled with maps, while others were domed and painted with phases of the moon or star charts.

There were living quarters as well, more than Kalleah would have expected, and a simple dining room where the devotees of Totoleon congregated for meals.

When Kalleah and her companions had first arrived, they had been shown to a set of rooms including a washroom where she and Baridya cleaned off their face paint.

Kalleah had been allocated a secluded room in the depths of the living quarters, which confirmed her suspicions that at least some of these people knew who she was, and in the morning they were given a simple breakfast before their hosts led them up to the temple.

Several small groups of people sat together beneath the domed roof, many perched on the edge of the steps leading down from the temple, and the space glowed a pale gold in the early morning light.

"I still don't trust them," Mellicante hissed under her breath when they were left alone beside the statue.

"Not all religion is evil," Baridya said, in a tone that said this was an argument they'd had before.

"Yes, but how do they know who we are?"

"They've saved us more than once," Kalleah said. "We ought to at least give them a chance."

Then she and her friends fell silent, because a robed man who reminded her uncomfortably of the Truthbringers was approaching. He was balding, his hair growing in white tufts over his ears, and his robe was at least a deep blue rather than the white of the Truthbringers.

Plagues, would she never be able to put that old fear behind her?

"Welcome," he said, his voice deep and resonant.

"Thank you," Kalleah said. She wasn't sure if he was part of the group that had brought her here, so she let him take the lead.

"You are Itreans?"

"Yes," Kalleah said warily.

"Then I must assume you are unfamiliar with the Gods of Light. May I introduce you to our benevolent patrons?"

This time it was Baridya who spoke up. "Please."

The man smiled warmly at Baridya. "Have you seen a Temple of Totoleon before?"

"No," Baridya said, "but I visited the Temple of Aurum when I was last in Desden."

Kalleah shot her a surprised look. They had captured Desden from the Whitish a couple spans back, and she hadn't realized Baridya had taken the opportunity to visit a temple of the Nine.

"I know the one you speak of," the man said. "A magnificent sight, is it not?"

"It is," Baridya said.

The priest turned back to Kalleah. "I can imagine your experience with Varonites has tainted your impression of religion in the Kinship Thrones. They can be quite forceful."

Kalleah made a noncommittal sound.

"I assure you, the Gods of Light are nothing like Varos. Our gods are positive forces in the world, encouraging scholarship, exploration, charity, and trade. They act as patrons to those who take up their pursuits, and the donations we receive are put toward furthering those causes, as a way of showing our devotion. The Gods of Light inspire us and encourage our curiosity and generosity. Without them, the world would be a grimmer place."

Kalleah could not help herself. "Before the Whitish interfered, Itrea was a wonderful place, even without the

467

influence of any gods."

"And how quickly were they turned astray by the influence of the Varonites sent by High King Warrow? People crave the guidance of a higher power. Your people feel a void in their lives, whether consciously or not, and seek to fill it with the first god they happen upon, however unjust."

Kalleah had just opened her mouth to argue when the priest waved a hand dismissively, giving her a sheepish smile. "Forgive me. My tongue has run away with itself. I am not aiming to convert you, nor to criticize your people. I simply wished to make the point that Dardensfell and Kohlmarsh are still devoted to the Gods of Light, on the whole, and our devotion is a very positive thing. Unlike in Whitland, where religion has become a twisted justification for endless power struggles and oppression."

"I did see evidence of much greater liberties in the Twin Cities," Kalleah admitted. "Tempered by the influence of the Lord's Men, of course."

The priest bowed his head, his expression grave. "We have all suffered greatly at their hands, and I am ashamed that they shaped your first impression of the Twin Cities. In the past, I am told we compared favorably with the Cheltish ports."

"And…were you involved with the group that brought us here?" Kalleah asked.

Now the priest lifted his head to meet her gaze, his eyes twinkling with humor. "Of course I was, Queen Kalleah. We have long awaited your coming."

A jolt of surprise went through her. "How do you know who I am?"

"We are well connected, Your Majesty. Our agent in

Eidervell saw your fleet turn east after the attack, and an ally in Stragmouth spotted that same fleet pulling into the harbor at the river mouth."

Kalleah took a moment to wrap her head around that. They must have some form of magical communication—there was no other way for word to have traveled across the mountains faster than her fleet had sailed. Were they using linked books, like the Whitish, or did they have some new invention her people had yet to discover?

And why had they followed her progress so closely?

Just then, Kalleah noticed something she had overlooked before. From his neck hung a chain with a diamond-shaped metal pendant engraved with stars, just like the one Baridya had described.

"You speak of agents—you are more than just devotees of Totoleon, are you not?"

His smile grew. "Of course. This temple is the base of the Prophet's Eyes in Dardensfell."

"The Prophet's Eyes?" Baridya asked, frowning. "I've never heard of them."

"You would not have heard of us. We operate in secret. Ours is a vast network of spies and devotees of Totoleon and other followers, spread across the Kinship Thrones as we work to destabilize Whitland."

"Why?" Kalleah asked.

The priest gave her a funny smile. "Has it occurred to you that your people are not the only ones suffering from Whitish oppression? The Kinship Thrones would be a better place if the Whitish high throne ceased to exist."

"And why should we trust you?" Leoth asked. He stepped

up beside Kalleah, his shoulder brushing against hers, and Kalleah saw in him the man she loved for the first time in many quarters.

"Our agents were protecting you throughout your stay in the Twin Cities," the priest said. "Bennett in particular. They followed their assignment loyally without being informed who they were guarding."

Kalleah remembered the distasteful way Bennett had spoken of Queen Kalleah—she could easily believe he had not known her identity.

"How are you plotting to overthrow Whitland, then?" Mellicante asked, her voice dry with skepticism.

"It is a complicated web many years in the making, and we will have plenty of time to explain its intricacies. For now, suffice it to say the conspiracy is headquartered at the Borderlands Academy, where we draw followers from all nationalities into our ranks. Ever since your attack in Eidervell, we realized your aims align perfectly with ours. If you would agree to work with us, we could liberate both continents simultaneously."

Kalleah looked sideways at her friends. Baridya's face shone with hope, while Leoth and Mellicante still looked skeptical.

"Give us time to think about it," Kalleah said. "We need to know more about what our involvement would entail before we commit."

"Of course," the priest said with a warm smile. "And in the meantime, I hope you will partake of our hospitality. Please explore the complex and speak to whomever you wish. We are all Prophet's Eyes, and all of our followers here are now aware of your identity."

"Thank you," Kalleah said. "We will."

Before she did anything else, she wanted to find Bennett. His straightforward manner would be easier to believe than the warm, kind, welcoming air of this priest who still reminded her too painfully of the Truthbringers.

58

Dreams of Victory

Once Daymin's army reached the camp they had left standing, the wary silence among his troops was replaced by a celebratory atmosphere.

They had, for the first time in this war, achieved a victory that meant something. With no harvesting machines remaining, and no captive Makhori on hand to create more, the forest was safe from any further large-scale assault.

And judging by the way the Whitish had captured Daymin's supply wagons long before they attacked the bulk of his army, the closure of the forest road had significantly impacted the Whitish army's ability to feed itself.

Maybe, if the forest held strong, the Whitish army's grip on Itrea would weaken.

For the first time ever, Daymin wondered if there might be a path toward re-taking Itrea someday.

It was a slim chance, but if the Whitish captured Baylore

and ate their way through the dregs of the city's dry stores, and if the troops from Chelt remained stranded on the Larkhaven coast, a weakened enemy might fall before a well-timed assault.

Daymin watched his army celebrate as if from a great distance, wrapped in thought. When he had first taken the throne, he would never have contemplated such a possibility.

But he was a warlord now. He had fought many battles now, testing the strength of the Whitish in different scenarios, and he knew how to lead his troops.

Besides, he had already lost everything. What was one more gamble compared to the decision he had made to abandon Baylore?

After dinner, his friends approached him, their smiles visible in the intermittent network of crystals glowing around camp.

"You don't seem to be reveling in our great victory," Zahira said.

"I've been thinking."

"About?"

He sighed. "Wishes and dreams."

"How specific," Zahira said drily.

Daymin gave her a wry smile. "It's foolish. We fought well today, and it's given me hope for the future for the first time in spans."

"We brought the towers down more effectively than I'd expected," Tarak said. "Do you think this means Baylore might hold?"

Daymin felt a pang at the thought of Idorii still biding his time in that doomed city. "I don't know. The Flamespinners were what finished the towers off every time, and at the city wall,

473

they'll have a hard time getting within range. Especially with so few of them spread around the entire perimeter." He looked at Tarak curiously. "You don't think I made a mistake, abandoning Baylore, do you?"

Tarak's mouth twisted. "Of course not. Still, I can't help but hope. If we lose Baylore, it feels like we've lost our whole reason for fighting. What are we without a city to our name?"

"Refugees," Daymin said. "That's how we came to Itrea in the first place, and that's how we'll continue forward from here."

"Maybe we can build a great city in the woods," Zahira said, glancing sideways at Lalaysha.

"Maybe," Lalaysha said. "If we can find a way to feed ourselves."

Daymin's thoughts were still tangled up in the logistics of marching from the mountains in one final, brutal assault against the weakened Whitish.

"I'm going to see if General Vask is willing to continue our lessons," he said abruptly.

"We'll join you, then," Zahira said.

So they threaded their way through camp to find the general, who was eating alone, his eyes on the nearby forest border.

They trained until late that night, until the revelry had subsided and most of the Weavers' crystals had been extinguished, until their muscles ached and sweat dripped in their eyes. Finally, finally, Daymin could tell he was improving.

And if he became a mighty enough warrior, he dared to hope his people would follow him willingly into that final, desperate battle to end all battles.

* * *

The next morning dawned grey and cold. Moisture hung in the air, eating its way through Daymin's layers, the humidity a foreign sensation. Baylore was never this damp.

At least the rain held off while his army packed up camp. Daymin worked in silence, his muscles burning from their late-night sword practice, his mind still spinning with possibilities. Nothing seemed as easy as it had last night, when he had been driven by that burst of triumphant optimism, yet the hope was still there, coloring his every thought.

His friends packed up quietly by his side, Tarak and Zahira exchanging the occasional brief word. Lalaysha kept glancing up at Daymin with a smile, and when his army moved out, she fell into pace beside him and said in Allakoash, "I still can't believe we defeated the towers so easily."

"I'm glad my army is good for something," Daymin said drily.

Then it started to rain. Daymin's Weaver's armor was enchanted to keep out the rain, but he had lost his hooded oilskin cloak in the river crossing, so his hair quickly grew drenched. The cold water ran down the back of his neck; he would be chilled through as soon as they stopped moving.

He had just opened his mouth to ask his friends how they were faring when he heard a chorus of groaning wood from behind.

Daymin whirled.

The forest border was a league behind them, individual trees blurring to a wall of green. But even from here, he could see leaves rustling as though a fierce wind had swept through.

His army pressed forward, forcing him a few steps back, but as the creaking sound grew louder, they came to a halt.

"What is it?" Lalaysha whispered.

Then he saw it—the leaves all along the border were yellowing, shaking violently as the branches writhed. Leaves began to drop off, leaving the branches bare.

One by one, the trees stopped moving. Soon the nearby forest border was nothing but a row of skeletal trees.

Further back, the forest was still creaking and groaning in distress. Trees bulged around either side of the line of dead trunks, trying to escape whatever was killing them, but even as their roots rippled forward, these trees died as well. The band of lifeless trees grew wider and wider, until Daymin could see no greenery behind their ranks.

Daymin stood frozen in place, unable to comprehend what he was seeing. Horror sank its claws into his chest, and his breathing grew ragged.

"The trebuchets," Tarak breathed.

It took a moment for the word to register in his panicked brain.

Then the truth clicked into place.

The Whitish trebuchets had scattered poison over the forest, dousing the trees as far as the throwing arms could reach. And the poison had needed water to seep into the roots and kill the trees.

It was destruction on a scale he had never seen before. Daymin's heart twisted as he watched the forest die, dozens of trees at a time, the creaking of wood and the screams of the Allakoash who had kept watch in the now-barren trees building into a single discordant cry of anguish.

He had never felt so helpless.

There was no enemy to defeat, no way to counteract the poison.

His optimism from the previous night now seemed a cruel irony.

"Can you stop the rain?" Lalaysha asked, voice shaky.

Her words broke through Daymin's horrified stupor. Cloudmages—he had Cloudmages.

With a terse nod at Lalaysha, Daymin pushed his way through to the edge of his army, where he broke into a run.

"Cloudmages!" he shouted. "Cloudmages, to me!"

Eventually a knot of Cloudmages, many of them familiar from the battle of Darkland Fort, extracted themselves from his troops.

"Can you stop this?" Daymin asked frantically.

"Not fast enough to help, Your Majesty," a white-haired man said gravely. "But we will do what we can."

Daymin stood watching for a few minutes, worrying at the hilt of his sword; when he sensed his presence was making the Cloudmages nervous, he retreated.

From behind, the ancestor trees were still creaking in anguish, lashing out with their branches and roots as they tried to escape their fate. And beneath the smell of wet earth, Daymin caught something acrid, something unnatural. The poison.

The line of dead trees now stretched several leagues in either direction along the forest border, and Daymin could only guess how far back the damage went. He had seen the remains of a trebuchet in the forest on his way out, following the scar of downed trees, so it must have penetrated deep into the woods before the ancestor trees managed to bring it down.

Little by little, the rain eased and the clouds tattered to reveal fragments of blue sky.

But it was too late. The damage had been done.

Daymin could do nothing but watch as the haze of rain parted to show the dead trees standing starker than ever. The rain had soaked his hair and seeped down the back of his coat, but he did not notice the discomfort. All he had fought for was crumbling away.

Then, from the north, he heard a resurgence of the rumbling, creaking sound of moving trees.

Far past the line of dead trunks, he saw the forest border bulging outward. The trees moved much slower when surrounded by such great numbers, so it was like watching honey spill from a jar.

Gradually the trees flooded the plains north of Daymin's army, engulfing the dead trees, roots rippling forward and punching through the grasses as the forest crept westward.

Daymin watched with a mixture of awe and confusion.

What were the trees doing?

At first he had thought they were closing in around the dead section of forest, preventing the Whitish from harvesting the wood, but the border was bulging further and further west.

Finally he spotted a group of Allakoash jogging from the dead trees toward Daymin's army. Daymin hastened over to meet them, Lalaysha at his heels.

"What are they doing?" he called in Allakoash as soon as they were within earshot.

No one spoke until the group was right before him. Slowing to a halt, a young man said, "The trees are marching on Twenty-League Town. The Whitish will taste our revenge, and they will never forget it."

Daymin's stomach swooped with something akin to hope. If the ancestor trees could bring down Twenty-League Town, his army had a real chance of taking back Itrea.

"Then we will march beside you," he said. "Let us hope this is the last time our people must go to war together."

59

The Prophet's Eyes

While she was grateful for the hospitality extended to her at the Temple of Totoleon, Kalleah felt she was always within earshot of some helpful, smiling priest or finely-dressed gentleman thief.

So, when she encountered Mellicante in the hallway on the way to an early breakfast one morning, they changed direction by unspoken agreement and instead left the complex to perch on a rock on the hillside. The morning air was brisk, and Kalleah drew her coat tighter about her shoulders, while Mellicante's hair—once cropped short but now growing into her eyes—was tossed about haphazardly in the breeze.

"Do you trust them?" Kalleah asked, resting her elbows on her knees and gazing in the direction of the Twin Cities.

Mellicante snorted. "Of course not. But if their aims align with ours, why shouldn't we work alongside them?"

"And what of their beliefs?"

"The vast majority of the Kinship Thrones follows a religion," Mellicante said. "If we were hoping to find atheistic followers, we would be searching for a very long time."

They were quiet for a long moment. Mellicante was a firm skeptic, so her willingness to go along with the Prophet's Eyes put some of Kalleah's doubts at ease.

"I'm just worried for the boys," Mellicante said eventually. She too was looking back toward the Twin Cities, where the smoke rising from the chimneys was whipped away by the breeze and small fishing craft bobbed in the steely water. "I hope Desh is with them."

Kalleah felt a twinge of guilt. She wished she had not brought them into the Twin Cities at all, young and inexperienced as they were. "They'll make their way well enough," she said bracingly, trying to convince herself as much as Mellicante. "We were the reason they were in danger, and now we're gone…"

Mellicante did not reply. She pushed her hair impatiently out of her eyes and leaned forward, squinting at something in the tall grasses outside Darrenmark; a moment later, Kalleah spotted the figure making its way toward the temple, following no path she could see.

"We should go inside," Mellicante said tersely.

Kalleah hesitated. There was something familiar about his gait. And indeed, a few minutes later, she recognized him.

"That's Bennett," she said.

"I've seen him before," Mellicante said. "Lingering around the waterfront."

"He was staying at The Lost Sailor," Kalleah said, though she suspected that had merely been a pretense to keep watch on her. "And he helped rescue us from the Lord's Men. He's the one I wanted to speak to."

"Do you want me here?" Mellicante asked.

"It might be easier if you weren't. He spoke very plainly to me in the past—criticizing my attack against Eidervell, not knowing to whom he spoke—and I would like to hear that same forthright opinion on the Prophet's Eyes."

"Look after yourself, then." Mellicante rose stiffly and watched the approaching figure for another moment before climbing back up the hill toward the temple.

Kalleah watched Bennett as he drew closer, gratitude that he had saved her from the Lord's Men warring with disgust for the way he had spoken of her attack on Eidervell. Yet soon her attention was drawn by the landscape sweeping out before her. Rays of sun penetrated the sheets of cloud, throwing pale golden light on the distant Andalls, and the Twin Cities lay half in shadow, half in light. The cities were more magnificent from a distance, Darrenmark in particular. Away from the stench of the waterfront and the closed-in feel of the streets, Kalleah could appreciate the delicate palace spires rising above the jumble of stone buildings.

When Bennett strode up to her, his footsteps rustling through the tall grasses, Kalleah gave him a distant smile, her thoughts still on the complexity and unexpected beauty of the Kinship Thrones. She had once dismissed this continent and its people out of hand—aside from those who would serve as trade partners—but now she wondered if the loss of meaningful contact between the two continents had been to Itrea's detriment as much as the Kinship Thrones'.

"So," Bennett said, a smile quirking up one side of his lips.

"Am I to address you as Your Majesty now?"

"Call me what you wish," Kalleah said. "I have questions for you, and I don't want you to dilute your answers with unnecessary formality."

"As you wish." He removed his hat and bowed with a flourish. "I gathered you weren't one to stand on ceremony."

"No." Kalleah frowned at him. "Why did the leaders of your little group choose not to share my identity with you?"

"They didn't want word slipping out before we brought you safely to the temple," Bennett said. "Besides, I'm a thief. As much as they rely on me, they don't place their full trust in me."

"Why work with a thief at all?"

Bennett dropped onto the rock beside Kalleah, draping his arms over his knees. The feather of his hat wobbled against the long grass. "The core members of the Prophet's Eyes come from the Borderlands Academy, but wherever they base themselves, they recruit thieves and smugglers and assassins."

"Why not reputable gentlemen?"

Bennett laughed shortly. "They are the ones who join us at the Borderlands Academy. But we reprobates serve a particular purpose. I move in many influential circles in Darrenmark, all without a residence or title for my enemies to trace back to me. As do many smugglers who conduct business with the wealthiest of households."

He paused, and Kalleah was suddenly, uncomfortably aware of how close he sat.

"I do apologize for my earlier comments about your attack on Eidervell," he said.

"It was honest," Kalleah said. "I appreciate that, even if it was offensive."

Bennett grimaced. "You can't blame me, can you? Totoleon's teachings tell us that magic is not something to be reviled, but even he warns us to be wary of the forbidden races."

"Because we are the original children of sin?" Kalleah said, recalling their previous conversation.

"Yes."

It was still so much nonsense to her, but she didn't want to come across as blunt and dismissive. "Well, in that case, you are to be commended for finding the courage to sit beside me. Especially since you know what I am capable of." She was unable to keep a note of sarcasm from her tone.

The corner of Bennett's mouth tightened; he must have forgotten the deadliness of her power.

"Forget about it. Please. I am no danger to you. I want to know more about Totoleon and the Prophet's Eyes, especially if they make allowances for magic. How did this movement begin?"

"Did they tell you about the Prophet?" he asked.

"Not specifically, no."

"He's the one who will lead us away from the mess we've become," Bennett said, and Kalleah was surprised to see a light of fanaticism in his eyes. "This whole movement started when the Prophet had a vision of Totoleon, the God of Stars. The vision showed him locked away in an underground pit, cut off from the light, unable to guide the Kinship Thrones. It was a message from the Nine—a message that Whitland has lost its way and is dragging the other kingdoms down with it."

Bennett's expression turned grim. "We believe Varos is a false god. A pretender. The original Nine were honorable gods, and when Varos helped destroy them, he turned the Kinship

Thrones to evil."

"If the gods were destroyed, how could Totoleon still be sending visions to this Prophet?" Kalleah couldn't help asking.

"It was a figure of speech," Bennett said. "Gods can't be killed, but the Nine are rendered impotent as long as Varos holds Whitland in his sway. The Prophet discovered that their fall from power coincided with the departure of Makhori from the Kinship Thrones, which means the two are connected. We believe the Nine depended on magic to guide the Kinship Thrones. When Varos forced out all magic, the balance was thrown off."

"How do you intend to rectify matters?" Kalleah asked.

"We're working on that," Bennett said. "We have a source of magic to tap, and our agents are stationed at nearly every court in the Kinship Thrones to—ah—guide the next stages of our plan."

Kalleah had a feeling he was concealing something, but she didn't understand their plans well enough to probe deeper.

"And how do you expect me to help you?" she asked.

"We need to weaken Whitland if we want to restore the balance between the Kinship Thrones," Bennett said. "Our plans only go so far. While High King Edreon maintains a fierce grasp on the continent, Varos may still be able to fight back against the Nine, even after we make our move. That's where you come in. If you raise an army strong enough to challenge Whitland, both of our causes will benefit."

"And where do you expect me to find such an army?" Kalleah asked.

"You stormed Eidervell with a significant force, didn't you? Can you not raise another army in the same manner?"

Kalleah frowned at him. "Perhaps, if I spend the next couple spans sailing back around the coast to Chelt and manage to arrive before King Edreon tightens his grasp on the remaining cities. And if I can convince those who have not been drafted that this maneuver aligns with their own aims."

"Does it not?"

Kalleah thought of the women who had surrendered to King Edreon, whose husbands and sons and brothers were stationed in Itrea at the High King's mercy. They had joined her in attacking Eidervell because they had thought it would weaken the Whitish hold on Chelt.

But she had failed. She had defeated only a small force of Whitish, and Eidervell was so vast that she had set a mere fraction of it aflame. And the women who had followed her were now under King Edreon's thumb.

She did not expect another civilian army to try the same reckless maneuver.

"No," she said at last. "It doesn't."

Yet as she rose from her perch on the rock and started up the hill, the grasses catching at her boots, her mind was swirling with possibilities.

60

A River of Trees

All through that day and the days that followed, the trees flowed past, forming an undulating river north and south of Daymin's army. The sensation of being engulfed by forest was very similar to what Daymin's army had experienced while traveling to Darkland Fort, only on a much larger scale, with trees stretching horizon to horizon.

Daymin kept to himself, caught between horror at what the Whitish had done to the forest and a twisted sort of gratitude that their actions had finally spurred the Wandering Woods to action. It would benefit the Allakoash as much as the Itreans if their peoples drove the Whitish from the continent, and if that was the result of this great march, the casualties might be justified.

But he would never say that out loud. It would feed the belief the Itreans had held all along that the trees were nothing but tools to be used as they saw fit.

They passed just north of Valleywall, the trees widening their corridor to leave the town unharmed, and two days later they came within sight of the river north of Pelek. The water shone golden in the late afternoon sun, the banks choked with willows north of the main road.

Daymin would need to lead his army north to the crossing near Ashton—that, or negotiate passage in the branches of the ancestor trees—but the trees seemed unaware of this. Instead they flowed down to the banks of the Elygian River, trapping Daymin's army against the reedy growth.

Daymin pushed his way to the edge of his forces, the ground soft underfoot, searching for someone who could direct the ancestor trees. But the Allakoash he spotted seemed no more than observers to the vengeful fury of the trees, clinging to branches like moss that had been swept along in the current.

Shouts rose from his own forces, and the mass of bodies pushed forward, jostling him. When he reached the edge of the column, he realized the trees had closed in around the back of his army, such an overwhelmingly dense forest bearing down on the river that it looked as though his soldiers were about to be shoved forward into the water.

Yet the trees were parting just in time, passing so close to his ranks that he could see soldiers staggering as roots forced the ground up underfoot.

Daymin could only stand and watch as the first of the trees slid their roots down the bank and started across the river, too tall and solid to be bent by the fierce current. He stopped above a steep section of the riverbank where cattails had overtaken willows, watching as the trunks were distorted by the clear water. Soon the roots stirred up the mud on the bottom of the river, turning the water brown. Through the columns of trunks, he could see where the spreading brown stain mingled with the clear current downstream before billowing outward to discolor the entire river from bank to bank.

"Orders, Your Majesty?" General Vask barked from behind Daymin.

Daymin turned. "We have to wait for the trees to cross. I can't command them to part for us."

Though General Vask saluted without question, Daymin heard muttering from his troops. The tight press of moving trees unnerved them.

And still the forest continued, unending. Even before the trees had begun plunging through the water, he had not been able to see how far they stretched to the north and south, and the wall of forest behind his army remained unbroken as hundreds of trees slid past. It almost seemed as though every ancestor tree in the Wandering Woods had lifted its roots to march inland.

Up ahead, Daymin heard a chorus of worried shouts from the Allakoash. Had the Whitish army looped back around to intercept them, instead of marching on Baylore?

Then he saw something that made his skin crawl.

Hundreds of paces beyond the river, the leaves on the first trees who had crossed were turning yellow and quaking as if in a stiff wind. He could only make out a few distant yellow branches rising above the nearby swath of forest, but as the forest slowed around his army, the blight spread closer.

"Are there Whitish archers ahead?" Daymin shouted in Allakoash, fear pricking at him.

He heard the question repeating itself through the treetops, until at last an answering shout came.

"No! The plains are empty!"

What could be killing the trees?

Then an icy knot of dread expanded in his chest.

The river was poisoned.

Daymin's mind was working too sluggishly to comprehend what he was seeing. How had the Whitish managed such a feat?

As the trees died, they formed a barrier holding back the rest of the forest, so no further trees could cross the river. Some tried to retreat but found their way blocked by the trees surrounding Daymin's army, and all the while the swath of dead trees spread eastward, closer and closer to the riverbank.

Soon the trees in the water were dying. As they drew up their roots in agony, several crashed over, pushed by the current, while others shuddered so violently they threw the Allakoash riding their branches into the water. The water churned with the flailing roots, and the fallen Allakoash quickly disappeared in the chaos.

From the bank where Daymin's army stood, trees reached out their branches to the people still clinging to the dying trees, and a handful were able to scramble over to safety. But more continued to plummet into the river.

Daymin's own army had fallen silent, all eyes riveted on the tragedy playing out before them. The river continued to churn as the last of the trees shed their leaves in a trail of yellow-brown. A great trunk close to where Daymin stood split in two with a hideous crack, and as the river flooded the hollow, the weight dragged the tree forward.

When the trunk crashed into the water, it sent up a frothy wave that splashed Daymin's boots.

Then, at last, the forest fell still.

Behind Daymin, the living forest stood motionless. Not a leaf rustled; all he could hear was the hush of breathing from his own army.

Ahead, stretching as far as he could see, dead trees clogged the river and stood in barren ranks on the opposite bank.

It was destruction on a scale he had never seen before. The trees doused in poison at the edge of the forest were a mere fraction of those that now stood lifeless before him. A crushing weight of responsibility bore down on him—even though the ancestor trees had moved of their own accord, he feared it was his entanglement with the Allakoash that had set off this chain of events.

Glancing back at his army, Daymin expected to find his soldiers impatient for direction, uncaring in the face of this tragedy.

Instead he saw his own despair mirrored on their faces. Whether it was sorrow for the Allakoash or for the way their last hope at saving Itrea had been snatched away, Daymin knew the two peoples were now bound together in their loss.

"So many trees," General Tria said softly.

"And to think we could have destroyed Twenty-League Town," Tarak said with a grimace.

"The Whitish knew what they risked in attacking the Wandering Woods," General Vask said gruffly. "We should have suspected they would take steps to prepare."

"But we didn't," Daymin said. He was still unable to move, unable to take charge. "We didn't, and now both of our peoples have lost everything. And soon Baylore will fall too."

61

An Army from the Mountains

After her conversation with Bennett, Kalleah couldn't put the idea of raising another army from her mind. With their influence in courts throughout the Kinship Thrones, the Prophet's Eyes gave any victory she achieved much farther-reaching consequences than before. She would not be trying to weaken Whitland to the point of withdrawing from Itrea this time; instead, she merely had to set things in motion before allowing the Prophet's Eyes to sweep in and enact their plans.

But where could she find a willing army?

She would not consider returning to Chelt, not after how badly the untrained women had fared in Eidervell. Besides, that would take too long. Itrea would have long since fallen by the time she sailed the long distance back to the Cheltish coast.

Were there other pockets of dissidents she might call upon?

The Prophet's Eyes had called a strategic meeting this

afternoon, and Kalleah had hoped to bring ideas of her own to the table. Instead, she would be digging for information as much as before.

When the time of the meeting arrived, Kalleah ventured belowground to find Leoth, Mellicante, and Baridya already waiting outside the conference room. The conference room door usually hung open, revealing an ever-changing group of people engaged in lively discussions over tea, but now it stood closed, voices echoing from beyond.

"Kalleah," Leoth said when she approached, giving her a sad smile. They had not found time to speak in true privacy since they had arrived at the Temple of Totoleon, and in the meantime were treating one another with a distant politeness that tore at her.

"Have you agreed to work with them, then?" Baridya asked with a hopeful look.

"To a point. Bennett said the Prophet's Eyes will do most of the work of stripping Whitland's power, but they first need an army to weaken his defenses."

Leoth's smile slid away as she spoke.

"And they expect you to raise that army?" Mellicante asked.

"Yes."

"I think it's exactly—" Baridya broke off when the door to the conference room swung open. The stale air that wafted from within was laced with lavender and chamomile, and indeed, a steaming pot of tea sat in the middle of the table.

The room was packed with unfamiliar faces. Kalleah recognized Bennett and Athamol, the priest who had first welcomed them to the temple, along with a few residents she regularly encountered in the corridors, but there were many others too—a handful of other devotees in dark blue robes; several well-dressed men and women who were either nobility or con artists of Bennett's caliber; and a number of solemn, scholarly men dressed in subdued tones.

"Thank you for joining us," Athamol said, nodding at Kalleah and her companions. "Please, be seated."

They sidled around the table to four vacant seats side by side. As they sat, another devotee poured tea and set it before them.

"To begin with," Athamol said, "you should be aware that everyone in this room knows your identity and your aims. We will speak openly here."

Beside Kalleah, Leoth took a sip of his tea and then quickly, discreetly swapped his cup for her own. Kalleah felt a rush of affection—he was acting as her taster. That brought her back to the first time she had allowed herself to trust him, when both had been poisoned at the same time and Leoth had saved her by discerning the taste of poison before she realized what was happening.

"Do you already have a population in mind that you could recruit to your cause, or are you looking for direction?" the priest was saying.

Kalleah blinked at him, returning to the present. "The only kingdom I know enough about to approach is Chelt, and the voyage there would take too long for that to be of use to Itrea. Besides, the last force I recruited from Chelt was quickly subdued."

"We agree," Athamol said. "And we believe the populations of Dardensfell and Kohlmarsh might prove an easier target."

Kalleah sat forward in interest. All along, she had been

hoping to find a few groups who might support her in Dardensfell, but Athamol made it sound as though there were enough who hated Whitish rule to form an entire army.

"Where?" Leoth asked. "Not in the Twin Cities, surely?"

"There are more who nurture anti-Whitish sentiment than you would imagine," Bennett said. "They were more vocal before the Lord's Men took charge."

Leoth shifted in his seat.

"But we have others we might approach as well," Athamol said. "In particular, the town of Brenvale."

"I've never heard of that," Baridya said. "Is it along the river, or…"

"In the mountains," Athamol said.

Baridya and Mellicante exchanged an excited glance.

"Brenvale is one of our largest towns, one that is unregistered in any Whitish records. They specialize in clockwork trinkets, including enchanted ones, and they are instrumental in our scheme to bring magic back to the Kinship Thrones."

"We saw some of their goods in Stragmouth," Kalleah said.

Athamol gave her a warm smile. "Very good. And there are other towns like them as well."

"What about in Kohlmarsh?" Mellicante asked.

"We are less acquainted with our potential allies there, but the marsh dwellers are thought to be descended from Makhori. Which means they could have a reason to sympathize with your cause."

"Do you have a map of the mountain settlements?" Kalleah asked. Ever since Hanna had first mentioned the possible existence of a string of hidden settlements in the Andalls, she had been intrigued.

A few of the devotees shared uncomfortable looks.

"If word of these towns got out, King Edreon could destroy them," said a finely-dressed man. "They are a significant source of our kingdom's wealth."

When Athamol continued to hesitate, Kalleah gave him a stern look. "You are asking a great deal of us. The least you can repay us with is your trust. Besides, if the Whitish manage to capture me, the information they will try to wrest from me will be on Itrea, not Dardensfell."

"Go," Athamol told one of the devotees. "Fetch the map."

They waited in tense silence until the man returned. Kalleah sipped at her tea, which was sweet and overwhelmingly floral, while Mellicante and Baridya seemed to be conversing in sidelong looks.

At last the priest returned with a rolled-up map under his arm. He circled the room to stand between Kalleah and Leoth before unfurling the map across the table.

Kalleah had never seen a map of any of the Kinship Thrones individually, and the level of detail was striking. She knew objectively that Dardensfell held close to the same landmass as the entire Itrean continent, but to see it displayed this way...

Where it was only fifty leagues from Baylore to the Icebraid Peaks, it was double that distance from the Twin Cities to the Andalls, and following the trade route from the northern coast at Stragmouth all the way to where it ended in Lostport, at the southern end of the continent, would be equivalent to starting fifty leagues north of Ambervale before traveling down to King's Port.

She remembered how daunting it had been to launch the trade route from Baylore to King's Port when she had first taken her throne. This was on a different scale altogether.

Of course, it helped that goods along this central trade route mainly traveled by water, but it would take a significant amount of time to make the journey nonetheless.

Then her friends drew her attention—Baridya and Leoth had stood to examine the map more closely, exclaiming over the string of mountain settlements Kalleah had not noticed at first.

There were more than she had expected—fourteen in all— and most lay near the sources of the rivers that fed the Lodren.

"There's Brenvale, then," Leoth said, pointing to a town that lay directly west of the Twin Cities. "Are there roads to these towns?"

"Not across the plains," Athamol said. "The roads begin at the foot of the mountains, but to find these, we follow rivers and streams. There are markers at their banks that only our people can decode."

"The journey would take a while," Kalleah said. "Not as long as sailing to Chelt, but similar."

"Not if you rode," Bennett said with a smile. "Our plains are home to the finest horses in the Kinship Thrones."

Kalleah chose not to mention the difficulties her power caused when riding, since Bennett had made it very clear what he thought of her magic.

"What sort of population do these towns have?" Kalleah asked. "How many would we need to visit to raise an army?"

"That depends on how large an army you would need to accomplish your aims," Athamol said.

Kalleah felt a spark of annoyance. "*My* aims? Are we not

raising an army on your behalf? I have no idea how large a military maneuver you will require to put your plans into action, seeing as you have not seen fit to describe the full extent of these plans. If you wanted me to bring Whitland to its knees, it seems there are plenty of princes and lords whose private armies are not fully occupied elsewhere, so we might need half the population of the Twin Cities to subdue these. But if you just needed me to execute a strike on one key location, especially one without fortifications, we can make do with a much smaller force."

"She makes a good point," Mellicante said sourly. "And what are we to expect from these mountain towns? Do the majority of their residents know how to fight, or are we recruiting only the small fraction that do?"

"That's right," Kalleah said. "We can't waste time training new recruits. Our attempts to train our Cheltish followers accomplished very little, especially when we were pitted against Whitish soldiers."

Chuckling, Athamol held up his hands. "Peace, my friends! We do have answers. First of all, you are correct. It would not be feasible to conquer all standing armies in Whitland with the force we can pull together. Which is why we need to make a smaller, more strategic strike to allow the other pieces of our plan to fall into place."

"Where?" Leoth asked.

"On Eidervell," Athamol said.

Kalleah and Leoth shared a grim look. Their previous attack on Eidervell had made it clear that this was a city too vast and sprawling to weaken without a considerable force.

"But you won't be alone," Athamol said. "King Edreon is

losing support among his own people. He wavers in his devotion to Varos, and as he does, others with a claim to the throne see their opportunity. Alone, neither force would be able to weaken Eidervell. But if we coordinate our attack to align with one of King Edreon's rivals, we will divide the city's defenses and cause enough chaos for our agents to make their move."

Kalleah did not like the idea of working with an army of religious zealots. Yet she said nothing.

"It sounds like a reasonable plan, provided the populations of your mountain towns are as willing to assist us as you make out," Leoth said. "But you must give us time to discuss the implications."

"Of course," Athamol said, inclining his head graciously.

Leoth drained his tea and rose, Kalleah and her friends following suit.

Instead of returning to their rooms, where all were still wary they might be overheard, they strode down the hall toward the door leading from the underground complex. As soon as they were outside, the light breeze whisking away the stale air of the tunnels, Kalleah turned to Mellicante and Baridya. "You were hardly able to restrain yourselves from objecting. What were you thinking? I know it would be a significant time commitment, but if the Prophet's Eyes are capable of toppling the Whitish Empire, is it not worth the risk?"

"I want to know why they're acting so guarded about their plans," Mellicante said darkly. "If they want us to spend the next several spans raising an army and attacking Whitland on their behalf, we need to know exactly how they intend to succeed. If they aren't capable of doing what they say they can, they're wasting our time."

"And if they do manage to dethrone King Edreon, who do they plan to put in power in his stead?" Baridya asked. "Their scheme might weaken Whitland, but it won't wipe the kingdom off the face of the continent. It will still be a significant player in the Kinship Thrones, and whoever takes over from King Edreon will determine what happens to Itrea."

"That's right," Mellicante said. "They might think it's easier to finish what King Edreon started in Itrea, since the troops are already over there."

Others emerged from the door behind them, talking and laughing, so Kalleah and her friends moved away from the entrance, looping around the hill until they were out of earshot once more.

With the grass rippling at their feet and the towers of Darrenmark rising in the distance, Leoth finally said, "What worries me most of all is their stance on magic. They claim they want magic to return to the Kinship Thrones, yet they haven't let on how they plan to achieve this. And I don't like the fact that they're willing to make use of your power while still believing the forbidden races are the source of all evil. Before we agree to their scheme, we need to know more."

"I agree," Kalleah said. That exact worry had plagued her from the beginning—without a clearer idea of how the Prophet's Eyes viewed magic, she could not be certain how her own people would fare with a different ruler on the high throne.

"And if they manage to satisfy our curiosity?" Mellicante said. "What then? Do we agree to go along with this madness?"

"I can't see any other way to destabilize Whitland," Kalleah said grimly. "We came in search of allies, and these are the ones we've found."

62

Ash in the Water

The bodies of a dozen Allakoash had been recovered from the river, and they lay on the bank, wrapped in blankets and hung with offerings. Other Allakoash had gravitated toward their dead, kneeling in a show of respect, some kissing the foreheads of their loved ones.

The ancestor trees had drawn back from the river, leaving a corridor in either direction for Daymin's army to pass, but none of his soldiers had retreated from their positions. A grim silence hung over his troops; all seemed aware, for the first time, of the magnitude of what the Allakoash had suffered.

Daymin stood motionless by the river, watching the last of the Allakoash who had been trapped on the opposite bank clamber their way through the branches. When he heard footsteps behind him, he expected to find Lalaysha or Renok approaching.

Turning, he instead saw an unfamiliar old Allakoash man

dressed in deerskin, his black hair hanging past his shoulders.

"What can we do for the trees?" he asked quietly. "I hate to think of the Whitish cutting them down and taking them for their own profit."

"We don't have the tools to cut them down ourselves," Daymin said, "but our Flamespinners could light those in the river on fire. They wouldn't be able to reach the trees on the opposite bank, so it would be more of a symbolic gesture than anything, but—"

"Please," the old man said earnestly. "We would be grateful for any send-off you could arrange."

It didn't feel right to shout orders, so Daymin made his way discreetly over to the nearest knot of Flamespinners and relayed the old man's request.

By the time the sun dropped below the horizon, everything was in place. Daymin stood back, not wanting to intrude, while the Allakoash farewelled their human dead. The bodies were laid in the hollows of ancestor trees, and as the trees sealed up around them, a haunting song rose from the forest, given voice by countless mourners.

"It's your turn now," Daymin told the Flamespinners, who filed toward the riverbank and lined up just before the reeds and willows overtook the grass.

When no one seemed willing to make the first move, Daymin approached Veesha and said, "Now. Do what you can."

She sent a bolt of fire shooting toward the nearest tree, the brightness searing across Daymin's vision in the deepening twilight.

The tree caught alight quicker than he had expected, the flames starting in the branches before eating their way toward the trunk.

As Veesha sent a second tongue of flame toward the next tree, the other Flamespinners joined in. Soon a whole line of trees was ablaze, the fires spreading north and south as the Flamespinners worked their way along the riverbank. The flames reflected off the water, the heat billowing in waves toward Daymin and the others standing near the bank. It was a great wall of fire, the flames leaping skyward, blazing like a beacon in the night. Daymin wondered belatedly if they would draw the Whitish toward them, but there was little the Whitish could do to worsen the damage already inflicted.

The crackle and roar of the hungry flames drowned out all thought, yet in the distance, Daymin could still hear the strains of song rising from the forest. The beautiful hopelessness of it sent shivers through him.

Still the fires grew, until Daymin's army was forced away from the riverbank, away from the heat and the falling sparks. He was taken back to the fires at New Savair, that dread inferno that had devoured the town and claimed Dellik's life.

There was something redemptive about the fires here. Instead of fighting, they were honoring the dead. Instead of destroying something living, they were trying to erase the harm the Whitish had done. Somehow, inexplicably, the gesture helped ease the guilt Daymin had carried ever since New Savair.

With the fires still roaring in his ears, Daymin did not hear anyone approaching until he felt a hand on his shoulder.

He turned, startled, and found himself face-to-face with Ilyoth, his foster mother.

Daymin drew in a sharp breath, his chest constricting. He had thought he would never see her again.

"Shonameeko," she said, smiling despite the tears that glistened on her cheeks.

"Mother." Daymin's voice was choked. He seized her in an embrace, surprised at how small and fragile she felt. Ilyoth gave a wet laugh and clutched Daymin close, pressing a kiss to his hair.

When he released her, Daymin found that his eyes were damp. He wiped them on his sleeve.

"Where is our tribe?" he asked. "Did they—"

She shook her head. "They're safe. We were further back, so we never made it close to the river."

Daymin let out a shaky breath. "Thank the ancestors."

"You brought your army to the forest," Ilyoth said. "When I heard you were coming, I couldn't believe it."

"Did you expect me to break my promise?" Daymin asked.

"Of course not. But I thought we were beyond that point. I thought, when we left Baylore, that was the end of our alliance."

"No. I'll never forget you and your people, as long as I live. Not that my army achieved much." He gave her a grim smile. "I might have been better off letting the harvesting machines do their worst."

"No," Ilyoth said firmly. "They wouldn't have stopped at cutting a path through the forest. They would have continued to threaten us as long as they remained standing, and we would have been forever cowering beneath their fury."

Daymin wasn't sure he agreed, but he was too wrung-out—too defeated—to argue. "And what happens next? Have you decided?"

"No. Once the fires burn down, we will make a plan. For

now…"

Daymin knew what she meant. He felt as though he was trapped in place, unable to think ahead, unable to strategize. Maybe when the raw ache of loss had worn off, he would come back to himself. But for now, he was adrift. There hardly seemed to be any point in continuing.

He and Ilyoth stood side by side as the fires blazed on, smoke choking the night sky. The last of the light faded, and still the flames lit the night, filling Daymin's vision with searing brilliance.

Soon he noticed that others had gravitated to his side. Tarak, Zahira, and Lalaysha stood close by, and there was Renok as well, and Veesha and General Vask. And beyond them stood row upon row of Allakoash and Itreans, the two peoples jumbled together, all watching solemnly with faces lit by the flames.

Daymin reached for Lalaysha's hand and gave it a squeeze, and Tarak laid a hand on his shoulder. Together they stood vigil as the trees crumbled to ash.

63

The Cathedral Bell

Idorii woke with an odd sensation in the pit of his stomach. He assumed it was worry for Daymin, since he hadn't heard from him in a while.

Ever since he had discovered the tunnels beneath Baylore University, he had spent his time racing around the city to round up all the books he could carry. It wasn't just books on Weavers' magic he was stashing away now, either. He had already emptied out all known private collections, along with the books stored aboveground in the University, and was now working his way through the vast repository of books in Baylore Cathedral.

Only the books in Baylore Palace remained untouched. He feared the holden monarchs would challenge him if he did anything to suggest he did not believe in Baylore's ability to weather the Whitish attack.

As Idorii came down the stairs from his grand bedchamber, his eyes fell upon the books still piled in the sitting room. He frowned. At least a hundred books remained in his manor; he was supposed to be narrowing them down to a number he could carry when he left Baylore, but he was having trouble with that.

Crossing to the kitchen, he hung a pot over the still-burning fire-twist and tossed in a handful of millet. Once his millet porridge was simmering, he returned to the sitting-room to scrutinize the collection. At least half of the books were on Weavers' magic, from the original piles he had been sorting through before he decided to hide the books, but now he had accrued volumes relating to Potioneers, Metalsmiths, Cloudmages, and Minstrels. He was trying to narrow down his collection based on the knowledge that would prove most useful in war, but he was not familiar enough with other disciplines to know what information was common knowledge and what might prove valuable.

Flipping through the books on Weavers' magic for the tenth time, Idorii set aside a few that were filled with fascinating, long-forgotten spells relating more to city construction than battle. By the time his porridge was ready, the sweet smell wafting from the kitchen, Idorii had managed to eliminate a dozen books.

He poured his watery porridge into a bowl and sank onto an armchair to eat, glowering at the books. This wasn't working.

Maybe he needed to start from scratch. Instead of eliminating, he should try packing his rucksack with only those books that seemed essential to the coming war.

As he ate, Idorii rolled up his sleeve and pressed at his tattoo, though he knew he would find nothing from Daymin. The same as yesterday, and the day before, and the day before that.

He didn't want to seem desperate. But he was truly starting

to worry.

Digging his pen from his pocket, he wrote, *Are you safe? I can't help but worry. And yes, I miss hearing from you.*

Ever since Zahira had written to him, and Daymin had told him that Zahira considered their means of communication romantic, Idorii had carried a warm, hopeful spark in his chest. Because it meant Daymin saw him in a romantic way. It was more than he could have hoped for.

How long ago was that now? Two quarters? Three? Time had begun to blur together.

When he received a reply just minutes later, giddy relief flooded him.

Idorii –

> *I'm so sorry for the silence these past days! I can't believe I haven't written since before we joined the battle in the woods.*
>
> *We have suffered a great tragedy—well, the Allakoash more than us—and we are still in shock. We defeated the harvesting machines more readily than any of us had expected, and we assumed it a victory, until a rainstorm activated the poison the Whitish had scattered over the forest. A vast swath of trees died, and thousands upon thousands more rose up in revenge.*
>
> *We were marching toward Twenty-League Town, ready to deal a blow that might have changed the course of the war, when the trees crossing the Elygian River died one after another. The river must have been poisoned as well. This happened yesterday, and last night we stayed up late to send off the dead. I am still reeling from the blow.*

To have hope again, and then to lose it as swiftly as it came…well, I can hardly see any point in continuing.

Yours,
Daymin

As he read, Idorii's joy at receiving word from Daymin slipped away. In its place, an ache clawed its way into his chest; the distance between them had never felt so unsurmountable. He wanted nothing more than to take Daymin into his arms and hold him. Nothing he could say would be enough to ease such a burden.

Daymin –

I don't know what to say. I wish you were not facing this tragedy alone. If you aren't ready to write to me now, don't feel obliged.

However, you are not allowed to give up until you rejoin the evacuees in the mountains. I am counting on seeing you there.

Yours,
Idorii

Daymin's reply came almost at once.

I'll write again this evening. For now, I must figure out how to move forward from this disaster. Our camp is beginning to stir.

Idorii left Daymin's writing on his arm and rolled down his

sleeve. Even though the last message was short, the very presence of his familiar handwriting was a comfort.

Thank the cloudy gods Daymin was safe. But Idorii's mind was still whirling through the implications of the news he had received.

The harvesting machines were gone? Then the spells had worked. Which meant their defense of Baylore had a slim chance of succeeding, as long as they weren't overwhelmed by ordinary siege weapons on top of the enchanted towers.

But a large swath of the forest was now dead. What did this mean? Had the Whitish gained any strategic advantage here, or would they continue as before, with the forest weakened yet no longer vulnerable without the harvesting machines to menace it?

And Daymin had nearly marched on Twenty-League Town…

If he was camped by the Elygian River, he was only a few days from Baylore. The closest he had been since he had left all those spans ago.

Idorii ached to leave the city now and track Daymin's army down. He had expected to wait several more quarters before he saw Daymin again; the prospect of a quicker reunion was almost enough to make him forget everything else he was working on.

Almost.

As he let his gaze fall to the floor, the piles of books confronted him. So much precious knowledge—enough, perhaps, to give their armies a chance to reclaim Itrea someday far in the future.

If he could sort through these books and finish hiding the collection in Baylore Cathedral quickly enough, maybe he would be able to slip from the city and catch up with Daymin before his army had travelled too far.

Then again, Daymin could still be far south of Baylore. Just because he had been marching toward Twenty-League Town, it didn't mean he was planning to cross near Pelek. In fact, hadn't he said he burned that bridge during his campaign?

Idorii groaned. As much as he wanted to see Daymin again, it wasn't realistic. But either way, he felt a sense of urgency he hadn't before.

He finished off the last dregs of his porridge, though he was growing weary of the bland taste, and knelt to confront his books once more.

* * *

By midafternoon, Idorii had narrowed his essential books down to twenty. They barely fit in his pack, and he would be straining under the weight, but he could not bear to leave any others behind.

He was just returning from a trip to the University to drop off the last of the books he had chosen to leave behind when the cathedral bell started ringing.

Idorii's head snapped toward the noise. Did that mean…?

He broke into a jog toward the main square, bypassing his manor.

Nearing the square, he heard shouts and footsteps slapping against cobblestones. Then he came around the bend and saw a flood of people descending the palace steps. Most were uniformed soldiers, but there were members of court as well, including Ellarie and Falsted. From the cathedral tower high above, the bell continued to toll, the sound reverberating through the square.

Idorii was not the only one who had been drawn to the square from elsewhere in the city. A cluster of people stood near the doors of The Queen's Bed, including several he recognized as members of the gang advocating violence against the Whitish; they wore no armor, enchanted or otherwise, but they brandished fine-looking swords and bows.

Idorii jogged over toward the people milling around outside the inn.

"What's happening?" he called breathlessly as soon as he was within earshot.

"The Whitish are coming!" shouted a scarred man with a vicious grin.

Though he had known as soon as he heard the bells what they meant, Idorii stomach still gave a giddy lurch at the news. After so much preparing, so much waiting and wondering, he could hardly believe the day had finally come.

Idorii hurried past the crowd at the inn and joined the army pouring down Market Street. Others joined the throng from side streets, swelling the flood of bodies, and when they finally reached the wall, Idorii could not see any space where he could possibly push himself up the stairs for a view.

Instead of shoving his way through the crowd toward the guard towers flanking the city gates, he ducked down Wolfskin Alley, hurrying past rows of dark, silent establishments, until he reached the next guard tower along the wall. This section was crowded as well, but at least he wouldn't be fighting his way up the stairs.

Breaking into a run, Idorii took the spiral stairs two at a time until he emerged at the top of the guard tower.

When he stepped out onto the exposed wall, he felt abruptly unsteady.

The Whitish army was marching over the rise of a distant hill. And it was vast—vaster than Idorii could have imagined.

He knew from reports that there were well over a hundred thousand soldiers stationed at Twenty-League Town, but to see those numbers descending on Baylore, armor glinting in the sun, still knocked the air from his chest. There were war machines as well—enchanted metal siege towers and wooden siege towers and trebuchets, rolling along in even ranks, as if an entire fortress had picked itself up and was now creeping its way across the plains toward them. Idorii tried to count the siege towers but got lost after forty; there were still more ranks emerging over the crest of the hill, until he thought the army might never end.

This was nothing like the previous battles they had fought. Those had been on a scale he could comprehend.

Idorii stood as if in a trance as the Whitish army marched steadily closer. Now that the time had come, he could not see any way for Baylore to stand against such a force.

Daymin had known. Even without seeing the numbers spread before him, he had understood how badly the odds were stacked against Baylore. What had seemed a great risk—evacuating before the city had fallen—now seemed the only possible course of action.

Glancing along the wall, Idorii was heartened to see more Itreans in plate armor than he had expected. Ellarie and Falsted's soldiers had spent the past quarters raiding the city in search of abandoned metal, and it had evidently paid off. Maybe that would give them the advantage they needed to defeat the enchanted towers.

Then his eyes were drawn once more to the approaching army. He was deluding himself. The sound of marching soldiers rose to him, a distant, rhythmic clanking, and beneath it the grinding wheels of those relentless towers.

64

Magic from the Old Lands

When Kalleah spotted Bennett heading back toward the Twin Cities, she leapt down the steps of the temple and took off at a run after him. The grass whipped against her boots as she picked up momentum down the hillside.

Bennett turned and looked at her when she was still a hundred paces away, his eyebrows raised in surprise. He looked more handsome than usual with his hair ruffled in the wind, his deep blue coat bringing out the color in his eyes.

Stopping in his tracks, he took a few steps back up the hill. "What's this?" he called out with a curious smile.

Kalleah jogged to a halt beside him. "I wanted to talk to you. Are you staying in the city for long?"

"I don't know. Why?"

Kalleah hesitated. "It's—I still have questions about this scheme of yours. How soon are we going to be expected to set out for the mountains?"

"Soon enough, I imagine," Bennett said, still looking confused. "We can't afford to waste much time."

She would speak plainly, then, if this might be the last time she saw Bennett before she was compelled to take action. "You seem to believe magic is the key to your success. But we have no idea what form this is going to take. Are you intending to invite the magic races to return to the Kinship Thrones? And how do you expect this to change anything?"

Bennett shoved his hands in his pockets, looking momentarily uncomfortable. "No. It's not that. We need the sort of magic that can lend strength to the Nine, and I don't think the Itrean magic races would do that. Especially since they don't worship the Nine."

"What sort of magic are you envisioning, then?" Kalleah asked in confusion. Did they know about the springs in Cashabree?

"Do you know about the barrier holding back the magic of the old lands?" Bennett asked quietly.

"Yes…"

"We've found a way to use that magic. Safely, I mean. In a way that allows it back into the Kinship Thrones without fully dismantling the wall."

Kalleah stared at Bennett in disbelief. The old lands had been sealed off because no one had been able to control the magic that had run rampant there, not even those with far more power than the magic races of modern times. And the last time someone had tampered with the wall, much of the Kinship Thrones had been leveled. How did a group with no magic of their own expect to harness this power for anything but chaos?

And Bennett seemed nervous as well—was he wary of

sharing these secrets with her, or afraid she would see how dangerous their plan was?

"This is folly, as far as I can tell," Kalleah said. "I have no intention of going along with such a dangerous scheme unless you can give me more specifics. Who is responsible for tapping the power beyond the wall? Is it someone with magic of their own? Someone who understands what they're doing?"

Bennett raked a hand through his hair. "Many different peoples are drawn into our fold at the Borderlands Academy."

"That's not an answer," Kalleah said sharply.

"It's—I'm not at liberty to speak of this." Bennett was twitchier than ever, and he kept glancing past Kalleah in the direction of the temple.

Kalleah gave him a stern look. "I am not about to waste the next few spans supporting a scheme I don't understand." Then she remembered something Athamol had said. "Brenvale. Your priest said the enchanted devices in Brenvale had something to do with your scheme. Is it a device, rather than a person, that is drawing on the magic?"

Bennett's hesitation told her she had guessed correctly.

"Where is the device kept? I'd like to see it, if possible. If it's in Brenvale, we can visit it before we start gathering supporters." She hoped to discern more about the magic that had gone into its creation.

"I—that's not—" Bennett cleared his throat. "It's not in Brenvale. The device is kept here, in the Twin Cities. Beneath Darrenmark Palace."

Kalleah blinked at him. "Does King Rodarin know of your scheme, then?"

"To a certain extent."

"I want you to take me there. If you can show me this device, I will be able to make my decision."

Bennett gave her a grim smile. "Of course. I'll see what I can arrange."

Then he shoved his hands in his pockets once more and started off toward the Twin Cities alone.

65

The University Tunnels

As rank after rank of soldiers crowded the wall, pushing Idorii further from the guard tower he had climbed, he realized abruptly that he hadn't sealed the tunnels under the University. All his work would be for nothing if he couldn't finish the job.

He shoved his way back through the mass of soldiers, encountering so much resistance from those in plate armor that he may as well have been trying to push his way through a solid wall. A few times he had to crawl along the rear parapet to get around an immobile mass of metal, his heart flying into his throat when he saw the long drop to the city streets below.

At last he reached the guard tower. A few soldiers were making their way up the stairs, but most continued to flood onto the wall from the two towers flanking the city gates. Idorii made it down without trouble and dashed back along Wolfskin Alley toward the main street.

Even when he came across the river of soldiers pouring down Market Street, he could tell it was a much thinner defense than before. Instead of filling the street, the soldiers walked four by four, leaving space on either side. There were no reserve soldiers rushing from their homes in the Market District to bolster their numbers, no civilians waving to their loved ones.

Idorii broke into a run toward the center of town. He was the only one moving away from the wall, but no one tried to stop him.

He was soon gasping for breath, a sour taste filling his mouth, but he couldn't stop. He didn't know how much time he had left. His legs were beginning to ache, shuddering each time his feet pounded against the cobblestones, and his scarf had slipped to show the markings on his face.

When he reached the main square, chest heaving, he stumbled to a walk and tugged his scarf back into place.

Only a handful of people remained. There were Ellarie and Falsted, each surrounded by a small complement of guards, and there were the Weavers and Flamespinners who had remained in the palace. Both holden monarchs were dressed in plate armor; Idorii thought it was the first time he had seen Ellarie wearing anything besides skirts.

"Idorii," Ellarie said tightly. "What is this about?"

"I need—to borrow a couple Weavers," he gasped. "Just for a few minutes."

"Any final advice for us?" Ellarie asked.

Idorii clutched at his shirt, chest searing as he gulped in air. "Our spells worked—against the harvesting machines. We still have a chance."

Two Weavers were already approaching Idorii, and Ellarie

waved them on, not looking their way.

"Have you heard word from Daymin, then?" Ellarie asked.

"Yes. His army was…successful in stopping the Whitish attack on the forest." Idorii didn't want to say more. Not when everyone in Baylore was about to die. Better they go thinking Daymin won a great victory for Itrea, and anything their own troops could do to chip away at the Whitish numbers could give him a better chance of reclaiming what they had lost, than fearing their sacrifice had meant nothing.

"What do you need us for?" asked one of the Weavers, a young woman whose silver hair was so badly depleted she would soon lose her ability to work magic.

Idorii gave Ellarie a nod of respect before leading the two young Weavers away. "We're going to the University," he said. "I've been hiding books on magic there, in the tunnels beneath the school, and I need your help to seal them so the Whitish can't harm them."

The young woman grinned. "Excellent."

Idorii glanced at the two—neither wore armor, and the swords they carried were hardly longer than daggers.

"Are you planning to leave the city before the Whitish arrive?" he asked.

"I don't know," said the young man, who was not much older than Idorii. "We had always intended to, but now it seems too late."

"I want to stay," the woman said stubbornly. "If we can hold out for a few days, they'll need as many Weavers as they can find to continue working spells."

Idorii's jaw tightened. He hated the thought of wasting so many lives. "And the other younger Weavers? Are they still here?"

"It's just us and Leedra," the young woman said. "Everyone else left a quarter ago."

Idorii let out his breath.

Then they reached the University gates, which hung open.

"I went here," the young man said shortly, "and I never knew about these tunnels. Where are they?"

Idorii led the way through the gates and pulled open the door beneath the archway. He had grown more frantic as the days had passed, filling in the space closer to the entrance instead of winding his way through to the storage rooms, and from here they could see several rows of books stacked at the foot of the stairway.

"Cloudy gods," the young man said in a hushed voice. "How far back does it go?"

"I think it follows the whole outer rectangle of the University," Idorii said. "I haven't explored the whole thing, but it seems to go on forever."

"Well, the Whitish certainly won't find this," the young woman said. "How do you want us to seal it?"

"I was thinking something with an illusion to cover the stairs, and then a spell to seal off the doors and make them disappear."

"I'll do the illusions," the woman said. "You work on sealing off the doors."

"Are there other entrances?" the man asked.

"I found one other set of stairs going up on this side of the building," Idorii said, "but the door was locked and I wasn't sure where it came out. Maybe you'll be able to figure it out."

The two got to work without any further questions. While

the woman hurried off in search of sheets to work her enchantment on, the man lit a crystal and ventured belowground to investigate any other entrances to the tunnels.

As soon as Idorii was alone, he rolled up his sleeve and wrote, *The Whitish are coming. The battle is about to begin.*

The other Weavers rejoined him soon, so when he felt the cold flash that signaled a reply from Daymin, he wasn't able to check it immediately.

Idorii helped where he could, sawing apart sections of a table to hold the illusion in place and removing the handles and latches from the doors they were preparing to enchant, but mostly he lamented the loss of his power. He realized the stairs leading down to the tunnels would be exposed if the University collapsed; he hoped the trebuchets wouldn't be able to reach that far.

At last they were ready to put the enchantments in place. They fastened the strips of wood to the walls to hold the cloth taut, and when the young woman finished speaking, the few stairs that remained in sight looked as though they ended in a shallow stone depression dampened by rank water and mottled with scum. Hopefully it would discourage anyone from stepping there, because the cloth had neither the strength nor texture of stone.

Next they sealed the doors and cast another illusion upon the outside to make them appear exactly like the stone walls on either side. If anyone touched them, they might discern the wood texture beneath, or the fact that the door was slightly set back in the wall, meaning the first fingerwidth of the illusion was not solid. But Idorii doubted anyone would linger in this archway long enough to encounter the inconsistency.

Just then, he heard a distant *boom*.

His head flew up. When he met the eyes of the two Weavers, he saw that the color had drained from their faces.

"The Whitish are here," Idorii said hoarsely.

66

The Attack on Baylore

I dorii left the two Weavers to finish sealing the other entrances and started back toward the main square, stopping to grab his rucksack along the way. As soon as he returned to the street, weighed down by his supplies and books, he pulled up his sleeve and pressed his tattoo. A moment later, Daymin's handwriting bled into place on his arm.

Get out of the city at all costs. I love you.

A lump formed in Idorii's throat. He pressed his lips to Daymin's words, leaving his sleeve rolled up just enough for them to give him courage.

Another thunderous *boom* echoed from the direction of the city gates.

Idorii picked up his pace until he was jogging, the books thudding against his back with each step. At least the city sloped gently downhill toward the gates, so he didn't tire himself out as quickly as he had before.

Market Street was eerily silent. Though he could hear a distant roar of voices from the wall, not a sign of life remained on the once-bustling main street, and the Market District lay dark and empty. Even the flowerboxes that had been bursting with color not long ago were now brittle and dead from neglect.

When he came within sight of the wall, the sound of battle grew to a deafening roar. Arrows flew erratically over the battlements, and as he watched, two soldiers plummeted backward from the wall.

Idorii winced at the clang of their armor as they struck the cobblestones.

He was desperate to see what was happening, but he had to stay away from the worst of the fighting. He had no helmet, and his fighting abilities were next to useless, so he would be an easy target if he climbed the guard towers here.

Another booming *thud* sounded from the gates, which shook beneath the impact. Idorii had expected to hear the crash of boulders launched from trebuchets as they struck deeper in the city, but he hadn't heard any yet.

After a moment's indecision, Idorii darted into a street leading to the left away from the main gates. He would find his way back to the wall eventually, somewhere he wasn't likely to be killed the moment he emerged from the stairs.

The street went on for longer than he'd expected, and the sound of the fighting grew distorted as he ran.

At last he reached an intersection and charged down the right-hand turn, which spat him out at the foot of the wall.

Even here, there were bodies of fallen soldiers lying on the cobblestones, surrounded by spent arrows and discarded shields. Idorii grabbed one of the shields and slipped his arm through the grip before dashing up the nearest guard tower.

As he climbed, the sound grew louder and louder, until at last he burst onto the top of the wall to a roar so overwhelming he could hardly think.

And there was the Whitish army.

For a moment, Idorii could do nothing but stare. The Whitish had thrown their might first against the city gates, and there were already several siege towers disgorging soldiers onto the wall on either side. One wooden structure was aflame, while the others seemed unhurt.

But the attack was spreading out in either direction, siege towers and trebuchets rolling toward Idorii, and it wouldn't be long before the next wave reached the crenellations. There were Whitish soldiers on the wall, pushing their way through the crowd of Itreans, and archers atop the towers were shooting as they moved.

Even though they weren't far from the gates, the defense was noticeably thinner here, only a single line of soldiers standing against the Whitish. Idorii didn't expect them to last five minutes once the towers landed.

As he hesitated, watching the worst of the battle, Idorii saw the Itrean force near the gates use one of their miniature trebuchets to crack open an enchanted siege tower. Before long, smoke was pouring from the inside, and the tower rolled backward a few paces before falling still.

At least the spells are working, Idorii thought grimly.

In the end, it would mean nothing.

The attack had nearly reached the section of the wall where Idorii stood, and the Whitish archers were getting more accurate. Idorii held the shield in front of his face, unable to tear his eyes from the slaughter all around.

Thwack.

An arrow struck the exposed neck of a man beside him. With a strangled grunt, he stumbled backward and collided with the parapet. For a moment he staggered in place, blood pouring down the front of his Weaver's armor.

Then he swayed and plunged over the back of the wall to the streets below.

Idorii swallowed back the sick feeling in his throat. Spurred into action, he took off along the wall away from the gates. When he glanced back, he saw the Whitish swarming from the new towers, not a Flamespinner in sight to stop them.

As he hurried along the wall, he spotted the trebuchets rolling along to his right, still a couple hundred paces from the city. Each was drawn by a team of oxen driven by a handful of soldiers. Eventually they stopped and turned to face the wall.

Idorii was right in their path.

The first trebuchet launched its boulder. Idorii froze as the arm swung, flinging the massive stone toward the city. It wasn't aiming for the stretch of wall he was on, so he waited, heart pounding in his throat, as it soared through the air.

With a resounding *crash*, the boulder slammed into the city wall. The stones underfoot shook, and Idorii staggered, grabbing the crenellations for balance.

Stones clattered as they fell, the top of the wall crumbling and sagging. The boulder must have been enchanted.

Idorii had expected the Whitish to aim for the buildings inside the city, hoping to weaken the forces they would assume lay in wait, but now he realized all of the trebuchets stood at the perfect distance to batter the city walls.

They know the bulk of our army is elsewhere, Idorii realized with a jolt.

He picked his way forward more cautiously than before. He wasn't even sure if he would be able to get past the damaged section of wall.

He should be looking for a way down, but he wanted to make it beyond the trebuchets first. Otherwise, he might become a target for the soldiers maneuvering the trebuchets.

Another stone flew, this time aiming for a stretch of wall behind Idorii. He picked up his pace, trying to keep his attention fixed on the way forward; when it slammed into the wall, he flinched and nearly lost his balance.

Pausing, he looked over the rooftops below. He had expected to see Whitish soldiers swarming through the city, charging up Market Street to take the palace. Instead the streets were empty.

Turning, he saw that the Whitish had overwhelmed the Itrean defenses on the section of wall over the gates, and as more siege towers dropped their drawbridges onto the crenellations, the last of the Itreans were forced back.

Then he saw something that sent a spear of ice through his chest.

Smoke the color of pond scum was billowing through the streets near the wall, sitting low to the ground and curling back upon itself as it spread. Soon it was churning its way up Market Street toward the main square, swamping the side streets as it went.

Though he had never seen the like before, Idorii knew it was a poisonous gas. Something designed by the Potioneers held captive at Darkland Fort, no doubt.

His first thought was of the Weavers he had left behind to finish sealing the University. Had they made it out?

No. They would still be somewhere in the city. Idorii drew a shuddering breath. It was *his* fault they had stayed behind. If he hadn't waited so long to finish his work…

Don't think about that. They wouldn't have lasted long either way.

Still, Idorii couldn't force back the nausea.

If Daymin hadn't compelled the city to evacuate…

Idorii could just picture it. Wave after wave of civilians falling to the noxious gas, running deeper into the city in a futile attempt to escape, screams piercing the sounds of battle—

Another thunderous crash shook Idorii from his thoughts. This time a boulder had hit the base of the wall just ahead of where he stood, and as he watched, stones crumbled inward, collapsing with a tremendous clatter.

He definitely wouldn't be able to make it past this section of the wall.

Idorii turned and dashed back to the nearest guard tower, where he ran down the spiral stairs. Close to the bottom, he sucked in a deep breath and held it. He could see no sign of the murky green gas, but he wasn't going to chance it.

Lungs searing, Idorii dashed from the base of the tower toward the ruined section of wall. He threw himself onto the pile of rubble and started climbing hastily, his pack dragging him off balance. The rocks slid away underfoot, trapping his boots and yanking him backward, and he grew clumsier as the urge to breathe overwhelmed him.

At last he cleared the top of the ruined wall. He sucked in a desperate breath. When his lungs filled with dust from the wreckage, he thought for a panicked second he had been poisoned.

Coughing, he staggered down the opposite side of the rubble. With the fresh air whisking away the dust, his head cleared, and he realized he was fine. Just winded.

From here, the trebuchets looked larger than ever, and closer as well. Idorii picked up his pace, hoping he wouldn't be a target for the soldiers at their base; then the rubble began sliding out from underfoot, and he fell heavily on his tailbone. It was hard balancing with the weight of his pack tugging at him and the cumbersome shield still strapped to one arm, but he wasn't about to abandon the shield until he was out of sight of the Whitish.

More cautious now, he started sliding forward in a crouch, raising a thunderous clatter as he sent stones skidding down before him. He grimaced at the commotion, sure someone would come over to investigate.

But he reached the end of the rubble without incident. Pushing himself to his feet atop the overgrown remnants of a farm field, Idorii started along the base of the wall, crouching forward in hopes the low farm walls and sparsely-leafed trees would hide him.

He continued this way for a long time, heart still hammering frantically in his chest, not daring to stop and look for signs of pursuit. Eventually he rounded the eastern side of Baylore and came within view of the Elygian River, where he could see no sign of Daymin's army. They were still a decent distance south of the city, then.

At last he made it past the northern end of the city. Here, the signs of battle disappeared altogether. He had made it out safely.

It was late afternoon now, and the city wall cast a deep shadow, chilling the air. Idorii slipped his arm from the shield and left it leaning against the wall. His shoulders already ached from the weight of the books he carried, and the Icebraid Peaks were many long leagues from here. He could just make out their snowy tops now, the craggy peaks streaked with shadow.

Even now, he had a hard time calming his racing heart. The brutal inescapability of the Whitish attack had been a shock, though he should have expected it; he would never forget the sight of wave after wave of enemies flooding onto the city walls and crushing the Itrean defense.

Yet he was alive. And if he wanted to remain that way, he had to pick up the trail of the refugees before the Whitish realized what had happened and chased them down.

Idorii hooked his thumbs under the straps of his pack, taking some of the weight off his shoulders, and trudged away from the only home he had ever known.

67

Retreat

Without any sign of a formal decision taking place, the forest began splitting in half the day after the send-off. Daymin watched from the riverbank as the trees formed two separate lakes, one moving to the north, the other south.

"What's happening?" he asked Ilyoth, who would be traveling with the trees but had lingered to say her farewells.

"We are retreating from the Whitish forces," Ilyoth said sadly. "Some of our number will shelter in the north, far from any civilization, while the rest will guard the sacred source to the south."

"You're opening up the forest road, then?" Daymin asked.

"Not just opening it. Abandoning it entirely."

Ilyoth clasped Daymin's hand tightly before releasing him and turning to rejoin her people.

A stillness hung over Daymin's army as the trees moved

away. All around, the groaning of branches and rasping of dirt followed the retreating forest, but he stood in a pocket of stunned silence.

The Wandering Woods had been the last of the Itrean flatlands to fully resist Whitish occupation, and now they were pulling back, leaving a dead, barren expanse where once a wall of trees had engulfed the eastern edge of the continent. The very geography of their homeland was changing irreversibly. Though many had feared to venture beneath the sentient trees, the forest road connecting Baylore to Larkhaven had been a piece of Itrean identity. Even growing up in times when such journeys were impossible, Daymin had heard many tales of the brave messengers who traveled the road, set upon by bandits and occasionally disappearing into the woods never to be seen again.

Now, in the absence of the trees, the Whitish would face no more resistance in resupplying their troops or bringing reinforcements across to Baylore. They would gain true control of Itrea.

"Why are they leaving?" Zahira asked quietly from beside Daymin.

He turned to look at her in confusion. "What do you mean?"

"The harvesting machines are gone. The Whitish might have exhausted their supply of poison. In all likelihood, the forest isn't in danger any longer."

"What happens when the Whitish chase down our refugees?" Daymin asked. "They'll capture more Makhori and start building everything all over again. They're sending the trees back to Whitland for timber—as long as they hold Itrea, they won't want to give up on such a valuable resource."

Zahira crossed her arms over her chest. "You say that like it will happen right away."

"Won't it? We have no fortress walls to hide behind in the mountains, and if our civilians can make it there with a train of wagons and carts, the Whitish will easily follow. We've bought ourselves a span or two at most."

"Then why did we evacuate at all?" Zahira asked crossly.

"I don't know," Daymin said. "I really don't know."

With a sigh, Zahira stumped away. Daymin watched her go, a sour feeling twisting in his stomach.

Ever since the river had poisoned the trees, he had felt as though events were spiraling out of his control. He had tried and tried to make a difference, and it had all played right into the Whitish army's hands.

The more he fought for his people, the more he hurt them. A few spans ago, he had thought he could make a difference if he bought more time for Baylore. Then he had done so, and what had it accomplished?

He had merely postponed the inevitable.

And in the meantime, he had killed countless civilians in New Savair, drowned many of his valuable troops while crossing the Elygian, and driven so many trees to their deaths that the Wandering Woods had given up altogether.

Maybe he should have stayed in Baylore. At least that way he might have avoided the losses his army had spread, plague-like, wherever they ventured.

A nudge from Tarak brought Daymin back to his surroundings. The trees were still visible, but they had retreated far enough that the sound of their passage had dulled to a distant rumble. And in their absence, Daymin's army was looking for him for direction. Waiting. Uncertain.

He swallowed hard. Where did he even go from here?

One step at a time. Where do we cross the river?

"We need to move north," Daymin said, his voice coming out unsteady. "March for the bridge near Ashton. We'll assess our strategy once we cross."

His army was already packed and ready to move, so his troops pulled together into columns and started marching north, leaving Daymin and Tarak standing to the side, in danger of being left behind.

"Daymin," Tarak ventured. "Is there anything I can do?"

Daymin shook his head curtly. "Let's go."

Then he stiffened his shoulders and fell into pace alongside his troops.

* * *

For several hours they marched, as the sun grew hotter and the disturbed earth gave way to grasslands underfoot. Daymin tried not to think, instead letting the rhythm of his army and the ache of his feet fill his mind.

He was yanked from his stupor when a message from Idorii flashed cold on his arm.

Pushing up his sleeve discreetly, he pressed a thumb to the tattoo. Idorii had written only a single line.

The Whitish are coming. The battle is about to begin.

Daymin pulled his sleeve quickly back down, a sick feeling clawing at the back of his throat. When tallying up his failings, this was one he hadn't considered—if he had abandoned the forest, he might have had time to return to Baylore and bolster their defenses. And maybe it would have been enough to tip the scales.

Instead, he had left Ellarie and Falsted to die, along with the foolhardy troops that had chosen to follow them.

When they passed a boulder rising statue-like from the plains, Daymin ducked behind it as though to relieve himself. Once hidden from his troops, he wiped away Idorii's message and wrote a hasty reply.

Get out of the city at all costs.

After a moment's hesitation, he added, *I love you.*

Pressing the tattoo, Daymin yanked down his sleeve. Then he fell back against the boulder, resting his head on the sun-warmed stone.

How had it come to this? His mother in the Kinship Thrones, his grandmother traveling to the mountains with the refugees, Idorii in Baylore—all of them trying to find some thread of hope that might save Itrea, while in truth they were just biding their time as their kingdom crumbled, piece by piece.

He wished he could give up. Just disappear one day and leave his army to choose a new leader. The holden monarchs could step into his place; now that the Allakoash were no longer depending on him, it would make no difference.

Yet the idea of putting his army in another's hands filled him with anxiety. As much as he hated it, he had grown accustomed to leading, and he would find it hard to relinquish that control.

Besides, he had started this, so he had an obligation to finish it. If he found some sliver of hope for the future of Itrea, maybe he could pass the throne to another. But as long as this death march continued, he was responsible for shepherding his people to their doom.

Daymin rubbed a hand over his face, hating his decision, hating the circumstances that had brought him here.

Then he pushed off the rock and rejoined his army once more.

After walking a few hundred paces further, he realized he didn't have to keep silent. His army would want to share his news.

"Baylore is under attack," he said, his voice too quiet to carry.

The soldiers nearest to him heard and began muttering to their neighbors.

Again Daymin spoke, his voice stronger this time. "Baylore is under attack. I've just heard word from my informant."

His army continued its forward progress, but the ranks grew disorganized as soldiers discussed this news with increasing agitation.

Soon Pollard pushed his way through the mass of soldiers to walk beside Daymin. He held himself upright, his expression stern and unreadable; beside him, Daymin felt like a child, unkempt and too beholden to his emotions.

"What of the attack?" Pollard asked. "How many troops have the Whitish sent? Have they deployed their enchanted siege towers?"

"I don't know," Daymin said hollowly. "My informant is trying to get out of the city, so I don't want to distract him with questions like that. I'm sure we'll have the answers soon enough."

Pollard gave him a short nod. Daymin wasn't sure if it meant he understood the circumstances or that he expected no better of Daymin.

As he let Pollard draw ahead once more, Daymin heard a question rippling through his army.

"Can we help?"

"Can we make it back in time to join the battle?"

At first he ignored the whispered voices, but when it seemed everyone within earshot was repeating the same question, he knew he had to respond.

Stopping abruptly, he turned to face his troops. Those nearest staggered to a halt as well, their fellows jostling them as the army tried to carry them forward.

"We're at least two days from the bridge near Ashton," Daymin said, grateful that his voice carried easily this time. "Provided the bridge is still intact, it would be another day from there to Baylore. The city won't hold that long. I'm sorry."

He had expected his soldiers to protest, but no one spoke. They knew.

"We'll set up camp soon," Daymin said. "Wait to hear how the battle plays out. There's nothing more we can do."

His army started forward again, but he could see their motivation waning. Soon they were making only halting progress, their ranks scattering as they gravitated toward friends and relations to talk in a low murmur.

Daymin finally gave the orders to set up camp, even though sunset was still hours off. He watched from afar as his friends set up his royal tent; they were still sharing with him, and he wanted nothing more than to be alone. Instead of joining them, he wandered down to the river and threaded his way through the willows and reeds until he found a rock to perch on. Then he sat there, staring at the water swirling past, trapped in a miserable stupor.

It felt like hours passed before a spike of cold from his tattoo roused him.

Daymin rolled up his sleeve and pressed the circular pattern with a trembling finger.

Daymin –

As you can likely guess, I made it safely out of Baylore. I am heading west of the city now, on my way to pick up the trail of the refugees.

The city has fallen. We hardly lasted an hour after the Whitish struck. Our spells were nothing compared to the sheer number of siege towers disgorging troops onto our walls, and as if that wasn't enough, they flooded our streets with a poisonous gas no doubt developed by our captive Potioneers. Thankfully there were few remaining in the city to succumb to the gas, as I'm sure it would have been a terrible way to go. I cannot imagine the casualties we would have suffered had you not evacuated the city. Your foresight saved every one of our civilians.

The Whitish hardly even used their trebuchets, except to weaken the wall; I imagine they knew they would take Baylore without trouble and wanted to move into a functioning city. Plagues. I still can't believe it's gone. We held on for so many years, and then in the space of a few hours, we lost it all.

I am desperate to see you again and hope you are planning to join the refugees directly, without too many detours. I am counting down the days.

Yours,

Idorii

Tears pricked at Daymin's eyes. He rocked forward, clutching his wrist with Idorii's message, the river blurring before him.

Abandoning Baylore had been a terrible decision to make, but knowing what he did now, it was the only possible route he could have taken. If his army had returned to support Ellarie and Falsted's troops, many soldiers would have been stationed throughout the city, and all would have died as the lethal gas spread.

It didn't make their situation any less bleak, but at least it helped ease his guilt.

He was vindicated.

68

A Great Victory

Edreon's wound was worsening again. After the brief reprieve the enchanted log had bought him, the infection had returned, this time digging deep into his flesh until he had a cavity beneath his skin. The very sight turned his stomach.

For a couple short quarters, he had felt well enough to return to court life and keep up appearances. Yet now he had returned to his bed, sicker than ever.

The one light that remained was the news that the attack on Baylore was underway. If that succeeded—if he was able to take the last Itrean stronghold without trouble…

Well, it would remind his court that larger events were unfolding beyond the drama of his own ill health. And it would reinforce the idea that he personally had orchestrated their victory in Itrea, making him indispensable.

He had shared the news with his inner circle, so when

Luvoli, Naresha, and Marviak visited him one morning with unconvincingly innocent expressions, he knew exactly what they were here for.

"What?" he grumbled, struggling to sit up. The pain in his leg had become such a constant that he often felt it sear through him even when he did not disturb the wound. Now was one such time, and he gritted his teeth, waiting for the ache to subside.

"We merely wished to enquire after your health," Luvoli said, settling gingerly on the corner of Edreon's bed.

"Of course," Edreon said sourly.

Marviak seemed to be fighting with himself; after a moment, he said, "And Baylore? What news of the attack?"

"Had I received word, you would be the first to know."

"When did you last check?" Naresha asked.

Scowling at her, Edreon tried to remember. Had it been a full day? Perhaps it had. He had descended into a feverish sleep yesterday, and had not roused until long after dark.

"Bring me the books, then," he snapped.

Naresha crossed around to his bedside table and sorted through the pile of communication books there. One linked to Twenty-League Town; one to King's Port; one to Larkhaven; one to Lord Juriel, formerly of Darkland Fort…

Naresha handed him first the journal linked to his commander at Twenty-League Town. He flipped to the most recent writing, sent four days ago, when his troops had begun moving out.

Nothing new had appeared since.

Frustrated, Edreon tossed the journal aside, the weight of the book dragging his covers across his wound. He hissed at the pain.

"Try that one," he said, pointing to the well-worn journal at the bottom of the pile.

Naresha handed him the journal linked to Lord Juriel, and he flipped through it, not expecting much.

When his eyes fell upon the full page of new writing, hope swelled in his chest. A quick glance told him there was nothing in Lord Juriel's report that he would need to keep from his closest supporters, so he beckoned the three close to read as he did.

Your Majesty,

We have received two pieces of news almost simultaneously—news of your victory, Your Majesty!

Firstly, we took Baylore with hardly a fight. Many of our number have relocated to the capital, while I have remained behind to direct those troops still in Twenty-League Town. Very few Itrean soldiers remained behind to guard the city, since the majority are still with King Daymin, east of the Elygian River. However, upon entering the city, we found virtually no civilian casualties. It appears the city was evacuated without our knowledge. The Itreans have nowhere defensible to retreat to, so we will be able to track them down and deal with them swiftly if you give the orders.

Now for the second piece of news. We heard from the troops sent to carve a path through the Wandering Woods that their mission succeeded in a way wholly unexpected. King Daymin's army disposed of our remaining harvesting machines before they had traveled more than a few leagues into the forest, but the poison killed off a large swath of trees. And when the trees were stirred to vengeance and moved as if to attack us in Twenty-League Town, many thousands more were poisoned as they tried to cross the river. You will have no shortage of wood for decades hence.

Seeing they had been defeated, the trees withdrew altogether. We have yet to receive word from Larkhaven, but from what our scout could see, it appears there is no remnant forest within twenty leagues of the old forest road. The route between Larkhaven and Baylore is fully open, with no further impediment to our resupply or movement of troops.

King Daymin's army remains intact, and those who evacuated Baylore must be dealt with, but I see this as a clear and indisputable victory for Whitland. All through Baylore, the streets ring with your praise.

I await your next orders.

Your faithful servant,
Lord General Juriel

Edreon looked up from the page to see Marviak and Luvoli grinning at each other, childlike in their glee.

"You've done it," Marviak said, gripping Edreon's arm. "No one believed you could topple Baylore, but you did."

"That was easy," Edreon said, though he could not hold back an answering smile. "The challenge was anticipating how the Wandering Woods would react and preventing their trees from overwhelming my army."

"And you did," Marviak said. "You foresaw their every move."

"This calls for a celebration!" Luvoli said. "Let your heralds shout the news from the battlements!"

"Indeed," Edreon said. He pulled aside the covers and eased his legs over the side of the bed, the pain dulled to a background throbbing. "Call a feast for the whole city! This is the greatest victory Whitland has won in centuries."

As Luvoli hastened off to do his bidding, Edreon let the news sink in.

He had won.

He had staked so much on the conflict in Itrea, and it had paid off. More thoroughly than he had dared to imagine.

Warmth coursed through him, lending him strength and vitality; in this moment, he felt he could walk again through sheer force of will. No, not just walk—he could don his armor and fight any who dared challenge him.

As he let the satisfaction of victory wash through him, he could almost forget the pain and doubt and disloyalty he had faced in recent spans. He was King Edreon the Great, conqueror of Itrea, greatest monarch ever to sit the high throne. He had climbed too high to fall.

69

Beneath the Palace

With the sun sinking over the distant peaks, Bennett led Kalleah back toward the Twin Cities. At her continued insistence, he had agreed to show her the conduit they were using to tap into the magic beyond the wall.

She had pretended to retire early, not wanting her friends to worry about her, and now she was dressed in a nobleman's suit borrowed from Bennett. The floppy hat covered the braid she had pinned to the top of her head, and the garish red-and-purple doublet drew attention away from her face—or so he claimed. She worried it would instead attract stares.

They walked in silence, boots swishing against the tall grasses as they passed. Bats flitted in the twilit sky, while a haze of smoke from cookfires had settled over the Twin Cities.

They reached the city gates just before they closed for the night. Kalleah felt a twinge of unease at the thought that she would be trapped inside the Twin Cities with Bennett overnight.

Where did he expect them to stay? Did he realize she had no funds to pay for an inn?

Yet she did not give voice to her concerns.

Quietly they slunk through the city, hugging the shadows, following the wall as it looped westward away from the river. Soon they were at the rear of the towering butte where the palace sat, and it was here that Bennett finally turned into the maze of streets leading away from the wall. This part of the city looked poor, but not in the dissolute way of the docks; rather, the homes were crammed one atop the other, narrow and grimy, and clothes hung like banners from laundry lines spanning the upstairs windows.

"Do you come this way often?" Kalleah whispered as Bennett ducked into an alley barely wider than her shoulders.

"Yes," he breathed. "No more questions."

They darted up a narrow flight of stairs, heading toward a keyhole of light at the top, and the alley narrowed even further as they climbed. Soon Kalleah's shoulders were scraping against the stones, and she had to turn sideways to fit through the final gap before the stairway opened onto the street above.

Coming out on this higher level, she was struck by the dramatic change. They had reached the part of town nearest the palace, dominated by manor homes and fine establishments, and the streets were immediately wider and cleaner. Oil lamps shone in many windows, and despite the chill, a few restaurant doors hung open, spilling their delicious smells onto the street.

As they followed this street around to the southern side of the palace, Kalleah realized Bennett had been correct—her colorful garments looked at home among the residents of this part of town. Perhaps the darkness helped.

Soon Bennett ducked into a shop selling bolts of fine cloth. He doffed his hat to the owner, who looked strangely familiar, before leading Kalleah through to the back room.

"What—" Kalleah began.

Bennett put a finger to his lips.

Behind a curtain that appeared to conceal a fitting room, they instead came upon a door. This opened to a narrow street running along the foot of the butte.

"Who knows of this place?" Kalleah breathed.

Bennett shook his head sharply. "Later."

The street only ran for a dozen paces before the buildings began jutting up against the rock once more. Where it ended, a man stood guard by a door leading into the cliff itself.

When he turned to look at them, Kalleah's heartbeat sped up. He was no Lord's Man, but he could cause trouble if he summoned King Rodarin's guards.

Yet he shocked her by smiling at Bennett. "Evening. Who have you brought with you today?"

"A new initiate," Bennett said. "We won't be long."

"Of course."

The guard unlocked the door and stepped aside, letting Bennett lead Kalleah into a dark, rough-hewn tunnel cut directly in the rock. Bennett reached for a torch just inside the tunnel entrance, its flickering glow the only light around.

Up a flight of stairs, they reached a row of empty cells. Kalleah faltered, skin prickling. Every sense told her to turn and run.

This would be a perfect trap. No one could have subdued her when she was free to escape, to carve a path through her opponents with her power, but down here she could be locked up as easily as any commoner.

"Just a little further," Bennett said, his quiet voice echoing oddly in the tunnels.

Kalleah hesitated. If she let on that she was suspicious, would Bennett turn on her? Would he force her into a cell and leave her there to rot? Or would the Lord's Men come and question her?

Maybe she would be able to fight him off before he trapped her. She had no sword, but her hidden dagger was strapped to her wrist, as always, and he would not be expecting that.

Or she could rip out his life, if he gave her long enough to summon her power.

"Milady?" Bennett asked, worry coloring his voice. "Are you well?"

"Of course," Kalleah said distantly.

As she followed him down the next stretch of tunnel, she began sinking into the state necessary to call on her power. It took longer than usual, since she was jumpy and kept thinking she saw movement out of the corner of her eye, but at last her surroundings blurred and Bennett's gold lifeline crystallized before her.

Resting one finger on the golden thread, she picked up her pace again. A single tug and he would die.

At last they stopped before a heavy stone door. Bennett pulled a key from his pocket and unlocked the door before pushing it open with a groaning of hinges. Why he had his own key to something hidden beneath the Darden palace, Kalleah could not say.

As the door swung open, Kalleah caught sight of something brightly-colored sitting at the center of the room. She couldn't make out the details with her power still blurring her vision, so she latched a hand onto Bennett's arm to make sure he would be trapped with her if the door closed and then reluctantly let the heightened state of awareness slip away.

Blinking as her vision cleared, Kalleah realized the item before her was a metal contraption painted in rich blues and reds. A set of exposed cogs were turning slowly on one end, while on the other, a short arm dipped and struck the ground before rising once more.

"How does it work?" Kalleah asked in a hushed voice.

"I don't know."

They stepped closer, and Kalleah knelt to examine the machine, dragging Bennett down beside her. She could see no evidence of the silver hairs that powered Weavers' magic, though they could have been hidden within…

"There is another one on the divide where the wall was erected," Bennett said. "It connects somehow to this. The wall isn't visible, of course, just a barrier that blocks anything from passing through."

"And the ancient Makhori somehow had the knowledge to erect such a structure," Kalleah murmured. She recalled the books she had seen in the library in Cashabree, full of knowledge her people had long since forgotten. Was it one of the familiar magic races that had created such a thing, or had a different brand of magic been involved? Perhaps something like the magic flowing from the Ma'oko springs?

And the people in the mountains, creating such marvels of technology and magic—what brand of power did they use?

One thing was certain—whether or not she managed to recruit an army, she needed to see Brenvale.

Kalleah rose and brushed dust from her hands. "Thank you. I appreciate this."

Bennett grinned, his face looking younger than usual in the torchlight. "Are you going to work with us, then?"

"We'll go to Brenvale. You've convinced me."

Bennett locked the door to the contraption behind him and led her back through the rough tunnels. By the time he deposited the torch at the door, she was wondering why she had mistrusted him so thoroughly. He'd had more than enough opportunities to take her captive before now. If he meant her ill, he would not have needed to go to such extremes to trap her.

Kalleah studied the guard on the way out, trying to tell if he looked familiar. She definitely recognized the man in the fabric shop—she must have seen him somewhere at the temple complex.

"Was that a Prophet's Eye?" Kalleah asked quietly as they followed the main street away from the fabric shop. "And the guard—why did they both know you?"

"As we said, our agents have been strategically placed around every royal court in the Kinship Thrones. We are very well connected."

For some reason, his words sent a shiver down her spine. She had already known this, yet this time she detected an ominous side to their influence.

She would find answers in Brenvale. She had to.

"Where are we spending the night?" she asked.

"A friend has agreed to host us," Bennett said. "A smuggler who moves in the highest circles."

Before Kalleah could question him further, he stopped before the door to a lavish brick townhouse with wrought-iron balconies, the structure sharing a wall with the houses on either side.

When he knocked, a woman in wide flounced skirts opened the door.

"Welcome," she said, clasping Bennett's hand. "What a delight. And this is your guest?"

Kalleah bowed, not sure if their host was aware she was a woman. "Thank you for your hospitality." She felt much less apprehensive to be hosted by a woman rather than a man. In Itrea, she would not have worried, but with her own rights so diminished here, she was forever expecting men to take advantage of her.

Their host led them up a flight of stairs to a plush living space with a sitting room, office, and dining room visible.

Another floor up, they came to a series of bedrooms, and Kalleah was relieved when she was given one on the opposite end of the flat from Bennett. It was always uncomfortable asking for a host to give her a room with enough distance from other occupants to keep them safe.

"I hope you'll join me for a drink," their host said to Bennett, smiling slyly.

"Of course." He tipped his hat at her.

"And you, if you wish," she told Kalleah.

"No, I'll retire early tonight. Thank you."

The two left Kalleah at her door; as they descended to the main floor, their laughter echoed back up to her.

Closing and bolting the door to her room, Kalleah crossed to the window. From here, removed from the stench and bustle of the docks and safe from the Lord's Men, she could finally appreciate the charms of the Twin Cities. Her window offered a clear view of the rear of the palace looming over this part of town, lamplight glowing from its many windows. Below, the streets were alive with taverngoers, finely dressed and laughing merrily. Perhaps the Lord's Men were less likely to harass those with money. Yet even here, she saw very few women on the streets, and those she did see were clutching the elbow of a man.

What were the Prophet's Eyes hoping to accomplish, embroiled as they were in every court in the Kinship Thrones? The ease with which Bennett had led her into the tunnels beneath the palace niggled at her. They were almost *too* influential.

If her own aims did not fully align with theirs, she worried she would be powerless to influence their work.

With a sigh, she let the curtains fall closed. At least she was taking action. At least she had not given up on Itrea altogether.

70

The Refugees' Trail

Idorii had barely left the city behind when he came upon the trail left by the refugees. The sight made his stomach cramp with worry—the Whitish would have no trouble tracking them down.

The grasses were flattened in a wide band, the ground rutted in some places by the passage of wagon wheels. The spring rains and new growth had left the plains more vulnerable than usual, more easily marked.

As he picked his way along the mess of tracks, Idorii found item after item discarded by those who had been too ambitious in their packing. A spinning wheel, a framed painting, a rolled-up Weaver's tapestry, a stack of cookbooks, even a chest laden with gold-plated dishes.

There were remains of cookfires, too, so close to Baylore that he was surprised no Whitish scouts had spotted them.

His first night out in the plains, he ate only the millet cakes he had baked a few days prior, the last of which he had shoved into his pack on top of the stack of books. Then he curled up beneath his cloak and tried to sleep, feeling very vulnerable here in the open, his thoughts still ragged with the horrors of the Whitish attack.

Continuing on the next day, he quickly discovered he had not stocked his pack well enough with food. He had enough water, thank the cloudy gods, and he soon came upon a small stream the refugees must have been following—small enough that it would run dry in summer, though it was now swollen with spring melt—but his food rations amounted to a small bag of millet and four potatoes. Not enough to last him to the Icebraid Peaks.

By noon, his legs were aching and his stomach was growling so persistently he could think of nothing else. When he came across an abandoned cart whose wheel had splintered, he perched on the back and dug in his pack for the millet.

At least he had a fire-twist, so he would not need to rely on the pungent buffalo chips that formed the remains of most of the fires he had come across.

He lit the fire-twist and poured a quarter of the millet into his pot, along with a generous helping of water from the stream. If he ate watery portions, he hoped he could be satisfied with less food.

While he waited for the millet to cook, he rolled up his sleeve and wrote to Daymin.

Daymin –

    I am on my way to the Icebraid Peaks and already dreading

the journey. I don't know how you and your army can march through an entire day like you do! I was up at dawn, and now that it's noon, my legs have decided they don't want to walk any further.

To make matters worse, I don't seem to have brought enough food. Perhaps I will starve before I reach the mountains. I'm sorry, Daymin. I will try my best not to perish in the wilderness.

The trail left by the refugees is painfully obvious, so at least someone will find my body, whether the Whitish or your own army.

Do you know of any food I might be able to scavenge without a bow or any other means of hunting?

Yours,
Idorii

He received no reply while he stirred his millet, nor while he burned his mouth eating the porridge, too hungry to wait for it to cool.

At last he was forced to admit there was no point waiting any longer. He rinsed his pot in the stream, extinguished the fire-twist, and continued on his weary way.

As the afternoon wore on, his boots began to rub painfully at his heels, adding to the already-constant ache of sore muscles. The meal had given him a second burst of energy, but it was quickly dwindling, replaced by a hunger more persistent than ever. Plagues, at this rate he would run out of food three days from Baylore. He did not want to admit it, but at this point he was counting on Daymin's army catching up to him before he starved.

Then, just as the sun was dropping low in the sky, he came across a pair of coyotes ripping at something hidden by the grasses.

Idorii broke into a clumsy run, his heavy pack slamming against his back with each step, and chased them away from their kill.

It was a hare. The coyotes had torn it into a mess of flesh and viscera and blood, but Idorii was too hungry to care.

Snatching up the carcass, Idorii washed it in the stream, staining the water red. Thank the cloudy gods for the stream. Hand still submerged in the water, he scooped out the entrails and threw them across the stream for the coyotes to enjoy.

Once the hare was in a less revolting condition, he pulled out his knife and set to work skinning the flesh. He had never done anything of the sort before, but he had worked with leather, and besides, it wasn't like anyone was around to care how much of a mess he made.

Soon he had salvaged a good chunk of meat, which he skewered on a reed and set to roasting over the fire-twist.

While he waited for it to cook, Daymin's reply came.

Idorii —

Please don't starve to death in the wilderness. I don't know anything more about foraging than you do, but if you can describe some of the plants around you, I'll ask my more experienced soldiers for advice.

Yours,

Daymin

Grinning, Idorii switched the skewer into his left hand and wrote his reply.

> *I am no longer in imminent danger of perishing! A pair of coyotes have done the hard work of catching me a hare, and I am about to enjoy a hearty meal. Alas, I can't assume this will be a useful strategy to rely on for the remainder of my journey.*
>
> *Let's see…I can see grass and more grass. Maybe some reeds?*
>
> *Oh yes, and I have been following a small stream that I imagine will lead me all the way to the mountains. So I have enough water to sustain me, at the very least.*
>
> *Where are you now? I miss you. It is very lonely out here.*

When Daymin did not reply for a while, Idorii finished roasting his hare and tore into it. Oil ran down his chin as he ate, the flesh juicy and perfectly charred. He couldn't remember enjoying a meal more.

When he finished, he licked his fingers clean and then leaned back against his pack, feeling more adventurous than he had before.

Daymin's reply came soon after, and Idorii had to light the crystal around his neck to read his writing in the growing darkness.

> *I've spoken to a couple scouts who have spent many spans stationed in the plains without easy access to supplies. One food they mentioned is the prairie turnip, which is apparently very*

hard to find when it is not flowering. It usually flowers in Reed-span, so we are a bit early for it, but you may as well keep an eye out. The flowers come in clusters of purple or blue, and the leaves in sets of five. I was given a drawing of it, which I can try to replicate, though my skills are abysmal.

Please, Daymin, I need to see this!

After a moment, his tattoo flashed cold once more, and Idorii pressed it to find a clumsy drawing appear on his arm. Daymin had sketched a very rough version of the plant as a whole—more just a mess of lines than anything recognizable— but he had illustrated the leaves more helpfully.

I am in awe at your talent, Idorii replied. *I can assure you, I haven't seen purple or blue flowers of any variety since leaving Baylore, but now I will be certain to recognize this prairie turnip if I stumble across it.*

I'm sorry, Daymin wrote back. *I know that was a mess. It was harder drawing on my arm than I'd expected.*

You're just making excuses. Don't worry, my own artistic skills are strictly handicraft-related. I can draw no better than you.

I doubt that. Anyway, you can eat the tubers, if you peel off the skin outside. You can either eat them raw or boil them. A bit like potatoes.
Aside from those, you may find crayfish in the stream. Look under rocks in the shallows. Apparently they aren't hard

to catch, and when you do, you can boil them in their shells.

Thank you, Idorii replied. *It's too dark to look for crayfish now, but I'll give it a try tomorrow. And in the meantime, no purple flower I encounter will be safe.*

He wanted to add something about how much it hurt to know Daymin was so close, yet they might not be reunited for another span, but he stopped himself.

He needn't have worried. Daymin soon echoed Idorii's thoughts.

> *I miss you too, by the way. Very much. I know I'm not alone, but I feel isolated from my army since the slaughter and retreat of the forest. I have lost all sense of purpose. When you were by my side in Baylore, it was a great comfort to be able to unburden myself to you and listen to your voice of reason. Now I feel as though I'm slowly going mad.*
>
> *Where do I go next? Is there any point in continuing?*
>
> *I know you don't need any further burdens added to those already on your shoulders, but the refugees need you. They have left such a blatant trail that the Whitish will be upon them in no time. If your army isn't there to protect them, it will be a slaughter.*
>
> *And besides, don't you want to see me again? Make that your reason to keep going, if you can find nothing else.*

Yours,
Idorii

71

A Race Against Time

Daymin fell asleep with Idorii's last message still on his arm, and before his army had finished packing up their camp, he received another message.

The Whitish army is already at my tail! I didn't realize it last night, but this morning I saw the smoke from their fires. They must be less than a day behind me.

Daymin's heartbeat started racing. At this rate, he wouldn't be able to reach the mountains before the Whitish caught up to the refugees.

He hoped they had made it safely into the foothills and found a way to cover their trail.

Kneeling in the pretext of checking his pack, Daymin wiped his wrist clean and scribbled a reply.

Keep moving as fast as you can. An army takes a while to set up and take down camp each day, so if you can walk from sunup to sundown, you should be able to stay ahead of them. We're only a day or two from the bridge at Ashton, so we should be close on their tail.

Even as he sent it, he remembered Idorii describing his complete exhaustion after a half-day of walking. He had felt the same way when his campaign had begun; only gradually and unnoticeably had he built up his endurance. At the end of each day, he was still ready to collapse, but he knew his army was making greater distances than they had initially.

Not that it would be enough to reach the mountains before the Whitish.

His soldiers were still securing the last of their gear as Daymin wove his way through the assembling ranks to speak with his generals.

He reached General Vask first. The swarthy man grunted when he saw Daymin and stepped aside so they could speak out of earshot of his company.

"More news from Baylore?" he asked gruffly.

Ever since Daymin had shared the news of Baylore's downfall, his army had been subdued. Almost in mourning. He had felt it, too—a strange, untethered sensation, as if the spirit of Itrea had suddenly ceased to exist. Its people clung to life, yet they were no longer Itreans, not without a capital to claim. They were landless, homeless refugees, now more than ever. Even his army seemed diminished somehow.

Daymin cleared his throat, pushing away these disconcerting thoughts. "It's my informant—he's on his way to the mountains, and the Whitish army is only a day behind him. They must have left Baylore as soon as they realized the city was empty."

Only the brief tensing of his jaw betrayed General Vask's concern. "And your orders?"

"We need to make it to the mountains before the Whitish do. I don't think it's possible, but…" Daymin swallowed. "We have to try. And we must stay out of sight of their army. If they engage us on an open field, we won't stand a chance. Not if they've sent the bulk of their forces. We need to reach somewhere defensible."

General Vask bent to rummage in his pack, pulling out a folded map with fraying edges. "Our refugees were heading directly west, correct?"

"Yes," Daymin said.

General Vask traced their route on the map. "If we follow a west-northwest angle, we should reach the mountains quicker than if we headed directly west, though that would put us north of our refugees." He ran his finger along another line connecting to the mountains where they began to angle eastward. "Then we can cut southwest along the front range. It will be a longer route than the Whitish are taking, but it will keep us well away from their army."

"Should we tell the soldiers we might not make it in time?" Daymin asked quietly.

"Yes," General Vask said. "We all have family and friends among the refugees. Worry will hasten your army's progress better than any orders you could give."

"Can I borrow this?" Daymin asked, picking up the old map.

The general's hand twitched possessively, but he stepped back. "Of course."

"Tell your own soldiers the news. I'll speak to the rest of the army as we move out."

Turning away from General Vask, Daymin started toward Pollard, who seemed to have aged ten years since the news of Baylore's capture. Or perhaps it was the long march that was wearing on him; Holden King Pollard was in his late seventies, and had perhaps not realized how grueling the campaign would be when he chose to join Daymin.

Daymin shared the news of the Whitish army's westward progress and asked Pollard to speak to his soldiers before moving on to Morrisse. Both holden kings took his orders with a hint of feverish desperation—he imagined they would push themselves to the point of collapse if they knew with certainty they would reach the refugees before the Whitish.

As his army started moving north again, following the shining ribbon of the Elygian River, Daymin could see his army's renewed purpose reflected in their pace. He lengthened his strides as well, soon drawing to the front of the column.

When he pushed on ahead of his army, the grasslands seemed to stretch on forever before him, the mountains to his left so distant they hardly seemed real.

Satisfying though it was to make progress, Daymin still felt he was deceiving his army. The Whitish army would surely maintain an equally punishing pace, which meant there was no legitimate way for his army to pull ahead. They would drive themselves to exhaustion, all for a fool's hope.

Plagues.

Daymin walked faster than ever, wanting to put distance

between himself and his army. Everything was falling apart. He was a fraud. He continued to stand before his soldiers, pretending they could make a difference, pretending he was still their king, when all he had done was bring ruin to Itrea.

Cloudy gods, he wished Idorii were here. He was good at pulling Daymin from the spiraling gloom of his thoughts.

More than that, he was afraid he would never see Idorii again. If Idorii joined the refugees and Daymin didn't make it in time to defend them, Idorii could die along with all the rest of them. The thought made his chest constrict painfully, and for a moment he couldn't draw breath.

Daymin clutched the tattoo on the inside of his elbow, the one piece of Idorii he still had with him. He had been such a fool, back in Baylore, to push Idorii away. He had been confused and frightened, and now he felt only a gnawing ache at Idorii's absence.

What if he left his army in the night and set off alone to intercept Idorii?

Daymin dismissed the idea at once. He was three days behind the Whitish army; he could not catch up and pass them by without a horse to ride.

But continuing at this pace, resigning himself to the likelihood that he would never see Idorii again…it hurt like the nine plagues.

Daymin's eyes stung, and he brushed the tears away furiously. He had no business being weak when so much rested on his shoulders.

Lifting his eyes to the horizon, he strode on, trying to crowd out the miserable clamor of his thoughts with the sensations around him. The warm breeze grazing his cheeks. The distant cry of a hawk wheeling in the sky. The smell of the earth and the grasses, bright green from the spring rains.

Then he heard footsteps crunching closer. Glancing over his shoulder, he saw Zahira plowing ahead of the army to catch up to him.

"Daymin," she said as she drew alongside him. "This isn't good, is it?"

"No." His voice was hollow.

"So we won't make it in time?"

Daymin shook his head.

Zahira fixed her gaze on the horizon and kept walking, keeping pace with Daymin. What else could she do? They would continue marching forward until they could no longer ignore the truth, until all hope was ground to dust beneath their feet.

Truthbringers and Lord's Men

When Kalleah returned with Bennett the following morning, she found Leoth waiting for her on the temple steps, face lined with concern.

"Kalleah," he said, an odd note in his voice. "You're well?"

"Of course."

Bennett inclined his head to Leoth before hastening off to the tunnels beneath the hill. Leoth watched him go, frowning.

Descending the steps, Leoth approached Kalleah. "Can I talk to you? Somewhere private?"

There was something sad and lost in his tone, and Kalleah felt a pang of guilt. He had saved her from the Lord's Men, yet she was still holding him at a distance.

"Of course," she said. "Shall we go somewhere private?"

They started walking down the hill, away from the doorway into the underground quarters, away from the Twin Cities. The stream that led toward Brenvale lay before them, and it was toward this they set their course. Neither spoke for a long time; the air rang with morning birdsong, the creek ahead burbling playfully as it raced toward the Lodren River. Kalleah realized she was still wearing the garish doublet Bennett had dressed her in, which made her self-conscious. She hoped Leoth did not think she had picked the outfit herself.

At last they reached the bank of the stream and sat on a large rock beside the water.

"I don't trust that thief," Leoth said in a low voice. "I want you to stop going off alone with him. Anything could happen."

Kalleah thought of how nervous she had been when Bennett led her into the rock beneath the palace, and how she had been wary of getting stuck in Darrenmark with him after the gates closed for the night.

"I could kill him at a moment's notice," she said instead. "He's the one who should be afraid."

With a sigh, Leoth leaned forward, resting his elbows on his knees.

"Why are you worried?" Kalleah asked. "Is there anything specific he's done to make you concerned?"

Leoth was quiet for a long time, staring at the water as it swirled its way past the grassy bank.

Eventually he said, "Is there something between the two of you?"

"What?"

Leoth's voice was hoarse. "He's younger than me. Attractive. And he's not—" He gripped his upper arm, where Kalleah knew his long, ridged scars were hidden by his shirt.

"Bloody plagues, Leoth!" Kalleah's heart twisted in sorrow. "No. I don't see him that way at all. Before we left the Twin

569

Cities, he went on a long diatribe about how evil my attack on Eidervell was—he didn't know who I was at the time, of course—and how he despised the forbidden races. He's since apologized, but I've felt very uncomfortable with his presence ever since. Anyone who feels that way about us is too close to a Truthbringer."

Kalleah reached out and gripped Leoth's hand, surprised to find his skin clammy. "Besides, I could never leave you for another. I love you too much for that."

"What were you doing with him last night, then?" Leoth's eyes held a desperate sort of hope.

"He was showing me the conduit the Lord's Men have set up beneath the Darrenmark palace to siphon magic from the wall. It's no magic I can recognize, but it looks real. I think we need to visit Brenvale, no matter what happens next." She hesitated. "I was nervous when he led me into the tunnels under the palace. There were rows of empty cells, and everyone seemed to know him, and…well, I was ready to kill him at a moment's notice."

Leoth chuckled weakly.

Both were silent for another long moment, but this time Leoth's hand was in Kalleah's, and he ran his thumb over her palm, sending tingles up her arm. It had been so long since Leoth had held her. Though the distance between them lingered, their hands formed a tether.

At last Leoth asked softly, "Why have you been so wary around me, then, if not for Bennett? It's as if you can't stand to be in the same room as me."

Kalleah swallowed the lump that rose in her throat. They had never spoken of what he had done while working for the

Truthbringers, and if she brought it up now, she was afraid his answer would forever change the way she saw him. She knew his father had pushed him to join, both overtly and over a lifetime of subtle denigration, but she still didn't know which of the Truthbringers' values he had believed himself and which he had only pretended to uphold.

But his stint with the Lord's Men had brought those long-buried fears too close to the surface for her to ignore. If she was going to move past this, she had to know the whole truth. No matter how much it hurt.

"I was afraid," Kalleah said faintly. "Afraid working with the Lord's Men would lead you back to who you had been when you were a Truthbringer. Afraid some part of you still liked their violence. Their brutality."

Leoth's hand stilled in hers. "That wasn't me. That never was me."

"You say that, but what does it mean?"

"Do you know why I started working for the Lord's Men?"

"Because we needed the money?"

Leoth shook his head. "I never would've considered it. But I was attacked by a gang of beggars one day near the docks, and when the Lord's Men came to break up the fight, they were going to arrest me. I couldn't see any way out, so I told them I had been attacked because I was on my way to join them. And when I showed them how good I was with a sword, they decided I was worth keeping."

Kalleah met his eyes, which were clouded with pain.

"I hated every day of it. I had a hard time even talking to you while I worked with them, knowing what you would think of the sort of things I had to take part in."

571

"What about the Truthbringers?" Kalleah asked. "Did you ever agree with them? Was there any part of you that liked what they were doing?"

"No." Leoth dropped his forehead onto his hands, staring at the ground between his feet. "You have to understand…"

He stopped and tried again. "When I was a boy, I didn't fully comprehend what I was or how much Curse-Weavers were despised. I had a close friend who was a year or two older than me, and I practically idolized him. He was confident and funny and seemed to know all the secrets of the palace, and I followed him around like a puppy.

"Then, when I was twelve, I stripped off my shirt in front of him after we had dueled—even though my father had warned me many times not to do so. When he saw my scars and realized what I was—" Leoth broke off, his voice ragged.

Kalleah brought a hand to his back and traced her fingers lightly over his shirt, passing across the scars that ran down either side of his spine. She continued to trail her fingers along his back as he resumed speaking.

"He was my dearest friend, and he thought I had been possessed by a demon. He—he tried to strangle me. I was saved by my parents' guards, and the boy was sent from the city to be assassinated."

Kalleah realized Leoth was crying, tears dripping silently down his nose. She wanted to fold him into her arms, but he kept speaking, his voice shaking.

"I've never been able to sleep well since then. And that was when my father started his campaign of belittlement, making it clear how evil I was. How worthless. He had protected me that one time, but it was only because I hadn't understood how important it was to hide my taint.

"So I buried it all away. I didn't speak for spans, and when I did, I was rude and dismissive of anyone who tried to approach me. I never wanted to have a friend again.

"As the years went on, my father decided to make use of me, still reminding me all the while of my inescapable evil. He pushed me to gain support at court, so I became witty and sarcastic, anything to protect myself from starting to care.

"When he ordered me to join the Truthbringers, I wasn't surprised. I had a deeply-ingrained hatred for the forbidden races by that point, and I had wanted to join their ranks myself. But after the first day of listening to them speak, I went home and threw up. I was still so scared. I still felt like that twelve-year-old whose dearest friend had nearly killed him. I felt so—broken." Leoth wiped his eyes on his shoulder. "So lost."

This time, Kalleah did gather him into her arms. Leoth buried his head against her neck, and she gripped him tight, afraid he would crumble to ash if she let him go.

He had kept this to himself all these years. He had admitted he was afraid of capture, of being discovered for a Curse-Weaver, but Kalleah had never guessed the root of his fear.

To be turned on so violently by a friend…

She felt like a fool. Her own fear of the Truthbringers was nowhere near as personal as Leoth's. In them, he had found the embodiment of the parents who despised him for what he was, the friend who had turned on him, the years of being told he was evil. Where she had found their intolerance foreign, he had accepted it as another piece in his tapestry of self-loathing.

"Leoth," she murmured, her own eyes damp as she pressed a kiss to his forehead. "Thank you for telling me. And I'm so sorry for not trusting you."

"It was my fault as well," he muttered. "I closed you out. I'm sorry."

Releasing Leoth, Kalleah wiped his tears away with a thumb and then kissed him fiercely. "I love you. Don't ever doubt that."

73

The Warehouse at the Docks

L uvoli's face was shining with enthusiasm when he burst into Edreon's room one evening.

"Have you heard the news?" he asked breathlessly.

Edreon took in his cloak and boots; he must have been somewhere in the city. "Obviously not." He shifted in his bed, too feverish to sit up.

"I've just been down at the docks. The new shipment of logs has arrived! There are dozens of the things, with more waiting in King's Port."

The news flooded Edreon like a restorative. This time he was able to drag himself into a sitting position, grunting at the effort. Excitement hummed in his veins; after so many spans of waiting, he could hardly believe the day had come at last.

And he was alive to see it. Thank Varos.

In the drawn-out spans of anticipation, he had devoted much thought to what he would do with the logs once they had arrived. He had contemplated commissioning a bed from the enchanted timber, as the easiest way to expose himself to the magic in constant low doses, but when he recovered abruptly and completely, he did not want anyone connecting it to his new bed.

Another ship would be easier to justify, and he could use it to feign a trip to a restorative seaside retreat. Yet the whole endeavor would take far too long, especially with the way his infection had made a resurgence. Even his trusted healer, the devotee of Tabanus, was now urging him to amputate the leg before it cost him his life.

There was only one way to do this quickly and in secret.

"Luvoli," Edreon said. "I need you to come to me tonight, after darkness falls. Speak of this to no one, not even your wife."

"Are you going to inspect the logs?" Luvoli asked.

Edreon shot him a warning look. "No questions."

Luvoli shut his mouth with a snap.

"Go now, and don't fail me."

* * *

By the time Luvoli returned, Edreon had fallen into a feverish doze. Much though he had tried to remain awake, his body had betrayed him.

"Are we going down to the docks?" Luvoli asked in a whisper. He was dressed for the night, with a stylish cloak and a warm scarf.

"Yes," Edreon said. "And you are going to get me there without use of a horse or palanquin."

Luvoli looked momentarily taken aback. "I'm not sure I'm

strong enough for this. Should we ask Marviak—"

"No," Edreon snapped. "I trust you with this secret, and you alone. Are the halls clear?"

"More or less," Luvoli said. "There are few events held in your absence these days."

"Then help me from this bed."

With careful movements that still sent agony tearing through Edreon, Luvoli helped him sit up and dress in a nondescript set of clothes and a hooded cloak. When it came time to stand, Luvoli's mouth tightened in worry, though he voiced no further concerns. He sat beside Edreon and pulled Edreon's arm over his shoulder. Then, on a count of three, he surged to his feet.

Edreon pushed with all the strength of his good leg, managing to rise from his bed, but once he was standing he swayed worryingly.

"Are you sure about this?" Luvoli asked quietly.

This time Edreon didn't snap at him. He could see Luvoli was genuinely worried. "I'll manage."

Together they stumbled from Edreon's quarters. Luvoli led the way down to a servants' entrance on the ground floor, avoiding the guards at the main doors, while Edreon leaned gratefully on the banister as they descended.

Then they were outside in the brisk night air. Leaving the castle was easy enough, as Edreon raised his hood to shadow his face and pretended to be Luvoli's drunken companion, but the steep back route down to the waterfront almost defeated him. There was no rail to lean on this time as he staggered down the stairs, and several times he nearly threw Luvoli off his feet. Luvoli was slender and shorter than he; recommending the burlier Marviak to help him had been reasonable.

Yet Edreon did not trust Marviak. Not in the way he did Luvoli.

And Luvoli did not complain. They rested whenever Edreon needed to collect himself, Luvoli murmuring soft words of encouragement, while Edreon gritted his teeth and did not voice the worry that he would collapse before he reached the docks.

By the time they came out on the waterfront, Edreon's eyes were streaming from the pain, his whole body trembling.

"Is there any way I can help?" Luvoli asked quietly.

Edreon jerked his head side to side and staggered on. He had been putting more weight than he should on his injured leg, using it more as a crutch than a limb since he could only drag it along behind him, and the wound was throbbing so fiercely he worried the flesh would rip free of his bones.

When they came in sight of the warehouses, a wave of dizziness swept over Edreon, and he leaned heavily against a discarded barrel.

"Where are the logs being kept?" he asked as he waited for the black spots to clear from his vision.

"In there." Luvoli pointed to a nearby warehouse.

It was close, but the distance seemed unsurmountable. What if he crawled the last fifty paces? He might lose the last shards of his self-respect, but if it was the difference between healing his leg and dying of infection, he would do virtually anything.

"Ready to keep going?" Luvoli asked.

Edreon pushed off from the barrel, leaning his weight on Luvoli's shoulders once more, and hobbled on. His vision swam, and the cobblestones seemed to heave and ripple underfoot.

Ten paces from the warehouse, his leg gave way.

Edreon fell roughly onto his hands, his cheek grazing the stones.

"Your Majesty," Luvoli gasped. "Are you injured?"

"No," Edreon grunted. "But I don't think I can walk any further."

Luvoli knelt beside him, lifting Edreon's head onto his knees, and Edreon lay there, breathing heavily, until he had gathered himself. He had never felt so wretched.

At last he pushed himself onto his hands and his uninjured knee. Swinging his throbbing head about to make sure no one was keeping watch, he started crawling painstakingly forward, the injured leg dragging behind him like a useless knot of driftwood.

When he neared the warehouse, Luvoli picked the lock—a trick he had learned from Naresha—and pushed open the door for Edreon.

Once they were safely inside, Luvoli whispered, "You put yourself through the Destroyer's fires to get here. What about these logs made that worthwhile?"

Edreon was too tired to be angry. "No questions. I want you to leave now and lock the door behind you. Come fetch me in the morning, before dawn."

Luvoli seemed to be fighting with himself, and he shifted his weight from one foot to another, mouth working.

Then he hissed out a sharp breath. "Fine. Do as you wish. I'll be back at first light."

Edreon did not move until he was alone. Once the door had closed behind Luvoli, the lock grinding back into place, he was plunged into darkness.

Edreon reached in his pocket for a flint and candle. Lighting the candle, he held it up before him to see the full glory of his harvest.

The warehouse was piled high with the enormous logs, and from Luvoli's description, there must be other warehouses along the waterfront converted to this purpose as well. Each was large enough to fit a bedchamber within the circumference of the tree, and the wood carried a soft, woodsy scent laced with brine.

On one end of the warehouse, he noticed a stack of wood that had already been cut into boards. Based on the weathering, his soldiers must have prepared the wood in King's Port so as to fit it more easily onto the ships. They must have known they would face Edreon's displeasure at tampering with the trunks, yet in that moment, he had never seen a more welcome sight.

Dropping back to his hands and one knee, candle gripped in his teeth, Edreon crawled across the warehouse to the stack of sawn boards. Then he dragged himself onto the pile, raising a small clatter as the boards shifted beneath his weight.

He froze, waiting for the sound to quiet.

Another shift forward brought him fully onto the mound of boards. Too exhausted to move any further, he extinguished the candle and lay back on the bed of wood. He pulled a few boards on top of himself, where they dug into his ribs, and let his eyes drift closed.

If this did not work, he doubted he would be capable of the return journey to the castle.

Varos, if you cannot heal me, let me die here, Edreon prayed. *Either way, let this suffering end. Surely I have endured many lifetimes of pain.*

* * *

He must have fallen asleep, because he woke with a jolt at the sound of shouting outside the warehouse. With his thoughts still muddled from sleep, it took him a moment to realize the sound was nothing more than dockworkers guiding a ship to its berth.

Sitting up with a groan, Edreon did not register at first that he would not have been able to do so the day before.

Then everything clicked into place.

Apart from the ache in his back from its prolonged contact with the mound of boards, he felt very little pain elsewhere. The fever had broken, leaving him refreshed and clear-headed, and his leg felt almost whole.

Pulling up the leg of his trousers, Edreon found the mass of bandages swaddling the infected gash. He unwrapped them with trembling hands, the smell of rot turning his stomach.

When he reached the skin beneath, he found nothing but a smooth patch of pink flesh where the wound had once been.

Lowering his legs carefully off the end of the boards, he tested his weight on the injured leg.

He winced as pain shot up his thigh, and his knee buckled beneath him.

So it was not fully healed. He still could not walk, but unless the damage was irreversible, he imagined another night in the warehouse would restore him to his full capabilities.

While he waited for Luvoli to return, Edreon surveyed the warehouse, imagining the fleet he could build from such a magnificent stockpile. Whitland would control the seas, dominating trade and policing the underhanded dealings he knew had begun to proliferate in the other Kinship Thrones.

At last the warehouse door creaked open. Luvoli's familiar tail of sandy hair was silhouetted by the grey light outside as he tiptoed in, peering around for Edreon.

Edreon pushed himself onto his usable foot and hobbled closer, leaning heavily on the ends of the logs.

"Your Majesty," Luvoli whispered, surprise evident in his voice. "Has your condition improved since yesterday?"

Edreon hushed him with a scowl. "Not a word."

Together they made the slow journey back up to the castle, where Edreon was forced to reveal his face to the guards to gain admittance. He hoped they would not gossip about his weakness.

When they reached his rooms, Luvoli left him in his bed, which now seemed rank with sweat and illness. Instead of lying in that accumulated filth, Edreon rose and hobbled over to his desk, where he spent the day going through his ledgers and correspondences, ensuring nothing had been overlooked or meddled with in his quarters of neglect.

It was here that Naresha and Odelia found him when they appeared with his lunch.

"You look well," Naresha said in surprise.

"The fever has broken," Edreon said. "No thanks to my healer."

Naresha shot him a sharp look. "He gave you his best recommendations. If he could not help, no one could."

Edreon grunted. "And what are you doing here, girl?"

Odelia dropped a curtsey. "I have been investigating the man who claims to train the best assassins in the land, Your Majesty, who offered to send thirty to serve you."

Edreon blinked at her. Lost in his recent fog of sickness, he had forgotten that offer altogether.

"Well?" he said belatedly.

"I discovered who had sent him. It was Prince Hosteran, Your Majesty. He claims it was a gesture of goodwill."

"I see." Edreon closed the book on his desk and turned to face the two women. "Prince Hosteran is an important player in Whitish politics, and if you are correct, this is the first gesture of loyalty he has shown me."

"Or a way for him to seed enemies in your court," Naresha said.

Edreon frowned at her. "I doubt he is as thick-headed as that. If he hoped to kill me, he would not have mentioned assassins. He could easily have disguised them as members of his own court, here to make alliances."

"Should we invite them here, then?" Naresha asked.

"Indeed. It would be useful for me to gauge their intentions."

Naresha gave him another searching look from head to toe, no doubt registering the fact that he was both clothed and sitting up without evidence of pain, speaking more coherently than he had since the fever had returned.

Then she took Odelia's arm and led her from his bedchamber without another word.

* * *

Again that night, Edreon and Luvoli made the trip to the docks, this time much more easily than before. Luvoli made no comment, thank Varos.

And when Edreon woke the following morning from his

bed of timbers, he stretched his injured leg and then curled it to his chest, warm satisfaction filling him when he felt not a single twinge of pain or hinderance of movement.

This time, when he stood, the injured leg took his weight with ease. It was weaker than the other, perhaps, but that was the result of spans of neglect. He passed the time until Luvoli returned pacing the warehouse to loosen his muscles, and when the leg was feeling less stiff, he transitioned to a series of sword positions.

When Luvoli pushed open the door, Edreon sat on the end of the stack of boards, feigning continued weakness. As much as he trusted Luvoli, he did not want to confront him with such a miraculous unexplained healing.

"Has the sea air done you some good?" Luvoli joked when he draped Edreon's arm over his shoulder. "The life has returned to your visage."

"Then perhaps it has," Edreon said, in a tone that discouraged further questions.

As they made their slow way up the stairs through the city, Edreon pretending he still could not bear weight on one leg, they came across a pair of guards in uniform walking down from the castle. When they drew closer, Edreon recognized them as two of his own personal guards.

"Bloody Varos," Edreon hissed. He couldn't be seen outside the city in such suspicious circumstances. His hood was draped low over his face, but if his own personal guards saw Luvoli accompanied by a man with a limp, they would easily make the connection.

The guards were approaching too quickly for him to escape their notice. Though they talked and laughed as they went, both scanned the street for any sign of danger.

Edreon withdrew his arm from Luvoli's shoulder. He had not wanted Luvoli to see the extent of his recovery, but if it was a choice between Luvoli knowing the truth and his guards catching him outside the castle under suspicious circumstances, he would choose Luvoli every time.

So he stood on his own two feet and strode toward a side street, where he turned and walked briskly until he was out of sight of the stairway. After a long moment, he heard Luvoli's heeled shoes clicking after him.

When Luvoli caught up to him behind a lean-to, he was wide-eyed and flushed.

"You—that was—how can you walk again?" Luvoli sputtered.

"You must guard this secret with your life," Edreon said in a low voice. "If I cannot trust you with it, then I must send you from court."

"So you're healed? Truly?"

"Yes."

Luvoli's face lit up with happiness, and he pulled Edreon into an embrace.

At first Edreon stiffened, not used to being treated so familiarly, but then Luvoli's enthusiasm caught up to him. Had he tried to recruit a spy to use for his schemes and instead found a true friend?

He thumped Luvoli on the back, a smile spreading across his own face. Though he had worried at first, he now believed he could trust Luvoli to keep his secret, however questionable the means of his recovery.

Holy Varos, it was good to be well again.

74

A Way Through the Foothills

Idorii had surprised himself. With the Whitish army close on his tail, the smoke rising from their fires each morning had spurred him to rise earlier and start walking with the first light of dawn. He often reached a state of near-collapse in the early evening, but after dinner, when those trailing threads of smoke appeared once more, the hairs at the back of his neck began to prickle. It was enough to give him one last burst of energy, to push him onward until darkness fell.

He had caught crayfish for dinner three times now; after a frustrating evening of searching in vain, he now knew where to look, and was able to scour all the likely-looking hiding places in the stream in short order. He had also stumbled across a sack of wayfarers' bread that must have fallen from the back of a wagon, and this was enough to keep him going without needing to cook except at night.

Whenever he stopped to rest, he wrote to Daymin, who

replied as often as he was able. Idorii still worried he might be annoying Daymin with his constant demands for updates, but after spending all day with nothing but his own thoughts for company, he was desperate for whatever Daymin was willing to give. It didn't help that the landscape was nothing but unrelieved grasslands as far as he could see. A bit more variety would be welcome.

Then, at last, the mountains seemed to be drawing noticeably closer. They loomed before him, the details of their rocky faces coming clear with each passing hour, and Idorii almost thought he could feel the chill air coming off the snow-capped peaks.

Closer still, the higher mountains disappeared behind the front range, which was cloaked in a pine forest unmarred by snow. There were great slabs of reddish rock rising from the face of the foothills as well, tilted against the mountainsides like the scales of a great beast.

As he closed the last distance to the mountains, Idorii found himself walking with his face lifted toward the hills, his thumbs hooked beneath the straps of his too-heavy pack. Something about the mountains called to him, sparking an urge to explore he had never felt before.

The land sloped up gradually to meet the forest, and as he climbed the gentle rise, Idorii looked back to see if he could make out the Whitish army.

All he could see were empty grasslands. He must have gained more distance on them than he had expected.

Further still, the land evened out again; here, with an abruptness that made him stagger, Idorii came across the refugees.

His heart sank. He had expected to find them already safely past the foothills, but he could see tens of thousands of people in the camp skirting the edge of the pine forest.

He had been hiking in only his shirt, the laces hanging loose, but now he pulled on his coat and turned up the collar, finishing by wrapping his scarf around his chin to hide his markings. The root-like tendrils that snaked across his face were impossible to hide without face paint; he hoped they would be mistaken for grime.

Then he shouldered his pack once more and broke into a jog, his pack slamming against his back. As he drew near, already sweating beneath his coat, Prince Calden emerged from the crowd and strode forward to meet him.

"You look familiar," Prince Calden said. "Are you King Daymin's informant who stayed behind in Baylore?"

"I am," Idorii said. He dropped his pack by his feet, feeling light enough to float into the air as he shed the weight.

"What news from Baylore?"

Idorii grimaced at the look of hope on Prince Calden's face. "The city fell almost at once. We were overwhelmed by numbers alone, and after they had gained an advantage, the Whitish flooded the streets with poisonous gases to kill any who were not stationed on the walls." He remembered belatedly that Ellarie was Prince Calden's mother. "I'm sorry."

A muscle at the corner of Prince Calden's mouth twitched. "Then we are lucky our population escaped well before the Whitish arrived."

Idorii nodded.

"And the Whitish army? We've seen smoke on the horizon, but we weren't sure whose army it belonged to."

"It's the Whitish," Idorii said. "Daymin was several days south of the bridge near Ashton when Baylore fell, and he's taking a different course to the mountains to see if he can cut off the Whitish army."

"He'll never arrive in time," Prince Calden said.

"No." Idorii looked behind Calden, running his eyes over the camp. "And what about you? Have you found a way into the mountains?"

"Not a very good one. Our scouts are still looking for a more reliable option."

"I want to see," Idorii said, shouldering his pack once more.

First Calden led Idorii to where the palace Makhori were camped. Idorii's mother hugged him fiercely, while the others clustered around him with feverish curiosity. Idorii was forced to recount Baylore's demise yet again, this time around mouthfuls of the delicious stew his mother had pressed into his hands.

Once he had finished the food, he said, "The Whitish are nearly here. We need to move into the mountains faster. I'll tell you more later, but first Prince Calden is going to show me the route you're taking through the foothills."

"Are you still reporting to King Daymin?" his mother asked.

"Yes," Idorii said. Then he hurried off to rejoin Calden, abandoning his pack with the palace Weavers.

When they left the refugees behind, Idorii caught the scent of vanilla rising from the forest.

"The foothills are more impenetrable than we'd expected," Prince Calden said in a low voice as he led Idorii beneath the trees. The smell was stronger here, and the mat of fallen needles

589

was soft underfoot. "It's easy to summit the low peaks from this side, but the mountains drop off steeply on the opposite side, giving us no way down. The only way we've found is through a narrow river gorge with a deer trail along one side, but it's very challenging maneuvering the wagons through. Most have been abandoned, and our soldiers are ferrying supplies through as quickly as they can."

"Why are so many people still camped on this side?" Idorii asked.

Calden glanced over his shoulder, expression grim. "We only found the route two days ago. It's not far from our camp, but from most approaches it looks impassable. You have to walk through the stream, stepping on the right stones to avoid getting swept under, before climbing to join the deer trail. We're trying to move the families with young children through first, so the remaining refugees are stuck waiting their turn."

They walked for another thirty minutes through open forest before reaching the canyon where the stream passed between two mountains. As they drew closer to the gorge, the trees receded, giving way to exposed red rock and a frothing creek that churned its way through the narrow divide.

A cluster of adults, many of them old enough to be grandparents, waited with the children on this side of the gorge. Where the river entered the canyon, Idorii could see a rope bolted to the rocks on both sides, zigzagging a few times across the water before disappearing around the corner.

Then, as they watched, a soldier waded down the stream, stepping carefully from one submerged rock to another. When he reached the group, he helped a young woman with a baby swaddled against her chest to step carefully down the eroded slope into the water. She went slowly, the rope swaying in her grip, while the soldier stayed close behind in case she fell. At one point, her foot slipped off a stone, and she would have been ripped free of the rope had the soldier not grabbed her around the waist in time.

By the time they disappeared around the corner, Idorii's hands were sweaty and his heart racing. The whole endeavor seemed far too risky. Had any been swept downstream, despite the best efforts of the soldiers? And what of the children who were too large to carry yet too small to reach the rope with ease?

"So you see why we're delayed," Prince Calden said grimly.

Idorii made a sound of agreement.

After another minute, they turned and started back toward camp. Idorii hardly noticed where he walked, too wrapped up in worry. They needed something to slow the Whitish, or the refugees would never make it through in time. But Daymin's army was too far behind to help, and the force that had traveled with the refugees was so small it would be flattened.

He could see no way to avoid their fate.

75

Too Late

The long, punishing days of marching had driven Daymin to such a state of exhaustion that his worries were trampled by fatigue. He simply kept walking, from first light to last, his legs and back aching worse with each league they crossed.

Yet for all their effort, the mountains remained stubbornly distant.

When he stumbled into his tent one evening, he pulled up his sleeve to see what Idorii had written earlier that afternoon. His messages were the one light that kept Daymin going, something to look forward to at the end of each interminable day.

But this time, Idorii had written so much it looped around the sides of Daymin's wrists and crowded the tattoo on the inside of his elbow.

Daymin lit his crystal and bent closer to read the cramped

writing.

Daymin –

I've reached the refugee camp. What looks like half their number are still camped at the foothills, because they have only just found a way through and the route is treacherous and slow going. They are prioritizing children and supplies for now, but there will be many thousands still on this side of the mountains when the Whitish catch up to us.

The way into the mountains is a narrow gorge with steep cliffs on either side. We have to walk in the water for the first part before joining a deer trail for the remainder of the distance, which takes at least three days given the difficult footing. And the wagons can't make the journey, so the soldiers are carrying supplies over by hand.

If we could get everyone to safety, it would be easy to blast away the side of the cliff and destroy the deer trail, which would make the camp in the mountains fully defensible. But without more time, the Whitish will pursue us into the mountains.

How far are you from our camp, by your estimate? We need your help. Without your army to slow the Whitish, I fear we will lose all hope of reaching safety. Either that, or half of us will need to stay behind while those who have made it through destroy the trail.

Please, Daymin. If there is anything you can do…your people have made it so far, and if they were to die at the last moment before reaching safety, all of it would have been a waste.

I hope I'm not pleading for help in vain. I hope you are close enough to make a difference.

If I cannot see you again before the battle…

Love,
Idorii

"Any news?" Zahira asked from the other side of the tent.

Daymin pulled down his sleeve, hand shaking. He had expected this, ever since his army had started toward the mountains, but receiving confirmation of their failure left him lightheaded. He had hoped the refugees had already found a way through, and his army would simply be reinforcing the pass they had taken. Not that half of his people would be stranded on this side of a narrow gorge, half on the other. How could he salvage a situation like that?

Zahira was still watching him expectantly.

"The Whitish are nearly to the mountains, and half of our people haven't made it past the foothills yet," Daymin said, voice hollow. "Our people won't be able to fight them off without our army, and there's no way for our army to make it in time to help."

Tarak and Lalaysha were staring at him now as well.

"What are we going to do, then?" Tarak asked.

"I don't know. I have no Varse-damned idea."

Rising, Daymin stalked from the tent into the darkness beyond, the crystal around his neck lighting the way through camp. Darkness had fallen, the stars beginning to emerge, and the only people still about were sentries.

He threaded his way to the edge of camp, nodding at a sentry as he stepped into the grasslands beyond. He didn't stop until he had left the tents a hundred paces behind, until he could imagine he was all alone in the vast emptiness.

Then he sank into a crouch, despair so thick in his throat he could hardly draw breath.

This was his fault. At the time he hadn't seen it, but choosing to help the forest had destroyed his chances of getting ahead of the Whitish army.

That was the tradeoff he had unknowingly made. It had never been a choice between Baylore and the Wandering Woods—Baylore's fate had been sealed from the moment the trees left. No, he had chosen to protect the trees over his own refugees.

And what good had his protection afforded? Thousands dead from the poison scattered over the trees, and countless thousands more killed as they tried to cross the poisoned river.

His whole campaign—all the long spans of marching, of losing more soldiers at each battle, of watching New Savair burn and pinning his army against the banks of the Elygian—all had been for naught.

He had given up hope long ago, yet still he had tried. Still he had pushed forward, because moving had seemed better than doing nothing.

And now…what?

He was too late.

Too late to save his people. Too late to make a difference. Too late to give Itrea another chance.

What was he supposed to do?

Should he keep marching onward, knowing it was futile?

Should he turn around and re-capture Baylore while it was lightly defended, leaving his civilians to die?

Should he attack the Whitish army from the rear, dashing

his forces against theirs until his army was gone, all to buy his civilians a few more hours to reach safety?

And what safety would they find, with no army to protect them?

Above, the stars glittered coldly, and all around stretched the vast, uncivilized grasslands. This was Itrea too, yet they might as well be in the Kinship Thrones for all the good his army could do.

Daymin clambered to his feet and started walking again, anger driving him faster and faster. He was furious at himself. If he had only struck out for the mountains a couple days sooner, he would have arrived in time.

He walked away from camp, toward the mountains he could no longer see, the crystal at his neck casting just enough light to keep him from tripping over uneven tufts of grass. He knew he might lose his way in the dark, but he didn't care. Not now. What difference would it make?

Soon he broke into a run, the grasses whipping against his boots, the breeze whistling in his ears. Maybe if he ran fast enough, he could forget it all. Maybe he would collapse somewhere out in the wilderness, and that would be the end of it.

He ran until his lungs burned, until his throat was coated with the sour taste of exertion. He ran until his legs were trembling and half-numb.

Then, when he could run no further, he dropped to his hands and knees in the grass. His breath rasped in his throat, and he coughed, his whole body shaking.

His eyes blurred, and he realized he was crying.

He had failed.

Everything he had done since taking the throne had led to this, and in the moment his people had needed him most, he had let them down.

There was no longer a refuge waiting for them in the mountains. There was nothing left of Itrea but death.

76

A Dangerous Path

When they returned to the castle, Luvoli followed Edreon back to his sitting room. Edreon was no longer pretending to limp; there was no reason to continue the charade around Luvoli.

Once they were alone, and Luvoli had locked the door to the royal chambers behind them, he confronted Edreon with arms crossed over his chest.

"What have you done?"

"I told you not to ask questions," Edreon snapped.

Luvoli narrowed his eyes. "I helped you sneak from the castle for Varos knows what reason, swearing to secrecy, and I saw how feeble you were two days ago. Yet now you can walk again? I deserve the truth. Have you made a bargain with the Cleaver? Were you feigning illness before?"

Edreon sank onto a chair, still marveling at the way his once-injured leg moved without the slightest twinge of pain. It wasn't that he didn't trust Luvoli. But if he admitted aloud what he had done—what he was bringing into Whitland—it would become true in a way it hadn't seemed before.

Luvoli took the chair beside Edreon, leaning forward with an unusually serious expression. "Please."

Edreon let out a long breath. Maybe it would help to share this burden with someone. Maybe he would be able to clarify his own thoughts if he spoke them aloud.

"Do you remember the voyage we took on the new ship built of Itrean wood?" Edreon began slowly.

"Of course."

"Did you notice anything strange when we returned?"

Luvoli frowned at him. "No, I can't recall…"

"I did. When I rose the next morning, I found that an old pain had vanished. It had needled me for years, yet suddenly it was gone, without a trace."

Luvoli's eyes widened.

"I suspected, then, that the wood from the enchanted trees had healing properties. And when I sustained my more recent injury, I hoped I would be able to avoid amputation long enough to allow the next shipment of trees to heal me."

"You gambled with your life," Luvoli said hoarsely. "You couldn't be sure they would do such a thing, and yet—"

"When the first shipment of trees arrived, all bound for my creditors," Edreon continued, as if Luvoli had not spoken, "I sneaked into the place where they were temporarily held, here in the castle grounds, and spent the night by the logs. It made no difference to the injury, but my fever broke, and the infection subsided. I knew then that I would need a more thorough exposure to finish the job. And so I bided my time until the next shipment came."

"The enchanted logs have done this?" Luvoli asked. "In two nights, they have accomplished what no human physician ever could?"

Edreon slowly folded up the leg of his trousers until Luvoli could see the place where the wound had once been. The patch of skin was hairless and smooth, pinker than the rest of his leg, but no other evidence remained of the injury that had nearly claimed his life.

Luvoli stared at it, wide-eyed, his mouth opening and closing without any sound coming out.

"You see why I swore you to secrecy?" Edreon asked, covering the patch of healed skin once more.

"You—that—" Though Luvoli looked horrified, Edreon thought he could see a spark of enthusiasm in his eyes.

"And now I must deal with those who sought to take advantage of me in my weakness. I will feign a slower recovery than this, of course, but I don't intend to hide away from court for long."

Luvoli found his voice at last. "But this means you're knowingly bringing magic into Whitland!" he whispered. "I might have joked about possessing magical items, but I would never take such a risk. I know the consequences. I can't believe you are going to continue importing logs, knowing what they do. People will find out. If you discovered their secret in a single night aboard an enchanted ship, others will do the same."

"I know," Edreon said heavily. "And I will regulate the use of the logs more heavily knowing what they can do. I think the magic only works if you are encased in the enchanted wood—in a ship or a house, for instance."

"Which is exactly what they are most likely to be designated for!" Luvoli hissed.

Seeing Luvoli's worry brought back all the fears Edreon had tried to suppress—of the priests discovering his heresy and burning him alive; of his people turning on him because he had dabbled too heavily in the magic they despised; of his rival claimants for the throne gaining support as his own popularity crumbled.

"I know the risk," Edreon said at last. "I just hope that whoever discovers the secret will be so eager to make use of it that they won't twist it against me."

"That's a dangerous assumption to stake your future on," Luvoli said. "Itrea was one thing, but inviting magic into Whitland? Even those who want to use the logs for their magic will be afraid they'll be implicated if the truth comes out."

"What would you have me do?"

"You could destroy the logs. Claim one of your priests discovered a dangerous taint on the wood, and stop bringing them across the ocean. Your soldiers in Itrea are already accustomed to magic and won't balk at using enchanted wood. Keep them for that purpose alone."

"And let Whitland fall to ruin once more? Our hold on Chelt is tenuous at best, and once we defeat King Daymin's army, we will have no excuse to keep the Cheltish draftees in Itrea. Our dominance of the Kinship Thrones depends on both the fleet those logs will become and the wealth that will flow to our coffers when we sell them on. You know exactly how dire our finances have become."

This finally quieted Luvoli's arguments.

"You see the position I am in?" Edreon said grimly. "I can't turn back, yet each step I take brings me closer to my own doom."

"And you would make that choice?" Luvoli asked. "You would continue to put your own life at risk in the hopes of bringing glory to Whitland?"

Though he had questioned himself many times, wondering how far he was willing to go down this dangerous path, Edreon said, "Yes. I would rather lose my life for this cause than settle for ruling a mess of squabbling princedoms."

* * *

It was getting near midday when Naresha called on Edreon, accompanied by the healer, the slight, grey-haired devotee of Tabanus. There was no one he wished to see less.

"Your healer wishes to examine your wound," Naresha said. "After how well you appeared yesterday, he dares to hope you might keep your leg."

Edreon was lying in his bed, after having changed the sheets himself and fed the old ones to his fire. Though the stench of burning fabric had taken a long time to clear away, he was relieved to do away with the last traces of his festering wound.

"It was but a temporary break in the fever," Edreon said. "I am worsening already."

"Please, Your Majesty. There may be something I can do."

"No," Edreon snapped. "I have had enough of your failed attempts. You were unable to heal my leg, and I see no further use for your ministrations. Go."

"Your Majesty," Naresha said, brow creased with worry. "If your fever has subsided, it might mean his methods are working.

What would you do in his absence?"

"I have arranged for another physician," Edreon said. "One who comes highly recommended."

The healer bowed. "Your Majesty, I—"

"Go! Leave my sight at once, and never return!"

Naresha sighed as the healer scurried away. Edreon had not intended to dismiss the man so harshly—he had done better work than the Whitish physician, after all—but if he was going to insist on examining Edreon so soon after he had recovered, there was no way to hide the work of the enchantment while the man remained at court.

"I've heard no word of another physician attending to you," Naresha said once they were alone.

"Do you imagine I share my every secret with you?" Edreon asked sharply. "When you kept the existence of your daughter from me for sixteen years?"

"Is this new physician the reason for your improvement, then?" Naresha asked.

"I imagine so. And speaking of your daughter, I have need of her. Send her to me at once. Make sure she is alone."

Naresha sighed once more, but she bent to kiss Edreon's cheek before taking her leave.

Once he was alone, Edreon ran a hand through his hair in frustration. He had been short with Naresha ever since he had learned about her daughter, shutting her out from his most dangerous secrets, and he missed the confidences they had once shared. Maybe it was time to give her another chance.

When Odelia joined him, Edreon beckoned her to his bedside. Now that he was well, it felt cumbersome to conduct business from this position. How long would he need to wait

603

before he could start receiving guests in his sitting room once more? He would have to plot his feigned recovery carefully.

"Your Majesty," Odelia murmured, dropping into a precise curtsey.

"What news from court? Have any whispers reached your pretty ears?"

"All the talk is of Prince Navaire, Your Majesty. He is marching toward Eidervell with an army at his heel, gathering support everywhere he goes. The priests of Varos are encouraging all devout followers to heed his call."

"Blast them." Edreon wished he could ride to meet them in battle himself.

"They are claiming you are unfit to rule given your illness, Your Majesty," Odelia said. "But my mother says you might be recovering?"

"I am certainly not on my deathbed," Edreon said sourly. "I don't intend to give Prince Navaire a chance to gain too great a foothold. And you will help me orchestrate his downfall. But in the meantime, I have a task for you. One that your mother must not learn of."

Odelia's eyes betrayed only a brief flicker of curiosity.

"This is a test of your loyalty, child, and if you succeed, I will entrust you with more crucial work. I have just sent my healer from court, since he failed in his duty, and I need you to track him down and assassinate him in a way that looks like a natural death. He is an old man, so this should not be difficult."

He saw the corner of Odelia's mouth tighten, so he added, "I am not doing this out of vengeance. It is crucial to my own plans, in a way that I am unable to explain to you at this time. Do not think me a monster. Everything I do is for the good of

Whitland."

Odelia curtseyed again. "Of course, Your Majesty. I will leave right away."

She turned and hastened from the room, leaving Edreon frowning at the weight of her judgment.

Why did he care what she thought of him? She was a child, a tool. Irrelevant.

Yet she could be so much more. And it was not just his trust she needed to earn—he had the strange feeling he needed to win her true loyalty in return.

77

Attack from the Rear

Daymin did not rise from the grasses until the sky lightened and the stars began to fade one by one. He had spent the night hunched forward, his arms wrapped around his legs, and he was now so stiff and exhausted he wasn't sure he would make it back to his camp.

Now that he could see the mountains, their snowy peaks catching the faint light, it was easy to put them at his back and trudge eastward once more.

He still had no idea what he was supposed to do. But he couldn't abandon his army; if they woke to find him missing, they wouldn't know whose orders to obey. Maybe the weary march back to camp would help him clarify his thoughts.

Yet the further he walked, the more he despaired. There was no way to reach the refugees in time to help, and no other way to make a difference.

When he returned, he would have to tell his army the truth.

That they were too late. That his decision to protect the forest had led to the deaths of his own civilians.

And if they turned on him?

He would almost welcome it. At least that way he would be relieved of the burden of deciding the next step.

At last he came in sight of his army. He had taken a different trajectory on the way back, but the camp sprawled so far in either direction that he could not miss it. He turned toward the sea of tents and trudged the final distance, legs aching, feet rubbing painfully against his boots.

Before he reached the edge of camp, where he could see his soldiers breakfasting and packing away their tents, Tarak jogged out to meet him.

"Where have you been?" he asked breathlessly.

"Walking," Daymin muttered. Exhaustion swept over him, and he stumbled over a prairie dog burrow.

Tarak grabbed his arm to steady him. "Are you okay?"

Daymin grunted noncommittally.

"Are you going to tell the soldiers?"

"I have to, don't I?" Daymin said. "But I have no idea what I'm supposed to do next." He started walking again, every bone in his feet aching. "What would you do?"

"Walk faster?" Tarak asked.

"As if that would make any bloody difference," Daymin grumbled.

When they reached the edge of camp, the soldiers nearby turned; spotting Daymin, they stopped what they were doing and stared. He must look a wreck.

"The Whitish have nearly caught up to our refugees, who won't make it into the mountains in time," Daymin said.

Then, because he had nothing more useful to tell them, he pushed his way past the circle of onlookers in the direction of his own tent.

He could hear the muttering that swept through camp as word spread, and by the time Zahira and Lalaysha greeted him with slack-faced relief, Pollard, Morrisse, and a few of his generals were visible making their way toward his tent.

"We've heard the news," Pollard said, coming to a halt before Daymin. "Do you have a plan?"

"We're too late to stop the Whitish from chasing our refugees into the mountains," Daymin said. Without fully intending to, he added, "But if we want to dash our army to pieces against the Whitish, we can change course and attack them from the rear."

Pollard frowned. "If it was enough to give our civilians more time, I would be willing to take that risk. Do you know anything about the size of their force?"

Daymin shook his head.

"They would have left reinforcements behind in Baylore and Twenty-League Town, not knowing where our army was headed next, so we shouldn't expect to face their full force."

Yet Pollard knew as well as Daymin that they were still unmatched against a much smaller Whitish force. Especially one in full plate armor. They had used the last of their enchanted explosives, and their Flamespinners would not be able to light the grass aflame for fear it would spread to the forest and catch their own people in the blaze.

"Are these your orders?" General Vask asked. "Are you certain?" Daymin could see his dissatisfaction in the set of his jaw.

"Yes," he said firmly.

And so they set off with the morning sun at their backs, now taking a southwesterly course designed to intercept the Whitish army at the foot of the mountains. Daymin knew he was throwing the lives of his soldiers away, possibly for no gain. Yet he welcomed the chance for one last fight. Better to throw away his life in a desperate battle than to admit defeat.

As they marched, exhaustion swept through Daymin in waves, making his footing clumsy.

They were moving too slow.

Plagues, he wished they still had horses. With a small cavalry, he could have ridden ahead and defended the gorge while his civilians made their way to safety.

He barely made it through the day. When they stopped at last to set up camp, the mountains seemingly more distant than ever, he collapsed in his sleeping roll without dinner.

The next day was as grim as the first, and to make matters worse, he had heard nothing from Idorii since his report on the refugee camp. He had failed, and the weight of his guilt was crushing him. He barely spoke, eating only as much as necessary to stave off hunger, each weary footstep carrying him closer to his army's demise.

Never had the situation seemed so hopeless. At least in Baylore, the wall had stood between his people and the Whitish. There had always been a chance—a slim one, to be sure, but a chance nonetheless—that the wall would hold.

Here, his people would be utterly defenseless. He had made a fatal miscalculation, and they would all die for it.

78

Into the Mountains

Jayna and Hanna had been following a trail left by the Itrean refugees ever since they skirted around Baylore. The going was much easier here, with a stream offering a dependable supply of water and a scattering of discarded goods to raid for food, and they made quick progress.

As they drew close to the mountains, they caught sight of trails of smoke rising from cookfires one morning. They had just started walking, and the evidence of another camp had come into view as they crested a small rise.

"Who do you think that is?" Jayna asked Hanna in a hushed voice. "Not the refugees, surely. They must have passed into the mountains by now."

"It must be an army, then," Hanna said. "We won't know whose until we can see the soldiers."

"What if they see us first?" Jayna asked. She wasn't eager to put herself in the path of the Whitish army again, especially since the army in Itrea was said to be many times stronger than what they had faced in Eidervell.

"Maybe we should skirt around them and try to find a different way into the mountains," Hanna said. "If the refugees are already waiting there, that's where we need to be."

"Except we were supposed to find King Daymin first, weren't we?" Jayna eyed the columns of smoke, wishing they would tell her something more useful. "Maybe we should skirt around them anyway, and then try to get a look at them from inside the woods, where they won't see us."

"Good idea." Hanna didn't seem any more eager than her to put themselves in the path of an unknown army.

They struck out at an angle away from the camp, and by nightfall, they had reached the forest at the foot of the Icebraid Peaks without catching a glimpse of the army to their left. The trees were different than she was accustomed to, with scaly needles instead of leaves, and the air in the forest was dry and scented with vanilla. From this angle, the mountains seemed much squatter than the Eldren Mountains in Cashabree, though she knew the peaks further back were high and snowcapped. Even so, their slopes were more gradual than the jagged peaks of her home, which made her think they would be easier to traverse.

Remembering how Queen Kalleah had described her initial encounter with the Icelings—a hostile confrontation the moment she stepped foot beneath the trees—Jayna hesitated just outside the shadowed forest. She would feel much more comfortable camping within the forest, where they wouldn't be visible from a league away, but only if it was safe.

Hanna must have been thinking along the same lines,

because she said, "I think any Icelings will be busy with the army. They won't care about a couple lone travelers."

"True."

Glancing at each other, they stepped beneath the trees together.

Nothing happened.

This forest could not have been more different from the Wandering Woods. Where the Wandering Woods had been so densely overgrown that they had spent their time climbing over enormous roots and skirting around bushes, this forest was open and airy; though there was no path to follow, they walked easily between the wide skirts of the trees.

As soon as they were out of sight of the open grassland, Jayna stopped and dropped her pack with a groan. "This is the perfect place to camp. Don't you think?"

* * *

In the morning, Jayna and Hanna set out directly up the foothills. They would at least be able to see where the refugees were positioned and whose army was camped below once they had gained a bit of elevation, and from there they could set a course for the refugee camp.

The climb was harder than Jayna had expected. The foothills were deceptively steep—in some places they could walk normally, but in others the ground gave way to eroded chutes where the dry dirt slid away underfoot. Here they grabbed roots and rocks to haul their way up, trusting their weight to handholds that seemed liable to pull free and send them careening down the slope.

But they made it to the top without too many scrapes and bruises. When they clambered onto a ridge, Jayna's eyes were immediately drawn to the high snow-covered peaks beyond the foothills. These marched away as far as she could see to the west, the sun reflecting blindingly off the snow, less jagged and sheer than the Eldren Mountains but no less imposing.

"Look," Hanna said. "There they are."

Jayna followed her gaze down to a valley at the foot of the peak they had summited, where the Itrean refugees had set up camp beside a narrow stream that glistened like the seams of rock in the Firehawk Region. It didn't seem like a very large camp, not if it was meant to fit the entire population of the vast city they had seen from afar, but she wasn't good at judging these things.

Turning to look back down the slope they had climbed, which looked far steeper from this vantage, Jayna caught sight of the army they had been following.

Her eyes widened, and she had to grab a gnarled branch for balance. The Whitish army was approaching the foothills in a column of gleaming silver, every soldier in full armor, their faces hidden beneath helmets. Now she understood why Queen Kalleah had dismissed the soldiers they had faced in Desden as amateurs. She could tell these were true elites, and the ragged, unarmored soldiers they had fought in the Kinship Thrones had been a different breed altogether. She had never seen anything so magnificent—or so daunting.

"Where is King Daymin's army?" Hanna asked softly.

"Maybe they're already down there," Jayna said, turning to the refugee camp once more. "I don't know where else we're supposed to find them."

"And how are we supposed to get down that?"

Jayna scanned the opposite side of the ridge, which dropped down much more steeply than the one they had climbed, with rocky cliffs jutting from among the few stunted trees that had managed to cling to the slope.

"You have experience with mountaineering," Jayna said, smiling hopefully at Hanna. "What do you think?"

Hanna raised her eyebrows. "I was climbing through snow, with crampons and ice axes. That's completely different from scaling rocks like these."

"But you have a rope in your pack, don't you?"

"Not one long enough to get us down this whole ridge."

"Can't we at least try?"

Hanna sighed. "Fine. Let's cut over to that saddle and see if we can find an easier way down."

Grinning, Jayna started off along the ridge, picking her way around boulders pocked with holes and past twisted trees. *This* was her sort of adventure.

Eventually they scrambled down a short distance to a saddle north of the ridge they had first summited. The saddle was flatter than the ridge above, and more densely forested, which made it hard to get a good look at the descent.

Just beyond the ridge, the ground dropped away, but the forest began again at the foot of a short cliff.

"I bet we could get down that," Jayna said.

"If the rope is long enough."

"How short is your rope?"

"We would need to double it over," Hanna said, "or leave the top half tied to the tree, with no way of pulling it down after us."

614

"Well, we may as well give it a try," Jayna said. "Are you going first, or should I?"

With another exasperated sigh, Hanna said, "I have to go first so I can belay you from the bottom."

She pulled off her pack and dragged out wads of untidily wrapped rope, which looked plenty long enough to Jayna. One end she tied to a sturdy-looking tree, the other around her waist.

"When I reach the bottom, I'll call up to you that I'm safe, and you can untie the rope from the tree and fasten it around your waist. Then I'll lower you down slowly."

"Right," Jayna said. "See? I told you this was a good idea."

Hanna's reluctant smile told Jayna she wasn't the only one enjoying this.

Gripping the top of the rope tightly, Hanna slid her feet over the edge of the cliff. Then, facing the rock wall, she walked her way slowly down, letting out the rope as she went. Jayna imagined it would strip her hands raw, but she made no complaint.

Hanna reached the bottom with plenty of rope to spare, but when she called up, "Safe!", her voice sounded more distant than Jayna had realized. The drop was longer than it looked from the top, maybe because the trees at the foot of the cliff were larger than the stunted things here on the ridge.

Jayna untied the rope from the tree and fastened it around her own waist, trying to cinch it up tightly enough that it wouldn't slide around too much. While she worked, Hanna looped the extra rope around a tree and pulled the slack tight.

When she was satisfied with her work, Jayna grabbed the loose rope and lowered herself over the edge of the cliff like Hanna had done.

"Let go of the rope!" Hanna shouted from below. "I need to lower you with that one!"

"What am I supposed to hold, then?" Jayna called back, a giddy sort of dizziness swooping through her as she realized she was dangling over a great drop with very little holding her in place.

"You can either hold the end of the rope that's attached to your waist, or you can try to climb down the cliff."

Jayna reached for the rock face and found a few likely handholds, which allowed her to take her weight off the other end of the rope. She managed to climb down a short distance before she got stuck, and as she scrabbled her hands across the rocks in search of another protrusion she could grab, she started thinking this wasn't a very efficient way to descend. Hanna had made it down in no time.

So, with another swoop of nerves, she leaned her weight into the rope and waited for it to pull taut. Then she let go of the rock and instead grabbed the rope connected to her waist.

"Good!" Hanna called. "Now walk your way down!"

The rope started descending before Jayna was ready, slackening in jolts that surprised her every time, and she walked and kicked her way off the cliff as she went down.

She was two paces from the bottom of the cliff when she stopped descending abruptly.

"I'm out of rope!" Hanna said worriedly.

"I can get down this last bit." Jayna grabbed the rock and pulled herself close, taking the tension off the rope. "Now let go."

It took a moment for Hanna to untie the rope from her own waist, and when she dropped the end, Jayna was surprised by the sudden feeling of vulnerability. She wasn't even far off the ground, but without the rope supporting her, the way down seemed much more challenging.

"There's a good foothold, if you can reach it," Hanna said, coming up behind Jayna and pointing. "And can you hold that knob there?"

Jayna slid her toe down, searching for the place Hanna was indicating, and Hanna helped guide her foot into place. With a solid foothold, she was able to grasp a small protrusion of rock and lower herself down further.

Soon she had closed most of the distance to the ground, so she let go and jumped the final half-pace.

"Hah! We did it!"

Hanna shook her head, smiling. "I told you the rope was too short."

"But it worked."

They bundled up the rope and tied it to the outside of Hanna's pack, in case they needed it again soon, and then they started off through the steeply sloping forest. Birds flitted through the trees, and squirrels chattered from high branches. In a few places, they had to squat and slide down a stretch of eroded ground on their feet, but they were able to skirt around the only other cliff they came across.

Soon enough, they had reached the bottom of the ridge, where the trees grew taller and the going was easy.

"Let's find King Daymin," Jayna said. "I hope we're not too late."

"I didn't see any sign of Icelings near the camp," Hanna said.

"No, but that didn't look like the full population of Baylore, and the Whitish army is right at their tail." Now that the excitement of their successful mountaineering experiment was wearing off, unease was beginning to gnaw at her. "Something is wrong. I just don't know what."

79

Imposter

Kalleah's party would be leaving the next morning. She and her friends would travel with six unfamiliar Prophet's Eyes: two devotees who lived at the temple complex and four others who traveled where they were needed.

Since she had very little in the way of belongings, apart from what she wore, she would be trusting the Prophet's Eyes to make the necessary arrangements for supplies; it made her uncomfortable to leave everything in their hands, but she was now eager enough to visit Brenvale that she did not want to impede their preparations.

The day was drawing to a close when Kalleah went in search of Leoth. He wasn't in his room, so she ventured outside the underground complex to find the sun casting long shadows from the temple above.

Then she heard shouts from the temple.

Had the Lord's Men tracked her down?

Heart pounding in her throat, Kalleah crept up the grassy slope. When she drew closer, she realized the shouts were all coming from Prophet's Eyes, many of them blue-robed devotees, clustered around something she couldn't see in the middle of the circular temple.

Kalleah's pulse raced as she closed the last distance to the temple. Bounding up the steps, she finally caught sight of what they were shouting at.

It was Leoth.

Fear swooped in Kalleah's stomach. He was restrained by two men, and his shirt was torn down the back; though she could not see his scars from this angle, she knew they were visible to the devotees.

Athamol was near the center of the ring, standing beneath the statue of Totoleon, the setting sun lighting his face with eerie bands of orange and black.

As Kalleah pushed her way into the ring of devotees, Athamol's eyes locked on hers. There was a spark of fury in his gaze, a coldness she did not recognize from him.

"He's an imposter!" Athamol shouted. "Look!" He pushed Leoth's shoulder roughly to the side so Kalleah could see the scars.

Kalleah breathed past her panicked fury, willing her voice to remain steady. "Did you think I was unaware my husband is a Curse-Weaver?"

"He is no king of Itrea, then! They would never accept a monster such as this on their throne! Are you an imposter, too?"

"I never claimed I was queen of Itrea," Kalleah said, still with forced calm. "It was you who sought me out. You who made the connection between the attack on Eidervell and the arrival of my fleet in Stragmouth."

"Are you saying you're not Queen Kalleah, then?" Athamol's eyes were bulging in his anger.

"What do you think?" Kalleah asked coldly.

"I—that's not—" Athamol glared at her. "You have shown us no proof that you possess Queen Kalleah's power."

"Would you like me to give a demonstration?" Kalleah asked sardonically. "I could rip the life from everyone standing here, if it would help."

Athamol paled. "No need for that."

"Unhand Leoth at once, then."

Athamol stepped between Kalleah and Leoth. "No. We won't release this man until we are certain of his identity. And if you attack any of our number, we won't work with you any further. We will set the Lord's Men on you, and you will lose your chance of toppling High King Edreon."

Leoth raised his head and met Kalleah's eyes, his expression dark with self-loathing. "Do as they ask," he said wearily. "We still need their help."

The bitterness in his voice tore at her heart. This was exactly what he had feared most.

But she couldn't get out of this without killing the Prophet's Eyes, and she wasn't ready for that. Not yet.

Drawing in a sharp breath, she nodded. "I won't stop you now. But if you lay a hand on Leoth…"

The men restraining Leoth marched him from the circle of onlookers. He held Kalleah's eyes, his expression lost, until he had stumbled past her. Soon they disappeared into the underground complex.

"I hope you know you have thoroughly lost my respect,"

Kalleah told Athamol coldly.

Then she stalked from the temple.

80

The Refugee Camp

Idorii had heard nothing from Daymin since he had written with news of reaching the refugee camp. The lack of response lay coiled in an anxious knot in his stomach—had something happened to Daymin? Had he run afoul of the Whitish army before reaching the mountains?

Or was he somehow angry with Idorii for sending ill tidings?

Whatever the reason, Idorii's tension grew each time he checked his tattoo to find nothing from Daymin.

In the meantime, he was kept busy helping the refugees move through the canyon as quickly as possible. Most of the children had entered the gorge now, though they might take more than three days to reach the valley on the other side given their size, which meant the Whitish would likely attack while there were still children in danger. The Makhori camped on this side of the canyon were working tirelessly to prepare whatever defenses they could from the materials they had on hand, while Idorii had joined the soldiers in ferrying supplies through the canyon.

He was close to the valley now—less than a day, according to the soldiers he passed going in the opposite direction—and he was already dreading the return journey. The canyon had been hot and dry, the sun baking the dark reddish rocks until the space felt like an oven, and the footing had been treacherous. Even where the deer trail was wide enough for him to walk comfortably, the dirt had a tendency to slide underfoot, so a single misplaced step would have sent him careening down into the river far below. And in some places, the trail became little more than a divot in a steep rock face. The soldiers had bolted ropes across some of these places to act as a handhold, but Idorii would have been happier with a rope spanning the entire length of the canyon.

The first night, he had camped along with a crowd of refugees in a verdant side canyon with a trickling stream. But the evening after that, he had simply walked until nightfall before curling up on his sleeping mat on the widest stretch of trail he could find. He had hardly slept, expecting to roll over the edge of the canyon if he let down his guard.

Now he was clumsy with exhaustion, walking slower than ever as he struggled to keep his footing. He had left his books and cookpot behind with the Weavers, instead loading his pack with dried goods and blankets, a large canvas tent strapped to the outside.

As he staggered around a bend in the undulating canyon, Idorii came across a line of soldiers he recognized from earlier that day.

"Nearly there," the woman in front called encouragingly.

Idorii forced a smile. They had been saying that for hours now.

He clambered up the slope to let the soldiers pass, balancing on a small rock and resting his heavy pack against the canyon wall.

When he started walking again, rounding yet another corner into a wider section of canyon with a well-formed deer trail, he caught the distant sound of voices. It was not just the chatter of soldiers and refugees making their way through the canyon; it was more of a low hum of noise punctuated by occasional laughter and shrieks, like Baylore's main square on a sunny day.

Hope swelled in Idorii's chest as he hastened down the easier trail. As it curved, the canyon widened further still, and he could see the slopes of the foothills dropping away before him.

Then, at last, the gorge ended and he came out on a grassy meadow surrounded in all directions by mountains. It was not a large valley, and beyond the meadow, snowy peaks rose steep and foreboding. He must have gained a good deal of elevation without realizing it, because the snow stretched nearly to the foot of the mountains. He could not see any obvious route deeper into the mountains—provided they even wanted to venture into that snowy wasteland when it was still spring—so it seemed this was the ground they needed to hold against the Whitish.

The refugees were camped on the eastern edge of the valley, along the banks of the now-placid river, and already the camp had the look of a more permanent settlement. There were laundry lines stretched between trees at the edge of the clearing, cooking stations set up near the water, and simple three-wall structures built near the foot of the mountains around what must be toilet pits. Young children ran barefoot through camp, laughing and calling to one another, while older children helped wash laundry and sort through newly-delivered supplies.

Idorii trudged over to the pile of new supplies and unloaded his pack, with much thanks from the older woman who was overseeing the movement of goods.

"There's stew for the soldiers over there," she said, waving Idorii toward one of the cooking stations.

"Thank you," he said, stomach grumbling at the prospect of hot food. While he hadn't missed foraging and cooking his own inadequate meals these last two nights, he was already sick of wayfarers' bread.

Idorii shouldered his now-empty pack and wove his way through camp until he reached a cluster of soldiers sitting on logs and rocks around a steaming cauldron of stew. All had boots and trousers caked in the same reddish dust that clung to Idorii, and some sat with their feet dangling in the stream to ease the ache.

Idorii took a polished wood bowl from the stack and helped himself to the stew, which smelled delicious. The refugees must have found wild foods in the meadow to supplement their supplies, because there were fresh greens he did not recognize mixed among the chunks of potato and meat.

As he scanned the circle of soldiers in search of a place to sit, Idorii saw with a jolt of surprise that Letto and Jakovi were perched side by side on a half-rotted log.

When he approached, they looked up and spotted him.

"Idorii!" Letto called, something like relief flashing across his face. He looked for a moment like he might jump to his feet and embrace Idorii, though he must have thought better of it. Jakovi just stared at him, openmouthed.

"I wondered where you were," Idorii said, smiling as he took a seat beside Jakovi. "How have you fared?"

"As well as any of the refugees," Letto said. "We've had a good time scouting the mountains, haven't we?" he asked Jakovi, elbowing him.

"I like it here," Jakovi said, his cheeks reddening.

Now that Idorii looked closer, he realized Jakovi was far healthier than he had ever seen him. His emaciated frame had filled out, which gave his features a softness they had lacked, while his black hair had been cut flatteringly in layers that fell around his face. And where he had once been pale and sickly, his skin had darkened from long days in the sun.

"And what about you?" Letto asked. "When did you leave Baylore? Is the city still standing?"

Idorii shook his head. "I left just as the Whitish army swept in and took the city. Our defenses hardly lasted an hour."

"So—"

"Their army is about to reach the mountains," Idorii said heavily. "And King Daymin is too far away to defend our refugees."

Letto paled, while Idorii saw a shadow of fear in Jakovi's eyes. In all his obsessive focus on guarding the knowledge of Baylore and reaching the mountains, he had almost forgotten about the boy's power.

"Don't worry," Idorii said quietly, glancing to the side to make sure the other soldiers couldn't hear. "We can't use your power here, even if we wanted to. We don't have any way to escape if anything went wrong."

Jakovi looked at Letto, who nodded. "He's right." Turning to Idorii, Letto asked, "How far away is King Daymin?"

"I don't know. We should forget about him. He won't be able to help." Idorii's heart twisted in his chest as he said this.

"Then what's the plan?" Letto asked.

"Hurry the refugees through as quickly as we can and pray to whatever gods you believe in."

They finished their lunch in silence, all three wrapped in their own thoughts. Then, without further discussion, they rose and shouldered their empty packs and started back toward the hot, dusty canyon.

81

The Prophet's Vision

As soon as Kalleah reached the musty halls of the underground complex, she broke into a jog toward Mellicante and Baridya's room. When she pounded on their door, no one answered, so she tried the knob. The door swung open easily to reveal two simple pallets pushed together on the floor and a few scattered belongings.

Though she knew there was no reason to worry, anxiety spiked in her chest.

Kalleah didn't want to face the Prophet's Eyes now, when she was ready to strangle them for their cruel treatment of Leoth, so she stalked back to her own room and slammed the door behind her.

Then she kicked at her sleeping pallet, which skidded to the edge of the room and flopped against the wall.

She wanted to fight someone. To make someone pay for the hurt in Leoth's eyes.

But she was furious with herself as much as the Prophet's Eyes. She had been wary of their religious leanings from the very start; how had she let herself get dragged so deep into their conspiracy? She still didn't know what their final aims were, what with their members infiltrating every court in the Kinship Thrones and channeling magic from the old lands, yet she had been let into their plans just enough to know she couldn't ignore them. If they held enough power to topple kings, their movements would affect Itrea. And if that device beneath the palace truly could draw on magic from the old lands, it was dangerous and volatile enough that its very existence could threaten all that lay beyond the wall.

Which included Itrea.

Yet their reaction to Leoth's scars had reminded her that the Prophet's Eyes were, first and foremost, members of a religious order. They might not agree with Varos, but the two branches of religion still married up in many ways. They would be overthrowing a Varonite High King and replacing him with an Alldrosant, and from all the Whitish history she knew, which religious branch held power made very little difference in how the kingdom was run.

She wished she had never ventured into the Kinship Thrones in the first place. If she had sailed back to Larkhaven after her attack on Eidervell, she would never have learned of the dangers brewing in the Kinship Thrones. With her power alone, she might have been able to take back ground from the Whitish; in her anger right now, she hardly cared that it would make her a monster. And maybe the conspiracy would have remained just that, a conspiracy without the means to grow into something deadlier.

Kalleah had been pacing her room without realizing it, turning with jerky movements around the cramped space. The more she paced, the more her anger grew, until she was desperate to lash out at something.

So she stalked from her room, slamming the door shut behind her, and went in search of Bennett. Maybe he would give her the answers she needed if she was persuasive enough. She fingered the concealed dagger at her wrist, almost hoping for an excuse to draw blood. If that made her a monster, she didn't care.

Bennett was in his room, dressed as though he was about to return to the Twin Cities. When he saw Kalleah's expression, his eyes widened and he took a step back from the door.

"What is it?" he asked.

Kalleah let the door fall shut behind her, crowding Bennett. "*Your people* have just locked Leoth up for his magic bloodline." She shoved Bennett hard in the chest, throwing him back against the wall. "I need answers *now*, or I'm going to kill every one of you two-faced bastards."

The color drained from Bennett's already pale face. "I-I don't understand—"

"Just answer my questions," Kalleah said, her voice low and dangerous. "What is your scheme aiming to achieve?"

"We're trying to weaken Whitland so the benevolent followers of the Nine can return to prominence," he babbled.

Kalleah drew her dagger with a quick motion and flicked the end against the soft skin beneath his chin. The knot in Bennett's throat bobbed as he swallowed. "You've told me that. Many times. But why does that necessitate your interference in every court in the Kinship Thrones? Why do you need to draw

631

on magic from beyond the wall?"

Bennett swallowed again.

"*Talk*," Kalleah growled. "Or I bleed you until the words come."

He drew a shaky breath. "The—the original prophet had a vision." He spoke quickly, as if his words would have less weight that way. "The Nine have languished too long in the dark, but his vision showed them re-born once magic returned to the land. They would take up human form, and if the nine thrones stood empty when they returned, the Nine Gods of Light would become kings of the Kinship Thrones."

Kalleah was struck momentarily speechless by the implications of this vision. "So," she said slowly, "you intend to flood the Kinship Thrones haphazardly with magic from beyond the wall, and simultaneously assassinate all nine rulers of the Kinship Thrones?"

"It would be a small cost to pay to have the Gods of Light walk among us once more."

And what happened when their imaginary gods failed to appear? Would they put their own followers on the thrones, pretending them to be manifestations of the Nine?

Moreover, she was depending on an alliance with King Rodarin to weaken Whitland. If he were killed, who knew what his successor would agree to?

"I've never heard of such an insane plan," Kalleah said coldly.

Bennett's confidence seemed to be returning. "You wouldn't understand," he said. "You and your godless land, long forsaken by the Nine. You don't know how much you have lost, and you can't imagine how much suffering the false god Varos has brought upon us."

"I can imagine well enough," Kalleah said, digging her dagger into Bennett's flesh until she elicited a gasp. "It is Varos who brought war to our land. Varos who tried to burn our magic races alive. Varos who has turned our once-proud people into a nation of refugees. But it is *your* people, under the guidance of the Nine, who have imprisoned my husband."

"Why?" Bennett asked breathlessly.

"Remember how scathingly you spoke of my attack on Eidervell? I should have known you were not to be trusted. Now get out of this place before I decide to sink this dagger into your throat."

Bennett lurched sideways, drawing a drop of blood from beneath his chin as he moved out of reach of the dagger. Then he fled the room.

Kalleah held the door open and watched as he ran down the hall with his coattails flapping behind him, not looking back.

Then, breathing hard with fury, she strode back to her own room.

She had almost killed him. When she had told him to go, it was to spare his life. If he had lingered, she might not have been able to hold back.

Alone once more, she threw her dagger onto her sleeping pallet. She felt trapped, with no way out.

She should have returned to Itrea while she still had a chance. Her dream of manipulating the war from the Kinship Thrones had never been more than a delusion; as an outsider, she would never be able to hold the political weight needed to make a real difference.

And now it was too late to help Daymin.

Bloody plagues. She wished she hadn't lost the book connected to her son. For all she knew, Baylore had fallen and Daymin was dead. She might return to find there was no one left to fight for.

Kalleah felt she was teetering on the brink of something dangerous. Something that frightened her.

How far was she willing to go? At what point would she lose her humanity?

Restless and agitated, she scooped up her dagger and jammed it back into its concealed sheath. Then she went in search of wherever Leoth had been imprisoned.

82

A Reckless Hope

Daymin had marched another three days in a miserable stupor, and at last they were drawing close to the foothills. Which meant the Whitish were on the brink of attacking his civilians—if they had not done so already.

Then, after another night of broken sleep, he woke to find a new message from Idorii. His heartbeat quickened as the writing appeared on his arm, partly out of relief that Idorii was still alive and well, and partly because he was afraid of the news he would convey.

Daymin –

I was hiking back through the gorge to carry another load of supplies through when word came: the Whitish have reached the base of the mountains. The man who ran the deer trail to bring word said he could see their camp stretched out on the plains, close enough he could make out the soldiers' weapons glinting in the sun.

The remaining refugees have reportedly packed up their camp and are filing into the canyon as quickly as they can, but I know how slow it is traversing the first section of the stream. They are abandoning any supplies they cannot carry.

The Whitish are undoubtedly going to attack tomorrow. There are tens of thousands of soldiers, fully armored, a smaller force than your own army but formidable nonetheless. If they chase us up the canyon, they will destroy us.

I'm afraid, Daymin. Why haven't you written? Are you safe? How far away are you? Selfishly, one of my greatest fears is that I'll never see you again.

Please tell me if I have any reason to hope. From here, I cannot see a way through.

With love,
Idorii

Daymin's friends had already left the tent in search of breakfast, so Daymin was alone as he slumped forward and hugged his legs, throat so tight he couldn't swallow.

Plagues. If his army attacked the rear of the Whitish force, he would likely die before he saw Idorii again. And what if his army wasn't strong enough to make a difference in the Whitish numbers? He would have thrown away the lives of his soldiers for nothing.

But they *were* getting close to the mountains. They were perhaps another six leagues from the foothills, which would take most of a day to walk, though it meant they had gained on the

Whitish.

What if there was still hope?

Daymin lifted his head, staring sightlessly at the canvas wall of his tent. He had been so quick to assume all was lost, first with the defense of Baylore and now with the refugees. And he had been right to abandon Baylore when he had, since no army could have withstood the poisoned gas the Whitish had unleashed on the streets. But maybe this time was different. Maybe he had to keep searching for a way to save his people, because with such challenging terrain between here and safety, their fate was anything but predetermined.

And his army was only a day's march from the foothills.

That might be too far, especially if he hoped to intercept the Whitish before they attacked, but it wasn't so far he would miss the fighting altogether.

Daymin rose slowly to his feet, a new resolve hardening.

He wasn't ready to dash his army to pieces against the rear of the Whitish force, when it might achieve nothing. But if he could give his refugees a chance to reach safety and cut off the route into the mountains, he would do anything to make it happen.

He strapped his sword to his waist and reached for his waterskin. If they wanted to make it in time, they would have to leave behind everything that was not essential for their survival.

When he emerged from his tent, he found his army quieter than usual, likely aware they were within a day's march of the Whitish army. Whatever happened, they would not be delaying any longer.

He found Zahira perched on a rock eating a bowl of millet porridge, while Tarak and Lalaysha finished packing away their

637

sleeping rolls.

"What is it?" Zahira asked when Daymin approached. She must have seen something in his face.

"Idorii just wrote." Even speaking his name made his throat tight. "The Whitish are camped at the base of the foothills, preparing to attack this morning."

Zahira's eyes widened. "So…"

Daymin strode past her without answering. When he spotted a boy in Morrisse's dark green livery, he asked him to fetch the two holden monarchs.

Soon Morrisse, Falsted, and several of his own generals had joined him at the outskirts of camp. Soldiers clustered nearby, pretending to check their supplies while listening in, and beyond them the camp bustled with a quiet intensity he recognized from the lead-up to their previous battles.

"We should catch up to the Whitish army by the end of today, according to our maps," Pollard said.

Daymin nodded.

"What are your orders, Your Majesty?"

Daymin paced before his audience, looking at the ground so he did not have to meet their eyes. "The Whitish are preparing to attack as we speak. The last of our refugees are piling into the gorge, leaving behind any supplies they can't carry, but they will be easy targets as they make the three-day journey to the other side of the foothills. Our soldiers will undoubtedly defend the rear, but their force is too small to hold for long. Especially if there are still refugees passing into the gorge when the Whitish attack."

"If we attack now, from the rear, the Whitish might be forced to turn and fight instead of pursuing our refugees,"

Morrisse said. "Wasn't that your plan?"

Daymin paused in his pacing and looked at Morrisse, whose face was lined with exhaustion. "By the time we reach the mountains tonight, it will be too late to draw them away from the gorge."

"Then why did we take this course?" Morrisse asked.

"Because it was better to have a plan than to give up," Daymin said baldly. "In all honesty, we've closed the distance much faster than I expected."

"So you never expected us to succeed?"

"No."

Pollard laid a hand on Morrisse's shoulder. "This has been true from the moment the Whitish laid siege on Baylore twenty-three years ago. Our people have never had a hope of defeating the Whitish, yet all along, we have planned and acted as though we did. What else could we do?"

Hearing Pollard say what he had felt all along lifted a weight from Daymin's shoulders. It removed some of the guilt he had shouldered for how the war had turned out; even though he had known the odds, he could not help but fear it was his own decisions that had doomed his people.

"What are you planning, then?" Morrisse asked Daymin, voice tight.

Daymin turned to face the holden monarchs and the generals, hands behind his back. "I won't make this decision without the support of my army. But I think we should abandon our supplies and our camp and run for the mountains, skirting around the Whitish army so they don't notice our approach and cutting them off at the entrance to the gorge. We would arrive exhausted and less capable of fighting, but we might be able to drive the Whitish back from our refugees in time to seal the way through."

For the first time that day, Daymin saw flickers of hope on the faces of his generals and holden monarchs. It was a small hope, a reckless hope, but that was all they could find, and it would have to be enough.

"My wife and daughter are among the refugees," Morrisse said, his voice rough. "Of course I think we should take that risk."

The others nodded, and from behind his generals, Daymin heard whispers as the news spread through camp.

By the time Daymin returned to his tent, the energy of the camp had changed, a buzz of frenetic excitement rippling through the soldiers.

"We're running to the mountains?" Zahira asked as soon as she saw Daymin.

"It appears so."

She grinned. "Plagues, I can't wait to fight again."

Daymin knew what she meant. All the long days of marching had left him restless with anxiety; it would be a relief to arrive and plunge into battle, no matter how poor the odds.

Preparations were swift from there. They would be diverting away from the stream they had followed, so every soldier carried as much water as their skins could fit, along with the last of their fire-baked and cured rations. They would have no time to cook, so they left behind their millet and lentils and oats and buckwheat. Half the tents were left standing, while those that had already been packed away were dragged out and thrown into the remaining tents, in the foolish hope someone might be able to recover the abandoned supplies after the battle.

Daymin's royal tent was packed, as were their maps and charts of battle strategy, but sleeping rolls and spare clothes were left behind. All dressed in Weavers' armor, weapons strapped to their belts, some carrying waterskins in hand while others shouldered near-empty packs.

Then, with the morning sun hot at their backs, they started running toward the mountains. Daymin's feet pounded against the earth, his heartbeat pulsing in his ears, as he breathed in the clean air sweeping down from the peaks. Behind him, the rest of the army stretched into a long column, curving as they set a course away from the Whitish.

Instead of tiring him, the relentless pace sent energy coursing through Daymin. He felt he could run for a hundred leagues if it meant finishing what he had started.

And maybe, just maybe, he would find Idorii waiting for him in the mountains.

Daymin bared his teeth in a grin, the sun hot on his black hair, the jolting of each footstep shaking him awake from the stupor he had been in. And he ran.

83

Rescue

Kalleah ran through the tunnels of the complex, anger and fear coursing through her in twin bursts of adrenaline. She listened at each door and tried each handle—most were unlocked—yet she encountered neither Prophet's Eyes nor any sign of her friends. She had never ventured this far into the complex, and she worried there were hidden branches of tunnels she had overlooked altogether.

At last, charging down a final flight of stairs to a poorly-lit tunnel that smelled as stale and mildewed as a cave, she caught a faint strain of voices.

Slowing, she crept closer, taking care to quiet the crunch of her footsteps on packed earth. The only light came from torches flickering in their brackets, the acrid smell of smoke intensifying as she passed each one.

Closer still, she recognized one of the voices as Leoth's. He was not shouting in pain, which was something, but there was a dull, hopeless tone to his voice that raised the hair on the back of her neck.

Rounding the corner, Kalleah was confronted by a burly guard standing before a door with an unsheathed sword held loosely at his side. When he saw Kalleah, he brought the sword up in a swift motion and fell into a defensive stance.

Kalleah could not win a fight against a man twice her weight with only her dagger for defense, so she did not even reach for it.

"Move aside," she said, her voice laced with threat. "I won't ask twice."

The guard leered at her. Either he was unaware of who she was, or he did not give her power credence.

Kalleah felt only the barest flicker of guilt as she reached for her power. With anger coursing through her veins, the power lurked just below the surface, waiting to be summoned.

The tunnel blurred around her, gold lines swimming into view, brilliant in the dim light—not just the guard's lifeline, but those belonging to people in the rooms to her left.

Plucking the guard's thread from the air, Kalleah gave it a rough tug, winding it into her hand like a fishing line. She hardly registered the moment when he dropped to his knees, lifeless, though she felt a heady surge of power as she consumed the last of his life force.

Then she turned to the first of the rooms, guided by two golden threads that disappeared into the stone wall.

To her surprise, the door was unlocked. She saw through a haze that Leoth was handcuffed to the wall, his torn shirt gone, his head slumped forward so his chin rested on his chest.

The man who was questioning him, a blur of pale skin and

deep blue robes, spun to confront Kalleah.

She yanked on his golden thread, reeling it in with both hands until the man collapsed.

Greed rose up in her like a shadow self, the monster ready to continue its rampage, to consume every drop of life in this room.

"Kalleah."

At Leoth's voice, Kalleah fought against the lust for power. She staggered away from Leoth, drawing out the thread, until at last she felt the grip of the madness easing.

Blinking, she let the power drop away. The room swam into focus, Leoth's face sharp before her in the darkness. With a jolt of surprise, she realized the man on the ground was Athamol, his skin paler than ever in death.

"Kalleah," Leoth said again.

She hurried to his side, pressing a kiss to his lips. "Are you safe?" she whispered. "Did he hurt you?"

"No. But if you hadn't come when you did—"

Kalleah swallowed.

"He had a set of keys in his pocket," Leoth said.

Kalleah dropped to her knees beside Athamol's body and dug in the pockets of his robe until she found a ring of keys. The smallest one opened Leoth's handcuffs, and he sagged into her arms as he fell free of the wall, burying his face in her shoulder.

"I'm so sorry," Kalleah murmured, digging a hand into his hair and holding him close. "I can't believe I ever trusted that man."

"It was our only hope of toppling Whitland," Leoth said. He stepped back, straightening and regaining his composure. "What are you planning to do now?"

"I'm going to find King Rodarin and talk to him, which means killing everyone who stands in my way." She searched Leoth's face for any sign of disgust. "I hope you won't hate me for it."

Leoth squeezed her hands, smiling grimly. "I could never hate you."

"I don't think you understand how many lives I'll have to take."

"Have you forgotten what I told you many years ago?" Leoth asked softly. "I am not a good man."

Yet he was, and the fact that he still believed in his own depravity broke Kalleah's heart.

But she had no time to argue. "We need to find Mellicante and Baridya." Still holding Leoth's hand, she dropped the keys into her pocket and tugged him from the cell. When they encountered the fallen guard just outside, Leoth knelt and took his sword belt, buckling it swiftly to his waist.

"Mellicante?" Kalleah called. "Baridya?" She didn't care who heard. In fact, if anyone emerged from the rooms down the hall to investigate, it would be easier for her to deal with them.

"Kalleah!" Baridya's voice sounded faintly through the door past Leoth's.

This one was locked, so Kalleah fumbled her way through the set of keys before she managed to push it open.

Both Mellicante and Baridya were waiting inside the cell, unguarded, and Baridya embraced Kalleah fiercely when she saw her.

"What's happening?" Mellicante asked sharply. "Why is Leoth—" She gestured his way, whether indicating his lack of shirt or the marks the cuffs had left around his wrists, Kalleah couldn't tell.

"Has Kalleah told you what I am?" Leoth asked in a hollow voice.

"What do you mean?" Baridya's eyebrows drew together in confusion.

Still holding Kalleah's hand, his grip tighter than before, Leoth turned to show them the scars—twin ridges that ran up his back and down both arms, peppered by smaller marks from the torture he had endured at the hands of the Truthbringers.

Baridya gasped.

"I don't believe it," Mellicante said flatly.

Leoth turned to face them once more, a sardonic smile twisting at his mouth. "Neither did the Prophet's Eyes. They think I'm an imposter, which is why they locked us up."

"But what does that mean?" Baridya asked.

"We are no longer working with the Prophet's Eyes," Kalleah said. "Bennett confessed that their insane plan is to kill all nine kings of the Kinship Thrones while allowing magic to flood back into the continent from beyond the wall."

Mellicante's mouth twisted in distaste. "*What?*"

"They believe the Nine Gods of Light will be reborn in human form when magic returns, and the gods will apparently claim the nine thrones if they are empty."

"Either that, or members of their group posing as gods," Mellicante said.

"Exactly. Anyway, we need to stop them before they break through the wall, or Itrea could be in danger as well. Which means destroying the device they plan to use."

"What's your plan?" Mellicante asked.

Kalleah described it roughly, trying not to pay attention to

Baridya's stricken look. She had always been much softer than the other two, horrified by the way Kalleah used her power.

"Now," Kalleah said, "I need you to get out of the temple complex and head toward the Twin Cities. I don't want you to be around me, in case—"

In case I lose control.

Mellicante had a vengeful gleam in her eye when she said, "Take your time. We'll be waiting."

Then Leoth squeezed her hand one last time, Mellicante took Baridya by the elbow, and they hurried away from the cells, away from the Temple of Totoleon, away from Kalleah.

84

Return to Darrenmark

An hour later, Kalleah strode from the temple into a deepening twilight, two spare swords beneath her arm, belts wrapped around the sheaths. She had killed everyone she could find within the complex, using a sword she had taken off a smuggler's body where she could, trying not to overindulge in her power. In Eidervell, she had been unable to draw on her power again after consuming the lives of the soldiers sent against her, and she hoped to continue her work in the Twin Cities without waiting to recover.

For all her caution, she had still ripped the life from at least twenty Prophet's Eyes, and when she had forced the excess power into the ground outside the complex, the temple itself had rocked on its foundations.

At least she was not feeling drained to the point of collapse. She was a touch lightheaded as she started across the grassy expanse between the temple and the city, and she began to wonder if she would need a rest before continuing her work.

She found her friends waiting within sight of the city gates, which stood closed. Leoth was now wearing a sword and a well-cut merchant's shirt that was a fraction too large; he must have taken them from an unguarded room at the complex.

"Kalleah," Leoth said, voice heavy with relief. He swept her into his arms, and as she leaned into his embrace, she felt the exhaustion more keenly than before.

When he released her, he searched her face, as though reading each death in the lines of her brow. "Is it done, then?"

"It's done." Kalleah was trying her best to block the scene from her memory. These were only the first of countless lives she would take before the war was over, and if she let each one weigh on her, she would lose her mind.

"Where are we staying the night?" Mellicante asked.

Kalleah hadn't thought that far. "I had intended to return to The Lost Sailor and see if we can find anyone who will help us. But with the gates closed…"

"Most of the houses along the riverbank have rowboats," Mellicante said. "We could borrow one of those, if you're willing to take the risk."

They would be more noticeable traveling upriver, though the darkness would hide them from all but the most vigilant guards. What Mellicante was really asking was if Kalleah would be able to deal with any Lord's Men they ran across.

Kalleah wasn't sure if she would be able to draw on her power again. Right now, it was far from her reach, and when she reached for it tentatively, she felt nothing. But she and her friends were now armed, and they would be unlikely to stumble across large numbers of the brutes at this time of night.

She took the two spare swords from beneath her arm and handed them to Mellicante and Baridya. "Let's find a boat."

They cut away from the narrow road, following the city wall to where it ended at the river. As they approached the row of simple fisher's houses lining the riverbank, Kalleah grew uneasy—there was every chance the river was heavily guarded where it passed beyond the wall. Apart from their Weavers' coats, they were undefended, which would leave them vulnerable to archers. She hoped it was not unusual for the fisherfolk to travel the river at odd hours, and that they would be captured rather than shot at if they caught the attention of any city guards.

Faint candlelight shone from the windows of the first house they approached, but Kalleah could see no movement from outside. So they crept through the little garden to the riverbank, where each house had its own small pier with a boat tied to the end. Strange, how she had managed to overlook such an obvious detail on their approach into the Twin Cities.

Without speaking, Baridya undid the knot and pulled the boat alongside the pier so the others could step in. The last light of day had faded, so they worked by the light of the half-moon that pooled and danced on the wavelets lapping against the bank.

Mellicante climbed in first, grimacing as the boat rocked underfoot, and Leoth stepped down next before helping Kalleah. She was grateful for his steady hand on hers, since she was still lightheaded. Then Baridya stepped in lightly, bringing the rope with her.

Baridya and Leoth found oars tucked beneath the benches, and they began stroking quietly through the obsidian water toward the Twin Cities. From here, the lights of the cities rose on either side of the bank, hundreds of reflected spots of brilliance leaping and wavering like flames on the water.

Now that she was sitting down, lulled by the gentle sway of their progress upriver, Kalleah was overcome by a wave of exhaustion. She wanted to curl up in the bottom of the boat and sleep for days. Fighting was beyond her, and she was almost certain she would not be able to call on her power in this state.

"I think I need a few hours of rest before we continue," Kalleah whispered to Leoth.

He missed a stroke with the paddle as he turned to look at her in concern. He knew Kalleah did not like to admit weakness, so he could likely tell she was more exhausted than she was letting on.

"We can gather support while you sleep," Leoth said.

"Thank you."

As they neared the city wall rising from the riverbank on their right, Kalleah sat up straighter, worry pushing away her tiredness. Maybe they should have waited for morning. If they were caught now…

But they glided past the wall without raising any alarm. Indeed, Kalleah could see other boats making the short trip across the river ahead of them, visible as pools of blackness against the reflected city lights, and she wondered what their business was that they wished to avoid the bridges.

Soon they reached a familiar stretch of riverbank. Leoth and Baridya guided the rowboat to a set of steps that dropped into the water, and Baridya jumped out, looping the rope over an iron bolt halfway up the stairway. The water slapped gently against the stone banks, a soft murmur beneath the voices rising from taverns along the waterfront.

651

Leoth helped Kalleah from the boat, and she found herself leaning heavily against him as they crossed the street to The Lost Sailor. The Lord's Men were nowhere in sight, so they entered the tavern unchallenged.

The bearded tavernkeeper was bustling around with a handful of drinks, and he did not immediately notice the new arrivals. As they crossed to the bar, Kalleah was reassured to see the same diversity in customers they had encountered on their first visit. The raid had only been a temporary setback, then.

When the tavernkeeper returned to the bar, he did a double-take.

"You're still here! I thought you'd given up and left our plague-ridden city ages ago."

"Not quite," Kalleah said. "We still have business here. But first, I'll need a room for tonight. Free of charge."

The man's brow furrowed, and he shuffled from foot to foot. "We're not a charity, I'm afraid. I can't be throwing out free goods to every return customer who comes through my doors."

Kalleah released Leoth's arm and drew herself up to her full height, glad to find she was steady on her feet. "Not even to the Queen of Itrea, who intends to rid your city of the Lord's Men forever?"

The barkeeper paled. "That's not possible."

"It is," Mellicante said pleasantly. "We'll explain everything thoroughly, but first, Queen Kalleah needs to sleep. She won't be any help to us if she collapses where she's standing."

With the expression of a fish that had been left flopping on the docks, the innkeeper fetched a ring of keys and led Kalleah up the stairs to a vacant room. She kicked off her shoes and fell into bed with her coat on, and she was asleep before she heard the innkeeper's footsteps retreating.

85

Down the River

Idorii hadn't known what to do when Daymin didn't reply to his second message. So he had continued walking back in the direction of the foothills, toward the Whitish army, passing countless refugees flooding in the opposite direction. He had sent Letto and Jakovi back to the refugee camp, away from the battle, so he had no company to distract him from his dark thoughts.

On the second evening after word had come from the end of the gorge, Idorii ran across a group of Weavers just as darkness was falling. He had intended to press on until he could no longer see, but he was too glad for a bit of company to abandon them.

It was while he ate a simple dinner of cured venison and wayfarer's bread, sitting with his back against the canyon wall, that his tattoo finally flashed cold.

Excitement and relief swooped through his stomach. He

pulled his oilskin cloak up to hide his arm and pushed up his sleeve, pulse racing.

Idorii –

> *I am so sorry for the long silence. I thought I had failed my people completely, and we could offer no hope for the refugees. I didn't know what to tell you.*
>
> *But we have run the final distance to the mountains, and against all odds, we have managed to reach the forest just north of the Whitish army. Our scouts report that the Whitish are already forcing their way up the gorge, but that they are likely to stop overnight since the terrain is treacherous enough in daylight.*
>
> *Our army has set up camp for a brief rest, but if there is any way to attack before this night is over, we would like to take advantage of the darkness. I need as much information as you can give me about the terrain and the position of the Whitish army, as well as any means we have of cutting them off from the valley without attacking from the rear.*
>
> *I don't know if I will be able to fight my way through to see you before this is over, but I cannot lose hope yet.*

With love,
Daymin

Idorii pulled down his sleeve and clutched his arm to his chest, buoyed and warmed by Daymin's words.

"How far is it to the start of the canyon?" he asked the Weaver on his left.

"Only a few hours," she said. "We were caught in the

fighting, so it took us much longer than that. It was only when our soldiers managed to push to the front that we could keep moving through."

A few hours…

"What enchanted items are you carrying?" Idorii asked the group of Weavers, leaning forward to look at those sitting on both sides of him. "Do you have anything that might help me travel down the riverbed without getting smashed to bits?"

"My oilskin cloak is a flying cloak," said a young man. "It would help if you had to get down any waterfalls."

"I converted a heating tapestry to a coat when it became too burdensome to carry," added an older woman. "That would ward off hypothermia."

"Does anyone have a pair of boots enchanted to adhere to surfaces?" Idorii asked.

The Weavers shared questioning looks.

"If you could wait an hour, I would be able to lay the enchantment in your boots," the young man offered.

"And a pair of gloves as well," another Weaver added eagerly. "For added stability."

Idorii hesitated. He had no time to waste, but without the right enchantments, he wouldn't make it down the river in the first place.

"If you can make it work, I would be very grateful," he said at last.

He pulled off his boots, hating that he couldn't do the spell himself, and passed them to the young Weaver. Usually the spell needed to be laid when the shoes were first being sewn, or it would have little effect, so he was curious to see how the Weaver would manage.

656

But the Weaver was more inventive than Idorii had given him credit for. He pulled a set of tiny nails from his pack and pushed them through a swatch of leather in a series of rows, the ends just barely sticking out the other side. Then he sewed them in place with a thread bound with an enchanted hair. He spoke the enchantment as he worked, his voice a low murmur that was almost lost beneath the rush of the river far below.

When he was done, he bound the leather tightly to the sole of Idorii's boot with the points of the nails facing out.

"It should work as long as this stays in place," the Weaver said, handing over the first boot.

"That was very well done," Idorii said, examining the man's work. There was no elegance to the needlework or the design, but he had come up with a clever solution to a problem that would have stymied Idorii.

Flushing faintly, the young man bent over a second piece of leather. While he worked, Idorii pulled on the first boot and tested it against the rock. When he got to his feet and took an experimental step up the sheer section of rock he had been leaning against, his boot gripped the near-vertical surface, allowing him to push his full weight off the ground.

A second later, he lost his balance and had to drop back to the ground, pulling his boot off the rock as he went.

"I'll definitely need the gloves as well," he said ruefully.

While the Weavers finished their work, Idorii readied himself. He traded his Weaver's armor for the heating tapestry coat, which was uncomfortably warm even in the chill night air, and draped the flying cloak over the top. Then he dug in his pack and pulled out a few strips of venison jerky. He wouldn't be able to carry his pack in the river, so he would have no spare clothes, no extra food, no sleeping roll. He had to find Daymin's camp before the night was up.

"There," the Weaver said, handing Idorii the second boot. The other Weaver passed over the gloves she had been working on; she had added a set of knots enchanted with the grip spell to the palms and fingers of each.

"Thank you," Idorii said. "Thank you all so much."

"You're going to look for King Daymin, aren't you?" the young Weaver asked, eyes glinting with excitement. "I recognize you from his court."

"Yes," Idorii said.

"Then all our hopes travel with you," the old woman said solemnly.

Idorii gave her a grim smile. "Safe passage. I hope to see you again on the other side."

Then he stepped into his second boot, pulled on the gloves, and turned to lower himself cautiously over the canyon wall.

For the first few steps down the sheer rock, Idorii's heart was pounding in his ears, vertigo holding him in its dizzying grasp. But as he grew accustomed to the grip of the enchanted gloves, the descent seemed less intimidating, and his nerves settled.

At last he reached the water. The darkness over the canyon was now absolute, but the stars overhead were bright enough that they provided a faint illumination, reflecting off the water and revealing the vague outline of boulders that lay tumbled through frothy rapids. The roar of the river filled his ears, making the army above seem distant and irrelevant.

Idorii started out skirting along the side of the canyon just above the water, clinging spiderlike to the rock, but a chute of loose rock soon forced him into the water. The first dash of icy spray was refreshing—his skin was damp with sweat from the heat of the enchanted coat—but as he lowered his foot deeper, searching for something to put his weight on, the numbing cold sent needles through his leg.

The river was deeper than he had expected, and when his foot finally collided with a solid rock, he could feel the current dragging fiercely at him.

Fear rose in him along with a rush of panicked adrenaline— if he lost his grip and was tugged underwater, the enchantment on his boot might hold him down until he drowned. He wasn't sure if it was better to remain trapped in place, battered by the current, or to let the river sweep him downstream, slamming him against boulders until he was too bruised to fight back.

Nerves racing, Idorii lowered his second foot carefully into the current, gripping the boulder tight with both hands to hold himself steady against the force of the river. Then, little by little, he shuffled his way forward until he had passed the eroded chute and was able to climb up the side of the river once more.

His heart was still pounding, the cold of the river making his legs clumsy, so he huddled there for a moment, breathing hard. He wasn't sure he could do this. The darkness, the force of the water, the cold…

Daymin needs you, Idorii reminded himself sternly.

Sucking in a ragged breath, he tried to force back the panic. Then he started down the river once more.

86

Battle for the City

When Kalleah woke, it was still dark. For a moment she didn't know what had roused her; then she felt Leoth's hand tracing her cheek, and he bent to press his lips to hers.

"Are you well?" he murmured.

Kalleah sat up, while Leoth fumbled to light the candle at her bedside. With a hiss, the flame took, and Kalleah felt a rush of relief to see Leoth's face shadowed with exhaustion but no longer twisted with self-loathing.

"I feel recovered," she said. "Whether I can use my power, I don't know, but I think I could wield a sword without trouble."

"Good. Because we've recruited enough help that we might not need your power at all, but we want to get moving before dawn."

Kalleah pushed aside the blankets, surprised to find she was still wearing her coat. She had even left her sword buckled to her waist.

When she stood and pulled on her boots, she found that she was still weaker than usual, but she hoped she would regain her strength once she shook off the last vestiges of sleep. And once she drew on the energy of whoever was gathered below.

As soon as they left her room, Kalleah heard a low rumble of voices from the main tavern. How many people had Leoth recruited to help with their work?

She gave him a curious look, and Leoth smiled.

When they descended the stairs and pushed open the door separating the inn from the tavern, a roar of sound rose up around them. Kalleah didn't have a chance to look at the room before Baridya pulled her into an embrace, her floppy hat blocking Kalleah's vision.

"You're awake!"

As Baridya released her, Kalleah finally saw the crowd that filled the tavern, packing the space so tightly there was hardly any room to move about. The barkeeper was handing around drinks, while others clustered around tables, conferring over roughly-drawn maps that looked like the street plans of both Darrenmark and Kohldar. The crowd represented a diversity of nationalities Kalleah had not seen reflected elsewhere in the city, and she wondered if these people had been in hiding. There were Varrilans with skin so dark it was nearly black, Ruunans who shared Baridya's sleek black hair and tan skin, brown-skinned marsh-dwellers, and many with mixed blood who could have been from anywhere. And there were plenty of Dardens and Kohls of Whitish descent as well, including a few women.

"Queen Kalleah has joined us," Leoth said, his voice projecting easily over the noise.

A roar rose from the crowd, many of whom turned and craned their necks for a glimpse of Kalleah.

"So," Kalleah said, heart lifting at the sight of so many who looked up to her leadership even here, in a tightly Whitish-controlled city. "Are you ready to overthrow the Lord's Men?"

Another roar sounded from the crowd. It was good they were moving out now, or the ruckus was likely to draw unwanted attention.

"You know your orders," Leoth said. "When you're finished, meet us at the palace gates, but stay hidden in the side streets until we approach the steps. The palace is likely to be the hardest place to breach, and we don't want this to escalate into a larger fight that sees civilians injured."

Little by little, the crowd started moving out from the tavern. Many downed the last of their drinks before they left, and Kalleah suspected more than a few were drunk.

"They'll spread through both cities and wait for the Lord's Men in the first places they usually patrol each morning," Leoth told Kalleah quietly. He approached one of the maps, and Kalleah noticed a set of marks on both sides of the river—information gleaned from his time with the Lord's Men.

"What about us?" Kalleah asked.

"We'll attack them at their barracks. If they're asleep, the rest of our recruits won't have much work to do."

"And if my power doesn't work?"

"If we catch them by surprise, we might be lucky."

Kalleah gave Leoth a skeptical look. They had virtually no chance of sneaking into the barracks housing dozens of Lord's Men unnoticed and then killing them all in their sleep without backup.

"They'll be joining us," Leoth said, indicating a group of around twenty who still lingered in the tavern.

"That's better. But it doesn't help us sneak in unnoticed."

"I have a key." Leoth reached in his pocket and held up a brass key. "I had only just earned their trust enough to get a copy before we left."

Kalleah wondered what he had done to buy their trust. Then she decided she didn't want to know.

"Good." Lowering her voice, she said, "I'd like to avoid using my power until we reach the palace gates, if possible. I'm not sure I've recovered enough to use it twice, especially not against larger groups."

"We'll do our best," Leoth said.

Then he, Kalleah, Mellicante, and Baridya led the way through the tavern door, their supporters falling in behind them. In some ways it felt like every other time Kalleah had gone into battle with her friends by her side, yet in other ways, everything had changed. Mellicante and Baridya knew Leoth's secret. They knew Kalleah had kept it from them for so many years, even though she supposedly trusted them absolutely. And while it had not been her secret to share, she had hurt them by keeping it from them.

Leoth was good at hiding it, but that shard of self-hatred, that enduring feeling of worthlessness, had returned to the surface, and Kalleah knew it was still eating at him.

And above all, her friends now knew that she would stop at nothing to save Itrea. She would kill anyone in her path, becoming a deadly weapon, no longer caring for her own conscience. She would push that aside in service of what needed to be done.

She would embrace the monster within.

As they started through the dark streets, following a route Kalleah had never taken before that avoided main throughfares, she felt strength seeping back into her as she drained energy from her followers. The stench of the waterfront was less potent here, which likely meant the buildings they passed were warehouses rather than residences.

Soon Leoth stopped before a nondescript block of a building constructed from wood. He inserted his key into the lock and pushed open the door, revealing a hallway lit by a single oil lamp.

"The bunkrooms are all along this hall," Leoth whispered. "Each sleeps twelve, and if we count the empty beds, we'll know how many are out on patrol right now."

"We need to move quickly and silently, then," Kalleah said, turning to the group of recruits as she spoke. "If anyone wakes before our work is done and raises the alarm, we'll be overwhelmed."

Several of the recruits traded nervous looks, and Kalleah wondered if Leoth had accurately described how risky this would be.

With a soft rasp, she unsheathed her sword, the others following suit. Then she and Leoth led the way silently down the hall. Pushing open the door to the first bunkroom, they slipped inside, each positioning themselves beside one of the twelve beds, swords raised like they were agents of some cruel god of death. The men looked as burly and intimidating as ever, even in sleep, and Kalleah did not like her chances against them if any woke.

"Now," Leoth breathed.

Kalleah responded by instinct, leaning her weight forward and plunging her sword beneath the chin of the man before her. He jerked in place but made no sound, his windpipe severed. Blood bubbled up from his throat, and his chest heaved as he fought to draw breath.

Then he fell still.

Some of the others had attacked their victims less cleanly, and Kalleah and her friends rushed to finish the job where the Lord's Men had not been properly decapacitated.

Soon all twelve men were dead with hardly a sound, their beds stained with blood.

A few of Leoth's recruits looked nauseous, and they averted their gazes from the sight. Kalleah could understand—there was no glory or skill in butchery like this. Even if their victims deserved to die.

As soon as the last of the men were dead, they hastened from the room, leaving behind the stench of blood that hung thick in the air.

The next room down the hall was half-empty, and as they continued down the hall, Kalleah made a mental tally of the Lord's Men they would have to track down elsewhere. The further they went, the emptier the rooms, until at last they found the final two bunkrooms standing empty. Forty-three bunks in total had been unoccupied.

"There should be more men here," Leoth said, brow creased with worry as he bent to clean his sword on a bedsheet. "They must know something is wrong."

"How?" Mellicante asked. "Unless they're colluding with the Prophet's Eyes, which would make no sense."

"Or they saw the commotion in the tavern," Kalleah said.

"They're more straightforward than that," Leoth said. "If they'd seen a disturbance, they would have gone directly to deal with it. But I posted lookouts while we gathered support last night, and they saw no trace of the Lord's Men anywhere along the waterfront."

"What are we supposed to do?" Baridya asked. "We can't waste all day tracking them through the city, can we?"

"No," Kalleah said. "We'll head to the palace as planned. If we run across them on the way, we'll deal with them, and if not, it won't matter as long as we can still speak to King Rodarin."

Their followers were subdued as they emerged onto the street once more. Some had specks of blood dotting their clothing, which hopefully would not draw attention in the faint light of early morning, and all looked grim and nervous, any trace of drunkenness long since worn off.

Leoth led the way up a narrow, winding route through the city, and again Kalleah was grateful for the time with the Lord's Men that had given him such knowledge. They encountered no guards along the way, which only increased Kalleah's anxiety. Where were the missing men?

Near the palace, they ran across the first of Leoth's recruits, hovering in the deep shadows of an alley that connected with the main square. The sun had crested the horizon, bathing the tallest rooftops in splashes of gold, while the streets below remained dark and cold.

"Did you find any of the Lord's Men where we expected them to be stationed?" Leoth asked the recruits in an undertone.

"Only two, at the open market," said a tall Varrilan man. "But the palace steps are overrun with the bastards."

Leoth shot Kalleah a worried look. How did they know?

But it was too late to stop now. With half the Lord's Men slaughtered in their beds, the city would face severe consequences if she didn't finish her work.

"And the rest of our group?" Leoth asked.

"Travin's gone around checking the nearby streets, and most of us are here. Except the ones who went into Kohldar."

"That will have to be enough," Kalleah said. "We can't afford to wait any longer, or the streets will fill up."

"And the Lord's Men will start wondering where their day guards have gone," Leoth said.

"This is going to be a fight," Kalleah said, "and not an easy one. Let us take the lead, and don't risk yourselves unnecessarily if you don't know what you're doing."

While Leoth organized their recruits, speaking more encouragingly than Kalleah had managed, she tried to slip into the state of focus needed to draw on her power. It wasn't waiting just below the surface, as it had been earlier, so she wouldn't be able to rely on it. Fighting might push her into the right frame of mind, but she had to approach this battle under the assumption that it would be a simple clash of swords.

"Ready?" she asked, stepping into place beside Leoth.

The murmur of agreement was in stark contrast to the cheers she had heard earlier that night. Most of these people had likely never spilled blood before, and she had forced them to kill in the worst possible way.

But there was no time to dwell on that now. The line of gold was creeping down the roofs, and the town would soon wake.

Kalleah and Leoth drew their swords and led the way up the alley, Mellicante and Baridya close at their heel. She had fought many unequal battles since reaching the Kinship Thrones, more often than not in the company of inexperienced recruits, but this felt like one of the most dangerous situations they had gotten themselves in. The population of Darrenmark was unlikely to come to their aid, and without numbers on their side, there was no escaping the fact that none of her recruits wore armor and many were fighting with daggers rather than swords.

Then they reached the square at the foot of the palace steps, and Kalleah stumbled.

At least forty of the brutish Lord's Men were arrayed on the steps, looking tense and watchful.

Nervous adrenaline surged through Kalleah. Against such a force, she felt naked and unprepared.

Too late to turn back.

Shaking off her surprise, she pushed herself forward, breaking into a run as she started across the square.

From behind, Leoth let out a roar, which his recruits echoed feebly. The noise swelled as her followers waiting in the streets joined the battle cry.

The wall of Lord's Men rose up before her, and she raised her sword, pulse thundering in her ears.

Then she slammed into the first of the Lord's Men.

Two men blocked her first blow, and before she could recover, strikes came at her from several directions at once. She darted out of reach of the first and caught the second on her blade, but it landed with such crushing force that her shoulders screamed in pain.

Kalleah yanked her sword free, her blade rasping against her opponent's, and danced backward. The Lord's Men were skilled swordsmen, but more than that, they were far heavier and stronger than she. It hardly mattered how well she fought when their blows slammed at her with such power.

Before she was ready, she was swept forward again as the rest of her followers joined the attack. This time, with a line of swords to reinforce her, she was able to push against the Lord's Men and hold her ground. Yet every strike rattled through her, and she could already feel her arms weakening against the onslaught.

She lost track of what was happening around her—all she could concentrate on was the blade that flashed through the air before her, always a hair too close to breaking past her defenses. Gradually the press of bodies around her eased, and she found herself fighting several men at once, whirling from one to the next as she countered with frantic speed.

She had no idea how the rest of her supporters fared. She could not spare a second to glance behind her; for all she knew, they might have given up and left her to face the Lord's Men alone.

But she knew this wasn't working. As hard as she fought, as many brutal blows as she threw aside, she was gaining no ground. Sweat prickled at her forehead, and she gasped for breath, lungs searing.

Plagues. She should have been less extravagant with her power at the temple. The Prophet's Eyes were no warriors—she could have killed every last one of them with her sword alone. She had used her power not because it was necessary, but because it had let her feel less culpable for their deaths.

And now she was paying for it.

In her brief distraction, one of the Lord's Men caught her

blade against his and shoved hard, sending Kalleah stumbling backward.

Abruptly she was enveloped by her own forces, who jostled her aside as they rushed the men Kalleah had been fighting.

She sucked in a breath, chest aching, and straightened. Free of the swords that had harried her, she was able to look around the square for the first time.

A few bodies lay at the foot of the steps, including one in the characteristic leather jerkin and silver wolf's-head buckle, while Leoth, Mellicante, and Baridya seemed to be holding the Lord's Men back singlehandedly, with only intermittent support from the rest of their recruits. Baridya's cheek was bleeding badly, and Leoth was fighting with a relentless fury that made Kalleah glad she was not his enemy.

They were making no headway up the steps, and even with the support of their recruits, they seemed close to breaking against the unyielding wall of Lord's Men. At least they had kept the Lord's Men from spilling into the square to attack the rest of their forces—or maybe they didn't intend to leave the high ground even if they had an opening.

Around the square, townspeople were gathering, drawn to the frenzy of the battle. None seemed likely to intervene.

Kalleah wanted to yell in frustration. If this kept up, they would dash themselves to pieces against the Lord's Men without gaining any ground.

Then, from behind Kalleah's recruits, someone shouted, "You need shields!"

Kalleah felt a flicker of hope. Had someone found a way to arm her forces better?

She pushed her way to the edge of the square, staying well

back from the fighting. When she broke free of the press of bodies, she saw a group of townspeople ducking into a café. They emerged a few minutes later carrying chairs and round tables small enough to hold one-handed.

Yes. This was what they needed.

"Grab a shield!" Kalleah shouted to her recruits. She jogged over and chose a chair, which she tilted so it sat on one shoulder with the legs pointing forward, keeping her right hand free for her sword.

Around her, others armed themselves similarly, until Kalleah was surrounded by a mess of wooden legs. The rest of her force parted as she led the way to the foot of the steps.

"Move!" she called to Leoth and Mellicante, who were blocking her way through to the Lord's Men.

Leoth glanced over his shoulder, blinking in surprise at the sight of Kalleah and a dozen others wielding chairs and tables as if they were shields.

When she broke through to the front of her recruits, Kalleah tightened her grip on her chair and shifted her weight so she could put as much force as possible behind the makeshift shield.

Then, with her followers jostling at her back, she charged at the foot of the steps, picking up momentum as she went.

A moment later, she slammed into the wall of Lord's Men. The legs of her chair connected with flesh, and as Kalleah shoved, she managed to gain headway. Someone was at her back, helping push forward, while Kalleah guarded her right side with her sword.

As the enemy was pushed backward, she stepped onto the first stair.

"Form a triangle!" Leoth shouted to the recruits at her back. "Shields out!"

Someone's hands were still on her back, pushing her forward, but others with chairs fell into place on either side of her, the wooden legs of the nearest covering her exposed right side.

"One, two, three," Leoth barked. On *three*, the wedge behind Kalleah gave a tremendous push, forcing her up another two stairs.

The Lord's Men were swinging at her, so Kalleah freed her sword from the tangle of chair legs and made sweeping motions over her head, warding off the blades that sliced her way.

Again the wedge of people at her back pushed upward, and again she gained a step, forcing the Lord's Men to the side. She didn't want to break into the palace without killing them, but while her power continued to elude her, it was the only way forward. Maybe if they could seal the gates and get King Rodarin on their side, he would send his own guards against the Lord's Men.

Another shove took her halfway up the steps, the mass of enemies thinning ahead of her. Kalleah couldn't make out what was happening behind her, but she thought at least one of the brutes had been thrown over the side of the steps.

Then, just as she started to believe the palace gates were within reach, she heard a horribly familiar *thwack*.

Someone behind her screamed.

"Arrows!" Leoth shouted. "Shields up!"

Kalleah raised the chair to protect her face and head, leaving her vulnerable to the Lord's Men. Again she reached for her power.

672

Nothing.

Nine plagues. She had to make this work.

Dropping to a crouch in the middle of the steps, the chair balanced on her shoulders, she tried to summon up the focus she had found aboard the *Sparrow's Flight*. She imagined the steady roll of the sea, the smell of brine, the smooth grain of the rail beneath her palm.

More screams broke her concentration, one of which sounded like Baridya.

Heart leaping into her throat, she turned and looked down the steps, searching the mayhem for her friend.

Her followers were being set upon from all directions at once. Without the shield wall, they were helpless against the onslaught, and the Lord's Men were stepping over bodies as they waded deeper into the throng. She couldn't pick Baridya out of the chaos, but there were Mellicante and Leoth, fighting at the foot of the steps without shields. Two men were swinging at Mellicante in concert, their heavy blows forcing her back.

Concentrate, Kalleah berated herself. She could see no way out of this without her power. Everyone here had trusted their lives to her, and she was going to fail them.

No. It's still waiting for you. Just…concentrate!

This time Kalleah closed her eyes, though the sounds of battle from every direction made her flinch. She summoned up the memories of the first time she had drawn on her power on her own terms—standing in a storm, the boat rocking wildly underfoot, rain pelting her face and chilling her skin. The shouts became thunder booming overhead, while the thwacks of metal against wood were the sounds of her crew scrambling to stow the sails.

As she sank deeper into the memory, she finally sensed the threads of gold hovering just out of sight. And she knew this would be the last time she could reach for them until after she had recovered properly—once she forced the power from her again, she would be left drained and weak.

Opening her eyes, she uncurled from her crouch and stood slowly. The shadowed steps faded to a blur, a web of golden threads emerging from the gloom.

"Allies! Retreat to the foot of the steps!" Kalleah called. She did not want to harm her own people once the bloodlust overtook her.

While they scrambled to obey, she turned back to the men crowding the steps above her. None of her followers had penetrated past the step she stood on, so the way ahead was clear for her.

Kalleah dropped her chair.

The men closest to her took the chance to strike, but Kalleah wrapped their golden threads around her hand and wound them in like a skein of wool. One man's sword connected with her arm, ripping her coat open, but it was a clumsy blow.

Then the men started falling to the ground one by one, like fish dropped from a net.

Power surged through her, a dizzying, heady rush, and she craved more with an urgency that had not diminished since the first time she had overindulged this way.

Turning, Kalleah found a mass of Lord's Men at her back, so she plucked their golden threads from the web and dropped them as well.

"The steps are clear," Leoth's voice called out, a single dissonant note in the harmony of light and power that thrummed before her.

It took a moment for the meaning of his words to register.

Then Kalleah scooped the rest of the threads greedily into her fists, tugging them until they snapped.

Ahead, only a few murky shapes remained between her and the palace gates. She charged up another few steps to confront the last of the Lord's Men, seizing their life threads as soon as they swam into view.

At last the way was clear. Power burned through Kalleah's veins, as painful as it was addictive, but she thought she could hold it in a bit longer.

"Into the palace!" she called. "The king awaits us."

She had only one chance to make this work.

87

At the King's Side

Through the gates and across the courtyard, Kalleah and her followers found the palace entrance unguarded. Kalleah had only a jumbled impression of footsteps and voices at her heel, her surroundings still blurred as she held onto her power. The pulse of lifeblood through her veins was growing fiercer; she didn't know how much longer she could hold it in.

Leoth and Mellicante dashed ahead of her, checking in each of the rooms lining the main hall.

"In here!" Leoth called at last, voice distorted by the vast space.

Kalleah turned to her followers. "Wait in the hall until we call for you."

Then she jogged over to where Leoth and Mellicante stood by the open doors of the throne room.

Kalleah let her power fade to the background so the room came clear before her. The excess energy she had taken in still burned through her, threatening to scorch her from the inside, and she knew she couldn't hold it in much longer. But if she pushed it into the ground here, the shaking could bring the palace crashing down.

As the throne room crystallized before her, she realized with a jolt that Bennett was standing beside the king, dressed convincingly as a nobleman, his doublet dripping with gold thread.

"No," she breathed.

Had she guessed wrong? Was King Rodarin working with the Prophet's Eyes?

Did he know most of their number lay dead at the Temple of Totoleon?

"I was expecting you," King Rodarin said grimly, his voice resounding through the cavernous space. "It seems I am the next target on your list."

"We would never harm you," Kalleah said, stepping forward.

Leoth grabbed her arm. Looking up, she spotted archers stationed along the balcony that lined the room, arrows trained on her.

"I know what you can do," King Rodarin said. "You're too dangerous to take alive. And King Edreon will reward us greatly if we do away with the thorn in his side."

"What reward could he give you that would mean more than the liberation of your city?" Kalleah demanded. Even as she spoke, she wondered if she could trust his words. There were forces at play here that she didn't understand—layers upon layers of intersecting factions. The way the Prophet's Eyes guarded the bowels of the palace; the fact that the Lord's Men had seemingly been warned about her approach, though they and the Prophet's Eyes were clearly working at cross purposes; the device deep beneath the palace siphoning magic to some distant source…

And she didn't understand how King Rodarin played into all of this. Was he speaking plainly? Or was he being manipulated?

Standing where she was, without armor or shield, she was as vulnerable as any common soldier. She needed to get closer to the king if she intended to use her power.

She slid her right foot a fraction forward.

"What are you doing here?" Leoth demanded of Bennett. He must have felt her move, and was trying to distract the king.

"You've never understood, have you?" Bennett said with a sneer. "You swept in here, thinking you could take control of a foreign kingdom, when all you've done is made a mess of things."

Kalleah didn't hear Leoth's reply, because the king's eyes had locked on hers. And she recognized the same look she had seen when she had danced with him—a desperate, impossible hope.

My hands are tied, he had said.

And that night, she had trusted him. That night she had believed he would support her, if only his city was freed from the Lord's Men.

Were the Prophet's Eyes oppressors of another form?

Was Bennett standing beside King Rodarin to protect him, or to control him?

Kill him, whispered the monster inside, the monster that flowed like molten steel through her veins, searing and boiling even as it lent her strength.

And this time, Kalleah listened.

She was still too far away from the throne, but she slid her foot another finger's breadth forward. If she made a dash for it, maybe she could reach Bennett before the archers hit her.

Bennett was speaking again, so Kalleah muttered out of the corner of her mouth, "When I move, get yourselves out of here. Away from the archers."

"But—" Leoth whispered.

"I can't do this if I'm worrying about you."

Then she tried to reach for her power once more.

Nothing happened.

Fear spiked through her. When she had let the gold threads fade away, she must have lost her last chance at summoning the power. She had pushed herself too hard.

But the energy she had drained was still burning her from within. Surely she could use that for something. Surely…

She eyed the twenty paces remaining between herself and the king. She wasn't too far out of range of her usual power. But if she wanted to use the power searing through her veins, she needed to be closer. Much closer.

She had read the theory. Every source had described how dangerous it was to feed power into another, how great a risk to the recipient, unless the Extractor was well-trained and controlled.

She was neither.

Drawing in a sharp breath, she broke into a run toward the throne.

She zigzagged across the room, not wanting to make herself an easy target for the archers.

After a second's delay, she heard a series of clicks as arrows hit the stone floor and bounced off.

Bennett drew a sword as she approached, while the king remained seated, unmoving.

Kalleah's sword had hung limp at her side, but she lifted it over her shoulder at the last moment. The *thwack* of arrows died off as she closed the last distance—no one wanted to risk catching the king in the crossfire.

She brought her sword down in a sweeping strike, powered by the energy raging within her.

Bennett blocked clumsily, staggering backward. He was many things, but it seemed he was no expert swordsman.

With her left hand, Kalleah grabbed his arm.

Then she closed her eyes, filling her mind with the fire raging within.

Drawing the power together into a restless bundle, like a tiny maelstrom tearing at her chest, she brought it to the surface.

Then, with a great shove, she forced the power down her arm and into Bennett.

As soon as the power left her, she staggered backward, legs wobbling.

She tripped over something on the ground—an arrow, she realized belatedly—and fell heavily to her knees, gasping for air. The room spun, colors blurring sickeningly, and she retched.

Footsteps rang across the marble floor, and someone was kneeling beside her, steadying her. Leoth.

As she drew in a deep breath, the dizziness subsided.

With the room clearing around her, she caught sight of the corpse at her knees.

Bennett looked as though he had been pulled from a funeral

pyre before it had finished its work. The skin from his face was charred and bubbling, part of his cheek melted away to reveal the bone of his jaw, and his hair had been reduced to ash. The sight was sickening—Kalleah retched again, Leoth holding her as she doubled over.

The sight—and the fact that Bennett was no stranger—made the weight of what she had done settle over her in a way the previous deaths had not. She was killing people, ripping out their lives as if they were nothing but sparks she snuffed out, and she *should* be horrified.

Someone knelt on her other side, and Kalleah blinked hazily over to see Mellicante by her side. Baridya was there as well, cheek streaked with blood, though she stood back from the corpse.

Mellicante and Leoth helped raise Kalleah to her feet, though she was still leaning heavily on them.

"Archers. Lower your bows," King Rodarin said. Though he spoke quietly, his voice resounded through the room.

He turned to Kalleah. "So. The tales are true."

She still wasn't sure where he stood, so she raised herself up to her full height, Leoth steadying her, and feigned confidence. "I could kill you at a moment's notice. Yet I haven't."

"No," King Rodarin said. "You knew that man?" He indicated Bennett's corpse lying at his feet.

Kalleah did not look down. "He led me astray with promises that he would help destabilize the High Throne and end the war in Itrea. But his conspiracy is meddling in affairs that endanger us all."

"I was similarly led astray," King Rodarin said. "And by the time I realized how deeply their people had seeded themselves in my court, it was too late." He lowered his voice. "They are holding my son hostage to force my hand. They want you dead as much as the Lord's Men."

"Those have been dealt with," Mellicante said with satisfaction. "And most of the Prophet's Eyes as well."

"Help me rescue my son, then," King Rodarin said. "And when he is safe, we can speak openly."

"My recruits are waiting in the hall," Kalleah said. "They can help."

King Rodarin threw her a searching glance, but if he guessed she was too weak to use her power again, he said nothing.

In the hall, King Rodarin's archers emerged and flanked him, Kalleah's forces trailing behind. She was still leaning heavily on Leoth, though she tried not to make it apparent.

They climbed a grand staircase and followed King Rodarin to the ornate door of what looked like a royal bedchamber.

"They might kill him as soon as they see our forces here," King Rodarin said hoarsely.

"I'll distract them long enough for your archers to deal with them," Kalleah said.

Putting a steadying hand on Leoth's shoulder, she stepped forward. When she let go, she managed to stay upright.

Legs shaking, she closed the final distance to the door and pushed it open, leaning on the handle for balance.

A grand bedroom met her eyes, resplendent with gilded furniture and silk bedding. For a moment she could not discern any people amidst the wash of color.

Then she spotted a boy tied to the head of the bed, flanked on both sides by guards. As Kalleah stepped into the room, one raised a dagger to the boy's throat. He was young—no older than ten—with a mop of blond curls and sallow skin.

"I am Queen Kalleah," Kalleah said in the most commanding voice she could muster, endeavoring to draw all attention to her. "I have destroyed your temple and killed your fellows. Surrender now, or you will be the next to taste my deadly power."

The *thwack—thwack—thwack* of arrows sounded from behind her, and a second later, the points were buried in the guards' throats.

As the men collapsed, the dagger clattering to the ground, King Rodarin rushed forward to his son. He used his own ceremonial sword to cut the ropes around the boy's wrists, and when he was free, the king pulled him into a rough embrace.

"You're safe," he muttered, hands running searchingly over the boy's head and arms.

"Father?" the boy said faintly. "Are they gone?"

"Yes. The palace is ours once more."

Dizziness swept through Kalleah, and her knees buckled. As the ground rose up to meet her, she felt hands grabbing her shoulders.

Then blackness claimed her.

88

The Forest Camp

Daymin's army hadn't reached the forest until nightfall, and it took them several more hours to tramp through the pines until they were a few hundred paces away from the gorge the Whitish were attacking.

The Whitish had already started up the gorge, from his scouts' reports, and their camp sprawled through the forest where the river left the gorge, which meant Daymin wouldn't be able to cut them off from the gorge without fighting the bulk of their army.

His army had been so exhausted they were on the verge of collapse, so instead of ordering the attack then, while they could take advantage of the darkness, Daymin had told them to sleep.

Where are you? he wrote to Idorii while his soldiers erected the royal tent. He felt guilty since he was the only one in his army with a shelter that night, but he had to admit it gave the camp a more orderly feel once there was a central hub for soldiers to gravitate toward.

Idorii's reply came soon after, the writing appearing in blurred streaks, as though Idorii's arm was wet.

Wait where you are. Don't attack yet.

Daymin frowned in confusion.

"What is it?" asked Tarak, who was standing nearby and eyeing Daymin's arm.

Daymin showed him the line of writing. "What does he mean?"

"Maybe he knows the Whitish have blocked the end of the gorge," Tarak said. "We weren't planning to attack for a few hours yet, anyway, so it doesn't matter."

"But why would waiting help anything?"

"No idea."

Once the royal tent was erected, Daymin and his friends helped carry the maps and charts into the shelter before settling onto the canvas base, their coats the only cushioning against the network of roots beneath their backs.

His friends fell asleep quickly, their breathing evening out, while Daymin lay awake for what felt like ages. The sounds and smells of this forest were too unfamiliar—he kept thinking he heard the swish of arrows in the hiss of wind through the needles, the calls of soldiers in the chirruping of strange insects.

Now that they had made it to the mountains, he hated waiting. Every minute they delayed put them further from being able to help—what if the entire Whitish army poured into the gorge before his forces could slow them?

But he could not send an exhausted force to attack the bulk

of the Whitish army. Not if he wanted to win back ground for his refugees.

As his mind turned over and over the day ahead, the impossible battle with stakes higher than any other he had waged, his heartbeat raced, adrenaline making him twitchy. He hated lying still, even though his legs throbbed from the long run.

Then, little by little, exhaustion won out over his anxiety. Daymin slept.

* * *

He woke to the faint light of dawn shining through the walls of his tent. He could already hear the quiet bustle of his soldiers rousing and preparing for the day, and a chorus of birds rang through the treetops.

Daymin rose and dressed slowly. His friends stirred as he did, and soon they had joined him in pulling on their boots and buckling their swords to their waists. None spoke, and Daymin knew they could feel the heavy tension that had settled over camp.

Now that they were here, his army was waiting on his orders. But he still had no idea how he was supposed to push the Whitish back from the gorge. If he had arrived a few hours sooner, maybe he could have cut off their access before the bulk of the Whitish army encircled the mouth of the gorge. Now…their odds were no better than they had been when he had considered attacking from the rear.

When he could delay no longer, Daymin emerged from his tent, glad at least to have his friends by his side.

His soldiers were gathering around the royal tent, many gnawing on jerky or hard biscuits; none had tents to pack away, so they were ready to move out at Daymin's command. Pollard, Morrisse, and General Vask stood nearby, organizing their forces, and the murmur of voices subsided as Daymin stepped before his soldiers.

Plagues. What was he supposed to say? Idorii had told him to wait where he was, but how long did he expect him to stall?

"Your Majesty," Pollard said, approaching Daymin. "Have you heard any further word from your informant?"

"He asked me to wait," Daymin said quietly. "He might be caught in the battle, trying to reach safety. I expect a more detailed report soon."

"What do we know of the battlefield thus far?" Pollard asked.

Tarak handed Daymin a map of the Icebraid Peaks that he had brought from the tent. It was highly inaccurate, as most of the mountains had been mapped from the front range, but at least the border of the pine forest was more or less true to life.

Daymin knelt and turned the map over, spreading it out on the springy mat of pine needles. Then he reached for the pen he always kept in his pocket.

"I just know the gorge is the only easy access into the mountains, and it takes roughly three days to walk from one end to another." Daymin sketched a rough set of mountains with a split between them. "The Whitish are camped here en masse and have already started pushing their way up the gorge. I don't know how far they've made it, but a significant number of refugees are still trapped in the gorge, trying to reach the other end before the Whitish catch up to them." He circled the area where his scouts had described the Whitish camp sprawling around the mouth of the gorge.

"And the gorge?" Morrisse said. He had knelt beside Daymin, frowning at the sketch.

"It's too steep to access from any direction besides the deer trail," Daymin said. "Our only option is to cut in front of the Whitish army and force our way up the gorge before the bulk of their forces can stop us. And…" He hated admitting this. Especially now, after all they had gone through to get here.

He took a deep breath. "We're too late to get ahead of them without fighting our way through their full army."

"What are your orders, then?" Pollard asked.

Daymin gripped his pen hard, hating this. What was he supposed to do? How could he salvage this mess?

Then, from the direction of the Whitish camp, he heard a faint voice calling, "Daymin?"

He knew that voice.

Daymin jumped to his feet, kicking pine needles over the drawing in his haste. Then he broke into a run through the trees.

When he caught sight of Idorii emerging from behind a pine bough, Daymin's heart flew into his throat.

Idorii's eyes locked on Daymin at the same moment, and the raw joy in his eyes made Daymin's chest constrict.

Idorii flew at him, and Daymin seized him in a fierce embrace, unable to believe he was truly here.

"Idorii," Daymin muttered feverishly, gripping Idorii's coat as he crushed him closer still. "Idorii. Cloudy gods. I thought— I thought—"

Idorii laughed weakly. "You came. I thought I'd never see you again."

Daymin pressed his face into Idorii's hair, breathing in his familiar smell. "I'll always come for you."

Idorii's hand threaded through Daymin's hair, and he pressed a kiss to his temple. "I'm here. I don't ever want to leave you again."

Then a low rumble of voices from behind reminded Daymin that his whole army was there, watching him. With a shaky laugh, he released Idorii. Idorii's eyes were glistening, his face shining with joy, and Daymin had to scrub away his own tears.

"I think they're waiting on your report from the battlefield," Daymin said weakly.

Idorii grinned. "Yes. That."

Daymin turned and led the way back to his waiting generals, giddy with joy. It was all he could do not to grab Idorii's hand just to convince himself he was really there.

Daymin's friends were beaming at him when he rejoined them, while Pollard and Morrisse gave him odd looks. Daymin ignored them.

"My informant has arrived with a more accurate report on the battlefield," Daymin said.

Idorii knelt and brushed the dirt off his sketch. "Gods, this is a terrible drawing."

Daymin laughed.

"But it does the job." Idorii reached for a stick and stood. "The Whitish are about a day's walk into the gorge." He indicated the place with his stick. "The going is slow, but our soldiers are falling fast. Soon they'll be fighting civilians. We need to get between them and the refugees before they make it to the end of the gorge."

"How?" Daymin asked, hoping against hope that Idorii would have a valid suggestion. Something better than he had been able to devise.

Idorii met his eyes and grinned. "We're going to use Weavers' spells to sneak up the gorge under cover of darkness and cut the Whitish off from above and below."

Daymin remembered the way Idorii's last message had looked as though it was dripping off his arm. Looking down, he realized Idorii's trousers were soaked, though his coat—an unusual garment woven of brightly-patterned flowers—seemed dry enough. "Wait. Did you walk down the river?"

"That's right!" Idorii pulled a pair of gloves from his pocket. "These and my boots are enchanted to adhere to any surface until I deliberately pull away, and the coat is made from a warming tapestry, to ward off the chill of the river."

A few of the Weavers in Daymin's army were pushing their way closer, and General Vask stepped aside to let them through.

"How do the boots work?" one asked. "What do you have tied to the soles?"

Idorii put a hand on Daymin's shoulder for balance, which sent a burst of warmth through Daymin, and lifted his foot to reveal a piece of leather strapped to the sole. "This is what's enchanted, not the boot itself. The coat was already finished, but it took less than an hour for the Weavers to prepare the boots and gloves."

This sent a wave of excited murmuring through Daymin's army.

"I don't think we have any warming tapestries to spare," Daymin said. "Do you think we could make it safely up the gorge without them?"

690

"As long as we stayed out of the water as much as possible. It's so icy it numbs your feet straightaway."

"And were you thinking of using flying cloaks to attack from above?" another Weaver asked.

"Exactly," Idorii said. "Is anyone here equipped with a flying cloak?"

"Most of us have enchanted our oilskin cloaks just in case," the Weaver said. "We brought those with us, thank the cloudy gods."

"And if we do manage to push the Whitish back," Pollard said, "how do we intend to cut off their access to the refugee camp?"

"I assumed we would blast away the deer trail," Daymin said. Then he shot a worried look at Idorii. "Do the refugees have more explosives? We've used our full supply, and we don't have the materials to make more."

Idorii shook his head. "The deer trail is narrow enough that we could destroy it with pickaxes, but that will take time. We need to hold the Whitish back long enough to chip away at it."

"And we'll want to destroy as much as possible so they can't find a way around," Daymin said.

He cast his gaze over his gathered army, buoyed by the hope shining on their faces. He had been right not to give up. To drive them to exhaustion pursuing the faintest shard of a chance.

As long as his people still lived, they had to cling to that hope. Otherwise, what reason did they have to fight?

"We'll camp here today while our Weavers prepare," Daymin said. "We should be able to equip several thousand soldiers to attack from above or below. Enough to break the Whitish line."

"And the rest of the army?" General Vask asked.

"We'll cross that bridge when we come to it," Daymin said. If he was unable to push the Whitish back from the mouth of the gorge, he might be forced to abandon more than half his troops on this side of the mountains. The thought was unsettling.

"Organize the Weavers," Daymin told Idorii, "and give me your best estimate of how many soldiers we'll be able to equip by nightfall. Find me in the royal tent when you've finished."

Idorii gave him a salute, fist to his chest, though the gesture was ruined by his broad grin.

Daymin couldn't help but smile back as Idorii turned to join the Weavers.

"Scouts, keep an eye on the Whitish camp," Daymin said, turning to the scouts who had reported to him the previous night. "I need to know how many remain outside the gorge by nightfall. Capture any Whitish scouts that approach our camp. And soldiers, sleep if you can. Rest as much as possible. We'll be fighting through the night."

When he collected the rough sketch off the ground and retreated into his tent, he heard soft footsteps as his friends followed.

"Gods, the way you looked at Idorii," Zahira whispered as the flap swung closed behind her. "I can't believe I never saw it before."

Daymin's face heated up. "We have battle strategies to plan," he said tightly. "Can we not discuss this right now?"

"We're just glad to see you happy again," Tarak said, squeezing Daymin's shoulder. "Right?"

Zahira gave him a mischievous grin. "Of course."

Daymin unrolled his drawing on the floor of the tent and then ducked outside to find a handful of rocks to mark troop movements. The Whitish numbers were smaller than his, but their armor would give them an advantage on flat terrain. In the gorge, it would be a liability, since they would likely die if they fell from the deer trail, but here in the forest, his troops would struggle to gain ground.

Maybe, if enough of the Whitish troops poured into the gorge before tonight, he would be able to overwhelm them with attacks from all sides and punch through the force that remained on this side of the foothills.

At what point would that strategy become viable? What sort of numbers could his army reasonably take on from this side of the gorge?

He started positioning rocks along the drawing, working his way through the various scenarios. Eventually his friends left him alone, and he mumbled to himself as he worked, trying to account for every eventuality. He had only one chance to make this work. Everything had to be seamless, or they would lose their sole advantage.

* * *

As Idorii talked the Weavers through the enchantment on his boots, he was so giddy with happiness he felt he could fly. For so many spans, he had feared he would never see Daymin again; to be able to embrace him now and see his own joy reflected back in Daymin's eyes had been such a gift he could hardly believe it was real.

And Daymin…his face was lined with burdens he had not

carried before, while his skin was darker than ever from the long spans of marching under the relentless sun, his arms muscled in a way that sent chills through Idorii. He was still the same scholar prince Idorii had fallen in love with, but he was now a warrior in equal measure.

Once the Weavers had settled in to their work, cutting apart shirts and vests and unenchanted cloaks to lay the new spell, Idorii stood and walked among their ranks, trying to get a rough idea of numbers. There were more Weavers with Daymin's army than he had expected—several hundred at least—and all were highly trained and efficient.

When he had finished his count, he threaded his way back through the forest to Daymin's tent to give his report. He wasn't sure of the correct protocol, but no one stopped him when he approached the flap and pushed his way in.

"Daymin?"

The king was kneeling in front of his drawing, frowning at a set of stones he had heaped along the gorge. At Idorii's voice, he rose swiftly.

"I've set the Weavers to—"

Daymin closed the gap between them and kissed Idorii fiercely, cutting him off mid-sentence.

Idorii's mind went blank. He dragged Daymin closer, kissing him with all the desperation of their many spans apart, unable to believe this was happening. Daymin's arm looped around Idorii's waist and dragged him close, and Idorii tangled his fingers in Daymin's beautiful hair, longer than usual after his time in the wilderness. After so much time spent doubting—wondering if he had been wrong—all his insecurities were wiped away.

694

Idorii could have kissed Daymin all day, drowning in his touch, in the softness of his mouth and the strength of his embrace. But too soon, Daymin released him.

They were both breathing hard, and when Idorii smiled and ran a thumb across Daymin's cheek, Daymin's face softened.

"I'm so sorry," Daymin murmured, callused hands framing Idorii's face. "I love you. I never should have pushed you away."

"That was my fault. I must have startled you."

"No." Daymin stroked Idorii's cheek, tracing the root-like markings left by the corruption. "I didn't realize, until that moment, how I felt for you—but I was trying to protect you. I was supposed to marry a woman who could give me an heir, and I didn't want to hurt you. I made that same mistake with Lalaysha."

"Then what has changed?" Idorii asked, throat tight. He knew he would agree to whatever Daymin asked.

Daymin gave a strangled laugh. "Our kingdom has crumbled. Any child I bear will inherit nothing but ash. I think we're past the point of worrying about tradition."

A rush of giddy joy swept through Idorii, and he kissed Daymin again.

"Now we just need to survive the night," Daymin said.

Some of Idorii's happiness drained away at that. "You make that sound easy."

Daymin pulled him into his arms and hugged him fiercely, and they stood that way for a long moment, neither one wanting to face what would come next.

89

Jakovi's Protector

After walking an hour up the gorge toward the refugee camp, Letto had gone against Idorii's orders and turned back toward the fight.

"They don't have many soldiers to bolster their line," he explained to Jakovi. "They need every sword they can find."

"Then I'm coming with you," Jakovi said—though he wasn't sure himself whether it was out of a perverse desire to see the fighting or an unwillingness to be separated from Letto.

"No," Letto had said at once. "You're supposed to be staying away from the battle at all costs."

"And you're supposed to be protecting me," Jakovi countered. As he grew more accustomed to interacting with ordinary soldiers, men and women who neither imprisoned nor feared him, he was learning to trust himself with decisions, standing his ground in arguments he would once have shied away from.

"It's not the same thing," Letto said. "There's nothing for me to protect you from while King Daymin is on the opposite side of the gorge and no one else with authority knows what you are. I'll be of little use to you up here, while we sit and wait to be attacked, whereas if I join the battle, I might be able to help hold the line long enough for help to arrive."

"And if you die?" Jakovi asked flatly. "Then where will my protector be?"

Letto did not reply at once, which told Jakovi all he needed to know—fighting at the front lines of this battle meant almost certain death.

"Let me go," Jakovi had said. "I promise I won't intervene. No matter the temptation."

He did not intend to use magic to twist the battle in their favor, but a tiny dose employed to protect Letto…he thought he could pull that off without unleashing too much corruption.

Letto had run a hand over his eyes in exasperation. "You do realize this is the exact opposite of what *you* claimed to want. But if you promise to stay out of the fighting…"

* * *

Now, after camping a night huddled on the narrow deer trail, they were approaching the fighting. The gorge did strange things with sound, carrying echoes from hundreds of paces away while muffling everything beneath the pounding of the river far below, so at times Jakovi expected to turn the corner and stumble across a Whitish soldier whose shout had resounded along the rocky canyon.

Letto kept throwing worried glances at Jakovi, seemingly

regretting his decision to bring him along, but he said nothing. Jakovi had planned to follow in secret even if Letto hadn't agreed, so he was grateful Letto had given him the chance. No matter the danger they faced, Jakovi felt safe with Letto in a way he never had before. He had not wanted to be parted from his protector.

Closer to the fighting, the clang of swords and shouts of soldiers seemed to come from every direction at once. Jakovi grew jumpy, clinging to the hilt of the sword at his waist that he could wield only with the barest of skill, and he hovered so close behind Letto that he kept catching the heels of his boots.

Here the deer trail was thronged with the last of the refugees, mostly older adults who had stayed behind while the children and the supplies passed through, and Jakovi and Letto were often forced to perch precariously on rocks looming above the trail to wait for a dense clump to pass.

"Where are the soldiers?" Letto muttered, throwing out an arm to slow Jakovi before rounding a corner. "We should have reached the army by now."

A chill went through Jakovi. Had they all fallen? Would Letto be the only one standing between the Whitish and the refugees?

Slowly, cautiously, they peered around the bend.

Ahead, just where the canyon rounded another corner, Jakovi caught sight of the Whitish army, a narrow band of silver that pushed its way forward step by step. And countering the Whitish was a small knot of Itrean soldiers no more than fifty strong. The Itrean soldiers at the front were clad in full plate armor, which explained why they had not been cut down yet, but they were being forced back little by little. And at their backs were soldiers in less protective Weavers' armor, and behind those, ranks of refugees who were bolstering the soldiers with nothing but the swords in their hands.

"Holy Varos," Letto whispered. Then he turned sharply to Jakovi. "You need to get away from here. *Now.*"

Jakovi gave Letto a panicked look. He didn't want to leave, not now, but he knew the Itrean line was about to break. When that happened, he would be caught in the stampede as the Whitish chased down the remaining refugees.

"Don't get yourself killed," Jakovi said hoarsely.

Letto gave him a pained smile. "I'm just another soldier. If I die, nothing changes."

Then he turned and shouldered his way forward, past the ranks of civilians, heading for the worst of the fighting.

Jakovi watched for a long moment, the abrupt farewell tearing at his chest.

Then the civilians who were bolstering the Itrean soldiers started jostling against him as the Whitish forced them back further still.

Jakovi darted away from the press of bodies, searching the canyon for a place he could hide and watch the fighting. They had passed a few side canyons earlier in the day, the incline shallow enough that he could have easily clambered up a hundred paces, but the last had been hours ago. He cast his gaze to the river below, wondering if he could climb onto a boulder in the middle of the churning flow and watch from there. But he wouldn't be able to see anything from that vantage, and he would be an easy target for any archers who spotted him.

Then he noticed the narrow runoff channel on the opposite wall of the gorge. It was not a proper side canyon, but the slope was shallower than the cliffs on either side. If he reached that, he would be able to clamber up until he was perched well above the fighting, within view of a long stretch of the trail.

The drop to the river was steep, but a boulder at the foot of the gorge would keep him from falling straight into the water, so Jakovi lowered himself over the side and skidded in a crouch down the chute of hardened dirt.

At the bottom, he collided hard with the boulder. Icy water sprayed him as it crashed against the stone, and a wave of nerves swept through him. The river was much wider and more powerful than it had appeared from above. He had thought he would be able to leap his way from one rock to another to cross, but the gaps between them were larger than he had realized.

Heart pounding in his throat, Jakovi pulled himself up so he was standing on the boulder he had collided with. The first two rocks would be easy enough to jump between, but after that, he had a deep, swift channel to clear.

Fear made his limbs stiff and clumsy, and as he readied himself for the first leap, he nearly lost his balance.

Arms flailing, he flung himself across the first gap onto a boulder that was thankfully dry and easy to grip. But his momentum threw him off balance, and he leapt to the next boulder to keep from careening into the water.

This rock was larger, and he was able to grab the side for balance, lowering himself to his knees to catch his breath. His heart was skittering in his chest, and he felt as though he had run a long distance.

From here, the next stretch of water looked wider than ever. How had he ever thought he could leap the distance?

Looking over his shoulder, he tried to find Letto on the trail above. But the canyon wall was so steep that he could only see a tangle of limbs over this stretch. He was able to see the Whitish army ahead, but he had no way of knowing how the Itreans fared.

That decided it. He needed to find Letto.

Jakovi got unsteadily to his feet. He didn't think he could possibly make the leap.

Drawing in a shaky breath, he rocked on his feet, trying to gauge the distance.

Then he flung himself recklessly across the churning water.

His feet grazed the boulder on the opposite side, but not high enough to find purchase.

The next thing he knew, he was falling backward into the water. With a shock of cold, he was plunged into the swirling white current.

He could see nothing. The river yanked him downstream, and he smashed against rocks as he went, unable to tell which way was up.

As his mind went blank with panic, his magic swept in, unbidden, and took over.

Abruptly he found himself sitting on solid ground, water swirling harmlessly around him. Jakovi rubbed at his stinging eyes and realized he had created a barrier in the air, forcing the river to part around him. He had been swept several paces downstream, but when he stood and trudged back toward the boulder he had tried to reach, the water parted before him.

When he reached the drainage channel on the left bank of the river, he climbed from the water and pushed his magic away. He hoped desperately that no one had been within reach of the corruption.

As the numbness and shock receded, the cold flooded back in, and Jakovi began shivering violently. He started climbing the runoff channel, numb hands fumbling on the loose dirt and rocks, his clothes dripping as he went. He could use magic to dry them, but he didn't want to risk it. What he had done back there…it had been too easy. Even if there were no consequences, it had formed a crack in his resolve never to use his magic again.

Higher he climbed, his shivering receding as the warmth of the canyon walls radiated back at him. The roar of the river faded to a hiss, and the sounds of battle flooded back in around him.

Eventually he reached a place where a boulder wedged in the runoff chute formed a comfortable perch, so he stopped there and turned to survey the canyon.

He was about twenty paces above the fighting, and as he had hoped, his location gave him an uninterrupted view of the deer trail stretching in both directions away from the front line.

There was Letto. He hadn't reached the front line yet— indeed, he seemed to be holding back, trying not to draw attention. But as he delayed, a Whitish soldier sent one of the armored Itreans tumbling down into the river, while another struck down a second with a mace to the helm.

They were the last of the Itrean force in plate armor.

The Whitish tore forward, making quick progress through the ranks of lightly-armored soldiers. Most went tumbling down the banks into the gorge as they fell, and from here Jakovi could see bodies scattered along the length of the gorge. Some lay where they had fallen, while others must have been swept downstream before getting caught on a rock. There were glints of silver showing through the less turbulent stretches of the river, as well—soldiers whose armor had weighed them down, pinning them underwater until they drowned.

Soon the last of the Itrean soldiers had fallen, and the Whitish were striking at civilians.

A shout came from the direction of the refugees, too distorted for Jakovi to make out the words, but Letto changed tactic abruptly. Instead of holding back, he pushed his way through the last of the Itrean ranks, sword held loosely at his side.

When he reached the front line, Jakovi held his breath, waiting for him to be struck down. Yet he didn't raise his sword.

Instead, Letto sheathed his blade and held up both hands in a gesture of surrender.

"Don't harm me!" he said, his voice just loud enough for Jakovi to make out. "I'm a spy for the Whitish army! I know secrets about a weapon the Itreans are planning to use against us, secrets that could change the whole course of this war!"

Jakovi swayed where he was perched. He hoped Letto was bluffing…but he couldn't be sure. His experience with people was limited enough that he had a hard time judging whether someone was trustworthy.

He watched, cold sinking into his bones once more, as the Whitish army closed up around Letto.

Letto had only gone a few paces from the front line when he flung his weight against an armored soldier and sent the man careening into the gorge.

As he drew his sword in a blur of steel, the air flooded back into Jakovi's chest. It was followed by fear that held him motionless, terrified that Letto would vanish if he blinked.

Letto swung at the soldiers around him, moving in a

dizzying rush. He used the weight of his body as much as his sword, throwing another three soldiers into the gorge, and Jakovi winced to imagine the way their plate armor would bruise Letto's flesh. He wore Weavers' armor—an enchanted coat over padded trousers—but he wore no helmet, and it was only a matter of time before the Whitish struck a killing blow.

As Letto fought, Jakovi heard shouts from the Itrean side. Daring to glance away from Letto, he saw a complement of Flamespinner children, led by Prince Calden, forcing their way past the refugees.

Letto must have known. He was distracting the Whitish long enough to let the Flamespinners arrive and reinforce the Itrean line.

Jakovi's throat was tight as he watched Letto hold his ground, strength visibly flagging. He took a strike across the back of his left hand, and another that grazed his cheek.

Then a mace came swinging down from the tangle of Whitish. Letto was too slow to block, and the mace slammed into the side of his ribs.

Letto gave a roar of pain as the blow threw him sideways.

His feet slipped over the edge of the gorge, and he dropped his sword as he flailed for purchase.

Another Whitish soldier kicked him in the leg, and Letto lost his balance, falling backward into the gorge.

He dropped silently, eyes wide with shock, and landed with a splash between two rocks. He was wedged in place, head above the current, but his eyes fluttered closed. Whether he was dead or unconscious, Jakovi could not tell.

Without thinking, Jakovi flung himself off the ledge he was perched on and dashed down the steep channel to the water. He didn't want to risk using his power where it might corrupt Letto, but panicked adrenaline lent him a surefootedness he had lacked before. Hugging this side of the river, he hopped recklessly from rock to rock, heart thudding against his ribs.

Before he reached Letto, a brilliant orange light flashed through the canyon, reflecting off the water below—the Flamespinners had joined the fight.

Closer to Letto, Jakovi found a safer place to cross the river, and he leapt to the opposite bank. By the time he stopped beside Letto, the man's skin had gone deathly pale, his lips a frightening shade of blue.

"Letto!" Jakovi said urgently. "Letto, stay with me!"

He wasn't sure if Letto was still alive, but he looped his arms under Letto's shoulders and started hauling him upstream, Letto's limp body colliding against rocks with each jolting step. He hoped he wasn't making the damage worse—but if Letto stayed in the water much longer, he would die of hypothermia before his injuries claimed him.

Jakovi's power nagged at him, reminding him how much easier it would be if he called on it to smooth the way forward, but he gritted his teeth and resisted. Even the tiniest slip would send corruption latching onto Letto, and that would be the end. His father was not here to contain the damage this time.

He managed, by some miracle, to reach the runoff channel and haul Letto up to a dry space flat enough for him to lie without slipping. It was harder to see the fighting from down here, but right now that seemed irrelevant. When he spared a glance up, he saw flames flaring and dying one after another, illuminating the canyon in bursts of orange. From his time with the army, he knew it took a great deal of training for

Flamespinners to learn to sustain and direct their fires, so these children could only send irregular flares at the Whitish.

And, worryingly, the Whitish line didn't seem to be retreating before the onslaught. They had stopped advancing, but the front ranks seemed unaffected by the flames. Was their armor enchanted to guard against fire?

Worry itching at him, Jakovi turned his attention back to Letto. The soldier's face was still chalky, his lips an unnatural blue, but when Jakovi leaned closer, he could hear the faintest hiss of air leaving his lungs.

"Stay with me," Jakovi muttered. He had no idea how to warm Letto up, especially since he had no dry clothes to change him into, but at least the sun was now shining into the runoff channel, baking the dark reddish rocks until they radiated heat. Jakovi pressed Letto's icy hand against one of the warm rocks, and then he lay beside him, shivering lightly himself as the sun gradually warmed his clothes.

Bursts of orange light continued to flash through the canyon, but they seemed distant, as did the rumble of battle on the opposite side of the river. None of that mattered while Letto lay here, caught between life and death, the last of his warmth bleeding away.

90

Leading Troops

Daymin had assumed he and Idorii would be attacking together, but as he ran through scenarios while his army's preparations fell into place, he began to realize there was no way to get the bulk of his army safely into the mountains without charging up the deer trail.

When Idorii approached Daymin's tent at sundown to report that the Weavers' enchantments were ready, he broke off at Daymin's expression.

"What's wrong?"

"Nothing specifically," Daymin said. "It's just…I had originally planned to join you in the attack from above and below the trail."

"Why can't you?" Idorii asked, alarm flashing in his eyes.

Daymin shook his head. "The numbers won't work out. We would be leaving tens of thousands of soldiers behind. So I need to stay back here and lead the rest of my troops on a strike up the gorge while your forces throw the Whitish army into chaos."

"Wasn't that what you had hoped to avoid at all costs?"

"I know," Daymin said heavily. "But I'm hoping your forces will be able to strike a heavy enough blow that we won't face too much resistance."

"What do you mean, my forces?" Idorii asked, eyes widening.

"I'd like you to lead the attack up the riverbed. You know the terrain best. I'll have General Tria direct the force climbing the ridge."

Idorii stared at him for a long moment, a dozen expressions flickering across his face.

At last he muttered, "I thought you weren't going to leave me again."

Daymin dropped the Weaver's coat he had been holding and pulled Idorii into an embrace. They stood like that for a long time, Idorii clutching Daymin's shirt, Daymin running a hand through his silver-and-black hair.

When they broke apart, Idorii ducked his chin, and Daymin realized his eyes were shining with tears.

"Idorii," Daymin murmured. "I'll find you on the other side of that gorge. I swear. I didn't come this far just to lose you again."

Idorii gave him a watery smile, and Daymin kissed him.

"Come on," Daymin said, brushing a thumb across his cheek. "It's time."

Daymin pulled on his enchanted coat and knelt to clear the piles of rocks from the map he had been working with. Then he and Idorii emerged together into the deepening twilight.

A hush lay over the army. Daymin's soldiers had clustered

around the royal tent, waiting, while his generals were trying to organize the troops as best they could.

"Our Weavers are now distributing the enchanted boots, gloves, and flying cloaks to the soldiers who will be attacking from above and below the gorge." Though Daymin spoke quietly, his voice carried through the still night. "My standing army will be carrying out this part of the attack, as they will be outnumbered and will need to fight fiercely to overwhelm the Whitish. Idorii will lead the troops up the gorge, since he is familiar with the terrain, while General Tria will direct the forces jumping down from the ridge.

"We will give these troops a three-hour head start to get into place and begin the attack. After that, I will lead the rest of my army in a direct strike up the gorge. With any luck, the chaos from our surprise attack will give us the edge needed to break through the Whitish forces."

His army knew as well as he how dangerous this would be, but no one spoke a word of objection.

Daymin met Idorii's eyes, hoping against hope that he could hold true to his promise.

"Soldiers, assemble," Daymin said. "May luck go with you."

He gripped Idorii's shoulder tightly for a moment before letting him go.

As Idorii and General Tria moved off toward the steepening slope of the foothills, soldiers broke away from the main body of his army and followed them, already equipped with the enchanted clothing.

Daymin watched them go with dread coiling in his chest. There was so much that could go wrong—especially for the troops traveling up the riverbed. Idorii was one of the only soldiers with a warming enchantment in his coat, so the others would be dangerously susceptible to hypothermia. And if the Whitish caught even the slightest hint of movement down below, Idorii's troops would be easy targets for archers.

As these first troops disappeared into the forest, soldiers came forward to pack up the royal tent and clear away the maps and charts. Tarak, Zahira, and Lalaysha gravitated toward Daymin, none speaking; he was both glad for their presence and sick at the thought that he would be risking them in this final, suicidal push through the gorge.

"Our scouts report at least ten thousand Whitish still camped outside the mouth of the gorge," Daymin told General Vask and the two holden kings, who were standing nearby as if awaiting further instruction. "We need to cut ahead of them before they can block our way through, or we'll be fighting a much bloodier battle that favors the Whitish."

"Should we approach the Whitish camp, then?" Morrisse asked nervously. "Then we'll be able to charge through as soon as word comes of the attack further up the gorge."

"Yes," Daymin said. "That's a good idea. But we need to wait here a bit longer first. We can't draw attention while our advance troops are at their greatest risk of being discovered."

Easy to say. But it hurt to wait, knowing the battle hung on such delicate threads. Knowing Idorii was risking himself while Daymin stayed back, unable to help, unable to see what was happening.

* * *

Idorii led the way through the trees to the place where he had left the river. As much as it hurt, he knew why Daymin had made the decision he had. And he knew he was the right person to lead this assault up the river—the soldiers would not have known where to enter the water otherwise.

Even after it left the deep canyon through the foothills, the river continued to carve its way through a shallower gorge until it flattened out at the plains below. The Whitish were camped in a tight knot around the canyon entrance, so Idorii had continued past their camp until he had turned a bend and was able to climb out unseen.

Now he searched for the same place he had left the river that morning. It was harder to find from this direction, but when he stumbled across the shallow gorge, he soon recognized the trail of eroded dirt from his scramble up the bank.

"This way," he whispered. There was no easy way down; he hoped the roar of the water would mask the sound of their entry into the river. Last night, the moon had been too low along the horizon to illuminate the canyon, but tonight it shone on the water, lighting their way forward. Idorii paused to wrap his scarf over his head, hiding the silver hair that might catch the light.

Then he crouched at the top of the bank and started sliding down the loose dirt slope. His enchanted boots offered little support without solid ground to adhere to, so he picked up momentum as he went, finally falling into the water with a splash of debris.

He hissed at the cold, muscles spasming. Even though he had spent the previous night walking through the same water, he hadn't been prepared for the numbing chill.

As he started up the river, he heard dirt and pebbles raining into the water behind him as the soldiers followed. This stretch of the river was the deepest they would need to walk through, rising past Idorii's knees—once they reached the canyon, they would mostly sidle along the rocky walls.

Soon the rush of water covered the sound of falling dirt, which meant Idorii would have to trust that the soldiers were still following him without incident. As the river neared the canyon, it narrowed and steepened, the roar growing so loud he couldn't even hear himself splashing through the water. Now the river cut through deeper channels between boulders, so he scrambled and hopped between rocks where he could, only stepping into the fierce current where he couldn't avoid it.

When they reached the Whitish camp, the only sign was the distant flicker of torchlight from the sentries posted around the perimeter. Idorii tried to move more cautiously than before, but there was little he could do—if the Whitish looked down right now, they would see a line of soldiers illuminated by the moonlight.

Ahead, where the river entered the deep canyon, the moonlight was blocked by the canyon walls. There Idorii's force would be safer.

Fear seemed to press at his chest as he leapt and waded his way below the Whitish camp, or perhaps it was the cold. Despite the warming coat, his hands were growing numb, his grip on the rocks clumsy.

Then, at last, he reached the dark safety of the canyon. Enchanted boots and gloves gripping tight to the rock, he clambered onto the steep wall of the canyon, where he huddled, shivering, until he could breathe again.

91

Breaking the Enemy Wall

Those first two hours of waiting seemed to last a year. Daymin paced and fidgeted and swung his sword at the darkness, knowing he was not inspiring confidence in his troops but unable to stop. His nerves were wound so tight he thought he would burst if he had to stand still.

Then, at last, it was time to approach the mouth of the canyon and get into position.

Daymin sheathed his sword and beckoned to his generals, and his army fell silently into line behind him.

Cautiously they padded through the pine forest, the dense mat of decaying needles muffling the sound of their passage. The Whitish camp was closer than Daymin had realized, and it seemed only minutes before he caught sight of a sentry holding a torch.

"This way," he whispered, veering away from the sentry and up the slope of the foothills. The moonlight was bright enough that it would betray his army if they stepped into view, but by hugging the shadows of trees, they were able to skirt around the edge of the Whitish camp and approach the mouth of the gorge from higher up the slope.

When Daymin caught sight of the river glinting in the moonlight far below, he dropped to a crouch behind a twisted pine, waiting. He couldn't see any sign of Idorii's troops passing below—but then, they should have left this stretch of the river long ago. That meant they had managed to reach the canyon without drawing attention.

Little by little, Daymin's army settled into place around him. Soon all was silent but for the hammering of his heart against his ribcage.

* * *

The further up the canyon Idorii climbed, the more he worried he would misjudge the furthest reaches of the Whitish army. The previous night was a blur—he had clambered for hours through the riverbed, half-dazed from the cold, and from this direction, none of it looked familiar.

Had he already reached the Itrean army? Did he dare climb the canyon wall to see what lay above?

No. That would be too dangerous.

On he climbed, hoping for some sign that he was nearing his destination.

Then, when he stepped into a deep pool to cross from one rock to another, his foot collided with something that shifted at the impact.

Peering closer, he caught a faint glint of metal illuminated by the distant arch of stars.

It was the body of a Whitish soldier.

Idorii's stomach heaved, and he scrambled away from the body, nearly losing his balance in the faster current as he did so.

He hauled himself onto a boulder, breathing hard. He had seen bodies on his way down the gorge, but he hadn't *stepped* on one. And now that he thought about it, most of the dead must have been unarmored Itreans who had been swept downstream, or he would have seen far more corpses the night before.

The fighting had intensified over the past day, then. The Itreans must be standing their ground instead of retreating—what did that mean?

Now that he was looking for it, Idorii started seeing fallen Whitish soldiers every ten paces. Some had sunk underwater, the weight of their armor trapping them beneath the current, while others lay wedged against boulders, their limbs bent at unnatural angles. There were Itreans too, sprawled atop the jumble of boulders like the Whitish, blood staining their Weavers' armor.

Idorii still didn't know how close he was to the front line, but a moment later, shouts rang out from the Whitish camped on the deer trail. The Itrean troops must be attacking from above.

* * *

A chorus of shouts dragged Jakovi from his restless sleep. His clothes and Letto's had dried over the course of the day, and Letto had briefly roused, long enough for Jakovi to feed him water from his cupped hands.

They had then fallen asleep in the runoff channel, huddled

together, Letto's breathing evening out as the night deepened.

Sitting up abruptly, Jakovi searched for the source of the disturbance.

The shouts were growing more frantic, and they were accompanied by scrabbling footsteps against rock as the Whitish army jumped to attention.

Then Jakovi saw what had alarmed the Whitish.

People were leaping from the top of the canyon, but instead of falling, they were drifting down like feathers to land amongst the Whitish.

Hope expanded in Jakovi's chest.

Daymin's army had arrived.

* * *

"Now!" Idorii called softly to the army at his back.

He heard the order passed down the line. Without waiting for his troops, he launched himself at the rock wall and hauled his way up, the enchantment letting him pull his way easily up the near-vertical face.

When he clambered onto the ledge with the deer trail, he drew his sword. He was standing on the remains of a camp—sleeping rolls sprawling along the trail, packs leaning against the cliff faces, and pieces of armor strewn throughout. Some of the soldiers were kneeling, frantically trying to pull on bits of armor unaided, while others stood with swords ready, wearing only boots and underclothes.

Up ahead, a mess of soldiers at the front line still wore armor, but they seemed unwilling to leave their defensive position between the two armies.

With the river thundering below, the soldier nearest Idorii had not noticed his arrival, his gaze fixed instead on the Itreans leaping from the cliff ahead.

Drawing in a shuddering breath, Idorii lunged forward and swung at his exposed neck.

To his surprise, the blow connected, sending blood pouring down the man's shoulder.

As the man's knees buckled, Idorii jumped aside and shoved him toward the gorge. He fell with a gurgling shout that cut off abruptly.

Nausea rose in Idorii's throat.

His footing slipped on the abandoned bedroll, so he kicked it off the ledge and pressed both gloved hands to the rock wall looming above the trail. There he remained for a moment, breathing shallowly as he tried to make sense of the chaos.

Even before his own troops had arrived, the Itreans jumping from above had thrown the Whitish into disarray. As Idorii's troops pulled themselves onto the trail, they were swiftly cutting down soldiers whose attention was focused on the attack from above.

Another Whitish soldier backed into Idorii, who yelped in surprise.

As the man spun to face him, Idorii recovered and stabbed his sword wildly in the direction of the man's abdomen.

The blade sank in deeper than he'd expected, sending hot blood pouring over Idorii's arm. After the cold of the water, it seemed to burn his skin.

Another wave of nausea choked Idorii, and he yanked his sword frantically from the man's stomach.

As the man staggered backward and fell into the canyon,

Idorii collapsed against the rock wall. His pulse was thundering in his ears, and he worried he would retch. He had never fought like this before, drawing so much blood—it was too much. Too oppressive.

Idorii watched dizzily as a soldier with a flying cloak managed to fell the next Whitish soldier who came near; then a shout from up the canyon drew Idorii's attention.

The armored soldiers at the front line had changed tactics and were now shoving their way toward the newly arrived Itrean forces.

* * *

When Daymin heard shouts echoing down the canyon, every sense went on high alert.

"Go!" he whispered to his troops, struggling to his feet. "No time to lose!"

Then he drew his sword and went charging down the slope, momentum carrying him past the first of the sentries guarding the Whitish camp.

When he skidded to the base of the slope and turned toward the mouth of the gorge, he found his way blocked by a column of armored Whitish soldiers. Their armor was illuminated by the light of the torches they carried, flames throwing off puffs of smoke.

He felt as though someone had punched the air from his lungs. It was not a significant force, but it would be enough to slow his soldiers. Enough to give the Whitish camp time to rouse and join the battle.

"Allow me, Your Majesty," came a rough voice from his

side.

Daymin was shunted aside by the powerful form of General Vask, who wore a helmet that protected all but his neck. He swung his way into battle without hesitation, throwing his weight against the column of Whitish.

After a moment, Daymin recovered himself and dashed forward to join the fight, soldiers jostling up the path behind him.

When Daymin fell into place beside General Vask, the general threw him a brief look.

"You shouldn't be here."

Daymin didn't respond. He swung and blocked as the Whitish turned their focus to him, his movements hampered by the narrow space. He knew it wasn't wise to risk himself at the front of this battle, but all he could think about was getting up the canyon to Idorii.

"You need armor if you're going to fight like this," General Vask said.

Then, catching Daymin halfway through a sword-stroke, he shouldered him back, out of range of the Whitish blades.

Breathing hard, Daymin lowered his sword. They were never going to make it through the column of Whitish soldiers at this rate.

Even now, he could hear clattering armor and shouts from the Whitish camp as the rest of the army prepared to join the battle. If Daymin's force was cut off from the gorge, that would be the end.

But maybe there was another way to break the wall of enemy soldiers.

* * *

As the Whitish pushed aside their unarmored comrades, Idorii realized with a jolt that he was the first Itrean standing in their path. He could hold his own well enough against men who had just dragged themselves from bed, but in a fight against armored troops in formation…he would be as helpless as a child.

Fear clawed at him as the Whitish marched closer. Though the moonlight did not shine into the canyon, it was enough to make their silver armor glow softly.

Idorii's eyes flicked back and forth as he searched wildly for an escape.

But what would his troops think if he fled? He was supposed to be leading this assault.

Bloody Varse.

His hands on the hilt of his sword trembled. From behind, he could hear the scrabbling of dirt and rocks as the last of his troops climbed up the side of the gorge onto the deer trail.

Then he had no more time to think, because the Whitish were upon him.

Idorii held tight to his hilt, brandishing the sword as if it were a shield that could hold back whatever blows rained down on him.

One jarring blow struck the blade, making his arms shake with the force.

The next caught him in the side of the ribs.

His coat was thick enough to cushion the impact, but the blow sent him stumbling sideways, toward the gorge.

As he fought to regain his balance, the rock beneath him gave way.

With a shout, he went tumbling down the bank toward the river that churned far below.

* * *

Turning away from the fight, Daymin started shoving his way back through his forces. Some gave him frightened looks as he passed, eyes glowing orange in the torchlight, as if worried he had already given up.

When he reached the gentler slope leading up the mountain, Daymin ducked away from his soldiers and dashed into the trees. The forest was sparse enough to let the moonlight shine through in dappled patches, though he kept tripping on unseen obstacles as he jogged up the steep incline.

Soon he caught the smell of smoke from the torches, so he crept toward the edge of the canyon, where the mountain slope gave way in a steep cliff.

Down below, General Vask was still holding out against the Whitish, but his strength seemed to be flagging as blows rained on him from two sides.

Daymin scanned the forest for something he could roll down onto the Whitish troops. He had hoped to find a boulder, but all the ones nearby were too large and well-buried for him to move unaided.

There—a half-rotted log lay trapped against another tree. He wasn't sure he would be able to drag it into position, but if he could, it would do some serious damage.

Daymin wiped his sweaty hands on his trousers and knelt beside the log. The top was intact, though when he reached underneath to roll it free of the tree it had caught against, his fingers sank into moist, spongy rot.

With a grunt, he shoved his full weight against the log.

It rocked in place, resisting.

Then, with a ripping of moss, it gave way and rolled.

Once the log was free, Daymin squatted near the front and heaved it forward. It moved slowly, only a finger's breadth at a time, but he was making progress.

Eventually he reached the edge of the gorge. Here he shoved the log until it lined up with the cliff. No one had thought to look up, so he paused for a moment to catch his breath, watching the fighting below.

Just then, a Whitish soldier managed to land a blow on General Vask's neck.

Daymin's breath snagged in his throat. In the darkness, he couldn't see how badly the general was injured, but the man stumbled aside and caught himself against the canyon wall.

With General Vask out of the way, the Whitish pushed past him to engage the next of Daymin's forces.

Heart pounding in his ears, Daymin gave the log a powerful shove forward.

It teetered for a second on the rim of the canyon.

Then it fell.

Time seemed to hang motionless as the log careened down the steep canyon wall. It bounced twice, shedding great clods of rotted wood each time.

Then it slammed into the Whitish forces.

A whole block of soldiers were thrown off their feet, some crashing down the wall of the gorge toward the river, others pinned beneath the log.

For a moment, Daymin stood frozen as he watched the

chaos below.

His own soldiers recovered from the surprise first, throwing aside the distracted Whitish soldiers and charging past those who had fallen. Several tore off Whitish helmets as they went, shoving them onto their own heads, while others quickly dispatched the men trapped beneath the log.

As his own troops reached the remaining block of Whitish soldiers, Daymin shook himself from his daze. He still had work to do.

He wouldn't be able to catch the Whitish by surprise again, but he could still deal damage from above. He scrambled back from the edge and went in search of rocks that were large enough to dent armor.

Soon he returned to the edge of the canyon with an armful of rocks. His own soldiers had pushed the Whitish back, allowing more of the Itrean forces to flood into the gorge, but the rest of the Whitish army was beginning to form up at the mouth of the gorge.

He had no time to waste.

Daymin dropped to his knees at the rim of the canyon and raised the first rock.

Then he hurled it toward the closest Whitish soldier below.

His aim was off, and he hit the man on the shoulder instead of the head, but it was enough to make him stumble.

While he was recovering, Daymin started throwing rocks one after another, hardly pausing to aim. Several hit Whitish soldiers on the head, denting their helmets or knocking them askew so they couldn't see, but even those that missed their mark added to the chaos below. Soon the Whitish were shouting and pushing against each other to escape the deadly rain of stones, while Daymin's forces pressed their way ever forward.

Daymin dashed around to gather a second armload of rocks, this time throwing them with less intention than ever, merely stirring the Whitish to panic.

Then, with a roar of triumph, his own troops broke through the last of the armored Whitish.

92

The Battle in the Gorge

Idorii splashed into a deep, turbulent stretch of river, his knee colliding painfully with a rock. The cold knifed through him, making his chest seize up.

When he forced his eyes open, he could see nothing. All was swirling darkness as the current swept him downstream.

His lungs were tight with panic, and instinct told him to draw in a breath; Idorii resisted, his chest burning.

Then he was flung against a rock. The impact knocked the last of the air from his lungs, but as he flailed against the current, he remembered the enchantment on his gloves.

He pressed his hands against the boulder, and as the enchantment adhered to the surface, he willed himself to think.

Up. He just had to claw his way up, and there he would find air.

Lungs heaving, he walked himself hand over hand up the boulder.

At last his head broke the surface.

Idorii drew in a great, shuddering breath. Water was still pounding against him, but he was alive.

Little by little, he dragged himself higher onto the rock, until he could grip the surface with his boots as well. Then he clambered out of the water and huddled there, arms wrapped around his knees, shivering violently.

It was several long minutes before his panic receded enough for him to remember the fighting above.

How were his troops faring against the Whitish who had charged them?

Plagues, he was useless in a fight.

Though he could feel the enchantment on the warming tapestry beginning to seep through his icy clothes, it did nothing to ward off the chill that had sunk deep into his bones. His body heat had been stripped away too many times that night—he wasn't sure if he would ever be warm again.

Just then, an Itrean soldier went tumbling over the edge of the gorge downstream of him. The woman's body splashed into the middle of the river and was swept away, quickly vanishing in the inky blackness.

Idorii had to do what he could. Maybe he wouldn't be any use on the front line, but he *had* killed a few Whitish soldiers. Enough to make a difference, he hoped.

Still trembling, he rose and reached for the canyon wall. Then he started climbing his way back up to the deer trail.

* * *

With his own troops sweeping up the gorge, Daymin realized he might be left stranded behind his army. He wasn't sure he had time to retrace his steps—not with the Whitish pushing against his forces from their camp—so he had to find a different way down.

He scanned the canyon wall, searching for a chute that would be less sheer than the cliff face. There—ahead, illuminated in the moonlight, he thought he saw a narrow side canyon leading off from the main gorge.

Daymin scrambled higher up the mountainside, hoping he wouldn't be too late. Another twenty paces took him to the side canyon, which dropped away steeply at first before sloping gently toward the deer trail.

Bracing himself, Daymin slid over the edge of the drop-off in a crouch.

He went careening down, picking up momentum as he skidded along the loose rock, the ground eroding underfoot. When he tried bracing himself with his hands, the rough surface of the rocks tore at his skin, leaving his palms raw and searing.

At last he crashed to the bottom of the chute, the momentum throwing him against the opposite wall. It was a narrow triangular split here, a thread-like runoff channel forming the base, so when he rose shakily to his feet, he had to walk with one foot on either wall, tilted at a precarious angle.

As he stumbled his way down the side canyon, the runoff channel widened until he could walk flat along the base. Here the canyon walls were steeper, trapping him in the narrow passage, so he had nowhere to go but forward.

Further along, the sounds of fighting grew louder. He wondered how far his troops with flying cloaks had gone—he had nearly reached the top of the foothills, but the gorge continued far past that point, so there must be several other layers of ridges before the steep ground gave way to the valley with the refugee camp.

Then he rounded a corner and came within sight of a clump of Whitish soldiers who must have camped in the side canyon. Most were still struggling into their armor.

"We're under attack!" one shouted, waving his sword in Daymin's direction.

Daymin had gone too far.

* * *

Jakovi had seen Idorii splash into the river, and had watched, stiff with apprehension, until he pulled himself out many paces downstream.

The urge to help the Itreans nagged at him, but he couldn't risk it. Not with the Whitish and Itrean troops tangled up together this way. And especially not with Letto beside him.

Letto seemed to be rousing, so Jakovi gave him a shake.

"Letto. Can you hear me?"

Letto groaned, and his eyes opened a crack. It was a moment before his bleary gaze locked onto Jakovi.

"I need to get you to the other side of the river," Jakovi said. "Before the Whitish push past us. But I need you to help me."

Letto groaned again. Then he stirred, and Jakovi realized he was trying to sit up. Jakovi grabbed Letto's arms and pulled, and he managed to lurch upright.

"My ribs hurt like the Destroyer's fires. I must've broken a couple."

"Can you move?"

Letto grimaced. "I have to, don't I?"

They started crawling their way down the runoff channel to the riverbed. Jakovi couldn't see a clear way up the opposite bank, but he would face that challenge when he got to it. First they would have to cross the river without falling into the powerful current.

When they reached the water, Jakovi called, "Help! We're Itrean soldiers trapped in the gorge!"

Someone leaned over the edge of the deer trail, and Jakovi waved.

The face disappeared, but a few minutes later, someone tossed a coiled rope across the river. Jakovi grabbed it and then handed it to Letto.

"You first."

"Are you sure?" Letto asked. His face was still unnaturally pale, moonlight giving him a sickly hue.

"Go."

Letto wound the rope around his hips and fastened it, gripping the loose end tightly with both hands. Then, once the soldiers on the trail above had pulled in the slack, he made a wild leap for a rock in the middle of the river.

He missed the boulder, so the soldiers above hauled abruptly on the rope. Feet trailing in the water, Letto swung across the river, finally colliding with a heavy *whump* against the opposite wall of the canyon.

Letto let out a grunt, but he quickly recovered himself. Planting his feet against the rock wall, he walked his way up as the soldiers hauled on the rope.

At last he reached the top, where several pairs of hands

helped drag him onto the deer trail.

As Jakovi watched below, he realized he couldn't follow. Not now.

With Letto out of the way, he might be able to use his magic after all.

Only if he had no other choice.

Only…

The rope came flying down toward him, slapping against his shoulder, and Jakovi jumped.

"Come on!" Letto shouted.

Jakovi didn't reach for the rope. "I'm staying here," he said, voice stripped of all emotion.

Fear flashed across Letto's face. "No! You can't!"

Jakovi shook his head. "I'm sorry."

* * *

Daymin had no idea how far away his own army was.

As the Whitish soldiers advanced on him, he took an involuntary step back. He wouldn't be able to climb back up the slope he had skidded down, so he had to stand and fight. For as long as he could hold out.

He drew his sword, this time shifting forward so his movements wouldn't be hampered by the narrow canyon.

At least he had broken through the Whitish line. At least his soldiers had a chance of reaching safety. It didn't matter if he died, now that he had done his duty.

Though he tried to convince himself of this, Daymin's chest was tight with panic.

Just then, the moon slid over the rim of the gorge, sending

silvery light pouring into the slot canyon.

"What are you waiting for, you fools?" one of the soldiers goaded, jamming a helmet onto his head. Though only his legs and chest were armored, he pushed past the soldiers surrounding Daymin. "Quicker we can get rid of this one, the sooner we can join the fight higher up."

When he launched himself at Daymin, his sword caught Daymin's in a ringing blow that juddered through his shoulder.

Two others lunged from behind him, thrusting their swords toward Daymin like spears, and he was forced to dance back to avoid being skewered.

Plagues. All they needed to do was push him back until he reached the narrowest part of the slot canyon, and he would be unable to fight. He had to end this quickly, while he still had a chance.

Daymin sucked in a breath through his teeth and tightened his sweaty grip on his hilt.

Idorii, send me strength.

Then he threw himself into the fight with everything he had.

* * *

When Idorii rejoined the fight, he found that the battlefield had descended into chaos. Enough Itrean troops had descended on the deer trail, quickly killing the unsuspecting Whitish, that they now outnumbered the enemy, but there were still large gaps in the Itrean forces. He had climbed into one of these, and found himself surrounded by enemies.

Arms heavy and slow from the cold, Idorii dragged himself onto flat ground and hoisted his sword onto his shoulder. He had barely been fighting, yet he was so weary he could hardly keep going.

These Whitish soldiers had given up on armoring themselves and instead pushed their way toward the fighting with swords ready.

When one turned and swung at him, Idorii dropped to a crouch, mind working too sluggishly to block the attack.

Then he caught sight of something shining faintly in the moonlight—an abandoned breastplate.

He lunged for it, dropping his sword as he did, and pulled it over his head like a shield.

His opponent's next blow glanced off the breastplate with a resounding *clang*.

As the soldier prepared for another strike, Idorii threw his full weight against the man's legs, slamming into him with the breastplate.

With a shout, the man lost his balance and caught himself against the canyon wall.

Idorii scrambled to his feet and slammed his shield against the side of the man's head.

This time his eyes rolled back in his head, and he fell to the ground like a sack of millet.

Gasping, Idorii knelt to reclaim his sword. When he stood once more, he felt lightheaded.

Ahead, one of the unarmored Whitish soldiers was busy fighting an Itrean, with his back to Idorii. So Idorii stumbled along the deer trail until he was close enough, and then he drove his sword into the man's side just below his ribcage.

He retched at the sight of blood pouring down the man's shirt, but there was no time to be sick—another soldier was turning to face him. Gasping, Idorii swung wildly at his neck before the man could engage him.

To his surprise, the blow connected; as the soldier swayed, he lost his footing and tumbled into the gorge.

"Thank you," croaked the Itrean who had been fighting him, a woman with blood smeared across one cheek.

Idorii could only nod, his stomach heaving.

How much longer could he stand this?

* * *

Every muscle in Daymin's arms was screaming, but somehow—miraculously—he was holding his ground. He had even injured one of the soldiers badly enough that he had retreated from the battle.

The longer he fought, the sloppier he grew, though he also started to see obvious gaps in his opponents' strategy. They had evidently trained in full armor, and were unaccustomed to guarding themselves properly without the heavy plate to catch stray blows. He had sliced a deep cut down one man's forearm, almost by accident, and had drawn blood from another's knuckles with a counterstrike.

And though his sword occasionally caught on the canyon walls, throwing him off, he was grateful that the narrow space prevented more than one soldier from engaging him at once.

Unfortunately, behind the handful of half-armored soldiers who had come forward to fight, the others hurriedly helping one another into the rest of their armor. When they were finished, he would lose any advantage he still held.

He swung and lunged, ducking out of the way when he

could not move his sword fast enough, avoiding disaster by the narrowest margins. Everything had faded to insignificance aside from the swords slicing through the air toward him, blades gleaming in the moonlight, his own instinct driving him to move faster than he could think.

As he parried and struck and whirled, he kept throwing his opponent's sword aside the barest fraction of a second before it bit into his flesh. Each near miss sent a spark through his nerves, putting him more on edge, until he felt as though he danced over a fire.

Then he heard something—a distant clamor building from outside the slot canyon.

Taking advantage of Daymin's distraction, his opponent slammed his sword into Daymin's shoulder.

Daymin roared in pain and stumbled backward, his whole arm throbbing.

When the soldier lunged again, Daymin caught his sword and shoved him back, shoulder screaming as he pushed with the bruised muscle.

Again they traded blows, but both were slower now, half their attention on the sound building like a distant rumble of thunder. Soon enough, Daymin could distinguish voices and the scrabble of footsteps coming up the gorge.

"It's the Itrean army," called one of the soldiers watching from beside the deer trail.

Daymin's opponent turned to look, so Daymin lunged at him and knocked him off balance.

He staggered, catching himself against the canyon wall with the hand grasping his sword, and Daymin drove his blade into his unprotected arm.

Before the next soldier could push forward to take the man's place, the first of Daymin's army jogged past the entrance to the slot canyon, their dark uniforms melting into the night.

Air flooded back into Daymin's lungs.

"Up here!" Daymin called.

Someone shouted a muffled command, and a knot of Itrean soldiers ducked into the slot canyon. Daymin's opponents must not have realized who he was, because every one of them abandoned him to face the new threat.

The fight was over in a few brutal minutes, the slot canyon ringing with shouts and the clashing of swords. Even the Whitish soldiers who had managed to don most of their armor were still hampered by missing pieces of plate, and the Itreans cut them down quickly, leaving their bodies sprawled on the rocks.

As the last one fell, Daymin picked his way forward to join his own troops.

"It's the king!" one of them shouted. "We've found him!"

A cheer spread up the gorge, and Daymin found himself buoyed by the sound. The soldiers who had rescued him were grinning, their faces glistening with sweat, and Daymin gave them a fierce smile in return.

* * *

Idorii dropped to his knees, retching over the edge of the gorge. He had killed three more men from behind, and his hands were slick with blood. It was too much. Too Varse-damned much. He was close to throwing himself into the river once more just to escape the fighting.

But as he paused to wipe his mouth on his sleeve, he heard a cheer from the direction of Daymin's army.

He got to his feet, swaying, and staggered back from the cliff in time to see a line of Itreans jogging up the gorge.

They must have broken through the last of the Whitish defenses.

93

The Outcropping

Y our Majesty!" one of Daymin's soldiers said breathlessly. "Was that you who dropped the log?"

"Yes," Daymin said. He peered out the slot canyon in the direction of the Whitish army, which was nowhere in sight. "How are we faring?"

"Our advance forces have already weakened the Whitish in this part of the canyon, Your Majesty. We're making quick progress. But the rest of the army is at our tail."

"Quickly, then," Daymin said. "We need to clear the gorge as fast as we can."

He paused to look back at the Whitish soldiers they had felled—some dead, some clutching their wounds and groaning—before joining the river of Itrean soldiers.

Up the canyon they jogged, passing countless bodies and the detritus of the Whitish soldiers' camp. Many of his own soldiers were pausing to snatch abandoned pieces of armor as they passed, while others shoved bodies into the gorge to clear space on the deer trail.

The moon was now shining directly into the canyon, bathing the trail in a soft silver light, and after the pent-up nerves of the previous day, Daymin felt he could have run straight through the night and into the morning.

On he ran, hardly pausing to think about his footing when the deer trail narrowed, the footsteps of his soldiers thudding like drumbeats through the canyon.

Then he heard a voice he recognized.

"Your Majesty!"

Daymin slowed, looking up from the trail to search for the source of that voice.

Ahead of him, Uncle Cal was pushing his way toward Daymin, hugging the side of the canyon to allow his soldiers to pass.

Despite their differences, and the sour note they had parted on, Daymin felt a surge of relief at the sight. If Uncle Cal was here, he didn't need to make every decision alone. He had someone to fall back on, someone to make the first move when Daymin froze.

"Uncle Cal," Daymin said, breathing hard. "Have you come from the refugee camp?"

"I have. It's good to see you safe. How are you planning to block the Whitish army's access up the canyon?"

"Is it true the refugees have no explosives?"

Cal nodded curtly.

"Then we'll have to chip away at the trail until it's impassable," Daymin said.

"And with the Whitish army at your tail, how many soldiers

would we need to sacrifice to hold the line?"

Daymin grimaced. "I don't know. How have we fared against them so far?"

"Badly. They cut their way through our small army in a matter of hours. The problem is, with such a tight space to fight in, the terrain will always favor the soldier in plate armor. And to make matters worse, at least some of their armor seems to have been enchanted to resist fire."

Daymin stepped onto a rock beside the deer trail to make more space for his army to pass. Looking back at the unending river of Itreans, it was hard to believe his forces were still in danger from the Whitish army.

"I'll wait here until the Whitish approach," Daymin said at last. "See if I can think of anything in the meantime."

"This way," Cal said, jerking his head back the way he had come. "There's an outcropping you can climb on to get a better view."

He and Daymin joined the flow of soldiers hurrying up the canyon, but this time Daymin found himself missing his footing every few steps, distracted by worry. If they couldn't close off the canyon before the Whitish pushed past his forces, everything they had done would be rendered useless.

Around another few bends of the canyon, Daymin nearly tripped over someone who was leaning against the wall of a narrow stretch of deer trail.

"To the valley!" Daymin said. "Quick!"

Then the figure turned, uncurling from his hunched position, and Daymin realized with a jolt that it was Idorii.

"Idorii!" he said.

Idorii's eyes were hazy and distant, and his face was streaked with blood. After a moment, he blinked and seemed to focus on Daymin.

"Are you all right?" Daymin asked.

Idorii nodded dazedly.

Daymin gripped his shoulder, scared by his expression. "I told you I'd find you again," he said in a low voice. "But what are you doing here? Why aren't you following my army to the valley?"

"I'm so tired," Idorii mumbled. "I just want to lie down."

"No!" Daymin said. "You can't give up. We're so close."

"Are we?"

Daymin realized Idorii was shaking, and he pulled him closer, sliding an arm around his waist for support.

"We just have to block off the canyon so the Whitish can't follow us," Daymin said.

But as he spoke, the truth slammed into him, tightening around his chest until he couldn't breathe.

They had no way of destroying the deer trail in time.

This whole battle—indeed, everything that had unfolded since Daymin had given the orders to evacuate Baylore—would mean nothing unless he could ensure the safety of his civilians.

And he was about to fail.

"Come on," he said numbly. "We have to get onto that outcropping. Then we can see what's happening."

Not that it would make any difference.

Cal was still waiting, back pressed against the canyon wall so the rest of Daymin's army had space to pass, and when he caught Daymin's eye, he beckoned impatiently. Daymin started forward, Idorii slumping against him as he stumbled after.

Soon they reached the base of the outcropping, which was

perfectly positioned to give them an elevated view several hundred paces up and down the canyon.

"What are your orders?" Cal asked, setting his back to the outcropping.

Daymin's brain was working sluggishly. Was there any point in trying, when he already knew how this battle would end?

Idorii's hand knocked against his, his skin icy, and Daymin threaded their fingers together. He had to keep going. Even when all hope seemed to be lost. It was becoming his mantra, yet it was no easier now than it had been in the wake of losing Baylore.

"Round up as many Flamespinners as you can find," Daymin said slowly. "They can help hold back the Whitish. In the meantime, we need soldiers to start chipping away at the trail. Have them work beside the outcropping—this is as good a place as any to make our stand." The trail curved away behind the small bluff, which would shelter their Flamespinners from arrows as they guarded the soldiers at work on the trail.

"Of course, Your Majesty," Cal said. His voice was strained, and for once he made no argument. "Don't put yourself in danger. Get off that outcropping as soon as the Whitish come near."

"I will," Daymin said, though he wasn't sure he could abandon his front line if it looked like his forces wouldn't hold.

As Cal darted back into the river of passing Itreans, Daymin released Idorii's hand and started up the outcropping. The rock was coarse underfoot, easy for his boots to grip, and he quickly scrambled to the top. Idorii climbed slower, his face pale in the moonlight. Daymin reached out a hand to pull him over the top, and once Idorii was safely on the flat ledge, he sagged against

Daymin.

"I'm sorry," Idorii muttered. "I'm just slowing you down."

"That doesn't matter," Daymin said. "Nothing we do now will make a difference anyway."

Idorii lifted his head to meet Daymin's eyes, and they shared a sad, hopeless smile.

When Idorii's shaking subsided, Daymin crawled to the edge of the outcropping to get a better view of the canyon.

To the east, in the direction of the Whitish army, he could see only a neverending stream of Itrean soldiers jogging away from the enemy at their back. Behind him, where the refugee camp lay, a few Flamespinners were already starting to push their way back toward the outcropping. And directly below, a handful of soldiers were slicing away at the deer trail with swords enchanted to cut through stone.

"They'll never finish in time," Idorii said, peering down from beside Daymin.

"I know." Even with the enchanted swords, it required brute strength to cut through the rock, and the soldiers were only managing to dislodge one small piece at a time. If the trail had been undercut by the river, their work would have been easier; instead, they had a solid wall of rock sloping down to the water to hack through.

Before they had made much progress, the first of the Whitish soldiers barreled into view, armor glowing softly in the moonlight.

Daymin's heart lodged itself in his throat.

The Whitish were still a few hundred paces away, but Daymin's forces were putting up only the barest resistance as they fled. As Daymin watched, one Itrean was cut down, then another, their bodies shoved over the ledge to the river that churned far below.

More Flamespinners were congregating behind the outcropping, but it wasn't going to be enough. A whole army couldn't buy Daymin's soldiers enough time to cut away the deer trail by hand.

The Whitish were coming closer, the clank of their armor resounding through the gorge.

Idorii reached for Daymin's hand again, and Daymin clung to him, tense with fear.

From behind, Cal's voice shouted, "Your Majesty!"

Daymin turned to see Cal pushing his way through the confusion of Itrean soldiers, a few more Flamespinners at his back.

"Get down!" Cal yelled. "You don't have much time!"

"I want to stay," Daymin told Idorii in an undertone.

Idorii nodded.

"I'm staying," Daymin shouted back to Cal. "The battle isn't lost yet."

The soldiers below were growing clumsy in their panic, chipping away only the smallest chunks of rock as they scrambled to finish before the Whitish arrived. They had barely made a dent in the trail—the gap was just over two paces wide and a few handspans deep, easy enough to clear.

"Daymin!" Cal shouted, anger tinging his voice this time. "Don't be a fool!"

"I'm not," Daymin yelled back. "I'm standing with my army until the end."

Ahead, the clanking of the Whitish was growing louder, drowning out the sound of his own army's passage. The moonlight was slipping away—soon the canyon would be plunged into darkness once more.

Then Idorii nudged Daymin. "Look."

Daymin followed his gaze to a figure crouched in a narrow split in the rock, nearly lost in shadow. Even though Daymin couldn't make out much, he thought he recognized the slope of his shoulders. "Is that…Jakovi?"

"I think so," Idorii said.

Alarm spiked in Daymin's chest. "What is he doing here? I thought he wanted to stay away from the fighting at all costs."

Idorii just shook his head.

Bloody plagues.

Daymin could see no way out of this. In a matter of minutes, the Whitish would be at the outcropping, and no amount of Flamespinners could hold such a force back forever.

Were they desperate enough to justify the use of Jakovi's magic?

Daymin ground his teeth, mind racing with panic. If he made this decision, he would be taking the first step down a road he wasn't sure he was willing to tread. Worse, Jakovi might not forgive him for breaking his promise, and the only thing worse than a Darkblood Heir in his army was one that turned against him.

Daymin's eyes flicked from the Itreans frantically chipping away at the rock below to the Whitish stampeding up the gorge. They were almost out of time.

Feeling faint, Daymin drew a deep breath and bellowed, "Jakovi!"

When the boy raised his head, the moonlight illuminated the familiar contours of his face.

"Come over here! Quick!"

For a moment, Jakovi hesitated, and Daymin wondered if he was planning something of his own.

Then he uncurled from his crouch and started crawling down the chute toward the river. He scrambled along the opposite bank, hands braced against the canyon wall, until he reached a place nearly level with the outcropping. As he started leaping from rock to rock, the river churning past, the moonlight slipped beyond the rim of the canyon, dragging a line of darkness swiftly up the rock face. While the silver Whitish armor still held the faint light from the vanished moon, Daymin could make out only the murky suggestion of movement from his own forces.

"Someone help that boy up!" Daymin called to his soldiers below the outcropping.

One paused in his work and lay on his stomach, reaching over the cliff, and a moment later he was helping haul Jakovi onto the trail.

"Are you going to ask him to destroy the trail?" Idorii asked softly.

"I don't know what else to do."

Idorii nodded, leaning his shoulder against Daymin's.

Below, Jakovi was sitting on the flat ground, breathing hard. Daymin wanted to urge him to hurry up, but he couldn't risk offending him when so much hung on his compliance.

The Whitish were now only a hundred paces away. Itreans were still dashing below the outcropping, but as they realized this was where they would make their last stand, more and more were turning to hold the Whitish back as best they could.

Daymin's pulse thudded in his ears, counting down the seconds. He didn't know if they would buy him enough time.

At last Jakovi clambered to his feet and started up the outcropping. When his face appeared over the rock, Daymin saw that he had lost the skittish, wide-eyed look from his days in Baylore.

"Jakovi," Daymin said as the boy pulled himself onto the top of the rock. "I haven't forgotten my promise to you. But we have no way of stopping the Whitish from breaking through our forces, and if we can't block off the canyon here, it will be the end of us. The refugee camp isn't defensible."

"I know," Jakovi said quietly.

Plagues. Jakovi was waiting for Daymin to say it outright.

Could he do it? Could he give the orders that would change everything, orders he could never take back?

Daymin realized he was still holding Idorii's hand, and he tightened his grip for a moment.

Then he drew in a shaky breath. This was his people's only hope.

"Jakovi," he said, "can you blast away the deer trail? Thoroughly enough that the Whitish can't find a way past?"

"I can," Jakovi said, his voice emotionless. He picked up a chunk of rock and ground it against the ledge by his knee. Daymin didn't want to push him, but after a moment he spoke again. "I used magic. Earlier. I fell into the river, and I was getting swept downstream, so—I stopped myself. Without meaning to." His breath rasped in his throat as he exhaled. "But nothing happened. No one was close enough for the power to corrupt. And there were no plants within range either."

Daymin realized with a jolt that Jakovi must have been contemplating using his magic well before Daymin brought it up, which explained why he had been watching the battle. It seemed Jakovi was beginning to care—he had spent time traveling with the refugees, and it was starting to change how he weighed the risks of using his magic.

Fear swooped through Daymin's stomach, but he pushed it aside. No time for that now.

"We'll clear the space around you as well as we can," Daymin said.

"And we'll gather Weavers to help with the counterspell," Idorii said. He sounded much more like himself, thank the cloudy gods.

Jakovi nodded mutely.

Then Idorii unstrapped the enchanted strips of leather from his boots and handed them to Jakovi, along with the gloves that had hung from his pocket. "Take these. They're enchanted to grip the rock even if there's nothing to stand on."

Jakovi stared blankly at the bundle of enchanted clothing. Daymin didn't know if Idorii's words had registered.

"Are you sure about this?" Daymin asked Jakovi in a low voice.

Again Jakovi nodded. Then something in his expression hardened, and he crawled to the edge of the outcropping. "Get away from here. Now. I'll handle the rest."

Daymin's eyes were drawn to the Whitish, who were now just fifty paces from the outcropping. Jakovi was right. They were running out of time.

Sharing a desperate, frightened look with Idorii, Daymin started down from the ledge.

When he jumped the final distance onto the deer trail, he was engulfed in chaos. Itreans pushed past him in every direction, some fleeing the oncoming Whitish, others returning to fortify their own defense, while a small group continued to hack away at the rock with their swords.

"Everyone back!" Daymin shouted. "We've found one last explosive! Clear the space around the ledge as fast as you can!"

For a moment, no one seemed to register his words.

Then a ripple of shouts spread out from where he stood, and all at once Itreans were shoving their way around the ledge toward the bulk of his army, tripping and falling against one another in their haste. Daymin and Idorii were pushed against the canyon wall, and they remained pinned there for several breathless minutes before they were able to plunge into the tide of bodies.

When they reached Uncle Cal and his small force of Flamespinners, Daymin flung himself out of the river of fleeing soldiers.

"What's happening?" Cal demanded.

"I need your forces to pull back," Daymin said. "I want the Whitish stopped at the outcropping, so retreat as far as you can while keeping that in range."

Cal gave him a searching look. "There isn't an explosive, is there?"

Daymin didn't have time to explain, so he shook his head jerkily before dragging Idorii back onto the trail.

Another fifty paces back, they scrambled onto a pair of rocks jutting from the canyon wall.

"We need Weavers!" Idorii shouted. "Any Weavers who know the counterspell, join us here!"

Daymin wasn't sure any Weavers were within earshot, and if they weren't able to assemble in time, he didn't know how he would stop the corruption from spreading. His stomach churned with guilt.

But it was too late to worry about that now. He had given the orders, and there was no turning back.

94

The Lure of Power

Jakovi crouched on the outcropping, hugging his knees, surrounded by an eerie bubble of calm. All around, soldiers ran in every direction, pushing past each other and shouting, but up here all was quiet and still.

Had he really just agreed to this?

He didn't think this one use of his power would unleash too much corruption, especially if he kept to a few careful incisions through the rock rather than a showy explosion, but it was more the principle of the matter that scared him.

Before now, he had refused to use his magic in even the smallest ways, insisting—to himself as well as those who might turn it to their advantage—that the risk was too high. But if he started using it here and there, in carefully controlled ways…where did it end? Who would decide he had finally gone too far and needed to stop?

While he warred with himself, the magic surged just below

the surface, tugging at him, begging for a chance to be unleashed once more. Was that why he had agreed to take the risk? Because he had already succumbed to his power once today, and it was influencing him more than usual?

Jakovi buried his face in his knees, wishing it would all go away. It had been a long time since he'd felt overwhelmed by the crushing press of humanity, but this was edging into that territory. He just wanted to be alone so he could think; instead his concentration was being assaulted by a dozen different sounds—scrabbling footsteps, clanking armor, shouts that echoed strangely from both directions, pebbles sliding off the deer trail to drop into the river below, and beneath it all the ceaseless roar of the river.

At least it was dark. That was a familiar comfort.

Eventually the chaos below resolved into a clump of Flamespinners hugging the side of the canyon not far behind the outcropping, with a small group of Weavers a ways behind them. The rest of the Itrean army was still hurrying past, but their numbers seemed to be thinning.

At their heel, the Whitish charged up the canyon faster than before, no longer slowed by Itrean soldiers turning to fight.

He needed to wait until the Whitish reached the outcropping. If he moved any sooner, the Itreans would be hit full-force with the corruption.

But it was a risk. If the Flamespinners didn't manage to slow the Whitish army's momentum, there could be dozens of people within range of his magic.

Closer they ran.

The sound of Itrean footsteps was soon drowned out by the rhythmic clank of metal, resounding through the canyon until Jakovi wanted to put his hands over his ears.

Just as the Whitish jogged up to the trail below the outcropping, a burst of flame seared through the air toward them. Jakovi could feel the heat wash across his skin, and he scrambled back without meaning to.

The Whitish slowed.

Several of the soldiers collided, their rhythmic pace shattering, as more flames joined the first. Soon a wall of fire blocked the deer trail, the heat searing Jakovi's cheek and driving him to press his back against the canyon wall in search of relief.

Earlier, when he had seen Prince Calden fighting with the untrained young Flamespinners, he hadn't realized how weak their efforts had been. They had sent small bursts of flame soaring through the air, illuminating the canyon wall, but they had been like wisps of cloud, and this was a towering thunderstorm.

A few moments of heart-pounding fear passed before Jakovi remembered that this was his chance. He had to move now, or risk giving the Whitish time to test their armor against the flames.

Drawing in a breath that seared all the way down his throat, he opened himself up to the magic once more.

Before, he had used it reflexively—involuntarily—and he had not been able to enjoy the way it flooded his veins with a delicious, tingling warmth.

Now he reveled in it.

Without thinking, he pushed against the air around him, warding off the oppressive heat of the fire. Cool air flooded back in, and he was able to step up to the edge of the outcropping without feeling any change in temperature. All around, heat distorted the canyon walls so they seemed to waver, and the firelight threw ominous shadows across the rocks.

He hoped these were the same men who had imprisoned him in Darkland Fort. Now was his chance to make them pay.

No! Jakovi thought frantically, though his fear felt muffled and insignificant beneath the power that raged through him. *That's not what I'm here to do!*

He looked behind him, trying to remember why this mattered. In the light from the flames, he could see King Daymin and Idorii clearly, standing with the Weavers. King Daymin was ushering the rest of his troops past while Idorii's lips moved rapidly; he was likely explaining what the Weavers would need to do.

He wasn't supposed to hurt them. They had saved him from his cell and cared for him, and without them, he would be lost.

They're out of range, his power urged. *You can do so much. No one can stop you now.*

That wasn't the only reason he was supposed to hold back, but Jakovi was having a hard time thinking straight.

The deer trail. I'm supposed to destroy the deer trail.

Jakovi latched onto this thought, the only thing he was certain of. He wanted to destroy the Whitish, but there was a reason he shouldn't. Even if he couldn't grasp it right now.

So instead he would shear away the trail directly below him, where it was engulfed in flames.

As he watched, the first of the Whitish soldiers stepped forward into the fire, flames swallowing their armored forms.

Jakovi aimed first at the ground below their feet. He sent his power slicing a careful line through the deer trail where the flames ended, gouging out the rock until a boulder the size of his body jolted free.

The boulder teetered for a moment before falling, two Whitish soldiers still standing on it as it dropped with a resounding *crash* into the river below.

Men shouted in alarm, shoving their way back from the space.

It wasn't enough.

The next soldiers took a running leap and cleared the gap, this time charging through the fire as if it were nothing but mist.

Jakovi had to work faster. More decisively. Maybe it was just his power telling him that, but right now he was having a hard time distinguishing the two.

He had told himself he wouldn't cause a large explosion. Nothing too showy or uncontrolled. But what he was doing right now would never work. The Whitish would find another way through.

It will be easy, his power urged him. *Hardly any effort.*

Jakovi gathered his power into a bundle, delighting in the warmth that uncoiled in his chest.

Then he threw it at the trail between the Flamespinners and the Whitish, unseen beneath the curtain of flames.

With a thunderous *boom*, the trail shattered.

Rocks flew into the air, smacking against the canyon walls, and soldiers on both sides shouted as they were hit.

The wall of fire flickered and then died.

In the sudden darkness, Jakovi sent another bolt of power slamming into the rocks below.

This time the entire canyon exploded.

Instinct drove Jakovi to throw himself against the rock wall, though no flying debris penetrated the bubble of cool air he had formed around himself. He flung his arms over his head as the explosion resounded through the canyon, boulders slamming against the walls before crashing to the riverbed.

As the noise subsided, Jakovi pushed away his power. It had dug its tendrils in deep, and was reluctant to let him pry it free.

Then, abruptly, he was alone in his body.

He felt drained. Brittle.

But at least his thoughts were his alone.

Shakily he pushed off the canyon wall and stumbled to the edge of the outcropping to see what he had done.

Below him, nothing remained of the deer trail but a cavity of newly-gouged rock. He had destroyed more than fifty paces of the deer trail—more than he had intended—and there was no way around the sheer cliff it had become. The riverbed was littered with boulders, and dust still hung thick in the air.

As the dust started to clear, Jakovi noticed a complement of Whitish archers pushing their way to the front of the army. It took him a moment to realize they would be aiming for him.

Jakovi's stomach clenched with worry. Were there soldiers from Darkland Fort here? Soldiers who knew what he was?

If so, they would be desperate to eliminate him at all costs. Especially now that he had demonstrated that he knew how to use his power.

Maybe they don't know, Jakovi thought, nerves thrumming with fear. *Maybe they just think I'm using explosives.*

Either way, he had to get off the outcropping.

He crept his way to the edge of the flat rock. Below lay nothing but a sheer cliff face, and a wave of dizziness swept through him as he tried to see a way down.

Then he remembered the enchanted gloves and leather

strips Idorii had left with him. They lay discarded on the rock, singed but still usable. Jakovi sat and pulled them on, hands trembling.

The first arrow flew before he had finished, and he threw himself forward, avoiding the arrow by a hair's breadth.

Hastily he pulled on the gloves and scrambled back to the edge of the rock. Even with the Whitish shooting at him, it took every piece of his resolve to stretch out a leg and trust the enchantment on his shoe to support him where no foothold existed.

Little by little, like a spider scrabbling across a wall, he edged his way along the sheared-off canyon face. When he glanced back, nerves swooped through his stomach—in destroying the deer trail, he had gouged away the rock underneath the outcropping so it looked as though the slightest gust of wind would tear the remaining shelf free.

At last he approached the Itrean army, which waited where the deer trail began once more. Jakovi's legs shook as he crossed the final distance, and when he came within reach of the Itreans, arms extended to pull him up onto the trail.

He collapsed onto the flat ground, gasping for breath.

It was done.

95

Slowing the Corruption

As the debris from the explosion clattered away and the dust wafted toward the Whitish army, Idorii and the Weavers pushed their way toward the destruction.

All was chaos, people shoving in every direction. The regular soldiers were fighting to get away from the wreckage, some so panicked they barreled Weavers out of their way as they passed.

Then Idorii heard a blessedly familiar voice rising above the clamor.

"Flamespinners and soldiers, to the valley! Clear the way! Weavers, come forward!"

At Daymin's voice, the soldiers fleeing the explosion seemed to register for the first time that the Weavers they passed were following orders. Now they took care to move aside, and Idorii's contingent made swift progress to the place where the deer trail was sheared away.

Jakovi had destroyed more than he had expected. Nearly fifty paces of trail were gone, the whole side of the canyon crumbled away to leave behind a sheer drop-off that none could pass. Most of the soldiers within range of Jakovi's magic would have died in the explosion…but as he looked closer, Idorii spotted a few soldiers lying on the ground with root-like markings spreading across their faces, the contrast illuminated by a Weaver's crystal hanging from a nearby boulder.

"These are the ones," Idorii said hurriedly. "We have to work fast. Their shirts have to come off—we need to find where the corruption ends and lay the spell there."

"Careful!" Daymin said, jogging closer. "I think it's contagious. That man wasn't within range, but he touched the markings on another man's face, and now it's affecting him too."

"Plagues," Idorii muttered. "Well, I should be immune. Let me handle them where necessary, up until the moment you lay the enchantment."

Some of the soldiers appeared lucid, while others writhed on the ground and lashed out at any who drew close. Idorii approached one of these men first, afraid he would be too far gone to treat if they waited any longer.

He fumbled with the buttons on the man's coat, but when the man threw himself at Idorii's face, he had to scramble out of reach.

Daymin pressed a knife into his hand. "If he's lost, move on to someone else."

Swallowing, Idorii darted close again, managing to slice the man's coat halfway open before he attacked again.

"Leave him," Daymin said quietly, laying a hand on Idorii's shoulder.

I was fighting like this, Idorii thought, eyes burning. *If Jakovi's father had given up on me, I would have suffered this same fate.*

But he obeyed Daymin and moved on to a woman who was still speaking coherently.

"Where does it hurt?" Idorii asked, kneeling beside her.

"It's my foot," she said, fingers digging into the arch of her left foot.

Idorii helped drag off her boot and sock to reveal a patch of scales spreading their way up her ankle. The pustules were beginning to swell between the scales as well; seeing them again sent a wave of nausea roiling through Idorii.

Idorii tugged up the leg of her trousers until he found where the scales ended.

"Here," Idorii said, beckoning the nearest Weaver over. "Lay the enchantment here."

The Weaver pulled on close-fitting leather gloves before beginning her work, slicing a delicate line in the soldier's skin and placing a hair into the bleeding line.

As she began to murmur the enchantment, Idorii moved on to the next soldier.

He soon realized the soldiers who were resisting the corruption best were those who had been affected lower down, while those with corruption spreading close to their heads or chests had succumbed almost at once. Idorii had been doubly lucky, then, that Jakovi's father had been able to contain the corruption before it destroyed him.

* * *

Daymin watched Idorii work from afar. As the affected soldiers had grown more violent and unpredictable, Uncle Cal had pulled him away from where they lay, saying he couldn't risk getting corrupted himself. Meanwhile, Daymin had sent Jakovi to the refugee camp under the supervision of General Tria; the boy had looked skittish and close to collapse.

"Are the whispers true?" Uncle Cal asked in an undertone. "Is the boy a Darkblood Heir?"

"He is."

Cal sighed. "Do you realize the implications of what he's done?"

"I do. Can we discuss this later?" Daymin was too weary to deal with the fallout from his decision right now.

"Of course."

"Your Majesty!" one of the Weavers shouted. "What should we do with the ones we can't treat?"

"Kill them. Quickly, before they can harm anyone." His voice sounded harsh to his own ears.

Many of the Weavers shied away from the corrupted soldiers—though they knew how to fight, they were no butchers—but Idorii stepped up to the first of the men writhing on the ground and plunged his sword into his chest.

Then Idorii staggered backward, and Daymin saw him slump against the canyon wall, coughing violently.

Without planning to, Daymin rushed toward the knot of Weavers to help.

"Are you okay?" he asked Idorii, brushing his hair off his forehead.

"Too much," Idorii choked out.

Daymin turned and drew his own sword. Then, before anyone could protest, he swiftly slit the throat of the next corrupted soldier. Working as fast as he could, before the reality of what he was doing caught up to him, Daymin killed one after another.

When the last of their crazed shouts died away, the canyon fell silent but for the rush of water below.

"To the refugee camp," Daymin said heavily. The choices he had made today would weigh on him, he knew, but right now he was too numb to think. Even the lives he had just taken had barely registered.

Turning away from the destroyed deer trail, he pulled Idorii to his feet and wrapped an arm around his waist for support. Then he started up the canyon once more.

96

The Valley in the Mountains

Once they had caught up with the bulk of his army, Daymin and Idorii had pillowed their coats beneath their heads and slept on the bare rock, so exhausted they hardly noticed the discomfort.

They had woken at the first light of day and continued on, and now, with the sun dropping in the sky, they were nearing the refugee camp.

Daymin could see the end of the canyon widening before the valley below came into sight. Mountains crowded into the space, their peaks towering and snowcapped, and the air carried the scent of new grass and pine sap.

Idorii walked by his side, with a crowd of Weavers and Flamespinners and Itrean soldiers at their front and back; he had been quiet and withdrawn ever since they had left the scene of the battle. Daymin thought it was the horrors of the battlefield that weighed at him, but they hadn't been able to talk in private in all the time they had walked, so he hadn't been able to ask.

At last they stepped from the deer trail onto a soft expanse of grass. Here the valley dropped away below them, and Daymin was able to see the refugee camp for the first time.

Tents and makeshift shelters spilled from the mouth of the gorge, filling most of the valley floor, and the mountainsides were cloaked in dark pines and aspens brilliant with new growth. It was a beautiful sight, bright with hope after so much ugliness, but Daymin was also confronted by the fact that the valley wasn't nearly large enough to sustain their population for long. They would need to venture deeper into the mountains to hunt and forage, which would almost certainly anger the Icelings.

As Daymin picked his way down the slope to the first of the tents, a soldier came jogging up to him with a worried expression.

"Your Majesty! There's an Iceling delegation that wants to speak to you."

And there it was. A wave of exhaustion crashed over Daymin, making him stumble. He had fought through the night and walked through the day, and evening was now approaching. Couldn't he just rest for a few hours?

Idorii grabbed his arm to steady him, and Daymin threw him a grateful look.

"I've told them it can wait for morning," the soldier added belatedly. "We're not going anywhere before then."

"Thank you," Daymin said numbly.

Then he followed Uncle Cal across the valley to a higher point, set off from the rest of the camp, where his royal tent had already been erected. Soldiers were cooking stew over a fire-twist, and the smell made Daymin's mouth water. He couldn't remember what it was like to eat fresh, hot food.

As he drew closer, he caught sight of his friends sitting by the fire, already digging into bowlfuls of the stew. Tarak's arm was bandaged, and Zahira's face was lined with weariness.

When Tarak caught sight of Daymin, he called a greeting, while Zahira clambered to her feet and jogged over to give him a hug.

"You're safe," she said. "Thank the cloudy gods." Next she hugged Idorii, who didn't seem to know what was happening. "And you. When I heard that explosion…"

"It's over," Daymin said. "The Whitish can't get through."

He and Idorii unbuckled their sword belts and cast them aside, and a soldier ladled up bowls of the delicious-smelling soup. Then they settled on rocks to eat with their friends, looking out over the refugee camp in companionable silence. The sun was beginning to set, throwing streaks of orange and crimson across the sky, and the snowy peaks glowed orange in the fiery light.

The rich, velvety soup was studded with venison and potatoes, and it tasted finer than any feast Daymin remembered eating in Baylore. With each bite, some of the numb exhaustion faded away, until he felt clear-headed enough to let his mind churn through what he had done.

He had only dared to use Jakovi's magic because Jakovi had suggested it first. Daymin would never have pushed him to do something he was uncomfortable with…

No. That wasn't true. If the Whitish had reached the valley and had begun slaughtering civilians, he likely would have unleashed Jakovi in their defense. And that would have been more dangerous by far, with so many bodies for the corruption to latch onto.

Daymin's stomach churned as the memory of slaughtering those poor corrupted soldiers flashed through his mind. He should never have expected Idorii to do the dirty work for him.

"You okay?" he murmured to Idorii, nudging their knees together.

"Mm," Idorii said noncommittally.

As they finished their dinner, a number of those who had fled with the refugees came by to thank Daymin and swear their continuing loyalty to him. Grandmother Ammeline visited as well, clasping his hands and telling him she was proud of him, though Daymin knew she would think otherwise if she was told of all the ways he had failed in his long campaign. As a child, he had often thought poorly of his mother for her brutish military tactics and undemocratic takeover, but he now understood exactly how she had felt. War necessitated many horrors, and sometimes the consequences of failing to take action were far worse than any tragedy he could bring about.

Gods, he wished he could see his mother again. He watched his grandmother's retreating back until she disappeared into the shadows of the refugee camp, heart aching. He didn't even know if his mother was still alive. He hadn't heard from her in spans now, so he had no idea how her campaign in Dardensfell was going.

Soon the last flares of sunset had faded, leaving behind a deep twilight peppered with stars. When Tarak, Zahira, and Lalaysha rose and took their leave, Daymin was surprised. He had grown so accustomed to sharing a tent with them that he had assumed they would camp nearby. But their families were here, and with most of the population of Baylore reunited, their place was with the Bastray camp.

At last he and Idorii were alone, clutching mugs of mint tea as the chill of night set in.

"You're very quiet," Daymin said, reaching for Idorii's hand. "Is something wrong?"

Idorii threaded his fingers through Daymin's; his skin was still clammy. "I've never killed people that—that way—before. There was so much blood. I…" He trailed off, giving Daymin a pained look.

"I'm so sorry. I shouldn't have thrown you into that."

"No one else would have known the way into the gorge. But—" Idorii shuddered. "I hope I never have to do that again."

"I hate it too," Daymin said softly.

They stayed outside, watching the Great Arch emerge overhead, until the dregs of their tea had gone cold and darkness had truly fallen. A chorus of insects and bats twittered from the forest at their backs, the sound startling after the quiet nights in the plains.

"You weren't being very discreet earlier," Idorii said abruptly, his face lost in darkness. "In the canyon. People are going to talk."

Daymin set aside his tea and pulled Idorii to his feet. "I'm not going to hide what you are to me. I won't do that to you."

Idorii buried his face in Daymin's shoulder. Daymin wrapped his arms around him and held him close, but after a moment he realized Idorii was shaking.

"What's wrong?"

Idorii shook his head, pressing closer into Daymin's embrace. When he managed to speak, his voice was thick with tears. "I can't believe you're here. You're alive. I never thought

I'd see you again, and it's been so—so—"

Daymin knew exactly what he meant. Neither of them were military men, yet both had witnessed enough war to last a lifetime. Idorii had seen Baylore fall, its people slaughtered, and had made the long and punishing trek across the plains alone. And for his part, Daymin's campaign had nearly broken him more than once. He had failed so many times and lost so much that he didn't know how he had managed to pick up the pieces and keep moving forward.

"I can't promise there won't be more fighting," Daymin said. "But I intend to keep you by my side from now on. I hope that will make it a little more bearable for us both."

"Definitely." Idorii pulled away to wipe his eyes, sniffing. "Sorry. It's been a really long couple days."

"I know. Come on—we should try and sleep."

Daymin collected their sword belts and tossed them into the tent before holding open the flap for Idorii.

"Are you sure?" he asked. "People are definitely going to talk."

"Let them."

With a watery chuckle, Idorii followed Daymin into the gloom of the tent. Someone must have scrounged up a new sleeping pallet from the refugees, because when Daymin lit the crystal hanging overhead, he thought for a moment that someone had carted a real bed all the way to the mountains. Instead of the thin sleeping roll he had used in his campaign, this was a thick wool-stuffed pallet, wide enough to comfortably fit two, and there were sheets and heavy furs tucked over the top.

"If I hadn't seen your tent on the other side of the gorge, I would have assumed you slept like this the whole time you marched through the countryside," Idorii said, grinning.

"Certainly not," Daymin said. "Though the other night wasn't indicative of our real camp, either. We left most of our supplies behind when we raced to intercept the Whitish."

"And here I thought most of your soldiers slept in the open through hail and snow."

"Didn't you?" Daymin asked.

Idorii made a face. "No hail, thankfully. But I got caught in a couple downpours. It wasn't fun. The biggest oilskin cloak in the world won't make up for the lack of a tent."

Daymin smoothed a lock of Idorii's hair off his forehead. He was so beautiful, with his warm brown eyes and elegant features. "Well, now we have this obscenely large tent to protect us from whatever comes."

With a smile, Idorii leaned forward and kissed Daymin, his cold lips soon warming against Daymin's.

Daymin gripped Idorii's coat and pulled him closer, losing himself in the moment. As Idorii's lips parted and their tongues tangled together, Daymin felt Idorii's arousal, and he dragged his hips against his own.

Daymin fumbled with the buttons on Idorii's ridiculous tapestry coat, which was far too thick and padded. When he dragged it off, he could feel the heat radiating from beneath Idorii's shirt.

Idorii broke off their kiss, breathing hard. "Wait. Can we turn out the light?"

Daymin's chest tightened with sorrow. Idorii must still be ashamed of the markings the corruption had left on his arm and chest.

"I've already seen you without a shirt," he murmured,

fingers starting their way down the buttons. "I think you're beautiful."

"But—"

Daymin forestalled him with another kiss. "I don't want you to feel like you have to hide around me. If you can be brave this one time, you'll never have to worry again."

"I suppose…"

Idorii stood motionless as Daymin finished working his way down the buttons, letting the shirt hang open to show a patch of scales spreading down the left side of his chest, a network of brown markings extending past the end of the scales. He watched with a pained expression as Daymin carefully slid his shirt off his shoulders and let it fall to the ground.

Daymin drank in the sight of Idorii standing shirtless before him. He was lean and smooth-skinned, with the slightest contours of muscles showing on his torso, and Daymin hadn't lied—he *was* beautiful.

Daymin kissed Idorii again and then ran a hand over the dark scales that extended from his neck down to his upper arm. They were smooth and cold, with black knobs protruding from them at irregular intervals. Rather than a disfigurement, it looked like a deliberate addition, a costume designed to be both fierce and alluring.

"You look like a dragon warrior," Daymin said, pressing his lips to Idorii's scaled shoulder. "These are dangerously attractive on you."

Idorii's face reddened, but Daymin could tell he was pleased.

"Your turn."

Grinning, Daymin let Idorii undress him with the same care

he had as his valet. Even then, before he had understood what he was feeling, he had delighted in Idorii's touch.

Once his own coat and shirt had dropped away, Daymin swept Idorii into his arms once more and kissed him greedily, delighting in the feel of his warm skin pressed against his chest. They collapsed onto the sleeping mat in a tangle of furs, desire running like fire through Daymin's veins, and for once he did not have to pretend it was an accident that he had ended up in Idorii's arms.

97

Troops

When Kalleah woke, she was lying in the most comfortable bed she had slept in since leaving King's Port. The covers engulfed her in a soft, feathery embrace, and she felt as though she might sink all the way through to the floor.

Rising, she found a set of clothes waiting for her at the foot of the bed—a deep blue velvet gown and slippers. She changed out of her grimy, bloodstained clothes and into this new garb, moving in a dreamlike daze. She had worn gowns like these for more than twenty years as she ruled Baylore, yet the weight and the fit now seemed foreign. Her adventures had taken her so far from the queen she had been that she knew she could never step back into the role. Now she looked the part, but she felt like a pretender. A sword whose sharp edges were hidden.

Outside the room, she found an attendant waiting. With a bow, the woman led her down the stairs toward a hum of noise that rose from an unfamiliar room; as they approached, she smelled fresh bread and roasted pork.

Entering the dining hall, Kalleah saw Leoth sitting at the high table with Mellicante, Baridya, King Rodarin and his son, and others who must have been his wife and attendants.

"Welcome," King Rodarin said. "I have not thanked you properly for your service to my city. King Leoth has explained what you accomplished in removing the Lord's Men from their posts, and my men have scoured the streets to ensure all are dealt with. The city is ours once more."

His court let out a cheer at this.

Kalleah circled the room to join her friends at the high table, noticing as she did that the light slanting through the windows behind her was pale and golden. She must have slept through the whole day and night.

"What now?" Leoth asked.

Kalleah settled into her chair before fixing King Rodarin with a searching look. "The Prophet's Eyes have hidden something beneath your palace. Something that threatens to destabilize the wall that holds back the magic of the old lands. We need to destroy it before the whole continent is thrown into chaos."

His gaze sharpened. "Of course. But first, enjoy your meal."

Kalleah dug into her breakfast gratefully. After the simple rations she had been surviving on for spans—first as she sailed around the coast, and then as she scraped by with meager funds in Darrenmark—she could not remember eating a more delicious meal. *Not even in Baylore,* she thought with a pang. Not while the city remained under siege, its rations dwindling.

Here she feasted on pork and pheasant and turkey, quail

eggs and smoked cheese, and crepes rolled with mushrooms and soft cheese and herbs. Though she had grown unaccustomed to rich food, she was ravenous, and she ate until her stomach ached.

As they feasted, Leoth explained what the Prophet's Eyes had been doing with the device hidden beneath the palace.

"But what was their end goal?" King Rodarin asked. "Why bother with the magic?"

"It's all part of their prophet's vision," Kalleah said darkly. "They believed that if all nine of the Kinship Thrones stood empty when magic flooded back into the land, the Nine Gods of Light would take up the thrones and guide the continent back into their fold."

"Does this mean what I think it means?" King Rodarin asked, staring at her with a thunderous expression.

"Yes," Kalleah said. "They were intending to assassinate all nine kings simultaneously."

"Holy Varos." King Rodarin's eyes flicked from Kalleah to Leoth. "But that means they must be installed in the Kohldar palace as well. We need to warn King Parvell at once."

"Please do," Kalleah said. "I don't know how close they are to carrying out their plans, since they were relying on us to raise forces to support their work in Whitland, but judging by what we saw here…"

"Their influence is far more extensive than it ought to be," King Rodarin said. "I ought to send troops to Lostport and Ruunas as well, to mitigate the threat."

He sipped at his tea with a distant expression, so Kalleah returned to her meal, noticing the tense silence that had spread through the room.

At last King Rodarin turned back to her. "And what of your kingdom? Do you expect us to pledge troops to your cause? What do you require in exchange for freeing Darrenmark?"

Kalleah glanced at Leoth. They had not discussed this, since they had planned to use the population of Brenvale to attack Whitland directly under the command of the Prophet's Eyes.

"I need to confer with my companions," Kalleah said. "I know you can't commit too great a force to a foreign war, so I don't intend to make unreasonable demands."

"And for that I am grateful," King Rodarin said.

* * *

After breakfast, while King Rodarin sent scouts into the tunnels beneath the palace to track down the enchanted device, Kalleah and her friends settled in a quiet sitting-room to discuss what they could reasonably ask of King Rodarin.

"I still think we should ask for troops," Mellicante said. "We don't need many, but if we combined your power with a dedicated force—a *trained* one, mind—we might be able to start taking back parts of Itrea."

"She has a point," Baridya said, though she looked troubled. "Before, we were fighting with civilians, yet we still managed to push through to the heart of Eidervell. If we had an actual army at our backs…"

Kalleah shook her head. "I want to reclaim Itrea as much as you do. But all of you are putting too much faith in my power. I'm not invincible, and I can only deal so much damage before it's too much."

"But Larkhaven has no wall," Mellicante said. "It's the

perfect target for exactly the sort of force we could pull together. And if we arrived quickly enough, we might be able to intercept the Cheltish draftees and win them to our cause before they join the fight for Baylore."

"There's very little chance of that," Kalleah said.

"Unless the forest road remains closed."

Kalleah looked at Leoth, who had stayed silent throughout, his mouth set in a grim line. "What do you think?"

"Brenvale worries me," he said. "That conspiracy is further-reaching than we had realized, and its members are dabbling in forces they don't understand and won't be able to control. If they see their plans through, I worry we won't be safe, even an ocean away."

"Maybe we would be better off worrying about that after we've retaken Itrea and have an army to back us up," Kalleah said. "If we can destroy this device hidden beneath the Darrenmark palace, the Prophet's Eyes won't be able to finish their work. That will buy us enough time to sail back to Itrea and start our campaign there."

"So you really think we can win back Itrea with your power alone, supported by a small force of Darden warriors?" Mellicante asked, a hint of sarcasm in her voice.

Kalleah frowned at her. She believed nothing of the sort, but she hoped she could learn to channel her power to other magic races, and thereby unleash powers not seen for centuries.

But she wasn't going to mention that until she knew it would work. She had to plan as if it wouldn't, since all the texts she had read cautioned that this application of her power required many years of study.

"Shall we see what happens after we destroy the device

here?" Baridya asked. "As much as I don't want to see the Kinship Thrones suffer for the conspiracy, I think it's time to return to Itrea."

"I think you're right," Kalleah said. "How many troops can we reasonably ask for?"

"That depends on the size of Dardensfell's standing army," Leoth said. "And on how many ships they're willing to provide to transport us to the coast. Given how easily they were overrun by the Lord's Men, I imagine they would balk at sending more than a couple hundred soldiers."

"That could be enough to re-take Larkhaven," Mellicante said.

Kalleah let her gaze drift to the window, which overlooked the western side of town. They were so very far from home. She worried they were deluding themselves into thinking they could accomplish more than they were actually capable of, simply because they were removed from the war. She could still remember the claustrophobic feeling of ruling Baylore while the Whitish continued conquering the countryside beyond the forest wall, sending refugees fleeing to the capital and crowding the streets, every day bringing them closer to the last of their rations.

Yet she had been unable to use her power in battle. If she could return now, knowing what she did…would it be enough?

"I think we need to return to Itrea," she said at last. "No matter the size of the force that accompanies us."

"That's what I wanted to hear!" Mellicante raised her teacup in salute as if it were a mug of ale.

* * *

776

That afternoon, King Rodarin's scouts brought news from the tunnels. They had found the hidden device, and had captured the two Prophet's Eyes who had guarded it.

"With any luck, they can tell us how to disable the device without injuring ourselves," he said.

"Maybe we shouldn't send the monarchs of two kingdoms to mess with something like that," Mellicante said drily. "I'd be happy to go, along with a few of your palace guards, and the rest of you can survey the work once we're finished."

Leoth looked like he wanted to argue, but King Rodarin said, "A wise observation. Guards, show the lady where the device is hidden."

They waited in the bowels of the palace for the group to return. Just below, the polished stone floors gave way to narrow corridors carved in the bedrock, and even here, Kalleah could smell the mildewed, cave-like air wafting from the tunnels.

While they waited, King Rodarin asked, "Have you decided what you would ask of me, Your Majesty?"

"I have a fleet waiting off the shore of Kohlmarsh, but I will require transport down the river to rejoin my own ships."

"Easily done."

"From there, I hope to return to Itrea and begin re-conquering the continent. But I can't do this alone. I ask for two hundred trained soldiers to travel with me, at least as far as Larkhaven. In return, I promise to send ten times that many troops—including Makhori who will outmatch any regular soldiers—to help track down and remove any remaining conspirators in the Kinship Thrones."

King Rodarin rubbed at his beard, which was speckled with grey. "It seems a fair offer. But how will I hold you to your promise once an ocean separates us, given the concerns of the Kinship Thrones have little bearing on your own campaign?"

He was right. The squabbles of the Kinship Thrones had seemed very distant before they spilled over into Itrea, and if she won back her own kingdom, she would have little reason to worry about what happened abroad.

"We will not disregard the importance of the Prophet's Eyes, even when we have left them far behind," Leoth said gravely. "We understand the implications of their work better than anyone else, and if they manage to destabilize the wall holding back the old lands, none of us will escape the consequences. No matter how far we run. Once we have secured a victory for Itrea, we will send our own son to lead the force we dispatch to the Kinship Thrones. This I swear, as the King of Itrea."

And Kalleah believed him.

King Rodarin's brow furrowed. "Very well. I will trust your word. But know that I count the monarchs of many other kingdoms as my close friends, and if you fail to honor your promise, your people will never find welcome in the Kinship Thrones again. Whether for trade or political alliances. Do you understand?"

Kalleah glanced at Leoth, who bowed his head. "Of course."

Before Kalleah had time to think on the implications of Leoth's promise, she heard footsteps approaching up the rough stairway, and Mellicante burst into the hallway flanked by King Rodarin's guards.

"The device has been dismantled," she said. "It was easier than we expected—almost too easy. Do you want to see?"

Kalleah, Leoth, Baridya, and King Rodarin followed them down the warren of dark passageways and narrow stairwells until they reached the familiar room where the device had been hidden.

The floor was strewn with mechanical parts—screws and bolts and cogs and plates of metal. There was no sign of any remnant enchantment; the parts lay still and quiet, and Kalleah could feel nothing unusual in the air.

"Well done," Kalleah said. "Send the parts to be melted down, for good measure."

"At once, Your Majesty," said one of the guards, scooping the metal scraps into a crate that had sat near the door.

"And I am once again in your debt," King Rodarin said, inclining his head to Kalleah. "Your troops and riverboats will be ready to sail north two days hence."

98

The Icelings

When Idorii woke to find Daymin's body molded to his, his heart swelled with a deep contentment. He was still sore from the journey up and down the riverbed, but those aches were dulled beneath the warmth of Daymin's skin against his, the soft tickle of Daymin's breath against his neck.

He had never felt so safe. So loved. Before Daymin, he had always valued his independence too much to let himself get tangled up in romantic dalliances. Yet this was different. When he was with Daymin, he felt complete in himself. He had found something he hadn't even known he had lacked.

Idorii twisted in Daymin's embrace and nestled in close to his chest, pressing his lips to Daymin's.

With a soft moan, Daymin opened his eyes and squinted at Idorii, his gaze fogged with sleep.

"Have I overslept?" he mumbled.

Idorii kissed him again. "The sun has just risen. I wanted to steal a few minutes with you before you met with the Icelings."

Daymin groaned. "I'd forgotten about that. Come with me, please?"

"Of course."

Idorii snuggled in closer still, nudging a knee between Daymin's legs and feeling his arousal.

Daymin ducked his head and kissed him again, hungrily, and Idorii tangled his fingers in Daymin's dark curls.

They might have remained there all morning if not for a snapping of canvas from the door.

Idorii broke off with a gasp and threw the blankets over his head.

"Who is that?" came a stern, matronly voice from the tent door.

"What are you doing here, Grandmother?" Daymin grumbled.

"The Icelings await your presence. More of them have gathered in the night—they may hope to intimidate us. I will send word that you are on your way."

"Fine," Daymin said grumpily. "But have someone bring me a couple new formal doublets. Our coats have yet to be cleaned following the battle."

Idorii held his breath. He still couldn't believe Daymin intended to make their relationship public—it would cause a huge stir for the king of Itrea to reveal he had taken a man for a lover. Especially without a wife or heir in place.

The tent flap rustled once more, and Daymin dragged the covers off Idorii's head.

"My bloody grandmother never leaves me alone," he said.

"I'd gotten used to doing things without facing the judgment of my court—having them back will take some getting used to."

Idorii had seen the way Daymin had retreated from the public eye while at court, and had watched him gain confidence in the less formal setting of the Queen's Bed. "I know. But remember all you've accomplished in their absence. They might try to push you around, but without you, all of us would have died when the Whitish captured Baylore. You've more than proved your ability to lead on your own."

"Thank you," Daymin said. As he climbed from bed, goose pimples broke out on his arms, and he hurriedly pulled on his dusty trousers and shirt. When he tossed Idorii's clothes onto the bed, Idorii dressed beneath the covers, making the most of the lingering warmth.

"You ready for this?" he asked Idorii as they tugged on their boots and buckled their sword belts into place.

"I hope so." Idorii gave him a nervous grin.

Then a guard bundled a pair of formal doublets through the flap, and they finished dressing in silence. Idorii dragged a hand through Daymin's curls, trying to tame them, while Daymin fiddled with the cuffs of his sleeves.

Giving Idorii one last, swift kiss, Daymin pulled back the tent flap.

When they emerged onto the sloping grass leading down to the refugee camp, Idorii was taken aback to find a crowd of Itrea's most powerful political figures waiting for them. Several threw him strange looks, which made his stomach flip over.

At the front stood Queen Ammeline, Holden King Pollard, Holden King Morrisse, Prince Calden, and a few generals Idorii didn't recognize. They were flanked by a couple dozen soldiers in gleaming armor, some of which must have been taken off the bodies of fallen Whitish.

"We have no suitable substitute for a crown," said Queen Ammeline, her disapproving gaze lingering on Idorii. He wished the tent would collapse on him.

"That's fine," Daymin said. "If they speak Whitish, they'll understand who has come to negotiate with them."

"Yes, there are a few translators among their number."

Daymin glanced toward the northern end of the valley; following his gaze, Idorii saw a group of perhaps fifty Icelings waiting at the edge of the forest. Even at a distance, they were unmistakable, with pale skin and brilliant white hair streaked faintly with blue.

Squaring his shoulders, Daymin led the way along the edge of the valley toward the Icelings, the soldiers clanking as they followed. Idorii trailed behind him like a stray cat hoping for scraps, feeling like a fool among such exalted company. The air was bitter this early in the morning, the sun just peeking above the foothills to the east, and birdsong rang from the trees.

When they neared the Icelings, a handful broke off from the group and approached. They wore no weapons that Idorii could see, and their deep blue woolen coats over deerskin trousers looked more like formal uniforms than fighting attire.

"One of you is the king of Itrea?" asked a tall man with deep lines beneath his eyes. His Itrean was heavily accented.

"I am King Daymin," said Daymin, stepping forward. "I come to negotiate on behalf of my people, who have been forced out of our homeland by the Whitish army."

"Slowly. Please," said the old translator. "You fight? Or you are civilians?"

"My army is here, but so are many thousands of civilians," Daymin said. "We had nowhere else to go. The Whitish have pursued us to the foothills, but we cut them off before they could follow us here."

"We saw," said a younger woman whose hair hung in an intricate pattern of braids.

The old man shot her a warning look. "We cannot allow you this place to stay. Too much danger for our people. From your fighters, and from Whitish fighters, if they follow here."

Daymin dropped to one knee, bowing his head. "Please. We have been cast from our homes, and we have nowhere else to go. If we leave the mountains, the Whitish will slaughter us. Let us stay here, at least until we find somewhere better to hide. If you allow us to remain, I promise I will give you anything that is within my power to provide."

The Icelings withdrew and discussed rapidly in their own tongue, their expressions dark with concern. While they spoke, a pair of foreign-looking girls pushed their way to the front of Daymin's company. Their faces were wide and flat, their straight black hair pulled back in tails.

"Your Majesty," one said, her words thick with a different accent.

Daymin looked up in surprise from where he still knelt. He clambered to his feet to study the girls, who must be in their teens.

"We are Mountain Lords, from Cashabree," the girl continued. "Your mother sent us to help negotiate with the Icelings. Our people are welcomed at their court, so they might trust us more readily than you."

"Thank you," Daymin said, looking between the two in

wonder. Idorii stared at them, not sure he believed their claim. If Queen Kalleah had sent them from Cashabree, how the bloody plagues had they traveled clear across enemy-controlled Itrea to join Daymin's army here?

As the girls approached the Icelings, they broke off their conversation abruptly.

"You are of the record-keepers," the old man said.

"Yes," the first girl said. "My name is Jayna, and my father is Councilor Ferrinon, one of our leaders. He and Queen Kalleah of Itrea sent us to negotiate on behalf of King Daymin. My people are isolated, just as yours are, but war is spilling over our borders. What the Whitish are doing here is only a small part of their move to bring the last of the free peoples under their thumb. Itrea is now Whitish-occupied, and even if King Daymin hadn't led his people to you, war would have come to you soon enough. The Allakoash have already been attacked and killed in large numbers—did you know that? Their forests are retreating."

"We hear whispers," the Iceling woman said, her face long with worry.

Daymin stepped up beside Jayna. "It's true. We fought on behalf of the Allakoash, but the Whitish were too strong to overcome. The forest that long divided the continent in two has split and withdrawn from the old forest road, leaving the Whitish the undisputed conquerors of Itrea. I regret that we drew the Whitish army to you so quickly, but maybe someday you will be grateful to have my forces here, ready to fight on your behalf."

Again the Icelings withdrew to discuss, but this time the looks they threw Daymin's way were thoughtful rather than hostile. Idorii dared to hope they might listen to reason.

When the woman approached Daymin once more, she inclined her head respectfully. "We accept that your words are of merit. However, we have not authority to make decision this. If you will travel with us to our home to speak with our leaders, as a guest under strict guard—"

"A hostage?" Jayna suggested pertly.

"Yes. We will allow you to make your case before the Most Honored. You come too." She indicated the two Mountain Lord girls. "While we are gone, we close off path to lowlands so the Whitish army cannot come to place this."

"Thank you," Daymin said.

"The king will need an attendant," Queen Ammeline said, stepping forward. "Perhaps Prince Calden will agree to serve in this role?"

Daymin turned to look back over the ranks of assembled royalty. "Idorii will travel with me."

Idorii's stomach swooped in happiness.

"But that is hardly—"

Daymin spoke over his grandmother's objection. "He is my partner and most trusted advisor. Meanwhile, Prince Calden, Holden King Pollard, and Holden King Morrisse will rule in my absence. I trust each of you to act in the best interests of our people."

Prince Calden dropped to his knee before Daymin. "I swear my unending loyalty to you in this and in all matters," he said gravely.

The two holden kings followed suit, Pollard leaning heavily on Morrisse's shoulder as he knelt.

"Then it is decided," Daymin said. "We will prepare to leave at once."

99

Icewrights

The next couple hours passed in a blur. Daymin was so busy making arrangements that he barely saw Idorii, which meant he had no chance to ask if Idorii was happy to be dragged along on a potentially dangerous diplomatic mission. But he had seen the spark of joy in Idorii's eyes when he had chosen him; he hoped it meant he wouldn't object.

While Daymin gave orders to his court, tracking down Jakovi and Letto and placing them under Uncle Cal's protection, several Icelings made their way to the mouth of the gorge. Even at a distance, their white-blue hair made them easy to pick from the crowd, and they drew curious stares wherever they went.

Daymin did not pay any heed to their work until he heard gasps and shouts of surprise from the far end of the valley. He jogged up the slope toward the edge of the forest so he could see above the refugee camp, and when he caught sight of what had elicited such excitement, he stopped in his tracks, staring in disbelief.

From the barren ground at the mouth of the gorge grew a network of pale, translucent vines that would have looked like ice if not for the supple way they moved. As they grew higher and higher, far above the heads of the Icelings who stood before them, the vines at the base of the tangle fused together to form a solid wall, smooth as a frozen waterfall. It looked exactly like the living ice that decorated the Mountain wing of Baylore Palace.

"Icewrights," he muttered, a smile spreading across his face. It was the antiquated term for Icelings, and he understood now that it was strikingly accurate. This was magic as he had never seen it used before, more elegant and powerful than anything the Itrean magic races were capable of.

As he started back toward the royal tent to make sure he hadn't forgotten anything, Tarak, Zahira, and Lalaysha intercepted him.

"I can't believe we got to see the Icelings using their magic!" Zahira said, grinning from beneath her flyaway curls. "I'm pretty sure no Itrean has had that privilege in centuries."

"It certainly was impressive," Daymin said.

"Do you think you'll be safe with the Icelings?" Tarak asked. "We don't know anything about them."

"I have to take that risk," Daymin said. "If this doesn't work, we don't have anywhere else to go. Besides, Cal, Morrisse, and Pollard will rule just fine in my absence."

"I'm a bit miffed that you didn't insist on bringing us along," Zahira teased.

"For your political power? Your diplomatic expertise? Your ability to defend me against foes?"

"And you think Idorii was a better choice for those?"

Daymin's face grew hot.

"Zahira," Tarak said sternly.

"I'm just teasing." Zahira pulled Daymin into a one-armed hug. "I'm very happy for you. I promise. Even though I wanted to see the Iceling capital for myself."

"Maybe Daymin will be so successful that the Icelings will welcome us to visit them freely," Lalaysha said.

"Wouldn't that be something," Daymin said drily.

When they reached the royal tent, his friends took turns embracing him and wishing him safe travels. As they started down the hill to the refugee camp, Daymin watched them for a long moment, trying to guess what his people would make of this new home. It seemed a very temporary settlement, with few resources to support such a large population—he could not plan for them to stay here forever. But at least his people were safe for now. It was more than he had dared to hope for.

A rustling from within the tent drew Daymin's attention, and Idorii pushed his way through the canvas flaps, a laden pack over one shoulder.

"I arranged a smaller tent for us," he said. Then he cast Daymin a wary look. "If that's okay? From what the Icelings were describing of our route, the royal tent would be far too cumbersome."

"Thank you," Daymin said. "Are you ready?"

Idorii nodded. After a moment, he burst out, "I still can't believe you claimed me as your partner in front of everyone!"

Daymin gave him a rueful grin, his face hot. "I only dared to make such a bold claim because we're about to leave. I'm not sure I could deal with the questions and whispers otherwise."

Idorii pulled him close and kissed his cheek. "I love you, Daymin."

Then Daymin fetched his own pack, and they were off, skirting around the edge of the valley to rejoin the Icelings at the northern end. The two Mountain Lords were already waiting, deep in conversation with the woman with the intricately braided hair, and Jayna jumped to her feet when she spotted Daymin.

A crowd had gathered to see them off, and when Daymin turned to wave at his people, a deafening cheer rose through the valley.

As they started up the slope into the fragrant pine forest, the bed of needles soft underfoot, Daymin was buoyed by optimism. The worst had happened—Baylore was lost and his people reduced to refugees—yet still they endured. Once, long ago, they had founded this great nation from the same humble beginnings. He had to believe it could happen again.

100

The Queen's Fleet

With the sun rising over the roofs of Kohldar, Kalleah and her companions made their way down to the riverfront. Kalleah had persuaded King Rodarin to provide her with a man's military uniform, so she and her friends were all dressed similarly in leather jerkins and black trousers, nothing betraying their status.

At the docks, they were greeted by their waiting troops, all two hundred dressed in uniforms of deep blue accented with red. None wore armor, but all were equipped with shields and spears.

Civilians had gathered as well, waving banners and cheering, and with the soldiers in what could be mistaken for the Reycoran colors, Kalleah felt a surge of nostalgia—almost as if this were a homecoming of sorts. Despite everything she had faced here, she felt a strong kinship with these people.

And as she let her gaze travel over the crowd, she realized

it was more diverse than she had expected. There were pockets of Varrilans and Ruunans, marsh-dwellers and people of mixed race; all were now safe to resume their lives, free of the oppressive presence of the Lord's Men.

Two long barges awaited Kalleah's troops, each with a single rectangular sail and a row of oars, and their captains saluted her with fists clasped together before their chests.

Kalleah and Leoth led the way up the gangplank onto the first of the two ships, the morning breeze that trailed down the river whisking away the stench of the waterfront. As her troops began filing on after her, Kalleah turned to address the crowd.

"I will never forget your hospitality!" she called. "Even under the shadow of the Lord's Men, we found those who were willing to trust us and to aid us in our work. I hope this will be the beginning of a new future, one where Whitland's stranglehold on our kingdoms loosens and Itrea and Dardensfell are able to cement a lasting alliance."

Kalleah heard a shout from the opposite riverbank, so she called, "And Kohlmarsh! The Twin Cities will receive equal attention from Itrea."

This drew a chorus of laughter and cheers from both banks of the river.

Soon the last of the soldiers had boarded, the decks of the two barges thundering beneath their footsteps. The gangplanks were raised and the lines cast off, and the barges drifted from shore, cutting downstream through the pearly waters of the Lodren River.

Cheers followed them as they left the Twin Cities behind, gradually fading until the only sound was the rhythmic splash and creak of the oars.

* * *

Two days out from the Twin Cities, Kalleah caught sight of sails in the distance. She stood at the bow, tense with fear, afraid King Edreon had sent a fleet to capture her.

But as the ships drew closer, she recognized them. There was Captain Jezwick's ship, with its grey sails and distinctive eagle's head bowsprit; behind it came the sleek, freshly-painted pirate ship from King's Port; and after that were the merchants and smugglers she knew so well. Kalleah's fleet had returned for her.

Leoth had joined Kalleah at the bow, and he squeezed her hand, face lit with hope. "Is that…?"

"It is," Kalleah said, a smile spreading across her face.

"Trouble ahead, Your Majesty!" their captain shouted. "There must be at least six ships approaching! We can't fight off numbers like that."

"We won't need to," Kalleah said. "This is my fleet. Make berth at the nearest dock, and my army can transfer to the ships."

The captain shouted orders and brought the two barges toward the left-hand bank, where they tied up to a long section of boardwalk at a fishing village. Kalleah barely paid heed to where they were going, as she was craning her neck to see who sailed aboard her fleet.

As they drew nearer, she caught sight of Triyam and Luc hanging off the railing of Captain Jezwick's ship.

"Your Majesty!" Luc shouted, waving frantically. "Look what we found!"

Captain Jezwick guided his ship alongside Kalleah's barge, and he secured the two together with hooks. Triyam and Luc jumped the rail before the ship had stopped moving, while Captain Jezwick climbed down with more dignity a few minutes later.

"How is this possible?" Kalleah asked, squeezing Luc's shoulder. She had thought the boys dead.

"We saw you taken by robed men," Triyam said. "Luc wanted to fight them off himself, but I persuaded him we would be wiser to bring help. So we walked and begged rides down to the coast, where we managed to track down your fleet."

"We were ready to fight for your freedom," Luc said with a grin. "We even picked up a few people in Stragmouth who wanted to join the battle!"

"You've done very well," Kalleah said. "Both of you. And Desh?"

Luc's smile slipped away. "We thought he was with you."

"No."

Leoth took Kalleah's hand. "He's likely somewhere in Dardensfell. He'll do well enough there, especially with the Lord's Men gone."

Kalleah hoped he was right.

Turning to Captain Jezwick, she said, "These soldiers have been sent by King Rodarin to fight on behalf of Itrea. I will sail for Larkhaven at once—how many of my ships are willing to follow?"

"We're all prepared to go wherever you command, Your Majesty," Captain Jezwick said. "We put it to the vote while you were away, and we can't see any other way to get ourselves out of this mess. We'll tie our fortunes to yours for as long as it takes to knock the Whitish back."

Kalleah stepped over and clasped the man's hand in both

of hers. "Thank you," she said warmly. "I don't deserve such loyalty."

* * *

It was that evening, after her ships anchored along a stretch of thinly populated riverbanks, when Abeytu and Nidawi boarded Captain Jezwick's ship. Kalleah had been dining with her companions on deck, perched on an assortment of crates and barrels, while a chorus of frogs chirruped from the reeds at the river's edge. It was a relief to be moving again—the very sway of the deck and the scenery drifting past on either side gave her the impression she was making progress for the first time in spans.

"Welcome back," Abeytu said shortly, stopping before Kalleah.

When Kalleah noticed her grim expression, she set aside her plate and stood.

"What is it?" she asked quietly, beckoning the women to the bow, where they would not be overheard. Stopping with her hip resting against the rail, Kalleah studied the two Ma'oko. Both had adopted a more conservative form of dress since arriving at Stragmouth, Abeytu in a simple Cheltish trader's blouse and skirt that were both too short on her lanky frame, Nidawi in a poet's shirt and trousers, her hair shaved close to her scalp.

Abeytu glanced over her shoulder at the circle of lanterns where the crew ate. "I will tell Nidawi's story as well as I can. She still only speaks a little Whitish."

"I practice much," Nidawi said with an earnest smile.

Kalleah nodded, her eyes flicking back to Abeytu.

"The girl slipped away from us in Stragmouth, before our fleet set sail. It was very bad of her."

Nidawi must have caught Abeytu's tone, because she dropped her chin to her chest, looking abashed.

"But she found something very useful, so we can't be too angry. I am worried what this means."

"What is it?" Kalleah asked.

"She followed the men from Stragmouth back to their homes," Abeytu said. "The ones with the little enchanted devices. They live up in the mountains, and Nidawi tracked them all the way there. No one ever saw her. This is lucky, because she is not good at disguising her markings. Elu and I practiced while she was away, and we are much better now. I think we could even walk through Stragmouth without anyone noticing."

"What did Nidawi find in the mountains?" Kalleah asked urgently. She wondered if these men were from Brenvale—she still wasn't sure she had made the right choice in turning away from whatever lay there.

"Magic," Abeytu said in a dramatic whisper. "She found people using magic in ways we have never heard of. It was war magic, too. Fighting magic. More dangerous than we could defeat, even with all these nice soldiers. At first she thought there was a spring, like we have, because she could sense a—how do you say it? A hum?"

"A vibration?" Kalleah said faintly. Cold was seeping through her.

"Maybe. So Nidawi tracked this to the source, and she found instead a very large metal device built into the side of the mountain. It was spilling magic everywhere, and some people were using it. But mostly it just leaked away. She couldn't get close, since men were guarding it, but she could feel how powerful it was. This is something very dangerous, Kalleah."

"I know."

Kalleah rubbed a trembling hand over her eyes, feeling weak.

The device in the bowels of Darrenmark Palace must have been a fake. She had felt nothing from it; the only sign of its supposed purpose had been the way it moved like the gears in a clock.

Somewhere in the mountains, forces were still at work siphoning power from the old lands, spilling it into the Kinship Thrones with no regard for the damage it could cause. Whether this was the work of the Prophet's Eyes or another faction, she couldn't guess, but the fact that someone had already put this magic to use for the purpose of fighting...

Nine plagues. She had barely made headway in using her own power, and already it seemed worthless in the face of this new threat.

Kalleah stepped to the rail, staring into the darkness in the direction of the Andalls.

A magic device stronger than anything her people had seen before...

The chill breeze raised the hairs down the back of her neck, and she shivered.

Would she defeat the Whitish only to lose her kingdom to a far deadlier enemy?

The Pretender

The court buzzed with rumors as Prince Navaire's forces approached Eidervell. They had been preparing to make a move on the high throne, so Edreon had gone one step further and invited them to his court for a feast. Many suspected Prince Navaire would seize the opportunity to discredit Edreon in front of his own court—perhaps even assassinate him for good measure—but those in Eidervell Castle had seen the way Edreon had begun to recover over the past two quarters, and they whispered that he was too clever to let a pretender defeat him so conveniently. Surely he was planning something.

Edreon delighted in the whispers. Now that he had regained his health and his mobility, he could seize the reins once more, dictating the way this would play out rather than letting himself be tugged here and there like a mule. And he had to admit, he enjoyed the drama of it all.

The day of the feast dawned bright and clear, the air still

carrying a bite of frost. Word came from the outskirts of the city that Prince Navaire's army had camped in the field beyond, and he had ridden into Eidervell at the first light of dawn, accompanied by twenty of his closest supporters. Less welcome was the news that the pretender was greeted by cheering in the streets, but Edreon's guard reported that an even greater number of townspeople tried to silence those who cheered. It seemed Edreon's popularity held at least in his own capital, then.

While the tables were laid out in the great hall, delicious smells wafting from the kitchens, Edreon sent Naresha, Odelia, and Luvoli to greet Prince Navaire's party and watch for any signs of foul play. Meanwhile, he arranged himself at his throne long before any guests arrived, accompanied by his guards. Prince Navaire's party would see no sign that he had regained the use of his leg when they first set foot in the hall.

Next his musicians took their positions near the high table, where they struck up a tune as the first members of his court filed in. All were on their best behavior, likely aware they were playing a part in his scheme. Marviak, Jormund, and Berrick took their places on either side of Edreon, leaving seats for Luvoli and Naresha; all three were aware of his plans and smiled to see the scene coming together so perfectly.

At last, a fanfare of trumpets announced Prince Navaire's arrival at the castle gates.

Edreon smiled at his court, catching many excited grins in return, before settling his face into a resigned expression.

The click of boots against marble heralded the approach of Prince Navaire's party. The prince wore military garb topped with a formal cloak and a circlet that was large enough to be mistaken for a crown.

"High King Edreon," said the prince, bowing stiffly. He was in his forties, handsome and brown-haired, with a long nose and sharp eyes.

"Greetings, Prince Navaire," Edreon said, remaining seated—exactly as the prince would have expected. "I thank you for answering my summons."

Naresha slipped away from the prince's followers and glided to her seat beside Edreon, whispering as she did, "They are equipped with vials of poison and concealed daggers. Just as you suspected."

Edreon gave no sign that he had heard her. "I have watched your growing popularity with interest," he told Prince Navaire. "As you are clearly well-loved by your followers, I suspect you have a number of promising ideas for the future of Whitland. I am considering appointing you a role in my court, so that we might share in the ruling of this great kingdom."

Prince Navaire stepped forward, lips curling in a sneer. "Oh, you poor fool. I have it on good authority that you are on your deathbed, with no heir to succeed you." He turned and spread his arms to Edreon's court. "With an army at my back and the Varonite priests pledging their full support, I am the only logical choice for your next king. And you would be wise to give me your loyalty now, before our empire crumbles from neglect. Already it has begun to decay."

Many of Edreon's court were looking between the prince and their king, eyes sparkling with curiosity.

Edreon waited for a long moment, letting the prince think he had won.

Then he pushed back his throne and stood.

"You are the fool, Navaire."

As Edreon strode around the high table to face the pretender, he drew gasps from his court, none of whom had seen him walk for spans.

"I am no invalid, and you are nothing but a traitor and a usurper. My suffering was drawn out at the hands of a healer who poisoned me, and I suspect you were behind this." That was a lie, of course, but no one would have a chance to discover otherwise. "Even now, you have come armed with poisons, ready to commit treason."

At these words, Luvoli drew a dagger and sliced at the coat pockets of two of Prince Navaire's followers, sending vials of dark liquid clattering to the ground.

Another round of gasps rose from Edreon's court—they were loving this.

Edreon drew his sword as he stalked toward Prince Navaire. The prince fumbled at his waist, but he was too slow. Edreon slashed at his cheek, drawing a deep line of blood, and then plunged his sword into the man's thigh.

Prince Navaire collapsed to his knees, shouting in pain and trying to stanch the flow of blood with his hands.

"I won't kill you now," Edreon said. "You don't deserve that kindness. No—you and your cronies will die traitors' deaths, burned alive in the main square. Your screams will resound through the streets of Eidervell."

Raising his voice, Edreon called, "Take them away!"

From the hall outside, his own soldiers filed in, quickly restraining Prince Navaire's followers and marching them from the dining hall. Prince Navaire was unable to stand, so he was dragged bodily toward the doors, leaving a smear of blood on the tiles. Edreon grinned fiercely at this—let the pretender spend his final hours as a cripple. See how he liked it.

Once they were gone, the doors fell shut with a thud, only the bloodstains marking the place where Prince Navaire's followers had once stood.

A deafening silence hung in the air.

Edreon strode back to his throne, where he turned to open his arms to his court. "You have been loyal through all these dark spans. I was weak, but no longer. I stand before you as the king you deserve, fit in body and mind, the Varos-chosen leader of the Kinship Thrones. And now that we have come into the light once more, your loyalty will be rewarded."

A few scattered cheers punctuated the silence. Little by little, more of his court joined in, until the hall rang with applause.

Edreon basked in their adoration, feeling the burdens he had carried all these long spans gradually slipping away. He still had challenges to overcome, but he would face them from a place of strength, not from his sickbed.

At last he sat and poured a goblet of wine, letting the cheering subside.

"And now," Edreon said, "we feast."

Glossary of Terms

The Itrean system of rule – Itrea has created a system of elected monarchy where five heirs share a thirty-year ruling cycle. Each heir is nominated by the current ruler from each of the five ruling families, and is usually a relative. When the ruling cycle switches, the heir of the king or queen currently in power takes the throne, and after three years, Baylore holds a vote as to whether that monarch should keep the throne or hand it to the next king or queen in line. If all five monarchs in the ruling cycle are voted off the throne after their three years are over, rule returns to the first monarch in line for that cycle.

Holden King/Holden Queen – The term for a king or queen in a current ruling cycle who does not sit the throne.

The five ruling families of Itrea – The original aim of this ruling system was to share power more evenly among the people, since the founders of Itrea had no royal blood. However, five royal families have now held power for centuries. These are the Reycoran family, the Aldsvell family, the Dellgrain family, the Vellmont family, and the Bastray family. Tradition dictates that all rulers and their relatives take the ruling family's surname, so these names have endured since the royal lines were founded.

Icelings – A race native to Itrea who live in the Icebraid Peaks. Little is known about them, so they often feature in fantastical stories.

Allakoash (Drifters) – A race native to Itrea who live in the Wandering Woods. They can choose to undergo a ritual to gain the use of healing powers.

The magic races – These are people born with one of a handful of magic powers. They are not closely linked by genetics (aside from Weavers), so anyone with even distant magic ancestry can end up with a magic power, and it can skip many generations. Also called Makhori (in the Kinship Thrones). The magic races include Weavers (who are born with silver hair that can be woven or otherwise incorporated into handmade objects to enchant them), Cloudmages (who can predict or even exert a slight power over weather), Minstrels (storytellers who pull named listeners into stories that feel like reality), Riders (who bond with animals), Potioneers (who create enchanted substances by channeling their magic into ordinary ingredients), Metalsmiths (who can sense veins of metal underground and use their power to forge delicate metal objects), and more.

The forbidden races – The forbidden races are not allowed within the walls of Baylore. The rationale is that these races are dangerous, especially in a heavily populated place like Baylore, but some magic races have been lumped into this category due to general mistrust or prejudice. Forbidden races include Extractors (who drain energy from those nearby), Braiders (who can fix the time and cause of a person's death), Curse-Weavers (who can curse people deliberately or accidentally unless the source of their power is cut from them), Dark Potioneers (who use less accepted substances such as blood and flesh in their potions), and Snake-Bloods (who can transform into snakes).

The Kinship Thrones – The name for the nine kingdoms joined under Whitish rule. Long ago, the expanding Whitish Empire was divided between the high king's nine sons, though some kingdoms had been settled long before Whitish influence. The Kinship Thrones are east of Itrea. They include Whitland, Chelt, Dardensfell, Kohlmarsh, Cashabree, Ruunas, Northreach, Lostport, and Varrival.

Whitland – The country that rules all nine Kinship Thrones (at least in theory). Whitland does not accept Itrea's autonomy and tries to curtail trade between Itrea and the Kinship Thrones. Most inhabitants of the Kinship Thrones are originally of the Whitish race, but are now known by their country of nationality (Cheltish, Varrilan, Ruunan, etc.). Whitish is also the official language of Itrea and most of the Kinship Thrones.

Makhori – A term used in the Kinship Thrones for those with magic blood (known as the magic races in Itrea)

Varos – A god worshipped in the Kinship Thrones, especially in Whitland. In Itrea, often shortened to "Varse" as a curse.

The Nine – The nine Whitish gods of light who pre-dated Varos. The days in a quarter and spans in a year have been divided up numerically to honor the nine gods (plus Varos, in the 10-day quarter).

The Seventeen Gods of Sin – According to Whitish religious teachings, the Gods of Sin birthed the magic races. Hence all Makhori are demons who represent the lingering presence of evil in the world.

Cloudy Gods – A joking term Itreans use to refer to things outside their control, sometimes as a mild oath. Itreans are not religious and have only adopted the parts of Whitish religion relating to general terminology (days/quarters/spans). However, some country folk genuinely believe in the cloudy gods, which causes no end of amusement to city folk.

Dravs – Stamped tin coins worth a small amount

Varlins – A varlin is worth twenty dravs. Varlins are stamped coins typically made of silver, with a gemstone in the center.

Span – A period of 40 days. There are eight full spans plus one incomplete span in a year.

Quarter – A period of 10 days. There are four quarters in a span. The days in a quarter are Aurumsday, Talonsday, Tensday, Tollsday, Samsday, Ilkayumsday, Tabansday, Daridsday, Varseday, and Sullimsday. These are named after Varos and the nine Whitish gods of light.

League – Equal to approximately 5 kilometers (3 miles)

About the Author

R.J. Vickers is the bestselling author of the Underground Academy series, the Forbidden Queen series, the Empire of Ash series, and numerous standalone works.

When she's not writing, she enjoys hiking, photography, and crafting.

Though she grew up in Colorado, she now lives with her family in New Zealand.

Connect with R.J. Vickers online at **rjvickers.com**.

Also by R.J. Vickers

The Forbidden Queen Series
    Forbidden Queen
    Innocent Queen
    Renegade Queen
    Usurper Queen
    Magician Queen
    Warrior Queen

The Empire of Ash Series
    Prince of Shadows
    Kingdom of Malice
    Lord of Battle
    City of Spears
    King of Ruin
    Empire of Ash

The Underground Academy Series
    The Natural Order
    Rogue Magic
    Lost Magic
    The Final Order

Standalone novels
    The Fall of Lostport
    Hunter's Legend
    Beauty's Songbook

Made in the USA
Middletown, DE
14 October 2023

40584372R00448